WOMEN

Twentieth-Century Continental Fiction

WOMEN

◆

Philippe Sollers

TRANSLATED BY

BARBARA BRAY

COLUMBIA UNIVERSITY PRESS
NEW YORK

Columbia University Press wishes to express its appreciation of assistance given by the government of France through le Ministère de la Culture in the preparation of this manuscript.

Columbia University Press
New York   Oxford

Femmes copyright © 1983 Editions Gallimard
English translation copyright © 1990 Columbia University Press

Library of Congress Cataloging-in-Publication Data

Sollers, Philippe, 1936–
  [Femmes. English]
  Women / Philippe Sollers ; translated by Barbara Bray.
    p. cm. — (Twentieth-century continental fiction)
  Translation of : Femmes.
  ISBN 0-231-06546-9
  I. Title. II. Series.
PQ2679.04F4613 1990
843'.914—dc20   90-39786
                                    CIP

Printed in the United States of America
c 10 9 8 7 6 5 4 3 2 1

Born male and single at an early age. . . .
Own and operate own typewriter.

WILLIAM FAULKNER

WOMEN

◆◆◆◆◆◆◆◆◆◆◆◆◆◆◆◆◆◆◆◆◆◆◆◆◆◆◆◆◆◆◆◆◆

I

In all this time . . . You'd have thought someone would have risked it . . . I look, watch, listen, consult books, read and re-read . . . But no . . . Not really . . . No one mentions it . . . Not openly anyway . . . Hints, mists, clouds, innuendos . . . In all this long time . . . How long? Two thousand years? Six thousand? Ever since records have existed . . . You'd have thought someone would have come out with it—the truth, the plain lethal truth . . . But no: nothing or almost nothing . . . Myths, religions, poems, novels, operas, philosophies, contracts . . . It's true there've been a few bold gestures . . . But most soon lapse into overemphasis, exaggeration, murderous exasperation or straining after effect . . . Nothing or almost nothing about the cause. The *cause*.

The world belongs to women.

In other words, to death.

But everyone lies about it.

Hold tight, reader—this isn't going to be an easy ride. Though you probably won't be bored. There'll be details, local color, one scene after another, mix-ups, mesmerism, psychology, orgies. I'm writing the Memoirs of a traveler the like of whom has never been seen before and who'll reveal the secrets of the ages . . . The origin of things unveiled! The secret fathomed! Fate X-rayed! So-called Nature unmasked! The temple of error, illusion, hidden murder, the very heart of things . . . Ever since I was brought into this bear garden, which can be terribly tedious, I've also quite enjoyed myself.

It's a woman's world. Only women exist. They've always known

3

it, and yet they don't know it at all. They can't really know it. They can only feel it, sense it. That's how it works . . . And how about men? Froth. Pseudobosses, pseudopriests, vague philosophers. Insects . . . Managers taken advantage of by the workers . . . illusory muscle, surrogate energy . . . I propose to tell how and why. If my hand obeys me, if my arm doesn't drop off, if I don't die of exhaustion en route. Above all if I can manage to convince myself this revelation is actually addressed to somebody. Though I'm almost sure it never can really get through to anyone . . .

Settling of old scores? And how! Schizophrenia? I should think so! Paranoia? I'll say! The whole thing has driven me crazy? I'll buy that. Misogyny? That's putting it mildly. Misanthropy? You must be joking . . . These pages will go further than all the great names of antiquity. Of yesterday in general, and of today, tomorrow and the day after that . . . Much further in height, breadth, depth and horror. But also in melody, harmony and inwardness.

Who am I, really? It doesn't matter. Better stay in the background. A philosopher in a darkroom . . . I've merely asked the writer who's going to put his name to this book to discuss a few points with me . . . Why did I choose him in particular? Because people hated him. I went into it, did a survey. I wanted someone reasonably well known but heartily disliked . . . A specialist in grudges and poisoned wells. I have my own ideas on the subject . . . A metaphysical theory . . . You'll see, you'll see . . . Why in French? A question of tradition . . . After all it's the French, some of them at least, who are most familiar with the dramatic world I propose to describe . . . Funny, though . . . It's as if they were also the primary inventors of what happens behind the scenes . . . The process still goes on, though on a more paltry scale, like everything else these days . . . Mutant on the one hand, Martian on the other . . .

I start from an elementary premise. If you're here, with your eyes scanning these lines, it follows that you've been born. Male or female? He or she? The action's beginning. You belong to one sex or the other, or at least you seem to. But is the appearance true or false? *Le cosi fallaci* . . . You don't exactly know. I say "exactly"

4

advisedly. Anyhow, there you are. And you don't know why, either. No, no, I'm talking about the old Mama-Papa puzzle which science cracked long ago. As Faulkner—him again—said to Ben Wasson in the spring of 1930: "Sorry, I haven't got a picture. I dont intend to have one that I know of, either. About the biography. Dont tell the bastards anything. It cant matter to them. Tell them I was born of an alligator and a nigger slave at the Geneva peace conference two years ago. Or whatever you want to tell them." No flies on him . . . All I mean is, a pig can't evaluate its own poke . . . Are you really in it? In your body? Does your thought exist in a body? Do we spend a season in the hell of the body and then ping! out of it? Into the void? "I have seen the hell of women there," said Rimbaud . . . What did he really see? To be? Not to be? Hell? We're going to rediscover hell — that's part of the plan. With a certain amount of pleasure in the process. Right — so where does it all come from? Mama? *Mama?* God-Mama? Her!! Behind him, her! The universal cell, the great atomic pile now run on the pill, the eternal mouth . . . Isis, Artemis, Aphrodite, Diana, Hecate! Cybele! Demeter! Mater! Athena! Gea! Geova! The frown, the pinch, the safety pin, the pyramid, the sacred triangle, the delta!

Kate arrives in her fancy cowboy hat. She takes herself for an Amazon now. Her head's full of the woman epic. Seething with it. "We women . . ." You can tell she never stops thinking about it. Excited, depressed, terrified. Obsessed. She's feeling awful, but has to hide it and pretend she's always on form, cheerful and decisive . . . No one must see her whole life is shot through with turmoil and fear. She has to keep on lying, trying to put people off the scent. Dissimulation isn't second nature to her—it's first nature, before nature itself. A spontaneous defense, a veil—but a distorting one . . . I can see she's gritting her teeth. She's about to approach me, Public Enemy No. 1, top of the black list, the man who knows ten times too much, who has inside information . . . She kisses me, switches on the stereotypes of seduction. Power struggle . . . I look at her. She's exhausted after a long day spent asserting herself and her rights. After an endless series of posturings—at the *Journal,* at the Agency, and at the press conference of the reactionary-progressive candidate whom she, as a progressive-reactionary, has to pretend to see as a moderate reactionary. Something like that. Her skin is greasy and shining, her breasts droop, her stomach protrudes as if in a permanent threatened abortion. Can it be her liver?

"You see, darling, you don't take women seriously . . ."

The old tune. She hasn't been here five minutes before she puts the record on again. Every moment counts, every situation has to be pressed into service. Nothing for nothing. I observe her surreptitiously. They're really crazy, women. Completely, fundamentally and systematically. That fixed leaden gleam in their eye. She doesn't see or hear anything. Yet the bar near the Etoile where I arranged to meet her is a pleasant enough place. Comfortable leather armchairs, table lamps, discreet piped-in-opera . . . But no—she's somewhere else. Like a sleepwalker. Frozen. Consumed by her passion.

"I often ask myself what you'd think or do about something. And I know right away what I ought to think or do. Exactly the opposite."

She's let the cat out of the bag. For her and her pals I'm the absolute negative yardstick. The funny thing is she seems to think the conversation can go on as if nothing had happened. It's as though she were so perverse she needed this kind of preliminary attack to get her going. But after spending a while first treating me to reams of gossip and being as nasty as possible about the friends she's going to meet later on, and then trying to gouge information out of me that she thinks might advance her career in the next few days or months, she'll suddenly lean forward and say, her breath already reeking of alcohol:

"I could tell you more . . . Quite a number of things . . . But it'll take time . . . For me to get used to it . . . In another two or three days perhaps . . ." Here we go. The trip trick again! She never misses . . . They all end up suggesting a trip . . . A change of scene . . . The better to eat you with when you get back . . .

Egypt, Greece, Rome, Venice, India, Singapore, Morocco . . . Just a weekend . . . Three days, a week. Of being together . . . All the time . . . Hotel room, *tête-à-tête*, cheek by jowl, walks, meals, museums . . . And then, perhaps, on the second day . . . Late in the afternoon . . . After some shopping . . . Shoes . . . A ring . . . A bracelet . . . A necklace . . . Fusion . . . We'd tell each other everything, absolutely everything . . . And the thing would be settled . . . Marriage, I mean. It always comes down to that in the end: settling down, sorting things out, putting things on a regular footing, having just one atmosphere for two . . . One bubble between you . . . Perfect understanding . . . A shared placenta . . . The little things in life, rather revolting but very touching; the real things . . . And it's then she'd tell me what I need to know . . . The dangers threatening me . . . Give me advice . . . Other people's intentions, what they really have against me, tittle-tattle, the plots being hatched behind my back . . . All the details I'm dying to know . . . I brace myself slightly against the shock . . . She mustn't see how disgusted I am . . . So I plunge in right away . . . Take her hand, lean forward, give her a little kiss under the ear . . . Nothing to speak of . . . Not that I wouldn't like . . .

"Yes, of course, we'll have to work it out . . ."

My voice sounds a bit feeble to me . . . Lacking in the proper enthusiasm . . . She'll notice . . . But no—women never notice . . . They're protected by a monumental, cosmic invincible narcissism. Either they're depressed in advance, whatever the situation, or else they're convinced of their irresistibility . . . And usually they're right . . . Vibes, spiritualistic vapors and so on end up confusing everything and casting a spell, a sense of unease, on any man, however homosexual or professional he may be . . . Better still, the mother effect! . . . Hidden causality. Always all or nothing, never perhaps . . . She wants me to want her, and it would never occur to her that I don't . . . Unless . . . One doesn't really know . . . She may have registered my instinctive recoil, my reticence . . . I can see a film of the whole thing already . . . Speeded up . . . The country hotel, the garden, the tables under the trees, the river, the bed, the bathroom . . . There might be a good moment at the beginning, my hand in the fly of her pants, my finger in her crack . . . Her, so sure of herself . . . And of them all . . . The certain damp something at the start . . .

But what can she do, actually? Pursed lips, incisor a bit crooked . . . I light a cigarette, finish my drink . . . Mumble something about a pressing engagement . . . She draws herself up . . . Another double black mark in my already sinister record . . . The Phèdre story . . . A hint of Racine starting to boil up . . . Bye, darling, we'll talk on the phone . . . I practically run out of the bar . . . A balmy June evening . . .

I have got an appointment, but not the one I alleged . . . Cyd opens the door. Always neat, punctual, discreet. The game is not to talk but to make love right away . . . She's naked under her black dress, and we go to it without more ado . . . We don't talk till afterwards . . . It's quite different once the physical crisis is over . . . Misunderstanding exorcized . . . Inability to communicate acted out and discharged . . . She's realized this and accepted the pattern . . . I know practically nothing about her life . . . That's what freedom means nowadays . . . Keep things separate, water-tight compartments, don't say anything, never admit and above all never complain, just engineer a change of scene . . . As many different scenes as possible, never get in too deep, here today and gone tomorrow . . . That's what I like about New York. The way you can change sets whenever you like, the flexibility of space, the distances . . . You raise your arm, hail a taxi, it's dusk, anywhere else is the center too . . . Whereas in Paris . . . Two or three lively focal points, and the rest periphery . . . Eyes everywhere, as bad as the provinces . . . A kind of brake on everything, psychological dissuasion . . . Not many people here who lead what can really be called a life . . . An existence, yes . . . But it's not the same thing . . .

Cyd has a lot of humor but she's also violent . . . She likes play-acting . . . The kind that helps you come . . . Useful artifice . . .

Magic, an ironical geisha, year two thousand style . . . Black stockings, garters, no panties, whispered preliminaries, intermittent obscenities . . . The retro manner . . . I must work out a theory of whispering one of these days, write a thesis, send it to my academic friends—I'll tell you who they are in due course . . . Casual, vague areas, staccato language, anything goes. Silly, old-fashioned beating about the bush, but exciting, in the end exciting . . . Don't you agree, *hypocrite lecteur*, lucid readeress? . . . Look at the audience in porno movie houses . . . Men on their own, embarrassed, gauche, obsessed . . . A few couples . . . If there's a foursome they laugh . . . They have to . . . As if to say there's nothing going on where they are, no one need come and stick their nose in, it's just a lark, the whole thing's ridiculous . . . Modern repression . . . In reverse . . . The women make them joke about it, while the image staring them blatantly in the face produces its subterranean effect . . . They don't stay very long, and when they go out they're pensive, stooping . . . Sometimes I look at a couple . . . She's gone to sleep with her head on his shoulder . . . He follows it all like a diligent schoolboy . . . She goes on sleeping . . . Typical of this day and age! It doesn't concern her . . . She just waits for it to be over . . . For her chap to have had his fill of cunts, thighs, asses, pricks and balls, from in front and from behind; of mouths outlined clearly against penises, sperm spurting over backsides or breasts . . . The actors have got some nerve . . . So earnest it only adds to the general despair . . . Every so often there's a peculiar, childish gleam somewhere . . . But never anything really out of the way . . . Nothing ever goes wrong . . . It bowls along like a puppet show, like clockwork, pictures on the one hand, sound track on the other . . . If it was real, that's to say happening in everyday life, it would be banned . . . Naturally . . . Cynicism and naiveté, the two main factors in everything now . . . Realism and foolishness . . . Abolition of death, intensive gynecologism . . . With the male in the middle of the maelstrom like a sort of circus animal . . . Either at work or sitting up and begging . . . Sometimes it's the other kind of sex: homosex . . . Murky writhings, gleaming queers . . . It comes to the same thing . . .

9

I look at Cyd in the dark. She's naked now, wearing only her shoes . . . Beautiful like that, fair but brown from her last trip to the south of France . . . She kneels down and sucks me off . . . At length . . . We become part of the universal movement . . . In the swing . . . I know what interests her—the mental instant, abstract domination by the within, the ritual of silent possession, yoga through concentration . . . Seeing if I can hold out, and how . . . That's what excites her . . . I lie down on the divan . . . She goes on going down on me . . . I can hear her now, the first time she said: "Do you want me to suck you off, you bastard?" . . . In a taxi at night on Park Avenue . . . There'd been some footsy during dinner, and I'd just kissed her, more or less out of politeness . . . And now here, at her place, in Paris . . . She's never minced her words . . . A language that isn't her own, that doesn't matter . . . These Englishwomen . . . Words like blows . . . Free for all . . . Transparent missiles . . . Sudden crudeness . . . I think I know the story she's telling herself . . . About a vampire, the switchback of death . . . The word "suck," louder . . . Why is she like this with me? I mean why doesn't she ask anything in return? Every time I expect her to name her price . . . Even indirectly . . . A word to someone here or there, some favor or other, a request for closer intimacy, the usual thing . . . But no, nothing . . . Everything remains smooth, frantic, enthusiastic, as if only the moment mattered . . . Even if it was only once or twice . . . As a matter of form . . . But no . . . It's free of charge . . . Unless she regards it as a long-term investment . . . I let her play . . . She must be as bored as I am in the ordinary way . . . Hence the scientific side of our meetings . . . She'll get pleasure from making me have pleasure . . . She mounts me, twitching, trembling . . . Straddles me, shudders running through her . . . Kundalini, the Indian books call it. I can feel the very snake of her sinews, from its coils to its head, and chromodynamically back again. Quantum chromodynamics, the physics of today, and of tomorrow . . . The varied resistance of the bedrock, matter vaporized and so more strong . . . With motionless catastrophes! . . . All the colors of the rainbow . . . Anticolors! A whole spectrum to experience . . . Cortex, spinal cord, the search for counterwaves . . . We're in the antiworld world now . . . And Cyd there dancing on the drifting raft. She comes down again, thrusts her mouth at me, tears at me . . . I'm starting to come . . . I let her come first . . . She eats me . . . Love . . . She devours me completely . . . Electrons, protons, neutrons, photons, leptons, muons, hadrons . . . And even the new ones, the gluons, which hold fibers together . . . She shakes substance by the scruff of its neck . . . A mane of atoms . . . As if she fed direct on the cogito . . . She murmurs as much . . . "It's your mind that excites me" . . . Her own invisible reconstructed image via my mind . . . She breathes me in entirely, collapses . . . She's lying down, sleeping, now . . . No conversation today? I get up and dress quietly. She utters an amiable little mmmmmm . . . I feel for the door in the dark . . . Am out on the cold stairs . . .

We must just get used to it . . . The world has changed its foundations . . . Or rather the eternal foundations have changed their world in passing . . . An operation performed under anaesthetic, a transplant, an overhaul of the circuits . . . It starts without your noticing, like a breeze . . . A few disasters, explosions, wars, a series of worsening crises, and then a slow, relentless tide rising to cover everything and sweep it away . . . When did it start? . . . Fifteen, twenty years ago? Perhaps latent much longer, with the final preparations completed only recently . . . Perhaps it was there all the time, but didn't come to light until everything was ready . . . I don't know . . . I don't know anymore . . . Sometimes I'm immeasurably bored . . . Not because of the absurd, or meaninglessness, those new literary chestnuts . . . No, but on the contrary, because of an unbearable, unsharable lucidity, an absolute knowledge of all about the chicken and the egg . . . A conscious ennui, with full knowledge of the facts . . . Nothing romantic or tragic about it . . . Nothing . . . The things that happen, the news always the same . . . Gray television, the papers, advertising, zombie-like processions, opening ceremonies, debates, speechifyings, protests, sermons . . . And nobody seems to suspect . . . At the end of history, said old Hegel, death will live a human life . . . Well, it's happened . . . The prophecy has come true . . . And I, here back home, sitting at my desk and writing this . . . Is death living me? Is it death that's filling these pages? Perhaps . . . A hard day, anyhow . . . It's completely dark outside, my window's a blue-black curtain . . . I'm listening to *The Well-Tempered Clavier* . . . *Das Wohltemperierte Klavier* . . . Zuzana Ruzickova . . . A Czech . . . It's perfect . . . delicate but full of energy, detailed yet massive . . . Women musicians . . . The only women I'd spare . . . Singers, pianists, harpsichordists, violinists . . . I remember that little brunette . . . Louise . . . We used to meet on Sundays . . . She was always working . . . Rehearsing the same phrases over and over again . . . Scarlatti, Haydn, Mozart . . . Her hands, her profile, flying fingers, shoulders swaying smoothly as a pendulum . . . I could have listened to her for hours . . . We flirted just a bit, nothing serious . . . Scales of nuances . . . Well-tempered temperature . . .

Yes, it's night-time, and another world is rising. Harsh, cynical, illiterate, amnesiac, revolving without reason . . . Spread out, flattened, as if perspective and vanishing point had been abolished . . . And the strange thing is that the living dead of this world are based on the world *before* . . . Their reflexes, their sensations, their brains are those of *before* . . . Hence the depressions, declines, suicides . . . The inroads of psychology . . . It's been like that with the Americans for a long time—a counterpart to social security . . . The shrink . . . Life interpreted, dubbed . . . Gurus everywhere, psychiatrists into everything, mad management of every poodle's lightest whim . . . Let the individual be aware of his limits, of the brick wall of reality; let him feel like Nessus' shirt, feel himself becoming useless before hurtling into the void . . . Triumph of free enterprise . . . Adaptation in all directions . . . In the East, as everyone knows, the treatment tends to be rather rough and ready . . . Is capitalism interested in your underlying ravings? . . . So is socialism . . . Your money suits me nicely . . . But I don't like your ideas . . . Your brain's very delicate: don't think without consulting us; stay with us; be coupled, diplomaed, urbanized, bound, mastered . . . For the benefit of what? Of whom? Science? Society? The human race? Progress? Of course not. For the benefit of the Idol . . . Of the combine-egglayer, the light of hearth and home . . . Regulation, manipulation, secret death by inches . . . Everywhere the same, the same old tune, with varying amounts of money and different means, that's all . . . And then there's chemistry . . . Should the person in question not be sufficiently in awe of the Widow . . . Die Witwe! La Viuda! La Vedova! The dream of sons and daughters alike . . . And of brothers who feel more and more as if they were their sisters' sisters . . . The ultimate "openness"—the elimination of original sin . . . In the beginning *she* was there, fertile, harmonious, nurturing, strong, gracious and complete, and everything related to her to produce unmixed good . . . Autogestation, autodigestion . . . In the beginning and at the end there was, and therefore will be, substance, and the essence of substance, and the substance of the essence of substance . . . Nature without a flaw . . . And Nature has been sullied! By whom? By what's-his-name, of course, the polluter, the doubter, the insinuater, the troublemaker . . . Notice in passing that the dogma with the most staying power is the one depicting virginity wounded and damaged by some vile and disgusting interference . . . No such thing as immaculateness . . . Ridiculous! If there were, the crime wouldn't exist, the contamination would be minimized, the responsibility of the marauding phallus would become relative . . . There *has* to be a Fall, over and over again—an accident, a hitch, a leading astray, a rape, a going off the rails, a rending apart, an infection . . . An external virus . . . Otherwise, my goodness, everything would be down the drain . . . You wouldn't be able to keep harping on the theme of infinite reparation . . . I remember Marie-Thérèse's funeral, at the church of St. Thomas Aquinas . . . Everyone who was in the swim was there . . . A gathering of free spirits . . . They looked as out of place at a mass as a school of whales in a goldfish bowl . . . Awkward, embarrassed . . . Why a religious service these days, not to mention all the rest of it, first-class burial, flowers, singer, cello, organ? I knew why . . . A posthumous message to me

. . . The last challenge . . . She'd even gone as far as that . . . She'd even dictated the insipid priest's sermon and chosen the readings . . . From the Apocalypse, no less . . . And the beginning of St. John, insisting on the translation "speech" instead of "the word." We'd argued about that . . . In the beginning—masculine or feminine? In French you have to choose between *la parole*(f.) and *le verbe*(m.) . . . The same thing? Not at all! They've got nothing to do with one another . . . And she kept it up until death! She dragged her cancer thus far . . . Awful and unremitting rectal pain didn't get the better of her in that respect . . . She might have to die, but she'd contradict me to the end . . . I didn't love her . . . She bored me, and she already smelled of death when I first met her . . . Not living death, which gives you a hard-on, but death that's dead and musty . . . She was too fat, and affected . . . I did screw her once, but only half-heartedly and because I'd had too much to drink . . . Never again, out of the question . . . She hung on to me in a frenzy of hatred . . . The more I avoided her the more eager she grew . . . She'd arrange dinners and I'd drop out at the last minute . . . Just send a note . . . Or a wire . . . Or phone . . . But she kept it up . . . The realism of women, their cynicism . . . Everything must be obtainable . . . They're ready to pay, to bribe, to corrupt, to arrange things . . . Once the fundamental anal force is unleashed in them they lose all moral sense, all modesty . . . Not a vestige of taste left . . . Just pure violence, relentless persistence . . . As obstinate as mules . . . She said to one of my friends: "I'm waiting for him to fall really low and then I'll get him." . . . She'd have arranged my fall if necessary . . . So that she could pick me up . . . A patient killed with kindness . . . Absurd . . . But it's a well-known peculiarity of their brand of eroticism . . . Their thing about clinics, hospitals, asylums, prisons, suburbs, morgues . . . What she wanted was to guide me and manage me, to organize what I saw and what I was influenced by . . . And in return I'd have been standing there in front of the genuine log fire whenever she threw a party . . . In a dinner jacket . . . Presentable . . . Horrible . . . Surly . . . Intimidating . . . Drunk . . . Aggressive . . . Witty . . . Inaccessible . . . What did it matter? . . . She wanted her unhappiness to come from me . . . And now the coffin . . . The sacred tests . . . *La parole* . . . Versus *le verbe*. Right to the finish! *Le verbe* has time on his side . . . But he's absent, more and more so, no one's for him any more, it's terrible . . . *Le verbe,* not *le mot* . . . *Das Wort* . . . Not *der* or *die — das!* . . . Neutered! The Word! Versus *el Verbo!* In the pulpit!. . . . The congregation went down the aisle and around the bier . . . The fashionable Left, most of them Jews or atheists . . . Masons, male and female, with their glassy, fishy, quartzy eyes . . . The guy in front of me didn't know what to do with the censer—it was the first time he'd held the celestial penis in his hand . . . Or perhaps he was just repelled by it . . . Anyhow, he gets rid of it by passing it on to me . . . I make the sign of the cross with the little leaden bone dipped in holy water . . . All the next chap has to do is follow suit . . . Goodbye . . . I catch sight of Kate in one of the pews . . . She said to me later: "The way you looked . . . I almost felt like coming over to cheer you up . . . But it's not as awful as all that, you know . . ." As if she felt sorry for me . . . But as usual she got it all wrong . . . In fact I found the whole thing quite pitiful . . . Fearfully false . . . And pathetic . . . And then on top of it all you're supposed to look on death as insignificant! Just part of the order of things . . . Hello and goodbye . . . The ebb and flow of the generations . . . Cosmic architecture . . . Birth, death . . . We know all about it . . . The cycle ad hoc . . . They find it quite natural, it doesn't overawe them at all . . . No judgment, no appalling truth, above all no *dies irae* . . . Both sexes ready to slip into their skeletons with a clear conscience . . . No nightmares . . . No shrieks . . . Fast asleep . . . Vague anxiety? Slight gnawings? Hear anything? No . . . Vanity, business . . . To bed . . .

Difficult moment . . . Last straw . . . Great puzzle . . . As if it were just after a war that never took place or just before one that never will . . . No need . . . What is going to happen already has . . . For the first time I feel as if I'd really come full circle . . . The same scene, but viewed from above . . . From the side . . . From the other side . . . Some funny things certainly have happened . . . Werth's accident; Andreas committing suicide; Lutz committing murder; Fals's collapse . . . All in a few months, like a long-drawn-out earthquake . . . In the middle of Paris, right at the center of power . . . Change of government . . . And of old friends . . . If the whole truth be told . . . The ramifications of the negative . . . The nervous system of conspiracy . . . The closets of perversion . . . The corridors of crime . . . I'm not one of those writers who go in for imaginary wonders and hide behind conventional scenery . . . Who withdraw into fairy stories—retroactive, regional, allegorical or mystical . . . No, no, straight to the subject, to the innards throbbing *hic* and *nunc!* The possessed . . . The special effects men . . . I wonder how the others do it, a bit of desert here, a touch of the provinces there, a few suggestions, some prevarications, long subordinate clauses, the imperfect subjunctive, everyone's happy, nothing has happened, it sells . . . They keep track of one another in the best-seller lists . . . Printed in blue in the weekly that knows . . . Written by those who count . . . Top people, as it says in the ad . . . Three or four palm trees, blazing sun, a little girl behind a dune, the sinister atmosphere of Paris under the Occupation, a love that dares not speak its name, a balcony in the forest, hold me up, I'm going to faint, my dream . . . So much for literature . . . Which has to be very well behaved, correct, anaesthetized, wrung out ten times, another place, another time, once upon a time, pastel-colored . . . Nonfiction, of course, has to deal with the "great questions of the age" . . . Is socialism compatible with freedom? Yes, no, not really, perhaps . . . Will the future of science be devastating? In a way, but there's another side to it . . . Will God make a comeback? What about surrogate motherhood? Inoculate fatherhood? The revival of the Couple? The lure of drugs? We're just like the rest of you — didn't you know? Weight problems, savings, trucks in the night, posters, T-shirts, shopping malls, discount stores! Promotion tours, book signings, local radio and TV, nonstop lectures, the thinker has thought, the historian has revised his views, the scientist has questioned his own findings . . . Right

. . . The only thing that's never discussed is: what are you, a speaking biped, doing here? Do you think this phenomenon is really necessary? Why you and not someone else? Why not nothing? Why does there have to be all this blather? Why does the ideal image of your mother have to be preserved at all costs? . . . Tut-tut . . . Touch of the brake . . . Icy silence . . . Biological embarrassment . . . Torpor . . . Taboo . . . Black hole . . . As if Nature had been shattered to the core . . . As if the Thread had been broken . . .

The person who knows something about it all is Flora . . . About the cauldron, the preparations, the herbs, the mandragora, all the chilling witches' brew . . . I first met her in the atmosphere of the late sixties and early seventies . . . In the middle of all the commotion . . . People thought this time really was it . . . Conflagration, fresh start . . . She was small, dark, quick . . . Above all, blue eyes with a dash of milk in them, never seen anything like it . . . Politics personified . . . A Cleopatra of intrigue, a queen of complication . . . Spanish, an anarchist . . . And at the same time, mysteriously, contacts everywhere—parliaments, newspapers, philosophers . . . Nomenklatura . . . A whiff of brimstone about her reputation . . . Two or three rather tart books . . . I mixed in circles of the far left at the time, playing the part of a kind of revolutionary extra, it was the thing just then, but my mind was on other things, including a bit of work on Shakespeare, but so as not to attract attention I used to say the first thing that came into my head as if I really believed it . . . That was a mistake . . . Amateurs are easily spotted, they overdo it in the wrong places and then people notice that they're irresponsible, their origins are suspect, they're not really serious . . . The hard-liner attitude struck me as the most amusing . . . I felt intuitively that the whole business was unimportant, so why bother with subtleties? . . . I liked holding forth dogmatically; still do, in the abstract, as a matter of form . . . I can't manage to be serious on the subject . . . But it's a mistake, a big mistake . . . In the first place because no one notices humor in that sort of thing, and then because even if they only sense it they regard it as unforgivably offhand, an offense only a spoiled child would be

17

capable of . . . So you end up with everyone against you . . . Believers, unbelievers, the right and the left, the rich, the poor, the half-rich and the half-poor, and morality itself, which is always in the right . . . Flora, despite her apparent irony, took this world terribly seriously . . . It was and still is her element, her passion, the very air she breathes . . . The relationships between everything, the dialectical maelstrom; economic ups and downs; the settling of scores even after years have gone by; the hidden pressure exercised by neuroses . . . Thanks to her I started to check up on my intuitions, to understand the spectacle presented by events and news of events, to feel that everything was subterraneously connected with everything else, just as it is in the theater, only better . . . Shakespeare "live" . . . Only more sordid . . . I mean more highly sexed . . . I shall come back to Flora . . . Fantastic "temperament" . . . Given to fantasies too . . . Bit of a medium . . . Inspired . . . Genuine . . . False . . . Frightful . . . Charming . . . But there are other actors I have to bring on . . . Other performers of both sexes . . .

Starting with myself . . . I suppose I'd better tell you a bit of my life history . . . After all, it's the only thing that's of interest, the details of the life of X or Z . . . Not of "people" in general, about whom darling Esther is always concerned . . . "Aren't you afraid people might think . . . ?" "Don't you think people will say . . . ?" "People don't realize . . ." For Esther, people are the great tribunal . . . You don't work out your own individual salvation . . . You act in relation to others . . . It's not exactly the conformist what-will-people-say; it's something more profound, and unconsciously religious . . . It implies a kind of universal biography or communal "story" . . . Funny she should be interested in artists . . . People who don't give a damn about people . . . Whose lives are based on not wanting to be mistaken for people . . . But that's what she likes . . . To stand for something with those who deny that very thing . . . She's rather like Kate . . . She comes and gives the family news of its enemies . . . And brings the protesters news of the family . . . Backwards and forwards . . . A fag, really . . . There's getting to be more of them all the time . . .

My life, then . . . The equation I started from and the point I'm
at now . . . I'm nearly asleep already . . . Telling my life story
bores me to death . . . You can never get it right, you can't help
oversimplifying, exaggerating, playing down, abbreviating . . . But
if I must I must . . . Let's try to stick to the point . . . The erotic
point . . . Let's see . . . What have we here? Ysia . . . Oh no, not
now! . . . Later! . . . China . . . The way she mews . . . No, not
Ysia, no digressions . . . Oh, well then, the last . . . We used to
meet briefly in the afternoon in a little studio rented specially near
the Champs-Elysées, near the embassy . . . An hour, an hour and a
half . . . One of my most daring affairs . . . A real detective story
. . . I'd met her at the Langues O., the Paris School of Oriental
Languages . . . She worked in the cultural section of the embassy
. . . Well, to go on, she was beautiful . . . Exquisite . . . Lacquered,
graceful, slim . . . Thirty years old, married, withdrawal symptoms
. . . Subtle perversion . . . The lot . . . Jade flute . . . Dream of the
red chamber . . . And the yellow . . . And the turquoise . . . Tales
told by the lake . . . The phoenix's tail . . . Dew in the moonlight
. . . Such precision, such appetite . . . The body of a child, almost;
one of my best experiences of feeling *inside*—membrane to membrane, I mean, in the abstract kiln of curved delight . . . Do you
understand? No? Too bad . . . I've always thought a cartography of
coitus would be a good idea . . . A sort of practical *carte du tendre*
. . . Narrators usually pass over the act in silence . . . Or else whip
the whole thing up . . . Various kinds of microsadism . . . Scatology, blow by blow accounts . . . But mostly they go in for the
ethereal style . . . She emerged from the bath and came and lay
down by my side. We switched off the light. She let herself go and
we rolled about on the feather bed . . . That day we read no further
. . . End of paragraph. No, what's needed is an exact record set
down by the hero of the inner sensations experienced by his scrap
of a sexual organ in contact with the comprehensive evasion of the
penetrated flesh . . . A whole new palette to be discovered . . .
Positive . . . Negative . . . Neutral . . . Galvanizing . . . Off-put-
ting . . . The usual descriptions are too external . . . Stiff, stilted,
and literary . . . Aggression is oversimplified . . . Scenes are too

much subjected to the eye, to the *idea* of the eye, to the optical stereotype . . . Ysia enters the narrative here because if I'm to tell the story of my life I have to say I owe a debt to her as regards touch . . . The gratitude of a painter . . . Or engraver . . . Two or three bamboos, four leaves, allusion to a slope, a stream, the density of the air, the brightness of the water . . . The universe in a brush stroke . . . Since I started this book, and as a result of my discussions about it with S., I've come to understand painters better than I did before. I seem to be able to enter into what they do, into their knowledge of what lies through the looking glass. To come back to Ysia . . . The studio once or twice a week . . . Outside, we didn't know one another . . . And even inside . . . *As if* we didn't know one another—yes, that was the secret of the beauty, the fascination . . . What will she have said to me, finally? A few things about the Chinese language, how to write certain suggestive words, bits of poems, passages from Lao-Tsu . . . While we smoked a cigarette . . . "The true Way is not the same as a constant Way" . . . "He who speaks does not know; he who knows does not speak" . . . "The greatest square has no angles" . . . I still have the little anthology of classical poetry that she gave me . . . Lingbao . . . *The Sacred Jewel* . . . Her crossed legs, her smile . . . She used to toss me off at length, standing up, and it was always marvelous because of her long, soft, cruel, insidious fingers . . . Then she'd ask me to lick her, and she'd concentrate completely on that . . . Then to buttfuck her . . . You see . . . And then to take her and make her come, and wait for her to come first before I came and shot my sperm into her wicked, crazy, severe little mouth . . . And then smile . . . And then a few poems . . . And then good-night . . . Never any politics . . . The Tao . . . Then one day, after a couple of months, nothing . . . A call to the embassy . . . Risky . . . "Mme Ysia Li has gone back to Shanghai . . . No, she's not expected to return for the moment . . . No, we haven't an address . . . Who is it speaking, please?" I hang up . . . Four years later, in Shanghai, I thought I saw her a dozen times on my solitary early morning walks along the waterfront . . . Shanghai . . . The Lady from Shanghai . . . Junks, heat, the light glinting from the river . . .

Was she there somewhere among those swarms of people? Had she been caught? Denounced? Anyhow . . . So that's how I came to be a bit of a Marxist for a while . . . Marxist-Leninist . . . Maoist . . . A question of skin . . . So there you are . . . You know it all . . . I went as far as China . . . I'm obstinate . . . When I have a sensation I really like, I'd go to the ends of the earth . . . To the moon . . . But Ysia was gone . . . One of the last brief conversations I had with her was about Confucius . . . For some reason or other the Chinese were getting all worked up about Confucianism then, although theoretically it looked irrefutable . . . "A woman-eater," Ysia said, laughing . . . Anti-Confucian slogans . . . She was against Confucius . . . I was against Confucius . . . A confused and convoluted name; an air of consummate bigotry; a kind of yellow Helvetius or Jansenius . . . Narrow wisdom, a cat is a cat, Kantian dilution, ancient potbelly . . . Sour old worthy of Antiquity . . . An inferior must obey his superior, a daughter her mother, a daughter-in-law her mother-in-law—that kind of aphorism . . . No doubt I'm oversimplifying . . . Outrageously . . . Be that as it may, a moral philosopher, advocate of the golden mean . . . Then presto! Eight years later, a big TV closeup of an official delegation visiting Confucius's tomb . . . So be it . . . The swing of the pendulum . . . Alternation . . . As when the ex-president found himself watching a performance of *Gisèle* in Peking . . . Chinese irony . . . Heads of state used as gadgets . . . Vive Adolphe Adam! Come back, Confucius! This time probably for good . . . Imagine France having a Pascalian propaganda campaign against Montaigne . . . Impossible! Anyway, I'd oppose it . . . Bordeaux, the wine . . . Best thing about this country . . . By far! And I notice the new president has had an official photograph taken reading the *Essays* . . . I find that reassuring . . . But what bothers me is his saying in an interview that he doesn't care for Baudelaire . . . What is it he doesn't like? *Carrion? The Lure of the Void? Lovers' Wine? Satan's Litanies? Women Damned? The Vampire's Metamorphoses?*

When she had sucked my bones to the marrow,
And languorously I turned toward her

21

To return a love kiss, all I saw
Was a leather bag, with slimy sides and full of pus!
In cold terror I shut both my eyes,
And when I opened them to the living light,
At my side, instead of a moving manikin
That seemed to have garnered stores of my blood,
There trembled a mess of skeleton remains
Emitting a sound like a weather vane
Or a shop sign hung on an iron rod
And creaking in the wind on a winter's night.

I like Baudelaire unconditionally . . . I think he's clear, musical
and irreducible . . . Very observant too . . . The marrow . . . The
leather bag with slimy sides . . . The pus . . . The manikin . . . The
skeleton . . . The sound of the weather vane, inevitably evoking the
shriek of an owl . . . The shop sign . . . The iron rod . . . Swept
away by the wind? . . . As fine as *Macbeth* . . . "Superior minds
are distinguished by a liking for the world of women. I am sure the
intelligent ladies listening to me forgive the almost sensual terms in
which I express myself." Baudelaire? Confucius? Comment, choose
and justify your choice, referring to your own experience . . . I can
understand, however, why a court of law got his number in 1857 . . .

Did Ysia really believe in all that — revolution and "the fundamental transformation of man," and so on and so forth? Perhaps
. . . Perhaps not. I still meet people today who talk to me about my
political "errors" . . . I nod . . . I roll my eyes . . . And I see the
studio again . . . The late afternoons . . . The rain on the window-
panes . . . Ysia's dancing body on the bed . . . I hear her brief
moans in the dark; I see the gleam of her teeth, her bird-like profile
. . . I feel her mouth, her tongue, the responsiveness of her neck
. . . My errors . . . Of course . . . All I've ever done is make
mistakes . . . Still do . . . Secret life . . . Ysia's face, upside down,
we must hurry, not much time, everything's temporary, hanging
by a thread, doomed . . . The attitude of a pseudo-aesthete! Immoral! Dandyism! Contempt for other people's suffering! The

steamroller of the censors . . . And censoresses . . . Sneers . . . Shrugs . . . I couldn't care less . . . Never have . . . I've got my orgasm notebook on my side, the black box recording my flights, my private record . . . I've always told myself there'd be evenings later on, much later on, when I'd look at my slides again and rerun my films . . . And here I am . . . Much sooner than expected, admittedly . . . Unless . . . "Ysia Li? Oh yes, that's right, Mme Li used to be in Paris . . . She's been posted to New York now . . . Yes, New York . . . Two months ago . . . That's quite all right . . . My pleasure . . ."

A jumble of images . . . Against the tide . . . Advantages and disadvantages of sexual precociousness . . . Advantages: you save a terrific amount of time; you find out early on what most people wear themselves out over, cut one another's throats for, too late; you acquire an unfailing sense of the relativeness of things, and a collection of ever-new sensations . . . You know what underlies people's posturings, you eventually come close to feeling compassion . . . Disadvantages: you get too used to immediate satisfaction; you're easily bored by calculation and continuity; you underestimate the importance of money (crucial) and the general ignorance (enormous). You've no time for psychology and splitting hairs about feelings; or in other words for the kind of stupidity necessary to anyone who wants to cut a figure in the world. You're too easily put off by obstacles or annoyances. You're too far in advance. In fact, you're not dishonest enough . . . That's a weakness . . . And you'll pay dearly for it.

Because it's absolutely necessary to cheat. Not that the species within which we're obliged to play our little parts is treacherous in itself, poor thing. It just isn't up to telling the truth on that score. And thus on any score. Sex is just too much for it. That's what makes it different from all the other species . . . The navel of nothing . . .

And so, from all these incidents, anyone born to ultimate disillusionment is bound to derive precocious revelations . . . Revelations that are strange yet only natural . . . Automatic . . .

Let's see.

What strikes me most is my lack of guilt. All my life I've been doing my best, as instructed, to *learn* to feel guilty . . . But I have to confess I can't . . . I feel innocent . . . Worse, I feel pardoned, redeemed, saved . . . It's strange . . . Am I devoid of moral feeling? On the contrary . . . But only on the intellectual level, people might say. I can't *feel* the *sin* involved in satisfying one's passions . . . On the contrary, I can see very clearly that they're meaningless . . . Pagan? Anti-Christian? Not at all . . . Present-day Christianity seems to me to be based on an enormous misunderstanding. A deliberate misinterpretation carefully maintained . . . Contrary to (dim) received opinion, I detect at its center a principle of subversion diametrically opposed to its general aura of cloying sweetness . . . A principle of radiation, of black awareness of radiation . . . And this just on the point where it seems weakest and most ridiculous, unfashionable, old-hat, leaking at every seam, caught up in its own contradictions, moth-balled, bloodless, hopeless . . . If only one could lift the curse, lift it just *there* and nowhere else . . . So, I've always come across women with characters corresponding to my own, adventurous women who create their own freedom as they go along . . . Or else—but it's the same thing—opposing me with peculiar, *very* peculiar violence . . . The same with men, but, as I've said, they're not so important—everything depends on the women . . . Their mother, their mother—they all, men and women, depend on their mother . . . It's the ever-fixed mark . . . Under any disguise you care to name, you inevitably come back to that . . . The primal Transvestite, the original Stele, the Rear-Mirror of the open tomb . . . In my very own family . . . *My* family, don't forget, not that of the person who's writing this book . . . No connection, and above all no comparison . . . . I swear it. I've said I'll explain the agreement between me and S. It's a technical alliance. Because I'm not French. Not used to the subtleties of the French language . . . So, in my very own family, mother, aunts, sisters, female cousins . . . You can see why I want to remain anonymous . . . I don't want to upset those of both sexes who are still alive over there . . . How am I to reveal in broad daylight what I experienced in my earliest childhood? What I saw, guessed, felt, touched, investigated? The hidden dark force that belongs to women . . . Their radar, their strategy, their constant underground calculation, their insane mystery, unknown to them yet implacably pursued? I have been initiated into the most secret of their rites . . . The Goddess has welcomed me into her own place, taught me her philters, shown me her snares . . . I know how each one of them, even if she's apparently and consciously the most sheltered, the most detached of women, is nothing but a mask concealing an elusive and inflexible reality, magnificently pathetic, that is detectable only indirectly, via attitudes that come to the surface at critical moments . . . You must never believe anything they say or try to show—it's always devious, always something else . . . Nor must you imagine they possess the key to their own key function . . . Not in the least . . . Maybe occasionally, for a few seconds . . . But that's all . . . Otherwise it's beyond them . . . They're left swooning . . . Hence their obsession with place, the nest, the fixed point, the home of one's own, legality . . . Hence the way they throw a nervous breakdown as soon as someone doesn't come up to par and relationships become too free . . . It's handed down from mother to daughter, or rather from grandmother to granddaughter, the burdensome and bewitched problem of how to keep things under control . . . The hidden face of the galaxy, the part that's hinted, suspect, misunderstood, stifled, unseemly . . . So good luck to the cosmonaut who ventures into these magnetic currents, into the intangible vegetation of the paranormal . . . Carnivorous flowers . . . Traps . . . Sudden whirlpools . . . Invisible craters . . . Secret castrations . . . Inexplicable inhibitions, paralyses, paraplegias, nervous haemorrhages, catalepsies disguised as epilepsies . . . Uncertain abysses . . . Shiftings, skids . . . Dark forest where the path of death-in-life cuts across our own brief shower . . .

My ancestors are there in the shadows, whispering to me to be careful . . . Father, uncles, grandfather, great-uncles, and the long,

vague sequence of faces consumed by murderous time . . . War
from the start, war forever, the rest is literature . . . Absolute,
total war, relentless and confused . . . Complete with smiles, scenery, lighting, acting, poetry, singing, films, magazines, diversions,
sham truces, renegades, spies, double games, poker, blackmail, false
exits, unavowed breaches, real trenches . . .

I can still hear my father getting up in the morning to go to work
. . . The ladies stayed on in bed . . . He washed and dressed as
quietly as he could, though he couldn't help singing a little song as
he shaved, he was probably so glad to be going out . . . He'd just
spent a typical masculine night . . . A night of undue closeness to
someone else, of sighs, of fatigue, and sometimes of pleasure; of
worries, addition and multiplication, suppressed snores and compensatory or accusing dreams . . . Out he went, a profitable ghost, to
spend his civilized day . . . When I think of him now I wonder how
he found the strength or the unawareness, the extra adolescence,
the spontaneous saintliness or infranervous genius to be always, or
almost always, in a good temper . . . Perhaps that was his revenge
. . . Demonstrating that nothing was happening . . . Nothing meant
anything . . . He was taciturn but cheerful . . . Stuck, but light-
hearted . . . Once he was out of the house the reign of the women
began . . . Lounging around, chatting, stretching, yawning, running about in their night-dresses to decide on the afternoon's shopping . . . I listened to them with a mixture of pleasure and fear . . .
Lucidity, superficiality, venality—all the qualities necessary for
sticking successfully to reality . . . At once horrible and enchanting
. . . The biological coil . . . But the crucial moment that I want to
tell you about, the supreme moment, came for me after lunch, in
the garden, near the greenhouse . . . By the orange and lemon
trees, under one of the two big palms . . . It's hard to imagine how
beautiful those gardens were, in the South of France . . . Wisterias,
magnolias, bays, acacias—a luxuriant climatic explosion . . . One
of my aunts, Edith, was in the habit of staying on after the rest . . .
She was a tall dark woman with a strange expression, thirty-six
years old at the time; I was fourteen . . . My mother's youngest

sister . . . Her attitude to me had always been aggressive, sarcastic, sharp . . . That summer she seemed bored and would read a lot . . . She'd sit on in her deckchair while the others went up to their rooms to sleep or slipped off to town to the stores or the movies . . . We were alone. I noticed a new intentness, a fixed gleam in her eye . . . I'd pretend I was going up to lie down too, but I came back and watched through the spindle-trees . . . White cotton dress, legs raised and parted . . . Brown skin which I guessed would be very soft, silky and sweet-smelling, like my mother's . . . Her white panties . . . I'm sure she saw me . . . And then one day a dark patch . . . It can't be, I don't believe it . . . No panties . . . The thighs wider and wider apart . . . And then the hand, slowly and expertly, head thrown back as if she'd fallen asleep . . . Eyelids opening from time to time . . . Shaft from the eye, black ray . . . In the end I took off all my clothes, there behind the dark green hedge, and moved close to a gap in the foliage through which I was plainly visible . . . Twenty meters away . . . She stopped for a moment . . . I started stroking myself, slowly at first, then faster and faster . . . She didn't move . . . Shamming dead . . . And then her hand went down again, trembling slightly, and we did it to-gether, eyes half shut, in the deafening blaze of July . . . I came when she leaned right back, before slumping forward a little with her head on her shoulder . . . I can still see my sperm on the leaves in the sunlight, it looked marvelous . . . I went back under the trees . . . She picked up her book . . . We did it again almost every day from then on, always in silence and as if neither of us knew the other one was there . . . In the evening, at dinner, we ignored one another . . . It was magical . . . God knows I've seen plenty of women masturbating since, in front of me and for my benefit . . . Or rather for their own via me . . . But for me Edith was the first, and the only one who seems to have done it for the love of the thing and because of the weather . . . She left eventually, and the next year it was as if nothing had happened. She was almost pleas-ant to me . . . But she didn't sit out by the greenhouse. And she read no more . . .

The world belongs to women. In other words, to death. Everyone lies about it. But one might as well put one's cards on the table. Though you could just as well say:

Lies aren't needed any more.
The world belongs to death.
So we might as well leave it to the women.

For a long time it's no longer been a question either of explaining the world or of changing it. It's *been* explained. It's *been* changed. We know all that! We know! You philosophers have been caught with your hand in the till! And so have you, you scientists, politicians of the harassed phenomenon! The world belongs to death . . . Isn't it obvious? Might as well leave it to the women . . . Isn't it natural? Like a rotten old bone for them to gnaw? Exactly! But what a cur, to say so! Too bad for the universal charlatan . . . The great everlasting charla-Satan . . . But Satan needn't worry—no one will listen to that piece of advice . . . It's been offered before, if I'm not mistaken . . . Not in the same form? Well, almost . . . Sinuous Socrates . . . Divine Jesus Christ . . . Enlightened Buddha . . . All men are mortal . . . And for good reason! Reason away! But Socrates is a man . . . Therefore Socrates is mortal . . . And for goodness' sake don't let him come whispering the opposite in our ear . . . By the way, do you know what hemlock really was, the potion drunk by Socrates, wonderful Socrates, who was starting to allow other people to doubt whether he really was a man and "therefore" mortal? Hemlock, the green brew of Hades . . . The Greek hell . . . A draught from the shades . . . Brrr! . . . Well, my dears, hemlock was first and foremost an unguent . . . An anaphrodisiac . . . Used in secret ceremonies . . . Ultraconfidential . . . Eleusis . . . When, in the sacred cave, in the depths of the mystic hole, the high priestess and the high priest performed their simultaneous simulacrum of copulation, guarantee of cosmic fertility, the high priest's penis used to be anointed with hemlock . . . This meant it remained in the sacred religious state of limpness . . . You

28

may say it was hardly likely, anyway, that a high priest would get a hard-on for a woman . . . Agreed . . . But still . . . You never know . . . In a sudden fit of ardour . . . The faithful had to be reassured . . . That papa and mama, or rather the two primal Principles, don't copulate on the sly like ordinary mortals . . . If you don't believe me, look it up in Frazer's *Golden Bough* . . . A mine of information on the nutty antics of the horde to which we have the doubtful privilege of belonging . . . Heaps of undeniable facts about the cult of the Mother whatchamacallit . . . Sacrifices here, murders there, and to crown all, offerings to keep the cycle of the seasons going strong . . . As Tertullian coolly summarizes it, quoted by Bossuet in his sublime Panegyric on St. Thomas of Canterbury (in 1668, when he was forty-one): "Our whole business in this world is to get out of it as soon as possible" . . . Suicide? Of course not . . . The world may be death, but death won't let you quit it . . . So you have to try to be there without being there; to feel as certain as possible that you're not there, while temporarily you are . . . Are you with me? No? Pity . . . Or so much the better . . . That's my experience, anyway . . . And it goes on like that, and even gets stronger, gets too much for me, installs itself inside me like a second life . . . I feel I have to express it before I too disappear into the silence of the infinite spaces . . . Or rather very finite spaces, incredibly finite and docile . . . Before I start to act as if I were dead . . . Of course, I *shall* die! . . . Of course! Of course! "So you do have a body after all!" as Flora yelled at me one day, exasperated beyond endurance by my amused detachment . . . Yes, of course, I have one, here it is, you can measure it, photograph it, film it, pinch it, stick pins in it, frighten it . . . And yes, it will die . . . What will that prove? Simply that I made a mistake in being born . . . Nothing more, nothing less . . . A mistake in being procreated, engendered, defined, imprisoned, obliged to follow the script that was forced upon me . . . My father never lied about this sort of thing . . . He would just never answer questions about it . . . Thus showing that the answers could only be vast, staggering, and ultradevastating . . . You'll understand later on . . . Each in his

29

own way . . . He used to sing to himself . . . It was my mother, of
course, like all the rest of them, who regarded it all as quite natural,
self-evident, justified, necessary . . . Why, though, apart from its
negligible value as propaganda? A kind of reparation . . . The truth
was too cruel . . . Compensation for the lack of a penis, that little
lump of meat which is the instrument of negation: hence the law of
gravity, the slope in the background, the killing power of corpses
. . . Indemnity . . . Amends . . . Otherwise death is greedy, sulks,
or has a headache . . . The frightful mystery of the family . . .
Men's expressions — scared, exhausted, always being disturbed, made
effeminate, debilitated, shriveled up, beskirted, domesticated, ma-
ternized, made into flabby mamas . . . And they're also the payers,
fetchers and carriers, chauffeurs, doers of odd jobs, stevedores and
general lackeys in the service of that endless, implacable bullshit
. . . Asphyxiated in double saucepans, on drips of insignificance,
caught in the lime of permanent house repairs . . . Families, I don't
even hate you, that would just be an indirect way of desiring you,
of believing in your secret, no longer of any interest except to
retarded homo naiveté . . . Mothers and homos, despite their seeming rivalry, are all guards in the invisible concentration camp; they
understand one another . . . In the beginning was the cold, next
you must keep the power plant going . . . Organic combustion . . .
The crematorium below . . . Spasms . . . Pregnancies . . . Desire
for same . . . Swelling, convex counterpart, filling in of crevices,
faults, cracks, fissures and their attendant tremors . . . The Womb,
The Prick . . . Gall bladder nearly full . . . We're getting there . . .
Anyhow, once you've started you've got to keep on, stick it out,
haven't you? Messianisms! Progress of projects and processes . . .
And now the fishpond is controlled; the prostitution is regulated;
the semen is selected and kept in banks . . . Discreet appointments
for females who want to step through the looking glass . . . Ting!
Abortion fee reimbursed! By the social security: there's the modern
novel for you . . . In other words, earlier literature is completely
out of date . . . No need to labor the point . . . Nothing has to be
altered except the technical details. There's nothing left to be explained but the camouflaged farce that's always the same. War,

however, is adopting a new slaughterhouse . . . Nice cozy nuclear power . . . Just imagine . . . No one's surprised or indignant anymore; they merely observe . . . What has become impossible is just the too subordinate, too proprietary phrase, the still photo . . . What we need now is uncertainty; the airy certainty of uncertainty; the grainy oblique . . . The hypo syringe and its dermic echo . . .

How bored I've been, when I come to think of it . . . The time I've wasted! Incredible . . . Amused as well as bored? Probably . . . Communicating vessels . . . Osmosis . . . Scales, balance, pendulum. Poetic justice . . . *Oisive jeunesse à tout asservie* . . . Idle youth enslaved by everything . . . *Plaisir d'amour ne dure qu'un instant* . . . The pleasure of love lasts but a moment . . . Whereas the chores last all your life . . . A touch of melancholy in your voice as you count up the costs . . . They've bored the pants off me, the ladies . . . I ought to give prizes. Flora comes first by a long way . . . Then Bernadette, she almost takes the cake . . . And then Deborah, with mitigating circumstances . . . Exceptions: Cyd, Ysia, Diane. No matter how much I cudgel my brains, they're the only three I can praise almost unreservedly . . . Usually I give them A^+ or A^-. Rarely A^{++}. Extremely rarely A^{+++}. Sometimes A^+? Occasionally A^+! Very often $^-$ $^-$. And I don't know how many !s. Pages of notebooks, little notches in time . . . What a stupid thing, and what a curse, to be attracted to women, magnetically, subterraneously . . . I'm waiting for it to wear off . . . Wear out . . . Physical need's a misfortune . . . A torture . . . An iron collar . . . But I think it may be beginning to loosen up a bit . . .

Let's start with Flora . . . What a jaw . . . You'd never suspect her of being a vampire . . . When I first knew her she had a reputation for absolute purity . . . A black diamond . . . Revolutionary fervor, no compromise, ideals, inflexible morals, the lot . . .

It used to amuse me to see men flock around her like choirboys around the holy sacrament . . . How she used to lord it over them, all those political windbags, those armchair theorists of the future! . . . She had poise, ease, decision . . . Her plump little body seemed driven by a hectic, tireless energy . . . Like her speech—jerky, broken, rapid, with little intermittent nervous laughs that made her voice go deeper . . . Disturbing laughs . . . And as I've said, her eyes were as guileless as those of a little girl taking her first communion . . . Or of a rather strange nun . . . There was something unbridled there in the background . . . Whenever she was worked up or wanted to put a point across, her voice grew shrill, an almost unbearable high-pitched vibration, a sort of squawk, no doubt developed in the course of many meetings in smoke-filled rooms and midnight cells . . . There was no interrupting her then; you couldn't get a word in edgewise . . . She'd just go on shouting louder and louder, not listening to anything, aiming at the psychological destruction of her opponent . . . Or at least of his eardrums . . . She often suffered from an earache herself, by the way . . . And from colds, bronchitis, and hoarseness . . . A walking mass of ravening blood . . . She rather reminded you of some sturdy female butcher . . . Young, and with the expression of a repressed madonna . . . A strange mixture of assumed interest in other people and contempt, coldness and calculated generosity, real cruelty and false genuine kindness . . . She was feared by men and hated by women . . . But she fascinated them all, sometimes to the point of obsession, nervous breakdown or slow yet feverish disintegration . . . She thought she was innocent and ingenuous . . . Pretended to adore Stendhal, though she'd never read him . . . She really saw herself as La Sanseverina, searching for her impossible hero, a master who would also be a servant, a human post-horse, a secular arm, a prince consort, an ideal manipulable double, a guide who could also be led . . . She had a detailed knowledge of nineteenth- and twentieth-century history . . . Of the vast and complex story of communism and everything related to it . . . Its motives, its secrets, its crimes . . . Not from books but from life . . . Everyday life . . . Whatever had nothing to do with that saga was for her unimportant, nonexistent . . . Vestiges of the Ancien Régime or of medieval obscurantism . . . Anarchism is a sublime enough doctrine, perhaps . . . Rather simple . . . With a fierce anti-god god, an implacable anti-Master Master . . . A Cynicism that, when you come down to it, has all the virtues needed to make it intellectually tenable . . . But Flora lived it as if it were an unquestionable religion . . . You could only see the same thing in a convinced Marxist, if such a thing still exists . . . In the third world? . . . Maybe . . . A Portuguese nun spawned by global expansion and the purulent, heady backlash from the charnel houses.

So Flora was at once marvelous and a bit ridiculous . . . Physically she was a fireball, not pretty but something more effective than that . . . Big nose; a sort of excitable twit . . . But sensually she was fantastic . . . That's where I came in . . . To give her professional help in clearing the bar of repression . . . A job requiring skill . . . Great skill . . . Like capping a burning oil well . . . Or like the work of a qualified exorcist . . . I think I can claim to be one of those too.

Anyhow, I maintain that the most interesting women come and will continue to come from continents or groups that have been brushed by the black wing of social upheaval . . . It's obvious . . . There aren't any more women aristocrats. The female from the bourgeoisie has told us all she had to tell. The petty-bourgoise is universal, but no more instructive. She's the same as her bourgeoise counterpart, only narrower or more harsh, with the same old psychological story already told a thousand times in the classics, plus an added element of frustrated social climbing. But I think, and the examples of Flora, Ysia and Deborah confirm it, that the exceptions will derive from the new steamroller . . . Change and strange discoveries will come from the East, from China, Czechoslovakia, Poland, and Hungary—and also from Iran, Angola, Cuba, Nicaragua . . . Or from the buried strata of Europe that still await their turn . . . It's there that the eroticism of the next century will explode . . . It's there, seething away, already . . . It creeps into the tired fibers of the old world, into its Bovarian languors: "Mademoiselle Albertine is gone!" Into the glands of the Western androgynate . . . It's not by arms, by bacteriological or meteorological warfare, or as between SS 20s and Pershing 2s that the fate of the modern temperate countries is being decided . . . It's in bed . . . Under the bed . . . In the hundred thousand ways of having it off at every hour of the day and night . . . In the brainwashing of the libido, masseur of the cortex, laser and scanner of anatomies . . .

A formidable stock of cells . . . A jumbled storm of muscles . . . I've seen only a few bits of the changing landscape, but I can tell you . . . A pubian apocalypse . . . An axial wiggle . . . A lick like a typhoon . . . You poor Frenchwomen don't know what's in store for you. Nor you poor American, German, English, Swedish and Dutch women. I think the Spanish women will come out of it a bit better . . . And the Italians . . . And the Argentines . . . But the thrust continues and it isn't going to stop . . .

Be that as it may, I managed to impress Flora almost at once . . . Though heaven knows she was suspicious . . . Rightly so . . . According to her standards I wasn't in the least serious—and that was just where she was in for a surprise . . . I'll say! . . . The fluency and accuracy of what I said! The way I said it! My humor! Sade versus Rousseau; Swift versus Bakunin; Jarry versus Trotsky; St. Augustine versus Marx . . . I upset her terms of reference . . . I stood for wild disorder . . . For a mistaken interpretation of history . . . For a strangely dynamic protest . . . And I was therefore an object of desire . . . She hesitated . . . She hesitated once more . . . She was lost.

I can see her now one summer day, lying on the bed . . . Our first time . . . She hardly knew how to make love. She kept shouting "No! no!" just as I was about to enter her . . . I was taken aback . . . How could someone so advanced, well-informed and subversive be so ignorant of the details? It was *too true* for her . . . But what astonishing progress soon afterwards . . . What amazing progress into vice . . . What a convincing proof that vice and purity are one and the same force, in which the devil immediately recognizes his own . . . The devil . . . That's to say, god's most valuable ally, his complete unconscious double . . . So very quickly Flora became an expert in passion . . . As earnest as if she were engaged in some special kind of ascesis . . . In a political or even a military campaign . . . Bravely into the breach . . . She started buying enticing underwear, which I imagine she tracked down through specialist magazines . . . She went to see films; she did research; she systematically set out to make up for lost time . . . I was the sorcerer's apprentice . . . The conductor unable to control his crazed orchestra . . . Now, hardly had I arrived at her place when she jumped on me, closed my mouth, came and sat on my lap, and attacked me as no doubt she supposed a man must do with a woman . . . I had to *be* a woman . . . What she wanted to avoid at all costs was not only thinking about what was happening, but also seeing me rather than herself . . . I was just a projection of herself . . . One of her pseudopods . . . The most problematic, of course, because of that inflatable appendage which seemed to intrigue her so much . . . She used to knead me at length with a kind of ever-new amazement, as in a fairy story, beauty and the beast, the pumpkin that turns into a coach, the mouse that becomes a mountain, the toad a unicorn, the ant a horse . . . Of course soon afterwards I could only turn back into an ant, a toad, a mouse, or a pumpkin . . . She was the one who thought, who understood what was happening . . . I couldn't, on top of all the rest, be cleverer or better informed than she was . . . Hence her resentment and fits of despair . . . And in short all the bitterness and reproach that usually, and today more than ever, end up governing the relationships between men and women . . . In reality, between women and their mothers . . .

The Plaint! The immense Complaint! Through steppe, tundra, Valhalla . . . Gusts . . . Groans . . . Gnashing of teeth . . . Oh, that almost imperceptibly tightlipped tone of voice vibrating with all the suppressed hatred in the world! Oh, those starchy accents, as of a sulky skeleton! I'd hear it still even from another galaxy. It's enough to make you want to disappear forever, when it doesn't make you shake inside with desolate laughter . . . How absurd! . . . How awful . . . I try to count up how many of them I've been able

35

really to laugh with, safely, the abyss taken note of and crossed . . .
Sometimes, at the beginning . . . But later . . . They have their
reasons, of course . . . Not all necessarily absurd . . . You have to
admit that men, including myself when it suits me, live in a permanent and facile state of illusion about them . . . Crediting them
with a power, with ulterior motives, sensations and a knowledge
about sensations they don't possess and shouldn't be expected to
possess, poor things . . . But one ought to try to clear the misunderstanding up . . . The great misunderstanding . . . It amounts to
believing in the Source . . . It consists in searching for the Treasure,
the Grail, despite all the evidence to the contrary, without realizing
that everything resides in the act of projection itself . . . Which, by
the way, is sometimes successful . . . In the case of "Open, Sesame!" the important thing is the word, the expression, the order,
the shaft of vibrations directed against the wall . . . It works in the
Arabian Nights, maybe . . . Otherwise, nothing happens . . . Two
and two make four . . . A breast is a breast; a thigh a thigh; a cunt
a cunt; an ass an ass . . . You have to transform the raw material if
you can wield the wand . . . Plunge in, get stuck into it, give of
yourself . . . Bengal tiger . . . Hindu tomb . . . Potions, talismans,
spells, amulets . . .

And that's just where the Plaint arises . . . Why have you deserted me, sighs the phenomenon when you withdraw, when the
magic's stopped working, when everything falls back to the everyday flatness . . . Why did you fill me with false hope by raising me
to a dimension alien to me? . . . Why can't you keep me afloat?
. . . One way or another every sexual act is an irreparable wound
. . . To the other person's narcissism . . . You impose an identification that can only lead to a fight to the death . . . You or me,
that's how it is, there can't be two of you, with sex. That's to say,
in time. That's to say, all the time . . . It's only women who think
it's possible. Who dream of having a lover who's become both
husband and mama, remaining a lover while accepting a mama's
cruising speed . . . The female *One* . . . The phallic mother created,
rediscovered at last . . . That's what's really expected of you, let me

tell you, gentlemen. You possess the erectile organ, you're passionate, you function, you screw; but at the same time you're stable,
faithful, affectionate, a good provider and minder of the store . . .
You sulk, but you make the jam . . . You ejaculate with one hand,
but with the other you look after the baby and dry the dishes.
That's their ideal: a man-cum-true-practical-woman . . . If you
object that all these different and indeed contradictory things can't
all be done at once, that the most highly evolved psyche can't stand
up to it, you get the Plaint . . . It's only natural . . . For the world
to be perfect at last, you ought to be capable of it, all of you . . . Of
this silence, gracious heroism . . . This triumphant dichotomy . . .
A world where men would at last be true mothers, young, mature,
always young and never-failingy mature, and women could at last
be eternal dazzled little girls . . . The socialism of tomorrow, perhaps . . . Who knows, it may be nearer than we think . . . To
judge, for example, from the report of the secret Committee which
met in Amsterdam five years ago . . . Flora unwisely showed it to
me . . . That's how I found out about FAM . . . The Front for the
Autonomy of the Matrix . . . The French section of WOMANN
. . . The World Organization for Male Annihilation and a New
Natality . . . Itself a part of the SGIC, the Sodom and Gomorrah
International Council . . . An old acquaintance . . . Far more advanced than the feminist liberation movements, including the French
MLF and Co., which have long been no more than its official
showcases . . . For a long time, countless symptoms have led me to
suspect the existence of another organization more secret, extreme,
intelligent and ambitious . . . And here it is . . . Kate suspects I
have a duplicate of the report . . . She'd like to know what use I
mean to make of it . . . When I first read it I could hardly believe
my eyes . . . I didn't know who to tell about it . . . Finally, the
situation grew so wild I went and showed it to Fals, the greatest
philosopher of our time . . . He read twenty or so typed pages,
threw up his hands, heaved four or five sighs, gazed wryly at me
over his glasses, and said: "I told them it would happen! . . . I've
always said so! . . . Of course it had to be you who copped it! . . .

Forget it, my boy . . . You weren't to know . . . Believe me . . .
It's inevitable . . . But forget it . . . Otherwise it'll do for you . . ."
A year later Fals himself had practically ceased all activity . . .

So what was it all about?

It was certainly a very strange document . . . Signed by delega-
tions from all over the world—Europe, North and South America,
the Middle East, Australia, Africa . . . It set forth a long-term
Program aiming at nothing more nor less than a secret takeover of
world power . . . Just another "Protocol," you may say . . . But
no, it wasn't a hoax, there was nothing crazy about it, it was all
perfectly reasonable and realizable . . . No violence . . . Nature
itself . . . Science . . . Control of reproduction, slant of same in
favor of women, placing of highly qualified agents in gynecological
sectors, suggestions for the education of children . . . As I came to
see later, this platform meant that the Gomorrah faction of the
SGIC had finally won out . . . But not without difficulty . . . For a
long while the hard Sodomite lobby had had the upper hand and
imposed its own plans and ideas . . . And then, especially from the
seventies on, the feminine element had gradually come to the fore
. . . Through persuasion, but the change also echoed to the new
balance of power . . . Which had been completely altered by the
contraceptive revolution and the great advances in genetics . . . It
was in the secret factions of the SGIC, as in all such official institutions as the Churches and so on, that the acceleration had been most
sudden . . . The effect was to demystify, demythologize, strip things
down . . . And indeed, what could stand out against this staggering
situation? Shouldn't one expect a laying bare, an X-ray, of all data?
A general change of direction, a universal sunflower effect?

Two things were especially striking in the Report . . . First, the
suggestion of a critical overhaul and sifting of the whole cultural
memory, with a recommendation that education, literature, and art,
together with all other elements regarded as sexist or macho, be
eliminated . . . Certain "geniuses" were to have their work either
extensively expurgated or else "relativized"—in plain language,
banned. Certain difficult cases (Mozart, for example) were to be
"presented"—i.e., set in the context of the age they lived in . . .

The second noticeable point: a merciless war was declared against "Judeo-Christianity" in general, held responsible for "patriarchal" tyranny, and against Judaism and Catholicism in particular . . . The Report claimed it wasn't in the least anti-Semitic, but insisted that the Bible be available in critical editions only where it couldn't be formally discouraged or suppressed (America and Northern Europe) . . . It was to be explained that it contained many unconscious traces of an earlier, sublime Religion which was maternal and tolerant, reassuring and ecologically sound, a Life Force maliciously slandered and suppressed by male fanaticism . . . The Catholic Church was a force to be destroyed . . . There was even mention of a terrorist attack on the Pope, with a suggestion that the blame be made to fall on Islam . . . Divide and rule was naturally the continual refrain . . . Jews against Christians, Jews and Christians against Arabs . . . Anything to do with monotheism was to be undermined, broken up and done away with . . . Anything that might stand in the way of a "free," scientific and "fulfilled" ordering of sexuality and of reproduction in and for itself was to be gradually reduced and abolished . . . The obviously out-of-date "opium of the people" slogan was to be replaced by "the poison of women" . . . This was to have a much more violent and profound effect, especially as the "people" were increasingly making use once more of abhorred religion to make their claims heard . . . (Shall we one day see women take up "Judeo-Christianity" again in order to preserve their elementary rights? That would be an amusing trick on history's part . . . But it would also mean that the problem had surreptitiously shifted its ground . . .)

The Report also dealt with the various philosophical systems, analyzing them in terms of their ability to accommodate the new religion. (There's no other word for it, even though the Report itself of course doesn't use it, and talks merely of facts and reason. But religion is nonetheless what it's all about, and Religion with a capital R—the oldest and most venerable known to man, unjustly overthrown and persecuted for two thousand years, but tunneling its way back into the daylight for the past two centuries . . . That's what is really meant by "the return of Nature," a phrase used in the Report . . . Used, rather, by the group of female Reporters who wrote it, and whose names by a strange coincidence included that of Bernadette, of whom more anon). Marxism? Yes, of course—it has done so much for the Cause . . . Still useful as a means of destabilizing the old world, as a hidden leaven in the lump, a law of evolution . . . To be encouraged, even, where physical conditions haven't produced a sufficiently raised consciousness in women . . . Elsewhere, to be supported only with reservations . . . As an internal aid, but not precluding other initiations and loyalties . . . Freudianism? Perhaps . . . Provided the more negative aspects are dropped . . . To be handled with care . . . Reformed, restructured . . . In particular, the ridiculous theory of penis envy was to be banned— an aberration, a veritable disgrace . . . A survival from the bourgeois Vienna of the twenties . . . Proof of Freud's own conformism and timidity . . . His jealousy of women . . . How could anyone imagine a woman wanting to be anything other than a woman? That her Completeness lacks anything? Another example of hidden patriarchal propaganda . . . It's well known that it's men who want to be women . . . Who are always dreaming of being pregnant . . . Of experiencing the infinite calm of gestation and the unspeakable joys of giving birth . . . In short, psychoanalysis if you insist, but only in the progressive sense, correcting its pessimism and other reactionary errors . . . Death is not to be mentioned . . . It's just another male fixation . . .

The Report ended by stressing the need to obtain the collaboration of as many men as possible, especially the most brilliant and influential. The first to be sought out were homosexuals, who by special adjustment of the statutes were to be allowed important privileges . . . They were really seen as the obvious priests of the organization . . . After all, *they* wouldn't oppose the restoration of the temple dedicated to the Great Mother, would they? . . . A long job . . . But despite ebbs, eclipses, accidents, setbacks . . . A great thing to strive for . . . A Faith . . .

Some further suggestions . . . Surveillance and restraint of boys' virility from their earliest years . . . Teaching of gracious and unfailing dependence on the mother, Japanese style . . . Devices for maintaining animosity between fathers and sons . . . Statistics to be kept on artificial insemination . . . Graphs, diagrams, forecasts . . .

Bernadette! Her name appeared at the foot of the page—a confirmation, for me, requiring no comment . . . I also knew the American, Dora . . . Formidable . . . An activist millionaire . . . She'd checked me out several times in New York . . . Two or three dinners . . . Was I friend? Or enemy?

Enemy.

As a matter of fact I'd spent all my time being sounded out . . . Watched . . . Approached . . . Studied . . . As a possible ally . . . A potential propagandist . . . A d'Alembert here, a Diderot there— you never know, he might come in useful . . . Even if I were more or less aware of what was going on it wouldn't have mattered . . . Money, favors, influence, passports, contacts, vanities, pleasures . . . WOMANN is remarkably well organized . . . It even has roving special agents . . . A traveler meets with inexplicable good fortune . . . Madonnas of the sleeping cars . . . Regular flights . . . Flirtations over the Atlantic . . . Easy crossings of the Alps . . . Coincidences concerning rooms in the same hotel . . . Brazil by night . . . Sudden interest by various people in your research, your character, your plans . . . Boys for some; respectable girls or women for the others . . . I've rarely had an affair that was at all known about without my girlfriend of the moment being contacted and sounded out . . . It forms a considerable part of the story of me and Deb . . . Deborah . . . My wife . . . What, didn't I tell you before that I was married? And father of a delightful little boy? Stephen? Of course! I'm a man of experience. I don't speak lightly or as an amateur. What is a man who hasn't had these experiences? A dreamer . . . It's true that anyone who has had this experience, this profound enlightenment, usually holds his peace . . . He can't say anything more . . . He knows too much about it . . . He's had it . . . He takes refuge in abstraction or modesty . . . What's the point? . . . No more illusions . . . And let us not despise the sublime kind of revelation you get from such acceptance of the common condition . . . In a way, the idea of the family is completely subversive these days . . . You've seen everything . . . Everything, and the opposite of everything, and the opposite of the opposite again . . . But you have to take a close look at it to understand how and why it still goes on . . . Instead of just repeating libertarian pieties . . . You need to evaluate the system, the wheels, the bearings, the slow and sometimes charming strings that help to work that all-powerful grinder . . . The penal colony . . . The supreme, mass-produced conformity . . . The charming, unwearying castratress . . .

Deborah has been criticizing me for a long time about my lack of inwardness . . . Of tact, sensitiveness, any sense of what's materially warm, colorful and interesting . . . To hear her you'd think she was the artist of the two . . . She looks at me clinically now . . . I'm someone who treats everything as a joke; a hardhearted caricaturist . . . I'm nervous, slow, clumsy, a bit of an elephant and a bit of a bear . . . Unlicked . . . Badly shaven . . . In too much of a hurry . . . Or else, to take the paramedical description further, I'm a kind of borderline case . . . If I understand it correctly, that's a vague kind of madman, an idiot lost between two worlds, a confuser of identities . . . Or else a nay-sayer . . . An autistic temperament . . . Mutic . . . Phobic . . . A big retarded baby, impassive and implacable . . . An egg . . . A ball . . . But with nice cheeks (yum yum!) . . . Or else a perverse polymorph . . . In any case, a nonadult, backward, obsessed with the imaginary breast . . . Unstable . . . Elusive . . . Unclassifiable . . . Too self-centered, incapable of opening up to anyone else . . . And stingy into the bargain! Or else thoughtlessly extravagant . . . Have I left something out? Probably . . . Anyhow, you don't want to believe all that, says he more or less sweetly . . . Marriage is a variable kind of purgatory . . . A school of sour affection . . . A monastery of consummate humility . . . A college of limitation . . . Anyone who's been able to stand that can stand anything . . . No quarter given . . . Ceaseless reminders of faults . . . Aura of nervousness, words out of place, examples of holding things back, of indifference, of developing protective antennae, of slyness . . .

Deborah deplores my casual approach . . . She thinks I ought to tell stories, take trouble over the plot, "set the scene" . . . Describe subtle sensations, unbend, lose myself, get involved . . . The characters ought to confront one another, size on another up, exchange looks, silences, meaningful hints and allusions heavy with desire . . . It ought to feel more like the cinema . . . For ages she's reproached me with never going out . . . With not wanting to see the latest film . . . With not knowing about the continuing great adventure of the screens . . . With not caring about the phenomena, the glitter, the shimmer, the made-up images of the moving stairway to nothing . . . In a nutshell, with not caring about life . . .

What's Deb reading at the moment? . . . Mishima . . . *The Golden Pavilion* . . . She sometimes shows me passages she admires . . . The hero stammers . . . Or has a club foot . . . Or only one eye . . . Or limps . . . Or has a hump . . . Or squints . . . Or has only one arm . . . I can't remember . . . He feels dizzy or has hallucinations looking at a tree stump . . . The moon-like countenance of his beloved appears to him between the quivering reeds in a garden full of nocturnal fragrance . . . A bird sings sadly in the distance . . . The hero is full of longing . . . He's waiting for something, he doesn't know what, he's always on the point of making a crucial discovery, the secret of love . . . He suffers . . . Others reject him . . . The countenance of his beloved seems to reject the universe . . . But he doesn't abandon his quest . . . Time passes . . . The vegetation grows denser . . . The misunderstanding also . . . There's talk of reincarnation, perhaps . . . No, that's another book—*The Sea of Fertility* . . . Or *The Decay of the Angel*. Unless it's *Confessions of a Mask* . . . The narrator's struck by a painting depicting St. Sebastian being transfixed by arrows . . . The elegant, muscular, effeminate body, unjustly tortured, is distorted with pain in the dusk . . . The blood flows from the cruel wounds inflicted on the beautiful milk-white body . . . The anguish is worsened by the rising tide (oh yes, it all takes place by the sea) . . . The waves come up and cover the naked body of the narrator, exposed to the sun . . . Not long after, he's stunned by a dragon tattooed on the chest of a perspiring young workman who's accompanied by some friends, while he himself is having a boring time with a young woman whom he doesn't even think he loves anymore and who is on the point of revealing some strange proclivities . . . Deb's very impressed . . . It must be the part of her that loves the heat, the beach, children, and plants . . . Her naive and admirable belief that something must be happening . . . That something is taking place . . . That all this is meant to lead to something . . . A Meaning . . . A dénouement . . . A plot, in fact . . . Ah well, they may not have been happy but there was always plenty of yelling in their apartment . . . Once upon a time there was the fact that once upon a time . . . Fairies . . . Folklore . . . Tales . . . Songs . . . I can see her with Stephen . . . Delighted to tell all the stories and tell them again in detail, and repeat the repetition, over and over again . . . Snow-White . . . Little Red Riding Hood . . . The Sleeping Beauty . . . Alice . . . Cinderella . . . Pinocchio . . . The Seven Dwarfs . . . Babar . . . The magic island . . . The enchanted pipe . . . The three little pigs . . . The fox . . . The grasshopper, the ant, the duck, ambiguity, the area between good and evil, the finding of the pearl, the pink whale, the kind-hearted crocodile . . . They enjoy themselves . . . They laugh . . . He asks for more . . . She starts again . . . Magic . . . Records, cassettes . . . One morning early I met the train . . . Little pine tree, king of the forest . . . *Alouette, gentille alouette* . . . They enjoy themselves . . . They do jigsaw puzzles . . . Stephen's happy . . . Papa? He's working . . . We don't quite know what at . . . Time will tell . . .

That was a grand passion, Deb . . . A splendor . . . A dream icon . . . A fire, an intelligence . . . The most intelligent woman I've met . . . Painting . . . Wisdom . . . Sophia . . . Mosaic . . . The black eyes alive everywhere in the face inside the cupolas . . . Looming up like a vibrant shade from Pompeii or Ravenna, with gestures that seem to belong to another world . . . She was a student . . . Came to interview me about something to do with linguistics . . . Byzantium . . . I couldn't keep away from her . . . Though I was leading rather a hectic life at the time . . . A life of debauchery? . . . I'll say! . . . No respite . . . Afternoons, evenings, nights . . . Three or four affairs going at once, one-night stands, hookers, the lot, all jumbled up together . . . Inspired insouciance . . . And I was quite right . . . Am I glad I did it! . . . Bars . . . Specialist joints . . . The one in the Rue X, with its little avenue of chestnut trees leading to a small private townhouse where the shutters were always closed; and the one in the Rue Z, with its majestic and soporific old elevator; and the one in the Rue E, like an aquarium; and the one on Avenue W, with its smooth, old-fashioned service . . . The Bois . . . Pickups . . . At twenty or thirty I did what men wear themselves out trying to do at fifty or sixty . . . Their evolution is from forced glumness to glossy-eyed and decrepit laxity; mine is from wild libertinism to mystical contemplation . . . Each his own way . . . I seem to remember I didn't have much money . . . It all went on enjoyment . . . And *they* didn't charge me very much either . . . Which only goes to show I had an innate sense of discontinuity and the preventive break . . . That's how you know you're getting old . . . When you hesitate about clearing out . . . When you have to think about checks . . . It's amazing how unconscious you can be of your own value in terms of raw flesh . . . I could have been a pimp if I'd wanted to, in those days . . . A girl even suggested it to me once, a professional with a bit of education, I thought she was joking, but no, I was twenty-two, a decent screwer, good at sucking, probably quite amusing . . . Maybe I *was* a bit of a pimp, actually, without realizing it . . . The way I never asked women for anything . . . Was never the first to call up . . . Never expected anything from them . . . If they want to they want to . . . If not, it's all the same to me . . . A question of independence, of intoxication with solitude . . . I'm always surprised when I see how scared other people are of being alone . . . For me it's always been the most fundamental pleasure, eyes open on the empty dawn, interminable evenings, the incredible beauty of walls . . . I like eating on my own in restaurants; I like going for three days without speaking to anyone . . . I like to feel time passing for no particular purpose, anywhere, to sleep, to *spend* time, to feel as if I were time itself hastening to its own destruction . . . I'm here, still more or less here, and one day I won't be here anymore, so I quietly mark out my own place in the comic strip, the swiftly moving atmosphere . . . I feel as if I'm passing through . . . Pleasantly, easily . . . I'm not afraid . . . Mankind's unhappiness comes from not being able to remain alone in a room? Yes, with Pascal on the bedside table, that ought to be enough for the long night of one's stay among men . . . Very strong coffee, whisky, tobacco, radio . . . And let them all come! . . . The pages! . . . And let time take its time! . . . Every so often I take a room in a hotel not far from where I live . . . I see everything as if I were a visitor to my own neighborhood, I feel as if I were researching after my own death into my own life in this part of the world . . . In Paris I tell myself I'm in London . . . In London, that I'm passing through Rome . . . But the best city for living on several musical staves at once is New York . . . A Chinese week . . . Another that's Puerto Rican . . . Yet another that's Italian . . . Chinese strippers . . . An art, an encirclement . . . I start thinking about Ysia again . . . The docks, the siestas on the pontoons on the Hudson, the way the planks heated up in the fierce sun, the gulls of Long Island . . .

Some of them understand this and avoid you from the outset, can't get away fast enough . . . They're the ones who have their own interests most at heart . . . And then there are the others— those who are curious, and the saints, the witches, the crazy ones and the half-crazy ones; that's to say the large minority, who cling and are hooked . . . There's a writer's syndrome just as there's a priest's . . . It's very different from that of the show-business star . . . More essential, visceral, in the bones . . . Connected with the basic nerve, with the reverse of the fabric . . . In direct competition with the oven of the womb . . . Mothers recognize it without fail . . . Sophocles' mother included . . . All important works of art are traces of this bitter struggle . . . To come out into the free air, be born, emerge from mere physical birth; too speak something more than the word that's been injected into you . . . To show one wasn't born just to make up the numbers; and that one doesn't die according to the prescribed arithmetic . . . That the crime of living may at least be known; that it may be noted and noticed . . . For a little while . . . For eternity . . .

Deborah's life with me is a strange kind of escapade . . . Not funny though, in a way . . . I love her very much . . . Courage, tenacity . . . She's great . . . For an American from the South, like me, even though I've long been Europeanized; for an American Catholic (the same as Flannery O'Connor . . . What, you don't know her work! A woman of genius! Read her *Wise Blood*, at least) she's really another continent, a perpetual discovery . . . Admittedly the Bulgarians are not just anybody . . . Communists now, or rather Russian, Russified . . . Deb "chose freedom" in 1966 . . . But, before, they were Bogomils . . . Cathars . . . A great tradition you Frenchmen may find among your Southern troubadors and Albigensians . . . No? . . . Perhaps the only revolt that has ever made French centralism shake in its shoes . . . Anyhow, you crushed it with particular violence . . . Monstégur . . . The marvelous civilization of the South . . . Dante . . . Pound . . . But that's enough literature . . . If now, down there, you manage to lever off the iron cowl of socialist education, you soon find underneath the orthodoxy the dark old vein of Manicheism . . . The basic dualism . . . A fabulous heresy . . . Perhaps heresy itself . . . Dogma's own hidden, repressed and shameful truth . . . The world was created; it is ruled, dominated and programmed by a Principle which is absolutely Evil . . . The good god has absolutely nothing to do with this sinister business—he's far away, somewhere else, above and therefore innocent of this frightful trick . . . The Negative Principle, the Demiurge, aided by a whole series of intermediaries each more grotesque, hungry, and narrow than the last, is permanently at war with the Principle of Good, the Father of Light . . . No reconciliation is possible between Darkness and Light . . . We exist amid a mixture of the two, but one day the great division will take place, when all that is pure is separated from all that is foul. In this world, the pilgrim or Perfect One must gather together his own sparks of light and rid himself of the murky darkness within him; he must

47

free himself from all will and desire and avoid compromising himself with the powers that be . . . His search for truth and liberty arouses fierce jealousy in the Achontes, the Master's henchmen of both sexes . . . They sense it when anyone is trying to escape their clutches, and do all in their power to prevent it . . . They use distortion, pressure, and mental stress in a continual attempt to cause the tumors and pustules of envy . . . The Manicheans have had a very bad press, and still do . . . They're seen as the source of all fanaticism . . . Of totalitarianism . . . Of the folly—which is, after all, very widespread—of believing in an absolute Good on the one hand and a no less absolute Evil on the other . . . "Manichean" is an insulting term, really meaning paranoiac . . . But is it a psychological trait that's universal? As it were, the reflection of an indirect truth? . . . But the problem isn't to impose a Good *in* the world, as everyone affects to believe . . . That's obviously impossible, unless you go in for fraud . . . A contradiction in terms . . . It's the eternal, ever-renewed mistake that's always being trotted out . . . But Good is not of this world . . . "My kingdom is not of this world" . . . Well, well . . . "I pray not for the world" . . . Well, well, well . . . "The prince of this world is judged" . . . Well! . . . The world is a vale of tears . . . *In hac lacrimarum valle* . . . Dust thou art, and to dust shalt return . . . How could a doctrine like that prevail and convince people? How could it be made to serve any kind of power? On the contrary, all powers are immediately up in arms against it . . . I don't recommend it . . . It's not tenable . . . Everyone has to manage as best he can . . . Keep quiet, say nothing, don't tell anyone anything . . . Above all don't let on . . . The slightest admission or confidence would be fatal . . . The Thing would pounce on you in a flash . . . Keep calm, say nothing, exercise self-control, follow your course . . . Keep quiet, and quieter still . . . Don't let anyone suspect you're trying to break loose or sneak out . . .

It's probably this "Manichean" aspect of things that gives Deborah her duality . . . Which would mean I didn't meet her by chance . . . On the one hand she's extremely realistic; I've rarely seen anyone so good at coping; at relying solely on her own strength and the application of her own will . . . *She* certainly believes absolute Evil is at work everywhere all the time and throughout the whole of history . . . On the other hand she's a complete idealist . . . So much so that it's often *I* who have to urge *her* to be more compromising and jesuitical . . . In order to confuse and foil the enemy. Deb and I actually shocked people . . . Merely because we loved one another, and what's more loved one another happily . . . Husbands, love your wives . . . Wives, love your husbands . . . But the effect is incredible . . . A cyclone . . . A storm in an anti-stoup . . . A challenge to civilization . . . Archaic . . . Dangerous conformism . . . The dreadful happiness of Laius and Jocasta was the cause of the tragedy . . . No more tragedy . . . Mama and Papa absolutely aware of the relative nothingness of the dark . . . My god, my god . . . You're triggering off mass Oedipus-ism, fully paid-up identification . . . Man a prey to woman's desires and inverted aversions; woman pursued simultaneously by men and women . . . Just as if you and she were the universal parents, the primal yin-yang couple, all possible misunderstanding converging upon you . . . People take you for her and her for you . . . I've had women who really desired only Deb; she's been adored by men who thought only of me . . . Masks . . . Masquerades . . . Ballets and lanterns . . . It's amusing for a while . . . Eighteenth-century ambiance . . . Then it gets downright tedious and exhausting . . . Roll on, Ithaca! . . . And now there are female as well as male suitors . . . You're up for grabs everywhere, and the market's a thousand times larger than in Homer's day . . . Crazy small ads! . . . Agencies! . . . Women are used to it . . . They've got an instinct for finance, investment, stocks, and shares . . . But we have to learn it . . . Wanted! — all the same things as *they* want . . . Girl, sensible, modest, enterprising; married woman anxious for a fling; senior woman executive with good portfolio . . . Dido . . . Nausicaa . . . But marriage always and everywhere . . . Never-ending publicity . . . Don't believe anyone who tells you different . . . Doctored surveys, rigged opinion polls, propaganda, jamming . . . And all the time and everywhere it's just a question of real estate . . . Where? . . . How? . . . Why? . . . I had a stunning revelation about it one day . . .

49

You'll say, what about children and so on? Yes, of course . . . They always want a child . . . *A child* . . . In one form or another it always tends toward that . . . In other words toward a fundamental negation of sex . . . But there's something else too . . . More extreme . . . Hidden — just . . . More monumental . . . More pyramidal . . . Crucial . . . It hit me right in the eye when Flora, a fierce advocate of free love for others, seeing I didn't want to get a divorce because of her, cried: "But that means we won't be buried together!" This was serious. Very serious. Appalling . . . The grave! The ashes! The bones! The vault! The mingling of miasmas before the shared eternal silence! The underground whisperings before the shinbones' meeting face-to-face! In the moonlight! Forever! . . . Women are necrophiles . . . Just scratch the surface and you'll see . . . A word to the wise! And good luck to you!

That a man should lead his own life as he wants and protect his own interests and those alone, that's what FAM can't bear . . . Or WOMANN . . . Or the SGIC . . . To mention but a few . . . It's a long time now since the Name, the Name of the Father, disappeared, to be dismembered and swallowed up in initials and references, social security numbers and the clacking of computers . . . A matter of principle . . . Mathematics . . . Regimentation . . . No free enterprise . . . No small farms or plots of land . . . General expropriation . . . No pockets of resistance against the great plan for the future . . . Supermarkets, hypermarkets . . . Cozy kholkozes . . . Checking up twenty-four hours a day . . . No clandestine endogamy . . . Keep it moving around . . . Impose exchange controls . . . No messing things up with anyone's own beliefs . . . Own ideas about death . . . As few individuals as possible . . . 1984? Yes, only of course much more subtle, less obvious . . . 1984 is really just the date when the global view of human time is revealed . . . When it emerges at last that things have always been as they are . . . Counted, measured, accumulated, nullified . . .

That they exist merely to move the tide forward . . . To hide the reprieved corpses, the torrent of slime . . . .

So they were after me . . . That's where Bernadette and her crew came in . . . And where admittedly a few things went wrong and Deb began to get on my nerves . . . Bernadette, Kate, Flora—a trap, a net with plenty of other nooses to it . . . Closing in . . . Sisters of the mist . . . Accomplices in the unconditional rehabilitation of Eve . . . Together when it's a question of *against*, but when it comes to *for*, no way they can really agree . . . All of them against us . . . But every woman for herself . . . And all of it full of theoretical, parapolitical justifications . . . And, as always, at the grassroots the poorer and not so clever ones are active, march, put up posters and have or think they have opinions . . . But at the top, also as usual, what you find is mere calculation . . . Administration, horse trading, deals . . .

Bernadette is one of the strangest and most repellent human beings I've ever met . . . One of the most fascinating too, in a way . . . It's difficult not to be attracted by perversity carried to an extreme . . . To an abscess of fixation . . . A point of no return . . . I can see her now in her black dress, always the same one . . . Hidden inside it, with her piercing glance; looking like a sick person finally cured . . . They say some people can't open their mouths without lying . . . She didn't need to open her mouth . . . Her very presence was a lie . . . Massive . . . Slippery . . . Frozen . . . Impregnable . . . Boris was the same, in a masculine version, as we shall see . . . Fals too, in a way . . . Something cunning, careful, almost imperceptibly "put on" about them all the time . . . A sarcastic air of long-suffering . . . Well-adapted madmen have a mysterious angle on things, whereas common or garden fools are more direct . . . There's a certain dirtiness about the former . . . Not physical—a moral or spiritual dirt . . . A kind of pale secretion, like that from a runny nose or a rheumy eye . . . A twist to the hair . . . Though no visible serpents hiss at you from their heads . . . An aura as of a Medusa of antimatter . . . In the case of Bernadette you had the feeling that a piece of chemically pure

51

wickedness had landed right in front of you . . . A meteorite . . .
She crouched in her hollow as in a machine-gun nest . . . Solidified
intergalactic matter . . . A lump of hate fallen as the result of some
obscure disaster . . . In her presence and that of a few others of
both sexes who are like her in the vampire world we're now entering, I'm filled with a kind of precarious admiration . . . One of
Sade's characters says somewhere, when faced with some excessive
monstrosity: this creature is too malevolent for us to hurt him . . .
He'll do mankind as much harm as possible . . . And as we're not
fond of the human race . . . Still, poor old humanity, it doesn't
know the kind of volcano it's sleeping on . . . One might add, more
loftily, that you can feel a certain respect for things that unwittingly
but evidently suggest that there's a law of divine vengeance . . . Or
if not divine, then logical . . . Acid seared by itself . . . Revealing
the foundations of things . . .

I've noticed that people have to have some kind of deformity in
order to be singled out for high negative office . . . Bernadette has
a bad limp . . . Boris has a glass eye . . . Or some nervous or
muscular hallmark . . . Magic . . . It's always disturbing . . .
Something missing, some scar, a hint of the other side of the canvas
. . . The mists of myth . . . Fals, who is or at least was for a long
time the master of them all, male and female, had to overcome a
lisp . . . A lisp on its way to becoming a case of paraplegic aphasia
. . . Various sorts of rituals and shamanism . . . I've been there and
I know what I'm talking about . . .

It was Bernadette who started FAM . . . It functioned secretly at
first . . . In specially selected drawing rooms and influential boudoirs . . . The usual story: the smart areas of town and the sticks,
and an ingenious link between the two . . . The apartment by the
river, the meetings in suburban cells . . . Unlike the others, Bernadette
always dressed the same way . . . Severe, black, white, no nonsense
. . . She wasn't at all well off . . . And then suddenly a lot of
money . . . American, of course . . . That was how FAM suddenly
acquired a luxurious office, started its own regular publications,
organized package tours and advertised for staff . . . The whole

thing had been seen to be viable . . . Bernadette had passed the test
. . . International devilry isn't open to just anybody . . .

I met her during the feverish, heroic period . . . We tended to
meet in secret because she was already quite well known . . . She
had to pretend to be a bit of a lesbian . . . A lesboid . . . No future
otherwise . . . I know something about it—I half kill myself trying
to seem a Sodomian . . . Otherwise it holds me back; it harms my
business affairs; it doesn't do my reputation with the public any
good . . . What a reputation I'd have as a writer if I could manage
it better . . . Be more ambiguous . . . More convoluted . . . More
Platonic . . . More subtle . . . Alas, coarse I am and in bad taste I
remain . . . Not in the least educational . . . Forsaken . . .

Bernadette was supposed to be a lesbian. She was anything you
liked . . . In other words, nothing . . . She wasn't interested in all
that . . . I don't think I ever met anyone with such a complete
block. Her libidgram was completely flat . . . For her it was all in
the intellectual spark . . . Total transfer into the will to power . . .
Frigidity is putting it too strongly . . . She was frigiform as well.
Nothing. Not the smallest sign of an involuntary twitch . . . Her
mouth open, letting itself be devoured . . . Awaiting penetration as
if it were some kind of medical formality . . . Corridor . . . Chimney . . . Tunnel . . . Entirely passive . . . After three or four times
I decided that was that . . . I behaved as politely as possible with a
view to calling it a day . . . But no, I was supposed to go on . . .
She had no idea . . . For her, that's how it was: a woman put up
with a kind of petrified rape, after which she was allowed to complain about it bitterly and at length . . . If I screwed her I ipso facto
"owed" her something . . . I had to screw her in order to owe her
something . . . It was there, I think, in a chilling cataclysmic light,
that I at last saw what the fundamental contract is . . . The trick of
tricks, the bond, the ropes . . . The others at least manage to put on
a show unconsciously. They instinctively go through the ritual
animal motions. They play on male gullibility, which doubtless is
unlimited in this connection. And consequently in all others. Just a
matter of degree or scale . . . But Bernadette—and this is what

made her in a way pathetic and sublime—was too proud to be able to force herself into any kind of play-acting. Lying there, black, glittering and accusing, she was like a witness at some immemorial and eternal trial . . . Testifying to the vile fate meted out to women. Demonstrating the torture to which they were subjected. So I could see passing across her face a whole procession of mothers and grandmothers muffled up in women's fated darkness . . . She was there before them, responsible for them, experiencing in her turn the brutal passion of the torturer and offerer up of sacrifice . . . I was supposed to enter into the part . . . To be the perfect Nazi. And, as a result, solvent, credit-worthy . . . She obviously didn't ask herself for a moment whether or not the act in question was agreeable to me on such conditions . . . As a man, I was assumed to like it for its own sake . . . They believe in men. They're prepared to undergo martydom to prove that men exist, that they function, that they never think of anything but sex, that they're utterly controlled and enslaved by it. For women the universe is shaken to its foundations when, having shown that you *can* go along with it all mechanically, you suddenly make it plain that you could also just as easily, and without regret, do nothing at all . . . Then they really are at a loss . . . It doesn't make sense . . . The only time I ever saw Bernadette really beside herself, saw her leap up and shoot out of the room like an outraged streak of lightning, was when, in the midst of a long silence, I said quietly: "You know, I can easily do without women altogether" . . . It was the absolute insult. Blasphemy. Murder in the cathedral. Desecration of the host. She fled that day, Bernadette, limping, wounded, shame . . .

I found all this horribly unpleasant, but at the same time I have to admit it produced a certain mental excitement . . . Bernadette was very much in love with a well-known, perfectly official, fickle as a butterfly homosexual. She was always talking about him. He was her god. The fact that *he* didn't desire her physically was intoxicating. A confirmation. Ecstatic suffering. The very basis of her belief in women. Strange? Not at all. You just have to get used to making out the real logic behind the opera . . . The tragedy, if you prefer . . . A laugh and the whole thing disappears . . . Mists, castles, graveyards, apparitions, bats, screeches, underground passages, oozing walls, tortures . . . Sheets swirling through the darkness . . . Pyres and pallets . . . Sighs, swoons, brooms, sabbaths and Goyas . . . . . . You could say I've floated my life along on that secret, permanent, exorcizing peal of laughter . . . Audible only to me . . . I daren't even say how enjoyably . . . Innate arrogance . . .

We did a lot of talking, Bernadette and I . . . We didn't really do much else . . . But the time passed quickly; she was clever, her ambition whetted her imagination and her inveterate mythomania produced plenty of waspish witticisms. She pulled everyone to pieces with steely unscrupulousness . . . She hated women, really . . . But she hated men even more for not seeing how hateful women were. And since the feeble males were stupid enough to be taken in by the equally stupid females, she had decided to back the second against the first, and lead them, proles of new hope, toward a fiercer and more conscious revenge . . . Not very wise of her to tell me all this . . . She must have thought of me as to all intents and purposes dead . . . Why? I've often wondered, and not only with her. I conclude, in the end, that they think the genuine reality of things can't be conveyed. And that even if it could be, no one would believe it . . . And that's not altogether untrue, not altogether silly . . . The immense duality . . . Sentimentality on one side, vileness on the other . . . *E cosi fan, fan, fan* . . . In all innocence . . . Ideals on top, shit underneath . . .

What strikes me most thinking about it now, is that she didn't once bother to find out if it worked for me . . . Didn't pay the slightest attention . . . Ejaculation? Never heard of it. Didn't want to know. Ever . . . Penis? A ghost . . . I've already told you what she wanted: for you to feel indebted. Indebted for the inestimable gift of her own person, if you don't mind! . . . One day, in a hotel lobby, she told me, with a shattered expression, that she'd forgotten to take the pill. Then as soon as we were upstairs on the bed she whispered, "And now make me explode" . . . That's the sort of situation that shows whether a man's been properly brought up or not. For a start he doesn't laugh. And then he does as required. No sperm? Her sort don't feel the difference. It's very common; com-

55

monplace, even. Flora was suspicious into the bargain. She absolutely insisted on seeing me produce a few drops, in front of her very eyes or into her mouth, to make sure . . . And then she'd start to complain . . . Because that proved I'd got something out of it too, and had therefore exploited her . . .

Another thing, surprising but essential, was that Bernadette and her female friends were all supposed to be being "analyzed" . . . And here's where we enter the latest lab . . . *Du côté de chez Fals* . . . In the psychical bubble chamber. The nuclear reactor . . .

Phew, what a relief! It's Cyd . . . I was afraid it might be Flora asking me to look over one of her articles . . . In other words, write it . . . It's always the same . . . Urgent . . . The *Journal*'s waiting for it . . . So you have to go and see her and improvise something on whatever the subject happens to be while she takes notes . . . Later on you have to go back again, sort out what she's written, then bash out something presentable on the typewriter . . . She always produces ten times too much, and all jumbled up . . . Involved, muddled . . . Slatternly . . . But with a few flashes . . . All this after we've made love . . . Payment in kind . . . Nothing for nothing . . . The number of incendiary proclamations I must have drafted for her in English—protests, outlines of lectures, chapters of books, prefaces, speeches . . . On all kinds of subjects, according to what happened to be going on in world politics . . . I always find an original angle, or course . . . Paradoxical, appealing . . . Aphorisms . . . Which then fly all over the globe, from Belgrade to Rio, London to Dakar . . . In Flora's sharp, passionate, scolding little voice, making (as she thinks) reactionary governments tremble . . . But what a bore . . . And what a chore . . . The elegant, unsuspected ghost writer . . . Professional lover and top stylist . . . Even so, Flora thinks I don't do enough . . . In her view I ought to take care of her correspondence, her shopping, the decorating of her apartments, her airplane tickets, her vacations . . . In short, to be her secretary. She's got the bossy, peremptory voice of a born employer . . . That's the only surviving form of the bourgeoisie . . . The pink and red middle-class . . . Busy with the latest revolutionary study . . . The third world . . . And a very effective network it is, from what I—at a distance—can see . . .

But if I ever let Flora feel she bores me to death, she starts to cry . . . I'd rather give her a quickie than listen to her whining . . . She whines anyway, but not quite so much . . .

But no, I'm spared—the call's from Cyd . . . Yes, okay . . . Be seeing you, then . . . I like it when she calls me like that, when it suits her . . . It suits me too; we get on well together . . . So here I am at her place. I look at her, lying there naked on her balcony in the sun . . . She's beautiful . . . She makes me want to be foolish and use the word "volupté." There I go—Baudelaire: *mon enfant, ma soeur . . . Luxe, calme . . .* It doesn't happen all that often now in this vile world of ours . . . Very vile, eh? More and more so . . . The apartment looks out over the Bois de Boulogne. It's hot. We have some champagne. Listen to some Scarlatti sonatas. Kirkpatrick 209 . . . When Scarlatti — may his name be blessed forever and ever — accompanied the Spanish Court on their travels in 1729 . . . Seville . . . Granada . . . The Sierra Nevada . . . I do love that sonata . . . Lively, snappy, rhythmical, the pang of senseless time, triumph over screeching death, joy . . . A farandole, a spiral, a puff or cuff of air   Isn't it a bit of a paradox that I can share my love of Spain with Cyd, who's English, whereas Flora, who's Spanish, is more or less immune to everything that makes up her own culture . . . Music just doesn't get through to her. Not a note . . . Hey, come to think of it, it's quite simple: I only love women who are capable of listening to harmony, melody, the unfolding fugue and particles of time . . . I ought to make up my mind on those grounds alone . . . As Shakespeare says, the man or woman who has no music in his or her soul is dark as Erebus . . . Music—in other words gratuitousness, magnanimity, tolerance, pearly indifference . . . Watteau? A little breeze, the leaves stir, the harpsichord twangs . . .

We kiss. Then we do it again. And again. And again. We lick each other all over . . . She sucks me, I suck her . . . She eats my balls,

57

chewing gently . . . Draws out my penis with her long slim fingers, lingers there on the tip, on the tip of the tongue . . . And then we take each other, really take each other, heat to heat, tremor to tremor . . . With some of them you come at the same time, rarely, madly, and then somehow, you don't know why, it goes, goes off . . . But with others it's not the same — when you make love to them it doesn't have the same effect on your breathing, on the way your days begin . . . You have to resort to the contortions of perversion . . . No vibes . . . Who's there, who isn't—how strange it is . . . "You're my silky dog," Cyd says, or some other idiocy . . . But one glance of her green eyes makes me come a bit more inside . . . We even play at cheap literature together . . . Cheap literature is marvelous—the pornographic stereotype . . . We stay like that, waiting, inside one another—I in her, but she in me too . . . She gets on top of me . . . We play with my prick, which becomes a sort of radioactive, hallucinatory third person . . . "I love you, I adore you." We know we're practicing magic—black, white, in color . . . A great act of exorcism . . . We laugh . . . We talk to each other again, the same little phrases . . . We know how ridiculous they are, how fragile and far-fetched, but never mind, we come . . . And we tell the whole world to go to hell, and our eyes tell each other that's what we're doing . . . We know what we're doing . . . We wish harm on other people, as much harm as possible on all of them whoever they are, whether they belong to the past, the present or the future . . . Just as others have done and will go on and on doing—that's what gives painting its dance of colors amid the drawing, and music its resonance beyond the silvery sounds . . . She turns over and presents her ass, and I take her that way . . . Her buttocks jiggle toward me, she parts and closes her legs to intensify the sensation, her fingers twist strands of her blonde hair against her cheek, she lets out a good yell, relaxes, draws in deeply, turns over and kisses me . . . Thanks me . . . She's just enjoyed making love to herself, close to me but in violent opposition . . . She's pleased with both of us . . .

"What are you up to these days?"
"Writing."

"Well?"

"Not too badly."

"What?"

"A novel. Ordinary things. The fever of today. Men, women. Boredom, thought, glimmerings."

"A realist novel? You?"

"Call it that if you like. Figurative. Emotive. Distorting and transforming. Not all Picasso's paintings were cubist. That may even be why—"

"Listen to you!"

"There are a few things I want to say straight out. Rub people's noses in them."

"Am I in it?"

"Of course."

"Bastard! All right, watch out."

And she kisses me. The idea of a writer arouses her. The word "novel" acts like magic. And what kind of a novel? American? Fitzgerald? Bellow? Roth? Mailer? Or is it more like a thriller— Mafia, drugs, dollars? In the great tradition? You'll see . . . Anyhow, it gets to her. It really does. Indirect effect, via physical influence, of the Muse on the hormones . . . But transposed, right? Idealized? Not too crude? Watch out or the women won't read it . . . Or won't buy it, which is much more serious . . . Funny, it has to be all or nothing in this. I mean it has to be love, more or less passionate love, or hate. The first, of course, usually followed by the second . . . But also, very rarely, love for love, love playing on love — as on a stage, as on a musical instrument. A kind of homage to art . . . All my life, just at the right moment, I've been given this kind of boost . . . Free subsidies . . . For love . . . Offerings . . . Cyd is one of the best . . . Along with Diane . . . Athens . . . Aegina . . . The boat . . . The mauve wake . . . The sun in the water.

"What are you thinking about?"

"You."

"Not true."

"No, but I wouldn't mind a drop more of champagne."

It's getting dark. We stay out on the balcony smoking, naked. Cyd claims a couple in the apartment to the right of hers watch us and make love at the same time as we do. She says the guy waves at her in the morning or in the evening. Perhaps . . . Ships that pass in the night once or twice . . . We're quite drunk now . . . Frivolously, gaily.

"Can I take you out to dinner?"

We get dressed. Go out. Cyd wears her nice dark-red dress. She insists on treating me. Muscadet, oysters, fish. She mentions her little problems. Editors, bosses, subeditors, colleagues. Publicity. The enormous boiler-room of make-believe. She knows all the ins and outs about news. How it's covered, "discovered," designed, put together, illustrated, diverted, cleaned up, slanted, timed, colored, plugged, intercut, cut . . . How and when to bring out some names rather than others . . . The formula for single appearances, and when continuous performances are better . . . The secret of winking, thumping the table, strategic withdrawal and comeback . . . All the steps in the choreography . . . The hint dropped in a million copies of a paper and understood by twenty, which makes the one person concerned shake in his shoes . . . The omission that terrifies, the praise of somebody that devastates somebody else, the "box" that kills . . . The right dimensions for a photograph . . . The proper size for a signature . . . The price of everyone . . . The greasing of palms . . . The financial repercussions of the briefest commercial . . . Whether the stock of current favorites is going up or down . . . Their illusions . . . As if they cared, ha ha! The old ones, the new, jealousies, intrigues, gossip, the daily dose of malevolence . . . Brainwashings . . . Underminings . . . Salaries . . . Interferences from above . . . Contacts . . . Television. She inhabits all this like a fish in the water, but at the same time as if she's outside it, not giving a damn . . . Anyhow, this isn't where her career lies. She's just passing through, to see how things are in Paris before she goes back to New York . . . It's the same everywhere. In Tokyo, San Francisco . . . the whole globe made one by the camera . . . An atomic trap baited with mirages . . . Secretions . . . Sham strip-tease . . . Maya of electronics . . . Pavlov . . .

Another world inside this one—the world of show . . . Everything is showable . . . What isn't showable doesn't exist . . . Politics, culture . . . And since everything is politics, or in other words economics, or in other words politics anyway . . . And since, in reality, Power . . . I've practically stopped listening. Does she belong to WOMANN? Of course not—she's too elegant, too independent . . .

And her girlfriends. And her girlfriends' love affairs. And her girlfriends' and boyfriends' girlfriends and boyfriends. The money connection, the way it affects things . . . Consumerism . . . I give my invariable opinion, which is that it will end badly . . . But I'm thinking about something else. Not really something else—rather a vision of the way the great engine works, with its vague wheels and its two-dimensional waves . . . If you could only get that down. Project onto a screen the mad, microscopic oscillations of that graph . . . What's needed is a suitable form . . .

"So tell me something about your novel. Have you got a title for it yet? Will you show it to me?"

"You'll see, you'll see."

Of course she's only too glad to change the subject. She's drinking too much. No doubt about it. I drive her home. Her hand on my thigh. Will you come up for a minute? No. Got to get to bed. Be seeing you.

I go back to my place. Lie down on the floor. Have one last whisky in the dark. I really go for Cyd, but I can still hear Diane's voice, whispering. "Greece is one big mess—didn't you know?" . . . The last time we met . . . The business of her abortion . . . The narrowing of her eyes . . .

I disconnect the phone and let myself drift away.

II

Gently . . . That's right . . . I'm floating . . . Floating upward . . . Emerging . . . I say hello to myself as I surface, as if I'd reached the end of a long voyage bound hand and foot in the hold . . . I've been dreaming . . . Dreaming I was the prisoner of my own heavy body. That the light couldn't reach me, that I was living in a waking, dreamless sleep. That time, like some cold wing, was going round in a circle in front of my face, without moving forward . . . The sides of the ship were of iron. Or steel. I couldn't see or hear anything. But the worst thing was that I was *thinking* my double, the one who was there at the opposite pole, on earth, walking, talking, moving about, drinking, eating and sleeping . . . I'd think: he's asleep. And I must have been sleeping. He's suffering—and something was probably hurting me. He's thinking—and my brain, in that other place, was meditating . . . But I didn't feel anything; it was as if I'd become a statue of my own life, a dead man living it. I think, therefore I'm dead. Or rather, death thinks me, and so like an idiot I think that I am. A spell . . . Bewitched . . . Was I really in the water, at the bottom of the sea, or was I, more horribly (god knows why) in space? In blind, spherical, silent flight toward Saturn, Mars, Neptune, Uranus, Venus? Or even further away? On the other side of the Sun — beyond all suns and their pointless, explosive, sick disintegrations, their mad decay into spurts of glittering poison? . . .

A traveler . . . In the floating whale . . . In Circe's galaxy . . . Circe, dispenser of drugs. . . . Terrible Circe, "endowed with a human voice," as Homer says in Book x of the *Odyssey* . . . Beautiful,

seductive, skillful, swift in the pouring of liquids that transform . . .
We mustn't forget that Ulysses yields to her secret caresses before
he resumes his eventful voyage . . . Ulysses, layer of goddesses.
Under duress, according to the primeval song, the great ship's log
of our ambiguous fate; and it stops there, it doesn't actually describe
the union of mortal and immortal . . . Ulysses of the thousand
tricks, of the hundred thousand wiles, the connoisseur of hard knots
. . . "Offshoot of the gods." Baccarat of the gods, yes, joker in the
pack, poker, ivory dice tossed in the air, roulette with a human face
. . . A glittering decoy accepted by the gods, yes, that's him, plotter
and foiler of plots . . . Look at him weeping and looking out to sea
when he's staying with Calypso . . . When he's caught, stuck whether
he likes it or not on some island, rock or promontory—in other
words, fixed sexually, tethered to his pleasure . . . But he refuses to
be a fetish of celestial delight, and to couple too long, through
nymphs, with the gods . . . He wants his own island, his wife, his
son, his house, his rights, his freedom, and when he says he prefers
Penelope, even if she is less majestic than some embodiment of the
divine seed, we must of course understand that it's himself he's
choosing . . . He doesn't want to be a mere transitory male mirror
reflecting females in general . . . Look at him performing sacrifices,
peering through the fumes that arise from the rams' black blood at
the wound at the heart of things . . . At the panorama of time . . .
Face to face, sword in hand, he challenges the menses of the earth,
of the earthen mother, menses full of hungry corpses, feeble heads
and hovering vampires . . . His own mother is there too—he speaks
to her . . . After Tiresias, thirsting for a chalice filled with the
bloody skins of the flayed . . . Animality, fertility, menses issuing
from entrails, castration within the clayey universal womb . . .
There isn't a death, is there, that doesn't in one way or another
silently recall that secret killing in the cave . . . They keep that
murder from us nowadays . . . Say there's no such thing . . .
Hygiene . . . Pharmacy . . . Neon signs of lying . . . And look at
Ulysses afterward, slaying the suitors and encouraging Telemachus
to hang the unfaithful servants . . . Cramming himself with crimes

. . . Domestic massacre . . . And fumigation by fire and brimstone! Some sailor! . . .

Between him and Circe it starts with a duel of drugs. . . . Ulysses is helped by Hermes . . . Of course, of course . . . Here come the crimson sheets, the silver baskets, the mead, the tripod, the fire . . . "The water heated up and sang in the gleaming bronze" . . . Anointings with oil . . . Silver-studded chair . . . The goddess is really gone on the man who's resisted her injection . . . So she has to give herself . . . She takes off her clothes . . . He is the hero who was foretold . . . The one who is to come together with her in human form, instead of, like the others, being changed by a single jab into a wolf or a swine . . . That is, into a slave . . . But the human body is still an animal, no? . . . And Ulysses, after that dream coition, looks ahead . . . He wants to die his own death, not be immortalized in the death of humanity . . . To die his own death and no other, the one he has chosen, at home, with his wife beside him . . . In his own bed . . . This must mean in something of his own making, in his own most personal style, in the art he practices in sleep, the most fabulous of all arts . . .

And yet, there's still Circe . . . And Calypso . . . "As Ulysses spoke, the sun set and dusk fell: and they went into the depths of the cave, beneath its high roof, to lie in one another's arms and make love." "The water heated up and sang in the gleaming bronze . . ."

The phone rings. It's Boris. As usual he goes on with a conversation we were having a week ago. He doesn't say who he is or ask if he's disturbing me—all that matters is signing something, expressing a view about some scandal, getting angry, answering back, attacking, striking a blow. He reads me his editorial. Waits with assumed nonchalance for my reactions. What impact his sentences make, the effect of his rhetoric. Gradually he gets me to correct something here and suggest something more forceful there. To quote Machiavelli or Chateaubriand or Kierkegaard—that always goes down well. Today he's on about the Irish . . . He takes notes . . . The tenth hunger striker is dead; the eleventh is at his last gasp

. . . "We both ought to go and lie down outside the prison," says Boris. "What a scoop! . . . The trouble is, we might have to go through with it . . . " Good idea, let's go and die together . . . I'm gradually going deaf . . . Then blind . . . My eyes shift from one side to the other and back again; I can't fix them on anything . . . I get more and more feverish; my body's devouring its own reserves; my cells are swarming over one another . . . I'm melting like wax in all directions . . . "I speak to the President about it every day, but he's very evasive." Of course—the President's got plenty of other things to worry about . . . Inflation, unemployment, the parity of the franc, the rise of the dollar, his left wing, his right wing, the threats to world peace, the disruption of international trade, the balance of payments . . . Boris goes on reading out his article . . . His voice swells, he's in the Assembly, the national one, the international one, the world screen, Radio Sinai . . . I throw him an adjective. A verb . . . One or two nouns . . . An idea for a photograph . . . I'm the ideal listener. Just like with Flora. My dear fellow, you ought to refer to this event, hint at that possibility, introduce such and such a threat . . . "Yes, that'll make them wince, won't it? Eh? What do you think? At least it's going to be on the front page? Naturally—and with an introduction by the editor! Terrific! A triumph!" The Irishmen won't be dying in vain . . . What a chore . . . A good quarter of an hour . . . Whereupon Boris: "Oh yes, and that novel of yours—what's it about? Love, I hope." "Love?" "Yes—it needs rehabilitating . . . Especially in the present state of society . . . Take it from me, love's the thing . . . Well, all the best, goodbye."

I go back to the Odyssey . . . Agamemnon stammering from among the shades: "Take heed by example and be harsh with your wife! Never tell her all you mean to do! You must be bold, but secret too . . . Yet not by your wife's hand, Ulysses, will you ever die. She is too sensible, and has too virtuous a heart!"

I look a proper fool, these days, with my pocket Homer or my little rice paper Bible . . . Or my microscopic edition of Shakespeare's *Sonnets*: *"You still shall live, such virtue hath my pen, / Where breath most breathes, even in the mouths of men"* . . . Ah,

English . . . That's something different again . . . It doesn't sound so good in French.

I'm too preoccupied with literature . . . The annoying thing about masterpieces is the way you feel they *had* to be written . . . But one should really train oneself to see them as still only potential, not yet formed, scarcely sketched out on chaos . . . To breathe amid the preliminary seething. People get to think they've existed from all eternity. That they're engraved on marble by marble . . . Where were we? I switch on the television. What a wonderful thing civilization is, to provide me instantly with the moving, gesticulating image of universal vanity . . . I switch off the sound . . . A new, mechanical Ecclesiastes. I put the set on the floor so that from time to time I can catch a glimpse of a face trying to look pleased or persuaded; a crowded road; planes; tortoises; ships; fires; dead bodies in gutted houses; some demo or other (they're all alike now); a commercial for chocolate, biscuits, or gleaming sinks; some nice soft toilet paper; some nice comfortable sanitary pads. I think the most real thing left in the world is the fish tank in the Closerie du Lilas, on the Carrefour de l'Observatoire: those quiet, majestic, irrefutable lobsters . . . The diners scarcely glance at them . . . It's they who X-ray the diners . . . Prehistoric, ironic, ready, in their aggressive artificial somnolence, to cast their precious pink and white flesh into the idly champing jaws of prattling couples . . . As noble as tanks or satellites . . . A fine example of the truth of false generalizations . . . Where was I? Oh yes—Homer, heroes, divination, gods . . . Masterpieces . . . Of how many people would we still dare to think that they're inscrutable, incomprehensible—and that therefore *they couldn't not exist?* Who must one be, or refuse to be, nowadays, in order to be as absolute as that?

A struggle to the death is being waged between self-interested stereotype and truly personal perception. Between deathly, flaunted repetition and inner experience . . . Or what's left of it . . . "The water sang in the gleaming bronze". . . Now, nothing holds out against flashy popularization . . . Not even obscenity. Everything's signposted. Entrails, groans, contortions, agonies, the various kinds of jerking off, ridiculous yells rehashed from private life, a mathematical desert . . . I think S. has expressed it all very well in *Comedy*, which apparently no one can read . . . Or wants to read . . . I notice that when his name is mentioned there's a strange lowering of the atmosphere . . . The magnetosphere . . . A kind of silent hiatus . . . A horrified reserve . . . So what has he done that's so awful and reprehensible, so fundamental, that only silence is appropriate? I'm intrigued by this almost unanimous rejection, this spontaneous bad-mouthing. The French are a funny lot . . . Terribly clannish, really . . . Much more so than they think, anyway: they believe they do nothing but challenge, fight and loathe one another. But just let a foreigner come on the scene, the genuine article, in other words someone *almost like themselves*, and they close ranks . . . But not against just any old foreigner . . . Not against an obvious one . . . In such cases their natural xenophobia is enough. Or else their paternalist attitudes on integration, suitably underlined: Look at us—originators of the rights of man, with a tradition of asylum . . . No, the one they turn upon is the foreigner within, or the infiltrator . . . The traitor, the one who kicks over the traces, the deviant, the mutant . . . Anyone who doesn't marry a Frenchwoman, for example . . . Quite natural . . . The crux of the matter . . . Controls on property, frontier patrols against genealogical corruption . . . A Jewess . . . A foreign woman . . . There you're getting too close to the bank safe, the identity card . . . To invisible miscegenation . . . To the mask that permits spying . . . And so it is with S., who committed the unforgivable sin of marrying a Pole. . . . Charming though she is . . . A friend of Deborah's . . . Sophie . . . Slim, fair . . . An actress . . . An aggravating circumstance in the case of S., already meat and drink to feminist France. . . . Because he turns literature upside down, takes the language to pieces and puts it together again, and is conducting a really extraordinary experiment in his *Comedy* . . . Worse still, he doesn't even come from humble origins . . . On the contrary . . . Good social background; good education; no contract with the women of the clan, or, ipso facto, with the great Ancestor, the Great Local Womb . . . And to crown all he indulges in the luxury of ruining our medium of communication . . . And it doesn't seem to do him

any harm . . . The absence of visible suffering is very important
. . . If only he *looked* crazy . . . Romantic, visionary, doomed,
surrealist, existentialist, fringe, punk, or anemic . . . But no. Even I
was surprised when I met him: he's a tall chap, rather on the heavy
side, easy, active, laughing, full of energy, intelligent, cultivated,
relaxed . . . A gambler . . . A bit of a lady's man, though some of
them put on meaningful looks and claim the opposite . . . But
from what I've seen . . . That counts as an additional fault . . . If only
he was a homosexual . . . But no luck, he's not one of them either . . .
He and I are different . . . Anarchists . . . And of the most dangerous kind—those who are on a correct footing with the established
order . . . But pursuing other aims . . . Rightists? Not even! Left-
ists, then? Too pessimistic for that . . . So we're completely on our
own. Despite the veiled hostility surrounding him, S. is very famous in certain circles, and there's something astonishing about his
isolation. He seems at ease everywhere, but in fact he's cut off from
everything, an alien presence everywhere, unable to find refuge
anywhere or belong to any band or group. Yet people accuse him of
having a closed circle of friends, a kind of sect or terrorist commando working more or less under his orders to promote his notoriety. But the two things are not necessarily mutually exclusive
. . . S. is really too explosive, too healthy for the half-tone salons of
the current intelligentsia: too violently forward-looking for what's left
of the conservatives; too full of genuine culture for progressive
gatherings; too inventive for the academic lobby; and too hetero-
sexual (to use the crass categories everyone still believes in) to fit in
with the ideas of the SGIC . . . A man who likes women is just
about tolerable if his excesses are in some way connected with the
family . . . If he's a bachelor, or one of a couple of gays, he's out
. . . The circulation of sperm. Short term. Medium term. Long
term. Bank. Short sperm. Termination allowed for. Reinvestments.
Subsidiaries. Distribution. Socialization. Regeneration. And so on
. . . The counterpart of the stock exchange . . . Shares . . . Bonds
. . . Expenses like valves, fans, and other spare parts for the engine
of the common airbus . . . Trompe-l'oeil . . . Buttocks, asses, breasts,
cunts, thighs . . . All heading for the invisible storeroom, Ali Baba's

cave . . . Let's stay with the planes: what's disturbing and very expensive, what needs watching and isn't easy to get delivered, is the swing-wing fighter . . . The F-14 "Tomcat" with air-to-air missiles . . . The 9L Sidewinder! With its own TV system. Able to take off from a moving aircraft carrier. The *Nimitz!* In other words, a fighter that's an apartment in itself . . . An operational 'studio, rather out of the way . . . With ejectable beds . . . Schedule open and unprogrammed . . . Capable of carrying out a raid in the morning, for example . . . No one makes love in the morning, do they? Or in the afternoon . . . Or at dawn . . . That's a problem with women, even now. They tend to be homebodies, don't they . . . You can't get them to move about as they used to do . . . When I think of Emma Bovary rising in the early hours and rushing through the fields to see Rodolphe, who's still asleep . . . "The bank was slippery and she clutched at tufts of withered wallflowers to stop herself from falling. Then she cut across some ploughed fields, where she kept sinking in and stumbling in her thin boots. As she went across the pastures the scarf she'd tied over her head flapped in the wind; she was afraid of the bulls and started to run. She arrived all out of breath, pink-cheeked, and redolent of sap, greenery and the open air. Rodolphe was still asleep at that hour. She was like a spring morning coming into the room." The good old days! Wallflowers! Greenery! The open air! And that wonderful semi-colon! 1857 . . . Now it's all been made commonplace, mechanical, hygienic; adultery compulsory for all . . . Women have become like shops in this as in other things . . . Security . . . Property . . . Minimum emotional wage . . . Guarantees . . . Economies . . . But the fighter sometimes finds accomplices . . . Among the radar people . . . The air-traffic controllers . . . In his own base on the ground . . . Even in his wife . . . Moreover, you never know when he's going to strike . . . Sometimes there's nothing for a long time . . . You say to yourself this is it, he's settled down, tired, old, worn out, dead . . . Obsolete . . . A has-been! And suddenly there he is again, cleaving the air — altered, repainted, refuselaged, and with technological improvements! New swiveling cannon! New rockets and torpedoes! Able to make short work of a dam or a

72

nuclear power station under construction . . . Mastery of the air
. . . R.A.F! Like in the last war, when people used to watch from
their gardens: boom-boom, puffs of smoke from the A.A. guns,
dipping of shining wings, black streaks, explosions over the sea . . .
I got this from S., telling me about his childhood in the southwest
of Occupied France . . . He was seven years old when he saw his
first American descending on him in a parachute among the spindle-
trees, at night, amid a tangle of tracer bullets and searchlights . . .

So we recognized one another as genuine members of the underground . . . Special Branch . . . Every man for himself, communicating as little as possible, special intelligence, very special, absolutely precise . . . Reports exchanged between researchers studying
elementary survival . . . An air corridor here . . . A roadblock there
. . . An act of sabotage somewhere else . . . Night operations . . .
Secret routes . . . An age of terrorism, yes, and more so than people
think, but also of counterterrorism . . . To the right . . . To the left
. . . Higher . . . Lower . . . Diplomatic bags . . . Enemy on the
warpath . . . Weather report . . . Down periscope . . .

S., like me, must have organized himself very strictly in order to
hold out. That's what interests me about him—the long and instinctive discipline of a man with only one object. The professional
attitude in the midst of imagination. Madness controlled and overcome . . . And all in the face of incessant and obsessive criticism;
continual and practically universal disparagement; easy sarcasm,
jeers . . . "Nit-picking" . . . "Hair-splitting" . . . "Clown" . . .
"Joker" . . . In all the papers, all the time . . .

I'm glad he's agreed to help me. He comes in the morning, twice
a week . . . I show him what I've written . . . He takes it away and
brings me back what he's corrected and arranged . . . We talk a bit
. . . About literary technique, politics, women . . . Especially technique . . . I ask him if he isn't overdoing the dots in the French
translation . . . I know, Céline, but can someone else go that far? . . .
Yes, he says, anybody can do it now . . . You have to move fast,
and lightly. Either no punctuation at all, or that. You have to show
that it's all in the voice hovering airily, dynamically, over the page.
. . . "It has to come off the page" . . . Be snatched up . . . He's a

73

strange fellow, S. I never hear any but ironical or pitying remarks about him. I wonder if he's aware of his reputation. Yes, he must be. But he's decided to pretend not to notice anything (I'm a bit anxious about his reactions to what I'm writing now). (Note, later: no reaction whatsoever.) What is it that keeps him going? What strength does he rely on? Why does he do it? Ultimately it's a kind of religious passion. One day he quoted a passage from Joseph de Maistre, a misunderstood author par excellence, conventionally regarded as the personification of reaction though perhaps a supreme humorist, and at all events Baudelaire's favorite philosopher: "One must say what one thinks is true, and say it boldly; even if it cost me dear I should like to discover a truth that was bound to shock the whole human race: I'd let them have it point-blank." "You'd think it was St. Paul who said that, wouldn't you?" said S. "St. Paul plus some studied insolence" . . . "But what if what you think is true is false?" . . . "That still leaves boldness . . . That's what people blame you for, never for being right or wrong." S.'s truth resides in his assertion of that style . . . Point-blank—I like that . . . He's always careful to invoke the classics . . . So where does that leave the avant-garde, modernity, the whole area to which he's usually consigned? I'm classical, classical! he cries. Strictly classical! Paradox comes naturally to him. I don't always understand him, but I'm very fond of him . . . And it's true, he can write in a perfectly classical style when he chooses. He likes Sade, Sévigné, Saint-Simon, Bossuet, Pascal . . . Stendhal? Not so much. Chateaubriand ? According to him *La Vie de Rancé* is the best example of swiftness achieved through compression, short-circuits, *montage* . . .

A ring at the door. I creep up and look through the keyhole. It's Kate. "Have you disconnected the phone? I have to talk to you." She comes in like a police raid. Looks around, breathing fast. Any women? No. Well?

"Fals has just died."

"Oh."

"Is that all?"

"At his age . . . And in his condition. It's a relief, really, isn't it?"

"I thought you were closer to one another than that."

She sits down on the divan. She's wearing a very low neck. Legs and arms bare. Rather tense. Breathless. Aroused? Yes, death always has that effect on them . . . Makes them open up like flowers. It's their invisible serum. Their secret vitamin . . . Fals dies, so Kate rushes to my place to tell me, to see how I react, find out if I'm upset for a moment and she can worm her way in . . .

"It turns out he had cancer.""Where?"

"The stomach."

"Didn't anyone know?"

"Practically no one."

"Did he suffer?"

"A good deal, probably. But he didn't let on."Here we go again —secrecy, dramatizing . . . Lies everywhere and in everything . . .

"You ought to write me an article, old chap," says Kate, with a smile.

"You think so?"

"Of course. Write about his influence in the United States. About the trip you made together there, the things that happened . . . I need an American's point of view."

"But you know very well nothing happened . . . Complete cross-purposes . . ."

"Say anything you like . . . I need it by the end of the afternoon. Please."

She smiles determinedly. News above all!. . . An obit. "Cold meat," as they say in newspaper offices . . . A death, a disquisition . . . Poor old Fals, dead under surveillance, just like everyone else . . . More than everyone else . . . He knew too much about what goes on . . . Did he tell anyone about our last interview? When I asked him what he thought about the Report? He was very tired and far away even then, and got mixed up about appointments and dates . . . Practically gaga, really, with lucid intervals . . . "Fals?

He's fine" . . . That was the watchword, though, with the family and the clique . . . He *had* to be fine . . . Had he spoken about it to Kate, whom he saw occasionally? "An idiot," he called her, but he said something like that to someone else about everybody. That was his game, the familiar one of divide and rule . . . Put people off, make them fear and curry favor with you . . . The trip to New York? You must be joking! A nightmare . . . Lectures to hostile or contemptuous audiences who scarcely bothered to listen—and anyway he kept stopping and starting and trotting out the same old points . . . Scenes in hotels. Tantrums on the part of Armande, mistress No. 1—his "pupil," as he called her . . . Ugly, up-tight, aggressive, and ready to turn nasty at the least little thing . . . A provincial shrew . . . A real pain in the neck . . . But Fals put up with everything, showered her with presents, groveled psychologically at her feet — and then would suddenly start smashing the crockery . . . He must have enjoyed it. A masochist, when you came right down to it . . . One night when we were together . . .

"You'll write something, then?"

Kate has leaned back on the cushions . . . Her legs very much crossed. But really very much. She gets up. Comes over to me as if to say good-bye. Then kisses me, feeling for my mouth. She finds it, and thrusts in her tongue, I disengage myself as gently as possible. It's plain she'd like to be screwed in a funereal setting . . . It doesn't seem a good idea to me. I edge her toward the hall . . . "Okay, then. Okay."

Yes, it was one night in November . . . I'd gone to see Fals about a trip we were supposed to be making, this time to India. I'd arranged some more or less underground contacts . . . He'd insisted that Armande should join us . . . Okay, Armande can come . . . We talk for a bit . . . Yet again about the beginning of the Book of Genesis, I remember. "I wish I could convey the depth of the lack," he said. He kept saying it over and over, dreamily, as he sat in his chair: "The depth, the depth . . ." His desk was covered with notes and mathematical drawings . . . He looked like a weary old Doge, wise and crimson and tense in his ruin, painted by Titian with finishing touches by the gold and brown pessimism of Rembrandt

. . . He had an absent look, but every now and then shot a piercing glance over the top of his glasses . . . Armande was supposed to join us for dinner in a restaurant . . . We went over the receptions we'd have to attend at embassies and in universities, and our contacts with the local Indian press, who weren't very familiar with his work. Then we go out and start having dinner . . . An hour goes by . . . No Armande . . . I can tell Fals is uneasy . . . He goes out twice to phone . . . Comes back . . . Goes out again . . . Comes back again . . . Each time a bit heavier, more tired and shrunken . . . At the same time he's getting more and more nervous . . . He goes out to phone once more . . . No answer? No. But she must be in . . . It's not far away. He pays the bill. We go there. Fals gets out a bunch of keys, about ten of them . . . He liked installing women in apartments near where he lived . . . How many? Three? Four? Anyhow, Armande was the chief one then, she must have monopolized his evenings . . . She used to have him to dinner at her place after seeing her patients there in the afternoon . . . He rushes up the stairs two at a time with an amazing access of energy, a third wind . . . She might have been taken ill, or one of her patients might have gone really crazy and attacked her . . . Because she must be there; she isn't answering the phone; and there are no lights on . . . I'm already imagining it: schizophrenia in action . . . Revolver, knife, pool of blood . . . Fals is thinking the same thing. He rummages about in the keyhole . . . Yes, it's blocked from the inside . . . Something really is wrong . . . We go downstairs . . . I go and phone, let it ring, no answer . . . Her floor is quite dark . . . We both start shouting up from the courtyard . . . Fals is getting redder and redder in the face, I'm afraid he's going to pass out on me, I can already see the frightful scandal and suggest I should leave . . . "No, stay!". . . He's seventy-three. . . . "Armande!" he shouts . . . "Armande! . . . Armande!" . . . I have an idea. I yell at the top of my voice, "We must fetch the police!" . . . The word "Police" has a satisfactorily loud ring . . . POLICE! . . . The effect is magical . . . Armande's windows light up . . . A man in his shirt-sleeves goes quickly past one of the windows . . . The murderer? "There's a guy up there," I tell Fals, who seems not to have seen him . . . "Armande!" he bawls. "Armande!" . . . It must be a terrible sight — the guy must have cut her throat . . . Disembowled her, perhaps . . . To revenge himself on Fals, who get at least ten letters a week containing death threats . . . Crackpots . . . Swarms of them, of all kinds . . . "Armande!" . . . This time a window opens noisily . . . It's her . . . Ugly-face . . . She leans over the balcony . . . And she yells too . . . "What's all this row? Have you gone crazy?" . . . Suddenly I understand . . . Once again I say I think I'll leave . . . "No, no—come up with me!" . . . He runs! He flies! Confounded old wretch! We reach the landing. Armande opens the door. She's very calm. Sitting on the divan with a little black bag on his lap is a chap from Fals's own college, perfectly at ease. Shades of Labiche and Feydeau! Armande has set the whole thing up to teach the Old Man a lesson! She must need a lot of money, fast, without any arguments. So she gets out the bazooka! And in front of me! She doesn't waste a moment—she weighs in . . . She makes a scene . . . An unanswerable move . . . Attack is the best mode of defense . . . She's the one who's yelling now . . . Says she phoned the restaurant . . . Looked for us everywhere . . . And anyhow won't have that hullaballoo in her courtyard . . . Even if she'd been dead it wouldn't have brought her back to life . . . We're a couple of children . . . Fals has collapsed into a rocking-chair, brick-red, breathless, apoplectic . . . The chap, a flashy type straight out of a Brazilian carnival, plays along and talks about having to catch a train . . . I attempt a diversion and ask Armande for a whisky . . . I don't know what to do . . . Perhaps they'll beat the Old Man up when I've gone, and pinch his money . . . Force him to sign a check . . . But then I'm struck by a suspicion . . . Supposing that's what he likes? . . . Supposing it's part of their erotic carry-on? . . . Perhaps the Brazilian acts as a kind of yardstick for the Old Man's voyeurism? . . . Perhaps he's used to these "surprises"? . . . Armande, standing there simmering, pretending to be furious, but more of a goose than ever, is still telling Fals off . . . Who finally hauls himself to his feet, takes me by the arm, and sees me out . . . But I listen for a while from the stairs . . . Nothing . . . They've gone silent . . . A peculiar kind of play-acting . . .

The next day I find out that Fals, without telling me, has canceled the trip to India . . . And then, the day after that, I meet him in the street outside Armande's place . . . "I'm just on my way," he says, looking exhausted, but knowing I'll understand what he means . . . Apologetic . . . On his way to what? To dinner . . . To his slippers . . . To Célimène's tender mercies . . . To an old man's wretched rubbings and suckings . . .

That was the last time we met . . . Or almost . . . I went to India without him . . . But I did speak about him in Calcutta . . . And in Bombay . . . About his very individual conception of discourse and speech . . . In terms of the local mumbo-jumbo . . . Sanskrit . . .

And now he's dead. *Sic transit* . . . He did get to be famous, in the long run . . . Very famous . . . After years and years of mostly solitary struggle . . . Very few people understood what he was saying . . . He had awful trouble with his colleagues, his pupils, the establishment, and the papers . . . He was accused of or held responsible for almost everything you can think of : charlatanism, dealing in favors, misuse of transference, withcraft, drug-taking, blackmail, suicides . . . His activities *were* pretty lively . . . But very interesting to watch and eminently romantic . . . If Fals was a kind of genius, he was also a bit of a crook . . . Was he forced into it because of the persecution he was subjected to? . . . It's possible . . . How can we tell? People's lives are inexplicable . . . He inspired both absolute devotion and implacable hate. That's quite a good sign . . . He destroyed or reshaped what was probably bound to be altered or done away with anyhow . . . He always had plenty of money, that's the main thing . . . A Swiss bank account . . . His consulting room was never empty . . . Very expensive . . . And quick . . . That was apparently what was held against him the most . . . Mass-production methods . . . An ordinary trained psychoanalyst sees each patient for forty-five minutes . . . Whatever happens . . . He or she comes in, lies down and recounts his or her dreams, etc. . . . Three-quarters of an hour is the necessary Time . . . The Unconscious Clock . . . One quarter of an hour for static and more or less repressed violence toward the analyst; another quarter of an hour for the heart of the matter, three minutes of which are crucial

79

and contain just three seconds that really count; then another quarter of an hour for tidying up, and presto, so long and on to the next . . . Fals changed all that . . . He thought it tedious and soporific . . . It sent you to sleep and didn't produce anything . . . Prevented rather than promoted revelation . . . Bottled it up, made it cunning, . . . Took the edge off what his disciples called the "virulence" of the operation . . . Virulence . . . Life seen as a virus . . . Be that as it may, he stuck his neck out . . . Three minutes . . . Hello and good-bye . . . That'll be so much . . . When shall I see you again? The International Association investigated . . . There was gossip, ins and outs never revealed . . . He was expelled . . . He made a great drama of it . . . Started his own Movements and Societies and Cartels . . . They all came to pieces in his hands, but he didn't care, he just carried on . . . It was very much like ecclesiastical controversy: orthodoxy, reformation and counterreformation. Or, with its regular explosions, even more like Marxism and Communism . . . Paul Fals could be regarded as another Trotsky, a neutralized prophet, a prophet in exile, a prophet of truth banished by the central power, Spinoza thrown out of the Synagogue . . . The myth took off of its own accord . . . Fals even claimed to be a heretic who'd eventually be proved right . . . Like Halláj, Luther, Calvin, Sabbatai Zevi, Jacob Frank, to mention a few . . . It was a merciless settling of scores between the Freudian Church and himself . . . The weapon he relied on most was his "teaching" . . . "Yes, I know the word makes you laugh," he'd often say to me drily . . . And the "Lectures" . . . Oh yes, the Lectures! . . . In them Fals can be said to have created a new genre . . . They were solemn, hermetical, logical, apocalyptic and comic . . . Great art . . . Oration, peroration, grandiloquence . . . People talked about them among themselves; dined discreetly with one another—there isn't anyone else quite up to this sort of thing . . . He didn't have very good taste, though, except in antiques, on which he'd occasionally spend a lot of money . . . I think he was generous to his women . . . Anyhow, FAM owes a lot to him . . . Directly or indirectly he was a major influence on most of those involved . . . Bernadette, Dora, Kate . . . It was in reaction to him that the movement took on its full meta-

80

physical dimension . . . Its restrictive initiations, its repressive secret intelligence . . . As in the Communist religion, or in underground sects — it comes to the same thing . . . For you must admit that not only does psychiatry derive from a system with coercive tendencies, but it also possesses vast potential data files on everybody who is or might one day be significant . . . People's connections with one another; their faults, eccentricities, weaknesses, obsessions . . . Fals had a few bankers up his sleeve . . . And two or three ministers, whatever kind of government was in . . . An archbishop . . . The head of the counterespionage service . . . The chief representative in France of the revolutionary Brigades . . . And a few pop and film stars . . . "What a saga," I used to say to him sometimes. "Just like a novel" . . . "My dear fellow," he'd reply loftily, "all that matters to me is the Truth" . . . And it really was so. He was fond of quoting a certain philosopher: "I always tell the truth. Not the whole truth, because that's impossible . . . There aren't the words for it. That's what connects truth with reality." I didn't agree with him about that. One day I said: "The novel's the only thing that tells the truth . . . The whole truth . . . Something other than the truth, and yet nothing but the truth . . . It does have the words for it . . . It's for that reason people regard it as unreal, whereas in fact it's reality itself . . . The nervous system of the facts . . . Anyhow, as someone you know very well has said, 'Truth is structured like fiction' " . . . He smiled. "All right, my boy, since it's you that says it . . . But drop it now and leave me alone. Just write . . . Write . . . That's all." He was right. Either you create a literary oeuvre or you don't. All the rest is claptrap, and he was right about the folly of passing claptrap around . . . Delusions, illusions, imaginings, distortions of the great lie of existence . . . But it's strange how just by manipulating the claptrap, by using it as raw material, with its silences, associations, interpretations, transferences, resistances, slips, lapses of memory, accounts of dreams, you can call the body so deeply in question, via sex, the tumor of the body . . . Incredible how that's the only thing that gets talked about . . . Pregnancy . . . What's that? . . . The Viennese waltz . . . Transposed by Fals into a veritable java . . . How long till the salsa? The rock, the reggae, the funk? There's no stopping deliberate decomposition . . . Fals was rather severe to begin with. . . . Aristotle, Heidegger, linguistics, topology . . . But I saw him gradually sink into a dark passion: the black pitch rose higher and higher, and his eye increasingly reflected the heavy tide. All his life he was amusing most of the time, and he got more amusing as time went by; but in a disturbing way, profoundly battered and broken. That's what you get for messing about with castration . . . And the inarticulate frigidity that lies behind . . . He was keen on money and immediate power . . . Obstinate, increasingly impatient and touchy. Perhaps he was already in great pain . . . Sometimes he came near to pitching into the guy he employed as a secretary . . . Incredible fits of anger . . . Insulting his nearest and dearest . . . I met a couple of his disciples the other evening . . . Frightful . . . Swollen up with vanity, unsociable, speaking entirely in code, obsessed by tiny sectarian details, unaware of how ridiculous they were . . . So what was missing? Music? Yes, quite simply and boringly that . . . Fals must have liked giving as good as he got—you could see that when you went to see his women . . . Grim and gaunt, they were, with malevolence darting out of their eyes . . . Did he drive them crazy? Probably . . . Or rather he revealed the cancer of madness hidden inside them. . . . Which ultimately he wasn't at all sure one really ought to meddle with . . . "Aesthetics! Aesthetics!" he used to growl at me. "You bother too much about the *Lustprinzip!* The pleasure principle!" Maybe . . . And why not? . . . A bit more despair, just one more step in that direction . . . I call to mind Bernadette's irretrievable madness, with its superficial dusting of psychiatry, and the flame of hatred burning inside her . . . Is Fals responsible for that? Of course not . . . I remember something Werth told me — he used to consult Fals sometimes during one of his neurotic periods. He said Fals told him to be careful of cars . . . Fals was run over by a car. "As I was telling him about myself," Werth added, "I suddenly realized I was a nutty old bastard talking to a silly old fool" . . . Wise words . . . Fals treated me quite well on the whole . . . As if he suspected I'd talk one day . . . A potential writer . . . Dangerous . . . But he did try to intimidate me once or

82

twice . . . It was part of the game . . . And he also tried to make a pass at Deborah . . . Ah well . . . I'd better get on with Kate's article since she's so keen on it . . . Only on the surface, of course . . . Mephisto . . . Moderato . . . Glissando . . .

It was Diane who one fine day took it into her head to find Fals irresistibly attractive . . . She ended up in analysis with him . . . She even wanted to translate his books into Greek . . . The good old days, 1968, if you can call it that . . . Diane's rather like Ysia— the memory of an excellent lay . . . Flavor, smell, taste, touch . . . A super yellow peach . . . A real case of love at first sight at some friends' place one evening . . . We arranged to meet the next day at Trocadéro . . . It was winter, everything was white . . . We pelted each other with snowballs . . . We kissed and kissed . . . She had a little apartment near the river . . . It's always the same . . . She wanted me to stay . . . And I had to get back . . . Because of Deb— I've never wanted to drive her too far, or lose her . . . That's how it is—I want to keep everything . . . Want to have everything . . . Childishness . . . Greed . . . Permanent long vacation . . . Fun . . . Everything fast and furious . . . I've always been like that and always will be . . . I'm wasting my life, I know, and I don't care . . . He that loseth his life shall save it . . . What on earth does that mean? I don't know, I've never known anything, I am what I feel, all I try to do is exist in what I feel . . . Diane was worse than me when it came to sensuality and narcissism . . . The way she fitted herself like a glove was something thrilling and terrible . . . Delight followed immediately by free-fall . . . I don't remember whether she was already on drugs . . . Maybe . . . We just smoked a lot of hash at her place, lying on the floor in front of a wood fire . . . A *lot* of hash . . . And screwed all the time . . . And what came next, for her? Morphine? Heroin? Snow? HMC? Just after me? During me? That would explain a lot . . . A kind of frenzy . . . A feverish, furrowed, *preoccupied* throbbing . . . She was on the small side, with fair hair and black eyes . . . Well-rounded and smooth . . .

Knees . . . Lips . . . The way she groaned when we made love . . .
Ai! Ai! You find that strange hoarse cry in Aeschylus and Sophocles
. . . At crucial moments . . . Anyhow, she was full of the sacred,
brimming over with it by her very nature . . . No man could stand
up to it; it scared them . . . As for the women . . . She wasn't all
that keen on sleeping with women . . . Just now and again, in
passing . . . What women liked in Diane was the image of wildness,
the rejection of all compromise . . . But what she had to have, and
plenty of it, was screwing on the grand scale . . . I used to emerge
in a state of magnificent exhaustion, covered in pleasant sweat even
after I'd taken a shower . . . She seemed in a hurry . . . It was she
who wanted us to leave almost at once for her place in Greece, to go
to Aegina and make love at night—all night—in the temple . . .
On the way back we slept side by side on the deck . . .

Diane's balcony had a view over Paris . . . She used to give me
coffee and honey at five in the morning . . . Summer dew . . . How
I loved her, now I come to think of it . . . Like some beautiful fabric
. . . But she was death too . . . A death made of velvet, and golden
. . . But death just the same . . . A swarm of bees overturned . . .
Oedipus delighting in Colonus . . .

> Stranger, you are in the land of fine horses . . .
> The best place in the world . . .
> White Colonus,
> Where the nightingale
> Utters the sweetest strains
> Amid the green valleys
> Of its ivied home,
> And the lush foliage of the god,
> Safe from sun and storm;
> Where orgiastic Dionysus
> Visited his divine foster-mothers . . .
> There, every day, wet with heavenly dew,
> Blossom fair clusters . . . . And so on . . .

Sometimes, as I kissed her, I could feel her heart like a distant
oven, a hive of blood seething with perfume . . . She concentrated

on, was absorbed in herself, like a stationary whirlpool, an intrave-
nous geyser . . . She seemed, really, to be performing a rite; to
come immediately and continually . . . Was it an illusion? But this
is a sphere where illusion is supreme—all you have to do is go
along with it, dive into it and disintegrate gracefully . . . Diana,
Apollo's twin sister, born in Delos . . . With her bow and arrows
and her doe, and the crescent moon on her brow . . . On earth she's
swift Artemis and the chase; in the sky the quiet, disturbing, vexa-
tious Moon, or Phoebe; in Hell the scintillating and peremptory
Hecate . . . Great is Diana of the Ephesians . . . Diane was quiet
and reserved, with rather a low voice . . . Detached . . . Preoccupied
with her own worship . . . It was her, and it wasn't her—a wave-
length of possession . . . Voodoo of the islands . . . It was as if she
were waiting for something to descend on her, some force, some
downpour, some hovering shroud, a tremor in the dark, a flash
rending the dark . . . But it was she who once told me, realizing
that after all she wasn't the only woman for me, "You're a high-
class whore . . . " Did I look a bit cross? She brought me some
flowers . . . We lived in a myth, but we never spoke of it . . . The
gods are there, lurking in the act itself . . . She was a magician, was
Diane . . . Those long nights in front of the fire, crammed with
grass, perhaps Colombian grass with its dry rustle and cool flash
which really makes you fly high . . . The fire glowed, became an
altar, a field of lava, a conflagration of water, a film about the Trojan
War, a rose garden . . . Indian music . . . Everything—drums,
tambourines, vinyas, long arpeggios . . . And we went to it . . .
Ghostly sleepwalkers . . . Through the looking glass, and through
that again . . . In the tunnel after the tunnel . . . I can see her now,
sitting cross-legged on the parquet floor (her apartment had nothing
in it but a bed, a lamp and some cushions), making the strongest
possible joints — careful, serious, warm, knowing exactly what to
do, and why and how . . . I was there . . . She liked me, and used
me to the full . . . When I arrived she concentrated all her attention
on making me share her own waking coma as fast as possible . . .
That inward, hurt, rather childish look she had—it was her strength
. . . Her laughter, the mouth and palate of laughter . . . I owe her

a lot . . . Either she was an outlaw, or she served some other law—she didn't know which . . . But pleasure was a must . . . It was really rather a bore in the long run, that silent, sacred imperative of bliss . . . Ecstasy, yes, but compulsory ecstasy . . . The other side of madness—benevolent, infinitely benevolent, vague, bewitching, implacable . . . Successful erotomania . . . Immediate identification and transfusion . . . Her little blonde head under my hand, her skull (really her skull), her hair damp with sweat, the hollow of her knees, her arms, the way she slept . . .

But like all the rest, she never really saw me . . . That's what they can't take: that one should be a body and also talk. That's the crux of the matter. The Church is right. They can't help it. Either what you say matters. Or you fuck. One or the other. But never both, or there's a crisis . . . A woman can't respect a man who fucks her . . . Who really fucks her, I mean—none of your vague tepid fondness. The only thing she can do is raise the stakes in proportion as she respects the speech in question, the words that strangely persist in emerging from that inexplicable male body, still — how weird! — living and thinking after the act . . . It must stopped . . . The organ, at once captured and repelled, must be transformed into a foetus; that which is trying to make itself heard in the voice must be negated . . . If you, a male, want to be taken seriously, to measure up, be admired, have real influence (for all society naturally follows suit), abstention is the thing . . . I said abstention, not inability, of course . . . But *they* can tell instinctively . . .

So the day came when Diane, as a tribute to my virtues as a long-distance runner, my endurance, decided to raise the stakes . . . She sold me to Fals . . . He agreed, natch . . . Came to see her at her place . . . It's funny to think they may have given each other a fix . . . It was as if she were asking for help . . . Not any old kind of help, but that which was likely, in her view, to impress me the most . . . It's not surprising it worked with Fals: he often used to sniff around after me, intrigued and entranced . . . The *odor di femmina*, that was me . . . Women are never more feminine than when they're with me, of course . . . Otherwise it takes a real professional, and they don't grow on trees these days . . . They're an extinct species . . . People look for them with a fine-toothed comb, but in vain . . . It's almost a mystical matter, not merely a physical one . . . And so, when a woman realizes you can be with her indefinitely and yet remain quite free, without either anxiety or guilt, she seeks help . . . The Group . . . The safety of the tribe; the common ideal of family or community . . . Or else a man you respect, a devious attempt by a father figure . . .

Fals was delighted: for once a man was more or less staying the course and putting the ladies in a flutter . . . What he usually got in his consulting room, as I have reason to know, was endless boredom, impotence and sexual disgust . . . After all—an obvious fact that one may underline in passing—you go into analysis because you're in the best of form . . . Right . . . In Diane's case (and in two or three cases of lesser importance), what interested Fals was finding out exactly what it was that had brought her "into analysis . . . " Imagine a woman, or women, being ill, or thinking themselves ill, just because some wretch stands out against the strongest whirlpool there is—nay, thrives on and swims along with it . . . A writer, damn it . . . Someone special . . . An artist where you never expected one . . . It worked . . . Fals started to look at me differently . . . I could tell by a number of little things . . . He was taken aback, his nose had been put out of joint . . . Diane would really have liked the plot to operate in both directions: after she'd left his consulting room she'd have come straight to my place and made love to me . . . That was aiming rather high . . . I refused . . . Perhaps I shouldn't have . . . Other people, too, have suggested I should be analyzed, of course; practically everyone does it nowadays, and as I'm out of the ordinary I can quite see why I should be the object of that kind of curiosity . . . But to put it bluntly, it means that apart from Deb—that's different—I avoid mixing with psychiatrists and psychoanalysts, and with academics in general . . .

It was at that point that Diane threw the time-bomb of the abortion . . . Was it my child? Quite possibly . . . Especially as the question hadn't even occurred to me . . . Of course, of course . . . That was the reason for the analysis . . . Back to square one . . .

She disappeared . . .

I didn't even see her at Andreas's funeral . . . He was one of her best friends among the Greeks . . . He jumped from the twentieth story of a tower block . . . A terrible mess . . . He was a Communist . . . People said his death was political . . . The crisis Marxism was going through . . . The end of the revolutionary hope . . . The things they always bring up to hide the yawning gap — politics on the one hand, psychology on the other . . . I knew Andreas slightly . . . We used to meet now and again at Marie-Thérèse's place . . . She's dead too . . . Andreas's wife, who was French, used to be a friend of Diane's too, but she joined FAM . . . She was close to Bernadette . . . Fanatically so . . . That wasn't the only suicide produced by the new religion . . . There was Guiana too . . . Jim Jones . . . The "People's Temple" . . . Could Fals, in his prime, have brought about eight hundred suicides at once? Out of unconditional loyalty? Why not? The cream of progressive society turned up for Andreas's funeral, as they did for Marie-Thérèse's . . . Very dignified and bursting with health . . . The secretary of one of the cells, a woman, made a speech over the coffin, complete with red flag and red carnations . . . The classic ritual, a bit worn at the edges by now . . . Then suddenly, to everyone's astonishment, a Greek Orthodox priest appeared in flowing black robes . . . And an old man, also dressed in black, and alone . . . Andreas's father, come all the way from Greece to bury his son . . . As strange and incongruous, as out of place and accusing, as a ghost in bright sunlight . . . I felt just as out of place as he was, and just as unreal as the priest, with his crucifix belonging to another age, to the quick and the dead of another world . . . And there in the middle, between the red and the black, was the broken body of that poor lad, so restless, loud and generous . . . A victim of the corrida of modern life, so much harsher than all the meetings, tracts, theses, analyses, and theories . . . Much more dangerous and subtle, much darker and more disguised than the class struggle of the good old days, when there was only one History, and everything was binary, clear, and rational . . .

Distinctions run much deeper nowadays . . . Good and Evil are

more than ever intertwined, inseparable, and difficult to recognize
. . . The difference runs through everything and everybody . . .
Whose side is one on? And against whom? Only institutions like
WOMANN know where they are . . . WOMANN and FAM have
the firm convictions that everyone used to have . . . They, at least,
know their enemy . . . Which they identify with the male organ
. . . There's a solid criterion for you! A vague source of everlasting
bitterness, an object of eternal resentment . . . And so, as always,
we come back to racism . . . Perhaps we never left it . . . All human
rumination ends in the brick wall of biology . . . Death requires its
fuel . . . In the beginning was the gene, like this or like that . . . X,
Y, XX, XY . . . In the long run the only real racism is between men
and women . . . All the rest is visionary chitchat . . . And racism
between the sexes is in excellent form—increasing, spreading,
flourishing . . . It's the ultimate driving force, the source of motion
itself . . .

It was in the cemetery that I saw Lutz for the last time . . .
Before he too fell through the window of propriety . . . Before he
killed his wife and "went mad" . . . Went mad? I doubt it . . . I
doubt it very much . . . Woke up at last, perhaps . . . The end of
Don Quixote . . . No more windmills or giants . . . No more
Dulcinea . . . No more fantasy about fighting . . . Just reality, all
of a sudden, that circumscribed gray blur with its endless vulgarity
and horror . . .

Flora knew Lutz very well . . . He was one of her old flames . . .
I think about him now, and about the dull, shrunken days he spends
in the psychiatric ward at St. Anne . . . Where Fals used to teach
and exhibit his patients, by the way . . . It's a small parademoniac
world—and always seems to end up about the size of a pinhead . . .
Magnetization and contraction . . . It never stops raining these days
. . . I look out of the window at the obstinately low Paris sky, just
as Lutz is doing, perhaps . . . The strange fate of people all living at
a certain time . . . As if they were linked together by the threads of

a novel in the process of being written . . . A novel no one would believe in if it really was a novel . . . And what am I doing in all this? Really I got here by chance . . . Or by the necessity that dictates that I write this book . . . I shouldn't have been here otherwise, that's for sure . . . Different interests, different background; a close and yet a hidden spectator . . . Or else there's a god, at least for writers . . . A strange, capricious god who reveals his plans gradually . . . A god of narrative within narrative, with a silent ethic that nonetheless spins the plot . . . A god who has an unpredictable way of choosing his witness, his private secretary, not necessarily, in fact never, the one you'd expect . . . Watch out for that little lad over there, the one with bright eyes who watches and never says anything . . . He's there just to see and hear, to record and decipher . . . S. agrees with me . . . He says there's a special life reserved for those destined to write about what really goes on . . . A life that's got nothing to do with life . . . A life that is death —death writing . . . That's why, according to him, the "woman" element is always paralleled, in such a life, by another kind of magnetic needle . . . Cherchez la femme—*and* the flame . . . The curve of the pole, where untruth—and therefore truth also—is most concentrated . . . So Lutz ended up by strangling Anne, the girlfriend he'd taken such a long time to marry . . . He'd just had an operation for a hernia . . . From what I was told, things were going from bad to worse with him . . . Complete disillusion, bitterness, red wine . . . He saw his whole life as an utter disaster . . . At this point we enter slightly more deeply into the important matter of communism . . . People think they know all about it, but they know nothing . . . Communism is not the same thing as communism . . . Fascism is different from itself too, and no one is prepared to poke about among its roots, amid the darkness where it renews its strength . . . And it's not happening somewhere else— it's happening here . . . It's got more to do with physiology than people think . . . A lot has been said on the subject, but it could amount to nothing . . . Laurence Lutz started off as a Catholic, a good Catholic . . . Then came the Resistance, the camps, scientific enlightenment . . . A human race that had grown up at last being shown the way by philosophy and science, etc. . . . Not so much the "new man" as an account of the overall system within which "man" exists . . . Taking the whole thing to pieces, mastering it, and putting it together again . . . When I first met him he was a star of the first magnitude . . . Who had no difficulty refuting feeble contemporary philosophies . . . And all philosophies were feeble in Lutz's eyes . . . His own thought was categorical, but it had elegance and style, as they say . . . So I saw quite a lot of him when I was dabbling a bit in politics . . . We talked a good deal . . . My penchant for literature had finally begun to strike me as superficial, inadequate, and reprehensible . . . What an idea! I'd caught the virus . . . The nihilist germ . . . Self-doubt, systematically injected by the philosophical attitude . . . So that one's ashamed of oneself, of pleasure, of egotism, gambling, liberty, and license . . . My God, what a mistake! How I regret having failed, even for an instant, to proclaim that I *was* "superficial" . . . Inconsistent . . . Irresponsible . . . "Polymorphically perverse," as Deb would say—she helped a lot, at the time, to make me feel guilty . . . But with her it was understandable; she had an excuse . . . She had to lure me into marriage . . . For that any kind of propaganda is allowed—in order to destabilize instability . . . The same was true of Flora, only in the opposite direction . . . I was caught in their cross-propaganda . . . But it all evens out . . . The best thing to do with women is to choose them as if you're selecting an orchestra—like a rose window full of contrasts . . . So as to expose yourself to every kind of criticism, and at the same time to all their opposites . . . It produces a fascinating kind of music, with each of them hammering away in support of her own interests . . . The thing to do is listen without saying anything, to enjoy it without letting on . . . The bass continuo of resentment . . . the violins of regret . . . The trombones of threat and dire predicition . . . The clarinets of heavy irony . . . the flutes of mockery . . . The trumpets of imprecation . . . The big drum, or cymbals, of a demand for money . . . The piano of melancholy . . . The pizzicati of automatic contradiction . . . And the voices . . . The one I like best is the booming voice of hysterics, when *they* try to invoke the Law that ought to be there, keeping this disobedient male in order . . . The soprano of slanderous insinuation . . . The contralto of denigration . . . In short, the whole rampant, ravaging opera . . .

Yes, that was the time when I'd been stung into showing them I too was a thinker . . . That if I felt like it I also could hold forth on the most complicated and significant of subjects . . . I read and took notes on all Hegel's works, I swear: *The Phenomenology of Mind, Logic* and the rest . . . Also Aristotle . . . And Plato . . . And Spinoza . . . And Leibnitz—I've still got a soft spot for him . . . And Marx . . . And Engels . . . And Lenin . . . Oh yes, all thirty-six volumes! I tell you! . . . And Freud . . . And Saussure . . . And so on and so forth . . . The girls got on my nerves with their worship of the philosopher-professors . . . I had such a backlog to make up, such a bourgeois existence to expiate . . . I wanted to know . . . What . . . Why . . . That was the way things were going —what a long time ago it seems when you come to think of it . . . Longer ago than the twenties . . . The Communist Party vision of the world has never been stronger that it was in the seventies . . . I talk about the Communist Party, but that's too sweeping . . . It would be better to speak of a great "leftish" nebula stretching from the United States to Japan, a whole galaxy, complete with its clusters, constellations and meteors . . . Marxism, psychoanalysis, linguistics . . . *"Nouveau roman"* Structuralism . . . Eruptions of local knowledge . . . Epidemics of dissection . . . Virtuoso performances in microscopic taking apart . . . Eczemas of X-rays . . . Endless changes of heart, with some examples of change of life . . . Returns to the nineteenth century, to the founding fathers, to the great refounders . . . The break occurred here . . . No, there! Interminable discussions . . . The thing that emerged most clearly from all this was a vast attempt to destroy the "Subject . . . " This was the enemy now, just as clericalism had been once . . . An unprecedented fascination with and greed for anonymity . . . A desire for suicide in the strictest sense . . . Or rather for a negation of the self, which is the ultimate affirmation of the self, brought to white heat . . . Of course, underneath all the thunderous declarations the same passions survived intact . . . It was a struggle for power among a few names who were trying to abolish names . . . Perpetual intrigue, jealousy and vanity . . . And was there any opposition? No . . . Not even that . . . The "right " and its musty old individualist values collapsed like a pack of cards, evaporated, dissolved . . . And that's how things remain . . . And will remain . . . I belong to the left, you belong to the left, we all belong to the left forever . . . But that's not the problem . . . What we need to know is if there's still anyone in the world with (1) a rich and interesting life; (2) real culture; (3) true originality; (4) style . . . But alas! If we limit it to the French—for I'm quite willing to believe there may be an American or a German, a Latin-American, or a Jamaican that fills the bill—what do we see? Disaster . . . Nothing . . . Take the authors published by Gallimard . . . Everyone knows they're the only ones that matter, and that it's no use trying to get yourself recognized as a writer in France outside of the Central Bank . . . Jean-Marie Le Creuzot? Eric Medrano? Louis-Michel Tournedos? Hey, their names all end in O! Oh! *Histoire d'O!* Perhaps they could all be joined together under the same pseudonym . . . Which one? Cocto? Giono? Corydo? As a tribute to Gide? To the nice, ultimate French ideal of not too little and not too much—allusive, naturalistic, aphoristic, moralistic, and, whatever happens, understated . . . What price the truth about women, i.e., the truth about our own time, there? Not a chance! I've just got a bit carried away in front of S., who listens and smiles . . . I don't really like to go on too much to him about the avant-garde's "experiments . . . " But after all, why not? He puzzles me, he's not where you think he is, he's looking for something else, it's incredible . . . That great contraption of his *Comedy*, tedious, unremitting, shapeless . . . But perhaps, after all, it's important—you never know . . . Classical! Classical! It's the only thing! He'll tell me that yet again . . . And the silly bastard won't even explain what he means . . . "I've explained myself too much already," he says . . . "Now mum's the word . . . Enigma personified . . . The mysterious passer-by . . . Hamlet . . . Legend . . . Pure will on two legs . . . " He laughs . . . He gets on my nerves . . . Avant-gardes? The "moderns"? What do I think of them? Illiterate gibberish . . . Monstrous pretentiousness . . . Distorted sexual obsessions . . . Every kind of scribble, regurgitation, and idiocy . . . And the airs they put on, too! The official secrecy! The masonic signs of recognition, the meaningful looks, the insufferable affectation of ignorance, the laziness, the unbounded self-satisfaction . . . You wonder where they get their justification and confidence from, what keeps them going, what maintains them like bungling parasites on a world that's prostrate and exhausted . . . Back and forth they go with their slim volumes, their moronic magazines, their plots always hatched by the same ten people, their petty perversities, their pathetic poetesses, their superghastly paintresses, their lavatory audacities . . . I think S. is too easy on all that . . . Lenient . . . Patronizing . . . "No, no," he answers, with the usual annoying smile, "it's very useful . . . " "How?" "It creates confusion . . . " "And what's the good of that?" . . . "One has to move forward in disguise . . . *Larvatus prodeo* . . . " "But why?" A vague wave of the hand . . .

But to return to Lutz . . . He did have charm . . . But he was very ill . . . Even when he was the intellectual beacon of potential revolution, the students' guide, the Party's hope of renewal (not only in France but in the whole world), he used to spend half his time in a mental home . . . Partly in analysis (not Fals's school, hence the friction between them), partly in electroshock or lithium treatment . . . Manic depression, the great psychosis of our age . . . Maybe the only true original one . . . Anyhow, the one that reveals want . . . "The density of want . . . " The primal and final Want that no junk can ever satisfy . . . Flora admired Lutz . . . Was jealous of, challenged, adored, hated, watched over, telephoned, bawled out, invited, telephoned again, attached, defended him . . . In short, he mattered to her . . . She was obviously in love with him, or perhaps not so much with him as with what he was . . . A guide to revolutionary theory . . . General secretary of concepts . . . Chancellor of arguments . . . He was a gentle sort of man, though, Lutz . . . But the way power has been distributed around the world until recently, a theoretical director of revolution might come into his own at any moment . . . I think he was fond of Flora, but at the same time frightened of her . . . She didn't let him get away with anything . . . She kept watch on all his comings and goings, on the articles he wrote, on everything he did . . . Despite being an anarchist, Flora always hoped—like every socialist, and like the whole of the left in general—that something would happen to transform the Communist parties . . . A purification, a conversion . . . Lutz might have been either the creator or the catalyst of this development, and gradually become the emperor of Marxavia, while she — why not? — became the red empress and gray eminence . . . A super-Tsarina . . . Catherine the Great and Voltaire . . . That sort of thing . . . Flora's passionate, naive, wondering love of power always fascinated me . . . For she wanted, and still wants, Power to be genuine, to be what it's supposed to be . . . That means she always finds herself to some extent in the opposition . . . That's what makes her what she is . . . She wouldn't be able to help making some sarcastic or critical remark to the Absolute Monarch of all the Universes . . . Just to let him know he was really usurping her position . . . Not that she wants to occupy it, either . . . "What does a hysteric want?" Fals asked one day . . . "A master to rule over . . . " A very profound remark . . . I told Lutz about it and he was impressed . . . But Flora is hysteria without hysterics, naturalness in broad daylight, the thing itself . . . She's very seldom wrong about a person or a situation . . . I always take some notice of what she says, even when she's at her most exasperating . . . She feels waves and forces; she senses beginnings and endings . . . I usually do the opposite of what she says, but that's because that's what really, unconsciously, she's telling me to do . . . You have to know how to read between the lines . . . Hear ditties of no tone . . .

We became sort of friends, Lutz and I . . . Pardoxically, my questions about philosophy and politics bored him . . . He'd have liked to leave all that — revolution, theory, Marxism — behind . . . What he wanted was to become more "cultured," to find out more about the other things that had been going on "outside" while he'd been shutting himself up in "scientific" abstraction . . . These things included literature, music, and painting . . . What had been going on in life all that time? In the end he'll merely have exchanged one prison for another . . . I noticed he didn't even have a television set

95

at his place . . . That, for a contemporary philosopher! And then there was his illness . . . And the illness of his illness: Anne, his wife . . . I only saw her once or twice . . . A gaunt little figure in a beret, older than he was, got up rather like a schoolteacher . . . Extremely disagreeable . . . I think he was scared stiff of her . . . In my experience they've all been frightened to death of their wives, these philosophers and revolutionaries . . . It's as if they were admitting that that's where real divinity lies . . . When they talk about "the masses" they really mean their wives . . . As a matter of fact it's the same wherever you look . . . The dog in his basket . . . Stuck at home . . . Kept watch over in bed . . . Lutz used to lower his voice when he mentioned Anne . . . I suppose she was nearly always horrible to him, in the usual style . . . Be a man . . . More . . . More again . . . Behave yourself, please . . . Just like you! . . . You forget who you are . . . What you stand for . . . What you believe . . . I don't understand how you can mix with such people . . . When I think how everyone believes that you're strong . . . etc., etc. . . . She drove him wild . . . And he strangled her . . . One night . . . But he'd probably been thinking about it for ages . . . The cohabitation of shame and hatred, repugnance, and contempt . . . The reverse side of old-fashioned idealization; when the other person becomes the unbearable sound of a snore, a tap, a toilet being flushed; when the other person's body is only a seeing, judging, irritable lump! . . . When space itself, and the slightest remark or movement, are all charged with the total, irrevocable, grim refusal of this breathing foreign mass . . . Close as can be, and cold as a glacier advancing millimeter by millimeter . . . When the sight of the other person's breathing is painful because it seems to steal something of the watcher's own existence . . . The rise and fall of the chest, the movement of the throat . . . She is asleep, he is still awake . . . Rereading an article devoid of interest . . . He looks at his books, stacked on a special shelf—all his works translated into every language . . . He'd like to burn them now . . . Yes, at that moment madness rises up, madness that's none other than a preternaturally sharp pang of awareness, lighting up his life as if it were some huge little crazy bubble . . . Swelling up . . . And about to burst . . . He picks up a scarf and goes quietly over to the sleeping woman to whom, after all, he owes so much: the woman who helped and encouraged him and looked after him in his neurosis . . . But who also gradually became a distorting mirror reflecting his defeat, his failure, his causeless guilt . . . All he wants is a boundless innocence . . . A great relief . . . To loosen the grip of imaginary duties . . . The Party . . . The Grass Roots . . . The Leadership . . . The Masses . . . The Class Struggle . . . The Historical Trend . . . Strategy . . . A fandango of capital letters on the chess board of applied thought . . . All those people waiting for him to produce the correct analysis of the situation . . . An explanation of the thousandth retreat that has to be seen as a relative victory, just one point in the long process of which one must never despair . . . Dialectic . . . Slogans . . . Easy enough to prove whatever you like . . . You can always find a suitable slogan . . . A leap forward . . . A tactical withdrawal . . . An indirect maneuver . . . The enhancing of inconsistencies . . . A period of transition . . . A turning point . . . The letters he receives every day from all over the world . . . His public . . . The heroism of millions of unknowns . . .

Anne sleeps on . . . She looks fragile, light, as if she were poised above her own sleep . . . Her face is serious . . . Even when she's asleep she's still unyielding and strong, as women are when they've managed to clutch on to some faith . . . It's thus because it ought to be thus . . . She is more of a believer than he . . . She hasn't been contaminated by casuistry . . . She's basically purer; irreproachable . . . And insufferable, because she's always insisting on vigilance, uprightness, intransigence, and fidelity from him too . . . Him and his worn-out body, his insides . . . He dreams of long holidays, sun, idle conversation, walks, swimming pools, and pretty girls . . . He doesn't believe in History anymore . . . He doesn't believe in anything . . . He's tired . . . Death no longer seems what it used to be, and as *they* have to think of it—a negligible detail, just a natural formality in the play that *has* to be acted out . . . Why? Because . . . He's seen everything . . . Censorship, condemnations, rehabilitations, new versions as false as the old ones, corpses

97

better forgotten, cries buried in ledgers . . . He knows, anyhow, that the machinery of the general and inevitable perversion is oiled down to the last little tooth of the last little cogwheel . . . Though on paper everything looks as if it will work as he's always said . . . He's never really been wrong about anything, except perhaps for a nuance here and there . . . But in the main he's always got it right . . . It's reality itself that's gone off the rails . . . And never gets back on . . . Stalin . . . Though of course . . . For now the Opium's making a comeback — religion itself . . . That really is the last straw! Where can such a crack in the edifice have sprung from? Such a terrifying leaking away of meaning? Vigilance must have been relaxed . . . God? No, Really! Anything but that! The Crusade of the present Pope . . . the Pole . . . Islam . . . The Ayatollah . . . All these revivals and throwbacks—the black tide must be mopped up again, calmly and patiently . . . We must show why and how the irrational recurs when Theory fails to supply the conditions favorable to reason . . . Deviation, regression . . . And then China flying the coop after the usual pattern . . . First you mummify the great man, then you cautiously disavow him and criticize his crimes so as to adapt them to the new era . . . In other words, you modernize them . . . They call it "liberalization" . . . We've heard it all before . . . The idea is, of course, in order to win more business contracts, to make repression less obvious and irksome, to make the police more efficient, more skillful, and incidentally more secret . . . Perversion everywhere . . . The trial of Qiang Jing . . . Everyone's in the wrong, everyone's a criminal . . . So what's one crime more or less? Perhaps Stalin was absolutely right in laying the foundations of the new universal religion: "In the end it's always death that wins . . . " Or maybe death tells you in person: "In the end it's always Stalin that wins. . . " Was Stalin the only one who succeeded? These new pamphlets in Arabic with his picture on them . . . Stalin the great survivor . . . With his laugh the size of this whole little pellet we call the world . . . The world seen from the cosmos as a speck echoing to Stalin's laughter . . . Or is it Arthur Baron who's right—that narrow, reactionay social-demo-crat economist, representative of the Americans? The so-called philosopher of the moderate—i.e., the most dangerous—right; a Jew who for all his intelligence is incapable of great thought . . . Who sticks to the facts . . . A "factalist," to use Lenin's pun . . . Baron was showered with honors . . . While there was Lutz, stuck in his poky, dusty little room, the study of a confirmed old bachelor, with an irreproachable and impossible wife . . . Who'd start creating the daily hell again over tomorrow's breakfast . . . You haven't worked hard enough . . . You ought to do something . . . I don't understand how you can lunch with that worldly reactionary . . . He's an opportunist . . . Probably mixed up with the CIA . . . And afterward you intend to see that scheming whore again!

At the same time of night Fals is in more or less the same frame of mind . . . He knows he hasn't got much longer . . . He too looks back with a weary, disillusioned inner eye on the long and difficult road he's traveled . . . Everywhere it's the little men who have triumphed . . . Those lice, that pack of parasites who flourished at his expense, battened on his blood . . . It's those intellectual ticks who've got the jobs . . . Who run the establishment . . . The establishment always wins . . . In the end it's always death, or in other words the establishment, that triumphs . . . The martyrdom of the true heretics—what a joke! What really matters is dogma, orthodoxy . . . But you can't say that . . . Especially to the young . . . The others, though, aren't surrounded by the young . . . False profundity, second-hand research . . . A thought for poor old Lutz who once came and interrupted him . . . Silly fool, he never did understand anything . . . These communists . . . The communist congregation . . . And to think one had sometimes had to make use of them . . . To overcome the scorn of the academic establishment . . . No one ever does understand anything . . . Little men, little men . . . Fals's and Lutz's apartments are only about half an hour's walk apart . . . It's three o'clock in the morning . . . If by any chance they set out to see one another they'd have plenty to talk about, there under the winter moon, near the Luxembourg Gardens . . . The lonely, chilly old park . . . How they watched, spied on, sabotaged one another . . . Sent one another false messengers and false traitors . . . Top secret! Microconfidences . . . Power struggles

. . . Students of both sexes . . . The younger generation . . . The influence of the future . . . How childish it was! How foolish! Then, almost at once, they'd start to quarrel . . . Pride . . . .

So it's better that they should stay at home . . . Gazing at the darkness . . . At approaching death . . . All that's left now is antique wisdom — there hasn't been the slightest progress on that front . . . The Stoics . . . Sartre died this year, after a strange act of autocritique . . . Sartre stopped halfway; he too was showered with all possible honors . . . But what they themselves had attempted was on a different scale, and had a much more rigorous aim . . . Marxism . . . Psychoanalysis . . . The without and the within . . . The without for you and the within for me . . . Absolute knowledge . . . Ah well . . . Who'd have come out on top is another matter . . . The Affair with a capital A . . . What will become of all that? . . . They'll all go drowsing on as before . . . Drift back and settle down again without the faintest idea of what's happened . . . The philosophers in one corner and the priests in the other . . . And no one will remember that it was actually found — the link, the join, the connection with the new age . . .

Fals isn't asleep—he's suffering . . . The worst kind of suffering, after all, is to have been forced to spend one's time on earth among imbeciles who are always lagging behind . . .

Lutz clutches his scarf . . .

He's going to do it . . . And then he'll do the same thing for himself . . .

Perhaps . . .

Anne's neck . . . Thin and wrinkled . . . She's breathing gently . . .

It must be done . . . The black blur that blocks out the air, that has always blocked out the air, must be put an end to . . .

He strangles her slowly . . . There's one supreme, terrible, crucial, ineffable moment when there's no turning back . . . A flowing arc . . . That has to reach its end . . .

And everything collapses . . .

Dust . . .

Next day Lutz is distraught, prostrate . . . The police come for him, he's put away, there's a great scandal . . .

Deliverance . . .

Fals dies a few months later . . .

It's at Anne's funeral that everyone suddenly finds out she was Jewish . . . There's a rabbi in attendance reciting the Kaddish . . . It's a pathetic litany . . . Jewish . . . Deported . . . Communist . . . Murdered . . . But absolutely antireligious . . .

Lutz is declared insane . . .

As insane as the truth . . .

I'm obsessed by that little strangled woman . . . What did I know about her? Nothing . . . Once, on the telephone . . . "I've read the letter you wrote to Laurent . . . I won't pass it on to him . . . You know he's not well . . . It would worry him . . . How can you defend that charlatan, Fals? It's intolerable . . . " That voice . . . Edgy and strident . . . Sure of being right, Right with a capital R . . . She hated Fals for calling attention to the part nerves play in Faith . . . She must have hated me as a matter of course . . . She couldn't stand Flora either, though in that case it was a conflict between two central powers, as you might say . . . Flora doesn't believe in anything except—fiercely—her own way of believing in nothing . . . I'm always astonished at how other women contend against her . . . Viscerally, crudely . . . As if she might give away the whole devious system they support . . . The heart of the matter, of exploitation from below . . . I should point out that Flora immediately places herself amongst the men . . . In her own eyes she's the only man anywhere near normal, and she's quite ready to be the only woman to all the men, the only man to all these women disguised as men . . . She loves women passionately . . . Unconsciously? Anyway, as a man would love them if he really did love them . . . If such a man existed . . . If there were still just one of them . . . Me? perhaps . . . That's really what Flora's looking for in me, what thrills her . . . What I do with women . . . What they do to me . . . Tell . . . Tell . . .

The murder Lutz committed was like a mirror image of the one shown in a Japanese film that Fals was very struck by at the time . . . In *the Realm of the Senses* . . . Where you see the insatiable prostitute, on top of her consenting partner, gradually strangling him in the course of an interminably long-drawn-out orgasm . . . She then goes mad, castrates him, and appropriates his inaccessible and sacred organ . . . The film ends with the two blood-spattered bodies clasped in each other's arms . . . He with a hole where his masculinity used to be . . . I think Lutz strangled Anne so as not to have to contemplate that hole . . . The hole of her castration, which he may just have begun to perceive . . . The great unbearable truth that women are first and foremost just poor women, worn out, weary, heroic, but still going on with the show . . . That they only manage to stay upright by constant effort, and then only just . . . That they're always on the point of collapsing into doubt and self-disgust and disgust with everything . . . It's as if by killing her he perpetuated her, beyond death, proof against all deterioration, in her incarnation of the Law . . . As if he made her live on forever as the embodiment of faultlessness . . . As if that was the only way he could find of putting himself once again, and for good and all, under the thumb of the Law . . . People kill others to make them live more . . . They kill themselves as a violent assertion that life ought never to end . . . Or at least ought not to be undermined by the suspicion that death is there at our endless beginning, mere apparitions that we are . . . Crime, murder, war are just rejections of death . . . Life at any price . . .

I remember Fals's "presentations" at the hospital . . . They were really something . . . The mandarin style . . . The master touch . . . The sudden changes of tone . . . The striking interpretations . . . It was almost as if Lutz had made a date with Fals in the lecture room . . . But Fals is dead, and Lutz is in the power of pure chemistry . . . The meeting never took place . . . Or did so all too well . . . Depending on your point of view . . .

The Realm of the Ignorance of the Senses! Two details in that really rather coarse film suddenly strike me as well observed . . . The first is when the heroine, playing with a little boy in the bathroom, gets hold of him by the prick, squeezes it and makes him cry . . . The second is when the hero, transformed into a supermale by his praying mantis of a partner, tries in vain to break away in order to go and pee . . . She wants him to urinate in and on her . . . She wants his member not to leave her, to stay there as if grafted on her . . . Or rather, she wants the man finally to be reduced to nothing, to dependency through that lively, irritating, superfluous little tube . . . "The prick's a parasite," Fals used to say . . . He thought the same thing about language . . . Language and the prick as elements in this world but belonging to another . . . Two functions outside nature . . . Two antithetical diagonals of antimatter . . . And it's around that that human activity centers . . . And learns as little as possible about it . . . And tries to exorcise what proceeds from it . . . The Phallus and the Word . . . An axis bisected, ruled out by the inertia of bodies . . .

The other film that impressed Fals, I remember (and goodness knows he wasn't any more easily impressed than I am, or any other gentle reader of Sade) was *Rosemary's Baby* . . . He saw it as a sign of the times . . . Another example of a sensational crime passing from fiction into fact . . . It was one of the rare attempts at representing demonic possession in its latest form . . . You remember what happened afterward . . . The director's wife was ritually murdered by some gang or sect consisting of a mad junkie leader and the young girls who adored him . . . The film itself raised the question of genetically manipulated reproduction . . . Strange, unexpected births . . . New possibilities of perversion . . . The girlfriend I went to see it with gratified me with a fit of hysterics when we came out . . . A sort of epileptic fit, with rolling eyes, foaming at the mouth and fainting on the sidewalk, the lot . . . The guy who caused that had touched some chord, no doubt about it . . . Another film to put down to the CIA—the Center for Insemination, Atavistic-style! At one point Bernadette invented an interesting slogan for the Front for the Autonomy of the Matrix: Get pregnant, then have an abortion . . . A kind of gymnastic exercise in aid of freedom . . . An initiation rite . . . The girls would trap the fetuses, experience the pleasures of the vital stoppage, the ultimate compensation, the primal refund—and then have the blessed things dislodged again

. . . A sort of game that would allow Bernadette to test her power . . . Medicine and black magic . . . They're more common than people think . . . Those who went *visibly* mad through such performances were whisked out of sight and no one really knows what's become of them . . . The rest have adapted completely to the new set of circumstances . . .

Such practical jokes can of course be carried to ever greater lengths . . . A publicity spot: "*Sexometer:* That's what the English papers are calling a small electronic device that enables a woman to tell whether she's in a fertile phase or not . . . every morning the sexometer reflects the temperature of a little sensitized plate placed briefly in the mouth, and shows either a green or a red light . . . "

RED!

GREEN!

THE NEW TRAFFIC SYSTEM!

It's up to you to decide if you trust the lady driving the taxi! The modern Eve, with a thermometer in her hand! And at so much a mile! It reminds me of Judith, and some others like her . . . She took it into her head to have a child by me . . . It struck her as quite natural . . . It always strikes them as natural to cause a baby, i.e., a future corpse, to become a descendant of the chimpanzee known as man, who after all only exists in order to be wiped out . . . That's really the most staggering thing about them—the cynicism, the utter desperate coldness, the determination, as of someone who has absolutely nothing to lose, the crudeness of the situations involved . . . The absence of Good and Evil when it comes to the crucial Thing . . . Modesty with a capital M concealing a complete incapacity for the quality itself . . . Even prudishness, when necessary, to hide every kind of trickery . . . I found Judith, radiant and excited, on the landing outside my door . . . I must screw her right away . . . It was the prescribed day . . . Hallelujah! The night of the calculation . . . The great night of the iguana . . . The Villa in the Mysteries of Pompeii! Red curtain, prostration, revelation! Hugo wrote an unintentionally funny poem on the subject: *Booz endormi* . . . "Ruth, a Moabite . . . . " Booz—what a name . . . All very Biblical . . . It's been going on since time immemorial . . .

The Bible talks about nothing else . . . That's why no one really reads it . . . Extortion of children, distortion of genealogies, transmission of property according to the effectiveness of insemination . . . The one fundamental epic . . . Stretching throughout time . . . In a way (though at the time everyone's teeth understandably chatter with terror) it's also sheer comedy . . . With Judith, as with the others, the suggestion was quite plain and even flattering . . . "I shan't ask anything of you, I'll see to everything, you won't even hear about me . . . " It's quite common these days . . . As one of the more influential leaders of WOMANN said recently (never having had any children herself, she never stops sounding off about parenthood): "Paternity begins after birth . . . " In other words, get started anyway and we'll see about the bills afterward . . . " Who knows, perhaps they ought to have to sign contracts . . . The new social contract . . . The rights and duties of the castrato in the age of the mother . . . Or else we ought to be paid at piece-work rates, so much a spurt, like a donor . . . A philosopher politician once said that S.'s airy, useless, experimental existence was only possible if ten children died of hunger every day in the Third World . . . S. offered to give his sperm to a committee of duly appointed women every morning by way of compensation . . . Almost no one laughed, except me . . .

Judith already had one child, a boy, by X . . . But that wasn't enough . . . Or perhaps she thought that if she had another one, with me, I'd take on both of them? If paternity begins with birth, if the Father isn't the "genitor" (a ludicrous discovery of psychoanalytic ideology), there's no reason to stop at that . . . Existence precedes essence . . . If we grow some existence the essence will always come along and fill it up . . . But because of the energy crisis *essence* (= gasoline) is getting dearer . . . The same thing happened when I became a father: I asked the *Journal* for a raise . . . Paternity begins with birth, if you like, but it also follows you in death . . . So family vaults will get overcrowded . . . The only answer will be common graves! Cemeteries will become museums . . . Children will be brought to see how those strange prehistoric creatures used to insist on being buried—meanly and mediocrely, in their own plots, under the same name . . . Everything's different, isn't it, in preparation for the final complete disappearance so much to be desired . . . A clean sweep! It will be more and more beautiful . . . A complete state takeover from the cradle to the grave . . . Forget about the past . . .

But, to be serious, for *them* it's a really dramatic experience . . . Madly so . . . Judith used to send me romantic little letters on fixed dates every month: "Darling, I waited for you all night . . . I burned between the sheets . . . You can't imagine now how I longed for you, your body, your lips, etc. . . . " The snaring of the spermatazoa! The Hunting of the Snark! There was a period when I was a kind of gold standard . . . Do these women pass addresses around to one another? And information? Is some guy designated every so often as being particularly vulnerable? Depressed? Free? Deserted? Worried? Be that as it may, for six months I was the Snark . . . A nightmare . . . Gorgeous girls . . . Lying there . . . There for the taking . . . No underclothes . . . Raring to go . . . Insinuating . . . The East! The temptation of St. Anthony! But I could already see them taking their temperatures . . . Plotting the graphs . . . Having the sort of injections that favor breeding . . . Gonadotrophine . . . Humegon . . . And yet there'd never been so much talk of abortion and contraception . . . I used to get ten gynecological booklets a month from Francesca, who thought I needed educating . . . (She's crazy about that sort of thing — a dedicated gynecophile who thinks human life is hell but that the hellishness should be multiplied . . . She's bored to death with herself, so everyone else has got to be miserable, to submit to the laws of realistic necessity and understand the human dilemma down to the last groan . . . She's tall, good-looking, sad, brave, meticulous, has trouble with her back, dresses very conventionally, and suffers in silence . . . Yes, it really was a revolution . . . They demonstrated in the streets, shouting and yelling, but at home at my place, between ourselves, it was quite different . . . They left their placards outside, folded up their banners, replaced their tights with black stockings and garters, and came in breathless to play their frantic roulette with me for the prize . . . You may say it's

106

only natural . . . It was as if I'd won a ribbon at a cattle show . . . I know France is a nation of peasants, but still . . . Bull No. 1? Or 10? Or 100? Perhaps I've got rivals after all? Of course—mustn't be conceited . . . They ought to write to me so that we can compare performances . . .

For if you screw them you soon notice something odd . . . A way of drawing up their legs or arching their backs . . . A suspicious hurry to be entered . . . The very opposite of the Ancien Régime . . . A sort of hygienic decisiveness, as if you were some kind of tube for administering an enema . . . The left wing of WOMANN and FAM issued another slogan: "The factory belongs to the workers, the womb belongs to the women . . . The production of life is our affair . . . " Bernadette's own inimitable style . . . More Trotskyist than ever . . . If I understand it correctly, men, the potential fathers, the bovine progenitors, had become the equivalent of coal and metal, wood and corrugated iron . . . We were to be recycled, put through the mill to provide material for the "production of life. . . " An inspired phrase . . . What a marvelous industrial landscape it conjures up . . . Sexual mines and penial quarries . . . Slavery to end all slavery . . . The vengeance of the ages . . . What a future! The new Stakhanovism! Under the eye of our great helmswoman, dictating the rhythm of the oars . . . It was very exciting . . . Perhaps even erotic, if you had strong nerves . . . Better, anyhow, than the purely medical proposition whereby the man was to be sterilized if the woman wanted to be sure he wouldn't go off begetting children elsewhere . . . Or even worse, heated underpants designed to made sure your spermatozoa are harmless . . . When your partner's ovulating she disconnects you, although the rest of the time you're functional . . . But that, if I may so express it, is for third-class heteros, those who really have no luck, the proletarians of love . . .

The Sodom and Gomorrah International Council must have found Bernadette's slogan too frontal . . . Too loud . . . Likely to provoke a revolt . . . To cause riots among the new slaves, whom there's no point in keeping too well-informed . . . So "The womb belongs to the women" didn't last long . . . Pity . . . It was starting to be quite exciting . . . Opportunities offered on all sides . . . A bit of discipline, on the yoga pattern, so that you didn't ejaculate too freely, and you could sometimes screw up to three or four a day . . . And if you take the trouble to fake it, as they do, you can learn a lot . . . You can, so to speak, cross over from your own sex . . . Judith didn't get her second child . . . At least not from me . . . Good luck . . .

Whole swathes of "fatherless" kids came on the scene about then . . . The mothers were, or at least seemed, very proud of this proof of "self-management . . ." At first, anyhow . . . For a few months they were bright and cheerful, megalomaniac, on top of the world . . . And then came the problems . . . Fatigue, nervous strain . . . Let's say no more about it . . .

Now things have calmed down again, with abortion finally reimbursable on social security . . . (This, together with the abolition of the death penalty, which of course I'm in favor of, is a supreme indicator of social change . . .) But it does puzzle me . . . What is it, actually, that the social security is reimbursing? What a wonderful commercial expression . . . Well, anyway, calm has been restored . . . And boredom? Come, come . . . A return to a certain element of secrecy . . . The SGIC is right—you must be careful not to frighten the fish . . .

Francesca has stopped sending me her specialist magazines with the latest products and gadgets . . . I'm out of touch . . . In danger of getting out of date . . . I'm going rusty . . . Or perhaps I've been denounced . . . Put under observation . . . No point in sending me any more presents . . .

Don't go thinking I'm disgruntled, though . . . That I'm a conservative, a traditionalist, a reactionary, a fundamentalist, a Papist . . . We Americans have known all about it for a long time . . . It's inevitable . . . And what's one bit of folly more or less on a ship of fools? . . . For all this is crazy, isn't it? I mean, horribly reasonable? Isn't it? I mean, rather ridiculous? . . . Isn't it? . . . Mankind had one last area of liberty left in that little, silent, forbidden thing— sex . . . And now it's all over . . . So let me tell you how you have to cope with the situation . . .

Let's just suppose Emma Bovary had come back among us . . . She's a hundred and twenty-five years old . . . But she'll always be thirty . . . She's still as beautiful, voluptuous and mysterious as ever . . . Her quest for the ideal may be less hopeful than it was, but she herself is unwavering . . . Everybody from the provinces has come up to Paris . . . Charles vegetates as a local doctor, running a clinic . . . Gossip has it that little Berthe isn't his child . . . He's given up on Emma—every time he goes near her she pleads a headache . . . She's cold to him, sulks over dinner, doesn't laugh at any of his jokes, and never misses a chance of saying something mean about his mother . . . The Apothecary has been a great success and is now a fashionable gynecologist, with a private nursing home in the smartest part of town . . . He's an influential member of the Party . . . Who hasn't heard of M. Homais, who is in with the government, writes every so often in the weeklies, works for the future of science and never wearies in the struggle to spread Enlightenment? It's true his diatribes in the press are no longer directed against "Loyola's gentlemen," though he does allude to them occasionally, as he did in his tempestuous youth in Yonville . . . His targets nowadays are the big monopolies, the greedy multinationals, American imperialism, the way his own country is losing its real identity . . . But he's still cautious . . . No point in indiscriminate nationalization . . . He's more than ever in favor of new experiments; the unsuccessful operation on the club foot was an unfortunate business, but it's all over and forgotten . . . What he's interested in now is biology . . . Genes, clones, grafts, the splendid jumble of substances that may at last make it possible to create a new human race . . . He says this is the magic materialism Diderot, his favorite author, spoke of . . . "Isn't it thrilling," he wrote in an article that made a great stir, " this final phase in the transfer of responsibility for creation? . . . From God to priest, priest to prince, legislator to couple, and lastly from the couple to the woman alone?" His wife, however, though an ardent feminist, is rather reticent on this point, as befits a partner in a marriage that's respectable as well as daring . . . But he gets worked up and holds forth, and wears a halo that definitely smells of alchemy . . .

He has read Freud and is (of course) in favor, but secretly delights in the works of Jung, who, say what you like, whether he's a spiritualist or not, is certainly a great visionary . . . Naturally the Papacy is as reactionary as it ever was, despite its flabby efforts to rejoin the course of history ("Do you realize they've waited till the end of the twentieth century to rehabilitate Galileo?"), but it has completely lost its influence, at least in civilized countries—one can't answer for Africa or Latin America, or backward crowds like the Spanish, the Irish, and the Poles . . . If you want my opinion, this last Pope, from the East, is bound to be a Soviet agent or a member of the CIA, as our friends in the East say . . . Bournisien, the priest, Homais's narrow-minded old adversary, has been vanquished, and is ending his days in some obscure monastery in the suburbs . . . But Homais, though he belongs to the left, is not a sectarian . . . Far from it . . . He disapproves of Totalitarianism in all its forms, including the Russian, which has long been an obstacle to science . . . He understands the views of his chief political enemy, who at least is a convinced rationalist and anti-Christian, classically educated and a great quoter of Marcus Aurelius . . . Homais and his enemy have similar ideas about genetic manipulation, though they differ about their application . . . Nonetheless, Homais sometimes finds himself thinking horrible things and contemplating possibilities that his mind firmly rejects . . . For example, that despite all that's rightly been said about them, the Nazis did have a certain nerve . . . Perhaps—such things do happen— they acted as crazy pioneers . . . These are only furtive little thoughts, mere sensations of thoughts really, that come to him when he gets tired of the human race's incredible timidity, when the future could be so wide open . . . "I'm a happy positivist," he likes to say . . . Every month he gives Emma a free consultation, examining her at length and prescribing a course of injections should she decide to dispose of herself freely . . . They discuss Charles's shortcomings: he's definitely a failure and is gradually growing bitter, especially since his mother died . . . "A classic case, really, of Oedipal fixation," Homais says . . . Emma agrees . . . She identified Charles's obsessional neurosis a long time ago, and after four years of analysis can laugh as she talks about her own hysteria . . . This doesn't prevent things from going on just as before . . . Léon is a young deputy belonging to the center-right group of the Opposition . . . Rodolphe is an influential literary critic . . . Instead of arranging to meet in Rouen Cathedral they go to the Closerie des Lilas or the Brasserie Lipp . . . But they still make love a bit on back seats, at night . . . A few years ago Rodolphe had a craze for swapping, and used to take Emma to parties where the lower-class style was sometimes a bit overdone . . . Emma took an interest just to please him, but she soon got bored . . . Financial affairs will always be the only ones that count, whatever people say . . . Emma has a great admiration for Flaubert, and much prefers him to Homais's Diderot or Stendhal, but they both think Sartre's *Idiot de la famille* (which neither of them has read) throws a remarkably interesting light on poor Gustave's illness . . . Flaubert's is a typical case . . . Quite obvious . . . Rather pitiful . . . When they think about the lawsuit that was brought against the novel they laugh as if at some relic of the Middle Ages . . . How conventional and ridiculous those people were — such a thing couldn't possibly happen now . . . Anyhow, censorship doesn't exist anymore . . . Of course not . . . Ernest Pinard, the prosecutor, has been retired long ago; he even got beaten hollow in the elections in the west of France . . . Marie-Antoine-Jules Sénard, the lawyer, whose speech for the defense is still remembered, is in line for the post of Attorney General, as is only right and just . . . Have you noticed, Rodolphe often asks— his observations are always shrewd and unexpected—, that Flaubert owes his acquittal to his social class? To his father's reputation as a doctor? If he'd been tried today he might have been found guilty . . . Panned by all the papers . . . They smile at the paradox . . . True, Emma criticizes Flaubert for describing the burgeoning of her love for Rodolphe in parallel with the agricultural show and the lowing of the cattle . . . She considers this passage somewhat labored, its humor rather forced . . . That's the right-wing anarchist side of him, says Rodolphe . . . The bad taste of a confirmed old bachelor . . . But Emma admires the journey on the boat with Léon as much as ever—it's so musical; and the ride in the cab with the curtains drawn; and the scenes at the inn . . . But she finds the description of the church very out of date:

> The church spread around her like a huge boudoir . . . The vaults leaned down in the dark to listen to the confession of her love . . . The stained-glass windows glowed to light up her face, and the censers would soon burn so that she might look like an angel wreathed in sweet-smelling smoke . . .

(This passage always makes Homais roar with laughter at its "terrible" irony; at the same time he sees it as naive evidence of Flaubert's unresolved Oedipus complex . . .)

Emma still gets a thrill, though, when she reads bits like: "She undressed hastily, tearing at the lace of her corset so that it hissed around her hips like the coils of a snake . . . She tiptoed over, barefoot, to make sure again that the door was locked, then let fall all her clothes at once;—and, pale, grave and silent, threw herself on his breast with a long shudder . . ."

They don't write like that anymore, says Emma . . . No wonder French is in decline everywhere . . . And that no contemporary writer is anywhere near as evocative . . . Name just one! Of course, some things in that paragraph have become outmoded (though whenever she reads it she wishes for a few seconds that she could wear a corset too), but the rhythms, the pivotal force of the semicolon and the dash . . . You feel everything, don't you, through the skillful suspense of the style . . . "Something extreme, vague and gloomy . . ." And especially: "He was becoming her mistress rather than she his . . . Where had she learned this corruption, so deep and secret as to be almost insubstantial?"

In fact, rigged out though she is in the whole paraphernalia of modern emancipation, Emma is Emma still, with the same tendency to brood, the same grief, rage, and disappointment at the sudden discovery that, strangely enough, only literature records . . . Namely, the lack of men worthy of the name . . . There aren't any men!

Not one! They're all puppets and cowards and braggarts and fools
. . . Forever, over and over again, in all her incarnations, Emma
always arrives at the same desperate and monotonous conclusion
. . . Men are all spineless . . . Except during the sexual act itself,
which reveals both their bestiality and their pointlessness . . . The
look in their eyes then is frightening . . . They really are radically
flawed . . . Pseudo-Emmas, in fact . . . Impostors . . . Mere sketches
. . . Why should we need them? And is it really so certain that we
do? Ultimately, Homais is the only one you can really take seriously, but he's drab and narrow, and you can't tell me he's a good
screw—anyway, ambition is all he cares about . . . Emma gets
hooked by FAM propaganda . . . She meets Bernadette and they
fall into each other's arms . . . There's a lesbian episode . . . But it
isn't really that . . . Even that isn't really genuine . . . And anyway
Emma soon suspects that Bernadette's only after her royalties . . .
So is everything just an illusion? The tubes of sleeping tablets are
ready to hand, supplied by Homais . . . She swallows them, hoping
she'll be rescued in time and Rodolphe will propose at last by what
was so nearly her deathbed . . . But he is unmoved . . . He still
won't get a divorce . . . He prefers to go on with his craven mixture
of marriage and adultery rather than devote himself completely to
her, who has given and sacrificed so much for him . . . He might be
cruel and unfeeling enough to give his wife another child . . . Have
her give him one, rather . . . Marie Curie had to endure the same
thing . . . That lucid, but sublimely passionate genius . . . Emma-
rie Curie, victim of a commomplace lover . . . Emma doesn't die
. . . She raises her two daughters, Berthe and Marie, in a spirit of
general vengeance that perhaps, one day . . . Later on . . . Some
other time . . .

Let's go on supposing . . . Where are we now? Country: the
world . . . Capital: Gomorrah . . . Chief town: Sodom . . . Inhabitants: the committed . . . Apart from them, there are a few exiles
in the mountains (like me now, in this clandestine apartment: I

can't write anymore — the letters swirl about before my eyes like a curtain flapping in the wind; I can't sleep either — I'm locked out of the chamber of sleep, which is full of harsh, blood-red light) . . .

It's easy to arrive at this incredible hypothesis . . . But it's clearly what Proust is leading up to, though no one seems to pay any attention . . . The SGIC's whole system of theories is contained in Proust, especially the crucial point that Sodom is in fact a "dialect" of Gomorrah, a branch, a subset, a separate but subordinate offshoot . . . The Bible gives both names, but you'll have noticed it only actually speaks of Sodom (Genesis 18 and 19) . . .

The three men—the three angels—visit Abraham . . . "And the Lord appeared unto him in the plains of Mamre: and he sat in the tent door in the heat of the day; And he lifted up his eyes and looked, and lo, three men stood by him" . . . They announce that by a miracle Sarah will have a son, she laughs incredulously, they promise to come back the following year, then go to Sodom . . . A brilliant transition . . . The men of Sodom immediately want to screw the Lord's envoys, who have taken refuge with Lot . . . That gives you an idea of their main preoccupation . . . They lose no time in scenting out the guys from heaven, and can't wait to get at them . . . But Gomorrah remains very shadowy—the story doesn't tell us anything about it . . . That's where Proust shows his genius —by starting to fill the void . . . By changing Emma into Albert, and then into Albertine . . . By giving a twist a further twist . . . He began to "see" the pattern as a whole . . . But what he really "saw" ("I saw the hell of women there") was that sex itself, the great insistent urge that agitates and torments men so, is ultimately determined by women, by remote control . . . There's a nonsexual form of sexuality that is much stronger, more insidious and unbeatable than that which appears openly . . . *Cosa mentale* . . . This intuition, arrived at by a homosexual, is central to the whole argument . . . The most virile homo is a woman to the very fingertips . . . *Like* a woman . . . *If* she were a man . . . Who *would be* a real woman . . . The circle is undoubtedly a vicious one—that's its nature and you have to get used to it . . . That's why the system as a whole resembles the mechanism of death . . . And why when the living God, the God of the Bible, intervenes, he can do so only through weird processes of procreation . . . He alters names, distorts and revolutionizes genealogies . . . Sarah is no longer a woman in the real sense of the word—it has "ceased to be with Sarah after the manner of women . . ." She's no longer part of the ebb and flow of reproduction, she's well past the menopause, but she gives birth just the same to Isaac, whose name means laughter and refers to Sarah's own laugh of wonder, disbelief and delight . . . "Is any thing too hard for the Lord?" (Genesis 18:14) . . . When I think how most people regard the business with the Virgin Mary as extraordinary . . . But, whatever the puritans say, it's exactly the same sort of thing . . . You think that's going too far? All right, if you're incapable of imagining any kind of relativity in these matters . . . The more extreme case, in this context, simply does without biological intervention, that's all . . . Is it more difficult to believe in god passing directly through a girl than in his managing things by some unknown means with an old woman? Admittedly Isaac, saved from the sacrifice, goes on to bungle his dying blessing, tricked by Rebecca, whose favorite is Jacob . . . And so on and so forth . . . Whereas the Other . . . Here, of course, I'm addressing myself only to the open-minded, who believe that despite everything the mind's vagaries always tell the truth . . . I'm not talking either to the believers or to the rationalists . . . So, anyhow, the beyond-nature of god corresponds to the counternature of nature; it brings it out and rectifies it . . . It's only the charming pagans, in other words everybody, who set limits to the marvelous by maintaining that there's a nature of nature . . . Which sometimes, as in Sodom and Gomorrah, may admit of exceptions . . . But above that there's only the function "god," the great glider of all time to whom this great mix-up below is all one and the same, or almost . . . A funny kind of a prick . . .

Speaking of paganism . . . And circles . . . And a nature of nature . . . And therefore of the *"eternel retour"* . . . Nietzsche, the son of a Protestant minister, said an interesting thing to Lou Andreas-Salomé . . . He wasn't speaking idly, and certainly not to her in particular: "One day, in the course of a conversation in which we were discussing the various changes he had undergone, Nietzsche said, only half joking, 'Yes, that's how the race begins, but where does it end? Where do you go when you've reached the end of the road? What happens when all the permutations and combinations have been exhausted? Wouldn't one have to go back to religion? Perhaps to the *Catholic* religion?' And he revealed what lay behind this remark by adding, quite seriously, 'Anyhow, completing the circle is infinitely more likely than going back to doing nothing . . .' "

Completion, infinite motion . . . "The hour-glass of existence will go on being inverted for ever—and you with it, dust made of dust . . ." One of his precepts on style is relevant here: "The richness of life is reflected in the richness of acts . . . One must learn to see everything as an act: the length and division of sentences, punctuation, pauses; also the choice of words and the ordering of the argument . . ."

I can still see Werth at the end of his life, just before his accident . . . His mother had died two years before . . . The great love of his life, the only one . . . He let himself drift more and more into complications with boys; that was his penchant, and it suddenly grew more marked . . . He thought of nothing else, though he dreamed all the time about breaking off, abstinence, beginning a new life, the books he ought to write, a fresh start . . . Did he know the nickname friends called him by now, surreptitiously, during the special evenings they organized to provide him with pick-ups? "Granny"! Granny! That said it all . . . We used to have dinner together regularly once a month . . . In the old days the conversation was about literature, authors, tricks of construction or narrative . . . Proust . . . His dramatic decision to cut himself off from the world to write the *Recherche* . . . But now the talk turned increasingly on the intrigues between so-and-so and so-and-so, and the little psychological annoyances arising from physical strain . . . There's nothing drives people to psychology worse than perversion . . . That's why, although with women I go along with it as much as they like, I'm virtue personified myself in that I can drop it at once whenever I choose . . . Really? . . . Yes . . . I keep a check on things . . . As I would with a drug . . . Why? No psychology, thanks . . . Werth was lucid and intelligent enough to see how stupid it was to get caught up, and what it was bound to lead to . . . But his late discovery of easy pleasure got the better of him . . . Though the conflict made him suffer . . . Now, in the darkness, on the window-pane separating me from the other side of life, I can see his face, small and shriveled, screwed down in his coffin . . . The bitter twist of the lips, the poor head like that of a stuffed bird, suddenly gripped in the talons of the thieving void . . . At one time or another many homosexuals have looked like that to me: as if they were being eaten up from within; as if some strange force in the brain or spine were gradually reducing them to premature ghosts . . . Contorted, sidelong apparitions . . . Dessicated, petrified . . . Turning into pillars of salt . . . It was very noticeable in Werth toward the end . . . Something crumbling, diaphanous, wan . . . Bloodless . . . A kind of suppressed fury and false gaiety . . . Envy, jealousy . . . A heavy, liverish ardor . . . To be someone else, like someone else; to ingest others so that others seemed not to exist . . . A continual touchiness . . . Although he had it very much under control, it was always plain to be seen and heard . . . A narcissistic padding out, ever more tense, of every imaginable boundary of identity . . . And it's precisely there that the more or less hidden dictatorship of women catches up with them . . . Like women, they'll never manage to see themselves, to catch their own infinite reflections, however much they keep on looking at them-selves in the glass . . . Homosexuals are to women as a chignon is to a head of hair, as the knee is to the thigh, an ornamental frame to the canvas or wood on which a picture is painted . . . A reflection of a reflection of a reflection reflecting the reverse of a reflection . . . The scattered vestiges of a mother . . . Kate told me about the other side of it—Bernadette's homosexual sessions . . . The Queen basking in the adoration of her maidservants, the hive humming and the anthill seething with images of images swelling toward the altar . . . Languishings, bulgings, coverings, curvings . . . "I made tracks when I saw Bernadette start fumbling in some girl's brassière . . . I couldn't take it" . . . And Deb, after she'd been picked up by

117

the Organization, told me about a weekend of that sort at Deauville . . . The slowness and passivity of women among themselves; the slow rhythms and gestures, the heavy bodies slumped in corners . . . Males among females . . . Females among males . . . But over both, the fixed but hidden gaze of an androgynous divinity who is ultimately feminine because the appendage has returned into its sheath . . . There's something very ancient about it all, despite the paltriness of modern cities—something Babylonian or Egyptian . . . The immemorial worship of Sleep . . . And that's the impression you get from being or moving or living among them . . . Trying, despite everything, to be like them . . . Rubbing up against them in the long, dreary, crowded corridors always filling up with fresh bodies, legs, hands, and faces . . . Fresh weariness wearing away because time passes so quickly it's as if no one took any account of it . . . No past, future, or present—nothing but sleep, or waking that's almost the same . . .

Werth couldn't quite make me out; I intrigued him . . . He sensed that I thoroughly understood the religion in question (which was far from clear to him), but that at the same time I remained outside it . . . Not because of any kind of complex, but from conviction . . . I even think that apart from the exhibitionist gratification he got from telling me things, he was more interested in trying to exteriorize them than in trying to disturb me . . . Here was at least one person who saw and wasn't particularly interested . . . In such situations I became almost a kind of priest or missionary . . . Understandably . . . All that empire of incense mounting up toward the unknown, impossible, inaccessible Father, as if to force him to exist and reveal himself . . . And nothing ever comes . . . And more and more sins are committed . . . And then one day the earthquake takes place and there's a whiff of brimstone—not only war, but sickness and death . . . Whole communities scattered and destroyed . . . Only to form again nearby . . .

There's nothing so hierarchical as the kingdom of perversity . . . It's a sort of clergy or counter-Church . . . With its own cardinals, bishops, and simple parish priests . . . Its poor sacristans without any future . . . It happens of its own accord . . . It's part of the

118

unwritten logic of sex . . . There are always fierce struggles going on for the top position . . . Queen of the termites, king of the rats . . . Nothing can be seen of it, except perhaps a few ripples in the curtain of secrecy; it all takes place in the dense phallic darkness . . . The king is the one who seems to have the sharpest experience of castration . . . The queen is the one most keenly aware of that fundamental ablation . . . Again it's all nonmaterial—physiological activities belong to a lower order of things . . . On the higher plane they assume the character of shadowy sacraments, seals set upon internal states . . . As if the whole system were a kind of hypnosis . . . Incidentally, hypnosis and drugs are both straits in that ocean . . . Have a good look at their eyes, men and women . . . They're asleep . . . Fast asleep . . . With their eyes open and shining . . .

Yes indeed, the old Manicheans were right . . . The Archontes or powers of the air are there all right, though intangible . . . They watch like sleepwalkers over the irrevocable burying of the bodies . . . S. is fond of quoting a saying—by Antonin Artaud, I think—to the effect that the world is nothing but a "*châtelet* or little castle of black magic . . ." An opera house with murder taking place backstage . . . I can still see old William Burroughs in New York, leaning against the wall and shifting from one foot to the other as he waited to speak at a conference . . . With his faded blue eyes blotted up by a thousand flashes . . . Stooping, thin, with hollow cheeks, caught on the rough hook of the counterbone . . . Then launching into a long, halting reverie on world pollution, the mutation of salamanders, an apocalypse of swamps and viruses in which what's left of the human race will have to leave the earth and scatter itself amongst the stars . . . Screwings, hangings, science fiction against a background of pirated recordings and damaged neurons . . . The golden age returns: naked young men run wild in gangs, and steal, kill, and fuck to their hearts' content, while the women, organized in Amazonian commando groups, merely act as a kind of police force . . . The American public—that's to say the nice fat old American ladies with their hairdos and their cheesecake—listen to the sermon in amazement and delight . . . They clap enthusiastically . . . Burroughs is wily enough, even if he does look like a hungry and exhausted old hound . . . He gets his fee . . . He survives . . . I open his most recent book, at random . . .

"In a dream I see Dink standing over me with the most perfectly formed erect phallus I have ever seen. Now he is fucking me with my legs up and as I wake up ejaculating, I find that he *is* fucking me. I can feel his face in mine and for a split second he disappears and I hear his fourteen-year-old voice in my throat: 'It's me! It's me! It's me! I made it! I landed!' "

I can see he doesn't do things by halves . . . He dedicates the whole thing, from the start, to every possible devil: "To the Lord of Abominations, . . . whose face is a mass of entrails, whose breathe is the stench of dung and the perfume of death . . . Dark Angel of the Four Winds with rotting genitals from which he howls through sharpened teeth . . . to *Gelal* and *Lilit*, who invade the beds of men and whose children ware born in secret places . . ." And so on . . . A horrid thrill! Marvelous! Emma's dumbfounded! Can't get over it! She devours the book . . . Rushes at Rodolphe, shrieking . . . He's in two minds about mentioning it in his column . . . It's so peculiar . . . Fringe stuff? Yes . . . Where do the Americans dig this sort of thing up? How could you recommend it to readers in Limoges or Mulhouse or Dijon? And doesn't he lay it on a bit thick? Wily old Burroughs . . .

Werth was at the end of his tether . . . Everything bored, wearied, and disgusted him more and more . . . The demands of some people, the entreaties of others . . . The atmosphere of unremitting malice in which amateur prostitution is shrouded . . . The stupid dependency of boys always wanting to be helped, mothered, pushed, have strings pulled for them . . . What a price to pay for a few pleasant moments (if that) . . . The phone calls to make, letters to write, favors to ask, quarrels to settle . . . The advice, the endless making allowances, the responsibility, the tips disguised as something else . . . By dint of all this resignation Werth had become a kind of saint in spite of himself, though he remained very reserved, with sudden bursts of rage . . . For him, unlike most of them nowadays, homosexuality wasn't something arrogant and aggressive, militant, open and uncompromising . . . Obscenity in the shop window . . . Sado-maso nightclubs, leather all over the place . . . Torsos, hair, muscles, swimming pools of clay, viscous seas . . . The flutter of groans and gasps . . . The one thing Werth was afraid of was that his mother might find out about his proclivities from the newspapers . . . That it might create a scandal and threaten his hard-won position as a leading professor . . . Already there was hostility from his colleagues—slander constantly put about by those who hadn't made the academic grade . . . No resemblance to the virile leftist stance of Pasolini . . . Among the underprivileged at work or on the beach . . . With the risk of getting murdered at the end of it, which is in fact what happened . . . No, the French are more reserved, of course—they suffer more and more subtly . . . Can you see Proust in a New York nightclub? Or Charlus and Jupien in the public baths on 72nd Street? What Werth was fighting for, without undue hopes of success, was a kind of attenuated sensuality, a variation of Epicureanism . . . Something rather Buddhist or Japanese, something rather limp . . .

His book, *The Fantasy of the Emotions*, produced the kind of stir you might have expected if Stendhal had come to life again . . . It arrived at the right moment, during a phase of unisex languor . . . The boys were rather like girls, and the girls tried to manage with that as best they could . . . Communicating vessels, the equals-sign . . . The women were pleased . . . Werth was surprised at this sudden and very public success . . . Flattered, then irritated . . . He wanted to be loved, certainly, what an idea, but without the hatred that inevitably goes with emotional demonstrations . . . Hate was always a mystery to him . . . He knew it was there, but he preferred not to see it . . . And he was forced to admit that it was everywhere . . . Jean Werth was a humanist, and it wasn't a time for humanism; it was an age for unbridled fury, with intervals of idealism . . . So was all that—love, pleasure, sensualism, perverse dalliance, temperate sex, a good self-image—just a flowery covering bound to give way and fling you down into a pit full of violence and filth, and death sought for its own sake? Such a thing struck him as philosophically absurd . . . Inconceivable . . . The end of the glory that was Greece, a subversion of all form, barbarism . . . He saw himself as a "Ghibelline"—someone belonging to the tradition of what he called "man's worship of man" . . . He considered me a "Guelph," and that's what I am—a "white Guelph" . . . In other words, pessimistic, casuistical, baroque, someone who's learned to his cost that you can only fight evil with evil . . . A Jesuit . . . Werth was a Protestant to his fingertips, and I'm a Catholic . . . There's no doubt that Protestants are morally superior to us—more naturally Christian, whereas we're not very Christian at all . . . We don't look up to our witches of mothers the way they do . . . The Virgin Mary's different . . . The same thing on a different level . . . On the other hand, we're better at understanding pagan cunning . . . What lies behind . . . Dionysus . . . Destruction, chaos . . . And now, perhaps, the Jewish Torah too . . . It's uncompromising challenge to all the tawdry devils milling about in the vortex of the pubis . . .

"Soon he'll be with his mother again," Deb said to me as we left the emergency ward where Werth lay dying . . . He was on a drip —almost naked, with tubes everywhere, like a great expiring fish still breathing . . . He made a slow, mechanical gesture with his hand, as if to ask to be disconnected and have done with it . . . Everyone had lied again, even then . . . He wasn't as ill as all that; the accident hadn't been so very serious . . . But it was all up with him from the beginning . . . His eyes had looked up at me, burning with fever and death, and his lips had muttered "Thank you, thank you" when I managed to stammer out a few words . . . I can't remember what they were . . . That he must hold on, that I was with him . . . With him a hundred percent . . . It was a warm spring day, disagreeably muggy . . . I could see him slowly drifting away, upright, like a drowned man . . . I ran over in my mind all the evenings in the past, autumn, winter, spring, and summer, when he'd come to meet me, with his cigar ready to smoke after dinner—elegant, sober, glad to see someone who was fond of him and of whom he was fond . . . In the old days we used to take turns talking about what we were writing; bringing one another up to date on the month's work . . . We were both interested in the voice, singing, the abbreviations of Chinese poetry, notebooks, pens, calligraphy, the piano . . . Werth used to ask me about American literature and let me run on about Melville and Pound . . . He found it strange that I was both American and a Catholic . . . I tried to explain the varied history of that minority, its virtues and its vices . . . We wrote little letters from time to time to cheer one another up . . . Each of us had his own adventures and trips . . . But he was the one who told about them; I never did . . . I never tell anyone anything about my life, as a matter of principle . . . A matter of personal aesthetics . . . Superstition . . . Transposition . . .

Several times, out in the hospital yard, I had to make an effort not to faint . . . Then I went up to him again . . . The intensive care unit . . . His heart was beating there, up and down, on the black screen . . . The last cabin of the cosmonaut . . . Journey's end, this time . . . He'd set out once more, very far, very near, millions of light-years away from his own body slumped there like a sack, a gray heap, with dried blood round his nose and lips . . . A tangle of wires . . . Tubes . . . Switches . . . Red and yellow flickers . . . The dying have become like submarines suspended day and night in some harsh blue medium of transition . . . Suddenly, as I stood there, I realized I'd started praying . . . In the name of the Father, and of the Son and of the Holy Ghost . . . In nomine Patris, et Filii, et Spiritus Sancti . . . It suddenly came back to me in the midst of disaster and despair . . . Of the horrible stupidity of this lonely death—like the death of a pauper or a tramp . . . And now in that featureless, functional room there burst forth for him the fervent entreaty and solemn magnificence of the mass for the dead . . . Requiem aeternam . . . Rex tremendae majestatis . . . The ultimate dusty, clayey, irrepressible plea for forgiveness, at the end of everything, beyond everything . . . I sang it silently of course, so as not to disturb or upset him . . . He couldn't hear anything anymore, but you never know . . . It was the most incongruous thing I could have done — the farthest from the habits of the circles Werth and I had lived in . . . But to me it was the only thing in tune with the great hazy uproar of his death . . .

III

I pack my case . . . I'm going away . . . Can't get a taxi on the telephone . . . Someone rings up . . . No! No! Boris . . . NO! "So have you read my last editorial? Terrific, eh?" "Absolutely—but I'm sorry, I have a plane to catch . . ." "What? You're going away? Again? What's got into you?" "This country bores me . . ." "Pooh, it's the same everywhere . . . Anyhow, I've started—I'm writing my novel . . . How's yours getting on? I heard you'd done a hundred pages—is that right? Anyhow, I've thought of a marvelous title for mine . . . Really fabulous . . . I've just registered it . . . This time it's the Goncourt, no doubt about it . . . Wait till you see the title—a real inspiration . . . Incredible no one's ever thought of it before . . ."

"Really?"

"Almost a commonplace," he says . . . "But it makes a wonderful title . . ."

"Really?"

"Yes! Far out! The sort of thing you could look for for a hundred years!"

"Really?" (An hour to get to the airport . . .)

"Listen: *The Eternal Feminine* . . . Fantastic, isn't it?"

"Yes, very good . . ."

"Your novel isn't too porno, I hope? One shouldn't go in for that . . . Affection, love—that's the thing nowadays . . ."

"Of course . . . Now you must forgive me—I'm trying to get a taxi . . ."

"Ciao!"

He's furious . . . How can anyone be bored in a country where he writes an editorial every week? In a paper you can't buy abroad . . . Foreign travel ought to be banned . . .

I get a taxi at last, and as we go along I think with some amusement (1) that Boris is undoubtedly very perturbed at the thought of my writing a novel with the provisional title, which he's just heard about, of *Women;* (2) that he hopes it'll be too pornographic to win a "prize" (be a best-seller); (3) that he's managed to put himself forward as my competitor, and to show me once and for all which of us is the "stronger" and the more "powerful," the two words that crop up most frequently in his conversation . . . *The Eternal Feminine* . . . Bravo . . . Go ahead . . . He really is something . . . Two years ago he failed to pull it off because a female character in his book kept defecating all over the place . . . Some eternal feminine . . . I think the book was set in Cambodia . . . Amidst the hell of the Vietnamese refugees, whom the heroine idly watched drowning or being eaten by sharks while she was being sodomized by the narrator . . . Something like that . . . By far his best book . . . But disgustingly sentimental, like him . . . He gave it all he'd got . . . There was one scene where she sucks the prick of a dying young Khmer soldier and swallows his sperm as he breathes his last . . . In the jungle . . . And another scene where, for love, she licks the pus from her lover's boil . . . He spends his time sticking two or three fingers up her rectum to enjoy the feeling of his nymph's warm shit . . . And so on and so forth . . . She ends up dying of cancer and asking for the shit of the Mekong red mullet, which feeds off corpses . . . The Lady of the Cacamellias . . . In short, a festival of the revolting . . . Pasolini's *Salo*, only with more bourgeois decadence, complicated and long-winded . . . But valiantly scatological, in the manner of the liquid diarrhea school . . . Still, not bad for Boris, whose writing up till then had been precious and allusive, smacking of schmaltz and fairy stories and the Arabian Nights . . . Highly praised then for his airy-fairy simpering, he was now snidely demolished for that coprophiliac mishmash . . . What was the thing called? *The Murmur of the Ages,* I think . . . Who got the prize instead of him? I forget . . . Of course, Boris tells me

I'll be the victim this time . . . He thinks I'm writing a best-seller . . . Why else would anyone bother?—I ask you! And if there's too much sex in it—wham! Meanwhile he, having had his fingers burned before, goes and concocts a chaste, inoffensive little thing, supposed to be "poetic," the revival of love, the quest for the Holy Grail, Morganic mists, elves, moss, moonlight . . . Good old Boris . . . Let him get his prize at last . . . Masterpiece . . . Great writer . . . The greatest of his generation . . . Anyhow, here we are, I see, eighteen months later . . . Seats being booked . . . Subsidies, scholarships and grants being handed out . . . Payments made into bank accounts . . . Share-outs, percentages . . . "I'm very powerful . . ." Oh yes, Boris is powerful, potent with all the general impotence . . . He has his "ins" and his outings . . . A skillful though exhausting network of pressures, counterpressures, discreet blackmail, indiscretion, gossip . . . Your genuine potent-impotents get so bored . . . Boris is their distraction, their latest little perversity, their comic opera saint, their dibbuk, the papier-mâché devil they pass from one to the other to give themselves a fright . . . Not too much of one, but a bit of a scare . . . Lest anyone should expose the underside of things . . .

Takeoff . . . Thirty thousand feet . . . Cornwall . . . Ireland . . . Cork, Shannon . . . The sea on the way to Halifax . . . Nova Scotia . . . Sleep . . .

New York . . . A fine day . . . Cyd's at the airport in her little white convertible . . . We zoom toward Manhattan . . . Verrazano Bridge . . . She's rented a studio for me in the Village—in Bank Street, a stone's throw from Greenwich Avenue . . . On the twenty-first floor, with a view over the Hudson . . . She leaves right away . . . See you this evening . . . I settle myself on the balcony . . . An Indian summer . . . Marvelous . . . Everything's mild, bright, sparkling, vibrant . . . Whisky? Whisky . . . Ice? Ice . . . Books? Terrific—all the classics, clothbound . . . Homer . . . Dante . . . Shakespeare . . . Milton . . . *Paradise Lost* . . . Yellow blind . . .

Blue chaise-longue . . . White armchair, white table . . . Inside, leather armchairs and settees, house plants, the sort of comfort you get in London . . . TV set on the floor . . . Radio . . . Tapes . . . Berg . . . Bach . . . Scarlatti . . . I get out my typewriter and type: "Takeoff . . . New York . . . A fine day . . ." Bath . . . I get up . . . I listen to the harpsichord as I watch the claret-colored sunset spread over the docks . . . Paris and Europe are suddenly far away . . . As if they'd been torn out of the book . . . Phone . . . Phonebook . . . The UN? The office of the Chinese delegation? "Mme Li? Who's calling, please? One moment" . . . A long moment . . . And there she is . . . Tomorrow evening? Yes? Tomorrow evening . . .

That's what you call wrapping up a trip . . . Cyd and Lynn this evening and Ysia tomorrow . . . Tomorrow morning I'll go to the Museum of Modern Art . . . We're getting going . . . I put down my instructions to myself: a week of *real* amusement . . . Then: regular hours . . . Light meals . . . No sex . . . Peace . . . Tennis . . . Swimming . . . As often as possible work till late in the evening . . . *The night* . . .

That's what I need—night!

The New York night—sheer, soaring, post-Gothic, shrill, cubic . . . The World Trade Center, like a luminous computer, with its two towers like tall visual amplifiers . . . And at the end of my street, the bustle of the harbor . . . The wharves, the trucks . . . The delicatessen, open till two in the morning, and the liquor store with its red fluorescent sign . . . The Puerto Rican bar; the dark, cheerful girls of easy virtue . . . I speak Spanish, and New York is a Spanish city, among other things . . . Channel 13 on TV . . . Or 17? And Reuter's News on cable, red in the middle, green at the bottom and blue on top, with the telex directly writing out dispatches, the exchange rate of the dollar, temperatures, weather forecasts . . . "Cloudy . . ." The dollar rises, goes down a bit, then up again . . . Rises, falls again, rises again . . . Taking the whole world with it, the four billion bodies living and breathing on earth at this moment . . . Meanwhile the history of the world is being written in detail . . . All against a continuous background of classical music, as if nothing were really happening at all, as if you were on Olympus and this was a concert for the gods, above the feverish, purely typographical activity of peoples, nations, governments, banks, criminals . . . *The Art of Fugue* . . . Or else CBS . . . Flushing Meadows . . . McEnroe's still winning, whirling and leaping about, covering the whole length of the net . . . He's just delivered an unanswerable first serve . . . An ace . . . One ought to write like that . . . The ball whizzes over the right side of the court . . . Just inside the narrow angle of the corner . . . He looks like a Caravaggio angel — aggressive, swift, subverting the laws of gravity . . . The American public loathes him . . . Or pretends to . . . "The Champ you Love to Hate," says the headline in the *Post* . . . In other words you really like him . . . A good comment on the human race as a whole . . . The embodiment of antifascism . . . The negative hero whose sins you applaud . . . But deep down you want him to lose . . . And in fact he wins . . . He sulks, rolls his eyes, throws down his racket, shouts at the umpire, falls to his knees, mutters, is convulsed with rage . . . What an act . . . Great artists are first and foremost actors . . . Mimes . . . It's innate . . . Imitation is the nervous basis of everything . . . In the beginning was assimilation . . . Despite what the fuddieduddies of all schools say, the root of originality lies in the intangible muscle of mime — in its plasticity, its swagger, its flow of nervous energy and air . . . It's the only thing that understands the fundamental emptiness of things, the pointlessness, the inevitable joke of every external manifestation, its death-deserving wrongness, yet its virtue, in excess . . . A spoiled brat? He can't be spoiled, so long as he's a genius . . . Insufferable . . . "The champ you love to hate . . ." A phrase aimed at the public, i.e., especially at women, and at men in the process of becoming women . . . At the whole world really . . . The universal gall-bladder . . . Bile . . . Envy . . . McEnroe has his own glandular thing: anger unleashes a flow of adrenalin in him that allows him to hover over the game and televise it in his head as if the whole court were relayed there . . . The scowls and grimaces are just to conjure up the hidden side of things . . . Poor Borg, facing him . . . The champ they love . . . Tall, upright, scrupulous, concentrated, decent, eminently moral . . . The perfect husband

. . . And indeed, when the picture moves to the stands, there's the explanation . . . The reason why Borg's losing . . . Ever since he got married . . . Mariana's there, a Romanian girl (watch out for Romanian girls!), sitting beside Borg's coach, who's obviously fed up at having to endure her . . . She's tense, tight-lipped, uptight, ugly . . . She's radiating ten million kilowatts of bad vibes . . . She wants her man to win, but above all, and she can't help it, she wants him to lose . . . And you know he's bound to feel these waves of inhibition . . . He tries to pull himself together, like a well-bred race-horse . . . But it's no good, the rays are too strong . . . Another ball in the net . . . Money . . . How to invest it . . . A child to produce . . . Children . . . Houses . . . In-laws . . . The lot . . . He'll end up owning a fashionable restaurant, or something like that . . . He's already in the midst of it . . . That's what's putting a spoke in his wheel . . . Tamed . . . Swedish . . . The champ you love . . . Because he's only a man, after all . . . Like all the rest . . . So, as you see, the viewers feel sorry for him, the ladies' eyes are moist . . . When he used to beat all comers everyone called him "an inhuman machine," "a cold piece of clockwork" . . . Will he ever smile? Does he at least feel something? Ah, now he's human — he's losing . . . Everyone loves him — in other words they'll be able to forget him . . . They love him to the extent that his body allows itself to be forgotten . . . McEnroe, the spoiled brat, the belated adolescent, hasn't yet reached the stage of being officially castrated . . . He hasn't got a woman . . . Or else he's got several . . . Or perhaps he keeps everything for himself . . . An irregular life, with nothing for anyone else and no contribution to the security of all . . . Exhibiting himself on the stage, in nightclubs, with rock singers . . . And what's more his father's there watching him, rather shrunken and feminized, like a mother . . . Father and son . . . It's generally understood that Mrs. McEnroe was eaten up by her son after she'd devoured her husband . . . He wins . . . It's a fable for all time . . .

I go out and walk up Fifth Avenue . . . I walk for a long time through the Indian summer, with the lofty sky still light, the wind

cutting the trembling ocean, the squirrels in the squares . . . I get
as far as St. Patrick's and go inside . . . A flood of lighted candles
. . . Here's the bridge between the worlds, the cathedral almost
crammed in between the tall office blocks . . . Opposite the "666"
—the number of the Beast in the Apocalypse—the top-floor restaurant with a view all over the city . . . Inside St. Patrick's the flags
of both the Vatican and the United States . . . The star-spangled
banner beside the yellow and white arms of the Papacy . . . The
tiara and the keys . . . I don't know if in Europe I'd dare say these
are my two favorite flags . . . That I feel at home with them
. . . At home at last . . . I can just hear the disapproving silence,
the rasping, wordless intake of breath, if I had the incredibly bad
taste to say such a thing . . . Here too . . . Needless to say, Catholics aren't very highly thought of, especially among the intellectuals
. . . I ought to avoid them all, men and women . . . Jane . . . Helen
. . . Paula . . . Dora . . . The Cell . . . The University, the periodi-
cals . . . As everyone knows, the United States is a fascist country
. . . American imperialism is the monster of monsters, and we
ought to campaign against the neutron bomb and in favor of unilateral disarmament, instant peace and genuine communism (not the
Russian version, of course, unless there's no alternative) . . . We
have to find a new path, a third, nonaligned way, not necessarily
like Cuba, but still . . . I can make up all the conversations in
advance . . . Talking of Cuba, I must ask after Armando Valladares,
the imprisoned Catholic poet, and find out if his long martyrdom is
still going on . . . Twenty years in a prison cell . . . Tortured by
inches . . . Meanwhile they hold the usual political meetings in
Havana . . . Gatherings of the intelligentsia presided over by the
"immense novelist," Gabriel García Marquez, tipped for the Nobel
Prize . . . Not a bad writer, true, though a bit too labored for my
taste . . . With little off-hand allusions between the lines to alchemy and the Kabbala . . . Well, well! A close friend of Castro's
. . . Whom he's always praising to the skies . . . He must have his
reasons . . . But it's Valladares who interests me, incarcerated and
suffering, while Marquez struts about in front of the journalists

. . . I'd give everything Marquez has ever written for Valladares to be able to read just one of his poems on television . . . Cut that bit, Boris would say—it'll lose you thousands of readers . . . Too bad . . .

It won't do us Catholics any harm to be persecuted again for a bit on this ailing planet . . . We've had it too good too long . . . Got away with too many crimes . . . Witches . . . Protestants . . . Jews . . . Only fair there should be a swing of the pendulum . . . Everything that happens now is uniquely, exclusively, passionately religious . . . Really it's the same as ever, but more violent now, with different excuses and disguises . . . we're becoming more and more, the suffering minority . . . Attempts to assassinate the Pope . . . Repression in Poland . . . Murky plots . . . From Robespierre to that ideal couple, Brezhnev and Qaddafi . . . But it's all very good . . . Excellent for the health . . . Just you wait and see . . .

I arrive at Cyd's . . . Her apartment looks out over the East River . . . A broad blue-black stretch of water in the blue-black window . . . She's wearing a clinging green dress with nothing underneath . . . That's what she likes, and what she knows I like . . . Short fair hair, green eyes . . . We make love quite quickly . . . Have dinner . . . Then Lynn arrives . . . She's Cyd's idea . . . For her . . . For us . . . She's tall, auburn, pretty, on the bony side and very English . . . She's a literary prof . . . In Los Angeles, just passing through New York . . . What's she working on now? Faulkner . . . His narrative technique, especially in *Absalom! Absalom!* We talk about the wistaria and the birds at the beginning . . . "There was a wistaria vine blooming for the second time that summer on a wooden trellis before one window, into which sparrows came now and then in random gusts, making a dry vivid dusty sound before going away . . ." And then the voice . . . And the "dim coffin-smelling gloom sweet and oversweet with the twice-bloomed wistaria" . . . The smell, the sound of the flight of the birds, Rosa Coldfield's voice . . . One of the best characterizations in all literature of an elderly spinster, a garrulous old maid . . . With her long monologue in italics in the middle of the book, practically without punctuation . . . "Talking of which," says Lynn, "I believe a book's just come out in Paris that's taken everyone aback . . . By someone called S.? It's called *Comedy*, I think . . ." Shit . . . I agree . . . Heroically . . . I say it probably is an event, but difficult, very difficult, to judge . . . "I read a very hostile article about it in a French weekly — *L'Express*," says Lynn . . . "It made me want to read it . . . Has anything else been written about him?" "S. is a charming guy," I tell her. "Very humorous and amusing." "They say he's quite young?" "About forty." I try to change the subject . . . Go back to Faulkner . . . *Sanctuary* . . . I'm brilliant for ten minutes about the way the rape with the corn cob is constantly evoked but never actually described . . . "The character of Temple," I say, "is really one of the modern novel's greatest achievements . . . The end, with his father . . . Temple's going back to his father . . . The profanation of the sanctuary of the vagina, ending up under the paternal authority once set at naught . . . As if at the end, in the Luxembourg, his father had become his mother . . . Without anything being said . . ." Lynn agrees . . . She looks at me curiously, warmly . . . She's just crossed her legs high up under her blue dress . . . Cyd, who doesn't give a damn about literature, says nothing and refills our glasses . . . We drink a lot . . . Cyd puts a slow disc on, it's dark, I ask her to dance . . . Lynn leans back a little, watching us . . . Cyd goes and sits beside her, kisses her . . . So . . . They dance together . . . We all end up, quite soon, naked on the bed in the living room . . . Lynn's skin is smooth and fruity . . . I take her gently from behind, while Cyd goes on kissing her . . . As I enter her she gives me her buttocks really generously and trustingly . . . She comes very fast . . . Afterward, Cyd shows her how she sucks me off . . . They must have talked about it . . . And then they have a game—they play at which of them's going to eat my prick, how to share it between them, hurting it, but not too much . . . They laugh . . . They're enjoying themselves . . . It's slow, intent, intoxicating . . . Lynn's the one who's going to drink my sperm . . . Cyd has just given her permission . . . I let myself come . . . She's very careful and affectionate about it, her distaste isn't perceptible, the earth moves just as it's supposed to . . . Then

Lynn conveys the milk to Cyd, mouth to mouth . . . They kiss at great length . . . And Lynn dives her head between Cyd's legs . . . She's sucking her now, slowly and skillfully . . . Cyd, lying back, gives me her mouth, her cool breath; she cries out and dies like that, onto my tongue . . . Right . . . That was the applied science of the threesome . . . The secret of gonorrhea unveiled . . . I have a special pass for this kind of performance . . . A well-known student, serious, pleasant, discreet, casual . . . We have a whisky, without switching the lights on . . . Etiquette requires that I leave them now . . . They're lying in each other's arms, pink and brown, the two blondes, in the October night . . . Relaxed, sated . . . Of course they'll go on making love after I've gone, in the vampire, plasma manner . . . Cyd will give Lynn an orgasm, it'll have to be better than with me . . . They'll talk about all kinds of things, including me . . . I get dressed, kiss them, and leave . . .

How long has the phone been ringing? The New York ring, slower and shrill, one-two, one-two . . . It's a violent day, the sun strikes right down on the blind, the sun they have here, ten times higher, searing, fixed . . . I pick up the phone . . . Yes? The distant voice surges into the room like a typhoon, sweeping away the apartment's bright silence . . . Flora . . . She got my number from the *Journal* . . . What am I doing in New York? I might have told her before I left . . . Who's with me? It's outrageous, insufferable . . . When do I think I'll be back? There to work—that's a good one! What?—a novel? There are other things now besides novels, and all this time she . . . etc., etc. . . . . She's literally shrieking . . . I do what I usually do with her—this is really what I'll remember later—and hold the receiver out at arm's length . . . Her voice twitters on in my hand . . . It's like one of those genies that come out of a bottle in a puff of smoke and swell up to gigantic proportions . . . Now it's reduced to a daintier size . . . Thousands of miles between us, and she makes a scene across them . . . It's no use trying to tell Flora scenes are outmoded as far as I'm concerned . . . That no woman embarks on them if she doesn't want me to clear off there and then . . . Flora wouldn't care . . . It's her we're talking about now . . . I hesitate to hang up . . . A mistake . . . True, she thinks she's in the right, and I can't really disagree . . . And I can't really be cross with her—she's horribly appealing . . . At the moment she's in Paris . . . But she'd be just as ready to phone me from Hong Kong, Manila or Buenos Aires . . . At any hour of the day or night . . . It's awful, but rather touching . . . Adventure . . . Nonconformity . . . Anarchy . . . They're a necessity . . . Perhaps on the whole I'm rather unfair to Flora . . . I tend to forget the sublime side of her character, her quickness, her courage . . . One must make the necessary allowances . . . It's very hard being a woman who's a bit creative, and independent, and so on . . . They overdo that kind of propaganda, but there's some truth in it . . . Allowances, allowances . . . The novel is only a balancing out of contradictions . . .

She's still shrieking . . . She's very annoyed . . . On this sort of occasion she goes from French to Spanish and back again in an incomprehensible jumble . . . I answer in English, forgetting she doesn't understand it . . . Anyhow she never listens to a word I say . . . Or hardly ever . . . When she does it's only to hear what she would say if she were me . . . She doesn't believe for a moment in communication . . . She's right, really . . . Women are nearly all like that some time or other . . . The balance of power . . . Will against will . . .

This time I'm not going to get off so lightly . . . There's a cobra at the other end of the line . . . Either I hang up or I have to put forward a proposition . . . An armistice . . . I produce my magic flute . . . It's a piece of cake . . . Travel! Together! Juntos . . . Los dos! Querida! . . . It's the magic spell, the irresistible incantation . . . Sesame! She stops dead . . . Her tone changes . . . When? Where? For how long? She's mellowed down now, charming, pleased, swaying gracefully at the other end of my voice . . . I leave it to her . . . No need to quibble about how many days . . . She's got to

go to Italy? Ok, Italy then . . . At the end of the month? Fine . . .
Milan? Meet in Milan? "In any case I'll call you . . ." Sweet . . .
Bueno . . . Hasta luego . . . Ciao . . .

Phew! Coffee, bath, work . . . Two pages a day — all right? I
negotiate with my own nervous system . . . Two pages at least . . .
Yes, yes . . . Good or bad . . . Work for work's sake, the travail of
labor . . . The sensations, colors, smells of books . . . The story of
a book . . . The opening up of time and space; of nonspace and
nontime . . . A light cool breeze . . . A yellow canvas and a yellow
vision . . . Coffee again . . . The Hudson sparkles; the gulls wheel,
glide, and dip down into the water . . . Get it onto the page, for
God's sake, onto the unruly conduit of the page . . . Always, all the
time, again and again . . . In earnest . . . Inner earnest . . .
Call Cyd though to thank her (a successful bout of sex helps pass
the time) . . .
Call Deb and give her and Stephen my love . . . Ten in the
morning here, so it's five in the afternoon in Paris (and already one
tomorrow morning in Tokyo) . . . I like to go to sleep thinking
about the time zones, and day simultaneous with night on the
checkerboard of land and sea . . . Experiencing different climates,
hearing different languages . . . Being a different person . . .
Deb's just having tea . . . It's raining there . . . She sounds
rather distant and indifferent . . . Some worry she doesn't tell me
about . . . A bad dream last night perhaps . . .
I've got it . . .
I leap into a taxi and am off to the Museum of Modern Art . . .
MOMA . . . I know what I want to look at . . .
And there they are—marvelous, uncompromising, blazing . . .
Women . . . Real women . . . Real women at last . . . Real women
at last seized bodily in a genuine and open declaration of war . . .
The magnificent destroyers, issuing from the eternal feminine . . .
Terrible . . . Wonderfully expressionless . . . Guardians of the enigma
of—of course—NOTHING . . . The gateway to the new void . . .

To living, superliving, indefinitely living death—this is at once its mask and its true nature, this picture devoid of anything hidden . . . Nothing behind or beyond or elsewhere . . . Just there, visible . . . Enjoyed, penetrated, hung up, exposed, giving and receiving homage, posing, caught by an expert on the subject . . . One of the few able to dare . . . The only one so capable in the twentieth century? I think so . . . The right man for the job . . . A major feat of exorcism . . .

The hand of the master!

1907 . . .

LES DEMOISELLES D'AVIGNON . . .

What a picture . . . How mad, how daring, how beautiful . . . And how angry you'd have to be with them to paint it . . . You'd have to want to smash everything in, break through the looking-glass and the great lie once and for all . . . Through all the "once upon a times" . . . How alone you'd have to be, cut off from everything yet at the same time sure of your own strength and of the fact that the previous haphazard, accumulated, artificial veneer was about to be exploded . . . The idealized, falsified, trivial but thick crust of feeble projections, musty sperm, worn-out psychologies, clichés . . . All the blandishments and prudishness of the nineteenth century—the parasols, the flounces, the respectable domesticity . . . How essential it was for him to back his own youthful experience (he was twenty-six) and the pleasure of prostitution freely dispensed just for him, the chosen one, their protégé . . . To back nudity, known, naked, and unadorned . . . *Olympia*, a widow horizontal on her divan . . . *Les Demoiselles*, vertical and single . . . From a pink and white coffin to death standing upright . . . *Olympia*: the black woman reminds us we were born in the plump-slim flesh of this money-grubber in her fancy slippers, with her black cat arching its back and the velvet string round her neck . . . The maid brings flowers to this insolent, man-killing tomb, this madam over the pettier Olympiads of intimacy . . . The *Demoiselles* are better still—great gawks spotlighted in every possible posture, their ecstatically stupid distortions open to every wind, to the African mask of the wind . . . What a bomb, what a grenade

. . . What a tiger among the pigeons . . . Picasso, like Manet and Goya and all great painters, is a whore . . . It's a biographical statement . . . Look at the eyes . . . Look at the self-portrait painted at about the same time . . . *Madame Bovary, c'est moi* . . . The young ladies from the brothel in Avinyo Street in Barcelona, *c'est moi* . . . Of course . . . These women never existed more truly than in the black scrutiny that they allowed to put itself in their place, in them, in the place of nothing; which ousts them from where they are visible and salable, and with their tacit agreement places them on the difficult other side of the act that undoes them . . . A deep and inadmissible act of treason . . . All their customers, of every age, condition and confession, come and die, grovel and get in a twist there . . . All, including those who'll never come anywhere near, the mere errand-boys of the great goddess . . . And here she is, new-painted . . . Reinterpreted . . . Rendered down . . . Made into five, like the fingers of the hand hovering above them . . . Prehistory . . . Egypt . . . Senoras . . . Packaging, shackles, red moon, menses, out of the bag . . . Hecate's inverted crescent . . . Furies, harpies, Erinnyes—flat and measuring 243.9 × 233.7 cm . . . A cave-cum-drawingroom, open to a sham sky and caught in ochre . . . They have neither past nor future . . . They're of all time . . . The moons of time . . .

It's like that, biblically, that you take an impregnable city . . . Paris, New York, Jericho . . . With a prostitute who knows everything for you and whom alone you save from destruction . . . You spare the brothel . . . The house of Rahab . . . Why? Because that's how it is . . . When the trumpet sounds and death passes over, cutting down a whole age with its hissing sickle and felling the wall of representation and all that went before, it cannot but spare its own image, its earthly incarnation . . .

Death doesn't see the whore . . . It can't see itself . . . If you manage to paint it, it's exorcised . . . And you sweep the board . . .

1907 . . . Two world wars . . . A third in progress . . . In fits and starts . . . And there they still are . . . People didn't really understand cubism . . . Picasso's version, I mean . . . There isn't any other . . . A direct, vigorous, superimposed way of both revealing and banishing the incubi and succubi in painting—in other words, those of reality . . . A way of bringing the forgotten vertebral into play . . . Lifeless . . . Confused . . . Unsexed . . . Heading straight for the inevitable grinder . . . If everyone had been a Cubist there wouldn't have been any wars . . . The dice . . . There wouldn't have been any crime if the Demoiselles had been seen, actually seen, for what they were . . . The shouting, cheerful, indifferent engine of illusion . . . People will look in blood and charnel houses for what is only a matter of montage . . . Collage . . . Décollage— taking off . . . They aren't there . . . No one is there . . . It's not worth trying to attain the almighty presence of absence . . . There's nothing but a shambles—and absence . . . Erection and the end . . .

Picasso and women—now I'm in my own field . . . Gertrude Stein, Fernande, Eva, Olga, Marie-Thérèse, Dora, Françoise, Jacqueline . . . And the rest . . . Nothing much has been said from the inside about all that . . . Anarchism, Cubism, Surrealism, Communism . . . In the end all these "isms" look as if they were made up to conceal the birth of new nouns . . . No one knows what to do with those nouns . . . Put them in museums? In safes? In the true unchanging bank of painting? If you like . . . But you know very well it's not just a question of painting . . .

The *Portrait of Gertrude Stein* is there too . . . No one had ever seen a woman in that way before, had they? To have deciphered her too would have meant, could still mean, understanding what followed . . . She too emerges from the recesses of prehistory, transferred directly from the bison into her apartment . . . Massive, oblique, infinitely watchful, infinitely malevolent, sitting amid her eternally mortuary skirts . . . Bernadette . . . He met her, understood her . . . She's the antivirgin virgin, yet virgin all the same, a demonstration of the law of gravity, the diametrical opposite of the Assumption . . . Frigidity rooted to the spot, ruminating, an anvil for lurking unhappiness to strike . . . A scribe ceaselessly negating Scripture . . . A stiff-neck, a turtle from the past . . . Impossible to lift . . . The Assumption really is a sublime dogma . . . The extra One screwed up against a falling moon that rules the leaden waves . . . Nothing new under the moon . . . A very belated dogma, by the way . . . November 1st 1950 . . . The Bull *Munificentissimus Deus* . . . Strange . . . Titian red in Venice . . . Go on, work yourself up, float, fly, enjoy it or at least look as if you do, really think about it . . . Picasso came to show the wretchedness of the age we live in . . . Grimaces and glaciation . . . The fierce and cynical solitude of the Minotaur, who nevertheless persists and gets his way . . .

I go home and look at the Catalogue . . .

Think of the Catalogue aria in Mozart's *Don Giovanni* . . .

But it's not as simple as it looks . . .

Mille e tre . . . A thousand and three . . . But that's only in Spain . . .

The real total is higher, more international . . .

In Italy: 640 . . .

In Germany: 231 . . .

In France: 100 . . .

In Turkey: 91 . . .

In Spain: 1003 . . .

If we add them all up it comes to 2065 . . .

Not bad for those days . . .

The fact that Da Ponte and Mozart let Austria off shows they didn't want to shock their immediate public, in Vienna and Prague . . .

Picasso . . . All those solid women's faces and bodies in motion . . . What motion? That of a kind of penetration, of course . . . An ocular gimlet that pierces right through . . . No blinking . . . If you keep your eyes open in love and in death you see the ultimate distortions of things . . . One eye . . . Three eyes . . . Thirteen fingers . . . Brow and chin unrelated . . . The rape of the image . . . Tongue shot out like a knife . . . The stationary whirlpool of a suffering face; cries, tears, agony, arrested decomposition . . . Each woman is herself plus her mother, and because of that a vast perspective of mothers . . . $2065 \times 2 = 4130$ . . . At least . . . It's within this torsion that a bold explorer must act . . . As if, becoming a paint-brush, he were dividing the waters that were under the firmament from the waters that were above the firmament . . . *Firmar* in Spanish, means to sign . . . No one signs as unmistakably as Picasso . . . His name's written all over it—the crime, the monster . . . It's your duty to hate it, all you women, and men too, who want to preserve the ideal image of motherhood . . . He doesn't just deform—he twists everything completely . . . It's not just a little local perversity . . . Nor is there any escape in color or abstract simplification . . . No, he understood it all perfectly, and also the fascination exerted by an exhibition of the act itself . . . Anyhow, Painting is nothing else but this old refrain . . . Though here it attains the truth at the heart of the whole performance . . . What a bear garden, what a dismantling of mythology, this mixture of identities and physiologies subordinated to the vertical that passes through them . . . Not to be overwhelmed by one's own pleasure, not to drowse and end in it . . . A treatise on prolonged ejaculation . . . Coming from the other side, a declaration and a route . . . *Commedia dell'arte* . . . Harlequin . . . The painter in three-dimensional disguise in the form of a colored chess game representing the human (so-called) condition . . .

> Harlequin, by his mask a black,
> A snake by his thousand hues . . .

Comparison: a man without fixed ideas or principles . . . Example: a political Harlequin . . .

By analogy with Harlequin's costume, the word is applied to anything made up of disparate parts . . .

In the theater the *Manteau d'Arlequin* or Harlequin's cloak is the name given to the framework supporting a simulation of open curtains, visible only when the real curtain is up . . .

Some writers trace Harlequin back to early antiquity . . . They see the origins of the character in the Greek buffoon, a satyr wrapped in a wild animal skin, with a wand in his hand, a brown mask over his face and a little black or white hat on his head . . . He represented the Athenian peasant, both coarse and shrewd, ridiculous and mocking . . . In Rome he became the *Macco* and the *Bucco* of the *Atellanes* . . . Later he was called *Sannio* (from *sanna*, mockery, raillery, grimace), and appeared on the stage with his face covered in soot, his head shaved, and wearing a garment made up of pieces

143

of different-colored cloth sewn together . . . So Italy called on its own traditions to create its Harlequin, adding the Greek buffoon's mask, hat, and wooden sword . . . The ancient name of *Sannio* even seems to have survived in *Zanni*, which is what the Italians call their Harlequin . . .

Harlequin seems to have been a personification of the Bergamasques, just as in earlier days he represented the Athenian peasant and the Roman slave . . . Just as Pantaloon and Scapino in their turn were identified with the Venetians and the Neapolitans . . . After delighting Italy the merry trio found a warm welcome in France . . . Harlequin brought with him his traditional costume consisting of a black mask, a gray hat, a wooden sword, and a motley suit made up of patches of green, red, yellow and blue . . . But he modified his language and his ways . . . In Bergamo, Harlequin was just a low-life buffoon, cheeky and often fiercely cynical, and in this form he became the *Hanswurst* of German comedy . . . But in France, where under the protection of Mazarin he was first seen by a brilliant and cultivated audience, he kept his faults but concealed them beneath an exterior that was less coarse, wittier and more amusing . . . See Marivaux's *Harlequin Civilized by Love* (1720) . . .

But no, no question of being "civilized by love" . . . Marivaux and Mazarin my foot! The humorous musketeer and the ironical bull go on wreaking havoc . . . A particular, unique, erotic situation . . . A particular woman (though different from herself) at a particular moment and in a particular attitude that is also unique, all in relation to the painter's brush-cum-laser . . . Two different women lying down in the same position during the same afternoon—the time it takes to dash from the apartment of one to the apartment of the other . . . Picasso's sense of organization: parallel houses and couples; removals; transversal adventures; accelerated points of view; technical variations; drawing, painting, and sculpture all at once, taking account of everything that comes and takes shape and disappears in smoke . . . The flame behind the smoke is the strange discovery of what's called the "cube," something beyond the sphere, the hellishly magnifying sphere, something that's really a dizzying work just getting started . . . A phallus that's phony, imitation phony, not with it . . . Picasso has been called the force fate chose to sort out at a blow the sticky mess of the visual . . . This business of the human race, of man-in-woman mixed up with children, and the animal renewals of animated matter . . .

I must go and have another look at his museum in Barcelona . . .

The musical chairs of *Las Meninas* . . . His great gamble . . .

I drowse . . . Wake up in the dark red of the sunset . . .

The *Liquors* sign is lit . . . The docks are growing quieter. . .

Cigarette . . . Whisky . . . Typewriter . . .

It's dark . . .

Mustn't forget Ysia . . .

It's an important date . . . For me, anyhow . . . Will she come? I think so . . . I asked her to meet me in a quiet little bistro on 33rd Street . . . Off the beaten track . . . Just the locals . . .

Here she is . . . Not changed—very beautiful . . . Paris-Peking-New York . . . So? Well, things are just the same . . . She's very firm from the outset: no politics, O.K.? Is her family well? Yes thanks . . . Her son? Yes thanks . . . We'd better eat right away . . . I tell her where I'm staying . . . She writes it down . . . She doesn't give me her home number . . .

I do all the talking . . . But I realize I've no idea what might interest her now . . . Conversation flags . . . I tell her about a film . . . Politics come up again, of course, but she either says nothing or just trots out the official Chinese line on the world situation . . . The danger from the USSR . . . I gather vaguely that her present job has to do with economic and financial problems . . . She keeps her eyes lowered nearly all the time . . . Smiles a little . . . Completely under control . . . As if she were seeing me for the first time . . . It's all an act . . . It could be she's smoking rather too quickly . . .

I try my luck . . . At my place? After dinner? She agrees . . . But let's take two separate taxis . . . Is she afraid of being followed? Perhaps . . .

And lo and behold it's exactly how it was in Paris four years ago . . . Right from the start . . . She arrives an hour after I do, just as I'm thinking she's decided not to come . . . And she gives the

doorman an assumed name . . . Mrs. Smith . . . My God . . .
Perhaps she changed taxis a few times and took the subway, as in a
spy novel . . . Perhaps it really is dangerous for her? Very likely
. . . How should I know? Perhaps it's dangerous for me too? That
would be funny . . . Anyhow, we've been standing inside the door,
kissing, for the last quarter of an hour . . .

She reaches for me . . . I haven't forgotten her wrist action . . .
I watched her fingers during dinner . . . She understood . . . She's
wearing a black skirt slit up the side . . . Ideal . . . She's very
horny . . .

We understand one another . . . We don't speak . . . Twice . . .
Both together . . . She stays barely a couple of hours . . . It's
midnight . . . She leaves tomorrow for Mexico . . . Cyd's leaving
tomorrow too, for San Francisco, with Lynn . . . By the time they
come back I myself will have left for Paris . . .

I love Ysia . . . A lesson in physics . . .

She leaves . . . She may be coming to Paris in three months'
time . . .

"But I'll see you again here, won't I?"

I hear her footsteps fading down the corridor . . . The sound of
the elevator . . .

I go back to my desk.

The typewriter again? Three lines . . . Out of duty.

I watch an old Bogart film on Channel 7, out of the corner of my
eye . . . Philip Marlowe . . .

I try to find words to describe Ysia's skin, her perfume, the inside
of her spicy body, the lingering feel of her back . . . Her lips . . .

Tomorrow.

Jane invites me to have a drink at her place in Soho . . . I get
there . . . A sixth sense tells me to be careful . . . She's alone amid
her neatly-kept bookshelves . . . Jane's a fat little girl of fifty-five
with slightly frizzy tow-colored hair, said to have been a beauty in
avant-garde circles in the old days . . . The formalist, experimental

sixties . . . Marxism, homosexism . . . Vertov, Malevitch . . . Sartre, Beckett, Genet . . . She goes to Moscow every two months . . . To do research on the twenties . . .

She gives me a whisky and sits down opposite me, gazing at me out of her big blue, innocent film-club eyes . . .

"So tell me, Will—what are you doing here in New York?"

I can tell straight away she's had a phone call from Paris . . . Flora? Probably . . . Or Bernadette . . . Or both . . . Anyhow, one of the network.

"Oh, nothing much . . . Resting . . . Writing . . . Having another look at the place."

"Writing what?"

"You're going to laugh . . . A novel."

"A novel? *You?* A real one?"

"Yes, I think so."

"But, I mean, with characters? *Scenes?*"

"Of course!"

"One that could be made into a *film?*"

"Take it easy . . . I shouldn't think so . . . But why not?"

"So no more philosophy for a while?"

"No."

"And is the novel going to be published here?"

"No, in French to start with . . . Probably in Paris . . . If I can find a publisher!"

"In *French?*"

"Amusing, eh?"

"Of course, you *are* bilingual . . ." She leans back in her chair . . . Looks at me in amazement . . . This is serious . . . It confirms what she's been hearing . . . But it goes much further . . . I don't think she knows about my agreement with S. . . . He certainly won't have said anything about it . . . She can't know the book's going to be published in his name . . . But now she's dying to ask me who I'm with, who's "taking care of" me, who I'm seeing . . .

"Deborah well?"

"Very well."

"And Stephen?"

"Very well too . . . He's keen on music."

"And the *Journal?*"

"As usual . . . The normal routine, you know . . ."

"And the events in France?"

"What do you think?"

"Rather exciting, aren't they? But it isn't the Revolution yet, is it? Pity! Anyhow, it's better than here . . . Terribly reactionary . . ."

"I haven't got the hang of it yet . . ."

"You never did understand anything about politics, did you?"

"Perhaps not . . ."

"And how about your new friend, S.?"

Now we've reached the nub of it . . . This is what really bothers them . . . That there should be an intellectual "bridge" between Europe and the United States that they probably can't control . . . That's the heart of the matter . . . Information . . . Influence . . . Appraisal . . . I keep forgetting that for reasons I can't quite fathom, S. is subject to close observation in this part of the world . . .

"He's charming . . ."

"Have you read his book?"

"Not really . . . Too difficult for me . . . But I'm told he has supporters . . . What do you think of it?"

"Oh . . . unreadable for the most part . . . Incomprehensible, even . . . And the parts you can make something of are awful . . ."

"From what point of view?"

"Well, he's obviously got a phobia about women! Don't tell me you haven't noticed! Very reactionary . . . Very . . . I trust you're not moving to the right too?"

"The right? Really?"

"Of course! Paula met him recently in Paris . . . He's going downhill fast . . . And he's very ill . . ."

Jane's getting into her stride . . . She knows about these things . . . Absolutely . . . Can't be mistaken . . . She's got her intelligence service, her card index, her flow charts . . . Her map of the world, with names . . . If she says it's the right it's the right . . . The same with the left . . . And with good and evil . . .

"Going downhill? That's not the impression I got . . . He's doing a lot of work . . ."

"What? That thing he did without punctuation? *Comedy?* You must be joking . . . The truth is he keeps on making speeches defending the Pope! The Pope! That Polish arch-obscurantist! Trotsky called the Bishop of Rome the last superdruid . . . Oh, I was forgetting you come from a Catholic background too . . . Don't you? But you don't carry it as far as he does, I hope?"

Jane, who's Jewish and ashamed of it, longs for me to agree with her . . . She'd like me to make a joke about the Pope, at least . . . But we'll still be friends . . . It's all between ourselves . . . At least there's something solid about the Pope . . . What can one do but agree? Pull a face . . . Roll one's eyes . . .

"Is this an inquisition?" I ask, laughing . . .

She bites her lip . . . I've gone too fast and too far . . . Silence . . . It's up to me to break it . . .

"And what about you, Jane? Are you well?"

"Of course . . . As you see . . ."

"Making headway with your Russian?"

"Yes, I can speak it almost fluently now."

Right, now we know where we are . . . She's got the message . . . We've said all we have to say to each other . . . Not quite . . . There's something else she's dying to know . . . Will she dare ask? She's just going to . . .

"I hear you know Cyd MacCoy very well?"

"Yes . . . She's a friend of mine."

"She's been a great success over here . . . She's English, isn't she?"

"Pure London."

"That's right . . . They say she's very attractive?"

"She's got a very good sense of humor."

"And what about Flora? Have you heard from her? Marvelous woman!"

"I see there's an article by her in the latest number of your review."

"Yes . . . 'The principles of the new international balance of power' . . . It's very good . . . Rather anarchistic, though . . ."

"You're an old pillar of orthodoxy, Jane . . ."

"Just loyal to my own ideas, that's all."

She says it quite dryly . . . But she's just called me a weathercock . . . A clown, a turncoat . . . In short, a Harlequin . . .

The interview is over.

Just a few more words about Fals's death ("Do you think his influence could spread to America?" Me: "I think so . . ." Her: "I don't"); about Werth's fatal accident ("He was very fond of you, but I could never understand his admiration for S."); and on the Lutz affair ("Is he really insane?") . . .

She's got her ear to the ground and no mistake.

Now she'll be able to file her report on me:

"Suspicious . . . Contaminated in Europe . . . Irregular and murky private life . . . Confirmed that he's writing a novel . . . So could give things away between the lines . . . It would be a nuisance if it got around too much . . . Ask all the publishers to be careful . . . Keep an eye on the papers . . . Is making it here in New York with an ambitious little middle-class English girl from a well-off banking family who knows a lot of people in advertising . . . In Paris, sees a lot of S. . . . and thinks he's 'charming . . .' That sexist! That pretentious creep! Who thinks he's another Joyce!" And so on . . .

"Thanks for the drink, Jane . . . Glad to have seen you . . ."

"So long, my dear . . . Work well . . . On your *novel!*"

She said "novel" as she might have said "shit . . ." With such contempt . . . Strange, that mixure of disparagement and fear . . . Yet Jane's own mental life is a continual novel . . . What people are doing, whom they've seen, what they've said, how they were dressed, their travels, their love affairs, a dinner here, a secret there . . . But for her that's life — it's not to be written down . . . People should

write in order to think, or, at a pinch, to poetize more profoundly
. . . No reflections of reality—that might make it look as if your
own life's a mere reflection . . . She herself is a character out of a
novel, but she won't admit it . . . She senses danger, the possibility
of catastrophe, the horror of a truth better avoided . . . Something
just like the hidden, patient, indestructible truth hatched in the
home . . . The family novel that haunts everyone's mind like a
primordial canker . . . All novels are to some extent detective novels, which is why they frighten all forms of repression . . . Not
only the obvious, visible police force but also and especially the
ceaseless and ubiquitous force that makes people watch themselves
and others, including their nearest and dearest . . . And as many as
possible of their contemporaries . . . Vested interests, rises, falls,
intrigues . . . For this reason the novel is the only verifiable, prov-
able criterion of freedom . . . Tell a story, and all is revealed . . .
Your position vis-à-vis events and the powers that be; your blind
spots; your room for maneuver; your implicit beliefs; the way you
look at yourself in the mirror . . . Tell a story and you'll give
yourself away . . . Describe things and you'll say much more than
you think about your own thoughts . . . Your way of dealing with
evil . . . The only evil there is—that of existing . . . With envy
and jealousy all-powerful . . . With grown-up childishness everywhere . . . For example, whenever Jane, who thinks she's operating
on the plane of pure theory, relates anything, she piles on detail
after detail about the geography of how it happened . . . "So they
were here . . . And I was there . . . They got nearer . . . I went a
bit further away . . . I saw she was standing there, quite close, to
listen to me . . . I could feel her eyes on me as I spoke . . ." All the
time, inside every individual, beating away like a heart, there's a
feverish attempt at presentation . . . Not even the greatest scholar
or most subtle mathematician escapes . . . It's obvious . . . Overwhelming . . . It emerges into the foreground despite all precautions . . . The philosopher reveals himself in a travel anecdote . . .
The politician by the order in which he introduces the points of
view in a story . . . Hysteria's there just lurking under the surface
—no need for a stethoscope, you can hear it dictating the briefest

sentence, seething within the smallest adjective . . . The immense perversity of the unconscious . . . What about me, what about me, what about me . . . Pure thought, c'est moi . . . Absolute allusion, c'est moi . . . Transcendance, c'est moi again . . . What I admire, c'est moi . . . And so is the sense of history, so is the indisputable good—it can't be anything else . . . A novel succeeds exactly insofar as, at a particular moment in time, it conveys the social comedy of that time, the endless web of narcissisms in which no one listens to anyone else and every living unit forms part of a general state of somnambulism . . . The only elements they all have in common are sleep and death . . . "We understand one another . . ." But not at all! Not in the least! Me, and me, and me . . . If I pretend to accept some existence other than my own it's because I think it's about to disintegrate and vanish, to my advantage . . . "Tell me about it . . ." Words that keep on being repeated, mannerisms, intonations . . . Always, beneath all appearances, quite audible, the utmost violence . . . A mosaic of paranoias . . . The novel is the art of the impossible: it makes use of it, it reveals that it alone is at the root of all bodies in transit . . . Imposture fears the novel like the plague . . . It *is* a plague . . . Balzac and Proust are terrible buboes . . . Hence the need, if you want to manage untruth properly, to manufacture a continual stream of the slight colds usually known as "novels . . ." And especially to nip in the bud if possible any attempt at really ambitious narrative . . . To devalue the novel, castrate it, so that it will be thought of as inferior or so that it deals only in the superficial . . . Listen, and you can hear the control exercised by authority . . . It's always a question of women, when you get right down to it . . . All the stories you tell . . . To keep *her* at bay . . . To avoid the question of questions . . . Not "to be" . . . Not "not to be" . . . But what about the Father . . . The taboo at the core of things . . .

The woman in the Father's stead . . . The ever insubstantial, elusive father, never coming up to scratch . . . In the eternal flow of the novel . . . The father forever being killed again, abased, put down, conned, staggering to and fro between sentiment and scheming . . .

Anyhow, for Jane, a novel by me is bound to be bad . . . Very bad . . . Terrible . . . Hopeless . . . It would be bad even if it didn't exist . . . It's written without permission or authorization of any kind . . . Its author neither can nor ought to be considered a writer . . . His outlook neither is nor can be of any interest . . . Signed: Jane, Paula, Dora, Helen . . . Advise all branches . . . Paris, Rome, London, Berlin, Madrid, Amsterdam . . . To all our officials, whether brothers or sisters . . . To all fellow travelers, male and female, and supporters of the SGIC . . .

Of course Jane won't actually write any such report, and none of all this will actually be said . . . But it will be exactly as if it had been . . . One of the mysteries about influence is that it works like that, without being spelled out . . . to lobby or not to lobby, that is the question . . .

What's it about? What are you capable of writing about?

As I leave Jane's place I wonder who she's calling up now on the phone . . . Helen, probably . . . I'm having dinner with her this evening . . . She's calling her just as I'm on my way there . . .

Helen is one of the system's real stars . . . A "lady" . . . She's much better known than Jane . . . And much better off . . . She's got what practically amounts to her own private town house in Gramercy . . . I'm really making my statutory rounds . . . It doesn't do any good, it might even make things worse, but it's the rule . . . As I'm not part of the homo network I belong to the dowagers' department . . . New York is even more cut-and-dried than Paris . . . Either you're a member of the official, organized homosexual countersociety or you're married—i.e., caught tight in the matriarchal net . . . What they don't seem to have envisaged, and I'm not exaggerating, is the case of the single man who has affairs with women . . . Or even just an affair with one . . . Outside the scope of matrimony . . . That's a vice, or rather a vestige of the old world, the *ancien régime*, of irrational relationships . . . The guys manage as best they can . . . Bob, for example, who teaches at the university, naturally does his best to screw his female students and secretaries . . . But that doesn't alter the fact that he's primarily his wife's husband, and each girl goes along only so as to capture the position in which he'll be *her* husband (only more manageable, she hopes, than he is with the present incumbent) . . . As for the wife, she puts up a barrage of scenes, headaches, insults in public when they're out to dinner, and so on . . . That's the law . . . He can only screw by dangling divorce and marriage in front of the girl . . . A man who voluntarily lives alone and has one or more girl-friends is regarded as a kind of dinosaur, an incomprehensible hero . . .

Bill de Kooning, the great artist of lyrical abstraction and inventor of action-painting, did a particularly severe, amusing, cruel series depicting American females, and called it *Women* . . . I met him two or three times in his studio on Long Island . . . A marvelous man . . . Quick, full of energy . . . But he embarrassed people by his consumption of women, which broke the basic rules I set out above . . . He lived frugally in a kind of gilded ghetto . . . Very expensive, but strangely out of the way . . . He drank a lot . . . Often had to dry out . . . In and out of the hospital . . . Frenzied production . . . It was he who mentioned Lilith to me in connection with his series on *Women* . . . Lilith! Isaiah 34:14,15:

> *The wild beasts of the desert shall also meet with the wild beasts of the island, and the satyr shall cry to his fellow; the screech owl [Lilith] also shall rest there, and find for herself a place of rest . . . There shall the great owl [serpent] make her nest, and lay, and hatch, and gather under her shadow: there shall the vultures also be gathered, every one with her mate . . .*

What a strange idea . . . The serpent's nest, the laying of the eggs . . . A tapestry illustrating the legend of Lilith, the female demon, double and predecessor of Eve, the secret center of the whole scenario . . . De Kooning showed me how he started a picture . . . He began with a mouth . . . A mouth, a kind of coil or slipknot, a circle or ellipse . . . And then the "all over," the direct action designed to exorcise the suggested abyss . . . He cuts photographs out of the papers . . . Models, singers, starlets . . . And ads . . . Mouths, lipstick, parted lips, the fascination of the hole, of its simulacrum

. . . The gaping entrance to the digestive system . . . He has a vast collection piled up in every corner . . . He looks at them, is stimulated, and suddenly starts to paint . . . Furiously . . . Antifellatio . . . Fellaction . . . The brush as penis . . . It's obvious he must identify completely with the mouths concerned, those that come to his studio to pose, so as to get as much as possible out of the unconscious aura and also to get a quick lay . . . It's this that produces those streaked canvases, that forced yoking together of colors, that crazy, violent style . . . Funereal lately . . . Mixtures of black and gray . . . He's old . . . Like a sailor on the bridge of a dismasted ship, driven before the wind . . . *The Flying Dutchman* . . . What Kate would call an "infantile dread of castration . . ." Or what nowadays any little suburban schoolmarm would describe as an act of "rejection" . . . Advice you read in the supermarket: Whenever you feel you're in the presence of a phallus that's too symbolic, get out your Freudtox, the concept guaranteed to do the trick! For use on men only, of course, ladies! Can you imagine? Culture simmered gently in a double saucepan . . . No more acts of aggression . . . Everything subtle, harmonious, and delightfully soothing, cooked up in little kitchens of allusion . . . I can hear Kate now, talking to me about S.: "You wait and see—the present situation will bring his class unconscious to the surface . . . The unconscious of a bourgeois Southerner, basically . . ." But why "unconscious"? On the contrary, conscious! A conscious candidate for castration! A clear-eyed Confederate! I suppose that for de Kooning, as for any free animal, castration is just unacceptable . . . And you have to say so . . . Not just hide in a corner and put up with it . . . Otherwise what's the point of art? Bernadette said as much one day: "What's the good of promoting art if it works against us women?"

I'm walking to Helen's hotel . . . Strange how, apart from marginal and more or less silent adventures (Ysia, Cyd), everything seems strangled now . . . Closed; brought to a halt . . . A kind of inverse conformism . . . Poisoned and poisonous . . .

Helen greets me with a pleasant smile in which I easily discern intense hostility . . . Her son is with her—a tall, gauche, awkward youth of twenty . . . Wants to be a writer . . . Like Mama . . . As soon as he goes out of the room Helen informs me he's just had his first homosexual experience . . . He's told her everything, of course . . . In detail . . . She looks at me avidly, delighted . . . I nod . . . Really? Really . . . He comes back . . . I try, because obviously that's what she wants, to put myself in the place of the perverter . . . But honestly, with the best will in the world . . . After which, Helen and I go out to dinner . . . What's happening in Paris? The latest books, plays, etc.; how they're rated and how much money they're making . . . The usual tirade against S. (I'm beginning to get tired of him . . . His rating's high . . . As one of my French friends would say, his N.F.R., or Name Flotation Rating, is excellent . . . People denounce him too, of course, but that's a good sign . . .) Helen ends up telling me her life story . . . Her love affairs . . . The relationship she had once with Jane . . . How hard it was to become just good friends again . . . We go back to her place . . . She wants to give me copies of her books . . . About ten of them; a huge parcel . . . As I'm in New York on vacation I'll have time to read them . . . Thoroughly . . . Then I'll be able to talk to her about herself . . . Better than before . . . Intelligently . . . My intelligence . . . Her voice softens . . . She kisses me . . . I sum up the situation fast . . . A brief vision . . . No . . . I give her a hearty kiss and thank her effusively . . . Then go . . . I'll phone soon, I promise . . . Taxi . . . Taxi . . . I get off at the end of my street, by the river . . . I throw the parcel into the water . . . There it goes . . . Helen's collected works . . . Ten kilos . . . A crime . . . They make a beautiful splash as they plop merrily into the impassive black waters of the Hudson River . . .

Cyd calls. I'm fine.
Lynn calls. I'm fine.
Deborah calls. I'm marvelous.
Flora calls. I'm O.K.

Ysia doesn't call.

Jane calls. I'm all right (wait, her voice sounds different—she must have heard something; my N.F.R. must be going up) . . . I've got all I want, thanks . . . No, really . . . I don't need anything . . .

You can say that again . . . On it goes . . .

Helen calls. I'm a bit under the weather. Flu. But everything's fine . . .

In fact I'm having the sort of days, and nights, that I really enjoy . . . Secret, out of sight . . . I've disappeared from view . . . My own included . . . I eat, drink, sleep, wash . . . When I want a girl I go down to the local bar at two in the morning . . . I catch the odd bit of news from TV, which I leave on all the time, on the floor . . . The weather's still fine, and New York seems to glide through the air like some great glittering bird . . . At eight every morning I play tennis with Bob . . . On Friday evening Mark drives me to Southampton, on Long Island . . . We swim . . . I have my own room . . . A handsome Colonial-style clapboard house by the water's edge, complete with lawn and flowers . . . Mark's a homosexual; there are three or four of them—pleasant, indifferent, lazy, greedy . . . Lobster . . . Ices . . . I just pick at everything . . . A bit of rustling on the landing at night, but they're very discreet in front of me . . . I probably make them feel awkward, being the odd one out . . . I sense sudden gaps in the conversation, and go off on my own as soon as I can . . . On it goes . . . Dora invites me for the weekend . . . She wants to sleep with me . . . Just to see . . . It amuses her . . . Why not . . . She's good-looking, quite elegant, tall, dark . . . She's either been asked to make a report on me, or else she's acting of her own accord . . . The result? Not bad . . . Frigid, of course, but imaginative . . . It really turns her on to do the opposite with me of what she claims in public to like doing . . . In the arms of the enemy . . . The kiss of death . . . Admitted to the secrets of the abominable snowman . . . So how's the novel coming along? But that's all . . . Except that, coming into my room unexpectedly after a swim, I find her rummaging through my papers . . . She throws her arms round my neck, weeps, takes off

157

her clothes . . . Perfect . . . I act as if I hadn't seen anything . . .
At least the homos couldn't care less what I'm thinking or writing
. . . Because I'm not one of them, not with it; I'm therefore square
and insignificant . . . Genet? No? Oh. They're always listening to
Verdi . . . Callas . . . Fassbinder . . . I avoid getting into argu-
ments . . .

Sometimes Barbara takes me to watch her ballet company rehearsing, near Washington Square . . . They practice their antics to
the accompaniment of a video . . . Barbara is a serious professional
. . . All she thinks about is her spacial geometry in five or six
dimensions, her muscles, her strains, her back, her joints, her ankles, her wrists, her knees, her elbows . . . It's in the great American tradition—cabaret, music-hall, cinema, song and dance in every
sense of the term, every sport you can imagine all rolled together
. . . India turned upside-down . . . I think what it would be like if
you tried to put it in a book . . . Dives, leaps, slow ellipses, reen-
trant diamonds, every limb performing its own score, the pelvis as
important as the head, thinking with the pelvis, the pelvis swinging
while the feet seem to do their own thing . . . Barbara answers
every comment with "If you say so . . ." Neither yes nor no . . .
Almost completely silent . . . Mad, but easy-going and knows her
own mind . . . So much the better . . . Physical mathematics go
with a play-it-by-ear attitude to life . . . Spirals . . . Loose knot,
figure-eight, dive, halt . . . Motionless movement . . . Another
body beside the one that's dancing . . . Weight's shadow . . . A
happy ghost . . .

The dance, not the dancer. Not the dancer, Time. No psychology
. . . Dots, not phrases . . . I let myself be permeated . . . Drawn
. . . Encoded . . .

We go and lie by the river, in the sun. She likes my way of
looking at things, I think.

We look at the seagulls.

So.

I have to go back to Europe.

Italy . . . Milan . . . And where do I go when I get there? You'll never guess . . . I go to see St. Ambrose . . . His mummy, in the little crypt of the basilica named after him . . . Milan for me is St. Ambrose and St. Charles Borromeo rather than La Scala . . . Rather than Stendhal . . . There lies Ambrose in his shrine with his crozier and his mitre, and beside him two other saints whose bodies he dug up and took around with him on donkeys in order to convert people . . . He wanted to show he wasn't afraid of death, and still less of grave-worship . . . St. Gervasio and St. Protasio . . . Roman law took a very poor view of digging up corpses! Ambrose was defying the authorities . . . That's one of the things he's famous for . . . And Theodosius, later . . . "Repent!" And the Emperor has to make amends . . . "On your knees!" That Ambrogio! . . . The same Christian name as Giotto . . . Ambrogio Giotto . . . The ambrosia of the gods converted into One-in-Three God . . . The sacred honey of discourse . . .

"Linguam vero pro sermone accipimus qui exultat in dei laudibus . . . Unde et illud sic aestimatur: *Lingua mea calamus scribae velociter scribentis*, sermo infusus prophetae . . . Quod si ex persona Christi dictum accipimus, vide ne scriba sit velociter scribens verbum dei, quod animae viscera percurrat et penetret et inscribat in ea vel naturae dona vel gratiae, lingua autem sit sanctum illud ortum corpus ex virgine, quo vacuata sunt venena serpentis et evangeli opera toto orbe celebranda decursa sunt . . ." (*Apologia of David*, verse 18) . . .

"By the word 'tongue' we mean the word that exults in singing the praises of God . . . That is why the text, 'My tongue is the reed of a swift-writing scribe,' is interpreted as referring to the word which God inspires in a prophet . . . If we interpret this text as put into the mouth of Christ, note that the swift-writing scribe is the Word of God, which pervades and penetrates the bowels of the soul and inscribes there the gifts either of nature or of grace, and that the tongue is the sacred body, brought forth by the Virgin, through which the serpent has lost its poison and the works of the Gospel have spread and been put into practice all over the world . . ."

Ambrose . . . *De Mysteriis* . . . *Treatise on the Gospel of St.*

Luke . . . It was after he heard him preaching in Milan that Augustine became a saint . . . Sermons and miracles . . . The tongue that becomes a body is stronger than the bodies of death . . .

I put down my bag and my typewriter and invoke him . . . His skeleton, covered with gray and green skin, lies loosely among the red and white fabrics; his soul is in heaven. I've forgotten what St. Thomas says about the numerical composition of saints' bodies . . . Oh yes, here it is: "The dead body of a saint is not numerically the same as it was when it was alive, because of the different form belonging to the soul; but it is the same as regards the identity of matter, which has to be reunited with its form." . . . The Angelic Doctor . . . Key questions . . . "Will the humors be resurrected with the body?" Delicate? Difficult? Unthinkable? Don't you believe it! "Our resurrection will be like Christ's. In the case of Christ the blood was resurrected with him; otherwise the wine wouldn't be changed into his blood now in the sacrament at the altar. Therefore the blood will be resurrected in us, and so for the same reason will the other humors."

Hic et nunc . . . I was reading an article on the plane about the Turin Shroud . . . The committee of experts has given its verdict . . . It's probably genuine . . . But they're still waiting for the result of the Carbon 14 dating . . . The prudence that's owed to science, of course . . . The photograph of the centuries . . . Galactic scoop!

If I accept Catholic dogma (which I'm quite prepared to do, because it's crazy, it's absolutely inexhaustible in the radiant absurdity it maintains against all comers; it's absurd and I'm absurd, though there are two kinds of absurdity—the negative and the positive, as far apart as one infinite non-sense from another infinite non-sense; non-sense is not single but double—it's just that which is rather difficult to understand);

if I accept Catholic dogma, then (no one else wants any more to do with it, which is one more reason for embracing it; I take everything, if there are no other connoisseurs left: everything—churches, statues, pictures, organs, dusty old libraries, kilometers of theology and archives—they've just opened the secret archives of the Vatican: fifty kilometers of them, underground);

I consequently have to believe that this shape in front of me, Ambrose's mummy; this graffito of dried skin and bone, dry as that of Ramses II (which they now have to treat with antibiotics and keep from being exposed to polluted air, just as they've had to close Lascaux because the magic bulls were being damaged by the damp and the microorganisms breathed onto them by bus tour visitors); that this mummy—(too bad about this long sentence, but the majesty, the profundity and the superconceivable grandeur of the subject calls for it; and it's necessary, gentle reader male or female, for you to see how I can adapt my style to whatever situation I find myself in); that this mummy, then, should arise one day in the glory of the universal resurrection and (according to Ezekiel's vision) be covered with a skin fresher than mine is now, though I am alive and looking at it with my living eyes; that the blood will circulate through those new and mysteriously transfused veins; and that Ambrose, here on this spot, Ambrose of Milan, after Milan is gone, will continue his ecstatic meditation, perhaps just feeling (if that!) a slight swirl in the air around his brow, an almost imperceptible break in its luminous flow.

It's very early and the church is practically empty . . . A mass is about to begin . . . For the repose of his soul? No, we know he's resting . . . For the repose of ours? Another three murders yesterday . . . The front page of the *Corriere* . . . Blood on the sidewalks . . .

The blue of the morning . . . Ambrose's boat, lying open upon the ocean of time, resumes its daytime speed . . . We are in the hold, like Jonah waiting to be cast up on the shore . . . An elderly priest totters up and kneels down not far away from me . . . He mutters to himself . . . I pick up my typewriter and my bag . . . *Lingua mea calamus* . . . The congregation starts to arrive . . . About a dozen of them . . . Old women with black scarves over their heads . . . Terrible poverty, dreadful abandonment . . .

What did St. Thomas say? That "When the end of the world draws near, the sin of lukewarmness will reign . . ." It won't be for some time, then, judging by the murderous passion raging everywhere . . . Or is it simply lukewarmness that lies behind all these murders? Death moving at cruising speed? Amid almost universal indifference? "Fire shall fill the world as the sea did during the Flood . . ."

We have been warned . . . I go off to my hotel . . . The Plaza . . . There are Plazas everywhere . . . The one in New York is one of the pleasantest . . . A maze of corridors, three or four restaurants, rooms that are more like apartments, spacious and comfortable . . . I forgot to mention Pat, with whom I spent three days there without going out . . . Where is she now? Rio, I think . . . She wanted to be shut away for a while with a "writer"—"writers" have all the luck these days . . . Some hotels are like that—liners where you can go on secret, invisible, stationary cruises . . . How many left now? In Paris? The Lutétia? Mmmm . . . The Ritz, more likely (the bar, in the summer) . . . Better still the Trianon at Versailles, out of season . . . All those corridors . . . The ideal place for a "writer . . ." Perhaps a bit too well-known . . . I think the Grand Hotel in Milan is better . . . Ah well . . .

Flora's message is duly waiting at reception . . . And scarcely have I opened my bag and put my typewriter down on the desk than the phone rings . . . "You took your time getting here! Where've you been? Don't tell me the plane was late — I phoned the airport!" But I'm not going to tell her about St. Ambrose — she thinks I'm crazy enough as it is . . . Some things I had to do . . . Anyhow, there's a change of plan — we're leaving for Venice right away . . . Really? We're due to have dinner there with Alfredo Malmora . . . The famous novelist . . . The great Italian . . . O.K. . . .

No time for St. Charles Borromeo! Straight to the station . . . Flora's in quite a good mood . . . Asks hardly anything about New York . . . Fills me in on her own latest intrigues . . . Elections all over the place; lunches; dinners . . . She reckons the situation in Spain is very promising . . . Despite the army's recent attempted coup . . . The parties . . . The unions . . . The rank and file . . . The press . . . She gives me ten papers to read . . . Two magazines . . . Three reviews . . . An interview with her in the biggest Madrid weekly . . . The situation in Paris? Complex, and changing all the time—you should see! The old familiar words come thudding out in time with the rhythm of the train . . . Communists . . . Socialists . . . The Right . . . Unemployment . . . Inflation . . . San Salvador . . . Poland . . . Afghanistan . . . The Middle East . . .

She finds me apathetic . . . Torpid . . . "America snuffs you out completely, doesn't it?" She doesn't like America . . . She thinks New York is neo-Gothic and dull . . . She's like progressives the world over; like all those who're viscerally and provincially attached to the grand and simple ideas of the nineteenth century—they can't appreciate the novel beauty of America with its love of excess, its silence in the midst of clamor, its flexibility and energy . . .

I try to talk to her about an article I've just read on the attempt to kill the Pope . . . The papers are beginning to discuss the possibility, obvious from the first, of an international conspiracy . . . But that doesn't interest her much either . . . The Pope, the Pope . . . An old-fashioned business sorted out long ago . . . I remember what Dostoievsky wrote in *The Possessed*: "As for the Pope, we relegated him long ago to the role of a mere metropolitan in a unified Italy, in the belief that in the present humanitarian age of industry and railways that ancient problem was no longer of the slightest importance . . ."

"'*Eppur si muove*,'" I say . . . "It's Galileo the other way around!"

"You shouldn't joke about Galileo," says Flora, with a religious twitch of the eyebrows . . .

"No, let's talk about him . . . First the Vatican solemnly rehabilitates him, and now they find that although he's still without question the founder of modern science and experimental method, he owes more than is generally thought or than has ever been said to contemporary Jesuits at the Sacred College in Rome . . . like Paolo Valla and Muzio Vitelleschi . . ."

Flora shrugs . . . My idea of light conversation . . . My provocations . . . My free-thinking sectarianism . . . Of course she has no means of knowing about the new experimental science I mean to initiate . . . The new telescope and microscope I'm preparing to set up . . .

We get to Venice . . . The Danieli . . .

I'm broke, but Flora pays (her last book, on Vietnam, has been a great success) . . . I'll pay her back in Paris . . .

She comes and knocks at my door . . . Rapes me very agreeably . . . There's no denying she's got what it takes . . . She wants us to make love in front of the mirror . . . I sit on a chair and she sits on my lap with her back to me, facing the glass . . . She puts my prick between her thighs, handles it as if it were hers, stuck out in front while she energetically fumbles my balls . . . She jerks herself off, insisting on seeing the sperm spurt out, then collecting it in a glass and drinking it in a theatrical manner with her head flung back . . . After that I have to suck her off while she lies on the bed . . . Her climax is intense: a brief high tide, a cry . . . A fiery little clitoris, an explosive little prick . . . She's suddenly beautiful, like that— dark, with her legs apart, her cheeks aflame, her big blue eyes wild and innocent . . . "Making love does suit you," I say . . . "Haven't you noticed yourself?" she says . . . It's true . . . Despite a nine-hour flight, the time difference, the two-hour train journey . . . It's three o'clock in the afternoon here . . . So still only eight in the morning in my studio back in the Village . . . The best time of the day, on the balcony in the sun . . . But an actor must be able to manage a change of scene, of setting and of role . . . And of breathing . . .

We have a cup of coffee and arrange to meet for a whisky at Florian's early in the evening . . . Then Malmora expects us to dinner . . .

Malmora's a national institution . . . He's old now, seventy-two, but lean and lively, with the face of an emaciated faun . . . A sexual best-seller . . . Two or three regular columns in the main dailies and weeklies . . . Television . . . Star of the *Mostra* . . . He's very nice to Flora, who's here to interview him for a Spanish paper . . . He's surrounded by striking and fairly good-looking women . . . Two actresses . . . A woman journalist from the *Corriere* . . . They're all dark and dressed in black . . . One of them asks me what I do . . . Philosophy? That'll do . . . In America? No, France . . . She looks at me as if I were a refugee . . . Pityingly . . . In Italy, and because I'm there in front of her, "philosophy" more or less automatically implies Marxist . . . It's a commonplace of the establishment . . . "I'm waiting for the revolution," she says, gazing at me out of her huge great velvety eyes, "but everyone tells me it's impossible now . . . Is that what you think?" Poor darling . . . We'd need to talk about it at more length, in private . . . Flora gives me a furious glare . . . The woman journalist sitting beside me keeps putting her hand on my arm or shoulder . . . There are a couple of vaguer types, too—a homosexual director and a socialist photographer . . . We're in a large apartment that's been renovated . . . We have to be taken around . . . To exclaim . . . The bathrooms really are luxurious . . . Ultragreen . . . We go upstairs . . . I lag behind a bit . . . So does the journalist, Lena . . . The others go on in front . . . Suddenly, at a bend in a corridor, Lena shoves me into a little study, shuts the door, pins me against the wall, just like that, in the dark, and kisses me . . . And how! "Lena!" the others start shouting after about five minutes . . . "Lena!" We come out and saunter nonchalantly up the stairs . . . We come to the living room . . . Everyone sits down to dinner . . .

Everyone congratulates Malmora on a couple of articles he's just written, one on Hemingway and the other on the neutron bomb . . . According to the first, Hemingway's letters show him to have been a complete mythomaniac . . . Malmora's settling an old score here . . . Hemingway was more famous than he was . . . More often photographed when he was in Venice . . . More sought after by the girls . . . The second article says the human race is in great danger . . . That's no news to anyone, but the danger is a new one and entirely unprecedented . . . Malmora quotes Ecclesiastes in order to refute him . . . He says that now there really is something new and more terrible than anything ever before . . . "I'm very worried," he moans . . . I think he doesn't give a curse, but the actress, overwhelmed with love, gives him a motherly kiss on the cheek . . . Alfredo is so sensitive . . .

Malmora looks at me . . . I'm supposed to say something . . . Hemingway? No . . . I ask him if he likes the Bible . . . He looks stunned . . . Yes . . . Of course . . . Not all that much, though . . . That's to say . . . I ask the actress the same question . . . "Oh yes!"

she says breathlessly, passionately . . . "You quote Wittgenstein at the end of your article on the bomb," I say to Malmora . . . He's flattered . . . "Ah yes," he says . . . "The last proposition of the *Tractatus* . . . 'Whereof one cannot speak, of that one should be silent . . .'" "Excuse me," say I, "but Wittgenstein puts it slightly differently if I remember right . . . 'That which one cannot say, of that one *must* be silent . . . The emphasis is on the 'must . . .' Being silent is an act . . . An imperative . . . Wittgenstein is adopting a mystical attitude here . . ."

He gives me a shifty look . . . He doesn't understand . . . He pretends he hasn't heard . . . Anyhow, the chatter is general now, and this is no time to start discussing formal logic . . .

With a wave of the hand Malmora calls for silence . . . He starts to give his opinion about international actresses . . . He's very severe . . . Buttocks, hips, breasts; the stupidity of one; the greed of another . . . Flora has already told me that although Malmora's very rich he's also very stingy . . . He can't even bring himself to buy anyone a coffee . . . He always pretends not to have any money on him and to have forgotten his checkbook . . . Apparently this quirk of his is notorious . . .

He goes on about his actresses . . . You think so-and-so is beautiful? Not a bit of it . . . You should see her, close-up . . . And on top of that, what a cretin . . . The women laugh . . . None finds favor in his eyes . . . He grouches on . . . When you get right down to it they're all ugly . . . Except perhaps the *tedesca* . . . The German . . . *Molto tedesca* . . . A drug addict, a lesbian . . . Interesting . . . Very interesting . . . The Italian women have stopped laughing . . . Malmora enjoys making his power felt . . . Flora resumes a serious discussion with the socialist photographer . . . European strategy . . . Lena plays footsy with me under the table . . .

Malmora now harks back to the neutron bomb . . . He says he's just read a ridiculous article by a French avant-garde author (his lip curls when he says the word avant-garde) . . . An article that was offhand, shocking, irresponsible . . . "Would you believe it, he claims to have found the answer to the bomb in language . . . *In language!*" Malmora throws up his hands . . . "That's where the ravings of these modern faddists get us! The current dry-as-dust formalist philosophy! You know what this guy suggests, to neutralize the neutron bomb? The 'neurone bomb'!"

"The neurone bomb? Oh, I like that," says the actress . . . "And what is it? A new heroin mixture?"

She looks at me, more velvety than ever . . . There must be plenty of doping going on around here, and that's for sure . . .

"The neurone bomb?" cries Malmora . . . "Just a literary gag! People will joke about anything these days! Anything!"

"But who is it?" says the actress . . .

"Some young French writer," says Malmora with a condescending grimace, "who's just brought out a huge tome without any punctuation whatsoever . . . Unreadable . . . It's called *Comedy* . . . Takes himself for Dante, I suppose! Anyhow, there are always a few snobs around who like that sort of thing . . . As usual . . ."

No, not again! Not S. again! But his name isn't actually mentioned . . .

The conversation trundles on . . . They've got onto Picasso now . . . Malmora's talking to me . . . "I've seen the New York retrospective—they organized a private visit for me specially . . . How about you?"

"I've seen it too . . ."

"It's curious," he says, "to see how much Picasso achieved, starting out from such a flimsy foundation . . ."

"Flimsy foundation?" say I . . .

"Yes, well . . . practically nothing, really . . . Anyhow, all that in general . . . Stravinsky, Picasso, all that lot—they spent their time composing music about music and producing paintings about painting . . ."

"Do you think so?" I say politely . . .

Malmora brushes aside the whole twentieth century . . .

"It's the same with Joyce, in literature," he goes on. "The same blind alley . . . Literature about literature . . ."

I'd better keep my head down—in the present clean sweep S. will probably turn up again soon . . . I'm going to have to read his blessed book in the end, I can see . . . But I can tell Malmora's in the grip of senile megalomania . . . Do they all end up like this? Apparently . . . Hemingway—no good . . . Stravinsky—no good . . . Picasso, Joyce—no good either . . . No one ought to talk about anything else but Malmora's books . . . Malmora's art . . . Malmora's view of the world . . . But they don't . . . And he knows it . . . And neither celebrity, money, films, actresses nor juries can make up for the wound, the anguish . . . He panders to the System, but the System isn't obliged to pander to him . . . As it has to the others, whom the powers-that-be have been forced whether they like it or not to recognize, to misrepresent, and to praise . . . Yet hasn't Malmora been a complete success? Won all the prizes? And the rest? And yet there are still some know-alls who persist in not recognizing his superiority . . . And what do they produce themselves? "Neurone bombs"! Eyewash . . . Waste of good paper . . . Fit only for imbeciles . . . And for academics, who'll swallow anything . . .

The cruel mysteries of fame! "Fame is nothing!" Malmora must say to himself as he's being made-up in the television studios or buying a paper with his name and pictures over a four-column spread . . .

But "Fame is the only thing that matters!" a voice whispers to him every night as he falls asleep . . . Not celebrity, not notoriety, not power, but real fame . . . Glory . . . The last judgment, the ultimate verdict, arrived at impartially, irresistibly, patiently . . .

The conversation veers back to politics . . . What do I think about the socialists in Europe? "I'm for them, of course," I say . . . "We're all socialists, aren't we? That's where the future lies . . ."

The irony appeals to Lena, whose foot grows more insistent . . .

Flora sticks her oar in . . . "But you won't admit you admire the Pope, and that deep down you see yourself as a Catholic . . ."

A Catholic! An American Catholic? A Persian with three heads?

Everyone turns and looks at me . . . There's a pause . . . A chilly one . . .

I give the signal to laugh . . . That's a good one!

Time passes . . . Lena's got tired of playing footsy . . . But she does give me her phone number . . . Everyone gets up . . . But

Malmora still has something else to show us . . . He goes and fetches a photo . . . A terrific girl, naked, kneeling, in profile . . . Everyone's in ecstasies . . .

"Yes," says Malmora, obviously delighted with his trick . . . "But it isn't a woman at all . . ."

What?

"No, no—*niente di donna!*"

He shoves the photograph under my nose as if we were a couple of schoolboys . . .

Oh yes, of course, a transvestite . . . A super-deluxe drag queen . . . South American, probably—they're fashionable at the moment . . . On hormones . . . Good old Malmora, he wants to show he knows the score . . . The women are impressed . . . Or rather they pretend they are . . . What a marvelous woman, though . . . "Yes indeed! Yes indeed!" Good old Malmora, what a kid . . . At his age, too . . . *"Vecchio porcellone!"* says Lena, affectionately tweaking his ear . . . "Little old pig!" echoes the actress, giving him a kiss . . . He's all flushed and excited . . . And happy . . . *Vecchio porcellone.* That must be how they get around him behind the scenes . . . Easy as pie . . . Just like all the rest . . .

It's raining . . . No question now of strolling around through Venice . . . We go back to the Danieli . . . In the bar there are at least three tables at which a pair of fashionable tarts sit pretending to read the papers . . . One of them's tall and dark and not at all bad . . . She looks at me . . . Flora fancies her, but doesn't dare . . . She's still all worked up about the transvestite . . . "Will you introduce me to some?" "Of course—no problem . . ." We go up to our room . . . She goes on asking questions while we're making love . . . What are transvestites' pricks like? They vary . . . Some have had an operation; some haven't . . . Are they or aren't they impotent? Most of them don't like women, anyway, I tell her . . . Are there any in Paris? But of course—loads of them . . . There are special nightclubs . . . The Cosmos, the Eden . . . Expensive? Quite . . . I'll arrange it for you if you like . . . Fantasies . . . She can't get over how lightly I take it all . . . I hadn't really noticed— it all seems pretty ordinary to me . . . True, I've met some transvestites who are very charming . . . "Transsexuals," to use the scientific term . . . And after all, I'm a peculiar kind of abstract transsexual myself . . . Unlike most of the other inhabitants of the planet that I know, I don't regard sex as a "problem" . . . No, I really don't . . . That's not where the problem lies . . . Nor a sin, either . . . What an idea, locating it there . . . What a load of crap, and what a comfort . . . Sin is much more a matter of going past Joyce and Picasso without even noticing . . . Without sensing that they're there . . . Or at least having an inkling of something *because* of them . . . A presentiment, a doubt, a suspicion, a fear . . . It's not a question of culture, either . . . Not at all . . . To be precise, sin consists in thinking that the only truth there is resides in the immediate, basic balance of power . . . In believing come what may in an origin . . . They're right to talk about original sin . . . In thinking there must be a cause, a meaning, an explanation, a purpose, a reason for everything! Whereas in fact there's nothing . . . Sin is terrorist and repressive . . . And contempt is its progeny . . .

And then there's the getting back home early in the morning . . . They're still in bed . . . Daddy! The first thing Stephen does is look to see what I've brought him . . . He heads straight for my bag . . . A musical train . . . A singing TV . . . A remote-control plane . . . A remote-control car with lights . . . A book . . . A disc . . . A jigsaw puzzle . . . Anything . . . I draw the curtains . . . Daddy! Deborah's smiling and calm . . . I admire her more and more as time goes by . . . I wonder how she manages it . . . How crazy not just to stay quietly at home with them . . . Not to just accept that particular death . . . The only one with any useful meaning . . . Daddy's a magic creature, full of adventure, beyond challenge, the diagonal of the square, the figure in the carpet, a vague atmosphere . . . In other words he exists only in the form of a hypothetical certainty . . . Does he exist, or doesn't he? He makes appearances, anyhow . . . By definition he's someone you don't ask questions . . . Who's supposed to be able to look after himself . . . Who isn't really of this world . . . And who can therefore quit it at any moment . . . Isn't he dead already? Isn't that what he's for? Unless he's just an ideal . . . An airy-fairy knight . . . A prince of the lost light, dead too in a way, or missing . . . Daddy *knows* . . . Or is supposed to . . . He's not like us . . . He's inexplicable . . . Out at sea somewhere . . .

It really is a strange function—an inhuman, trans-human role . . . And we don't know very much about it . . . It's the other side of the picture, and a part of it that's particularly shadowy . . . And with good reason . . . It's an algebraic function, way beyond geometry . . . Joyce has a good phrase in *Finnegans Wake:* "Father Times and Mother Spacies . . ." Father equals times and Mother equals spaces and the species . . . The Father gives the time, or even temporizes; the Mother arranges space and the people in it . . . Father-sound and Mother-image . . . Difficult to synchronize . . . To represent both time and the tempo of time, and also the one who beats time in time; to be at once an individual and a universal counter; to embody, as you pass through space, the vanishing point of space . . . No easy matter . . . So what is a father? Silence . . . Embarrassment . . . Stammering and stuttering . . . Religion . . . And as the idea of the parents is the product of the children's imagination . . . As, from start to finish, the only meaning in it all *is* the children . . . And as children die calling for their mother . . . And the mother herself is only a child . . . So it just doesn't stand up to examination . . . And that's the reason for my reasoned Catholicism, which is ever more internalized . . . I take my investigations seriously . . . The combinations and permutations of sex . . . The various kinds of metaphysics . . . The latest scientific discoveries . . . East . . . West . . . Catholic, Apostolic, Roman, post-Roman . . . I narrow down, assert, persist, insist . . . It's here the drama is thought through in its greatest complexity, in its atomic dimensions . . . All the rest is merely approximation, a dream of substance, a fantasy void, poeticized babblings, vague hallucination, silly fetish . . . I'm subjected to two simultaneous temptations . . . Judaism, a grandiose idea of creation in which the

Father question can't even be formulated . . . And out-and-out materialism, like that of Democritus, but which only the best disciplined minds can understand . . . Otherwise it's just a welter of organs, dubious visions, neurosis, psychosis, desiccation, and desultory sacralization . . . Which soon turns into maternalism . . . Matter isn't Mater, but it's very close, and you can easily revert to it automatically . . . I must admit to a weakness for Taoism . . . The genius of the brush-stroke . . . But whenever Westerners talk about it they usually do so out of the back of their necks . . . So it's Catholicism, then . . . With Judaism standing by . . . Reciprocal borrowings . . . Revival of Hebrew, which has been scandalously neglected . . . Taking on board of Galileo . . . Vatican II? O.K. Yes, of course . . . Back to the primitive church . . . Roll back two thousand years . . . A phoenix from the ashes! Let's play down Latin and Greek—we'll keep them, of course, but we won't be too strict about them . . . We'll reawaken Aramaic once more, and above all the great marvels of Hebrew . . . Do you know what I think? I think the real breakup of paganism is taking place now . . . The fall of the Roman Empire is a contemporary event . . . Thank you, Hitler . . . Thank you, Stalin . . . Thank you, Mao . . . And Khomeini . . . And your very good health, Wojtyla! An excellent trick on the part of history . . . I read an interview with an English Catholic writer, Anthony Burgess . . . Some interesting intuitions, but what confusion . . . He criticizes Vatican II and says it spells the end of the Church . . . What a mistake . . . He reveals that he broke with the Church over the "stupid" proclamation about the Assumption . . . What bosh! How Protestant he still is! Blind sexual repression! The Assumption is a sublime piece of folly . . . An extravagant comment on the invention of feminine orgasm . . . He refers to Aquinas and St. Augustine, but not a word about the excellent Duns Scotus, subtlest of the subtle on the subtlety of subtleties! Not a word about St. Bonaventura, not even a mention of St. Francis of Assisi! I note in passing that he says he doesn't know anything about women . . . *Naturally!* His book's called *The Power of Darkness* . . . A great best-seller . . . His hero's a homosexual . . . He himself isn't . . . He tries to understand . . . In short, he gets it all muddled up . . . He says homosexuality is hereditary . . . Better still, he says it's a biological defect . . . God! Just let Burgess come and see me—I can tell him a thing or two . . . He sees only one of the Devil's horns . . . And His Nibs must have played him one or two lousy tricks along the way . . . I'd say his soul's in danger . . . He isn't careful enough in bed . . . These Anglo-Saxons . . . He overvalues the papacy in order to oppose the primitive anti-Popery of his own society, then falls into anti-Popery himself . . . Best-seller, best-seller! The Devil's delighted! I notice he doesn't say a word about the Jews, either . . . Or about Israel . . . Or the Old Testament . . . So there you are . . . Ignorance is always with us . . .

It's a matter of death . . . The world is death . . . And the world belongs to women because they give it—give not life but death . . . No truth is more basic than that . . . And none is more systematically hidden and ignored . . . Write it out a hundred times . . . But it won't do any good . . . How strange it is . . . The purloined letter . . . Look at yourself in the mirror . . . No, you don't see yourself . . . You don't see the grin you were born with . . . That's a shock you get only in a dream sometimes, or in a brief flash just as you're waking up . . . Three-tenths of a second . . . Not even . . . You trip over yourself, over your own poison-sac . . . Spittle of the void . . . Snot of the ages . . . Final shit . . . Pus of time . . . Discharge of duration . . . Vile mush to finish with . . . Add it up . . . Fall . . . Curtain . . . If you've never had a snootful of your own lousy stuffing, forever hold your peace! Silence 'neath these solemn vaults, or else you'll end with a whimper!

Farewell, sight, hearing, breathing, light; farewell, pleasures, perfumes, and most beloved, desired and savored of peach-like skins! Farewell, freedom! There you sit on the latrine of truth! Is this really you? This shapeless thing that "no longer has a name in any language"? No . . . no! Ah, but it was . . . It was you there on the surface, over the waves that engulf, the concrete that closes forever over your black, effervescent, stinking visage . . . It was you, talking, eating, copulating, calculating, heedless of the real truth that was becoming more and more real and getting ready to kill you . . .

It was you in your triviality, you in your lust—but ridiculously not in them enough . . . It seems to you now that the hour has struck . . . The hour of steel, falling like the blade of a guillotine with a sound like that of a drain . . . Not enough! Not enough! You amid all your sins, of which perhaps the fatal one was to have waited, to have put things off, not to have been in any hurry . . . To do what? To measure exactly the waste you flaunt . . . It was you . . . It *is* you . . . In the midst of your transitory story . . .

Open your eyes for once, on the street, at home, in the subway, the bus, the train, the plane, the theater, the movies . . . Look at the ghastliness of the greasy skins and unwashed hair, the great weight of tedium and worry on the end-of-day faces . . . The prison bars of twilight . . .

O potential skeleton, walking corpse, painted purulence! O living brain still riding a mount doomed to dusts and vomit!

O dressed-up, jabbering toad, cowardly and frantic! Dyed-in-the-wool meanness, fly in a ballet skirt, lead-assed swine who doesn't even know it's you doing it when you shit!

Gormandizer, miser, liar! Envious, jealous, sly, deceitful! A mollusc clinging to the breast, to the penis, to turds in the bank, to honors!

Media zombie! Acrobat ready for any treason or compromise in exchange for a touch of glory! And not even for glory . . . For a daily fix of narcissism . . . Cocaine moistened with pride!

Great soft-head and impostor, trembling before you're hurt, muzzled by the slightest pressure! Made effeminate by security! O family allowances! O all those registration numbers! O coward! O scholarship boy! O pseudo-civilized and fettered ghost!

O ex-thinking reed, turned into a safety-pin! O docile driver, born victim of traffic jams! O wearer of bibs and diapers! Believer in the masses or the unconscious . . . Irresponsible, ready to let your neighbors be killed and to stop your ears if your friends were tortured . . . Patient, timid, half-hearted, resigned, depressed . . . Above all lazy—lazy as the drip you dream of being in a world of drips, thrilled to sink into lifelessness . . . O absolute washout! Lout!

That's my prayer . . . Needless to say, it's addressed to myself
. . . Every morning and evening . . . Nothing in the least to do
with you, of course . . . Just to keep myself in trim . . .

Where were we?

Oh yes, death . . . The subject to end all subjects . . . We used
to talk about it . . . We don't talk about it anymore . . . Psst!
Gone! Or rather, present everywhere . . . It's as if we'd managed
to isolate it in the past, and then it suddenly slipped out of our grasp
into thin air, invisible, the inhabitant of the naked fabric . . . Dissolved . . . Faded . . . Absorbed . . . "Natural" . . . I can hear
Bernadette saying it: "DEATH" . . . *LA mort* . . .) The feminine
particle . . . If anyone died anywhere, by some coincidence Bernadette would always turn up . . . One of her friends dies . . . She
dines with the husband a few days later . . . It gives her a thrill . . .
It really is her trip, that and masturbation . . . She makes no secret
of it—it really makes her feel she's playing with herself . . . Death
. . . She looks almost beautiful then: feverish, her eyes shining, it's
her religion, she's almost completely hypnotized . . . She's in the
chimney, the soot, the tube of the shining serpent . . . Instead of
earth, fuel . . . There must have been, there must still be, women
like her in the camps . . . *Anus mundi* . . . Unfuckable rectum . . .
She goes to meet herself in death, *LA mort,* and gives herself
entirely, white and suddenly fragile, open-mouthed, her breathing
deep and frantic . . . That's how she produced her daughter Marie
—Bernadette and *LA mort* . . . Together of course with the supreme fantasy of her mother; and, to be sure, some guy who
happened to be passing; but above all, she admits, she will admit,
yes, with *LA mort* . . . Death . . . She's the only one of them who's
dared, or been able, to tell me . . . She thought of it as she was
giving birth: Now I've done something for death . . . The others
won't admit . . . Pooh, what's all this? You and your obsessions!
Are you feeling all right in the head? There's a cure for that sort of
thing . . .

They don't want to know about *this.*

Nor do the men.

Nor does anyone.

And yet . . . The eye of dreams . . . The knowledge of what lies unseen . . . The secret, wordless revelations of sleep . . . Cauldron of nightmares . . . Incubator of fear . . . But also joy from somewhere else . . . None knows where . . .

So for the moment I'm at home . . . I like Deb . . . As I've said before, there's nothing more subversive these days than to love and desire one's wife . . . It shocks the present age . . . The enormous Oedipus complex society has nowadays . . .

I take her out to dinner . . . Once, before Stephen was born, we used to go out practically every evening . . . Quite freely . . . More than freely . . . It was as if we were both still students . . . It seems to me we had a lot of fun . . . Not much money, but very happy . . . And then there was pressure from all sides, especially from WOMANN and FAM . . . Deb gradually grew worried and withdrawn . . . Faintly bitter . . . That was when she started seeing Bernadette, more or less in secret . . . Bernadette, of course, wanted not only to get her own back on me but also to extend her influence . . . Soon after that Deb started in analysis . . . She had Stephen . . . And now she's a psychoanalyst herself—in other words she's gone over to the other side of things . . . But she's still sensible and intelligent . . . She still has the "inspired" touch that's always been so striking . . . She's always reading some book no one else has read, or learning another language (at the moment it's Japanese), or thinking up some new philosophical approach . . . She has the *Complete Works* of Freud on a shelf over her desk . . . An astonishing combination of qualities when you see her like that, so dark and cool . . .

So we're having dinner together in a little restaurant in the Champ-de-Mars . . . I set myself out to please her . . . I think she's given up on a lot of things with me . . . Above all she's stopped trying to persuade me, as she used to in her aggressive period, that I'm neurotic, subject to phobias, perverse, and so on . . . I pay attention to Stephen; I make a proper practical, i.e., financial, contribution; I'm not a nuisance . . . I'm actually quite attractive physically . . . I make her laugh . . . I can't talk about psychology, but psychology bores her as much as it does me . . . So this is the night Papa and Mama come home arm in arm slightly drunk . . . The night Papa lifts Mama's skirt up as they come up the stairs . . . The night Papa screws Mama as he used to do, passionately and with skillful excesses . . . The night Mama groans and murmurs words both loving and obscene, twists and arches, rolls about, offers Papa her ass . . . Not nice, not nice at all . . . Frightful, as a matter of fact . . . Parents don't do that sort of thing, do they? Jocasta and Laius—how horrible . . . Jocasta and Oedipus is one thing, but that! Really, I'm disgraced before the whole of society . . . Before History itself . . . I feel I've committed a crime without a name . . . To be erotic in one's own home; to have an orgasm with one's own wife, and to give her one too—can you imagine anything in more outrageous bad taste? The end of the world! The ruin of the novel! Imagine if Charles Bovary were attractive . . . A writer . . . And Emma a psychoanalyst giving herself to him willingly and with enthusiasm . . . No more Flaubert! No more University! No more theses! The perfect crime! A real revolution, a new era . . . And *I'm* the implacable revolutionary, the hero, the bringer of unprecedented good news—strange but quite simple, inaccessible, enviable, tremendous . . . Nonsense proclaimed! Absurdity made euphoric! Values transmuted! I'm a superman, or rather a post-man, a post-human, an *être*erosexual, the opposite of a monosexual . . . I've overcome the ancient curse, got the better of inevitable tragedy . . . No, really, it's the height of human experience . . . The origin and end of all myths—they're as simple as that! Great outcry from the audience . . . Howls! Hisses! Convulsions! Rages! More hisses! "How pathetic, how vulgar," says those who are still searching . . . But that's the point—there's nothing to search for . . . Yes, but what are you to say if you've solved the problem? If you know the key to everything? Yes, everything—each object and each part of each object . . . The ever visible, ever audible crucible and melting-pot of things . . . The moment out of time . . .

177

The curse . . . We were going to lift it together . . . I remember saying that to Deb one afternoon by the Thames . . . It was a strange way of saying what I felt then . . . In the sun . . . The dazzle . . . Sometimes, rarely, there are moments between a man and a woman that oughtn't to be judged in time . . . Moments belonging to a part of duration that can't be measured . . . That remain there, apart . . . Not to be included in the settling of scores that always comes . . . Painting . . . Figures . . . What were we doing in London? I forget . . . All I remember are her light brown eyes very close, widening, blind in a fervent caress . . . The rooms in the British Museum, Egypt vibrating in the very stones . . . And us there by the river, enclosed in the circle, the ring . . .

"It doesn't work, between men and women," Fals always used to say . . . That was the cornerstone of his doctrine and he kept on repeating it . . . As if, after him, he didn't want anyone to experience the fundamental shaking of the earth; as if he wanted to confiscate pleasure, show it didn't lead anywhere . . . But who ever said it was meant to "work"? What's interesting is that it should take off from time to time . . . Before it explodes . . . Anyway, if it ever has really taken off once, it still goes on working a bit . . . Unless it gets stuck in hatred . . . But that can be avoided too . . . I think Fals never soared enough . . . I think that's what made him ill . . . Did any woman ever swoon over his anatomy? Not very likely . . . Not really . . . Not madly . . . Not enough to make him not care, afterward, whether it "worked" or not . . . Hence his mission, to be a parasite on the lives of others . . . A great vocation . . . To infiltrate, interfere, stand in the way, seek out the cause of the discord, then settle in there, urging, undermining, making things worse . . . I remember how he used to hang about at our place . . . Gazing at Deb over his glasses . . . Poor wretch! It was painful to watch . . . But that was all . . . We had to be polite . . . But why does one have to be polite, one wonders? Given all the pests, male and female, going about seeking whom they may devour . . . Relying on your good manners to let them keep bawling out their botherations, get between you and yourself and lap up what's left over, launch out on their scatty maunderings . . . Vampires on all sides . . . As if they were multiplied electronically . . . Background noises . . . Animal noises . . . Take my advice—if you've managed to create a bit of civilization for yourself, defend yourselves and don't make any concessions . . . You're surrounded by the living dead . . . They're swimming toward you . . . Their half-rotten jaws hem you in . . . They're coming nearer . . . Throwing their grappling hooks, their rope ladders . . . Clambering up toward the light they dimly discern in their musty, dark-encumbered minds . . . You are Moby Dick . . . The white whale . . . They'll hunt you through the whole world . . . In the air and under the sea . . . To harpoon you . . . Cut you up . . . Eat you in slices . . . In extracts . . . In oils, perfumes, creams . . . You are regenerative, stimulating . . . Spermaceti! The perfect massage . . . The coveted eucharist . . . "Oh man! admire and model thyself after the whale! Do thou, too, remain warm among ice. Do thou, too, live in this world without being of it. Be cool at the equator; keep thy blood fluid at the Pole. Like the great dome of St. Peter's, and like the great whale, retain, O man! in all seasons a temperature of thine own . . ."

Marvelous Melville . . . Comparing the whale to St. Peter's in Rome . . . Fabulous *Moby Dick* — my favorite novel . . . Call me Ishmael . . . Or Queequeg . . . The Parsee . . . Ahab . . . Stubb . . . Starbuck . . . Whichever you like . . . Something of all of them flows in my veins . . . On the bridge of the narrative . . . Sails, masts, ladders, hatches, dinghies, rigging . . . The open sea . . . On watch in every paragraph . . . Monologues strewn on the water . . . From the Atlantic to the Pacific . . . Manhattan to China . . . Jonah rewritten by Shakespeare . . . Father Mapple's sermon . . . Meditation in mid-ocean . . . "Born of earth, yet suckled by the sea; though hill and valley mothered me, ye billows are my foster-brothers!" And so on and so forth . . . Five hundred pages for a shipwreck . . . Of which nothing survives, finally, except the printed book . . . Saved, like a fatherless bastard or an extra page of the Bible, by a passing ship, the *Rachel* . . . Which picks up the narrator from his floating coffin . . . ". . . for almost one whole day and night, I floated on a soft and dirge-like main. The unharming sharks, they glided by as if with padlocks on their mouths; the

179

savage sea-hawks sailed with sheathed beaks." . . . A typhoon of ink . . . Arrow phrases launched into the spray-filled wind . . . And then nothing . . . The story swallows up everything . . . The abyss and its whirlpool both put into words . . .

What is there in French to compare with that? Lautréamont? Of course . . . But the French look on him as difficult . . . Baudelaire? Often . . .

And sleep in oblivion like a shark in the waves . . .

That's from *Le Mort joyeux,* I think . . .

But to get back to the novel . . . No one's really interested in it anymore . . . Not really deep down, as they ought to be . . . "I'm sure," S. once said to me, "you couldn't find one critic today who could tell you how *Anna Karenina* begins . . .

I bet you couldn't.

Not one.

Don't bother looking . . . Here it is: "All happy families are alike; every unhappy family is unhappy in its own way."

"Everything was upside down in the Oblonksky house. The lady of the house had just found out that her husband had been having an affair with their former French governess . . ."

Come, come . . . What's interesting nowadays is exactly the opposite of what's said in that first sentence . . . A happy family? Just as hard to find as a good novel! More extraordinary than a whale that can't be caught! More fantastic than an invasion from outer space! Unique! An extinct species . . . Tell us about it! Please! That must be something! Go on, tell!

"All happy families are alike . . ." Good old Tolstoy—there's another one who couldn't tell the truth . . . His appalling wife . . . The opposite of Dostoievsky's, who was instinctively aware of what was going on . . . He tells how she begins to cry whenever she sees his face covered in blood after an epileptic fit . . . As he fell down he used to hit his head against tables and so on . . . It could happen at any time—in a corridor or on a staircase, and especially while he was asleep . . . Or writing . . . He comes into the bedroom carrying a lighted lamp . . . She props herself up on the pillows and looks at him . . . It's through seeing her in tears that he realizes he's had a fit . . . Were the Dostoiesvkys a happy family? Completely . . . He takes on himself the ultimate tension and strain . . . Playing his own nervous system like a hand at poker . . . The spasmodic hazard of births . . . And of deaths . . . And between the two, the electric shock of coition . . . The radiant absurdity of being here, with this head, these hands, these legs, this particular chest, this sex equipment . . .

We got to be happy again, Deborah and I, after we'd weathered the Tropics . . . It was a difficult voyage . . . We saw everything . . . Now we've emerged . . . Enough to have some idea how to live afterward . . . Still . . .

That is, to face up as far as possible to fate and the fall . . . The fact that there's nothing men and women can do together but perpetuate misunderstanding . . . That men haven't got anything to talk about to one another either, nor women to other women, except the scenery, and that's always subject to jamming or interference . . . That everyone is forever alone on his canal between two locks, two crazy cataracts . . . All these millions of eyes, each in its own nights, thinking they see the same light or the same story . . . In short, all the obvious things it takes you years to see clearly, inside you and out . . . All that men invent to escape from what they see: even wallowing in the shit, though the shit itself isn't the bottom of anything . . . Sometimes they think they've arrived at the ultimate in cynicism . . . Like dogs, with their pricks, their balls, their dirty anuses, their swiveling noses . . . A few little faded blasphemies . . . The mockery of suicide . . . The determination to show off even inside one's gaseous carcases . . . Poor perverse peripherals . . . Meanwhile the women, for their part, go on cooking up their romance . . . What's fascinating about marriage is its closeness to incommunicability . . . An irremediable impossibility . . . Nothing has been so rarely described; nothing is so little understood . . . And what comes out silently on top nine times out of ten is the beginning of nausea . . . A kind of desperate drowning in the bath of the subject . . . When you're at the end of your tether . . . With disgust, pointlessness and boredom . . . Overcoming that takes superhuman discipline, rigid ritual . . . Every morning we have a brief session of martial arts . . . Between Stephen and me . . . I wear the navy blue and white kimono Deb brought me back from Japan . . . I let out Kabuki yells . . . We bow respectfully to one another . . . I teach him the strokes . . . Roooooo! He hits me . . . Hand flat, arm out straight, imaginary sword flashing down . . . I reply by pushing him about a bit . . . He laughs . . . At five years old he's learning to kill Papa . . . Seriously . . . With all his strength . . . Deb watches us, amused but rather uneasy . . . We've just had breakfast . . . Tea for her, coffee for me . . . We eat our croissants, we chat . . . Papa must always be calm, rather distant, humorous, but not too much so . . . Yes, yes . . . No, no . . . Papa's a stake for unruly climbing plants . . . Not only the tone of the whole day and the following night but also the general atmosphere depends on his nerves being able to take it . . . Fathers, sacrifice yourselves . . . That's the price you have to pay for civilization . . . Be ready to die and to lie . . . Reject openness . . . Don't say anything . . . Never confide in anyone . . . Don't be ill . . . Go on till you drop . . . Stay easy, relaxed, ironical, even if you're trembling with dread inside . . . Be generous, understanding, enthusiastic, apparently naive, exemplary . . . Empty . . . Your role, set from all eternity, is sublime: you have to be the axis of the world, the spine of the cosmos, the pillar of harmony . . . But for heaven's sake don't talk about it . . . Silence . . . No statements . . . No complaints . . . No proclaiming of values . . . Just pay up! Rooozoooo! Zen improvisation . . . But since we're in the West— in Europe, in France, in Paris—I take Stephen round the churches on Sunday morning . . . Notre-Dame . . . St. Germain-l'Auxerrois, St. Séverin, St. Jacques-du-Haut-le-Pas, St. Etienne-du-Mont, the Val-de-Grâce . . . We look in on the masses in passing . . . Catch bits of gospel and epistle and sermon . . . A shred of Apocalypse . . . A fragment of Prophet . . . A gust of organ . . . A few flowers of song . . . "Papa!" says Stephen, "let's go to another church now!" I can't remember who it was that told me about seeing Werth drop into a chapel one morning, after looking round to make sure no one had seen him . . . And someone else was amazed to come upon Fals deep in prayer in a church in Italy . . . As for Lutz, philosopher of the enlightenment to the end, he's said to have gone back to the religion of his childhood when he was in St. Anne . . . "That proves he really was insane, doesn't it?" Malmora quipped to Flora . . . She looked thoughtful . . .

Stephen's very fond of these excursions . . . Candles . . . Statues . . . Stained-glass windows . . . Deb's not very keen . . . She's an atheist . . . At least she thinks she is . . . Science . . . Freud . . . Very well . . . Women ought to be against god . . . So ought those who worship Woman . . . It's only logical . . . Woman is the true god . . . The other one's false . . . How foolish to have backed the mingling of the two religions . . . Poor old Church . . . Mystification . . . Waste of time . . . Women can't but be hostile to the worship of the Father . . . In the form of the Son . . . And of the Holy Ghost . . . Eve . . . Original Sin . . . The lot . . . Women realize it's all secretly designed to keep them down . . . You can't stop reproduction, but you can make it invisible . . . And if you make women believe in that piece of eyewash it takes the pressure off . . . You end up with syrup and prettification . . . Or with fanaticism . . . They're the same thing . . . In frigidity it's rigidity that counts . . . Of course, of course . . . So let women be scientific . . . Realists . . . Interested in society . . . Security . . . Rationality . . . The best possible thing, instead of sham ecstasies, raptures, dizzy spells, blushes, and attacks of modesty . . . The *Spiritual Torrents* of Madame Guyon . . . Fénelon . . . The row over Quietism . . . Bossuet putting it down . . . Good old Bossuet . . . I see some fashionable old French philosopher refers to him in a newspaper as a silly ass . . . He loves Guyon and Fénelon . . . Love . . . No one seems shocked . . . On the contrary . . . S. says, "Imagine the howls of outrage if I wrote an article calling the old boy a cretin for saying such things . . ." And goes on to quote Bossuet on Fénelon: "I recoiled in astonishment to see so fine a mind admire a woman whose intelligence was so limited, whose merit was so slight, and whose illusions were so obvious; and who pretended to be a prophetess . . ." On the other hand, S. adds, you have the harshness of Port-Royal, which very nearly finished off Pascal . . .

No, no, let women be modern, calculating, in business . . . And fond of sex . . . And let us turn to music! Diversion! Mystery! The circus! A new Middle Age! An enlightened one! Complete with *son et lumière!* That's where subversion lies! The women are free, they work, they contracept, they have their own money, their own little amusements . . . Just like men, only even better . . . That's perfect . . . But the men must make one more effort . . . They must learn to amuse themselves . . . To sublimate everything . . . Metaphysics is back in fashion . . . The art of dying gracefully . . . Everyone's amazed . . . Transcendence is a brand-new idea . . . A new kind of bingo . . . Lotto . . . Lotto-eroticism . . . The more hopeless and tragic the situation is, the more you need to enjoy yourself . . . Bring on the Dances of Death . . . The Passions in the church porch . . . Carnivals . . . Videocassettes . . . Fancy dress . . . Skeletons . . . Hemp . . . Brimstone . . . Resurrections . . . Paradise . . . The other world is open once again . . . Let's go! Leave this vale of tears to the dames! The maternity homes, the clinics, the cemeteries! The ovules and the urns! All unified at last! Let's put out propaganda on the television! Let's have a program! Let the dames run everything! Let them have their finger in the pie, let them make decisions! No resistance! It can't be any worse than it is! But in exchange there must be a deluge of mystical gratuitousness, otherwise there'll be no solution . . . The bomb in less than no time . . . From within . . . Nuclear decay guaranteed . . . Cancer and the rest of the bag of tricks . . .

I meet a woman journalist just back from San Francisco . . . She's going to write an article for the popular press—"Hell for Women . . ." About San Francisco . . . Why? The invasion of the homos . . . Fags everywhere . . . A deluge of gays . . . Polk Street . . . Castro Street . . . Golden Gate Park . . . Fisherman's Wharf . . . The women are panicking . . . Their husbands are going over to the other side . . . In droves . . . The women are being deserted more and more . . . Sodom City! They're forming therapy groups

. . . Weeping on one another's shoulders . . . The mothers buy colored T-shirts with "Gays' Mothers" written on them . . . The gays kiss them in sympathy . . . What a to-do . . .

And then there's that lawsuit in New York . . . A stewardess suing a steward who screwed her in the air over Iran . . . She's pregnant . . . He only ejaculated once and has never seen her again since . . . She wants him to support the baby . . . He refuses . . . Accuses her of just using him as a sperm bank . . . The feminist lawyers say if he doesn't want children all he has to do is get himself sterilized . . . The sound of cash registers! Chemical warfare! Stand and deliver, cuckolds! A racket in test-tubes . . . Dirty work in the laboratory . . . Funny business . . .

I hear the pill is suffering from deflation . . . Apparently women have started to mistrust what they once demanded at the tops of their voices . . . Abortion, deletion . . . It's no longer acceptable . . . They fall ill . . . Or think they do . . . Something wrong with the works . . . Their daughters' freedom scares them . . . They complain of being programmed . . . Depersonalized . . . Categorized by computer . . . But of course!

What a huge joke, all of a sudden! What a farce! And what predominates in the end—horror or laughter? Take your choice . . .

Anyhow, things have never been so clear.

"Man is a useless passion," Sartre said. A mere portion . . .

A portion is what's left of a pig after conception tax has been deducted . . .

I look at us, the three of us, in our room near the Luxembourg Gardens . . . Foreigners, no doubt—as we'd be anywhere . . . And yet at the same time so much at home . . . Our families are far away, almost forgotten . . . Savannah, Sofia . . . We're suspended in mid-air . . . In the evening Deb and Stephen go to bed and I continue alone into the night . . . Red light . . . Silent streets . . . I can't make out what's going on in this country anymore . . . Their television's unwatchable . . . You can't even leave the picture on without the sound as I used to in New York . . . The French are mainly interested in the jabber . . . There aren't really any pictures . . . S. keeps me up-to-date with what's going on . . . Not much

. . . For some time he's been looking fed up too . . . Problems? No . . . Trouble getting on with the work? Not really . . . Well then? Oh, *you* know . . . The new government? No, no, something more fundamental than that . . . It's true the world has never seemed so stuck, so much of a garbage dump . . . Trash-can of the stars . . . No more credible plans . . . No way out . . . Is this the first time it's been so bad? Yes . . . The final disillusion . . . Not even the end of the world—that would be too much to hope for . . . Just the revelation that there's neither beginning nor end, neither sense nor nonsense, only pleasure, suffering, and attrition of attrition . . . A bit of liver eating itself up . . . A face-lift for the cells . . . S. reminds me of a little medical story . . . What are the only two diseases transmitted by women to men? I've forgotten . . . Only to men? By women? Yes . . . Myopathy and hemophilia . . . Progressive atrophy of the muscles; and tendency to bleed, with absence of the factor necessary for the clotting of the blood . . . A regression . . . Circulation overflows . . . The fetus dribbles . . . Resorbed, spongy . . . A little sponge at the bottom of the sea . . . A dull gleam . . . Green senility . . . Nothing to be done . . . They can throw out their chests for all they're worth . . . Dress in leather . . . Ride motorcycles, hold board meetings, chain themselves up, indulge in sado-maso writhings . . . Or prettify themselves up to the nines to escape the teacher's eagle eye . . . But whether they swell themselves up like frogs or go in for little curls, it all comes down to the same thing . . . Myopaths or hemophiliacs . . . A little shriveled-up bit of grooved flesh slowly macerating in its own juice . . . That's what drives people to drink . . . Or to settle down . . . They have an inkling of the bottom of the crater . . . They anticipate it, superficially . . . Flabby, exhausted . . . Slack, shapeless . . . The various fascist or totalitarian carry-ons are only ridiculously bloodthirsty attempts to stave it off, which merely accelerate the process . . . A steely hand behind . . . A rampant womb . . . St. Matrix, sword of god . . . A curly Caesarean . . . Abscess trap . . . A good jab, there in the arm, held out in the wind of waves . . .

All this reminds me of the indecent larks Cyd and I get up to . . .

When she has her period and we don't screw . . . We amuse ourselves in other ways . . . Whisper things to each other as disgusting as we can make them . . . She's going to castrate me . . . Slice my prick up lengthwise . . . Stick a pin in it . . . Bandage it up . . . This gradually gets her going . . . All that's needed is to bring hatred into it . . . Carefully, slowly, in a sustained murmur in time with the rising tide of the cells . . . The eternal desire to efface and destroy . . . Morbid, perverse; as insistent as a nurse or a masseuse . . . She jerks me off as she speaks . . . She likes talking . . . She says she's going to collect my sperm in a bottle . . . Put it on her chapped lips . . . Let her girlfriends dip their fingers in and taste . . . How horrible . . . I want to make her come unseen, inside her blood—the lukewarm, languid blood out in the open, being lost . . . I want her to feel my prick low down against her body, hemmed in, wasted . . . I want her to become a flower . . . To feel herself flowing like a flower . . . Drinking her sap . . . Or else I'm supposed to be dead . . . Or going to die . . . And she makes me shoot just before the end . . . Last breath . . . Very last sigh . . . What trivialities . . . Look again at the French nineteenth-century novel . . . Balzac . . . *The Girl with Golden Eyes* . . . "The Girl with Golden Eyes was drowning in her own blood . . . On all sides she had tried to cling on to life, on all sides she had tried to defend herself, and from all sides she had been attacked . . . The marquise's hair had been torn out, she was bitten all over—some of the wounds were still bleeding . . . And her torn gown left her half-naked and showed her breasts covered with scratches . . ." Zola . . . *Nana* . . . *La Curée* (The Quarry . . . Or, The Scramble for the Spoils . . .) The adroit and anonymous Gamiani, probably de Musset, describing his amorous goings-on with George Sand . . . "She touched me up gently, projected her saliva into my mouth and slowly licked me, or else nibbled at me so delicately and yet so sensually that the mere memory of it makes me ooze with pleasure . . . Oh, what delight transported me, what fury possessed me! I shrieked unrestrainedly; whether I collapsed in ruins or rose up wildly, always the sharp swift shaft reached and pierced me . . . Two thin lips, catching hold of my clitoris, nipped and pressed it until my soul took flight! No, Fanny, it is impossible to feel, to enjoy such ecstasy, more than once in one's life! How tense my nerves were! How my arteries throbbed! What ardor filled both flesh and blood!"

And so on . . .

Those Frenchmen certainly put their backs into it . . . *The 120 Days* . . . *Juliette* . . . You'd think it was the sole business of a whole nation and its language . . . Sade . . . It's the best thing about them . . . They're tattooed with it through and through . . . That's not to say they know much about it . . . Or want to know . . . Heaven forbid . . . But underneath . . .

In any case, that's not the problem . . . The interests of the human race as a whole lie elsewhere . . . In another dimension of the black lining . . . I can hear Lutz now, in his Marxist heyday, saying over and over again, as if to convince himself: "It's the masses that make history . . ." But every time I couldn't help hearing, echoing the word "mass," the word *hommasse*—a mannish woman . . . This asexual organic cut-out now seems to watch over universal boredom . . . So that you're surprised these days if you actually meet someone, really someone, instead of a mere hypnotic influence . . . But when you check it out . . . No, there wasn't anyone there at all . . . It was an optical illusion . . . Or you misheard . . . It was nothing . . .

Deb and Stephen and I are like fleeting apparitions to one another . . . And we know it . . . We smile at each other fondly and regretfully as we proceed on our exodus . . . "It's sad that we have to die," says Deb . . . No, the masses don't make anything—it's time that manipulates masses of masses, at full tilt . . . Like an unnecessary hourglass, endlessly inverted . . .

Paris, then . . . I've spent my day making phone calls . . . Kate, surviving amid the rotary hell of the *Journal* . . . Flora, frantically active trying but failing to hide from herself the void that's coming, that's already here . . . Cyd, drowning her sorrows as best she can in advertising . . . Boris, in a panic, a megalomaniac on an ever more trivial scale . . . Robert and his dealings with boys . . . They've all got through the day, gripped in the vice of news . . . Political

developments . . . A microscopic shift here . . . A sexual slide there
. . . A popular subject of conversation in Paris at the moment is a
book that reveals what goes on behind the scenes in publishing and
the media in general . . . *Money and libido,* it's called . . . The two
authors have chosen some funny names: Mammon and Rutman
. . . You learn about the battles that rage over a publicity spot
lasting six seconds . . . But on television that's a lot . . . Who
lunches with whom . . . Who screws who . . . The way various
rivals watch one another . . . Scandals about literary prizes . . .
Mild interest on the part of the banks . . .

I have a cup of coffee near my place . . . The waiter likes people
to talk to him about current events . . . He's a nice man; high
strung . . . "It can't go on like this, sir, you know . . . You'll see—
something'll happen, take it from me!"

I think it's just the winter . . .

It's pitch dark by six in the afternoon . . .

And what about the women, in all this? They're worried . . . It
isn't working out according to plan . . . Backlash . . . Control . . .
Model henhouse . . . Organized laying . . . And what about seduction, fantasy? Vanished! And desire? Chloroform . . . Weariness
. . . Work and weariness . . .

I go on, in the light of my lamp . . . What for? Nobody gives a
damn . . . No one reads anymore . . . To keep in form? That's it—
stick to form . . . The technique of meditation . . . Every man to
his yoga . . .

IV

There's a ring at the door of my studio . . . Flora . . . "Aren't you answering the phone these days?" She rushes in and looks around everywhere . . . No one . . . She's taken aback . . . I must be with a woman . . . What can I be doing if I'm not with a woman?

Hence the scene . . .

"The Englishwoman, eh?"

"What do you mean?"

"Don't deny it! The whole of New York saw you! You flaunted yourself everywhere! What a joke! You didn't stop screwing!"

"Really?"

"If you want my opinion I don't think you're capable of writing a novel . . . Not a real one . . . For that you have to be able to tell a story, my dear . . . You have to be true to life, forthright, close to reality, seeing it as it is . . . You mustn't shy away . . . You mustn't be abstract . . . Or hazy . . . It's not at all like the sort of thing your literary friends write . . . Elitist, decadent . . . And cultured—oh yes, three quotations to every page . . . Take S., for example . . . Anyway, I'm sure *you* couldn't set a scene or manage a simple plot . . . Malmora talked to me about it . . . You and your gang . . . Little bunch of snobs . . . Sixth arrondissement . . . Saint-Germain-des-Prés . . . No life, no energy . . . Except for screwing . . . And even that . . ."

Flora's all worked up . . . She must have just seen someone . . . Checked up on me . . . Someone has said . . . Someone has hinted . . . Someone has really set her off . . . Kate?

"Have you seen Kate?"

"What does it matter who I've seen? The thing is you never stop lying . . . Inventing sham timetables . . . Pretending you're working when all you're doing is sleeping around . . . Going from one bed to another . . . Don't you ever get fed up with it?"

The eternal scene . . . As it was in the beginning, is now, and ever shall be, world without end . . . The truth of all the ages is the awfulness of a scene like this on a wet morning . . . I look out the window . . . I vaguely hear Flora's outpourings . . . I concentrate on the rain running down the window-panes . . . I suddenly feel as if I were $N+1$ in an infinite series of numbers, living through this moment, these words, this pointlessness . . . Always the same performance . . . Ridiculous . . . Women on the one hand, men on the other, all rushing ignorantly after and through the bodies opposite . . . A steeple-chase . . . A feverish game of leapfrog . . . And they go round and round, and they ponder, and they get steamed up, and they reassure one another as best they can . . . They can think themselves lucky if the moment of mental agitation ends up in a screw . . . There are a few exceptions . . . But very few . . .

"Anyhow, women only take an interest in you because of me . . . I suppose you realize that?"

Flora paces to and fro . . . Sits down, gets up again, throws my papers on the floor, riffles frantically through my diary . . . I know the routine . . . Tears . . . Then arousal . . . Then seduction . . . In ten minutes she'll wind up on my lap like an innocent and perverse little girl . . . Start kissing me . . . Check whether I'm having an erection . . . The whole scene's designed to produce an erection in anyone she can't castrate . . . I can decide then whether or not to go along . . . Why not?

Flora's quoting names now . . . "The Englishwoman" has vanished . . . Flora doesn't know Cyd, so she can't use her as a symbol . . . But everybody's like this—can't imagine anything can happen except in relation to themselves . . . This principle has a corollary: no one can conceive of what sex means to someone else . . . All anyone can do is project his or her own attitude onto others . . . It's obvious Flora thinks I spend all my time trying to lay some woman or other I've met at the *Journal* or one of the other circles she knows I move in . . . She tries to make me give myself away . . . She's absolutely convinced . . . Whereas in fact it hasn't even crossed my mind . . . I find most of them quite unappealing . . . No accounting for tastes . . . All that matters to Flora—or to any woman, for that matter—is that everything should be among acquaintances . . . Problems, but family problems . . . A definite plot . . . An affair should have a beginning, a meaning and an end . . . The technique of water-tight compartments throws the whole system . . . A man capable of keeping his own counsel is unthinkable . . . A man who can refrain from boasting . . . Even indirectly . . . Who can be silent . . . Stay alone . . . Very present yet completely absent . . . The effervescence is doubled . . . No outlet . . . But then how can there be any story? If the characters never meet? If they don't have any relationships except those known to the narrator himself? Inadmissible liberty? The end of society as we know it?

Flora, still reviling me, manages to reveal that she's wearing her special gear of black stockings and garters . . . Her combat dress . . .

I think with some amusement that exorcists in the dim distant past must have been familiar with this kind of performance . . . The insults hurled at them by the "devil," the accusations so mysteriously relevant to their own weak points, the semblance of second sight and divination, were of course only meant to induce a kind of complicity . . . They were an invitation to yield to the spasm . . . To the Law . . .

Then it's back to politics again . . . Contemporary preoccupations . . . Pacifism . . . Neutralism . . . Poland . . . American missiles . . . Russian ditto . . . Pershings . . . SS 20s . . . But she's less emphatic about it than usual . . . As if she realized that it too will soon be a thing of the past, out of date in five years' time . . . The old topics of the '60s and '70s . . . China . . . Berkeley . . . Italy . . . Germany . . . '68 . . . Feminism . . . Terrorism . . . The something "brigades," the something else "fronts . . ." Still, you have to pretend to take an interest . . . I make a vague sort of contribution . . .

"Have you become a Buddhist or something?"

Talking of Buddhism, I've just seen Helga again . . . She's back from Calcutta, via Berlin . . . Her description of Berlin is wild . . . Concerts with two thousand punk-funks and the usual paraphernalia: chains, red and green hair, tattooing, sweat, unisex . . . Raising their arms and bawling things like:

> Geh in der Krieg!
> Tanzt den Mussolini
> Tanzt den Adolf Hitler!

Or:

> Deutschland
> Deutschland
> Alles ist vorbei!

They're at it again . . . In the "Let's have us a ball" manner . . .

Helga is tall, fair and quite good-looking . . . Her eyes are rather glassy and she's not very fresh—fish that's been marinated for too long in heroin and coke . . . She's finally found herself a guru, a visionary Indian preacher with whom she undergoes "rebirths . . ." She's already "rebirthed" two or three times . . . She has trouble, she says, getting her head out between the imaginary legs of her great personal womb . . . She thinks I haven't yet experienced real "enlightenment . . ." But it could happen . . . If I was more self-disciplined and not so casual . . . I'm not far from the light, but I need to make an effort . . . I've noticed for some time that everyone keeps telling me the same thing: I'm too this and not enough that . . . The theme changes but the reproach is always the same . . . Something about me isn't right . . . No question of screwing with Helga . . . She's beyond all that . . . Stabilized . . . Refrigerated . . . I have to listen to the same old song as ever: sexual fulfillment, immersion . . . The same great suffering as ever, imagining its own causes and compensations . . . She shows me some of her guru's sermons . . . Candy from a baby . . . I ask myself what the hell I'm doing writing my novel when there's all that credulity waiting to be exploited . . . The tone is all of the "beyond" . . . And the beyond is here and now . . . The Absolute, *c'est moi* . . . Nothing else . . . A sea of serenity . . . The fact that you ask the question shows how far you fall short . . . Your suffering is due merely to the restrictions of your mortal frame . . . The guru looks like somebody's overwrought old mother up to the gills in opium . . . Shit-bang . . . And indeed there's nothing more "luminous," more sure in its "knowledge" than a certain type of basic ferocity . . . Struggle for expanding space . . . Deathly mumbo-jumbo . . . The same tricks handed out to everyone . . . All-purpose slogans . . . the void, nonduality, an ounce of Buddha, together with a pinch of Jesus to bring in befuddled Westerners . . . And off we go for a return trip on the ghost train . . . Rebirth!

Helga's going to Texas, where they're opening an "ashram . . ." They think the Americans are ripe for Revelation . . . A question of money, I suppose . . . I tell Helga they'll have plenty of competition down there . . . Gurus two a penny! Raptures every five minutes! Trips by the million . . . But it doesn't bother her — she adores her primitive Aryan . . . Wears a photo of him around her neck . . . Like a dog . . . He's the best . . . The only . . . Her expression hardens . . . That's how she survives . . .

I manage to get Flora to leave without incident . . . It's an art . . . You have to promise to meet again as soon as possible . . . Dates . . . Write them down . . . Go over them half a dozen times . . . Always the same sigh of relief when one of them takes herself off . . .

At last I can open my mail in peace . . . Charles Bukowski's latest book . . . *Women* . . . Good Lord, my own title . . . Fortunately the French publisher has left it in English . . . Anyhow, it doesn't matter . . . The more experimenters there are the better . . . Let everyone tell his own story . . . Anyway, he's only adopted the title De Kooning used for his great series of pictures . . . Grinning specters . . . Vampire cover-girls . . . I like Bukowski . . . right on target . . . Good . . . Excellent . . . The French remember him all right because once, in a live literary TV show that everyone watches religiously every Friday—everyone in the big little world of publishing and the media—he started to fondle the thigh of the lady psychological novelist he was sitting next to . . . Then he uncorked a bottle of white wine . . . And started to drink it . . . Out of the bottle . . . They chucked him out . . . Gently but firmly . . . His book? Very good; a bit repetitive . . . But that's because of the subject . . . How he boozes, screws, gives lectures at the universities . . . He meets Burroughs on the same circuit . . . All the rather difficult authors are reduced to doing it . . . They don't speak to each other . . . Different publics . . . They take the money and run . . . Bukowski always picks on some woman . . . There's always one who wants to make the guy or the girl she's with jealous . . . His earlier things were good, too — *Tales of Ordinary Madness, Notes of a Dirty Old Man* . . . A Frenchman would never dare . . . Bluish horizons . . . Quibbles . . . Dreams of alchemy . . . Merlin's forest by night . . . The land of myrtles . . . The secret of the Pyramids . . . Mme de Rênal's hand under the table . . . Elsa's sighs . . . The child and the spells . . . But Buko has realized one thing: you mustn't hold things up . . . The author's mental maunderings are no longer of any interest . . . You must go straight for the kill . . . The primal scene in front of everyone . . . Between Proust and Bukowski the novel has taken a leap . . . Relentless bad taste . . . But actually he does believe too much in women's omnipotence . . . He lets his belly blow up; beer; decomposition . . . He refers to his prick as his "carrot" . . . His "wick" . . . Is it a mistake in the translation? No . . . He "jets his juice" . . . In the "pussies" . . . He "plants his carrot" . . . He "dips his wick" . . . When he's not too tight . . . Nine times out of ten he rolls over before he's finished . . . Too much beer . . . He can't do it . . . Really what the feminists would once have called an MCP . . . But what are they going to do now with a brazen, desperate, deliberate pig — glad to be what he is, *wanting* to be a caricature?

And yet they write to him . . . A good wheeze: pick-up by publication . . . Well, he's asked for it . . . They're writing to the right person . . . They come by plane from all over America to jump him . . . Secretaries, sales assistants, hairdressers . . . And right away: to bed! Let's do it! Not bad . . . Whereas with me — complete cross-purposes . . . Women idealize me . . . They love me . . . And put on airs . . . Act like schizophrenics . . . Paranoiacs . . . Everything has to be distinguished . . . A question of image . . . "Social class" . . . Whereas with him . . . He's practically a tramp . . . But there's something in that alcoholic eye, some touching twist in the veins of that reprobate's nose . . . They dream of taking care of him . . . It's either that or frantic identification . . . The eternal you and I are one . . . They write to me too . . . All the time . . . But never anything out of place . . . They get him with porno snaps and shredded panties, but with me they poetize and go into raptures . . . They want to show me they're much crazier than anyone would ever dare imagine . . . My favorite lives in Switzerland . . . She doesn't ask to meet me; she's quite happy just telling me how she thinks of me when she makes love to her husband . . . Of course I never reply . . . But sometimes I find myself wanting more details . . . *Physical* details, *physical* details! But it's no good, they *will* wrap everything up . . . They have a penchant for curtains . . . Not for words — words are for men, for animals . . . No, what they like is veils, gauze, shadows, allusions . . . My appearance leads them astray . . . Keeps them at a distance . . . Except for one or two who phone up from time to time . . . A few ruderies . . . Nothing much . . . Or else rather breathless, rather promising silences . . . Are they really masturbating? Hard to say . . . It would surprise me . . . The thing's always based on a lie on one side or the other . . . It's very unusual to find one of them who knows how and why to set the scene . . . Cyd . . . When she whispers that she's been to buy a "string" with me in mind . . . Or that at some friend's house she's shut herself up in the john to play with herself and think of me . . . True or not, it doesn't matter — it's truer than the truth . . . She works herself up working me up . . . But that's a special case . . .

Still, Bukowski isn't Bataille . . . Everything's external with him, and without variation . . . A quick screw and that's it . . . What's

really new is that he records the way women have been transformed
. . . The tidal wave . . . Not only American women — we know
about them . . . But it's happening everywhere . . . Their aims . . .
Their new hygiene . . . The underlying influence of the SGIC . . .
The no-nonsense side there is to them now; straightforward, de-
poetized, ready to take the initiative . . . They go straight at it . . .
Nothing to lose . . . So they think . . . No more preparations . . .
That, and money . . . Matter-of-fact! The chaps are left far behind
. . . Tangled up in images . . . Just as the women used to be . . .
General post . . . the other way around . . . Funny . . . More and
more, women are becoming open-eyed realists, cold, sexist, exchanging men as they might exchange household gadgets . . . They
pretend to accept the most shocking situations . . . Ménages à trois
. . . A cinq . . . A sept . . . A mere matter of tactics, as Bukowski
shows . . . Behind it all, and more than ever, there's always the
same virulent jealousy . . . The yelling will soon begin . . . It's
coming . . . It's here . . . The women are trying to break down any
male who's left himself open, gone to sleep, dwindled, dropped his
guard . . . Opened the door . . . Never! Don't forget: never! Not
on any account! Keep your eyes open! Gun under the pillow! Quick
on the draw! On your feet in a second!

Being on your feet, vertical, that's the important thing . . .
Otherwise you become their mother — it's inevitable . . . They
curl up inside their dear old mother — which is what you imperceptibly become for them . . . They have an automatic tendency to
become electric fires . . . Toasters . . . It strikes me particularly at
cocktail parties . . . Women and their mothers . . . Men turned
into mothers . . . Unwittingly . . . They totter into it without
realizing . . . It's incredible . . . Not a single man . . . Only
women — yet, at the same time, not a single woman! It's there in
front of us, obvious, an open graveyard . . . Old stuff . . . The
homos manage things a bit better . . . They've made a preemptive
strike, if you'll forgive the expression . . .

Here's another book . . . *The Ceremony of Farewells*, by Simone
de Beauvoir . . . Sartre's last years . . . That subject again — can't
get away from it . . . I can still hear Fals: "My dear boy, we've now

embarked upon the really important thing . . . You're still young, but you understand . . . Surprisingly enough . . . So there are at least two of us . . . As for me, I'm on the way out . . . I've seen and heard and exaggerated enough . . ." A brief suppressed laugh . . . A quick glance over his specs . . . "This is the turning point . . . The middle of the voyage . . . Don't be surprised at anything . . . Seriously—I warn you . . . Not at anything . . ."

What exactly did he mean? A change of bearings? Something wrong with the compass? New objects of worship? New crimes?

It's curious, though, how fascinated Beauvoir is by the physical decay of Sartre at the end . . . She discovers the shriveled body of her great man just as he's making his exit . . . Keeps a detailed record of his decline . . . An irreproachable settling of scores . . . The best of intentions . . . His lapses of memory; how he starts to pee all over the place . . . The dubious company he kept . . . Former revolutionaries now turned toward god and learning Hebrew . . . It's as if that's what shocks her most—god and Hebrew . . . She publishes a long conversation, the last, that she had with Sarte in Rome . . . This sort of thing: "You don't believe in god, Sartre?" "Of course not." "Are you sure?" "Naturally." "So you believe only in Man?" "Of course." . . . Phew, what a relief—we were quite nervous for a moment . . . It's essential, when it comes to present-day Religion, to make one thing clear . . . The cornerstone of out-and-out humanism . . . God doesn't exist . . . All men are mortal . . . The greatest suffer the same as the least . . . Liberty . . . Equality . . . Fraternity . . . Once Sartre's dead, in the hospital, she wants to lie down beside him under the sheet . . . The nurse on duty won't let her, because of the gangrene . . . As Kate says, "Despair justifies anything . . ."

To be with him in the grave; to mingle remains . . .

If god doesn't exist there's at least a chance that corpses meet again in the Great Whole . . . The Cycle . . . In the sexless dust . . . Whereas if they were resurrected, you never know, a vestige of difference might survive . . .

Every morning on my way to the *Journal* I pass a maternity home . . . There are words on the pediment forming a triangle:

MATERNITY

The three that add up to four . . . The French all over!

Sartre's last act of generosity: even if he'd had a passing doubt about god after all, he wouldn't have gone and shocked Beauvoir about the very foundation of things . . . Thoughtful and discreet to the end . . .

It's true women inevitably make for investment, bricks and mortar . . . Paraphernalia in general . . . Household goods . . . Fitted carpets, armchairs, chests of drawers, closets, sideboards . . . Lawyers . . . When they realize, one fine day, after having made a lot of effort for nothing, that they didn't clear the hurdle a long time ago . . . The hurdle? Yes; puberty . . . Just look at them—it hits you in the eye . . . Mentally they're always about thirteen or fourteen . . . Twelve or thirteen . . . The time when the landslide, the disaster, happened . . . The failure represented by the solemn communion . . . The bleeding . . . Flagrant . . . Beyond all possible doubt . . . Shattering . . . And recurrent . . . The moon . . . Increased irritability a few days before . . . "The body plagued and ready to burst," I remember Diane saying . . . Embarrassment, pain, obstruction . . . The feeling of being crushed beneath it, bowed, humiliated . . . You have to understand them . . . Realize to the full what's involved . . . The condition of our existence . . .

How should one approach this basic shambles? This bloody crucible?

How can one be detached from this renewal of devastation?

I look at my own sex this morning . . . Meditate a while on its adventures . . . Urine and sperm . . . Two different mechanisms . . . Two unrelated lives . . . Two separate identities . . . At rest;

in erection; jerked off; sucked off; penetrating; ejaculating; resting . . .

One day it will decompose and disappear . . . With its own stock of memories . . . Ill said, ill transcribed . . . It's never really like that . . . Superfluous man . . . Useless . . . Except as a temporary refill . . . A battery . . . A little locomotive on the rails of the generations . . . Toot-toot!

It's difficult to describe the life one leads in this gutter of time . . . On the roof of time . . . A lump in your throat . . . Meetings . . . Illuminations . . . Vibrations . . . I'd never finish if I tried to describe the hidden side of it all . . . Incredible, what you pick up whether you want to or not in this realm of commotion . . . What remains . . . All the rest is nothing . . . "Pensées" . . . Thoughts . . . Ashes . . .

That's why the truth of sensation is always religious . . . To deny it is to reduce the panoply of the senses, to make them pale and insipid . . . To unplug the human radar, out of stupidity or insensitivity (the two are the same) . . . To cut off one's own antennae . . .

This is what rites, rituals, all of them, say . . . Even if they're performed or experienced as if in a dream . . .

In my mind's eye I see again a circumcision I once attended . . . Anyone who's never done that has never seen the fundamental structure of existence . . . The male baby, all dressed up in its cradle . . . The family, the friends, the witnesses . . . The arrival of the officiating rabbi, suave, in his element . . . With his little medical kit . . . The anxious agitation of the women . . . Ready either to swoon or to exchange inquisitive whispers . . . The men with their hats on . . . The Pass . . . The Great Passage . . . "Hebrew" means "One who crosses over . . ." The going forth out of Egypt . . . Cutting the hieroglyph into the flesh . . . A leap out of the stars . . . Over biology . . . The Red Sea . . . Sailors on land . . . Coming from afar and going far . . . It's the year 5741 . . . Quite recent compared with the pyramid dynasties . . . Cheops' ear listening to the spiral axis of the Milky Way . . . The Colossi of Karnak . . . The pillars of Luxor . . . A slash with the scissors in all that . . .

The Mila . . . The Môhel . . . "Blessed are You, O Lord our God, King of the Universe, who has sanctified us by Your commandments and ordered us to perform circumcision . . ." The cut is made . . . "Qôdesh!" The baby cries . . . He is received into the Word . . . The congregation answers: "May this child, who is entering into the alliance, grow up in the Torah, the Khoupa, and good deeds . . ." Sublime violence . . . Butchery converted back to lightning . . . From the sex to the throat . . . Opening of the larynx . . . Separation from the Mother . . . A nexus of sound . . . It's said the Prophet Elijah is always there unseen, watching over the operation . . . He'll have seen oceans of blood . . . He'll have heard plenty of prayers . . . The same as at Passover, when a glass of wine is set out ready for him . . . In case he might really be there, all of a sudden, just ahead of the Messiah . . .

Fabulous nervous tenacity . . . Just the thing to worry the neighbors as the centuries rolled by . . . You can understand the whispers, the rumors . . . The tales of murder and witchcraft that impressed the not so bright . . .

Concierges . . . Chambermaids . . . Delivery men . . . Inevitably, because it's a question of the ultimate lock and key . . .

Which doesn't mean that those who use the key necessarily know what they're doing . . . Far from it . . . It's just repetition, that's all . . . The same as with our own baptism . . . I remember Stephen's . . . A stormy day . . . In a little village church on the southwest coast of France where Deb and I go on vacation . . . It was my doing . . . Deb wasn't keen . . . All the more reason for me to insist . . . I knew it would seem odd . . . "What? You had your son christened?" I could already hear them saying it . . . In their schoolteacher voices . . . "Your son? christened?" And they did say it too . . . Their faces went sour and distant . . . As if it were something indecent . . . Yes, funnily enough, that's what's regarded as indecency now . . . What a joke . . .

So, as I said, there was the father and mother of a storm . . . Raging sea . . . Huge green breakers . . . Gulls screaming . . . Stephen scared and crying . . . The priest in a hurry . . . These foreigners . . . The little church like a boat swept adrift . . . And no one there except us three, and some local sailors' children as godparents . . . Thunder and lightning . . . "In nomine Patris, et Filii, et Spiritus Sancti" . . . Water and oil . . . Water and fire . . . And I, to the great astonishment of Deb, the priest and the children, starting to read aloud from one of St. Paul's Epistles: "God sent forth his Son, made of a woman, made under the law, To redeem them that were under the law, that we might receive the adoption of sons . . . And because ye are sons, God hath sent forth the Spirit of his Son into your hearts, crying Abba, Father . . ."

I must say it was an impressive scene . . . Voices and din . . . Because, as is only right, the priest had the bells rung . . . The two little rustics were given a few sweets . . . We went home along the beach . . . The sun was shining again, the wind was still blowing . . . Stephen had stopped crying . . . I was carrying him, all muffled up and quiet . . .

Perpetuity . . . Exodus . . . The revolving door of the generations . . . Circumcision or baptism . . . Two different logics . . . Two different ways of dealing with the inevitability of physical reproduction . . . Of not regarding the body as "natural . . ." I tried to talk to Fals about it . . . These little questions of symbols . . . A part of the physical body removed, the part for the whole . . . The whole referred back to its vibrant source . . . But it left him cold . . . He preferred to think about burials . . . Funeral rites . . . Prehistory . . . The worship of the dead . . . An Egyptian, really . . . Sarcophagi . . . Double mummies . . . What strikes me is this surprise intervention, these strong verbal shocks in the midst of birth . . . And at the other extreme, "Let the dead bury their dead . . ." A bit of incense . . . May they rest in peace . . . Ressurection? Second birth? As you like . . . But we must get rid of the fascination with remains . . . Graveyard hallucinations . . .

Where did Fals get that proclivity from? I think it was from his living continually in the cemetery of psychoanalysis . . . Latent hypnosis . . . Lying down in the half-light . . . The sinister to-ing and fro-ing between couch and chair . . . They can never really wake up any more . . . Too many dreams . . . Too many conjurings up from below . . . Too many semicomatose states . . . Too many

205

ghosts . . . Look at Freud's office as it appears in the photograph taken in 1939, just before the Nazis entered Vienna . . . It looks like a fortune-teller's lair, with cushions, glass-fronted cabinets, children's photographs, embroidered rugs, statuettes in every nook and cranny . . . Passion for archaeology . . . Excavations . . . Miasmas from the other side . . . Concrete objects with evocative powers . . . Thebes . . . Obsession with temples . . . The stoic tragedy of his face at the end . . . And to think all that rises up again via the negative slopes of clouded perception, and whispers from the folds of a curtain of morosity . . . As time went by I understood Fals's sudden rages better . . . His red and speechless explosions . . . The way he'd sometimes boot everybody out . . . Clobber his patients . . . Aim kicks at the furniture, much to the terror of his ancient cleaning lady . . . Or, on the other hand, the way he'd suddenly go silent, numb and depressed . . . He oscillated between the two extremes . . . With the fury of someone who, though he was very well paid for it, felt as if he were fixed there, stuck there for the ceremony of the lost souls, screwed in his chair by the whole cunning weight of human detritus . . . He survived because of his lectures . . . His masses, like sacred ceremonies . . . All the repressed religion returned in them . . . "Fals a great rationalist?— you must be joking," his closest followers used to say . . . A father is never clever to his sons . . . "A high-ranking initiate, a 'shaman,' " said others, with Pythagorean knowingness . . . But finally, what? A poor man just like anyone else, worn out by all that somnambulist repetition; always having to listen to the same demands, emotions, nonsense, ravings, sham revelations, interpretations, and confusions . . . Yes, how bored they must all have been — Werth and Lutz too . . . How hard they must have had to pretend in order not to give the show away and *admit* . . . Admit what? That even there where they'd managed to get to, in that position so much desired by others, there was nothing . . . Nothing to see; nothing to understand . . .

Here we go . . . Poland! Military coup . . . Communications cut . . . Tanks in the streets . . . Soldiers at the intersections . . . Arrests . . . Curfew . . . Identity checks . . . A Sunday morning, naturally . . . Paris asleep; everything dull and gray . . . I'm in the bathroom . . . Deb yells out to me . . . The phone rings . . . It's S. . . . His wife has already gone out . . . He doesn't know where she is . . . I'd forgotten Sophie's Polish . . . Her parents are there . . . I tell S. to come over . . . He comes . . . He's furious . . . I've never seen him so worked up . . . He paces up and down . . . "I'm sorry," he says, "I'll go . . ."

He stays . . . We were supposed to be working today, but instead we just stay there waiting for Sophie to phone . . . Appeals for donations . . . Demonstrations . . . News flashes . . . In short, just what we expected . . . Ever since the attack on the Pope in St. Peter's Square . . . The Turkish killer lying in wait in the crowd, shooting over their heads . . . A professional . . . The red stain spreading over the white cassock . . . The red and the white . . . John-Paul II slowly subsiding in his jeep as in a great painting by Rubens . . . The Kennedy assassination . . . Martin Luther King . . . Sadat . . . Marksmen from the shadows gradually appearing in the light . . . That's war . . . Contradictory versions . . . Indoctrination . . . Jamming . . . Cubans, anti-Cubans, Mafia, Libyans, Iranians . . . Destabilization . . . Force . . . Warsaw . . . Polish names start spluttering out everywhere: Gdansk, Katowice, Posnan, Lublin, Stettin, Pomerania, Silesia . . .

Hell, what a mess . . . Never as bad as this before . . . A general seeping away . . . The Church left more than ever alone in the darkness . . . Come, let's be serious, the Church is all that's left . . . Irony . . . Infinite guile . . . The old Church, belonging to two thousand years that went by like a dream . . . The Church of the calendar . . . Not always easy to make it work, is it, the trick with the calendar? Moon . . . Sun . . . 1789 . . . 1917 . . . Two upheavals . . .

"It's not generally known," says S., "how fiercely determined the French revolutionaries were to replace the Gregorian calendar . . . And do you know the name of the person who drew up the reform, adopted by the Convention on October 1793? You'll never guess . . . Romme! With two m's. It was he who introduced the divisions of time to be used in the new era . . . The era of the

207

Supreme Republican Being then gushing forth its torrent of egalitarian heads . . . The words themselves were invented by one of France's worst poets ever . . . Fabre d'Eglantine . . . *Il pleut, il pleut, bergère* . . . He himself was topped in 1794 . . . Moderantism . . . Danton . . . Oh, that obsession to have done with Rome! The Luther alternative on the one hand . . . Antiquity on the other . . . Back to Nature! *Bergère!* Shepherdess! The time the world has was spent revolving around that — always much more than is generally thought . . . The axis and spring of universal revolution . . . If "Hitler" hadn't rhymed with "Luther" it wouldn't have worked . . . Keep on going around and around, little puppets, something of it will always be left . . . And so the new months at the end of the eighteenth century: Vendémiaire, Brumaire, Frimaire, Nivôse, Pluviose, Ventôse, Germinal, Floréal, Prairial, Messidor, Thermidor, Fructidor . . . And the days: Primidi, Duodi, Tridi, Quartidi, Quintidi, Sextidi, Septidi, Octidi, Novidi, Decadi . . . Huh! How awkward they are to say . . . Social revolution and linguistic regression . . . Strange . . . New rights and tongue like a parrot's cage . . . Murders . . . Mumblings . . . "But that's not the worst of it," S. goes on . . . "The saints have had to be got rid of . . . But what's to be put in their place? Christianity has been officially abolished . . . The *infâme* has been *écrasé* . . . Substance reigns again, a transparent Héloise . . . The Vicaire Savoyard has won . . . Geneva exults . . . Emile will tell us all we need to know . . . So, the saints will be replaced by everyone's personal image of the country, rehabilitated . . . By rusticity pure and simple . . . Just listen to this! (He consults his notes . . .) There'll be a day of the grape, of saffron, of the chestnut, of colchicum, of the carrot, of the potato . . . So much for the plants . . . Then there are the animals: a day of the horse, the donkey, the ox, the goose, the turkey, the pheasant . . . Next come the implements used by the peasant who works this new and inspired land: the vat, the press, the cask, the plough, the spade . . . And the sickle! The hammer! And do you know all this has been taken over just as it stands by the USSR? Linear Judaeo-Christian time is wiped out, making way for cyclical time—exactly as under the Nazis! The feast of the tree, of the Russian birch, of the first furrow, of the harvest . . . Solstices! Equinoxes! Slav paganism! Nurse! Baba!"

"The original intention was rather charming," I say . . . "Utopian . . . Poetic . . ."

"Yes, indeed! Rose-colored spectacles floating on blue blood . . . Anyway, it lasted thirteen years . . . On the 22nd Fructidor of the Year XIII a Senate committee under Laplace opened the way for the humiliating return of Gregory XIII . . . Napoleon decreed it should happen on January 1st 1806 . . . The new religion was officially repudiated and people reverted surreptitiously to the old . . . But let me read you the actual document—it's marvelous, incredible:

" 'Senatus Consulte
on the reintroduction of the Gregorian Calendar
22 Fructidor, Year XIII
(Bulletin no. 56)

" 'Napoleon, by the grace of God and the constitution of the Republic Emperor of the French, to all present and to come, greetings . . .

" 'The Senate, after hearing the speakers of the Council of State, has decreed, and we ORDER, as follows:

" 'Article 1: As from next II Nivôse, January 1, 1806, the Gregorian calendar shall be used throughout the French Empire . . .'

"So! If ever the Papacy won a famous but little-known victory, this is it . . . The time and the signatures are just right . . . Perfectly judged . . . Can you imagine yourself dating a check 'Decadi Pluviôse Year 190? Poor Robespierre . . . But listen again . . . This is Octave Aubry in his book . . . *The French Revolution* . . . I think it'll come in handy for your novel . . . 'On 20 Prairial' "—this was in 1794—" 'reveille was sounded at five o'clock in all sections . . . The sky was splendid, already pierced by the rays of the sun . . . The houses were decked with leaves and garlands, and the streets strewn with flowers . . . Every window was hung with flags and banners; the boats on the Seine likewise . . . At eight o'clock the gun on the Pont-Neuf summoned all the sections to the Tuileries garden . . . The men, carrying branches of oak, took up their position on the terrace of the Couvent des Feuillants, while the women and girls, dressed in white and carrying roses, occupied the terrace by the river . . . The youths were massed on the path which runs through the middle of the garden . . . The deputies arrived gradually . . . They wore their official dress of leather breeches, blue coat with red collar and lapels, tricolor belt and big plumed hat, and most of them carried a bouquet of roses and ears of wheat . . .

" 'Vilate, an unfrocked priest, member of the revolutionary tribunal and fervent friend of the Incorruptible, met the latter in the Tuileries, in the Hall of Liberty . . . Robespierre had arranged for him to have lodgings in the Pavillon de Flore, and Vilate invited him to lunch there . . . There was a good view from the window . . . Maximilien accepted the invitation . . . He was dressed in a purplish blue coat and breeches made of *basin* . . .' "

"What's that?"

"A sort of cotton twill . . . 'He wore a jabot and cuffs, and his hair was carefully powdered as usual . . .

" 'He ate very little . . . He never had much of an appetite . . . Every so often he would look out of the window at the merry crowd milling around in the sun . . . His face was softened and warmed by genuine feeling: "The whole world is here today!" he cried . . . "O Nature, how sublime and delightful is thy power! Tyrants must grow pale at the thought of this celebration!" ' "

S. intrigues me yet again . . . He's sure this kind of event has an almost mystical importance . . . That's the surrealist in him . . . As he read the passage aloud he entered completely into the scene it described . . . I expected to see him rise up in front of me in a blue coat and powdered wig . . . He's more of a Frenchman than he thinks . . . Anyhow, he considers that period of history crucial for the understanding of everything since . . . Even the current situation in Poland, even the so-called agreement made at Yalta . . . From Rousseau to Marx and beyond . . . From Nature to Science . . . He reminds me that Sade just escaped the guillotine then . . . He shows me the document, signed by Fouquier-Tinville, condemning him to death . . . Also police reports of the period . . . Three different kinds of citizen were denounced: aristocrats and their accomplices, "fanatics" (Christians), and free-thinkers . . . All in the name of Virtue, of course . . . This reminds us that a French philosopher, a friend of Lutz's, has just been arrested in Prague for drug trafficking . . . Someone had put a few little packets of heroin in his case . . . "The rights of man . . ."

"You, as a foreigner, can't imagine," says S., "The educational dictatorship that's prevailed over the period we're talking about . . . I don't even know if you ought to write about it . . . The present régime is very hot on the French Revolution . . . It's getting ready to commemorate 1789 with great pomp and circumstance . . . But that subject is sacrosanct, and if you start criticizing it there'll be cries of 'Fascist!' and 'Pétain!' "

"All the more reason to talk about it," say I.

"Yes! That wouldn't stop us! We're "English" Catholics, aren't we? But you'll shock people . . . Disorient them . . . Repel them . . . The essential telephone number in France is DANton 17–89 . . . Very rarely ROBespierre 17–94 . . . Or only in secret . . . No more NAPoleon 18–04 at all . . . You have to be discreet . . . Too many suspicious deaths . . . Pointless ones . . . Megalomania . . . No, the ideal number is REV 17–89 . . . Pure idea . . . True, when it comes to the macabre it runs LENin 19–17 pretty close . . . And TROtsky 19–36 . . . Not to mention BAKunin 19–68 . . . Hello? Hello? There's a lot of static on the line from HITler 19–33, MUS-solini 19–22, FRAnco 19–37 and PETain 19–40 . . . And STAlin 19–42! Is the line still functioning? Hello? Hello? The lines really are swamped . . . Bombarded . . . And what funny voices!"

"But," I say, "do you really think it all revolves around Rome? Isn't that a bit wild?"

"No! Yes! Rome . . . A reflection of Jerusalem . . . A projection . . . Whether you take the Jewish year (five thousand years and a bit), the Islamic Hegira (for Moslems this is the year 1398), or the people who fantasize some esoteric descent for themselves from the Egyptians or the Sumerians, the great problem is the date . . . The magic date . . . 1981 . . . After Christ, as the Anglo-Saxons say in their conciliatory manner . . . BC! AC! All this gives rise to considerable differences of interpretation . . . Of categorization . . . Anyhow, the paradox exists: people say 1981, but they no longer know what they're talking about . . . Orwell was really spot on when he picked on 1984 . . . Do you know why?"

"No . . . Why?"

"1984 = 5744 in Hebrew . . . And the letters that form 5744 are Tav, Shin, Mem and Daled . . . And that means "destroyed . . ." But what about when it's 5984, the Masonic year of the 'true light,' the first month of which is March?"

"But you're not in favor of the Ancien Régime, surely?"

"Of course not . . . What's dead is dead . . ."

The radio tells us what's happening in Poland . . . Thousands of pilgrims flocking to see the Black Virgin . . . "The Black Virgin is Isis!" Boris has just informed me, on the phone . . . "The same old attempt to avoid facing up to things . . . Everywhere, all the time . . . And in this respect Jahweh too is only a sublimated Babylonian image . . . Anything will do so long as it conjures up the past and something different . . ."

"Imagine the *Te Deum* in 1802," says S. . . . The year when *The Spirit of Christianity* was published . . . An immediate best-seller . . . A stroke of genius . . . Have you read it?"

"Not really . . ."

"You should . . . The whole nineteenth century imitated it . . . Including Proust . . . Do you know what Chateaubriand himself says about it in *Memoirs from beyond the Grave?* He says that when it came out 'Voltaire's empire let out a shriek and rushed to take up arms . . .' Nicely put, huh? This is what he says about the effects the book produced: 'People no longer felt obliged to remain mummies of the void, wrapped up in philosophical bandages . . . They allowed themselves to examine every kind of system, however absurd it might seem, even if it was Christian . . .' And he made one observation that's very relevant to our own age: 'The new literature was free, but science was servile . . .' "

"And what about your de Maistre?"

"The writer, together with Poe, that Baudelaire most admired? It's hard to think of anyone so underrated . . . And yet he's one of France's greatest writers, in the same class as Bossuet, Pascal and

Sade . . . As you'll soon see if you get over the Rousseau prejudice
. . . But listen to this—I brought it specially for you . . ."

We start on the whisky again . . . Sophie and Deb are whispering
in a corner . . . S. starts to read:

" 'There's something *satanic* about the French Revolution that
distinguishes it from anything that has ever happened before and
perhaps from anything that ever will happen after . . . Remember
the great meetings! Robespierre's speech against the priesthood, the
priests' solemn act of apostasy, the profaning of religious objects,
the inauguration of the Goddess of Reason, and all the incredible
scenes in which the provinces strove to outdo Paris . . . All this is
outside the ordinary scope of crime, and seems to belong to another
world . . .' "

"Not bad," say I . . . "Surprising."

He goes on.

" 'The present generation is witnessing one of the greatest spectacles ever presented to the human eye: a struggle to the death
between Christianity and philosophy . . . The lists are open, the
two enemies are grappling with one another, and the whole world
is watching . . .' "

Sophie came in a little while ago, pale and breathless . . . She
spent the day with Polish friends . . . She says what shocks them
the most is that in order to show their sympathy people have been
coming round with red flags and singing the *Internationale* . . . And
then defending it all in the name of the French Revolution . . . Or
of the true Russian Revolution . . . The revolution that oughtn't to
have gone off the rails . . . But did it? Anyhow, what's the difference . . . It's still a revolution . . . One religion versus another . . .

Anyhow, what everyone watches on television this evening is the
Pope's speeches and the party given in the Kremlin in honor of
Brezhnev's seventy-fifth birthday (the System having just made
him a present of Poland again on a silver platter) . . .

Reagan speaks too, in his B-movie cowboy style, of course . . .
How far away New York suddenly seems . . . I see myself walking
along Madison Avenue hardly a month ago . . . The sun right in
my face . . . The lightness of the air . . . Is it on the same planet?

The sun; the soft warm breeze; the light, vertical sea . . . Cyd's happy-go-lucky ways . . . Being free to do as one liked . . .

The Kremlin . . . The mechanical, dreamlike crowd of faces, chests covered with decorations (you can imagine what Chaplin would have done with them: that scene in *The Great Dictator* where he tears off Goering's medals and tramples them underfoot) . . . The practically paralytic line of old men representing the greatest military force in the world today . . .

The Pope . . . A white survivor, poring over the text of his speech . . .

They say that for a long while Brezhnev has been having treatment from a Georgian clairvoyant, a female "medium . . ." He does rather look as if he's under hypnosis . . . Novocaine . . . Opium . . .

"But you know very well," I say to S., "most people will tell you all you have to do is send both of them packing . . . Brezhnev and the Pope!"

"I know, I know! It's the easiest thing in the world to say . . . We've all said it some time or other . . . Not to mention our rational friends . . . The anarchists . . . Critics . . . Anglo-Saxons . . . Of course, of course . . . But things have changed . . . And as you must realize, when they say it now—with less and less conviction, as if they had a presentiment of something breathtakingly horrible—in fact they actually do choose one of the two . . ."

"Brezhnev as capable of improvement? Stalin a little local accident? The evolution of the system? Socialism all right in itself? One day? One fine day? The inevitably slow pace of history?"

"Of course . . . For them Brezhnev is just a trick of Time . . . But the Pope is an out-and-out mistake . . . In a world of his own . . . Brezhnev could be educated philosophically . . . But listen to this: 'The most striking thing about the French Revolution is the overwhelming force that crushes all obstacles . . . It is a whirlwind that sweeps away like a straw any opposition human strength can offer: no one could stand in its way with impunity . . . An opponent might be distinguished by the purity of his motives, but that is all. And that jealous strength, marching steadily toward its goal, rejected Charette, Dumouriez and Drouet alike . . .' "

"De Maistre again?"

"Yes . . . 'It has been rightly said that the French Revolution rather leads men than is led by them . . . This observation is very just, and though it may be applied in some degree to all great revolutions it has never been more striking than it is now . . .

" 'The very scoundrels who seem to conduct the revolution are really its mere instruments, and as soon as they claim to control it they come to an ignoble end . . . Those who set up the republic did so unintentionally and not knowing what they were doing . . . They were led into it by events: at an earlier date the plan would have failed . . . These extremely undistinguished men imposed on a guilty nation the most dreadful despotism in history; and they themselves were certainly more surprised than anybody at their own power . . .' "

"You'll make the Panthéon come crashing down on our heads!"

"You never spoke a truer word . . . Someone should write a book about the secret battles that have been waged over getting into the Panthéon . . . To begin with, as you know, it was a church dedicated by Clovis to the apostles . . . The church of St. Genevieve . . . The musical chairs with the corpses started as early as 1780 . . . Voltaire . . . Rousseau . . . Mirabeau . . . He was replaced by Marat on the orders of the Convention . . . And then in February 1795 Marat was removed too . . . And so it went on . . . It finally settled down with Hugo . . . Deism . . . Lofty sermons . . . Everyone falling asleep . . . But as de Maistre says: 'I can understand how Marat can be de-Panthéonized, but I don't see how the Panthéon can ever be de-Maratized . . .' Anyhow, don't let's get lost in the mysteries of Paris . . . The wars of the obelisks . . . But you'll notice it's the same in Moscow and Peking . . . Mausoleums . . . They leave Lenin . . . They take away Stalin . . . They demausoleumize Stalin, but how can you de-Stalinize the mausoleum?"

"And the Panthéon still exists in Rome?"

"Oh yes . . . Transformed by Boniface IV into St. Mary and the

Martyrs . . . Lorenzetto's *Madonna del Sasso* is there, with Raphael's remains underneath . . . They were found in 1833 . . ."

"Corpses, corpses . . ."

"That's just it! Graves opening up! Spirits tapping out messages! How about a bit more Chateaubriand? . . . 'The Revolution is quite happy to serve those who have emerged through its crimes; it's an innocent origin that is an obstacle . . .' "

"The most interesting theory is that of an unconscious impulse . . . The idea that they were all asleep . . ."

"Yes . . . Chateaubriand looks as if he's awake, but he fought the war with Homer in his luggage . . . Look how he stresses the contradictions in the revolution . . . Blood flows, but pastorals flourish . . . Marat is adored like Jesus Christ . . . 'Fathers point out to their children the gee-gee that draws the tumbril to the scaffold . . .' People philosophize as they kill . . . Everything takes place against a background of flowery, right-thinking speeches: the "sepulchral mechanism" the "murder machine," the "blood machine . . ."

"Anyhow, the death penalty has just been abolished; the guillotine's a museum piece now . . ."

"Yes, but by decree, like the Gregorian calendar . . . The polls show the greater part of public opinion is against the abolition of the death penalty . . . Analysis? None whatsoever . . . The sleeper rolls over, that's all . . ."

"And Sade's the only one really awake?"

"Exactly . . ."

A few days later it's Christmas . . . We decide to watch midnight mass on television so as to see how Wojtyla's making out after getting two bullets in the stomach in May . . . I think of St. Patrick's in New York, where there are Polish demonstrations on the steps and on Fifth Avenue . . . With banners saying the swastika = the hammer and sickle . . . "Isn't that rather an exaggeration?" said the editor of the *Journal* . . . "Ought we to publish it?" We publish it . . .

There's St. Peter's . . . The genius of Bernini's . . . The baobab baldaquin . . . Spirals . . . Baroque gone mad . . . Close-ups of African faces . . . Japanese faces . . . There seem to be more of them than of the whites . . .

John-Paul II seems to be himself again . . . It reminds me of when he went to Auschwitz . . . Another date — perhaps the most important of them all . . . He circles around the altar with the censer . . . Recites and chants in a firm voice . . . Elevates his host and his ciborium vigorously . . . Makes a 360-degree turn . . .

Sophie is kneeling on the carpet, crying . . . I sense that Deb's rather irritated . . . S. is very intent and quiet . . . There must be awkwardnesses like this up and down the whole block . . . "To hell with your Pope!" I had a note from Helga in her ashram: "Will your precious Pope shift his big ass a bit to help the Poles?" She thinks she's shocking me . . . Poor thing . . . All these male and female idiots still think a person is a Catholic out of sexual repression . . . Two centuries of propaganda . . .

"Benedicat vos Omnipotens Deus, Pater, Filius, et Spiritus Sanctus . . ."

Good . . . It's over . . . It was the war of the airwaves . . . Litanies against tanks and rockets . . . Sophie leaves . . . She has another meeting . . . Deb goes to bed . . .

"But tell me," I say to S., "how could you be a fellow-traveler of the Communists even for a moment?"

"Fellow-traveler!" he roars. "As if I wasn't a road in myself! A highway, even! But I can see you don't know much about French society . . . Pure balance of forces at a particular moment . . . I'll explain . . ."

His casualness disarms me because it's so like my own . . . He always declines to perform any autocritique . . . The whim of the moment is paramount . . . That's what people hold against him . . . And yet I know he's right . . . Scorning to justify oneself . . . Making no deals . . . But what if it were meaningless? If the mask were all there is? If the appearance of truth were only a lie? If to borrow the clothes of untruth in passing were the highest of truths?

"Right," I say . . . "But what has all this got to do with women?"

217

"It's essential," he answers . . . "Wars of religion mean nothing more nor less than the control of women . . . In other words, of reproduction . . . And with the religion of Woman it's the same as with the rest . . . Except that in this case it's a privileged class of women who will control the rest . . ."

"From that point of view," I say, "Judaism and Christianity have had it . . . No one has any use for them anymore, have they? I've just read an article by Bernadette that says the Bible was intended by men for men . . . The same line of argument as in the famous 'report . . .' "

"Always the same old tune," says S. "The Bible is the code of exploiters, capitalists, obscurantists, colonialists, and so on . . . And now of men too . . . And opposite you have Nature, innocence, science, and women . . . Good . . . And so what?"

"Brezhnev and women—the same struggle?"

"Poor old Brezhnev . . . He's only a transitional figure . . . Don't forget he's just a bit of froth on the surface, and what we're working on is the basic hypnosis . . . Brezhnev's the name of a lobster who dreamed it was Brezhnev . . . Watched by Andropov . . . Androgynopov . . . We must get used to the dimension in which the organs live; to their silence; to their stirrings around in the depths . . . Look at the present tactics of the Communists, and through them at the Tactics pure and simple of the most religious of religions . . . That of mere animated matter . . . On the one hand, open violence, helped on by terrorism . . . On the other, pacifism, neutralism, ecologism, gynecologism, tranquility, little birdies . . . This second aspect is crucial . . . That's how you catch the women, especially if you promise them a world as desexualized as possible . . ."

"But you could say that's the Christian message as well?"

"Oh yes, and that's why the competition's so fierce . . . But it's not the same kind of desexualization . . . Not at all . . ."

"What's the difference?"

"The point of departure . . . From the theological point of view sex, and therefore reproduction, is Evil . . . But it's a transcendent and unassailable Evil, a prowler within . . . In the totalitarian reduc-

tion it's an aberration that's perfectly amenable to treatment . . .
Totalitarianism is simply belief in adjustable castration . . . Reasonable . . . Bearable . . . Dedramatized . . . Hence the constitutional
anti-Judaism . . . Why? Precisely because the Jews reject 'universal'
castration . . . It belongs to them, with their kind of exclusiveness,
the right kind, and they can't compromise about it . . ."

"What about Christian anti-Judaism? The Catholic kind?"

"That was different . . . At least in theory . . . The trouble is
that despite Vatican II, the most important Church council ever,
Catholics are still riddled with various kinds of paganry . . . But in
my opinion it's starting to wear off . . . I'm not going to start
reading you St. Paul again, but I do think we're seeing in current
events what he was talking about two thousand years ago . . . 'For
if the casting away of them'—the Jews—'be the reconciling of the
world, what shall the receiving of them be, but life from the dead?' "

"Was the Inquisition just in a hurry to get there?"

"We still haven't finished paying for the blood that was shed
trying to convert people by force . . . It's only fair . . . Why didn't
they understand what Paul meant, the perverse fools! 'And if some
of the branches be broken off, and thou, being a wild olive tree,
were grafted in among them, and with them partakest of the root
and fatness of the olive tree; Boast not against the branches . . .
But if thou boast, thou bearest not the root, but the root thee . . .
Thou wilt say then, The branches were broken off, that I might be
grafted in . . . Well; because of unbelief they were broken off, and
thou standest by faith . . . Be not high-minded, but fear . . . For if
God spared not the natural branches, take heed lest he also spare
not thee . . . Behold therefore the goodness and severity of God:
on them which fell, severity; but toward thee, goodness, if thou
continue in his goodness: otherwise thou also shalt be cut off . . .
And they also, if they abide not still in unbelief, shall be grafted in:
For God is able to graft them in again . . . For if thou wert cut out
of the olive tree which is wild by nature, and wert grafted contrary
to nature into a good olive tree: how much more shall these, which
be the natural branches, be grafted into their own olive tree?' The
Christians being the unnatural and the Jews the natural! You couldn't

put it more clearly, could you? It's always worth coming back to Paul . . ."

I notice S. always carries a little Bible with a dark red leather cover about with him now . . . He takes it out every so often and scans it like a computer . . . He seems to know it almost by heart . . . It's a kind of mental conjuring trick . . . Very funny to watch . . .

'Olive-tree . . . Olivier . . . Doesn't Malachi say there's going to be a Pope called that just before the end of the world?"

"Yes," says S. "The next to the last . . . 'Gloriae Olivae'—the glory of the olive . . . For the moment we've got 'de labore solis'— the work of the sun . . . Yes indeed . . ."

"Oil, unction, the name . . ."

He starts reading again . . .

" 'As concerning the gospel, they are enemies for your sakes: but as touching the election, they are beloved for the fathers' sakes . . . For the gifts and calling of God are without repentance . . . For as ye in times past have not believed God, yet have now obtained mercy through their unbelief: Even so have these also now not believed, that through your mercy they also may obtain mercy . . ."

"The last encyclical talks about mercy . . ."

" 'Dives in misericordia . . .' "

Deb suddenly comes back into the room . . . One way of telling us enough is enough . . . "Would you like some beer?" No, we've finished . . . Low mass . . . Masculine whispers . . . More or less homosexual goings-on, no? That sect of nut cases . . .

S. laughs and puts on a special voice.

" 'O the depth of the riches both of the wisdom and knowledge of God! how unsearchable are his judgments, and his ways past finding out! For who hath known the mind of the Lord? or who hath been his counsellor?' Here Paul is quoting Isaiah 40:13, a very good telephone number these days! 'Or who hath first given to him, and it shall be recompensed to him again? For of him, and through him, and to him, are all things: to whom be glory for ever . . . Amen . . .' "

Deb, looking exasperated, has gone off to bed again . . . It is very

late now . . . Three in the morning . . . The divine child is born
. . . Oboes and trumpets . . . Conversation flags . . .

We go on drinking for a while . . . Technical details . . .

S. leaves me his notes . . . Takes a chapter to revise . . . Goes . . .

Let's call her the Chairwoman . . . A strange escapade . . . I dine
with her—alone, though at some friends' place . . . She arrives in
the middle of the evening . . . Sorry to be late . . . Her work . . .
The ministry . . . The burning question of the X committee . . .
The famous Y lawsuit, still in progress . . . She scarcely looks at me
. . . A little, though . . . And a lot, for a couple of seconds . . .
After a moment she wants to know what I think, as a foreign
journalist . . . I improvise . . . The Chairwoman seems to follow
. . . She's not at all bad-looking . . . A bit on the heavy side, lovely
deepset black eyes . . . Chanel suit . . . Strong jaw . . . Thick lips
. . . She gets up to make a phone call . . . I wait for a while, then
take the opportunity to go to the john . . . Kate, observing me out
of the corner of her eye, throws me a look of disgust . . . Now here
are the Chairwoman and I both in the hall . . . She's leaving . . .
Her driver . . . "Can I drop you?" she says, overdoing the casualness . . . Very kind . . . No, really . . . We go in and tell the others
. . . They look rather surprised . . . Nothing more . . . Kate's
look . . .

Together in the back of the car . . . Yes, we must talk some more
about all that . . . I'm very interested in your point of view . . .
But no, we often get Americans quite wrong . . . Phone me some
time . . . Won't you?

It's practically an order . . . The day after next . . . Breakfast at
her place . . . Apartment overlooking the Seine . . . She's in a sky-
blue négligée . . . All silky . . . Dreamy . . . Orange juice, tea,
coffee, boiled eggs, toast, soft rolls, butter, jam . . . It's hot . . . But
there's an icy wind outside; gusts sweep over the gray and yellow
water . . . I look at her—mature, massive, sure of herself, large

brown chignon, rather petite herself, compact . . . A tactful maid appears . . . Madame has everything? I may go?

So here we are, obviously alone . . . It's half-past eight . . . Nothing happens in the evening anymore, or at night; the morning's the time for everything now . . . A reversal of pleasure . . . The Chairwoman doesn't pay any special attention to me . . . She talks about the current situation . . . Does her nails . . . Slowly and at length . . . We talk about New York . . .

"I think I know one of your friends . . . She told me some very nice things about you . . ."

"Really?"

"What was her name, now? Her Christian name? The same as that musical comedy star, the dancer . . . You know, the one with the legs . . ."

"Cyd?"

"That's it! Cyd MacToy, isn't it? An Irish girl?"

"English . . . MacCoy . . ."

"Cyd MacCoy . . . She works in television, doesn't she? We met at a friend's on Long Island . . . Charming . . ."

At Dora's . . . Of course . . . The network . . . I should have known . . . So they picked Cyd up after I left . . . It figures . . .

Now the Chairwoman's smiling at me directly . . .

That's the best moment, after all—just before space turns upside down . . . The Chairwoman knows that too . . . Green light . . . Time suspended . . .

She leans back slowly among the blue cushions on her divan . . .

"Why don't you come and sit beside me?"

Her voice was an almost inaudible moan . . .

I practically leap . . . Her mouth is half open . . . Her muscular tongue is ready . . . The négligée doesn't last long . . . The East . . . Perfumes . . . She has big, vibrant thighs . . . Soft, heavy breasts . . . She swiftly puts my head between her legs . . . She's all on fire . . . Then she suddenly gets up and draws the curtains . . . Comes back in the half-light . . . Stands motionless, then kneels and opens my fly . . . Seizes hold of my prick . . . Sucks . . . Looks up . . .

"Cyd is really very pretty, you know . . ."

Good god, they must have screwed one another . . . I can just see it . . . The Chairwoman blows me a kiss . . . She's thought a lot about all this . . .

"Cyd really loves you, doesn't she?"

Now's the moment . . . She's ready and willing . . .

The Chairwoman is concentrating hard . . . She's panting . . . She's going to come . . . She comes . . . I come with her . . .

A quick one . . . A bit old-fashioned, but that has its points . . . Louis XV coziness, pearl necklace . . . When I think she's a socialist . . . And bisexual too, from what I can see . . . When she's at home!

The Chairwoman's bold . . . The Chairwoman's wild . . . I like her . . .

A brief bathroom session in the background . . .

Then more tea and coffee . . . Cigarettes . . .

"And it seems you're writing a novel?"

This takes me by surprise . . . Though I ought to have expected it . . . You must be slowing down, dear boy! . . . But everything moves so fast now . . . Faster than my novel anyway . . . It's hanging fire a bit these days . . . The winter . . .

"Uh . . . yes . . ."

"How interesting . . . Oh, do forgive me—I must get dressed . . . I have a meeting in a quarter of an hour . . . I shall be late again . . . Call me in a week or so . . . Won't you? We'll talk about your novel then . . . And I've got other things to tell you, too . . ."

Hell, the "report . . ." Of course . . .

How should I say goodbye?

I kiss her hand . . .

She strokes my cheek . . .

"See you soon!"

I find myself out by the river again, rather stunned . . . It's windy . . . Not far from Notre Dame . . . I think I'll drop in and stroll around . . . Brush up my mediaeval history . . . Media . . . Eval . . . Several shots at once . . . Moving and still . . . Carnival . . . Things are happening one after another, grotesque, sardonic, sublime, inward . . . Don't let anything surprise you . . . Be prepared for anything . . .

The cathedral's empty . . . Only ghosts . . . January 6, 1482 . . . Esmeralda . . . Frollo . . . Quasimodo . . . Oh oh, Hugo! Gothic bat . . . Arches . . . Vaults . . . Rose-windows . . . Gargoyles . . . The lanceolated High Gothic style . . . Must pursue this today . . . No need for gipsy girls or archers or archdeacons . . . Everyday life will do . . .

Kate on the phone . . . "So what did she say to you in the car?"

"Nothing special . . ."

"Liar! Are you going to see her again?"

"Not exactly . . ."

"You know she's a terrible hot pants?"

"Really? She doesn't look it . . ."

"She's very secretive . . . Very! What are you doing on Saturday?"

"Nothing . . . Working . . ."

"Oh yes! Your 'novel'?"

"Yes."

"But you might work better in the country, mightn't you?"

"No, I need to have my books handy . . ."

"When are you going to let me see a bit of it?"

"Well . . . No . . . I'm superstitious . . . When it's finished . . ."

"I'd try to see her again if I were you . . ."

"Who?"

"The Chairwoman . . ."

"Do you think so?"

"Don't be silly . . . But mark my words—be careful . . . O.K. —Ciao!"

I call Cyd. She's not in New York . . . San Francisco . . . But she'll be passing through Paris next week . . .

Is it likely, an affair between the two of them? Just in passing? Some unplanned evening? Why not? What really surprises me is that Cyd should have mentioned me . . . Now if it had been Dora . . . Or Helen . . . Or Jane . . . Unless the Chairwoman's lying . . . And she got her information elsewhere . . .

What's interesting is when life starts to resemble the novel you're writing . . . Magic? Yes . . . As soon as you start to write a book the whole landscape shifts . . . An insidious ballet . . . The real people start to move about . . . As if they were trying to escape what they suspect you're writing about them . . . As if they were engaging in parallel diversions . . . To correct your memory of them, make it more favorable, more flattering . . . Women are particularly flexible in this respect . . . They have a sort of radar . . . A ninth sense . . . They sense what you might be writing, and interpose, interpropose themselves . . . You'd think there was a tacit agreement between them to restrain the man concerned, or rather the hand that might write . . . A word is enough for them to understand one another . . . A wink . . . A hint . . . A meaning silence . . . A pressure of the fingers . . . Do they do it consciously? No, no—by instinct . . . Suddenly they need money from you . . . Or time . . . They take time from you as they might take blood . . . A conspiracy that doesn't need to be spoken . . . Or even thought . . . Anyhow, a genuine conspiracy doesn't need to exist as such—it's hatched in the atmosphere, in trifles . . . Spontaneously . . . Secretively . . . It mustn't be written down . . . Or as little as possible . . . I mean in black and white . . . The true inscription must be in reality . . . Three dimensions . . . Children, presents, bricks and mortar, connections . . . You need to be able to break down a woman's appearance in a flash . . . Fabrics, metal, leather . . . Clothes and signs of conspicuous consumption . . . Shoes . . . Handbags . . . Jewels . . . Maya revolves and gleams . . . The veil . . . It's beautiful and fascinating . . . Or else suddenly absurd and empty . . . A woman is as good as at least ten unwritten books . . .

I sometimes drop in for a drink at the Ritz Bar, just to make notes and sketches . . . From the life . . . Bars, beaches . . . Festivals of narcissism . . . There are two of them, simpering away just next to me — wearing at least a hundred-thousand-francs-worth of rings, necklaces and bracelets . . . They're glittering for one another's benefit; their men are reduced to mere extras with checkbooks . . . Pure and innocent looks . . . Display of dimples . . . Covert smiles . . . Right, they've seen how I'm looking at them and they're putting on an act for me . . . Repair their makeup . . . Lizard-skin bags . . . Mother-of-pearl compacts . . . Gold lipstick cases . . . The blonde's tongue on her lips . . . Her mock-helpless, little-girl look . . . Hand on the arm of one of the men . . . "No! — I don't believe it!" She catches my eye sidelong, swivels away . . . They both drink their iced vodkas . . . Chat to each other . . . Light one another's cigarettes . . . Cross their legs . . . Uncross them . . . Not forgetting the ritual twitch of the skirt over the knees . . . For emphasis . . . The knee says it all . . . Always . . . A kind of initiatory elbow . . . All the unseen in the knee . . . Perfume on the nape of the neck . . . Behind the ears . . . On the lobes . . . Between the breasts . . . The men have gone now . . . The women instantly become more serious . . . Count up . . . How much did yours give you? What about yours? They almost forget me . . . But remember every so often . . .

At another table, a young couple up from the provinces . . . She has a surprised, fierce look in her eye, a look that speaks of screaming children, dolls, toys, apartment, car, house in the country, furs, diamonds, gardens, dresses, happy Mama, Mama's Mama in her glory . . . A lover later on . . . Via him . . . He's the one that sets everything in motion . . . Everything . . . Husband-mother . . . Father Christmas . . . Lawyer . . . Doctor . . . He takes out his credit card . . . She adores him . . . No charm, though . . . But that's just the point . . . Beard . . . Monotonous voice . . . What does it matter? It's not the bottle that matters, it's the effect of the wine! No competition in the mirror! Security! La vráie vie! Income . . . Isn't she worth all that? And more? I stare at her . . . She doesn't even see me . . .

Or in the summer, by the sea . . . All the skins on exhibition . . . The ordeal of bare breasts, thighs, buttocks, superfluous flesh . . . The enormous indifference of the ocean . . . The mould starting around the edges . . . Cream this, recream that, forehead, eyes, nose, little taps . . . Mechanisms of anxiety . . . The image . . .

Getting a tan . . . Mirrors everywhere . . . Indispensable . . . Pharmaceutical sirens . . . Meticulous octopuses . . . Sun-lotion squids . . . Greek vases for supermarkets . . . Discount bacchantes . . . Sacred cows . . . An improbable cult . . . But one that you must prepare for all the time . . . Why? No one knows . . . You just must . . . That's how it is . . .

What is it that gnaws at them, drives them? The feeling of being there to serve nothingness, the abyss, the shimmering periphery of absolute darkness? They sense something . . . But they can't know . . . By definition . . . Even when they say the word "death" the meaning escapes them . . . The meaning of the meaninglessness . . .

Black virgins . . . Suburban Venuses . . . Kleenex . . . Cotton . . . Sanitary pads . . . "I'm not well" . . . Women's bodies are hypothetical . . . You have to navigate them by guesswork . . . Permanent approximation . . . You can make one of them suddenly come by stroking her shoulder blade, licking her eyelids, touching her navel . . . If you've never had that happen to you, you don't know anything about it . . .

Cosa mentale . . . Hysterical elasticity . . . Or just a knack . . . But nothing is certain . . . It depends on the interests involved . . . On the magneto-imago . . . What makes a woman feel pleasure? Her own mental image of the social relationships involved . . . That's how you can tell whether or not you've become the knight in shining armor . . . *The* man . . . Or it could be the woman . . . A question of power . . .

Now I understand . . . The Chairwoman has taken it into her head to educate me . . . I realized it when she started talking to me about music . . . And that's why it's all suddenly become rather a bore . . . Flora all over again . . . Institutionalizing . . . She wants me to help her . . . Think of "ideas" for her . . . In return she'd use her influence . . . And she'd introduce me to culture . . . Mozart . . . *The Magic Flute* . . . Or rather she'd introduce herself, though me, to the infinity of culture . . . Painting . . . Literature . . . The rise of the middle classes . . . The Chairwoman is of humble origins . . . A dazzling rise . . . Pink wave . . . She's one of the French lower middle classes trying to take the state system by storm . . . It draws her irresistibly . . . Corridors, palaces, paneling, ceilings and gilt . . . The taking of Versailles . . . What's to be done? How to deal with the situation? Have as good an "Appearance" as possible? Manufacture a memory? A family tree? A "class"?

I soon see that for the Chairwoman screwing was merely a bait . . . it doesn't interest her . . . Just a technique for making contact . . . Her husband has disappeared into a minor role . . . She's looking for a close collaborator . . . I shall just bow out . . . She'll understand . . . Discretion guaranteed . . .

She hasn't asked me, even indirectly, what I know about WOMANN or the SGIC . . . I was worrying unnecessarily . . . Or else she changed her mind and thought better of it . . . But what decided things for me was hearing her say of a journalist colleague that he's a "fanatical anti-Communist" . . . That's the test that sets the alarm bells ringing . . . The unmistakable password . . . A vision of the world . . . A dialectic . . . A subtle progression . . . The lever of time . . . The pump that primes whole series of phenomena . . . "Fanatical anti-Communist"—the kiss of death . . . Like "Communist" in other days, other places . . . At home in America during the McCarthy era . . . Now in Argentina . . . To tell the truth the two reactions are similar and exert the same fascination . . . History . . . Purification . . . Everything else in the trashcan . . . All they ask is not that you should be for or against, but that you should understand and accept the way the real world has to go . . . Above all not to react, and especially not to show any reaction . . . Not to remark, as I once did to Kate and Boris, a 1930s liberal could have been accused of being a "fanatical anti-Nazi . . ."

"You can't put Nazism and communism on the same plane!"

"Really? Perhaps Nazism didn't have time to adapt? Perhaps, if it had, it would have been as presentable today as 'advanced' communism? Not the kind you see in Cambodia, of course, but what about in the West? Where it's based on something that's it and not it at one and the same time? Efficient; madly scientific; preoccupied with 'modernity'; open to all the new trends in philosophy and art; increasingly concerned with biology and genetics; defending the workers against the oppression of international finance; and not anti-Semitic, merely anti-Zionist . . ."

"Out of the question! Disgraceful! Inadmissible!"

And so on . . . No point in entering these debates that are all written down in advance . . .

"Nihilism! Despair! Nothingness!"

Ah yes, I was forgetting . . . You absolutely have to have a purpose, a meaning, a direction, a hope . . . Don't you see? The young! The young! Round tables! Forums! Discussions! Live broadcasts! Arguments! Scandals!

No . . . Silence . . . For behind all the din there always lurks the old dark question no one ever asks . . . Ever . . . "Why something instead of nothing?" Then it's incumbent on everyone to make a gesture of philosophical impotence . . . We don't know the answer . . . We can't know it . . . We shouldn't know it . . . Does anyone know it? Yes! Me! Well? No, I've nothing to say . . . It would be too painful . . . For women . . . For public opinion . . . For the fabric . . . For Mama . . . All the Mamas . . . Especially the expectant ones . . . And what is the future but one huge potential expectant mother? Here, for the moment, they're just little girls full of hope . . . And so advanced compared with the boys, aren't they? Yes indeed, and with good reason . . .

"But tell me—perhaps you want to monopolize the future for your own ends? It's all very well to say all this is meaningless! But you have to be able to make it good! The bodies are going to keep on pouring in, and we're going to have to do the best we can with them . . . And get ourselves elected by them somehow or other . . . So forward! Or else back! Reactionary! Is that what you want?"

Very well . . . Silence . . . Never come out in opposition . . . Just look for the gifted individuals and make do with that . . . Those men and women who don't need any explanations or theories . . . Who try to live in the present . . . And who know they're being fooled in the present . . . That's why the answer is always erotic

. . . Mystical? Yes, if you like, but only if confirmed by eroticism . . . Confirmed? Yes . . .

I disappoint my Chairwoman . . . Amicable separation . . .

Cyd arrives in Paris . . . The Chairwoman? Yes, she has a vague recollection . . . A dinner party in Easthampton . . . A pick-up? I must be mad! Of course not . . .

We're in the apartment she stays in now when she's in Paris . . . Near the Luxembourg . . . Close to where I live . . . Very convenient . . . She's just out of the bath . . . Blue robe . . . Four o'clock in the afternoon . . . She looks at me . . . "Everything all right?" But she's in a hurry to make love, that's what I like best about her, not a minute to lose, incommunicability, off we go . . . It's true, she does love me, really . . . That's to say I provide her with a good image of herself, a female prick, the best way (there are others, and why not?) for her to revolve around herself . . . The ritual's always equally precise and successful . . . I stroke her fair hair . . . I eat her skin . . . She keeps kissing me today; wants to have done with breathing, she says . . .

She loves the untruthfulness of life, does Cyd . . . Delights in it . . . Never tires . . . Constitution of an ox . . . She's just rereading *Juliet, or the prosperities of vice,* to see if it can at last be adapted for television . . . Closed circuit . . . Special cable . . . She wants to know what I think . . . Here and now . . . I say I don't think it's doable . . . Doesn't lend itself entirely to film . . . Everything takes place through hearing, before it's seen, or rather in a kind of invisible, vibrant, visibility . . . If it's made too visible, with cuttings up and blood, brains exploding and shrieks, the effect will be the very opposite of the arousal produced by the book itself . . . Inhibition . . . Repression . . . You must only "see" what you hear . . . Silently . . . An orgy of pen and ear . . . Sade was very sensitive in real life . . . Repelled by realistic violence . . . Of course . . .

Cyd shows me a passage: "La Durand's spasms of pleasure were something unparalleled . . . I'd never in all my life seen a woman ejaculate like that . . . Not only did she shoot her spunk like a man, but she accompanied it with such furious cries, such vigorous blas-

230

phemies and such violent convulsions that you would have thought she was having an epileptic fit . . . I was entered as if by a man, and experienced the same pleasure . . ."

"Well," she said, getting up . . . "Are you pleased with me?"

"Fuck it," I cried, "you're delicious—a real model of lechery! Your passions set me on fire . . . Do for me what I did for you . . ."

"What? You want to be beaten?"

"Yes . . ."

"Slapped in the face, whipped? "

"Certainly . . ."

"You want me to urinate on your face? "

"Of course, and be quick, for I'm getting horny and can't wait . . ."

We laugh . . . Military dialogue . . . Souped-up Marivaux . . . But we're aroused as well . . . Cyd wants to pee . . . We go into the bathroom . . . I lie down in the bath . . . She squats over my face and releases a warm jet over my face and eyes . . . How beautiful she looks like that, tender, excited, groaning, flushed, giving her most intimate self, warm and drowsy . . . She sighs, goes over to the toilet, starts to play with herself, thighs apart . . . I come over and take her, kneeling, strongly . . .

We get washed . . . She makes us some tea . . . We look at the trees in the park . . .

"What would you have to do to transpose Sade and his energy?" Cyd asks.

"Best to find something else for nowadays," I answer.

"Have you heard about the Mafia films?"

"Sexual murders shown live, you mean? Yes, that's been used to shock people . . . But eroticism is entirely internal . . . And it's passionate inwardness itself, not entertainment, that's censored the most . . ."

"So you believe eroticism has to be confined to literature?"

"I think so . . . It's verbal, at any rate . . . That's why it's so difficult and so rare . . ."

"And do you see writers in terms of it?"

"Oh yes, always . . . I turn straight to the scene about sex, if there is one . . . But all readers do that . . . A reader is a child . . .

Even if he pretends otherwise . . . Also all an author's vulnerability is there . . . His naiveté, his obsessions, his limitations . . . His relationship with sex is of exactly the same order as his relationship with words . . . That's what's so extraordinary . . . Have you seen the passage that Sartre left out of the final version of *nausea* because of pressure from the publisher? Hell—as if there was anything there to make a fuss about! A newspaper account of the rape of a little girl seems to give the narrator a bit of an erection, and there's no punctuation for a while . . . Sartre can't keep it up for more than fifty lines . . . Rhythmical stimulation is not his line . . . Politics comes in by way of compensation . . . As does the puritanical and punctilious dictatorship of Simone de Beauvoir . . . Writers under surveillance by women . . . To break away and write musical smut in spite of that is pure heroism . . ."

Cyd comes and sits on my lap . . . Kisses me . . . She's dressed now . . . White blouse and black pants . . . Looking very pretty . . . Scented, graceful . . .

"And is your novel erotic?"

"I think so . . . But not in the way you think . . ."

"Is it a philosophical novel? Like Sade?"

"Sade is applied philosophy, rather . . . Philosophy broken down and pillaged . . . The fundamental object is to make the woman involved in an escapade say 'I' . . . That's impossible in action . . . It requires extreme guile . . . But Sade's philosophy is old now and needs to be reversed . . ."

"How do you mean?"

"God was still holding out then . . . He could still take some knocks . . . He was beginning to weaken, but just the same . . . Whereas now! My god!"

"There are still a lot of people who believe in him . . . The 'moral majority'!"

"Yes, but they don't matter . . . They're not exciting; not worth shocking . . . Pitiful . . . It's only worth scandalizing a force that's strong, scientific, serious, complex . . . Read Sade's *Travels in Italy* . . . Look at all he knew . . . Florence . . . Naples . . . Rome . . .

Everything happened in relation to an Italy that was still flamboyant
. . . In relation to the Church . . . To the monarchy . . ."

"So what would be the equivalent today?"

"That's the question . . . It's all completely different . . . Politics
. . . Sex reduced to money . . . Compulsory sex! You might say an
erotic book nowadays would be a defense of detachment . . ."

"The misfortunes of vice and the prosperities of virtue?"

"A laughable Sodom and an absurd Gomorrah! Virtue treating
vice with vice! Evil with evil! Good where you expected it least!
That's a very Jesuitical notion, by the way . . . Sade was one of the
Jesuits' best pupils . . ."

"Pleasure only by contradiction?"

"Of course . . ."

"And so?"

"You take the modern world . . . The 'liberated' world . . .
Money, sex, violence, publicity, cynical politics, spiritualism, occult-
ism, pornography . . . And you introduce a character who mixes
with that world and shows the stupidity and emptiness of the
religion that lies behind it . . ."

"But sex is still the driving force?"

"Of course . . . Insatiable childish curiosity . . . Only excitement
will no longer be aroused by crime, because crime, selfish intrigue
and organized and perverse malevolence are everywhere . . . No,
arousal will come from a dizzying apprenticeship in modesty . . .
The perception, gradual or immediate, of good in the midst of the
blackest orgies . . . Can you imagine? The world turned Sadistic
overturned by a Sadian stroke of luminous negation! Sex described,
decanted, demystified! The key to the abyss! End of film!"

"But it'd probably be horribly boring! Unsalable!"

"Not necessarily . . . Because it would be *evil* . . . And seen to
be so . . . Imagine a prostitute, i.e., almost any woman nowadays,
discovering passion and delicate reserve in the middle of a brothel
. . . And god too, why not? And Faith?"

"God through vice? Complete surprise?"

"That's right!"

233

"Sounds interesting . . ."

Cyd ponders . . . Her cigarette burns away without her . . . She kisses me again . . .

"Would *you* write it for me?"

"Haven't got time, darling . . ."

"It would be good, though . . . *The Mystic Boudoir* . . . What a film!"

She puts her face down between my legs again . . . Reopens my fly . . . Gently turns me on . . . She must be screening some rushes in her mind's eye . . . *Bande-sonore* . . . Moves . . . Colors . . . She persists . . . Insists that I come . . . Amply, and into her soft mouth, and her throat, whose silky brown skin I stroke as it vibrates . . . I want everything I've been saying to be for her . . . To be made concrete . . . Swallowed . . .

S. phones. He wants to tell me about a poem by some Polish prisoners that Sophie has just translated for him . . . It was written in the camp at Szczblinek . . . It's a Christmas carol . . .

> *A loud voice breaks the silence of the camp*
> *Young and old stand by the bars*
> *We're spending Christmas at Szczblinek*
> *And we shall remember it all our lives*
>
> *The trees of the forest sleep under the snow*
> *The wind blows our song away into the darkness*
> *Poland that flows in our veins*
> *Is not dead and will not die so long as we live*
>
> *We implore you through these walls, newborn King*
> *Open the gates for us and awaken all Poland*
> *Awaken each town and village*
> *Your power can end the darkness*

We believe in you, Lord who is in heaven
And we believe you will help us drive out the men
  from Moscow
Poland that flows in our veins
Is not dead and will never die, if only for your glory . . .

S.'s voice is strangely shaky as he reads this to me . . . I'm
moved too . . . I suddenly realize how much he loves Sophie . . .
And how sentimental he can be, he who is usually so casual . . .
I'm reminded of a conversation I had with an Israeli woman friend
in New York . . . "The Poles have done us Jews a lot of harm . . ."
"But it's different now, isn't it . . . The Jews and the Catholics are
both in the same boat . . ." "But how can you expect us not to
mistrust the Catholic Church? Too much harm, too much harm
. . ." "Things will sort themselves out — you'll see . . ." "How
many Catholics are there, actually?" "Eight hundred million . . ."
"Really?" "And they're not anti-Semitic anymore, or at least they
haven't any dogmatic reason to be so anymore . . ." "You think
not?" "That's what I'd like to think . . ." Her terrible disillusioned
smile . . . "I like you very much myself. But I can't conceal that
the Jewish community itself is very doubtful . . . I hear some very
harsh things . . . Such as 'The Poles can drop dead!' " "I understand, but that doesn't stop things taking their course, as I've said
. . ." "Do you really believe that?"

Two thousand years . . . The business of Pius II . . .

There's something new about him, as a matter of fact . . .

This is what I read in a weekly called *Regards* (Glances), "The
only French-language Jewish weekly in Belgium, produced by the
Jewish Lay Community Center": *"Pius II and the Jews, a new version:*
In 1943 two German diplomats serving in Rome deceived the Nazi
authorities in order to help Pope Pius II protect the Jews there, says
Father Derek Holmes, a British historian and priest, in his book,
The Papacy in the Modern World, just published in London . . .

"According to Father Holmes at least half the Jews in Rome were
sheltered in Vatican City and various blocks of flats belonging to
the Vatican, while the two German diplomats put up a screen of

'tactical lies' to deceive Berlin . . . In this way the Holy See, the nuncios and the Catholic Church as a whole are said to have saved some 400,000 Jews from certain death . . ."

The article appears on page 11 of the number dated 2–8 October 1981 . . .

I've just been listening to Bach's Cantata No. 6, *Stay with us for the night is nigh* . . . I seem to hear that Polish poem against the shifting background of the choir's great solemn protest:

> *Stay with us, Lord Jesus*
> *For night has fallen*
> *Let not the light of God's word*
> *Be extinguished for us!*
> *In this hour of great affliction*
> *Grant us, Lord, the gift of constancy*
> *That we may keep alive till our last breath*
> *Your Word and Sacrament . . .*

One hears the music . . . What one takes to be the music . . . But the words? the words *of* the music? Which are like different words, beneath the others, in the living throats . . . Who hears them, inwardly? Truly? Constantly? Who really experiences what takes place in the living breath of song?

Or take the St. John Passion—the sinister slow opening, soaring and wheeling, and then the great unanimous cry . . .

S. is talking to me . . . "The heart of the mystery . . . The heart of the crime . . . I seem to hear a vast groan echoing through the darkness . . . The tortured bodies, the broken bones . . . Death trembling at itself, indifferent, relentless . . . Most of the time I feel like a survivor from a catastrophe that happened somewhere else, on some parallel plane . . . Settlements, deportations, trains, cold, snow, camps, gas chambers . . . It happened, it took place . . . and we're still calmly here . . . Calmly? Only just . . . I don't know if you can understand . . . You weren't living in Europe at the time . . . Your relatives weren't caught up in that great sickening grimace . . . Even a Frenchman has great difficulty in feeling it genuinely, viscerally . . . We were "protected" . . . But at what price! I must tell you about it some time . . . Anyhow, one must find a way of breaking absolutely with all that . . . Absolutely, do you understand?''

Well, well, he's stopped joking . . . He's told me more in the last ten minutes than in conversations lasting over a couple of years . . . Perhaps that's the source of his *Comedy?* Perhaps that's what he's always getting at? I must write a quick biography of him one of these days . . . Anyway, he's entering into my novel more and more . . . Making himself a strange but insistent place in the story . . .

Cyd writes:

"I'm delightfully alone and comfortable this evening . . . I long to hear you talking about my ass and whispering that it always arouses you . . . Darling, I'd like you to be coming now . . . Please, let your spunk flow and think I'm swallowing it . . . Why haven't I made you jerk yourself off over my face yet? You absolutely must . . . Imagine my cheeks streaming with your milk! I think I'd writhe with pleasure, and open my legs and thighs and ask you to see how easily I get juicy . . . I adore you, and as soon as I start to feel your prick up against me, even when I'm still dressed, I feel I could lie down on the floor and groan . . . But I love the feel of your lips too much for that . . . I long to feel your tongue, your breath, and picture again the almost childish pleasure I experience when I kiss you . . . I want you to know I love you like a little girl, a little sister reading in the garden in the afternoon, troubled by an unknown desire but sure its strength will one day be felt in reality . . .

Cyd . . .

"Think about my project!"

She's left for New York now . . . She posted the letter the next morning at Roissy . . .

So there it is . . . The age we live in . . . You just have to get used to the way it keeps changing . . .

Now it's dark . . . A long evening . . . A blue-black tide . . . Everything muffled . . .

I don't want anything . . . I don't expect anything . . . I'm quite

237

happy to vanish all alone into any nook or cranny . . . I don't even require anyone to check that my breath doesn't cloud a mirror anymore . . . I know I'm dead . . . At this very moment I can see the mist Cyd's breath makes on the mirror in her hall as I screw her from behind, standing up, her skirt turned back showing her black stockings, her silky skin beneath my hands, her mouth open as she leans back slowly to kiss her own reflection . . . She looks at herself . . . Photographs the image of herself with her eyes open and a prick inside her . . .

It's a fine thing, a woman who's not afraid . . .

I say: "Remember this moment—I want you to remember it . . ."

She: "Yes . . ."

I: "Why are you laughing?"

She: "Because I feel so light . . . Floating here like this . . . No tragedy . . . Nothing . . . I'm laughing at the lies people always tell about it . . . I want all you want . . . And all I want too . . . It's of no consequence . . . I love you very much . . ."

I: "Come onto the bed now . . . Take your revenge on my prick . . ."

She: "I like it when I possess your cock . . . I like to feel it swell up when I choose . . . To dictate when you're to lose your sperm . . ."

She likes *bite*, the French word for cock, better than the English, and keeps on saying it . . . She looks at herself again . . . Her green eyes are slightly bloodshot . . .

Bad literature will always be the best . . . The most inarticulate will always be the most excellent . . .

I must get some sleep . . .

Everything is gray this morning; I'm alone . . . I fall back into ordinary unhappiness; absence . . . I don't have any friends; can't have any . . . No one to call . . . Perfect . . .

What happened yesterday? Oh yes, my prick inside Cyd, her hand over her fur and moving down to play with herself at the same time . . .

Right . . . I've had all that . . . And the rest . . . And the others . . . And nothing . . . The physics of antimatter . . . Nothing serious . . . Immediate unreality . . . The road to knowledge! Every time, negation a bit more intense . . . Sex is our dematerializer, our instrument for piercing through things . . . It's only natural . . . Where do non-children come from? Non-men? The non-world? Yes . . . If we have to screw women it's so that we may come as close as possible to this negation . . . Most avoid it . . . Remain within the circle and the sphere . . . No breaking through . . . No shattered narcissism . . .

The last time we spoke S. said to me, "I think it's time for you to pop over to Rome . . . Take Rome! Take the novel!"

All right, I will.

Rome . . . The Hotel Raphael . . . Near the Piazza Navone . . . Bernini's fountain . . . A dream . . . Now he was somebody . . . I go from one marvel to another . . . From one dazzling sight to the next . . . Headlong . . . Bernini . . . "The mists of the Counter-Reformation . . ." I've just read this hyper-idiotic phrase in a preface to Michelet's *Renaissance and Reformation* . . . God, everything needs to be done over again . . . Rewritten . . . Reexplained . . . What a job . . . And what's the point? Stereotyped education everywhere . . . Either you *feel* baroque or you don't feel anything at all . . . An inner dimension . . . A whirlwind within . . . Private waves . . . In the blood . . . In the veil blowing about inside you, the curtain of desire . . . A window, the air of the open sea . . .

As everyone knows, Bernini was summoned to France by Louis XIV . . . If he'd stayed the Louvre would have been different . . . Rounded, filled out, lightened, opened up . . . The Louvre! But that was not to be . . . Regal, anti-papal rigidity . . . "French classicism . . ." *L'Etat c'est moi* . . . Insidious Protestantization . . . Swedization . . . Kremlinization . . . Colbertism . . . Perrault's intrigues . . . Bernini thrown out . . . Too lively . . . The coziness of secrecy wins the day . . . Gloomy façade . . . With fairy tales behind . . . Whereas baroque consists in flaunting, exhibiting, exceeding, twisting, varying, veering . . . The "mists of the Counter-Reformation" — don't make me laugh! *Truth revealed by Time* . . . There she   is

239

at the Villa Borghese . . . Lying back, laughing, as if suffused with joy . . . Her left foot on the globe, her left hand holding off the mask of the sun . . . The statue was begun in 1646 . . . But left unfinished . . . Unfinishable . . . Is it a discreet, ambiguous tribute to Galileo? It's something more . . . The discovery of some other law of gravity . . . Gravidation . . . A matter not of the stars but of the invisible, or rather of that which is too visible to be seen . . . One pays too much attention to women—or not enough . . . Difficult to judge the correct distance . . . Curve . . . Silent hollow . . . Contained contorsion . . . She laughs to herself . . . To the angels, as the French say . . .

St. Peter's . . . The air seems to be made of a different substance once you've passed the gates, the colonnade, and the obelisk and gone up the magic staircase . . . Silvered lightness . . . As in New York . . . The canopy . . . Bees and branches of laurel . . . The apostle's tomb a cupola, with the inscription "Thou art Peter, and on this rock, etc . . ." And between the two, and above the altar where solemn masses are said, Bernini has struck . . . The columns that rise up in the middle are *his* . . . His permanent offering, his clouds of incense transformed into solid whorls . . . His rocket, vision, meditation, prayer . . . His Pope and friend, Urban VIII, Maffeo Barberini, paid him this tribute: "A rare man and sublime artist, destined by the divine will and for the glory of Rome to illuminate the age he lived in . . ." The dove on high with outspread wings . . . And at the far end of the Basilica, the glory of the Holy Spirit . . . A trickle of golden semen . . . An empty porthole . . .

I make for the chapel of the Holy Sacrament . . . Perpetual adoration . . . There are always about fifteen nuns there . . . Unprepossessing, doomed . . . Except for two, in ecstasies . . . Vietnamese girls dressed in blue . . . Frail . . . Rapt in contemplation of the golden monstrance . . . The bunches of red carnations . . . They're beautiful . . . I sit down near them . . . Watch them . . . They look as though they're about to take flight . . . Really, they almost levitate . . . They become almost as thin and transparent as the disc of bread there, so far away, so near, that they worship as the true body of god who descended here below, then went back up on high, and who is incarnated in that little stamped edible token . . . Yes, that's what it is, a little round transcendent ticket that falls like a snowflake . . . Exaltation . . . The body on the tip of the tongue . . . But now the silence is deafening . . . As if it broke out everywhere because of the endless prayer within . . . I'm thinking of Diderot, of course . . . The *Philosophical Thoughts . . .*" Commenting on the phrase, "Tu es Petrus, et super hanc petram aedificabo ecclesiam meam," the pun on which the Church is based, Diderot writes: "Is this the language of a God, or is it rather just a *bigarrure,* more worthy of the Lord of Rhymes?" The latter was Etienne Tabourot, born in Dijon in 1549, died in 1590 . . . His *Bigarrures* (1572) was a collection of rebuses, plays upon words and puns . . . Truth is revealed in ambiguities . . . Slips of the tongue . . . Witticisms . . . I imagine Diderot being with me now, after philosophy and science have conquered two-thirds of the world . . . A victory unavailable to two billion of its inhabitants . . . I talk to him about Freud . . . Tell him to look at the two rapt Asian nuns . . . He's worried . . . How things have changed! And changed again! And keep on changing! We go back through the Pincio to the Villa Borghese . . . He looks at Byron's statue . . . And at Goethe's . . . Seems rather taken aback by Chateaubriand's . . . And here we both are back again in front of *Truth revealed by Time* . . . "But Time isn't shown at all," he says . . . "Of course not," I answer . . . "It's the absence of Time that's the answer . . . Its universal nonpresence is what unveils the topsy-turvy nakedness of the world . . . And the incredible drollery of ever having thought there was one . . ." "One what?" "One world!" "You mean you think there's an infinity of them?" "Not even . . . Nothing . . . Simply nothing" . . . "What do you mean, nothing? No earth, no sun, no galaxies, no cosmos, no infinitely small or infinitely great, not even d'Alembert's dream, no life, no species, nothing? Just a woman laughing at nothing? My dear fellow, you must be crazy!"

Diderot vanishes . . . I go back down into the city . . . The clear winter light falls red and blue between the strong lines of the trees . . . I'm always surprised by the vigor of the vegetation in Rome

. . . Sap amid all those stones . . . Determined, vertical dark green . . .

The Piazza Navona . . . Bernini's fountain of the four rivers again . . . I never tire of it . . . The cave of the entwined horses . . . Weights reversed . . . Necks, legs, and heads all mingled . . . The vibrant toils of a dragon . . . The tiara of arms and keys over the broken rock . . . The pink obelisk rising up like a space rocket covered with hieroglyphics . . . And the water . . . Drops in the wind . . . The wrinkles . . . A happy jumble . . .

"So! We're in Rome!"

A voice behind me.

Kate.

She's with an Italian friend . . . A man . . . For the weekend . . . So's she's found at least one to spend three days with her . . . He's short, dark, stocky and looks exhausted . . .

"Shall we have lunch together?"

Can't refuse . . .

The man leaves us . . .

"So what are you doing here?"

"I came to have a look at the shapes . . . I'm taking notes . . . Bernini . . ."

"Oh! The *St. Teresa*? Are you following in Fals's footsteps?"

"Not especially St. Teresa . . . There are lots of other things . . ."

"Really?"

Kate doesn't know what I mean . . . One day she heard Fals improvising in one of his Lectures about the St. Teresa in the Church of the Victory, and that's enough for her . . . Fals saw it as an image of "female pleasure," not at all as a sculpture reflecting the extreme of the male equivalent . . . A strange mix-up, very frequent in histories of art . . . The subject instead of the artist: the theme promoted at the expense of the source of its expression . . . Fals's audience didn't really care for that business of St. Teresa in ecstacy, her draperies pierced by an angel with a golden arrow . . .

They were put off by his dubious, religious sensuality . . . His casual, cranky excursions out of science and into the maze of metaphysics . . . Kate doesn't like people going too deeply into phenomena . . . Not those to do with the Church anyway . . . A bit of the occult is all right, but not in that connection . . .

"Are you putting Rome in your novel?"

"Yes! I'm going to show that all romances lead to Rome!"

"Do you know that people in Paris, on the *Journal*, think you're getting very strange?"

"Tell me all, my angel . . ."

"Stop talking to me like that! My dear, my pet, my sweet, my child, my angel—it's not funny and it makes you sound ridiculous . . ."

"I don't really mean it . . . It's just a joke . . ."

"I don't like it . . ."

"Sorry . . . So tell me what people are saying about me . . ."

"Well, that you're not interested in anything, that you're letting everything go . . . That you're obsessed with commercial success . . . That you don't think about anything anymore . . ."

"What does that mean?"

"Politics . . . Business . . . You're withdrawing . . . Getting old . . ."

"I suppose it's true in a way . . ."

Kate looks at me pityingly . . . It's as if I were fading away in the distance under her very eyes, dwindling into a tiny, faraway, unimportant speck already swept away by history . . . Kate's dream: that all men should be either very young or else definitely old . . . Either about to be or a has-been . . . Still looking for the key to the mystery, or having withdrawn into the impotence of wisdom . . . Hectic, ardent and idealistic, or philosophical, slow and resigned . . . If they're young you can "initiate" them . . . If they're old you can become the eternal little girl . . . But a fellow of forty, free and in good form . . . Frightful!

"They even say your novel isn't up to much . . ."

"How's that? No one's read it!"

"Yes, they have—Boris says he's seen a few pages . . . He says it's the poor man's Céline . . . Full of all your obsessions against women, apparently . . . If that's true you're going to get it in the neck, old boy . . . Flora's talked about it to Robert, too, in Madrid, and he told me about it . . . Ravings against women! Weininger—the man who inspired Hitler! Are you writing a Nazi novel? You? You're going to come unstuck, mark my words!"

Wham! You learn something every day! So it's war! Attack! Counteroffensive all along the line! Dinner parties! Cocktail parties! Meetings! Whisperings! Apparently . . . Poor guy . . . Has he gone crazy? What could have caused it? It's very strange . . . Mind you, he always *has* been a bit odd . . . He doesn't like women? So it's like that . . . Completely fanatical on the subject . . . But where does it come from? His mother? His wife? A recent disappointment? Who? Which? The little blonde he was seen with in New York? Flora's taking steps already . . . Not surprising . . . She smells a rat . . . She's getting ready . . . But hasn't he always been a homosexual, really? Oh no, but are you sure he really is going on about women? Perhaps he's talking indirectly about something else . . . Do you think so? But what? *What?*"

"And what does Deborah think?"

This is one of the few times Kate has ever uttered Deb's name . . . Usually she just ignores her . . . Pretends she doesn't exist . . . This must be serious . . . When the social network in person talks to you about your wife it's because there's something it can't make out; it's trying to find out if you've become unstable, what your real intentions are, what's come over you . . .

"I believe she quite likes it . . . Thinks it's fun . . . Exaggerated but fun . . . Anyhow, she's only seen bits of it . . ."

Kate turns pale . . . He and his wife have fun together! What a crime! I observe her compressed lips, her chin, her nose . . . All the resentment in the world is gathered there, in a pale patch three centimeters square . . . Spite . . . As clear as if it were written in so many words . . . a moment . . . Look more closely at the unconscious basis of our condition through the ages . . . Watch the intangible poison start to flow, on which we float and dream . . . The retractile rim of oysters . . . The eyelashes of reproach . . .

And it's happening quite outside of her—always has, always will, at least so long as this animate matter lasts . . . It's my turn now to be struck by the pathos of it . . . A torrent of pity and tenderness for all of us, failures and potential corpses that we are . . . Weininger! It's true he did get rather excited . . . A Kantian . . . A Jew converted to Protestantism . . . Vienna 1903 . . . Self-hatred . . . And then the shot at dawn when he was twenty-three . . . What was it he said? That one ought to be for women in the plural, against woman in the singular . . . That the problem is to allow for individuality as against the species, the race as a whole . . . But you need to read him—it isn't as simple as that . . .

> Every individual case is an enemy of the community spirit, as can be seen by the way a man of genius, the highest form of individuality, experiences his own sexuality . . . All great men, whether artists, who are free to express it, or philosophers, who are not (which is why they are regarded as cold and passionless)—all great men, then, without exception, insofar as their sexuality is developed at all, are perverted . . . They all suffer from either sadism or masochism—the latter, probably, in the case of the greatest of them . . . Now what all perversions have in common is an instinctive *rejection* of physical union—a *determination* to *avoid* coitus . . . For a really great man can only see it as a brutish, disgusting and filthy act, and certainly not one to be celebrated as a divine mystery . . .

Weininger's against copulation, contact, fusion, "pimping . . ." But finally too cerebral, too Protestant and puritanical . . . He observes that there aren't any women composers, architects or sculptors . . . People are shocked . . . But isn't it true?

"Won't you let me see just twenty pages?"

Kate practically yelled that . . . She wants to be able to give her own bad opinion of my book, not just pass on the guesses and gossip of others . . . "*I* know, *I've* seen it . . ." Let *me* sabotage you! Let *me* cut you down to size! Just *me, me, me!*

"No, really—it's very kind of you to ask . . . But when it's finished . . . After all, it may just be a mistake . . . I may not even publish it . . . But anyhow, even if it is a mistake, I might as well go through with it . . ."

Her expression changes . . . Seeing me like this—hesitant and weak—she softens . . . Gives me a sidelong glance . . . Am I becoming exploitable again? Malleable? Manipulable? Am I uncertain? Suffering? Am I short of something? Do I need anything?

"Are you all right for money?"

"Just about . . . This is my sabbatical year, you know . . . My year with the witches . . ."

"You really are a nasty brat . . ."

"I am, aren't I?"

"And hysterical with it . . ."

"Yes!"

"But why?"

"I'm made like that . . . People ought to pay me whenever I'm nice . . . There's no reason why I should be . . . Do you know what I'd really like to do, seeing the point we've reached in the war of the sexes? Now that everything's going to be more and more just a matter of embryo banks? I feel like asking a fee for every ejaculation! Otherwise simply chastity, meditation, and prayer . . ."

She's getting horny . . . They always do when they sense you're really outside of it all . . . Bring that one back! Back into the fold!

"Okay, okay . . . How long are you here for?"

"I leave tomorrow."

"Me too. What plane?"

"Eleven o'clock."

"Me too . . ."

"Terrific."

She's doing some quick thinking . . . Her Italian doesn't seem to come into it much . . . She's here to "cover" some conference or other . . . On psychoanalysis . . . "Politics and the Unconscious . . ." That sort of thing . . . "Sex and Culture . . ." "Democracy in Crisis . . ."

"It's a pain in the ass," says Kate, "but very well organized . . . Fals's philosophy is in good hands . . . There are lots of Japanese this time . . . And a couple of Russians! And some very good-looking Brazilians . . ."

Fals . . . His "philosophy . . ." The legacy . . . How far away it all seems now . . . Did it ever interest me? In the past? The race to control the mind . . . The backstage gossip of castration . . . The test-tubes of hysteria . . . I remember one of our last dinner parties . . . He was with one of his women "pupils . . ." Quite pretty, tall, well-dressed, black leather . . . He looked tired and said pensively at one point: "It's strange how, when a woman stops being a woman, she can squash the man she happens to be with at the time . . ." A sigh and a laugh . . . And the girl, slapped right in the face, asked: "Did you say *squash?*" And Fals answered, assuming the foolish smile he sometimes wore, answered, "Yes . . . For his own good, of course . . ." And raised his glass of champagne . . . It all comes back to me now . . . And what strikes me is that she didn't ask what he meant by "when a woman stops being a woman . . ." As if there was no need to ask . . . As if anyone knew what it means when a woman *starts* being a woman . . . Although she's one already . . . I'm not talking, of course, about her reaching puberty or losing her virginity . . . Nor of the transition from girl to woman, or from woman to old woman after the formidable journey through the menopause . . . Nor of the red sea episode . . . No, I'm talking about a more profound change . . . Might a woman be a woman only from time to time? For a while? Not during pregnancy . . . Oh no . . . A strange interlude . . . Unforeseen . . . According to whether or not she encounters her Mission . . . As a man does at a certain point . . . When it unexpectedly alights on him . . . Mana . . . Phallus . . . The mission, then, encountering a woman, uncovers *a* woman *in* a woman . . . And upsets the sleepwalking mechanism she's been caught up in from mother to daughter, grandmother to granddaughter, great-grandmother to granddaughter's granddaughter . . . Let me make my purpose clear: this book is of course an apology for women . . . For women as special, single individuals . . . Assuming there are any . . . Who've escaped the production line . . . Not women "in themselves," but women-as-happenings . . . As rare as the phallic sparkle itself, so fitful and

247

fading . . . The phallus isn't "cratic" . . . "Phallocracy" means weakness. Whereas the function of the phallus is to make a man one of the elect . . . As for women "in themselves," they're just a reservoir of "women-as-moments . . ." Have I made myself clear? No? It certainly is hard to explain . . . It would be better to dramatize it . . . Admittedly it takes a special kind of perception to understand . . . Aesthetic sensibility . . . The eye of liberty . . . Women are waiting for liberty . . . I see it at airports . . . The grim, locked-up, family faces . . . Or else the feverish eyes . . . Because of women we are alive, or in other words subject to death . . . And yet without them it's impossible to find the way out . . . They're all together when it comes to the great crusade against men . . . But as soon as there's one on her own . . . All the rest are against her . . . A woman has no fiercer enemies than other women . . . But even she will join the rest again against another . . . How they watch one another! Envy and spy on one another! Lest one of them should suddenly, without warning, take it into her head to become a woman . . . And what does that mean? The echo of infinite gratuitousness; of the secret, irreversible vanishing point . . . The passing by of the Evil One! Devilry!

I leave Kate . . . I know what I want to see again . . . The Triton fountain . . . The bas-relief in the sacristy at Santa Maria Maggiore . . . An *Assumption* by Bernini . . . Flight portrayed in marble, nothingness captured . . . Then I rush back to the Villa Borghese to have another look at his *Rape of Proserpine* . . . The same thing . . . The art of abduction . . . Trouble in the underworld . . . Hands, thighs, feet, the marks of fingers in the shrieking, petrified flesh . . . The three-headed dog below, with gaping jaws . . . Good old Pluto . . . Heavenly Bernini . . . Kidnap! Kidnap! Uproar! Exclamation! The lock of the harem's been picked!

He died on November 28 in his mansion in Rome, at number 12 via della Mercede . . .

I dine alone and happy . . . Scampi, Valpolicella, a murmur of Mozart . . . My hand skims over the paper in my notebook . . . The notebook throbbing over the heart . . . The heart of the sentences . . . A last salute to the fountain of the four rivers, lit up now . . . I'd like to sleep there, in the ceaseless cool torrent . . .

The journey back . . . Kate chattering over the Alps . . . Her talk's as restless and frozen, as limited and inexorably confused as the snowy peaks . . . Apparently when Hegel, the Himalayas of philosophy, found himself looking at the Alps for the first time, all he said was: "That's how it is . . ."

Kate is unique in her way: she gets everything the wrong way around . . . Everything . . . Without hesitation . . . But she thinks the same thing about me . . . Her Hercynian hostility toward me is the best compass I could possibly have: if I vex and am vexed by her I'm sure I'm going in the right direction . . . The reader would like to know if I ended up screwing her? No! Of course not! I slithered out of it . . .

Ysia! She phones from Roissy . . . She's just got in from China . . . A few days in Paris with the Peking Circus . . . "Cultural exchanges . . ." There's just been a production of *Carmen* there . . . With a Chinese cast . . . And a French conductor . . . *L'amour est enfant de bohême* . . . Love is a gypsy child . . . Things are certainly moving faster all the time . . . Shambles! Howls! *Il n'a jamais, jamais connu de loi.* . . . It has never known restraint . . . Ah, *Carmen!* Ample provincial dames cooing away after lunch in gloomy drawing rooms, leaning back against grand pianos . . . The thirties . . . Advancing on the fat, red-faced gentlemen in the front row . . . The lawyer . . . The doctor . . . Carmen Bovary . . . *Si tu n'aimes pas, je t'aime; et si je t'aime, prends ga-a-a-a-a-arde à toi!* . . . You may not love me, but I love you, so watch out! They're still trembling in their graves . . . The flame of the South . . . In China now! Panic among the Party secretaries . . . *Prends ga-a-a-a-a-arde à toi!*

Shall we meet after the circus? Right . . . She'll pretend to go back to her hotel with the company . . . She's supposed to be acting as their guide and adviser . . . A marvelous company it is, too . . . Swooping about like swallows . . . Acrobatics on bikes . . . Balancing on balls . . . On see-saws . . . Balancing jars on their foreheads

. . . Patterns diving . . . Pyramids of all kinds built up and collapsing . . . Such skill . . . Such ease . . . Like reeds . . . Like a breeze
. . . The women, especially, are incredible . . . Light and pearly . . .

I wait for Ysia in my studio at one in the morning . . . She
arrives . . . Out of breath . . . Throws herself into my arms . . .
Darling . . . She smells nice . . . Her whole body smells nice . . .
Her whole slim body, ready, warm and nimble, and too often
deprived of love . . . She kisses me over and over and over . . .
Feeds me with saliva . . . How bored she must be most of the time
. . . Visits, minor details, courtesies, tricks, administration, supervision, checks . . . Is she a member of the *Gong'anju,* the GAJ, the
Chinese KGB? Perhaps . . . But we never talk about public matters
. . . Never say a word about China . . . I've hidden the books I've
got about repression, the camps, and the prisons . . . Worse than
ever, espionage everywhere, arrests, summary trials, beatings-up,
"reeducation" . . . But she throws all that off for the time being
. . . That's my role . . . As if she were visiting a brothel . . . The
man-as-brothel, a new kind of being that needs to be invented . . .
Once again I'm amazed by her spontaneous skill . . . Almost better
than Cyd . . . As though she carried about inside her the living
roots of the *Tong-husan-tse* . . . The postures and positions . . .
The basic movements . . . The mimes . . . Unwinding silk . . .
Dragon coiling up . . . Four-eyed fish . . . Mandarin ducks . . .
Butterflies fluttering . . . Ducks soaring . . . Pine with low branches
. . . Bamboos near the altar . . . Dance of the two female phoenixes
. . . Gulls flying upside down . . . Wild horses gamboling . . .
Charger galloping . . . White tiger leaping . . . Brown grasshopper
against a tree . . . Phoenix in a vermilion cleft . . . Roc flying over
the sea . . . Monkey groaning and embracing a tree trunk . . . Cat
and mouse in the same hole . . . Dogs running on the ninth day of
autumn . . .

All that . . . All told and embroidered through tangled limbs . . .
Ysia doesn't speak . . . She mounts me, then goes right down me,
fluttering her fanatical little mouth over my sex . . . She sighs and
moans . . . Envelops me, shatters me . . . Sways, arches . . . Breaks
free and dives in again . . . Grabs . . . Comes back for more . . .

Where are we now? Paris? Night? Shanghai? Peking? I, the tall White, get up in the dark at one point, go into the kitchen for a glass of water, glance out of the window at the plane trees in the courtyard, bare and black in the moonlight . . . Yesterday's papers are lying on the table . . . The headlines, the stories . . . Scandals? New revelations just beginning? Others ending? No one any the wiser? As never before the papers strike me as already yellow and old, piled up, burned and forgotten . . . The dollar at more than six francs still . . . The main news item . . . Politics a distant murmur . . . Far away, in the past, left behind . . . A gust swallowed up in the current void . . . X's serial . . . Y's column . . . Z's editorial . . . And Kate's article, describing the latest ultraidiotic female volume as "heartrending," "deeply moving," "shatteringly authentic . . ."

I go back into the bedroom . . . Ysia is already dressed again and smoking . . . She'll have a bath back at her hotel . . . Taxi . . . See you soon . . . As usual she has avoided any discussion or intimacy . . . She's certainly taking great risks . . . Dream technique . . .

Exclamation from S. . . . In the sequence about St. Peter's in Rome I ought to have gone for a stroll with Sade! Of course! That's the whole key to *Juliet*! What no one will admit, he tells me, is that the entire novel is constructed around that central episode . . . The mass of the black masses! Which means that Sade understood the main thing . . . It's true . . . He realized better than anyone that the climax had to come there . . . At the true point! Where the supreme negation of matter takes place! The omega of the journey! Trigger off the release of the repressed! Supressed religions! The more archaic the better! archaic! Retell the story of coitus! Since remotest prehistory! With majestic dinosaurs! Insatiable! Ravening! Human sacrifice! Mayas! Trips with tripes! Oozings in charnel houses! Innards all over the place! Brains blown out! Fetuses trampled underfoot! Conveyor belt fucking . . . Mass produced lesbianism! Decapitations! Long-drawn-out monstrosities! Hairraising! It's amusing the way the word they used then for "penis" has become out of date . . . The *vit* . . . The Pope's *vit!* Unmasked by philosophy, which escaped from the boudoir and entered the basilica in triumph! Nowadays, S. says, the Church ought to be replaced by the University—the Sorbonne, or Paris VIII . . . Or better still by a television news room at night . . . This is how you have to screw if you want to be screened at peak viewing time tomorrow . . . Everything changes . . . We could keep Juliet herself . . . The philosopher in action . . . The wretched Pope depicted by Sade is Pius VI, Giovanni Angelo Braschi, born in 1717, died in Valence, in France, in 1799 . . . Sade makes him a blasphemer, a queer, a piss artist, a butcher . . . He, the delightful Marquis, seems to take a particular furious pleasure in showing it all happening under the canopy in St. Peter's . . . With consecrated hosts placed on erect *vits* and thence transferred into the ravished asses of the victims . . . What a hymn to transsubstantiation! What a staggering practical analysis of the Eucharist! What intuition about the functioning of the great human Tube, of the digestive snake itself! What a prodigious attempt at resistance just where the human peripeteia is utterly revealed! What a vision! Endless masses mingled with repeated sacrifices! Incredible! Sade, or Theology *malgré lui* . . . Bodies immolated while tied to the four columns . . . In short, Bernini made a great impact on the imagination of our best and most honest writer . . . And Rome! And Italy! Vesuvius! Naples! Olympia Borghese! Princess! The Duchess Grillo! Cardinal de Bernis! Albani!

Sade's skill . . . The Father Superior raped by the frenzied little girl . . . The Father goes green . . . The great Pervert stripped naked by the wild paranaoiac in person! The very heart of the Story! Burning curiosity! We thought as much! We thought as much! Even if it's completely false, it's true just the same! The Devil "live"! Terrible, unanswerable cynicism!

I grant S. all this . . . He's full of his subject . . . It's better than Diderot . . . Fiercer . . . More symptomatic of the tornado that shook first France, then Europe, then the world . . .

" 'A man like me is never sullied, my dear girl," the Pope told me. 'As the successor of God's disciples I am cloaked in His virtues. I am not a mere man even when I temporarily adopt men's failings.' "

And Sade has himself screwed like a Pope . . . Insulted, whipped, covered with filth, he never loses his sovereignty for a moment . . . He gives himself the appropriate female demon . . . A luxury rationalist succubus! Juliet is implacable! She steals the cash! Loots the treasure! Strips all pretense from the hypocrite! From the *infâme!* What she wants is total frankness . . . Truth! Virility! Cato! Brutus! You can just see those two in this setting! Their faces! Antiquity in its birthday suit . . . Amid universal sodomizing! Plato and Aristotle having an orgy!

Let's see what Sade has to say about Christ, summarizing the spirit of the age and immediately raising it to a peak: "Let us examine this rascal, then . . . What does he do, what does he think up to prove his God to us? What are his credentials? Frolics, supper parties, whores, cheapjack cures, puns and swindles . . ." As Goebbels was to say so sinisterly later: "The grosser the deception the better it works . . ." There's nothing more credulous than the human race, especially when you're preaching incredulity! That's the tactic to follow . . . Quite simple, really . . . You take whatever's most respected, most sacred, and then you deliberately go for it . . . You show it's a complete and utter lie . . . That its virtues are there only to hide its vices . . . And the trick works! Without fail! So strong is latent Resentment! You make the gall-bladder pee . . . The spleen overflow . . . How? You use the heroine? The female light-bearer! Lucifer! She has nerves of steel! She's unstoppable! That's where the stroke of genius comes in! A woman screwing screwing! As if that were possible! Towering credulity! It's impossible, therefore it's the reality we dream of! When I think of it!—Fals used to say Sade had no sense of humor!

"The more wit a man has the more he breaks free from restraint; so a man of wit will always be more inclined than another to the pleasures of libertinism . . ."

The Pope's *"vit"*! A gift from vice to virtue! Thanks very much! Only real bastards think Sade is "unreadable," "monotonous," "boring . . ." When you hear people say that, watch out! You're among a lot of wits who think it's all for real! That the Pope keeps on screwing the masses!

S. goes on . . . "Sade is visibly repelled, or pretends to be—who can say which?—by two things . . . The first is that anyone should have dared to restrain nature in its most sacred aspect: sexual susceptibility . . . He feels it as a kind of unbearable castration . . . He tries to show it's unthinkable—that the process of making semen through murder is as infinite as space and time . . . Incidentally and valuably proving, too, that murder lies at the root of all sexuality . . . The second thing Sade resents, and here we're on common ground with the Philosophers, is that the god in question speaks through plays upon words . . . 'The imbecile Jesus,' he writes, 'who speaks in nothing but logogryphs . . . ' The whole Christian religion—like the Jewish one too, by the way—is based on 'insipid allegories in which places are heaped on names and names on places, and facts are always sacrificed to illusion . . . ' The other world suggested by substitution . . . No more limits to the body—whereas we only really vibrate on those limits . . . Hence the business of Peter *(Pierre)*, the rock *(pierre)*, upside down on the tombstone *(pierre tombale)* where people have orgasms, strikes Sade's detractors as a joke in the worst possible taste . . . But what is it really? An affirmation of names and places and above all of facts . . . Philosophy is always, deep down, a kind of policeman . . . It has to challenge equivocation, the metaphorization of sex . . . It cuts short . . . It cuts out . . . Why? Because it cannot doubt for a moment that everything can be reduced to one simple term . . . A literal one . . . Hysterics! And if the term par excellence isn't Idea, then at least it's Sex . . . Isn't that so? Appetite! The Drive for Power! Come, come—we're not so easily taken in! We know what's what! Behind the appearances . . . The fine speeches . . . And Sermons . . . And processions . . . And confessions . . . Balls! Lollipops . . . Trickery everywhere; a passion for deceiving in order to exploit . . . Strange, isn't it, to think men have been crazy enough to believe in a conscious desire for untruth, for a vast, deliberately organized theater of dupes . . . Note that this seems to derive from a woman at last become lucid, and thenceforth bearing the torch of truth . . . You've only to look again at *D'Alembert's Dream* . . . Which ends with thoughts on genetic manipulation . . .

254

This quite titillates Mlle. de Lespinasse . . . The reference is to Dr. Bordeu . . . Man descending from monkeys . . . The orangutan that was shown at the St. Germain fair in 1720 . . . The creation of man-monkeys to serve as porters . . . Well, why not? And why not distinguish between different races? First, second and third class . . . After all, WOMANN in its famous Report talks about classifying reproducers . . . There'll be the house-man; the nanny-man; the suitcase-carrying-man . . . The sperm donor, through whom the capital of generation circulates . . . And then the eccentric types, a possible lover for moments of relaxation . . . Of course, you and I are to come into this last category . . . Additional 'help' brought in to entertain the ladies . . .

"Sade is incredible," says S. "What a novelist! The challenge he flings down is so enormous it will always remain ambiguous . . . A great pause . . . Before the infernal machine goes off . . . So long as bodies exist . . . The height of unawareness is to have inhibitions about reading Sade . . . And I mean not only the inability to read him, out of revulsion or disgust, but also the habit of taking him literally . . . Like that unspeakable cretin, a painter I believe, or rather a Surrealoid dauber, who had the name SADE branded on his chest during some wretched fetishist ritual . . . Surrealism! What about that then? Breton's occult pruderies . . . Aragon's mincing imposture . . . Artaud's antisexual raving . . . Out of all that repressive shambles only Bataille has some appeal . . . Sartre is an example of what I'm talking about . . . Nausea . . . I'll say! Genet . . . In a word, sexually there's nothing . . . A disaster . . . The *"nouveau roman"*? You must be joking . . . Nothing, nothing— not one plausible woman . . . And so nothing . . . Not one book . . . Not even one passage that's really erotic . . . But let's move on! Music! Let's get into the swing of it!"

He plays what according to him is the best accompaniment to Sade . . . Boccherini's *La casa del diavolo* . . . Dramatic, flamboyant, full of curlicues, extremely violent . . . Boccherini . . . Underrated . . . Died in Madrid in 1805 . . . And then Scarlatti . . . Domenico! Furious harpsichord, cold passion . . . He died in Madrid too (well, well), in 1757 . . . I think about little Louise going over and over his *Sonatas* . . . I feel like ringing her up to find out how her fingers are doing . . . Whirlpools, stirrings in the depths . . . Piercing of nerves . . . Commotion collapsing . . . Bonfire—blaze of joy . . . Scarlatti! A god! The scarlet letter!

"Because of the radio and records," says S., "the harpsichord's making a comeback . . . Through sound we can get back into the drawing-room intimacy of the past . . . A château in the abstract! Aristocratic sensibility! For all! No need for declamatory pianos and vast concert halls as in the nineteenth century . . . Like a public meeting . . . No, just listen to this storm of little pluckings! If only one could write like that! Go straight into each syllable! Patter away like that, without an atom of psychological fat! Or of pseudoromantic organology! Imagine what sort of women that must come from! Let's have them again and again! No vapors whatsoever! *Verdurin, avaunt!* Her famous migraine would turn into a tumor if she had some Scarlatti hurled at her head! The dance, old boy—clear tumult! Away with the future! Everything now! Compact and severe! All here in front of us—the essential sarabande!"

And now Flora . . . I'd completely forgotten about her . . . A breathing space . . . Pulmonary reflex . . . And now she's here . . . Back from Central America . . . Mexico . . . She'll tell me about her trip in detail, I'm sure . . . Must be polite . . . Fasten your seatbelt . . . Put a good face on it . . . Surely she's going to ask how I am? No . . . Marvelous . . . They really are monstrous . . . Pregnant with, i.e., full of, themselves by themselves, and with themselves in themselves . . . Out of nervousness? Of course . . . And so it starts up all over again . . . The Caribbean . . . The poverty of the people, pollution, corruption, revolution . . . Salvador, Nicaragua, Guatemala . . . Cuba's strategy . . . Maya temples . . . Olmec, Toltec, Aztec . . . Politics and tourism . . . She seems to have had a shock . . . Great cult of the void in the virgin forest . . . Walls built of skulls . . . Tennis played with death's-heads . . . The past, the

immense past, and the future . . . The cycle of plant decay . . .
Evolution echoing it . . . Demagogy and demography . . . Graves
that are cradles, blossoming corpses . . . Coups d'état looming
ahead . . . Plots . . . Flora's in great form . . . Or at least wants me
to think so . . . Her strident little voice sputters away at full tilt
. . . It's going well out there . . . New people arriving all the time
. . . Naive, fiery . . . Susceptible to propaganda . . . Enthusiastic
. . . Ready to sacrifice themselves . . . Nothing to lose but their
chains . . . Capable of dying for an ideal . . . And it's true the
powers that be are horrible . . . People disappearing . . . Rape . . .
Torture . . . Women and children massacred . . . Plenty to be done
. . . Plan the horror . . . Rationalize it . . . Democratize it . . . Oh,
if it weren't for the priests, as usual, diverting and hindering progress with their other-worldly timidities . . . Not that they're on the
wrong side, any more than in Poland, but they're so backward . . .
All that effort just to go backward, to cardinals and croziers, incan-
tations and genuflections . . .

Flora looks at me . . . I don't turn a hair . . . I sense there's
something wrong with her sermon . . . A doubt, a hesitation . . .
Fatigue . . . Yes, that's it—an immense weariness . . . Doubt with
a capital D . . . The hypnosis isn't working so well . . . She's not
actually going to wake up, but she can't sleep as deeply as before . . .

"And did you see Robert in Madrid?" I ask.

"Yes . . ." She hesitates. "He talked to me about your book."

"He's heard about it then?"

"Of course."

Silence. Impasse. Flora doesn't like to attack me head on . . . Nor
does she feel she can suggest screwing straight away, as in the old
days . . . The spring's gone slack . . . The mechanism's seized up
. . . Before, it was quite simple: she'd talk, I'd answer for a bit,
she'd get bored with that and come over and shut my mouth . . .
Then we'd get down to work . . . Ideas for her lectures and speeches
. . . Felt pen in hand . . . Page after page . . . Any old how . . .
Realism . . . Not relaxing for a moment . . . On with the conspir-

acy all the time . . . But I can see this doesn't suit her anymore . . .
The symbiosis has stopped working . . . It's as if I'd lost my magic,
as if I were out of range . . .

"Robert agrees with me. He doesn't like the title."

"*Women?* It's only provisional . . ."

"But it's really no good. Too general. Common. Magazine-y.
Soppy. A touch of the Virginia Woolf."

"Virginia Woolf?"

"Anyway, he says it's a lousy title. And I think he's right."

"It rather depends on what it's about, doesn't it?"

"The title's very important. And yours is no good."

"But that's what the subject is. At least ostensibly."

She pulls a face. She knows. Knows those who know. But it isn't
really a question of the title. Any title would be lousy in her eyes.
In truth I shouldn't be writing a novel at all. And especially not this
one. The whole thing is clear and undeniable. I'm not cut out for it.
I shouldn't. I ought to stick to the place the intellectual community
has been good enough to assign me. That of foreign journalist and
philosopher. And, vis-à-vis Flora herself, that of fucker-cum-ad-
viser. The rest is pointless. Fiction is pointless. Except the kind
that's predictable, that can be programmed, that swims with the tide
. . . I know too much, and say it . . . But I don't know what one
really needs to know, and what *I* need to know is to shut up . . .

"Do you want me to tell you what Robert says?"

"Please do."

"Well, he says you're treating women the way Céline did the
Jews . . ."

"But where does he get that from?"

"He heard it from someone who's read bits of it. You've gone
over to the extreme right, that's for sure."

"But really! No one's read any of it at all!"

Flora yawns. This conversation strikes her as pointless . . . She
already has her version of the matter . . . It's official, if occult: she
believes in it, and that's that. She's probably longing to get back to
Nicaragua. And perhaps, in spite of everything, she'd like me to
help her write a "think piece" about it for the *Times* . . .

First, Weininger, then Céline! Of course . . . Any monster will do! So now I'm a mass murderer . . . Propounding genocide—the only genuine kind, by the way: gynocide, against women! Back to the source of things! To the heart of the dark triangle! It's terrible . . . I'm finished . . . Unmasked . . . Judged . . . Sentenced to be shot and hanged ten times over . . . Banned . . . Confiscated . . . "Disappeared" . . . Cut up into a thousand pieces . . . Consigned to a sinister oblivion . . .

I think of *Mea Culpa* . . . All Céline's troubles came from that, in 1936 . . . It's his worst diatribe, and his most lucid . . . "The world is rabid, convulsed, superfused with envy . . . A creative person has only to open his mouth to be crushed with hatred, ground down, vaporized . . ." Back from the USSR, i.e., from the future . . . Blasphemy . . . Afterward he charged straight into anti-Semitism, a superficial idiocy . . . Forgetting evil itself . . . Trying to find a cause . . . Fixing on the Jews, as if they had anything to do with the origins of the mechanism! He starts to defend health, authenticity, women! A huge error! A wrong diagnosis! Suburban doctor! Genius of the ring-road! You got it back to front . . . On the contrary, on the contrary—if it hadn't been for the Jews and their determination to point out the universal vanishing point, the slope, the chink, we wouldn't have known anything about imposture a priori! About its perpetuation through illusion! About the Fall itself! I who live with a Bible under my pillow! Who am absolutely for Peter and Paul, a branch of the Moses bank . . . Itself a subsidiary resulting from Abraham's takeover . . . Making up for Adam . . . Produced by God in person! I whose only aim is to make women light and pleasant! Who spend all my time helping them, calming them, smoothing them down, reassuring them, praising them . . . Who regard it as a metaphysical mission . . . As if I didn't pity them . . . Pity their terrible fate . . . As if I wasn't moved by their courage . . . Didn't have the deepest sympathy with their difficulties . . . Their "problems . . ." As if I'd ever once admitted to any of them she bored me to death! Or that her mouth was too big . . . Or not big enough . . . That her voice was painful to listen to . . . That she made the most frightful blunders . . . No, no, never! A gentleman! As if I didn't weep every day when I see their efforts to exist . . . Better still: as if I didn't offer to give them the keys to existence, openly and for good—on condition, of course, that it's well understood and made known everywhere that existence is a curse . . . The only amelioration is through sexual pleasure, music, the science of coition . . . My god, how misunderstood one can be! Slandered! Belittled! Written off! I can just see what Rodolphe will write: "A crib from Céline. Monsieur X, who is said to be of American origin, has recently published a book about women in just the same style as Céline . . . Like his friend S., who has translated the work into French, Monsieur X has an astonishing talent for mimicry . . . The reader will recall S.'s own labored *Comedy*, the most unreadable gibberish ever perpetrated till now, and written without any punctuation whatsoever: S., who is never afraid of pretentiousness, appeared to be taking himself for Joyce . . . And now here are our two experts collaborating in further plagiarism . . . That's all we needed . . ."

Flora's reaction doesn't surprise me . . . Only natural . . . Women are so literal . . . Can't understand a metaphor . . . Always want to scale you down, reduce you to a doll, a babe-in-arms, a package-sized infant . . . As soon as a woman sees you, even before you've seen her, you can be sure she's already adjusted her lens . . . She never sees you as you are—only, as Goethe says in his priceless Faustian ragbag, a vague mass of dots . . . The Mothers . . . Who see around their tripod but forms as yet unborn . . . A sort of future abstraction . . . Grains of caviar . . . The necessary alchemy —of which Goethe's preaching can naturally say nothing—consists in transforming the lens in which you appear as a sooty little homunculus into a magnifying glass that focuses the invisible rays of passion on your penis . . . Optics! Microscope! High precision! Telescope! Astronomy for the fingers! Jewelry in the mouth! Let their mouths fall in love with your prick! Let them be mad about it! Let them find in it the lost breast that has to be changed at all costs into a child! Magic! A wave of the wand! A potential baby carriage there in the cock! Be sure you make the miracle seem possible . . . Conceivable . . . Otherwise nothing doing . . . If a woman's convinced that (1) she's not going to have a child, or another child, by you; or (2) that you aren't or won't become her child; or (3) that you're not even her wandering substitute phallus, bringing back to her thrills it's had with other women (or, better still, other men: if you're a homosexual she'll be terribly fond of you) — then she stops loving you . . . Completely . . . You're nothing to her anymore . . . Except to supply influence or loot . . . Or perhaps as a nanny . . . Loot, man! Or else help! entertain! buy! earn! The managing-director-cum-nanny is the ideal. . . . How to make them respect you? It's possible, just so long as you haven't gone to bed with them . . . That, as everyone should know, is unforgivable . . .

So where's the offense in what I've been saying? It's all true, verifiable, run-of-the-mill and of the bedroom; it flaunts itself everywhere . . . What's the remedy? There isn't one . . . The way out? None . . . The only solution, it seems to me, is to amuse oneself a bit more . . . Everyone agrees we're bored as never before . . . The atmosphere's stifling . . . At least in these parts . . . Perhaps it's different in the third world? In the "developing" countries? In Caracas? Beirut? With all the shooting? Singapore? Damascus? Dakar? In secret, inside hotels and embassies? There perhaps, amid the anxiety and insecurity, you can still find both the warmth and the coolness of good old intrigue . . . Insecurity and lack of freedom are excellent for giving you a hard-on . . .

But I see Flora's drowsing off . . . We go out . . . Have a cup of tea . . . She doesn't even try to interest me in her plans anymore . . . I think that for once we're both equally relieved to part . . .

Women . . . Is it really a bad title? For a comprehensive judgment at a certain point in time and space? On the social situation? The extent to which humanity has evolved? Come on now, it's a great title! A landmark in the history of literature . . . Of the novel . . . Of reality-vérité pure and simple . . . Of the thing in itself . . . Of the mystery of the superself . . . Of the open secret no one can fathom . . . Of the word on the tip of the tongue that everyone's looking for, seeing there's supposed to be a problem and all that claptrap . . .

What does Marx have to say, then? The giant with the beard who never fails? The only tough expert on bank notes? The great man-of-all-fortunes? The only really fashionable philosopher amid the universal obsession? The frightful, inhuman materialist? The galley slave? The tireless scribbler with boils on his bottom? The great visionary? The capital contemporary? The dreadful terrorist? The too well-known yet underrated dictator of situations? The one who knows about prices? And taxes? And value added? And quanta?

Yes, what has Marx got to say about all this, then? Now that his books are either mummified or challenged everywhere, it's not easy to use him . . . But he is an authority . . . And he'd have impressed Flora . . . Yes, I remember now—in a letter . . . Yes, here it is: London, December 12, 1868, to Kugelman: "The last conference of the American Labor Union is a great step forward, in particular because it treats working women on a basis of absolute equality, whereas from this point of view both the English and even more the gallant French may be described as extremely narrow-minded. Anyone who knows any history is aware that great social upheavals are impossible without the ferment provided by women. Social progress can be measured exactly in terms of the social position of the fair sex (the ugly ones included)." Marx! American prophecy! Ten years after the publication of *Madame Bovary!* Flaubert is writing *L'Education sentimentale* . . . That's it! That's it! Nowadays the upheaval, *c'est moi!* The "fair sex"! What an expression! How embarrassed Marx is about it! But let's see . . . When were Breuer and Freud's *Studies on Hysteria* published? 1895 . . . A new era . . . Observation . . . Theory . . . The nucleus . . . The strata . . . As important as Galileo and Copernicus . . . Memories . . . Forgettings . . . Energy . . . Probing . . . Anatomy of the nooks and crannies . . . Resistances . . . Discovery of various currents . . . First mapping of the black triangle . . . Exploration of Namibia . . . Marvelously precise, Freud: "To represent the logical sequence involved, we may think of a rod reaching via the most tortuous paths from the periphery to the deepest levels and vice versa, but usually going from outside to the central nucleus, stopping at all stations in a pattern that recalls that of the knight on a chessboard . . ." And all that while talking . . . On divans . . . Moses' Rod . . . Fool and knight's mate! Directly from the uterus to the brain . . . In the nerve lining . . . The body of the ages now expanding . . . Everything explained! Original sin! Why you're here! Transfixed . . . In transit . . . Your inability to breed . . . The same old story . . . Proust is coming . . . Still not enough . . . Jimmy Joyce! Céline! The modern knights! Bernini 2000! Here I come! At the gallop!

But you mustn't think Flora left me just like that . . . "By the way, Malmora was very nasty about you . . . He thinks you're very disagreeable . . . He hates you . . ." Or "This time you really have put on weight . . ." The usual little niggles . . . Designed to sting, cut, unbalance; and to trigger the need for the painkiller, the pill, the soothing jab of sex . . . According to her I must need her . . . Can't do without her . . . But nothing doing . . . No reaction . . . Tired . . . Next time perhaps . . . We'll see . . .

V

So now Robert's joined in . . . Bloody old queer . . . Reliable instinct . . . Subtle alliance with my women . . . Against me . . . I thought he seemed rather strange lately at the *Journal* . . . Only natural . . . Friendship? Yes, but not enough to call in question the sub-penial creed! Mama! The law of Mama! The great fear of Mama! Stimulation, idealization, depression . . . A whole psychoaffective conception of the world . . . Envy! Diabolical envy! Vigilance bound . . . Immediate frown . . . Sodom, province of Gomorrah . . . I'd forgotten . . . But of course . . . The whole network lights up . . . Mistrust . . . To the defense of the capital Mama! The Principle! The SGIC!

Robert falls in love about once every three years . . . With a soul incarnated in a body . . . A spiritual palpitation . . . They're usually pretty uninteresting youths who all of a sudden strike him as sublime . . . He drops hints about them . . . All his conversation comes back to them . . . Olivier . . . Alain . . . Jean-Claude . . . If they utter a few platitudes he's in raptures . . . Knowing looks . . . Avid glances . . . Not that that stops him, of course, from cruising all the time everywhere . . . Can't fill in the time any other way . . . But the object is still the union of the Idea with the Identical . . . Thought *à deux* . . . Initiation . . . Plato . . . Secrecy . . . Utterly loony esotericism . . . You are me . . . All that exists is Me in You . . . Very jealous of women, only thinking of one thing, but on the women's side at the least threat of danger . . . Protect the Androgyne! The Herma and the Phrodite! And danger is quite simply a man that's worth two of them . . . An anti-invert . . .

One who understands himself . . . What a horror! One who doesn't need any educating . . . Any philosophy . . . A very rare bird! But it does exist! The complete atheist! The Creator! Or his ghost! How apt is Proust's expression about "the bachelors of the Art . . ." The Bride kept warm by her Bachelors . . .

I've noticed there's a cliché that keeps recurring in Robert's articles: "Beings and things . . ." "Beings and things"! It's like a password, a sign of recognition, an esoteric gesture shading off into nostalgia . . . But Robert doesn't write very much . . . That's his trouble . . . He thinks I write much too much . . . Without distancing, without dimension, without enough allusions, without enough obscurity . . . I think he really considers me vulgar, too apt to call "beings and things" by their right names . . . Too casual . . . I don't make enough use of ambiguity . . . To the veiled, the velvety, the antiquated . . . In short, to the climate in which "beings and things" really flourish . . . Indirectly . . . Biologically . . . It's as if I rejected the vegetable and animal kingdoms . . . As if death left me cold . . . That's putting it mildly . . . They're always bringing up death . . . How fond they must be of it! How it must reassure and legitimize them! Death! It reminds me of Bernadette's fiery expression when she said to me: "I don't understand how you can measure eroticism in terms of a feeling of Evil . . . I think it's enough that *death* is present . . ."

I tackle Robert.

"Did you see Flora while you were in Madrid for your article?"

Slight grimace. Calculation lasting a hundred thousandth of a second. Should he tell a lie? No.

"We had lunch together . . . Did I forget to mention it?"

"Did you talk about me?"

"No . . ." Microgrin . . . "Or rather yes, a little, vaguely. She's worried about what you're going to say about her in your novel . . . Given its subject . . ."

He pronounced the word "novel" within a millimeter of the way Kate did in New York a few months ago . . . I remember it distinctly . . . I look at him . . . He's leaning forward in his chair over his cluttered desk . . . His green eyes gaze at me frankly . . . But in the word "novel," as he said it just now, there was a brief but violent storm . . . Digust . . . Contempt . . . A degenerate form . . . Unworthy of a superior mind . . .

He lights a cigarette.

"It seems you don't pull any punches."

"But no one's read it!"

"Really? But . . . Let's see . . . What about Boris? Haven't you shown it to him? He says there are at least four potential lawsuits in it . . ."

"What does he mean?"

"Relatives . . . Families . . . Organizations . . . Individuals who are recognizable . . . He says no publisher would dare print it . . ."

"But this is crazy! Boris hasn't set eyes on a syllable of it . . . He just wants to demolish me because he's writing a book aimed at the literary prizes . . . And anyhow, what about the novelist's privilege? The license allowed to fiction? So long as there are no real names, can't you write what you like?"

He looks at me, smiling. His tall, rather limp body is now all nervous and tense. He, too, obviously knows. No, you can't write what you like! No, imagination isn't allowed free rein; it must be kept under strict supervision if the secret isn't to leak out . . . Of course the novel's the most dangerous thing there is . . . And the risk doesn't lie in calling "beings and things" by their right names, or in poeticizing them for some mythical purpose, but rather in causing them to exist under other names that are more real than the real ones . . . The magic of the novel lies in its dealing with magic itself . . . The black magic of doubles, the baleful invisible work of permanent substitution that causes life to be lived by other characters than those who think they're alive . . . The novel is diabolical . . . It's the devil par excellence—the devil in the service of truth . . . And truth is nothing else but an ever deeper understanding of universal possession . . . Unconscious possession . . . *The Possessed* . . . I can see Robert here, before my very eyes, literally *caught*: self-satisfied, worried, unsuspecting, unconsciously thrilled, sure he's part of the occult power, sleepwalking, scarcely even annoyed at having someone in front of him who doesn't *know*, doesn't *understand* . . .

It's the end of the afternoon at the *Journal* . . . I've been finishing off a few pieces on foreign affairs . . . I feel Robert's been a 'bit distant toward me lately in this connection too . . . He didn't almost immediately share my feelings about Poland . . . Or about the desperate situation of the Christians in Lebanon . . . He made a stiff and sarcastic remark about my defense of John Paul II, although it was quite impartial . . . He looked at me without saying anything when I said I was going on a trip to Jerusalem . . . He strongly advised me against publishing that article against Cuba . . . I know he still sees intellectuals close to the Party . . . Oh, of course, they're critical, very critical . . . Human Rights and all that . . . But even so, among themselves . . . "Historical trends . . ." Necessity . . . Reality . . .

"Would you like to cover the conference in Milan?"

"What sort of conference is it?"

"Some socialist affair . . ."

"Why not?"

"You ought to show yourself a bit, old boy . . . Sabbatical year, 'novel'—all very well, but you ought to put in the odd appearance from time to time . . . You know how people are always plotting . . ."

Robert never misses an opportunity to remind me how precarious my position is . . . No one's indispensable . . . Not even I, it's implied, even if I do have all these qualifications and am so cultivated . . . Everyone spies on everyone else, from one office to another . . . From one page of the paper to another . . . How much space? How many columns? Who has his photo in? Who's allowed to write the intros, printed in bold and signed with his initials? Who really runs the "supplements"? Wars over square millimeters . . . Nibbling at someone else's space . . . Trying to increase one's own cubic volume of print . . . Mutual fraternal hate . . . Day by day, minute by minute . . . Concentrated jealousy, the battle of images, with all the pancreatic and hepatic passion that goes with frenzied

me-me-ism . . . And then there are the young ones . . . Shoving
from behind . . . Their move . . . When Robert talks about "the
young ones" he does so with his whole nervous system and idealistic soul . . . The same as Kate . . . What they both like best is to
have a "young one" in their office asking for a job . . . Or a
promotion . . . Or merely some advice . . . How to get on . . .
Make one's mark . . . Get to sign what one writes . . . A long
business! Tortuous paths! Trials and tribulations! All sorts of accidents! Tricks! Connections! Smart moves! Useful lays! Business, in
short . . . The great thing is to know how to sort the young ones
out . . . Lead them on . . . Let them flounder . . . Sack them . . .
Give them another chance . . . Sack them again . . . Give them
another chance again . . . Keep them waiting . . . Forget . . . Promise . . . Allow them a glimpse . . . Shut the door . . . Leave it ajar
. . . A cyncial shadow show . . .

But I have a certain amount of sympathy for Robert . . . He
went through it all too when he was a "young one . . ." Initiation
. . . And now it's his turn . . . He's in charge of his own particular
cult . . . The Sodom tradition . . . The candidates arrive . . . Plenty
of what it takes . . . Mountaineers of the Idea . . . Ascent via the
west face . . .

So I fly off to Milan . . . The Grand Hotel in the via Manzoni
. . . The bar's charming—big, old-fashioned, comfortable . . . This
is the hotel where Verdi used to stay . . . I've brought Deb with me
—she quite likes a couple of days away like this . . . The white,
bristling Duomo, dedicated to *Mariae nascenti* . . . La Scala? No, a
quiet dinner at Savini's . . . We're having a rest . . . We go back
and go to bed early; we sleep . . . I like sleeping with Deb; she
floats lightly in her sleep, like an echo . . . A warm feather . . .
Nice skin . . . Women are to be judged at night, when the petals
are turned back . . . Everything comes out . . . Either peace or the
quota of resentment . . .

I go to my conference the next morning . . . The usual crap . . .
Then of course Deb wants to do some shopping . . . Shoes . . . We
meet for a stroll in the Victor-Emmanuel Gallery . . . Under the
great glass roof . . . And what do we suddenly see in front of us? A

grayish, shapeless, slumped and quivering mass borne along at arm's length by a couple of bodyguards, "ex-young-romantic-poets-and-members-of-the-Party . . ." Aragon! Himself . . . As into himself the absence of eternity changes him, to adapt the quotation . . . Glassy-eyed Surrealism . . . Exhausted communism . . . Seeing nothing . . . Perceiving nothing . . . An old man of straw . . . A puppet out for a walk . . . A muffled-up witch . . . They're taking him on a trip . . . To see the fraternal Italian Party . . . Sidelong propaganda . . . Poems read aloud in the presence of the author, on the brink of the final disintegration . . . I can still hear his shrill, mannered, emphatic voice . . . "I have trod on the va-a-a-sty vine of your gown . . ." Nasal delivery . . . Some lines by Henri Bataille, I believe . . . It was at his place . . . He'd read an article of mine on Surrealism and wanted to see me . . . I was twenty-two . . . S. had the same sort of experience when he was twenty and was put forward as a young writer with a future by Mauriac and Aragon both at the same time . . . He doesn't like talking about that time of his life very much . . . He's ashamed of it . . . As he is of the little novel he published then and that he's done all he could to withdraw from circulation . . . Personally I think it's much better than any of the first efforts you see nowadays . . . A style and a flexibility . . . Stendhal . . . "No, no!" S. protests . . . He's absolutely uncompromising about his present experiments . . . Doesn't he realize he's in a complete wilderness? That everyone's laughing at him? That they think it's crazy? Pointless? Perhaps, but he takes pride in it . . . In being an incomprehensible monster . . . Someone peculiar . . . Ready to die of arrogance for his unrecognized masterpiece . . . Written in his own rhythmic scrawl . . .

What a show Aragon put on! He kept on reading his things out loud to me . . . Poe-e-e-e-ms . . . I thought he'd go on for ever . . . He couldn't have cared less whether the listener was tired or indifferent . . . He was used to lording it over crowds mesmerized in advance by the CP . . . Thorez's automatic writing . . . Duclos's Ouija boards . . . Stalin's speeches to Women — before he let it out that he preferred boys . . . "Woman is the future of man . . ." I think that pearl is one of his! Elsa! Love! Writings interlinked!

Fates intertwined! Doting crowds! Match to the finish with Sartre and Beauvoir! To be the genuine ideal couple! The genuine left! The most successful left-wing androgyne! Result: Beauvoir won hands down, as was only right . . . Why? The reason's simple . . . The Name . . . Simone de Beauvoir . . . Aristocratic . . . Return of repressed monarchism . . . And then . . . Of course! Beauvoir? Bovary! The absolute triumph of Flaubert!

What are Sartre's most famous words? Those at the end of *Words?* Those the schoolboys of the future will have to write out a hundred times to make the new humanism sink in? "A whole man made of the whole of mankind, as good as any, and to whom any is as good . . ." In the French there are a lot of repetitions that happen to suggest "poodle" and "sheep."

It's the key to both totalist and antitotalitarian theory . . . Totalitarianism exemplifies the totalist philosophy that's supposed to cry out against it . . . Every man worth every other man . . . Poodle . . . Sheep . . . Golden calf? Sartre won in terms of dollars . . . They say Aragon's sales are falling . . . A mistake to bet on the ruble . . .

Let's put it differently:

Socrates is immortal.

And Socrates is a man.

So all men deserve to be famous . . .

My eardrums remember Aragon . . . I was at the end of my tether . . . Pinned to my chair by the would-be Hugoesque voice (come to think of it, Hugo himself must have been just as tedious . . . Those evenings in Guernsey, with the jabbering tables and droning alexandrines!), I shifted about as best I could under the bombardment of false prosody . . . What a ruminant! What a pontificator! What a bore! I observed him surreptitiously as he wound himself up into his hollow lyricism . . . Was he wearing makeup? No! Impossible! But yes . . . Foundation, anyway . . . And big reddish patches on his cheeks and hands . . . And Elsa coming in and out of the study all the time to fetch some scissors . . . Some glue . . . Some envelopes . . . A lighter . . . Odd . . . Very nervous . . . As if she . . . But of course, why didn't I think of it before? No! Yes! Me? No, but really! Checking up . . . What a hell . . . Love! What was she afraid of? Hoping for? That he might try to blow me off in between a couple of epic flights? Perhaps she'd have joined in? If it had been my style? But it didn't dawn on me! Robert will laugh when he reads this bit . . .

What novel was it she autographed for me that day? No idea . . . I must have thrown it away when I left . . . All I remember is the side-splitting dedication: "To so-and-so—maternally . . ." They'd got some nerve, those stars! They took themselves for the universal Father and Mother! *They* didn't have any children either . . . Who will deliver us from these imaginary father- and motherhoods? The little mother of the people . . . She was hunchbacked . . . Apparently she wouldn't let Aragon go swimming . . . Wouldn't let him put on a swimsuit . . .

He's pathetic now, a blind and broken Oedipus in the Milan afternoon . . . Deb is appalled . . . When she was a high school girl in Sofia he was for her *the* French poet . . . The genius of the language . . . Heir to Mayakovsky . . . Only more civilized . . . The beacon of feeling . . . The hope and star of world redemption . . . But she preferred Dostoievsky . . . And she used to read Baudelaire in secret . . . Then Freud . . .

One of the two bodyguards recognizes me . . . Waves . . . Bye-bye! . . . He hoists his puppet up again . . . Pitiful . . . They go off . . .

In the evening Deb and I have dinner at Alfio's . . . We talk about all and sundry . . . Laugh a lot . . . Go back to the hotel . . . Gently make love . . . The delights of marriage . . . Deb's very tender, really . . . Very wise . . . What's it she says? That people are usually broken up by their passions . . . That they're astounded if you stick to your own position . . . We smoke together in bed . . . Once again I love her intelligence . . . On the other hand, she doesn't understand a thing about music . . . Or, consequently, about metaphysics . . . There's nothing more amusing than having religious arguments with your wife . . . Something new . . . She's not really a Catholic at all . . . And I'm one more and more . . . For aesthetic reasons? Of course . . . Stephen and I are Catholics

. . . Father and son . . . Versus Mama . . . Whom we love very much—that's not the point . . . But admittedly it reverses many centuries when the opposite was the case! When it was Mama who defended the faith out of prudishness, while the men tried to get out of it on the sly . . . But the guard's been changed . . . What a joke! Rome seen as the embodiment of fantasy! If I could go back into the past knowing what I know now, I'm sure I'd join the Papal army . . . Fight for the yellow and white flag . . . Against Garibaldi! Against Cavour! Stendhal, disgusted by that hardened profaner of the sacred, winks at me from the shadows . . .

Amandine! That's all you hear! The *French* test-tube baby! The little *French* Jézutte or female Jesus! A victory for Science! For national pride! We now produce ourselves! The new religion glorified! Lourdes licked! Fatima behind the times! The dawn of a humanity identifying itself as human and controlling humanity's future in uniquely human terms! A great moment! What about changing the calendar? Oh yes, of course, there was an English one, before . . . Louise Brown . . . And others on the way all over the place . . . Two in the United States . . . Three in Mexico . . . Four or five in Canada . . . All girls? The first two, anyway . . . The finger of God! I read in our own *Journal* that the mother, pleased but a shade disappointed, is supposed to have murmured: "And now I'd like a boy!" Like Emma, turning her head away when little Berthe is born . . . Archaic prejudice . . . Nothing to be done . . . Emma! Emma! And what about me? I'm sure no one else has ever dared to hear the "ovary" in Bovary . . . Nor has anyone else really paid attention when the noises made by the "bovines" or cattle tell the truth about the amorous atmosphere . . . There's no literary criticism anymore! You'll only have to read what will be written about this book! The women are in charge everywhere . . . Publishing . . . Newspapers . . . Television . . . Radio . . . But, you'll say, X, Y and Z are men, aren't they? Do you think so? Are you sure? Yes, they may be, but they're completely encircled by the ladies

. . . Bromided without realizing it . . . Caught up in the pleasures of the table, vanity, the line of least resistance . . . Carefully bridled . . . Or else terribly repressed . . . Harmless! Spiritualized! Taking refuge in the rumblings of the Absolute, the last resort!

Anyhow, Amandine's picture is on all the front pages . . . The minister for scientific research sends his best wishes . . . The priest on duty says vaguely that he greets her with love, but warns everyone to be careful about this sort of excess . . . And there she is, bloated, irrefutable, the new baby, the new Eve, Mary of the immatriculated conception! A genuine appearance of the Virgin at last! I work it out: when she looks at herself in fifteen or twenty years' time she'll think of how she was studied in her cradle in millions of copies! She'll say to herself: "Was that really me?" Doubt . . . I'm willing to bet she and the others will be my belated allies . . . I'll be old . . . My daughters! Come! I'll tell you everything! Come and see your real Papa! . . . If I'm still there!

But as Bernadette yelled out one day at a public meeting: "Why do they have to have a father?"

Yes, why?

You can't help wondering . . .

But look how marvelous it is: nature, schizogenesis . . .

Well, they'll want a father, I assure you—all of them, male and female . . . A prophecy . . . None of them, male or female, will be able to breathe for long in your incubator . . . Take it from me . . . There'll be a depression . . . Wars . . . A deeper and deeper unease . . . The males will want to know . . . The females will want to see . . . All of them will be bound to ask why . . . How . . . What does it mean exactly? No how? No why? Oh no, that would be too easy . . .

What is all this? What the hell are we doing here?

I note that there's a new society called NADRHAI (National Association for the Development and Recognition of Human Artificial Insemination).

Forward!

I read that new methods are being used:

"Steroid vaginal rings, which after insertion produce progestogens hostile to spermatozoa . . . This method avoids the bothersome manipulation involved in the use of a diaphragm and works more efficiently."

"LHRH, now administered by nasal spray, is a hormone secreted by the hypothalamus which inhibits ovulation." This anti-baby squirter seems to be superefficient.

"The contraceptive vaccine requires one injection a year . . . Experiments have been carried out in India, but nothing is yet known about the risks of intolerance, failure or sterility . . ."

"Finally the RU 486, the supreme ruse, the universal Easter egg, the new antiprogesterone pill which makes the little fertilized sac bite the dust!"

But it's the other aspect that's interesting, though people don't talk about it . . . The science of samples . . . The art of implants . . . The new agriculture . . . Kolkhozes . . . Hothouses . . . Not necessarily sperm . . . One day it will be saliva, you'll see . . . The slightest sneeze will be put to use . . . The fait accompli . . . Progenitors in spite of themselves . . . Pay at the desk!

Since people's only subject of conversation has become this little basic thing that propels mankind into its fourth dimension, it's as if history had begun to misfire . . . As if nothing was happening anymore . . . As if everything was repeating itself . . . And indeed . . . Cars keep blowing up all over the place . . . Gloom spreads everywhere . . . England attacks Argentina . . . Inspiration isn't up to much . . . Whose fault is it? Voltaire's? Rousseau's? No . . . Mine . . . It's staring me in the face . . .

And what about the women, the poor women, in all this mess? They're interviewed, surveyed, displayed on every page . . . As if it went without saying . . . As if that's the only thing they could think about . . . Like a cattle market! Bovines! Bovarized! Bovulated! But not one refuses . . . Not one rejects the violence of being reduced to her mere physical function . . . Is that really you there? Is it really you in your body? Well then, say no to Science! Which claims to be on your side into the bargain! Offers you the freedom of the market! And they answer! Make foolish shows of themselves . . . Go along with it . . . Anyhow, they're got so little to lose . . .

Bitterness . . . Ideal consumers . . . Polls . . . Profiles . . . Portraits . . . Statistics . . . TV programs . . . Encounters . . . Solidarity . . .

I see them in the morning when I'm taking Stephen to school . . . Half awake, faces drawn . . . Shaky on their pins . . . Crazy with boredom . . . Yesterday evening was terrible again . . . Gloomy dinner . . . TV . . . Husband a pain in the ass . . . More and more withdrawn . . . Still, he pays . . . That at least . . . A lover? What for? As if I hadn't got enough problems already . . . Women friends? Even more depressed than I am . . . So there they are in the early morning with their squalling brats . . . A few fathers, silent like me . . . Shadows . . . Stephen and I take the bus; he always wants to go on the platform to avoid the others . . . "Papa—the trumpet!" Papa pretends to play the trumpet . . . "Papa—jump!" We jump out at the stop . . . "Papa—a croissant!" We go to the bakery . . . "Papa—a gee-gee!" Papa pretends to be a horse . . . "Papa—sing!" What? *"Depo!!"* . . . That's how the tenor aria begins in Bach's *Magnificat* . . . One of the first things I sang to him in his cradle . . . "Deposuit potentes de sede, et exaltavit humilies . . ." Voice down to suggest the fall of the mighty . . . Up to indicate the raising of the humble . . . Very moral . . . Divine Justice . . . I think he'll remember . . . Perhaps one day things will be reversed . . . Sometimes, if we're a bit early, we go into a café . . . It's still dark in the winter . . . Stephen has a glass of milk . . . I read my papers . . . Paris is getting itself organized: circulating, revolving, vibrating . . . I go back to my studio . . . Shut the curtains . . . Get out the typewriter . . .

Just one evening! One little night all on my own . . . To breathe . . . I do that from time to time . . . Say I'm going on a trip . . . Then stay where I am, or go to a hotel, or don't sleep at all, just walk around Paris all night . . . Meditate till dawn . . . Enjoy the sensations . . . This evening for example . . . Bliss . . . I treat myself to a good dinner in a district a long way away from home . . . Honoring the artist at work . . . If I don't do it who will? No one knows how to entertain anymore . . . How to organize a meal and talk for the sake of talking . . . No woman, or almost none . . .

The end of civilization, in short . . . They haven't got the time anymore . . . Nor the money . . . No more frills or double meanings or
indiscretions or salons . . . No more play . . . Stodginess everywhere
. . . It would be fun to bring parties back into fashion . . . Gowns,
flirtations, sidelong glances, wit, witticisms . . . What is the middle
class? That's what Werth used to ask, I remember, at the end of his
life . . . He'd have liked to "go out . . ." Get ready . . . Then shine
. . . Try unobtrusively to get off with the girls . . . I haven't been
to a decent dinner party in Paris for at least ten years . . . For ten
years I've been eating and drinking badly wherever I go, drowned
in talk on utilitarian subjects and the business in hand . . . Publicity
. . . Profit . . . Not a single "hostess" left . . . It's finished, over, as
far away now as châteaux and brocades . . . Proust sitting down to
dinner in someone's apartment today . . . I shudder at the thought
. . . And not a wisp of an undie . . . What is the middle class now,
all over the world, from Leningrad to Los Angeles, from Stockholm
to the Cape? I don't mind telling you: pantyhose . . . Pantyhose
and hairspray . . . Pantyhose covered in hairspray . . . A woman in
pantyhose — asphyxia! Just thinking about it makes you gasp for
air . . . Pantyhose stands for the ultimate functionalization, the
complete separation of the without and the within . . . It assumes a
woman knows in advance what *isn't* going to happen in the way of
the ambiguous, the iridescent, the lightly brushing . . . Mme de
Guermantes in tights! Odette! Mlle de Vinteuil and her girlfriend!
The curtain would come down on perversity . . . Send for the dust
covers and the moth-balls! . . . And I'm only talking about the
consequences for contemporary culture, conversation, way of life
. . . Food, women's underwear, language — they're all affected . . .
Knowledge of wine . . . Know-how in trivia . . . The role of the
writer . . . Lady reader who by some miracle has got as far as
this — if you possess a pair of pantyhose you're not worthy to read
this book! Nor any other! You may laugh, but you're wrong . . .
Your own interests are more deeply involved than you think . . .

Machiavelli, after all his adventures, living in the country in
disgrace . . . He used to invite himself to dinner . . . Dressed up
like a prince as if to meet Thucydides, Livy, and Tacitus . . . Ac-

279

cording to him, barbarism had come again . . . The Courts were in a state of collapse . . . But it picked up again later . . . And will do so again . . . Already some women are complaining . . . In secret . . . A spark could set fire to the whole plain . . . They sense that something's wrong . . . They try to improvise a little . . . Awkwardly as yet . . . It's only a beginning . . . They need time . . . Little panties . . . A touch of irony . . . Being able to tell the difference between a Pomerol and a Médoc . . . Totalitarianism, as they modestly say these days to avoid the thought that it's just mankind's inevitable tendency, will only be overcome by elegance . . . A systematic and fierce elegance . . . Not by noble feelings . . . Absolutely not! Don't go in for statements . . . Keep quiet . . . Defend your private life like a tiger . . . Improve it all the time, for no particular reason, just on principle . . . The only danger lies in a growing disgust for and renunciation of life in and for itself . . . Be monstrously withdrawn . . . Don't join in the absurd belief that the world is absurd . . . Don't believe that it has a meaning either . . . Not the slightest! Don't let yourselves be helped, maternalized, or soothed by the specter of society . . . Go home, don't show yourselves, don't waste your strength, don't hang about, talk about perfectly useless things . . . It doesn't matter what, so long as no one else has mentioned it for a month . . . Seep out in words . . . To no purpose . . . But in the strictest modesty . . . And then go to bed . . . You'll see, in the morning . . . Already an improvement . . . A great improvement . . .

Be careful of the all-conquering cybernetic death wish! The later to coffin or crematorium the better!

I have spoken . . .

The head waiter finds me very peculiar, sitting here by candlelight all alone, drinking champagne and writing things down in my notebook . . . Tonight I go back to the studio . . . As I sometimes do, I pick up the phone and ring some numbers at random . . . Sampling moods . . . Swift said a clever government would have its citizens' excrement examined every morning . . . I believe just the sound of their voices saying "hello" is enough to reveal their basic attitudes . . . I make a present of the idea to the party leaders . . .

Judging by this evening's "hellos" things are going very badly . . .
The currency's shaky, morale is twenty thousand leagues under the
sea . . . The future is meaningless . . . Eighty percent react loutishly,
especially the women . . . Admittedly I'm disturbing them . . .
Ringing up and then not saying anything . . . But people who are
enjoying themselves never sound put out . . . Which of them shall
I ring just to see, just for a lark? To hear how she's getting on?
What about Judith? You remember—the one that was so keen on
having a baby . . . Who loved me so unconditionally . . . Three
years ago . . . It's not nice, what I'm doing . . . It's beastly, really
. . . Too bad . . . The phone rings at the other end . . . She answers
. . . I don't breathe a word . . . Just listen . . . And she starts to
talk all by herself . . . "Hello? . . . Hello? . . . Pablo? . . . Pablo?
Is that you? Are you there?" She's absolutely sure it's Pablo . . .
"Pablo? I know it's you . . . Funny that every anonymous call
coincides with your landing at Orly . . . Are you well? . . . And
your aunt? . . . Pablo? Aren't you going to say anything? . . . You
might just say something! . . . Pablo? What about your cousins?
Are they all right?" Silence . . . A bit of irritation now . . . "What's
the matter—have you gone to take a shower?" Silence . . . "Do
you need some vaseline? . . . Finished in the bathroom yet?" Silence . . . Depression . . . "Pablo? So you're determined not to say
anything? . . . Well, I'm on my own now . . . Since my abortion
. . ." A quiver . . . "So there it is!" Silence . . . "Well then,"—
voice on the brink of tears—"if you're not going to say anything
I'll hang up . . ."

She hangs up . . . Pablo's a nice one! It's all rather touching . . .
Lamentable vulgarity, but real suffering . . . I didn't remember her
having such a common voice . . . She must have put on a posh one
for me . . . Was she beautiful, Judith? Yes, very . . . They all talk
like that nowadays: "Let him go and toss himself off in the can!"
"Hi old cock!" Sweet talk like that . . .

There are twelve million women between fifteen and forty-nine
in France today . . .

The graph of going through the mill . . .

But the really new thing is their appearance on the terrorism

scene . . . Germany . . . Italy . . . Pistols . . . Machine-guns . . .
They jump out of cars and mow down Christian Democrats . . . An
attaché at the Israeli Embassy in Paris . . . Killed at point blank
range by a little dark girl in trainers . . .

I turn on the television . . . The news . . . The christening of
Maria-Victoria, Walesa's daughter . . . He's still in jail . . . The
church is surrounded by the police and the army . . . There's an
enormous crowd . . . Catholic baptism seen as subversion . . . "Long
live the Pope!" Phew!

I turn it off . . . Look out at the other apartments, the little
families sitting watching their screens . . . Just an ordinary night
. . . The lights go out one after the other . . . Nightgowns . . .
Pajamas . . . Tablets . . . Teeth . . . Rectums . . . WCs . . . Sighs
. . . Digestions . . . Millions and millions of abandoned bodies . . .
Illnesses . . . Worries . . . Euphorias . . . Menses and heartburns
. . . The blue light of hospitals . . . Nightclubs with ear-splitting
audio systems . . . Sweat . . . Swaying . . . Musing . . . Little
Nineveh . . . Strip joints . . . Homos . . . Dope . . . Call joints . . .
Patrols . . . Suburbs . . . Subway . . . Bois de Boulogne . . . The
president can't sleep . . . The minister's thinking about his speech
. . . The banker about the downward trend of the mark . . . The
professor about his colleague . . . The analyst about his own former
analyst . . . Bernadette about the new publicity drive about women
and that girl who needs watching . . . Flora's thinking she's angry
with me . . . Cyd's forgetting me . . . Ysia's flying to Peking . . .
Diane's walking about somewhere in Athens . . . Kate's got her
eyes closed and is seeing a three-dimensional version of her own
signature at the end of the article that's coming out tomorrow . . .

"Oh, you're there!"

Boris is delighted . . . He's got some important things to tell me.

"You're out of the running for the prizes, old man . . . Pity . . .
A great pity . . . You shouldn't even enter . . . I've seen So-and-so
and he's quite definite about it . . ."

"Really?"

"Not a chance! Not the slightest! Someone mentioned your

name, to see . . . Icy silence . . . Backing off . . . I *am* sorry . . .
Funny thing, though, how they all loathe you . . . Ouch!"

"But why?"

"You know very well . . . Wrong image . . . How are you
getting on, by the way? Making progress?"

"It's difficult . . ."

"It *has* got a plot?"

"A plot?"

"A story . . . That you can follow . . . That develops . . . That
you can tell . . . Summarize . . ."

"Yes, I think so . . ."

"What do you mean, you think so? Aren't you sure? Are there
scenes? Dialogue? Real characters?"

"I think so . . . What about you?"

"Oh, I've almost finished . . . It's called *The Eternal Feminine*,
did I tell you? Sublime! Enough to bring tears to all those simple
eyes! And moving the woman in the street is the whole secret . . .
Yes, yes, take it from me . . . Three hundred thousand copies
ordered by the book clubs already . . ."

"I heard you were telling everyone you'd seen my manuscript?"

"Really? No! What an idea! I just mentioned our conversations
. . . Perhaps—"

"What conversations?"

"Anyhow, I'm on TF1 tomorrow evening at eight-thirty . . .
Will you be watching? I'm preparing a terrific stunt . . . I must tell
you about it . . . Brilliant! Have you seen my interview in *Scratch*?
. . . No? Not yet? Four pages! Three photographs! And I'm very
good—excellent! Shall we have lunch?"

"I'm leaving tomorrow . . ."

"Again? But what's got into you? We never see each other anymore . . . When will you be back?"

"In a week or ten days . . ."

"Right, I'll call you, and we'll meet right away . . . I've got a
real stunt up my sleeve . . . No, really . . . A terrific scoop . . . It'll
amuse you . . . Ciao!"

And Boris springs on another victim . . . Three hundred phone calls a day . . . On an average . . . Blanket propaganda . . . Rule the waves . . . Visible and invisible . . . Confuse, hint, disinform, find out, re-disinform . . . Real secret service stuff . . . Never at rest . . . Rest and it would all break down . . . He's a whole telephone exchange in himself . . . By the end of the afternoon he knows everything . . . Quotations, variations, oscillations . . . He's quarreled . . . Made it up . . . Quarreled again . . . Made it up again . . . Not that it matters . . . Pure fiction . . . Media madness . . . Any publicity's good publicity . . . No alternative . . . The image race . . . Treachery by guesswork . . . And as everything's false, everywhere and all the time, he's always bound to be telling the truth . . .

"The eternal feminine . . ." That suits him down to the ground . . . So long as it's taken to mean something that's always changing! The force of change! Not this, not that, and not the other . . . Mad rush forward, sideways, in all directions . . . "The eternal feminine that draws you ever upward"? Poor old Goethe . . . Faust is nothing compared with Boris . . . The Devil himself is only an amateur . . . "The prince of the powers of the air," as St. Paul says . . . Yes, but do devils know that's what they are? It's not certain . . . Still, perhaps . . . I've seen Boris tremble sometimes . . . A strange tremor passing over his face, suddenly frozen with exhaustion and a fleeting awareness of the futility of all his agitation . . . An attack of stony weakness . . . An old stump . . . A cast-off lizard's tail . . . One of Macbeth's toads . . . Emasculine . . . The eternal feminine? Ever upward? White goddess? Beatrice floating high above the world? Hidden Venus? No . . . Women are very solid and weighty now: faces, mouths, makeup, hips, thighs, legs . . . Determined to drag you *down* . . . Ever downward . . . Is it true, what people say? That Boris once had cancer of the testicles? That he only just survived? That they sterilized him with radiation? That afterward his wife played the I.D. trick on him? Scores settled by ultraviolet . . . Little incidents from modern life . . . Flourishes . . . Curlicues . . . Patches . . . *Rosemary's Baby* . . . If you look closely at people's lives . . . Every time something strange . . . I can understand his wanting to tell himself stories . . . I pity him for wriggling about on the grill . . . I silently pray for him . . . If he wants to spend his time doing me down, so be it . . .

"A most original English novelist: Angela Lobster!

"Evelyn, a young English university professor already burdened with a name that is both masculine and feminine, leaves England for a disintegrating America that is prey to vandalism, anarchy and rats . . . There he meets a Czech alchemist who succeeds in transmuting base metals into gold but is beaten to death in a supermarket . . . He sleeps with a marvelous girl he takes to be a black prostitute, whom he forces to have a bloody abortion . . . He then takes refuge in the desert . . .

"There he meets the women of Beulah, an underground city run by Amazons who themselves are ruled by the Mother (The Earth-Mother, the Castrating Mother, every possible item in the litany of Woman-as-Mother) . . . The Mother is enormous, embryonic, with several breasts; she is also a surgeon . . . Evelyn's sperm is collected and, after a remarkable operation that changes him into a woman, he is inseminated with it, in order to produce the first child created in this manner . . . The operation also involves psychological conditioning, so that the new Eve also *feels* like a woman . . . Eve then meets a one-eyed, one-legged phallocrat by the name of Zero, who has a bust of Nietzsche on his desk and a harem of seven (one for each day of the week) . . . This arrangement is thrown into disarray by the arrival of the eighth female . . . Eve is brutally deflowered and becomes a real woman, spending her time either servicing Zero or performing household tasks . . ."

And this is put out as publicity! At last a real novel! *"The Hormones of the New Eve!"*

"Note on the author: Angela Lobster, already well-known in her own country, is quietly developing into one of England's best woman novelists . . . She has seven novels, two collections of short stories and one work of nonfiction to her credit, and has won three prizes . . . She is equally at home in all these forms as well as in poetry and literary criticism . . ."

I want her! I want her! Bravo, Angela! An Englishwoman?

285

That's not surprising . . . So bold! And the French publisher's got some sense too . . . Bringing out this fantastic thing along with *The Jesus Question, The Roots of Nazism,* and *The Blunder of the Eucharist according to the New Testament,* and *Socialism at the Bar of History* . . . Vestibule Publications . . . That inspires confidence . . . Supernatural anonymity . . .

Anyhow, this Angela is for me! I can feel it! I'm sure of it! I could roll on the ground for joy . . . On the earth . . . Mother Earth . . . She's bound to be a member of WOMANN . . . Militant tendency . . . I must drop a note at once to Cyd in New York and tell her to buy the original . . . You can never tell with translations . . . It'll make her laugh . . . An Englishwoman, like herself . . . What a film it would make!

What else do people want in a novel now except everyday life, lived carelessly and to no purpose? Take the small ads . . . The situation's quite plain . . . Hits you in the eye . . . *Libération* for the victims who travel on the subway . . . The *Nouvel Observateur* for the lucky ones with wall-to-wall carpeting . . . Clerks, workers, middle executives, senior executives . . . One glance and you've got the whole thing . . . The detail that reveals the truth . . . Sado, maso and uro on the one hand . . . Sentimentality and billing and cooing on the other . . . Orgies or lousy poetry . . . Scatology or soppiness . . . Organic detail or lyrical flights . . . And between the two the permanent feminine requirement: stability, security, and insistence on "affinity . . ." Affinities! Elective and electoral! Homos, lesbians, bi- and trisexuals, couples who claim to like swapping (it's the men, really), outright loneliness, brief encounters, games, obsessions, fantasies . . . I take one at random . . . Gosh, Rouen must have changed since Flaubert's day . . . "Young man, good physique, keen ham fetishist, would like to meet young woman with same tastes with view to ham-woman lovemaking . . . Meet next Thursday afternoon between three and four by the big clock . . . I shall be carrying a knuckle of ham under my arm . . . Ask 'Is it ham or bacon?' "

Is it a daft joke? A highly elaborate code? A typical contemporary artist . . . A post-Surrealist . . . Comfortably off . . . Disillusioned . . . Cultivated . . . "Fresh pork of my thoughts," Sade wrote to his wife . . .

Another one . . . "I was on the métro at about seven o'clock last Friday evening, the 12th, between République and the Gare de Lyon . . . You were standing next to me in the first car of the train, holding onto the same pole . . . I have auburn hair, brown eyes and very white skin, and that evening I had my hair up . . . I was wearing a red coat, and, as you noticed, a black slit skirt . . . Your soft hand made me tremble . . . You were quite tall, dark and manly-looking . . . I'd love to correspond with you about my fantasies . . . Write soon but discreetly . . ."

Tut-tut . . . White skin . . . Slit skirt . . . Hair up . . . Unless it's a homo trying to ensnare the deep-down hetero of his dreams . . .

Or, more simply, one of thousands of military communiqués: "Young man, 23, dark, 5 foot 7½ inches, seeks guy between 18 and 30 with view to having fun (f., fell.). Nude photo if poss., utmost discretion . . ."

And so on and so forth . . . No end to it . . . No matter . . . These are the poems of today . . . The novels . . . Instant, like lightning . . . Bedlam gleams . . . Little bottles cast into the raging metropolitan sea . . . Hectic prostitution . . . Shades of ancient Rome . . . What happens to them, these dilettantes for a day or a few months? What sort of old age do they have? How do they end up? In what hell of boredom? How do they gradually drop out of the underground rotary market?

It's not difficult to see that the whole bag of tricks, male homosexuality included and perhaps that most of all, revolves around women as business and women as hell . . . All an act . . . Panic fear of discovering there's nothing there . . . Nothing at all . . . Just a projection . . . But what energy! What faith! What sacrifice! What self-denial! An inverted monastery . . . Visionary exercises . . .

Meditation . . . Prayer . . . Expectation . . . Ecstasy . . . Intimations of the divine . . . Offices . . . Workshops . . . Buses . . . The girl who wants someone to rescue her from Mantes-la-Jolie . . . The boy who hopes for other mental horizons beyond Vitry . . . The boy who only saw her once . . . The girl who'll collect his letter from the poste restante . . . The immigrant . . . The Black . . . The Arab . . . The thug . . . The shy young bourgeois . . . Wondering if this time he'll have the nerve to be fucked . . . All, male and female, hoping something might happen at last . . . Smile if you like—I find it ten thousand times more interesting than all your modern philosophical treatises . . . The phenomenology of perception . . . A critique of dialectical reason . . . The millionth commentary on Kant . . . But these others are live people in extremity . . . You can hear their voices through the sound of trains and ambulance sirens . . . Glory to you, dear placers of small ads! Honor of the age! Diehards of the game! Fanatical dreamers! Guardians of comical freedom in action! Do you find contemporary literature and theater pointless? Do you not give a damn what happens on the respectable upper floors? You're right! I'm with you! Don't weaken! Keep demanding more room! May the papers be full of you and only you . . . Drive out all other subjects . . . Let it all become so boring and absurd that everyone is put off and a new era begins! Let instant truth, let low sensation be set out constantly before all eyes . . . Tenderness, filth, love! The whole gamut . . . Ranged through forever by the Great Goddess Illusion . . .

Paris! Yuk! City of light? City of shite! Capital of papier-mâché vice! The Great, or rather Gross Tradition! But crumbling away with age . . . It's as if the French can't get used to having become Holland . . . At best . . . Or perhaps Finland? Who knows? Provincial anyway . . . They really were had by the Second World War . . . Then a jump into the Sartre-de Gaulle dimension . . . Enlightened tyrant . . . World philosopher . . . But by the seventies it was all over . . . All that was left was Technology and Science . . . Another régime . . . It was then that the women's movement really began to take off . . . To fill the gap . . . Wide and irresistible . . . Cat almost out of the bag . . . People might wake up . . . Find out

about everything . . . Oh no! Certainly not! The upheaval naturally masked something else at a deeper level . . . It was really the
most remarkable sign of the transformation of hard into soft . . .
This is S. talking now . . . For him the real revolution has been
taking place over the last ten years . . . Color television . . . Cassettes . . . Video . . . Video recorders . . . Even McLuhan didn't go
far enough . . . A fabulous mutation . . . A reshaping of inside and
out . . . New bearings . . . Everything in audio . . . Anticipation of
the last judgment . . . Transition to the trans-world . . . Material
and immaterial at the same time . . . Superhuman . . . Soft! The
wave-length of the angels! Or the devils . . . The death of man?
Plenty of blather about that, but it's only a detail . . . Heidegger?
Yes, yes, but too slow . . . A new Counter-Reformation . . . An
explosion! The power of hearing! All that belongs to before is
overemphatic, ponderous, awkward, arthritic, rheumatic, ridiculous
. . . Fascism, Stalinism and terrorism are just desperate attempts to
slow down softization . . . Death throes of a hysteria pierced to the
heart . . . But defending itself fiercely . . . Against relativity . . .
By means of loud voices . . . And the Law . . . But no good — the
white tide has started, pirate radio is unstoppable, broadcasting right
around the clock, it's the maelstrom!

  S. tells me how he recorded the whole of his *Comedy:* it took
him twelve hours reading aloud as fast as he could, and that's only
the first volume, he said proudly . . . He's crazy . . . He thinks he's
performed some kind of great liturgical act . . . A sort of exorcism
. . . He's going about all over the place now, reading the beginning
of the second volume . . . Still no punctuation, and surrounded by
eight television screens . . . On six of them a film in which Venice
is quickly succeeded by S. playing tennis, flashes of porn, the head
of a sleeping baby, fountains . . . On the other two screens he has
himself shown live, in color, as, perspiring and cataleptic, he spouts
his voodoo prose . . . I went to watch him . . . You could call it an
amazing feat of virtuosity . . . No one understands a word . . . The
audience is staggered . . . They vaguely gather he's calling for
the end of human reproduction, for enthusiastic experimenting with
the void and an ironical cult of the Virgin Mary . . . After an hour

of this barrage of eloquence you feel as if you've been sitting through a summary of the last two thousand years . . . He's reviving the apocalyptic form . . . In a sportswriter's style . . . The strange thing is that what seems opaque and monolithic to the eye strikes the ear as clear, polyphonic, harmonious, melodious . . . He moves about inside it as if playing a sprightly score, sometimes comic and sometimes lyrical . . . With guffaws, accelerations, protestations, lowerings of tone, bursts of song . . . A new troubador . . . The jongleur of Notre-Dame . . . The composer interpreting his own work . . . He likes Miles Davis . . . In short, heady stuff . . .

The gist, if I heard it right, is a violent denunciation of the ascendancy of sex . . . Of ascendancy pure and simple . . . A kind of gnostic hymn . . . It's significant that he refers to the Manichean "noria . . ." The wheel that sifts souls, letting some through and rejecting others . . . Salvation and damnation . . . Perpetual motion . . . That sort of thing . . . The Manicheans used to believe human beings could be divided up into three classes: hylic, psychic, and pneumatic . . . Corporeal, spiritual, and metaphysical . . . To become a pneumatic was a difficult business . . . The Archontes, the authorities of Evil, were always there, lurking behind a bound and bewitched world of whose darkness we see only the dimly lit peak . . . They were waiting to take the living corpses prisoner . . . The overseers of primeval wickedness seem male to females and female to males . . . At least in theory . . . Ha ha! . . . The main thing is to get the humans to disgorge their seed . . . To feed the machine . . . The great duplicating machine? Photocopying duplicity? The uterus in itself? Yes, says S., listen to these lines from Baudelaire:

> Blind and deaf machine, fertile in cruelty,
> Salutary instrument, drinker of the world's blood . . .

Salutary? Solitary? The grinder? The reconstructor? The female wolf that Dante mentions at the beginning of his journey to hell? Anyway, the important thing is this absolutely wicked intention at the beginning . . . Jealous desire . . . Matter . . . Al-Hummama . . . The female instigator and inspirer . . . The spirit of darkness

. . . The fetid breath that rules the world . . . And the little pawns on the chessboard . . . Moving about in the smoke, the fire, the air, the water, the darkness . . . *"Iram in facinoribus, libidinem in flagitis,"* as St. Augustine says . . . "Anger in infamy, lust in debauchery . . ." You can only escape by hearing a kind of fundamental cry or call . . . Drawing you up to the bright milky way of singing and prayer, recitation and psalms . . . A column of glory and praise . . . Permanent *sanctus* . . . Animated spiral . . . Harp and lute . . . And if you do escape, it's called "being reconciled with the right hand of peace and grace" . . . *Ad dexteram Patris* . . . A strange figure, this *Jesus Patibilis,* showing that the whole world is a cross of light . . .

S. is carried away by his subject . . . He's a pneumatic in action . . . Hence his style, he says, laughing . . . He claims that hylics and especially psychics are particularly active nowadays . . . And that rampant psychoanalysis is reducing their numbers . . . To finish me off he quotes his precious St. Paul again . . . 1 Corinthians 2:14: "the natural man receiveth not the things of the Spirit of God: for they are foolishness unto him: neither can he know them, for they are spiritually discerned . . . But he that is spiritual judgeth all things, yet he himself is judged of no man" . . . The Spirit, he says—that's what we always forget . . .

But what about all this playing with words, the changes and permutations of syllables . . . The Kabbala? If you like . . . S. lends me some articles by Gershom Scholem, who's just died in Jerusalem . . . And he reads me this passage about the infinite: "The eye of the Kabbala can see all worlds, even the mystery of the *En-Sof,* in the place where I am now . . . There is no need to speculate about what is 'above' or 'below': merely"—merely!—"to penetrate the meaning of the place where you are yourself . . . To this metaphorical eye, to use the expression of the great Kabbalist, all the worlds are nothing but 'names written on paper by the very essence of God.' "

Yeah, yeah . . . While we're at it . . .

Here. Now. Really here . . . Really now . . .

I have a date with the Chairwoman . . . Breakfast at her place
. . . What does she want? Nothing . . . Just to screw . . . To relax
. . . She's in a good mood . . . We have a good screw . . .

"And so how's your novel doing?"

"So-so . . . Getting rather metaphysical, I think . . ."

"Oh dear! In what sense?"

"Biblical!"

"Biblical? What an idea! Nowadays? Are you interested in
God?"

"I find it a strange business . . . Not really explained . . . Perhaps there are some new things to be said about it."

"But come, come—you're not saying you're a *believer* in it?

She's not the first one who's asked me that, with an undertone of
amazement in her voice. Of fear . . . This is where you're faced
with a choice. Where you're a coward . . . Where the cock crows . . .

"No, of course not."

"Why, then? Fashion?"

"Maybe . . . Why not? Fashion is often true . . ."

"It's incredible, though, this return to God! Isn't there a serious
philosopher left among the intellectuals?"

"Philosophy isn't attractive any more."

"And politics?"

"That isn't attractive either."

"What is, then?"

"Nothing . . . Art . . . Metaphysics . . ."

"Or terrorism, perhaps? Anyhow, present society doesn't share
your views, my dear."

"Who knows?"

"Do you think women are going to put up with it?"

"No, but if the phenomenon occurs they must have had something to do with it . . . Something must have slowed down somewhere . . ."

"What about their liberation?"

"If that's what it really is!"

"Well, it's better than what *God* has to offer, isn't it? I saw a film recently about the way the Soviet revolution has liberated the women of central Asia . . . It's extraordinary . . . All those women throwing their veils on the fire . . . Their chadors . . . Think about Iran . . . Frightful . . . How can *you* have any hesitations about it? Or else what are we talking about?"

"Of course . . . I just wonder if we're not always changing from one false god to another . . ."

"Well, the so-called real one has spoken . . . And what he says is eloquent enough to justify any kind of oppression . . ."

"Is god a woman-hater, then?"

"And how!"

No doubt . . . No doubt . . . Nothing's more obvious . . . But how can I explain to her that the much-vaunted absence of god could be just as misogynous . . . In another way . . . With the inevitable updatings . . . She'll never admit it . . . Nor will anyone else . . . But I can hardly tell her she's just enjoyed making love thanks to god's indirect, discreet, and professional intervention . . . Bad taste . . . Must be a gentleman . . . But that's the idea of which I've just given a practical demonstration . . .

The Chairwoman leans toward me over her tea:

"Tell me, did you take part in any political movements ten years ago?"

"A little . . . From a distance . . . Verbally . . . The 'Maoist' affair . . ."

"But I've been told you were really committed! Very 'red'! The complete Stalinist!"

"It was the way people amused themselves at the time . . . China . . . Romanticism . . ."

"But some of them took it very seriously . . . I think you're being rather frivolous . . ."

"I suppose I must have signed or written some pretty incendiary stuff."

"Exactly! That's what I was told . . . You've been trying to hold out on me! Anyhow, it seems you made some fierce enemies in those days . . . Who are now, as you may suppose, close to the powers-that-be . . . I've heard some very severe things said about you, my dear . . . Amusing though, I must admit, for anyone who knows you . . . Things about you and that friend of yours—the avant-garde author . . . What's his name, now?''

"S.?"

"That's it . . . The hermetic one . . . Unreadable . . . The one who writes without any punctuation . . . People call you both all the names they can lay their tongues on, you know . . .''

Ah, so there *was* some reason behind our date . . . It wasn't totally disinterested . . . I screw, but I'm kept under observation . . . It's understood that I'm free to come and go, but I'm supposed to need support, my social life is vulnerable . . . And who is it who's been looking out for me? Yes, I see . . . Michel, the banker who's also a leftist and a poet . . . That episode with his wife's girlfriend . . . And the nonepisode with the wife herself . . . "The men toss off the laws," Céline said, "and the women shape public opinion . . .'' Marie-France . . . Was I still a bachelor? Or was it when no one knew yet that Deb and I were married? Anyway . . . Marie-France took a shine to me . . . We went out together, with her husband and various friends . . . She was a middle-class girl from *Alsace* with pale tow-colored hair, peevish and a martyr to migraines . . . She was trying to get off with me . . . I remember dancing a slow foxtrot with her one evening in a night club, and her driving her right knee straight into my balls . . . Persistently . . . A declaration . . . Urgent . . . I thought she was going to stave me in completely . . . As for me: nothing . . . A big mistake! The ignorance of youth! However, Marie-France had a friend . . . A fat, curvaceous little girl with chestnut hair . . . I forget her name . . . Oh yes, I believe it was Martine . . . And late one night I find myself dead drunk on her bed . . . Naked . . . I open one eye . . . She's in the bathroom . . . Super-chic apartment in the avenue Foch . . . Her riding clothes are strewn over a chair . . . I can't remember anything much . . . She comes back in a nightgown . . . I see everything in a flash and shut my eyes again . . . She settles down and goes to sleep . . . And the next day, lo and behold, she has a set of hi-fi equipment delivered at my place . . . We must have talked about music over dinner, what sort of system have you got, oh just an ordinary setup, and so on . . . Three days later she booked a couple of airline tickets for a weekend in Cairo . . . The Pryamids! *Son et Lumière!* Honeymoon chez Isis! I decline . . . She writes to me . . . Makes a date in a bar . . . Where who should arrive but Michel and Marie-France . . . Mediation—Marriage! But it doesn't work! Marie-France looks daggers at me . . . She and Martine had arranged it all between them . . . Together with all their acquaintance . . . I was to marry the one . . . To satisfy the other . . . And be the husband's friend . . . I'd liven up their anemic relationship . . . And then the apartments I'd have! The tennis courts! Longchamp! Providing an intelligent background . . . Golf! Juan-les-Pins! The Mamounia in Marrakesh! The Sahara Palace! And the left into the bargain! Since I tended to belong to the extreme left . . . A brilliant and promising young man of the extreme left must join with the left . . . Understand! Mature! See where his responsibilities lie! With the trend of history! The moderate left . . . The genuine left . . . An open Communist Party! Trotskyism with a difference! Evolutionary! Planned! Socialism properly understood! My god, the life I might have been leading now, instead of being automatically classed as belonging to the right but without the slightest support from it . . . And for good reason . . . Never the least offer from *Le Figaro!* Yes, that's what the Chairwoman was getting at . . . What a silly ass I've been! Incorruptible without even knowing it! Not for moral reasons, just out of boredom! Improvidence! Arrogance! The grasshopper having sung all summer . . . Constantly wasting my energies all over the place, at random . . . When the wind began to blow . . . And the worst thing of all! I go and marry a foreigner! For herself! Without any financial cover! And from the East! And beautiful! And intelligent! And not Triolable! And I don't even join that lot! Fit into that slot! The Aragonian! The Sartreuse! And I still go on wasting my energies! And always on women! Curse it! The Furies! So I immediately become a fascist! Drieu la Rochelle! Nazi! Anti-Semite! Underminer of the Republic! Not to be touched with a barge pole! Fanatical! Perverted to the core! All right, that amuses me for a

while . . . I'm giving them what they want . . . I play along a bit
. . . But then everyone starts to take the joke seriously . . . The
little faction, made to look silly, moves heaven and earth against me
. . . I'm the most awful swine ever . . . A virtual Beria . . . A
potential Himmler . . . I'm never invited out any more . . . Quarantine . . . Cordon sanitaire . . . Protect the women! Lock up your
daughters, sisters, sisters-in-law, cousins, aunts, grandmothers! That's
what you get for not being a homosexual! When society gets cross
with you! No excuses! A threat to morals! Raper of Joan of Arc!
Polluter of Elsa! Blasphemer of Simone de Beauvoir! Murderer of
Marie Curie! Torturer of Louise Michel! Corrupter of Mme. de La
Fayette! George Sand! The Princesse de Clèves! Mme. de Sévigné!
Louise Labé! Mme. de Stäel! Christine de Pisan! Rosa Bonheur!
And the Queen's secret lover! An Austrian! A conspirator! We'll
teach you to refuse the Social Contract! Rousseau! France itself!
Rotten Yankee! Half-breed! Imperialist! Irrationalist! Obscurantist!
You'll see what the French spirit is made of! It may have been
hidebound once . . . Now it's progressive . . . Same old story . . .
Catholic scum all converted to masonic-contraceptive trips! From
taking the consecrated wafer to doing pills! Symbolic shoplifting!
Live! Masters of fates! Eternal dreamless bourgeoisie . . .

But let's keep calm . . . What's really happening is that the
Chairwoman is giving me a friendly warning . . . My position at
the Journal isn't good . . . If I understand her correctly, the ground's
being cut from under my feet . . .

"You know," I say, "literature's the only thing I'm really interested in now . . . Everything else strikes me as vague and pointless . . ."

"Literature? What kind of literature?"

I give her a little lecture . . . On the twentieth century . . .
Ulysses . . . 1922 . . . The advent of the protons of perception . . .
Minute shocks . . . Thought by means of feather-light shifts . . .
Molly's monologue . . . The revolution of making a woman talk,
for the first time and in the first person, from within her period . . .
The new art of the word caught as it flies . . . The "spot" . . . The
immediate epic . . . Faulkner . . . The last Céline . . . *Rigodon* . . .

1960 . . . Language after the Second World War . . . Until the next one, which started a long time ago . . . And is spreading before our very eyes . . .

I can see this soon bores her . . . Right, that'll do for today . . . So long . . . We'll meet when we're back . . . After her journeys . . . And mine . . .

This time the Devil comes to see me in person. And talks to me as follows, until further notice:

"Here I sit this twelfth day of August 1766, in scarlet waistcoat and yellow slippers and neither cap nor wig . . ."

Have you recognized him? Laurence Sterne . . .

He's here forever. It's a fine day. He's writing.

The novel's at home with him.

You should bring it back to the same unrestrained lightness . . . Enough of nihilism! Of glumness! Of would-be poetic evasions! The dawn! The sun!

I adore the sallies of these old authors. For example, the "declaration" at the beginning of Lesage's *Gil Blas de Castillane* . . . :

"As there are some who cannot read a book without equating any depraved or ridiculous characters in it with real people, I hereby declare to such ingenious readers that they would be wrong to do so with the portraits in the present work . . . I publicly confess that I have tried to do no more than represent human life as it is . . . God forbid I should have meant to point to anyone in particular! So let no reader apply to himself anything which may apply equally well to others; otherwise, as Phèdre says, he will make himself untowardly conspicuous . . . *Stulte nudabit animi conscientiam.* Anyone who recognizes himself in my portraits will lay bare both his conscience and his folly."

You could use that as an epigraph to your novel even today, couldn't you?

But seriously, perhaps you ought to draw back? Change tack? Confuse the issue? Throw people off the scent? Walk through the

water for a bit? Let's see . . . This book . . . That embarrassing title
. . . Why don't you change it? *Women* is too particular and provocative . . . And at the same time too general . . . Which is limiting,
because after all you don't deal only with women, do you? That
would be at once too much indignity and too much honor . . . Poor
things . . . Why bug them? No reason . . . Especially as they're the
ones who buy books . . . It's not really about them at all, is it? Not
as such . . . It's enough to make people think you've got an obsession . . . What is it you say right at the beginning?

      The world belongs to women.

      In other words, to death.

      But everybody lies about it.

True; very true . . . And no one knows it better than I, the father
of lies . . . Who arranged all this setup so that they may never be
found out . . . So that everything should seem to point in the
wrong direction . . . Especially on this particular subject . . . But
that's the point—it's *too* truthful! Much too rough! A merciless
analysis! They won't swallow it . . . You should never have put
that right at the outset! All the signs are against it . . . Your book
will fall flat . . . Tell a story! Tell a story! That's all—not a word
more! Ragbag! Loading every rift with ore! You were all worked up
when you let that out . . . A bad beginning! And what about the
plot? What exactly is it you want to say? But here—a good idea for
another title! On the same lines, but broader and more ambitious!
"Deeper"!

The End of the World

    Why not? A good peg for the sales people: cashing in on the
modernized version of Nostradamus . . . An appeal to gullibility
. . . There's a sucker born every minute . . . Science fiction sells
like hot cakes . . . People want to know . . . They feel more and
more vulnerable . . . As if they were in some dubious theater that
might burst into flames at any moment . . . Around 1998 . . . Or
1999 . . . Or 2020 . . . Or 3040 . . . It might depend on the latest
preparations going on in the background . . . On the whims of the
atoms here in my hand . . . On the fancies of the quasars . . . On a
dictator with the bomb . . . On a madman . . . On chance . . . Or

—I was forgetting—on the coming of the Messiah . . . Or his second coming! Take your choice . . .

The End of the World
a novel

Bang on!

What? Hasn't anyone thought of it before?

A la recherche du temps perdu . . . The Trial . . . The Sleepwalkers . . . The Man without Qualities . . . The Voyage to the End of Night . . . The Sound and the Fury . . . The Unnamable . . .

So. What about *The End of the World?*

Perfect.

It's clear and comprehensive . . . It covers both crisis and change . . . It's inevitable . . . Surprising you didn't think of it before . . . Especially as it fits in with your plan, which mustn't be revealed to the reader on any account . . . The truth about the woman secret, the secret that comes out through women and does away with the belief that there really is a world or any necessity for it . . . The unmasking of the power of death! Ssh! Don't let the news get out! The good news! The very good news! The Gospel according to St. Discreet!

No more world! No more death!

No more humanity! No more universe! No more anything!

The story ends with you! Last performance! Electrons! Curtain! Thunders of applause! Salvoes!

Or else perhaps *The Key to the Abyss?*

Or *Bordel? Bacchanale? Bliss?*

Or what about *Truth revealed by Time,* as a tribute to your precious Bernini? . . . On second thought, too long.

No, *The End of the World,* fair and square in red capitals in every shop window, just before the end . . .

What about *Apocalypse,* you say? Yes, of course . . . If anyone ever went straight to the heart of the subject it's him . . . With my assistance, by the way . . . And to think I never get any royalties . . . How unfair . . . *The Second Apocalypse?* No. One's enough . . . It still has to be proved; the suspense is a bit dated; but he made an effort . . . Mustn't have any unfair competition . . . *Apoc-*

alypse Now? Hollywood? No, *The End of the World* may seem a bit farfetched and pretentious, but just think of the effect in the middle of all the other books . . . The end of all books . . . What? *The End of the World?* Neither more nor less? Just that . . . You'll be sitting pretty . . . And it'll hardly have cost you anything . . .

We all look up to St. John . . . Are you surprised to hear me say that? If you only knew! Listen: "So he carried me away in the spirit into the wilderness: and I saw a woman sit upon a scarlet colored beast, full of names of blasphemy, having seven heads and ten horns . . . And the woman was arrayed in purple and scarlet color, and decked with gold and precious stones and pearls, having a golden cup in her hand full of abominations and filthiness of her fornication . . . And I saw the woman drunken with the blood of the saints, and with the blood of the martyrs of Jesus . . ."

"Hey! Steady on!" say I.

The Devil stops . . . I can't see him . . . Only hear . . . He's got a soft but energetic voice . . .

"All right," he says . . . "Stick to *Women,* if you insist! But don't say I didn't warn you! It won't help sales . . . But don't expect any help from me! And remember I control all the media and the publicity . . ."

He disappears.

I wake up . . . Open my *Book of Revelation:*

"And the angel saith unto me, The waters which thou sawest, where the whore sitteth, are peoples, and multitudes, and nations, and tongues . . . Reward her even as she rewarded you, and double unto her double according to her works: in the cup which she hath filled fill to her double . . ."

The apostle's certainly worked up! There's no stopping him! A really radical novelist . . . In the beginning was the Word . . . And at the end, the victory of the Word that was at the Beginning . . . Despite all the plots and "ends" thought up on the way . . . Showing on every screen . . . The Beast, the Dragon, the False Prophet . . . And the flower that blooms on their triple grave: the Whore . . . A single force from beginning to end of the alphabet . . . "I am Alpha and Omega, the beginning and the end, the first and the last

. . . Blessed are they that do his commandments, that they may have right to the tree of life, and may enter in through the gates into the city . . . For without are dogs, and sorcerers, and whore-mongers, and murderers, and idolaters, and whosoever loveth and maketh a lie . . ."

That's a hell of a lot of people thrown out!

And more and more!

Why do you authors write? That guy at least had an answer.

But that reminds me of something . . . A sequence from an orgy in New York . . . I found myself with a girl in the can; she was sitting on the toilet, naked . . . She'd just made me come, and her right hand was full of sperm . . . She bent over her hand and brought it slowly up to her eyes as if in some mystical delirium . . . Cocaine? Probably . . . But I can see her drawn face now, suddenly lit up, transmuting and worshipping the whitish liquid . . . Her features were incredibly contorted, as if she were being transported into another world . . . As in an epileptic fit . . . My sperm had become her saliva . . . She was crazy . . . It was one of the few times in my life I've been frightened . . . Really frightened . . . In case she didn't come back . . . In case she was completely consumed by what lay beyond . . . She belonged to a rather curious group . . . A nameless sect . . . A second-hand prostitute, at the service of her mistress's guests . . . I had to wipe her clean, there, with my handkerchief; to wake her up, almost by slapping her . . . It's at times like that that you see; that you glimpse . . . Briefly . . . The twisted features of the Other . . . Unconscious . . . She was asleep . . . Sitting on the john fast asleep . . . And at the same time miming an ageless ritual . . . Priestess-of-the-great-other-side-of-the-picture . . . Now, in the present, right in the middle of town . . . I carried her to the bathroom, moistened her face, found an empty bedroom and laid her on the bed . . . People were screwing all over the place: murmurs, panting, groans . . . I stole away . . . Full moon over Broadway, I remember . . . Babylon . . .

Traveler, give me a summary of your impressions of the world . . . Well, angel, I never met anyone anywhere except barely dis-guised gangs of madmen or potential murderers . . . There—end of survey . . . They certainly *are* crazy, too . . . Raving . . . It happens of its own accord . . . But you mustn't think they know what they belong to . . . What it is they're members of . . . Do you want a dictionary definition? Clear and mathematical? Here you are, then: you can recognize someone who's possessed by the devil by the fact that he thinks nothing is external to him . . . Is that madness? Look at it and see . . .

I rerun them . . . Try to go over them in my mind . . . See if there isn't one here and there that might be saved . . . I hesitate a little . . . No . . . Vanity . . . Mist . . .

They're hooked . . . Dope . . . Toss of the chin at eye level . . . Pose . . . Impose . . .

And I'm sorry to say that behind this arrogant, insistent, grotesque illness you always without exception find the old, so old, anonymous feminine thing . . . Its innate hollow swelling . . . Hysteria is only a detail, a tiny blister on the deep enveloping surface . . . It's here that they endlessly look at themselves in the glass, bask and embrace . . . Themselves and nothing but themselves, more and more, forever . . .

Hence the symmetrical accusation leveled at anyone who tries to escape from this business of the egg . . . That he's a monster of egotism, heartlessness, and pride . . .

I can see Bernadette now, always blaming me for being narcissistic at the same time as she, with a mixture of anxiety and satisfaction, continually seeking her own reflection in the mirror . . . An emblem of the whole epic . . .

It's enough to make you die laughing . . . Just because I don't enter into the game . . . The empire of debt . . . Of alleged reciprocity . . .

Whenever some mannered stereotype gives free rein to his own self-satisfaction and naiveté, just open your eyes and watch . . . It's terrible . . . Funny . . . Indescribable . . . Yes — it's Her making her appearance again, even in the case of the most self-controlled man . . . Not a shadow of doubt . . . The great imaginary Whore is there, preening and showing off, not suspecting for a moment that

302

she might be observed and reduced to atoms . . . The great immortal Peacock! Léon!

Queers or not, it's all the same . . . They all reach the same point of feminization at one time or another . . . It's the Law . . .

There's nothing but women . . . You might equally well say there aren't any women at all . . . That would be amusing, wouldn't it?—all this talk for nothing . . . All this sound and fury for a stolen handkerchief!

You can see why the Chosen People and the Church call themselves, in their different ways, the brides of god . . . The laments of the prophets . . . Infidelities . . . Is god a woman-hater? Yes, insofar as he tries not to be just human . . . The least he can do . . .

What about the order in which the Prophet himself lists his preferences? Mohammed? Peace be upon him! "Women, perfume and prayer . . ." That which is intangible, immaterial . . . *An-nisa* . . . Quickly over . . . In ascending order of importance, I presume . . . That's quite amusing . . . The Koran is full of humor . . . For example: "If a husband repudiates his wife three times he may not marry her again until she has married another husband and been repudiated by him . . . There is no sin then for either husband or wife if they are reconciled in the belief that they can keep God's commandments." Or again: "Husbands are superior to their wives. God is mighty and wise." Let us pray that the Prophet may once more be listened to on this subject! Pious hope! Shakespeare! Molière! The Shrew tamed! The Précieuses made less ridiculous!

Anyhow, I can take my stand on Sura 113, the one before the last, *The Dawn of Day:*

I take refuge in Allah, Master of the dawn,
Against the evil of that which He has created,
And against the evil of darkness when it falls,
And against the evil of the women who breathe upon the knots
And against the evil of the envious man when he envies.

I'm struck by the fact that the Arabic word *falaq* means both "dawn" and "slit" . . . God, master of the slit, the female genitals

. . . The witches breathing on the knots, the penises . . . Envy as the principle of evil . . . And that opening . . . No need to keep on about it . . . He that hath ears, let him hear . . . That's my favorite sura . . . It protects me . . . God is compassionate and merciful! He knows my heart . . . He knows everything . . .

I leave for New York again . . . This time Lynn is there to meet me at Kennedy Airport . . . Cyd's in San Francisco, she'll be back tomorrow; we go to her place . . . Lynn's just passing through too, giving a lecture on Faulkner at the university . . . I go for a walk on my own . . . Find my pier on the Hudson . . . It's winter, a fine day but cold . . . I run . . . I come to the end of the great empty raft . . . I start to shout, and go on for a quarter of an hour, yelling all by myself . . . The sparkling gray water laps against the wooden piles . . .

I invite Lynn to dinner . . . We go and have clams at One Fifth . . . Then go back to Cyd's place . . . We don't make love; we listen to some music . . . We do kiss a bit, though . . . I like her light brown hair, her hands . . .

Next day Cyd takes us to see some friends of hers . . . Cocaine and heroin right on the table . . . White streaks . . . Little lines . . . Celluloid straws . . . They sniff . . . Stuff their sinuses . . . Three punk guys and three punk girls . . . Cyd's brought some good hash with her . . . Afghan . . . Long live the Afghan resistance! Someone talks about the war there . . . Chemical weapons used by the Soviets . . . Biological warfare . . . One of the guys has read some articles . . . The next world conflict really will be fun . . . The bacillus of pulmonary anthrax . . . Encephalitis . . . Botulism . . . Typhus . . . Various fevers . . . Yellow . . . Brown . . . Paralysis . . . Asphyxia . . . Aerosols causing millions of deaths in ten minutes . . . Sprayed from the air . . . Death by diffusion, respiration, suggestion . . . Experiments already being carried out in Asia . . . Laos . . . Cambodia . . .

The conversation drifts on to communication . . . "They talk about whales singing," says one of the guys, "but we still don't know what it really is or means. The sounds cover a wide range of frequencies, and go down below what the human ear can hear. A typical song lasts about fifteen minutes; the longest lasts an hour. They often repeat themselves exactly, bar for bar and note for note. Sometimes, when the whales leave the waters where they spend the winter, they break off in the middle of a song, and then, when they come back six months later, take it up again at the exact note where they left off. But usually they change their tune after they've been away. Members of the same group often sing the same tune, all together."

"Old Melville would have loved that," I say.

"Melville?" says one of the punk girls.

"And do you know," continues the whale expert, "how many units of information a virus needs? About ten thousand. A page in a book."

"It depends which book," I say.

"And a bacterium?" he goes on. "A million. A hundred printed pages. And an amoeba? Four hundred million—eighty volumes of five hundred pages each. And a human being? A hundred thousand billion, corresponding to the number of connections between the neurons in the brain. Twenty million volumes."

"So when a biped dies it's like the loss of the Alexandria library?" I say.

"Worse!" says the guy. "Fantastic, isn't it?"

"The Alexandria library?" says the other punk girl . . .

And so on . . . What an evening . . . Cyd and Lynn and I go home . . . We all go to bed . . . Cyd is tired, and leaves it all to Lynn . . . She sucks us both off at length, one after the other, while Cyd makes love to me . . . She comes first, while Lynn is licking her . . . Then Cyd pushes her away and takes her place, and Lynn starts kissing me, looking straight into my eyes while I come in Cyd's mouth . . . Then it's my turn to suck Lynn off . . . She comes very fast, very juicy but discreet . . .

We all fall suddenly asleep . . . Then I'm having coffee in the bright sun . . . They talk about their own little concerns as they drink their tea . . . Natural and goodhumored, as if nothing had happened . . . So it can be like this . . . One time in a hundred thousand . . . Shade, peace, quiet river . . . Brief encounters . . . Fortunately we all have to part . . . That's the whole secret . . .

Lynn shuts herself away to revise her lecture . . . "The revolution of time in *The Sound and the Fury*" . . . Faulkner's letters to Joan Williams, his last young woman friend, have just been published . . . 1951, 1952 . . .

No comment . . . The classic pattern . . . Lynn showed me her lecture . . . Correct and academic . . . The quotations are the best parts, of course . . . Sublime and inimitable Faulkner: "The paternal blood hates, full of love and pride, while the maternal blood, full of hatred, loves and cohabits." Or this: "It is this that one wants to say while one talks of time's bosom: the agony and despair of the bone that grows, the rigid circle that encompasses the outraged entrails of events." Parallels, balanced phrases, sweeping ellipse, sexual awareness of death . . .

I go shopping with Cyd on Fifth Avenue . . . We lunch at the 666 . . .

"Why do you stay on in Paris?" she asks . . . "It obviously suits you better here . . ."

"I'm practically French now . . ."

"No, you're not! You know very well you're not!"

"Maybe . . . Anyhow, that's how things have worked out . . ."

Her "no!" was very emphatic. She laughs and kisses me.

"How's your novel coming along?"

"Not too badly, but I wonder if I'll ever really be able to tell a story . . ."

"In that case, drop it! The story's crucial . . . Beginning, development, continuation, end . . . Otherwise no point . . . A novel is a film . . . A film is a certain number of dollars . . . The dollar prescribes the sort of novel it wants . . . Period . . . The rest is literature! Sorry!"

"I know . . . What's the rate of the dollar today?"

"Six francs eighty . . ."

"Nearly twice what it was three years ago!"

"Right . . . Anyhow, darling, you don't have anything in common, do you, with all these sophisticated intellectuals they invite over to ornament the University? What do they call it? The "nouveau roman"? That old gimmick for the profs? Why don't you really do some work? Life is very livable here, you can take it from me . . . You'd be a great success . . . People would recognize you right away . . . Everything is physical here . . . And you *are* physical . . ."

It's true I do breathe more freely as soon as I'm back on this side of the Atlantic . . . And that here no one bothers you too much about where you come from and what you think . . . Apart from the "European" requirement, of course . . . Presence is what matters . . . Either you have it or you don't . . . Presence and eloquence . . . Originality, energy, and conviction inevitably attract attention . . . Whereas in France . . . Reserve, thrift . . .

"The French will never really accept you," Cyd goes on . . . "They're the most xenophobic and naturally racist people on earth . . . Despite appearances and noble principles . . . So don't forget it . . . The coldest, sourest, and most unwelcoming of nations . . . France is a very agreeable place to live, I agree . . . But they're prejudiced against us . . . Especially us English . . . Joan of Arc . . . Napoleon . . . St. Helena . . . Fashoda . . . Mers-el-Kebir . . . Hello, London calling . . . The French speaking to the French! They're embarrassed as soon as an Englishman appears . . . Like a ghost . . . Guilt . . . Superiority and inferiority complex . . . Shakespeare . . . I expect it comes from their going over and over their famous Revolution at school . . . My first is French . . . My second is German . . . My third is Russian . . . And my whole?"

"Yugoslavian!" I say . . . "Yugoslavia is the ultimate form . . . Do you know what Chateaubriand says? 'Malevolence and denigration are the two chief characteristics of the French mind.' "

"But seriously, don't you think you're wasting your time in Paris?"

"Perhaps . . ."

"It would be easy to get you transferred here, you know . . . I can talk to the *New York Times* . . ."

Hmm, this is the first time Cyd's taken such a close interest in my future . . . Watch out . . .

"You know," I say, "everywhere's as livable or unlivable as everywhere else these days . . . New York . . . Paris . . . Rome . . . It's moving about that matters . . . As if you lived in the TV news . . ."

"Okay . . ."

We go on walking for a bit . . .

I pick up a taxi outside St. Patrick's . . . She stands there, slim, fine and golden in her gray suit . . . A wave of the hand . . . The taste of her skin is still in my mouth . . . Shall I tell the driver to stop? No . . . She vanishes into the crowd . . .

A cocktail party in Paris . . . For Burgess . . . So his book, *The Power of Darkness,* has caused a stir . . . My subject . . . Which he's approached from the other point of view . . . I suppose that's what they're fêting him for . . . He predicts the fall of the Papacy . . . Vatican II an instrument of the Devil . . . I go over to him . . . He looks strange . . . Hunched up . . . Doesn't look people in the eye . . . Absent . . . I ask him what in his opinion is the most important thing that's happened recently . . .

"The hundredth anniversary of Joyce's birth?"

"Certainly," I say . . . "But there's probably something more important still . . ."

I show him a page of the *New York Times,* which I've brought with me . . . The news I mean is the resumption of official relations between England and the Vatican . . . For the first time since 1534 . . . When Rome refused to recognize Henry VIII's divorce from Catherine of Aragon and his remarriage to Anne Boleyn . . . We're moving toward the reunification of the Christian Churches . . . The Protestantization of the Catholics? On the contrary! The Roman

Church is making great strides everywhere . . . The end of the Reformation . . .

He pulls a face. He's furious.

"I don't like this Pope," he says. "Too political!"

"Yes, isn't he?" says Kate, who's just joined us.

"Do you think so?" I say.

"Too political! Too political!"

"Yes, isn't he? Yes, isn't he?" yells Kate.

Burgess slips off. He wants to drink his cocktail in peace. He couldn't care less. Oh yes he could. He's had enough trouble already, being accepted despite being a Catholic. He apologizes for it. Spends all his time doing so. It's fashionable now to be nostalgic for the splendid Latin liturgies from before the Council . . . The fundamentalists? No, it's the progressives who feed you that, adding that the Church has gone too far in accommodating itself to the world . . . Strange . . . Right in the middle of the Polish affair . . . Of the sweeping away from the hierarchy of the old anti-Semitic fuddy-duddies . . . Of fire and slaughter everywhere . . . Strange, strange . . .

Burgess looks at me suspiciously . . . He thought I'd be interested when he mentioned Joyce . . . I'm a confounded nuisance . . . Trying to provoke him . . .

"But it *is* interesting, isn't it," I say, "that the whole of the Reformation turns on fusses about marriage . . . Luther . . . Calvin . . . All wanting to get married! What an idea!"

"You're not against priests marrying, are you?" Kate bawls at Burgess. "And you don't agree with the Church's attitude to contraception, I hope? Or on abortion? Or homosexuality?"

I move away. The usual script. The Roman, Catholic, Apostolic Church, sprung from the Gospel and Peter, is supposed to approve of mankind's fiddling with its genitals . . . Whereas the Church's basic principle is to lay down limits in the matter . . . As if that were the most important thing! As if sex wasn't a disability! Whether severe or slight depending on your talents . . . Admittedly we have to put up with it . . . And have to get around it as best we can . . . But to turn it into a value! And then to ask the institution concerned

309

with celestial things to legitimize the error! Curiouser and curiouser . . .

I leave and drop in at the bar of the Port-Royal for a drink, on
my own . . . More writers . . . Gabriel Garcia Marquez, sitting
between a great dark cow of a woman with an imperial expression
and a crouching and respectful little reporter who's interviewing
him . . . William Styron's at the bar with a tall redhead . . . Garcia
Marquez looks like an ex-*vaquero* who's acquired a hacienda . . .
Navy blue peacoat, sailor's cap, respectable . . . Styron's in a lum-
ber jacket, like an elderly student, relaxed, a bit soft, feminine . . .
Plenty of charm . . . We met at some friends' place in New York
. . . He gives me a wink . . .

Burgess's success is based on Rome . . . Garcia Marquez's is
based on the third world — Latin America and Cuba . . . Styron's
on the South, and more recently on Auschwitz . . . Best-sellers . . .
I look at them with interest — and with liking . . . Writers are
likable . . . When you know the effort it takes to stay on the page
in spite of everyone and everything . . . Of the three, Styron is the
one who's safest and most comfortable . . . America! Dollars!

There are also some Swedes, talking loudly and without a pause
. . . A bit drunk . . . Ya! Yo! Yow! and Ya again! And Yow! Yô!
In every possible tone . . . Officials . . . I keep catching the word
"Nobel . . ." It must be a summit meeting . . . The names of some
French writers crop up . . . They laugh . . . Grimace . . . Yô! Yow!
They talk about the Archbishop of Paris . . . His Jewish origins . . .
Lustiger! Lousstiguerr! Yô! Yow! Yewd? Yô! And then off they go
again, back on literature, I suppose . . . The Nobel Prize . . . Yow!
Yô! Ya! Yao! Yô . . .

But hey, who's that over there on her own in the corner? Yes, it
is . . . It's Diane . . . Tragic, splendid, black dress, blonde hair . . .
My heart misses a beat . . . Our eyes meet . . . She turns away
. . . A couple of minutes later she's joined by a guy . . . A former
student of Fals's . . . The shrink network . . . They leave . . .

Well, so here I am, more on my own than ever, huh? A surge of
delight . . . I'm slightly tipsy . . . Another glass of champagne in
honor of the mixing-up of time zones . . . Of the tribulation of the

absurd . . . Of role-swapping . . . Of whirligig of identity . . . Everything breaking down? Good! At last we'll find out what holds up . . .

Another glass of champagne . . . Then I go back to my studio, get up again about midnight, work till three in the morning and go and have dinner in my night spot in Montparnasse . . . A kind of bar-cum-snack-bar that stays open till dawn . . . Long and narrow, murky as an aquarium, patronized almost exclusively by the local tarts . . . No intellectuals here . . . Not a sign of a "personality" . . . That's the way to approach Paris—in the depths of the night . . . Never mind the days and the evenings . . . I go home at about four in the morning through the narrow, deserted streets . . . After an omelette and a half-bottle of Bordeaux . . . This is the time for the drag queens in the boulevard Raspail . . . Just after that of the one-night hotels in the rue Sainte-Beuve and the rue Chaplain . . . The Wistaria . . . The Hydrangeas . . . Small places, comfortable and discreet . . . Shutters fastened on the ground floor . . . Everyone asleep . . . Men and women . . . At the Vavin intersection, Rodin's statue of Balzac, lit up . . . Balzac keeps watch . . . No one sees him . . . There he is, recoiling like another Moses amazed by an apparition of God . . . At the foot of Mount Sinai . . . The mountain of books he wrote . . . Against the stream of all Paris, rushing toward the Seine along the darkened river of the boulevard . . . A bronze monk . . . Every so often a kid comes and pees on his plinth . . . Great nineteenth-century phallus . . . The human comedy . . . In the rustle of paper . . . Ah yes, the "courtesans"! Another word that's disappeared, together with the thing it denoted . . . Like "splendor" . . . Though "woe" survives all right . . . The splendor and woe of the courtesans . . . The disappearance and woe of the disappeared . . . "Woe"—there's a word with a future . . . And not only in the physical sense . . . Never obsolete . . .

What's novel in New York is the way the intelligentsia of the pro-Soviet lobby have run out of steam . . . Or at least become less vehement . . . Change of fashion . . . Helen has even made a statement about Poland . . . She's discovered there's no longer any excuse for communism . . . That after all it may only be another form of fascism . . . Hallelujah! Storm among the skyscrapers! Devaluation of the ruble-rouser! It's difficult to imagine how much cultivated Americans doted on Russia . . . The Russian revolution . . . Think of the trouble Nabokov had in the States with the local celebrities, journalists, and academics . . . In the fifties . . . And how Jakobson objected to his teaching at Harvard . . . I knew the good old linguist, and so did S. . . . He often used to talk to me about Mayakovsky . . . A whole era . . . Formalism, futurism . . . The Moscow circle . . . The Prague circle . . . The science of literature . . . Phonology . . . The same thing in painting, sculpture, and architecture . . . Malevitch, Lissitsky . . . The modern age . . . A new alphabet . . . A clean slate, go back to the beginning and build a new world that's more harmonious, more democratic, more spiritual and more fundamental . . . Minimal art . . . Anonymous . . . Each individual being everybody at once . . . The life of the atoms . . . Icons replaced by cones . . . Puritanism . . . As if Italy had never existed . . . The negation of Rome, Florence, Venice . . . That's the whole point! The American revival . . . Civilization ex nihilo! Functional . . . Culturism, machinism, scientism, mysticism . . . Visionary nuts . . . Trans-mentals . . . Rhetoric taken for truth . . . Pure contemplation . . . The Immaculate Concept . . .

All this has been endlessly thought over, meditated, sold . . . And thought over, meditated, sold again . . . But it seems the prices have got stuck . . . Have even started to fall . . . Under the impact of television! The first signs have been seen at Sotheby's . . . Kandinsky stationary . . . The Mondrian market saturated . . . Malevitch falling . . . Counterattack by Picasso . . . Italy via Spain! It was bound to happen . . . Rembrandt stands firm . . . El Greco is back again . . . A boom in Delacroix . . . Yes, yes, *Sardanapalus* . . . "I've been told," writes Baudelaire, "that for his *Sardanapalus* Delacroix made a number of marvelous studies of women in the most voluptuous attitudes. . ." A crimson miscellany on the imminent pyre . . . The paintbrush twisted in the bodies . . . A scarlet meditation on the vanity of the senses . . . The Thinker contemplating the chaotic flood of the libido . . . The great drowning . . . Sade's fevered nonchalance . . . Sadanapalus! Go to the Louvre! Reread Baudelaire! Jump to it!

VI

IV

The first thing I see when I go out next day are the big headlines! Boris kidnapped! By FRAW, the Front for Revolutionary Action in the West . . . So that was his scoop! He certainly organized it all in a masterly fashion . . . Just after a prime time appearance on television . . . He disappears during the night . . . The next day the media are full of it . . . The police are on alert . . . The telexes splutter . . . Fame! Exactly what he wanted . . . Fantastic! FRAW issues its demands . . . The government must resign . . . Notre Dame is to be transformed into a countercultural center . . . All religions are to be abolished immediately . . . Diplomatic relations with the imperialist United States are to be broken off . . . Russia is to be asked to finish off the Polish clergy once and for all . . . The State of Israel is to be dissolved . . . There are photos of Boris everywhere . . . The TV news bulletins show extracts from his interviews . . . His wife appears, in tears . . . His mother says the kidnappers needn't expect a penny from his family, and that he himself is ruined . . . His elderly father, who has a bad heart, is dragged along to press conferences . . . In three days the thing has grown to international proportions . . . The President is questioned about it during his visit to Gabon . . . "Monsieur le Président, ten years ago, when you were still a member of the opposition, during your long, long march to power, you wrote that Boris Fafner was a dazzling poet, another Rimbaud . . . Do you still think that? And will you allow France to lose such an important personality? Will you sacrifice the greatest writer of his generation to political considerations?" The President gives a little cough, "live" . . . Says everything possible is being done to find Boris . . . That every citizen has equal rights . . . This is a bit cool vis-à-vis Rimbaud . . . Still, the media hype has been launched . . . The grosser it is the better it works . . . Boris Fafner was just finishing his sixth novel, *The Eternal Feminine*, a book glorifying the rediscovery of love . . . Influenced by Wagner . . . A great song of tenderness and gratitude to the eternal woman . . . "Yes," he told us, "I want to go against the tide of an age in decay . . . To bring back the old, timeless values . . . I'm thinking about the younger generation, mocked and deceived . . . I want to give them back the right to hope . . . And despair that is lucid and positive . . . Gide lied when he said you couldn't make good literature out of noble sentiments . . . I prove the opposite is true, by reconciling life with the ideal . . ." Magnificent! The supreme provocation . . . Passing himself off as a Holy Joe . . . The typist's Parsifal . . . The women's magazines are behind him immediately . . . A man who lays down his arms . . . Who acknowledges his fundamental impotence in face of the unfathomable mystery of life . . . The police soon say FRAW is probably a small group belonging to the extreme right . . . Better and better! Boris is now a victim from the left . . . Despite the protests of the intellectuals, who maintain it's all a hoax, Boris is on the front page for a week . . . He eclipses the real news . . . The Falklands . . . The fluctuations of the franc . . . The President's visit to Africa . . . The terrorist attack in the rue Marboeuf, and its genuine victims . . . The triumph of fiction over fact . . . I tremble for a moment when I read that when Boris came out of the Brasserie Lipp, just before he disappeared, he had a date with an American journalist . . . A hint aimed at me! I expect to be questioned by the police . . . But no, nothing happens . . . At the *Journal* everyone thinks it's a great gas, but it helps sales . . . Just like the French!

After ten days, when everyone is starting to get rather anxious just the same, or afraid his charming old old-school Papa might get one of his big toes through the mail, he coolly reappears . . . Makes a number of contradictory statements . . . Issues various confused explanations . . . This time the reporters get angry . . . Insult him a little, as a matter of form . . . That starts it all off again . . . Froth of ages . . . Good prepublicity for *The Eternal Feminine* . . . The eternal pubicist . . .

"Hello? Hello? Will you write an article defending me? Say I'm first and foremost a great writer?"

"Sure, sure, old boy . . . But it'll have to be later . . . I'm just leaving . . ."

"What, again? But surely you've time for three or four pages before you go?"

"Afraid not . . ."

"Manage it somehow and I'm your friend forever! You can ask me anything!"

"Terribly sorry . . . But I think I've got a good title for an article about you: *In praise of Imposture* . . . In an ultrafalse world, only the height of falsehood can tell the truth about falsehood . . . You get the idea . . ."

"Splendid! Write it! I'll have it picked up tomorrow! For *Scratch!*"

"Unfortunately I'm just leaving for the airport . . ."

"When you get back, then?"

"Yes, yes . . . We'll see . . ."

Boris redeploys his efforts in other directions . . . The case becomes confused . . . He sues his detractors . . . Issues further noble statements . . . Attacks the commentators . . . Talks about god . . . Implicates the Syrians . . . The Libyans . . . The Palestinians . . . The Armenians . . . The Israelis . . . The Cubans . . . But it all dies down a bit just the same . . . The usual old subjects revive . . . Cinema . . . Unions . . . It's pathetic, really . . . Boris and his mania to be recognized as a "great writer . . ." By fair means or foul . . . As if it were still possible for the masses to worship someone who's the incarnation of literature . . . Like Victor Hugo! He's very nineteenth-century, Boris . . . But that's all over . . . Forever . . . Though it goes on more than ever in the form of farce . . . He's still stuck in the groove you go for when you're fifteen . . . The modern Rimbaud! Junk! The grimy, ignorant purity of adolescents that thinks itself sublime . . . He struggles . . . And a whole backward society struggles with him . . . Horrified to discover its own accurate reflection . . . But all is not lost . . . He only needs to play the suffering child . . . Not to mention the touch about feminine mystery . . . *Le Lys dans la vallée* . . . The Lady of Shalott . . . It works like a charm . . .

S. has known Boris for ages . . . They were friends when they were twenty . . . No one knows more about French literary and political circles than S. does . . . But he's left all that behind now . . . He leads a life that's quite remote . . . But he doesn't complain . . . Or only a little, sometimes . . . He can't be bothered . . . True, he's finished up in a sort of ghetto, scarcely tolerated and not even well off . . . Internal exile . . . But he considers that natural and inevitable . . . Still on his everlasting *Comedy* . . .

There was some murky affair between him and Boris at the time of the Algerian war . . . When they started their little avant-garde revue . . . Which is now, thanks to S.'s grim perseverance, a kind of international institution . . . It has published the best work of Werth, Lutz, Fals, and many others . . . Established their reputations . . . And it still goes on, thus ceaselessly incurring the resentment of the establishment . . . At the time I mentioned Boris did all be could to get the revue away from S. . . . Including (in collusion with his own father, a prefect under the Vichy government) getting him sent into the Algerian desert . . . On the Tunisian frontier . . . Where people were dying like flies . . . It was only Malraux's personal intervention that got S. out of that . . . One of his closest friends was killed out there in the mountains . . . S. often tells me there are two key periods in the history of modern France: 1940–1942, the great secret, and 1958–1962, the discreet cancer . . . But there are links between the two . . . anti-Semitism, nationalism . . . Censureship, silence . . . Equivocation . . . According to S., Boris is the product par excellence of the bourgeoisie than . . . A bourgeoisie in rapid decline . . . And replaced by nothing . . . That's the whole problem . . . Hence the crisis in "values," the prevalence of corruption, the increase in intellectual and spiritual emptiness, the rise of technology . . . Add to that the crash of the great Stalinist bank, and the circle's complete . . .

S. shows me an article in which he's attacked by Frank Cressel, the leading writer of *Le Jour* . . . Yet another . . . Cressel is the ladies' favorite writer . . . They find him touching, sensitive, marvelous, madly witty . . . He likes to talk about his own fads, the sort of cooking he likes, his visits to provincial hotels . . . He's so *French* . . . And as he's also Jewish and has a sense of humor—i.e., slips in subtle touches of anti-Semitism—they're in raptures! Like Proust! Just like Proust! they all cry . . . Sooner or later everything ends in "like Proust," in France . . . Perhaps one ought to write in Proustspeak . . . This time Cressel complains that S. is in Larousse . . . Or Hachette . . . Or Robert . . . He thinks it's not fair that he, little Frank, isn't in the encyclopedia too . . . With his photo . . . In color! That's what's always the hardest to get . . . The equivalent of a portrait in oils . . . Like Proust, painted by Jacques-Emile Blanche! The camphor oval of the face . . . The dandy drained white by his knowledge of night . . . The pervert who has given it up because it's too tiring . . . The nonchalant, detached observer looking down on the doings of humanity, knowing exactly what to say, and when, and to which shockable, postwar little petite-bourgeoise . . . A sports car whenever required . . . Two or three country houses . . . Little bursts of stifled laughter . . . A way of swallowing one's words, as people used to do when there really was a sixteenth arrondissement . . . Cressel is the local good Jew, one with the right kind of moderate self-hatred and self-pity . . . The living proof, almost stuffed already, that there won't be any reprisals over the great question that preoccupied French literature in the late nineteenth and twentieth centuries . . . You know what I mean . . . The question that culminates in the Vel d'Hiv'—the rounding up of the Jews in a sports stadium in July 1942 . . . It's a salubrious weekly pleasure to see how much Frank Cressel loves our beautiful country . . . Its native refinement . . . Its moralist tradition . . . An adapted Saint-Simon . . . An oddball Saint-Beuve . . . An instant La Bruyère . . . Chardonne! The gratuitous little dig that goes pschttt! A skipping Voltaire . . . Giraudoux! He can count on the affection of all the den mothers of the "supplements" . . . The "launcher of books . . ." He conquers them like the nice, harmless bachelor that he is . . . With his whims . . . Goodness, how unpredictable he is! And so funny! Sometimes grumpy and grouchy, and then all of a sudden inexplicably sweet . . . A writer to his finger tips! Of course he hasn't written anything—that's the whole point . . . "Works"—how vulgar! No, an extended childhood is better . . . And pouting . . . Intellectual pouting . . . He really is delightful . . .

You have to understand, says S., that it all operates on closed circuit, carefully supervised . . . The column in *Le Jour* . . . The series in *Le Temps* . . . The colored photo in *Scratch* . . . The relaxed and daring interview in *Male* . . . The sly article in *Peristyle* . . . The exhaustive article in *Retina Magazine* . . . Rightish press masquerading as leftish . . . And vice versa . . . On the right you're supposed to take an interest, whether serious or seemingly frivolous it doesn't matter, in things occult . . . The same on the left, but here it really depends more on whether you belong to the male or female network . . . Woe to anyone who isn't properly resigned or suitably lax . . . Woe to anyone who is too cultivated, or a troublemaker, unless he's a foreigner and lives somewhere else . . . Latin America or South Africa . . . An admirable symbol of universal emancipation . . . Of long-distance humanism . . .

In this little world everyone knows everyone else and everything about them, and makes sure this state of affairs is kept up by means of a day-to-day record of movements, prizes, illnesses, extramural affairs, marital crises and "crushes" . . . As I've said, there's only one condition for being allowed to join in, and that's to have no private life . . . You're just supposed to look pleasant and take part in some way or another in the enlightened prostitution . . . Oh, nothing special . . . Just life . . . The sort of life that hides nothing and leads nowhere . . . Modesty . . . Living and partly living in common . . . One big not very happy family . . .

S. talks lightly about all that for a moment . . . It's of no importance . . . Let's get back to the point . . . He's just home from a festival on the Côte d'Azur . . . Full of enthusiasm about a nightclub called the Divan, where, as happens everywhere at the same time, allowing for date lines, bodies writhe about in the crossfire of spotlights . . . A big screen shows animated cartoons . . . Mickey Mouse . . . The height of fashion . . . S. watched the girls dancing . . . The men don't count any more . . . Just weary robots . . . Clumsy props . . . Overwhelmed by the plants they're supposed to support . . . They only sit around, or, if they dance, try to be girls . . . The opposite of the old wallflower scene . . . The women have taken over; it's they who lead the dance . . . The men are just jerks . . . "But what about the films?" I ask . . . "What films?" "The ones at the Festival!" "Oh yes," he says . . . "No one gives a damn about them, they're just the occasion for making a quick buck, but of course there has to be plenty of blather about them . . . Here, old sport, I've brought you back a gem . . . An article on Antonioni, about his film *Identification of a Woman* . . . Our subject! Our subject! Listen: 'Of course Antonioni's film doesn't succeed in identifying a woman, or women as a whole, completely . . . The character mixes women he comes across in real life with those he meets in his imagination . . . For him, a woman always inhabits the realm of the incomprehensible . . .' According to Antonioni, a man can't understand the whole of a woman's behavior rationally . . . I'm not Stendhal, but I believe the relations between the sexes have always been the central subject of literature . . . And it still will be even when people go and live on other planets! In my view, women probably have deeper powers of perception than men . . . Perhaps what I'm saying is silly, but I think this may be due to the fact that women are used to receiving, in the same way that they receive men inside them, and that pleasure for them consists in this taking in . . . So I suggest women are ready to take in reality in the same wholly feminine way . . . They're better than men at finding solutions to fit different problems . . ."

"Perfect!" I say. "No comment! First prize! Oscar! Palme d'or! Silver penis! Platinum clitoris! Bronze anus! We'll add it to our collection . . . It sums it all up!"

The discriminating reader will have been startled just now to hear

S. use the expression, "old sport . . ." He'll have recognized Gatsby
. . . *The Great Gatsby* . . . Fitzgerald, of course . . . Hi! . . .
Tender is the Night, . . . *The Jazz Age* . . . *A Diamond as Big as the
Ritz* . . . *This Side of Paradise* . . . And the great brief masterpiece,
The Crack-up . . . Francis Scott Fitzgerald . . . The charm of the
twenties . . . Of Irish Catholic origins, by the way . . . Every time
I see Long Island I think of the end of *Gatsby:* "The old island here
that flowered once for Dutch sailors' eyes—a fresh, green breast of
the new world. Women and money . . . Money in their very voices
. . . Daisy . . . The death of Myrtle . . . And that comment on
Jordan—probably the most accurate ever made on a woman: "She
was incurably dishonest. She wasn't able to endure being at a
disadvantage . . . It made no difference to me. Dishonesty in a
woman is a thing you never blame deeply—I was casually sorry,
and then I forgot." Another one who knew better than anyone else
about looking down the barrel of a gun and setting public opinion at
naught . . . His own wife . . . Zelda . . . She wanted to write . . .
To outdo him . . . She went mad . . . Was put away . . . Fitzgerald
died completely forgotten, an alcoholic . . . Posthumous fame . . .
Charm . . .

"And what else have we got in our encyclopedia, my dear Pécuchet?" I ask S.

"Would you care for some recent statistics?"

"Why not?"

"Here you are, then: men die on an average at the age of sixty-
nine; women at seventy-seven. Men commit suicide three times as
often as women."

"Quite understandable . . . Is that all?"

"Would you like to hear the list of treatments available at a
beauty parlor? I regard it as an example of a perfect paragraph.
Linguistically and semantically."

"Go ahead . . ."

"It's a scream . . . The prices are in francs . . .

Cleansing, with face mask or astringent 70
Complete treatment: cleansing, mask, astringent, eyebrows,
    makeup 100

Please inquire about complete sun-tan in VULVA cabin.
Special terms for regular treatments."

"Thanks, my dear fellow . . . Our book's becoming really serious —well documented, sound, indispensable . . . I can hear the protests already: gratuitous monomania, idée fixe, obsessive machismo . . . A propaganda novel! You're right—that list is a poem in itself, truer and more beautiful than all the works of Paul Eluard, René Char, and St. John Perse put together . . . Shall we call our book *Elsa's Beauty Care?*"

"Let's do that, Bouvard, and make our readers really furious! Uncompromising bad taste! History will thank us for it . . ."

"Only in the long run, I fear . . . I can already hear the gnashing of teeth, the writhing of spleens, the hair standing on end . . ."

"What does it matter? We're the pioneers of the new liberty! Poquelin is with us! Molière approves! How well the Jesuits brought him up in their school at Clermont! Molière, or the essence of Jesuit humor! Like Bossuet! What a wilderness it would be without them! What an Orient of boredom!"

"Ready for more, my dear Darwin?"

Now S. really does finish me off . . . He's brought about fifty children's books with him . . . And twenty records . . . Each one more idiotic than the last . . . The Bible for the kiddies . . . Revised by FAM . . . Commissioned by the ministry . . . With an introduction by Eve! "The first Mama in the world!" The whole thing couldn't be more moronic . . . All about how wonderful Mama is

. . . Wherever you look . . . Propaganda . . . Drawings, colors, choruses, and affected, pompous, overemphatic voices: MAMA! MAMA! . . . Enough! I can't take any more . . .

S. collects up his evidence.

"I thought we were working," he says rather stiffly.

"Okay," say I. "But not too realistic, huh?"

"You'd like something more theoretical?"

"I don't know."

"Still," says he, "you could write a chapter on the first commandmant in the religion of psychology . . . The desire of the son for his mother . . . And consequently his hatred of his father . . . Imagine if someone were to explode the idea of the mother as desirable . . ."

"Out of the question," I answer. "The whole of civilization is based on it."

"Yes! Yes! You're right! Incest! The desire for incest! The main thing is to concentrate on that! And whatever you do don't tell us the mother is pitiful and not desirable! Anything but that! The supreme sin! Unforgivable! The law to end all laws! You mustn't reveal that your mother has never been anything but a little girl, doubtful and lost and frankly comic . . ."

"I'm taking this down, Pécuchet. But you really are awful . . ."

"Of course! Especially as after that I saddle you with the SCIG, and in no uncertain manner!"

"We'll cut this bit out before the book's printed, Pécuchet!"

"Oh no, we won't, Bouvard! Science must have its martyrs!"

"You haven't got a bit of publicity to pep it all up?"

"But of course . . . The perfect toilet water! Just the thing for the active narrator. Listen:

" 'The freshness of Z Man revolutionizes all the usual notions of freshness . . . It's smooth . . . Voluptuous . . . Full of crinkly mint, juniper berries, sage, coriander and ylang-ylang . . . A storm of woodland notes with a wicked dash of amber and spice . . .' "

"I like it, Pécuchet! Ylang-ylang! The magic potion! The primal

scent! Sinanthropus! Homo Pekinensis Erectus! Our Bantu progen-
itor! From Lascaux! You win!"

"That's the spirit!" says S. "To work! *Novelist!*"

Deb must be right . . . The book is too rambling . . . I can see
she reads it with pleasure, and without skipping a page or even a
paragraph, but she's stopped talking to me about it afterward . . .
She forgets all about it . . . Is it because of the subject? The way it's
written? She's just told me again that one really does have to have
a story . . . The characters need to *meet* . . . The women characters
ought to see one another. Discuss things . . . Give their opinion
. . . About me? Yes, actually . . .

The narrator ought to be looked at a bit more objectively . . .
Relativized . . . Ridiculed . . .

I try to imagine the scenes . . . The meeting between Flora and
Kate . . . Cacophony! Or between Ysia and Kate? The conversation
wouldn't last three minutes . . . Diane and Deb? I ask you . . .

There's such a thing as a gift for women, just as there is a gift for
languages . . .

And isn't the converse true too? Could a woman "do" men? Yes,
probably, but only if she savagely reduced them to their common
denominator . . . But I must stop you there! Isn't that just what
you do yourself? Yes and no . . . I'm prepared to bet the women
couldn't see one another in terms of me . . . I may be wrong . . . A
kind of tribunal? Frankly, I don't see what they'd have to say to one
another . . . A few platitudes about my most obvious faults? After
which there'd be two separate camps . . . Those who quite like me
and those who loathe me . . . Those who quite like me are fond of
themselves . . . Those who loathe me can't bear themselves . . . It's
of no interest . . .

The plot? The story? But what I have is Plot with a capital P and
Story with a capital S! Infinitely transposable in the whole of time
and space! Illusion! Disillusion! Illusion again! And once more

disillusion! The art of going endlessly from one to the other . . . Motion . . .

There's an amusing idea in S.'s *Comedy*, though it's so buried in his linguistic lava I shouldn't be surprised if nobody else had noticed it . . . It's the idea of turning the Gospels upside down . . . Expounding the other side of them . . . Instead of producing a message for twelve disciples to perpetuate (in the same version, with a few variations), the hero would work out a method by which he was criticized by twelve women in twelve different ways . . . Each in her own style and language . . . A diabolical device . . . A jigsaw of silences, spites, interrogations . . . Mental devastations . . . Ineffable moments . . . Hatreds . . . Unsuccessful identifications . . . Successful shudders . . . Implosions . . . There you are . . . Clues for some future researcher . . . Who'd gradually notice the inconsistencies . . . Was he nice? Oh yes! . . . Nasty? Very nasty! . . . Generous? Magnificently! . . . Stingy? Incredibly! . . . Was he genuine and sincere? Oh, nobody like him! . . . A liar? Deception personified! . . . Highminded and disinterested? Absolutely! . . . Calculating? Never stopped! Never thought about anybody but himself . . . And his fiddle-faddling writing . . . Superb as a lion? Yes, yes . . . Crooked as a camel? I'm telling you! . . . Strong? Very strong . . . Weak? Unbelievably . . . Handsome? Extremely handsome. Not bad. Rather ordinary . . . Brave? Yes! No! . . . He had to have everything practical done for him . . . No! Yes and no! . . . Did he help you? A lot! Never! . . . Did he exploit you? Not in the least—just the opposite! I should just think he did! All the time! . . . And so on and so forth . . .

Neither Christ nor anti-Christ . . . The Parachrist . . . Elusiveness in person . . . Beyond good and evil . . . Beyond definition . . .

There are plenty of new things to be said about Christ, actually . . . Take the Judas episode . . . One of the most controversial . . . The most staggering . . . The heart of the crime . . . You'll always find some clever dicks who coolly maintain they were more or less in cahoots . . . Judas and the Son of god . . . A put-up job . . . A master stroke . . . He had to be crucified on that particular date . . .

In time for Passover . . . Or, scarcely more elegantly, they'll tell you Judas understood his Master's intentions better than anyone else . . . His secret voice . . . Judas is the subtlest and most intelligent of the disciples . . . The most cultivated . . . A sort of contemporary Renan . . . He sees in a flash of illumination how the new angle can be established . . . Though it amounts to making Jesus an accomplice in his own death . . . Supermasochism . . . Hyperautosadism . . . With incomparable triumph at the end of it . . . All becomes clear . . . Just a bit of pressure . . . The trifle that produces the well-known to-do . . .

Personally I think it was simpler still . . . Simpler and more horrible . . . And that old Melville guessed the main outline better than anyone else in his story of the handsome sailor, *Billy Budd* . . . It tells in veiled terms of what he calls the "mystery of iniquity" . . . Judas is sexual passion itself, raised to the highest degree of frenzy . . . Of mania . . . I love him therefore I am he, in all his beauty, wisdom goodness and desirability . . . So he must die . . . For each man kills the thing he loves . . . After all, he's only a man, isn't he? Divine, yes, but a man . . . And if you want my opinion, a man like that ought to be immortalized by death . . . By the shining seal of death . . . Made permanent as an apparition . . . Forever . . . Never losing any of his perfection . . . And Judas will have him all to himself, in secret! Judas has become a real woman! *Vénus tout entière à sa proie attachée!* He can tell Jesus doesn't really want to love him . . . That he didn't really choose him . . . That he prefers any prostitute he happens to come across . . . He even let himself be anointed by one of them, in Bethany . . . He! . . . From head to foot! All that oil trickling down! And so expensive! That ointment! The metaphor is unbearable! He! . . . Lending himself to adoring female vulgarity! Wasting the petty cash on perfumes . . . With that hysterical whore . . . Ugly as sin into the bargain! An ex-sinner playing the hypocrite . . . Don't think no one sees you, Jesus! Sees through you! I'll teach you! I, the most scrupulous of men, the most loyal . . . I who know all the details of the sublime spectacle . . . To whom you've assigned the lowliest of tasks . . . I'll teach you to take your foot away like that, in public, from the hands of a floozy . . . So calmly . . . So indifferently . . . As if you didn't feel a thing . . . And anyhow, shouldn't sacred things be kept between men? Anointing? Shouldn't it to be kept between members of the Council? Judas is deep in the confusion of love . . . Satan has entered into him, just as the evil spirit of Yahweh fell upon Saul at the sight of David's grace and musical genius . . . You want to kill something because it's too beautiful . . . You know you can't kill it . . . But the attraction is so strong, you try to anyway . . . And John, like another Jonathan, seeming to understand everything . . . With his visions of the end of the world, as if the world really were going to end . . . The lamb! . . . The idiot! . . .

What Judas really wants is to talk the whole thing over man to man . . . It's not a question of money . . . No, the thirty pieces of silver don't come into it—they're just a little touch of anal irony, in passing . . . The Reality Principle, don't you know . . . But these fools don't understand anything about the Passion . . . They'll execute the Great One as if he were just some two-bit crank or rowdy . . . The fools! Instead of giving him a spectacular death! In front of everyone . . . At sunset . . . In the glory of light . . . Something you can enjoy without having really wanted it, because it's so beautiful, so true . . . Can you tell me what could be more worthy of him than death? The Ideal . . . Spoiled . . . Spurned . . . Shattered . . . Now let the Excess Homo go and hang himself . . . Go and at least mingle his corpse with that of the Other . . . Shall we love one another in the grave, Master? Shall I at least have you all to myself among the bones of Sheol? Of Hades?

Someone who understood all this very well from the inside, afterward, was of course Saul . . . Shaoul . . . Paul . . . Judas converted . . . That's why he laid such stress on the resurrection of the body . . . Paul? He is the depths of Judas in broad daylight . . . We know the result . . . It was inevitable; only to be expected . . . A proof as dazzling as the flame of truth . . . "The thorn in the flesh . . ." Yes, yes, we get the point . . . Damascus!

How could it be otherwise?—it's in the air . . . El Greco is back in fashion . . . A great retrospective at the Prado . . . I dash to

Madrid . . . God, how beautiful! The articles that appear all over the place are marvels of right-thinking naiveté . . . Hey, here's one by Kate in the *Journal* . . . Poor thing, she hasn't a clue about painting . . . And can't see anything in music, either, beyond the din of Puccini or Verdi . . . She couldn't tell a Fragonard from a Watteau . . . Anyhow, El Greco is evidently the thing . . . So here's Kate with her usual performance . . . Whatever you do don't go thinking El Greco threw himself into that frenzy of distortion out of religious or mystical conviction . . . What an idea! Absolutely not! True, he does seem to have applied all his morbid energy to supporting the Church during the Counter-Reformation, but that was only by chance . . . Circumstance . . . No one can choose when they're born . . . What he was after, of course, was Painting within painting . . . Painting in itself! The evolution of painting! The limits of painting!

It's so embarrassing, isn't it, that the Council of Trent resulted in thousands of masterpieces, whereas applied Progressivism has produced only so many daubs! What a bore that the beastly Inquisition should be coupled with so many marvels, and Goebbels and Ghdanov with so much crap fit only for the rubbish-heap of time! What a trial for the philosophical spirit! What is to be done? Who will rid us of this irksome paradox? Name me one great revolutionary artist . . . David? The Oath of the Horatii and the Curiatii? Tsk! Marat in his bath? Tsk! Tsk! Picasso! There you are—him again! The sly one! The clever one! Exploiting the realm of the naive! But as a matter of fact he died a monarchist . . . Didn't you know? Well, take it from me! Velasquez! Brecht, then? A novel by Brecht? No . . . Let me reframe my question . . . Can you name any great novelist who has subscribed to the progressive-revolutionary ideology? Let me see now . . . Not from the third world . . . You'll quote me Garcia Marquez again . . . Wait a minute . . . Yes, I have to admit it's not easy . . .

El Greco is ecstasy, pain, the trickle of joy and pain . . . He's the convulsion and elongation of a faith that's stronger than pain . . . The light of tears; a vision, through tears and the storm, of the voice of god; the suffering that comes from having a body doomed to death, together with the incredible joy of being the only one to possess that body caught up in the fourth dimension of flames . . . That Assumption! Those lost and bloodless Christs! Those swirls of saints! Ten Johns! Twenty Peters! Fifteen Jameses! Eight Philips! Thirty Dominics! Fifty Francises! An optical defect? My eye! A crucified eye, yes, like the one St. Ignatius recommended . . . Imagine yourself on the cross . . . Nailed . . . Breathe as best you can . . . See Golgotha distorted below you . . . Enter into the ill-fated rib-cage . . . Feel your lungs . . . The fierce burning of your brow . . . The crown of thorns . . . The burning bush . . . Like a very bad toothache . . . The tearing at the wrists . . . At the feet . . . Tell yourself it's forever . . . For ages upon ages . . . Here, now, forever . . . Asphyxiating . . . *Eli, Eli, lamma sabactani!* Jerusalem in Toledo . . . The sky like the curtain of the Temple . . . The thunderbolt of judgment . . . The meditation in the wilderness . . .

I tell you—painting comes into being of its own accord . . . So do literature and music . . . The colors and movements summon up themselves . . . Reds, yellows, greens . . . Phrases like the rhythms of breathing . . . Only you have to go right at it; let yourself go with your eyes open; suffer the thing to pass through . . . Oh, so Your Highness is defending inspiration now? You don't mind being an obscurantist? Yes, yes, the Lesson of the Darkness! More light! Always asking for more!

I rush to Barcelona . . . The Peking Circus is giving a couple of performances there, as no doubt you've guessed . . . I know Barcelona like the back of my hand . . . An old habit from my youth . . . To go there and vanish is child's play to me . . . Three days with Ysia . . . I won't tell you the name of the hotel . . . A dream . . . We go and have dinner outdoors at Montjuich, on the hill . . . Spring already . . . Oleanders . . . The city glittering below . . . I've got memories about all this . . . Another time . . . I only hope Flora isn't in Spain just now . . . She'd be out of her mind if she knew I was on her territory . . . But no, she's still in Holland on a lecture tour . . . About Peace . . . How entertaining life can be with these comings and goings, trips, detours and masquerades, this farce and endless playacting . . . What Deb, with an irony that's half amused and half bitter, calls my "larks" . . . "Don't you remember? It was during another one of your larks" . . . Larks; nonsense . . . "Nonsense" comes into *Alice in Wonderland*, which Stephen's just reading . . . The Cheshire Cat! Which disappears, leaving only its grin . . . "It may kiss my hand, if it likes," said the King . . . "I'd rather not," the Cat remarked . . . "Off with his head!" cried the Queen . . . "But how can they behead him," said Alice, "when all that there is of him is his grin?" "Anything that has a head can be beheaded!" said the King . . . "All the rest is nonsense . . ." Or Kate, when I come back from one of my trips: "Well, still flitting around?" Kate's whole strategy now consists in making me out to be nice but unstable; superficial, restless, a leaf carried away by the slightest breeze, a cork on the water, a Cartesian diver, an hourglass that keeps on reversing itself . . . Not serious . . . Shallow . . . Well, if the ladies like to say so . . . It pleases the men . . . It's very convenient . . . Oh, him—just one of her passing whims and fancies! Nothing of any importance! And anyhow, these Americans . . . That's fine by me . . . Let them all just leave me alone . . . I don't count, I'm not to be counted on—okay, okay! That's the price you pay for being allowed to live . . . I lark, I flit, I turn my coat and my hourglass more and more . . . I waver, I zigzag, I take off, I'm not there, I don't exist . . . A weather-vane . . . No ulterior motives, don't worry; no consequences . . . No problems . . . When I think of what they've managed to turn Fals into; one of the funniest guys I ever met . . . A monster . . . A bogeyman . . . For pharmaceutical conferences . . . At the universal Hilton . . . Hiltonization is the disease of the century . . . You should just see them, with their symposia, their conferences, their simultaneous translations, their earphones, the hundred thousandth Party meeting . . . What Party? *The* Party . . . Always the Party, the one and only, with its typical smell of carbolic . . . What narrowness! What a caterpillar! Party? That's right—I'm *parti* . . . Gone . . . The flesh is sad, alas . . . ? On the contrary . . . Not sad at all! Bye-bye!

Ysia and I are walking in the tropical garden near the Citadel . . . I took a good look at her over dinner—her black suit, white blouse, short black hair and beautiful black eyes . . . Like a couple of bold and brilliant brush strokes . . . The other diners were looking at her too . . . So Chinese . . . We're in the dark now, though, and no one any the wiser . . . I embrace her burning little black body under the leaves . . . I keep saying the word "black" to myself . . . There are plenty of other couples among the trees . . . The plump Spanish girls, fresh but slightly sweaty, are naked under their dresses . . . We find a little terrace out of the way, and exchange fierce kisses . . . Saliva, biting . . . *Femme*, the French for "woman," is close to *fame*, the Italian for "hunger" . . . You need to be able to turn a woman into hunger . . . Into a veritable appetite for lust . . . Transsubstantiation . . . Otherwise . . . Ysia said a little while ago that she was rather hungry . . . And now, lo and behold, on this unfrequented terrace she leans against the warm stone parapet, turns her back to me and lifts her skirt . . . I screw her here, up above the harbor . . . Screw Columbus's caravel there below, and the docks, and the carefree milling in the streets, and the bluish nighttime mist above the trees . . . Ysia turns her face toward me; I feel her slantwise twisted tongue . . . She likes Barcelona . . . It reminds her of Shanghai . . .

Why is she so terribly reckless, all of a sudden? She'll tell me after a while . . . For the moment I don't think she knows what the "unconscious" is . . . Ysia's like me . . . What interests her is simply the possibility of getting time to herself, time when you can get away, find kindred spirits, breathe, float . . . In an animal kind of way . . . We're horribly superficial . . . It's disgraceful . . . It reminds me of a letter Freud wrote to Jung on September 19, 1907: "When I've completely got the better of my own libido (in the ordinary sense of the word), I shall write a treatise on 'The Love Life of the Human Race . . .' " What an idea! And above all what an idea to write like that as man to man . . . No screwing! says

334

Balzac . . . It costs you thirty pages! . . . Strange . . . And what about Flaubert's letters? Better still . . . Nineteenth-century version of pitch!

Ysia gives little groans as she wiggles her sweet little bottom . . . I can tell she's enjoying herself . . . She too . . . She's about to come . . . We both do . . .

> *What a pleasure to walk in the garden*
> *All the plants exhaling their perfumes*
> *While I take a stroll around infinity . . .*

We stay out in the dark for some time . . . She tells me she's going to be transferred to Tokyo . . . No more America . . . No more Europe . . . For the moment . . . She's rather worried . . . In the hotel, before going back to her room, she gives me a lengthy manuscript written in Chinese . . . She doesn't say anything . . . She doesn't need to . . .

When she was last in Paris I lent her some books on Taoism . . . The great tome by Maspero, the French researcher of genius who by some strange chance died in Buchenwald . . . I wanted her to explain to me about the *Lingbao* or "sacred jewel . . ." A fascinating mythology for a writer . . . Like the Bible . . . She gives the Maspero back to me . . . She's marked a passage in it . . .

While the works claiming to belong to The Book of the Great Depth can be dated without too much difficulty, it is hard to be precise about those which claim to belong to the Sacred Jewel, the *Lingbao* . . . The latter consists of the sacred books themselves, created spontaneously, when the world began, by the congealing of the Pure Breaths into tablets of green jade inscribed in gold . . . The gods, who are not pure enough to contemplate them directly, heard them recited by the Celestial and Venerable Yuanshi Tianzun of the Original Beginning . . . He alone may read them, having been likewise formed spontaneously, when the world was created, by the congealing of the Pure Breaths . . . And the gods in their turn had them engraved on tablets of jade, which they keep in their celestial

335

palaces. I do not know when the term Lingbao first began to be used. The most ancient books of Lingbao texts, which seem to have recorded the rituals of certain religious ceremonies, go back to the third century at least. The doctrinal books of the group seem to me to have appeared later. The most important of them, the "Book of the Salvation of Innumerable Men, by the Celestial and Venerable One of the Original Beginning," *Yuanshi wuliang duren jing*, must date from around the turn of the fourth and fifth centuries, the period when the Lingbao tradition seems to have started to spread and to occupy the most important place in Taoism.

Imagine the man who could mediate about all that in a Nazi concentration camp . . . Or in a psychiatric hospital in the USSR? Tbilisi, for instance? Or in a reeducation camp in China? Ysia stiffens . . . A taboo subject . . . She merely glances at the manuscript she's just given me . . . Silence . . . But I can tell she's more than a little intrigued by this old stuff about her own culture that's banned where she comes from . . . And that reaches her through me . . . Stories . . . Legends . . . Poems . . . Techniques for attaining immortality . . . Scrolls and paintings . . . Like the tale of the tortoise emerging from the river *Luo* with the Chinese-characters carved on its shell . . . The water . . . The Breaths . . . The jade containing all . . . I can see the Luo now as I saw it on the flight— a thin dark streak below . . . Embankments, a glaring expanse of yellow light, and a trickle of ink deep down . . . A suspension bridge of bamboo . . .

The *Sacred Jewel?* You don't need a drawing, do you? It wouldn't make a bad title, either . . . Better than Diderot's *Indiscreet Jewels!* More profound! Encyclopedic! Asia!

"Listen," says S. "Suffering or not suffering—that's what it all comes down to . . . Or rather back to . . . Think of the great shrieking yet silent throes; the unconscious rattle of the dying when palfium treatment doesn't work anymore . . . Start off every morning knowing that death is a spongy mass . . . Remember what the most sensitive nerve feels on the rack of pain . . . Burned all over . . . Just think about that for a bit . . . And then get down to your phrases!

"The main thing is to face up to stupidity . . . The enormous, crushing weight of it . . . The way it's automatically renewed . . . Almost every night I wake up in a cold sweat, so stupid are the things I think about while I'm asleep . . . The realization has me starting up in bed . . . If I succeed in registering the permanent factory of foolishness that I am, things go a bit better the next day . . . More distanced . . . You need to be crushed by the crap you yourself produce . . . Absorb . . . Reproduce . . . The stereotypes . . . The tiny vanities . . . The vermin of self-interest . . . Oh, ours is a moral function, there's no denying it! You can say what you like!"

"But that's ghastly!"

"Don't let's exaggerate," says S. "At the moment I've got a young mistress of twenty-five who's well-behaved, beautiful, lecherous, and delicious . . . It's quite bearable, as you well know . . . So long as one's not wasting one's time . . . One must be absolutely uncompromising about that . . . But let's go on . . ."

"It's as if I were at least three people at once," I say. "The real live one, the writer, and his sex . . . A strange trinity . . . One, but separate . . . Sharing a life that's the same yet not the same . . ."

"That feeling is the very basis of experience . . . Given that, the important thing is linking them all together . . . Smoothly . . . Into one story . . . You become the submarine of yourself, the explorer of what has just happened to you, the author of what you've just done . . . You grow more and more wide awake . . . You notice you spend your time under a spell . . . Under your skull . . . In the bony crypt . . . Your body is your grave . . . There is no other . . . Your composition—your work—will be as good as your own skill at decomposition . . ."

"Do I still keep women as the subject?"

"Of course! More than ever! The guardians of the sepulcher, don't forget! Do you know the best thing that can happen to a man and a woman?"

"Tell me anyway . . ."

"To be able to pretend they hate each other . . . And to laugh about it . . . It's very difficult . . . It's the ultimate . . . I manage it rather well with Sophie . . . You have to admit these new women from the East are very advanced . . . Once they've got the message! How about you and Deborah?"

"I think so . . . Don't you?"

"There you are, then . . . Hence your simultaneous defense of the family and philandering . . . Of love and debauchery . . . Of the greatest fidelity and the greatest infidelity . . . Once you get to that point all is well—you shock your contemporaries, you get their backs up, you're famous . . . You become Oedipus in reverse, you overturn Antigone, Jocasta, Tiresias, the Sphinx and Co., the oracles and the whole menagerie . . . You abolish tragedy, you're comedy personified, Thebes is terror-stricken . . . But watch out! You have to discipline yourself every second . . . Money . . . Time . . . Watch how more and more men let themselves get made pregnant . . . And it gets more and more expensive, they're exhausted, they collapse before term . . . Don't forget that's what the women have to aim at . . . To make you collapse within . . . It's up to you to resist . . . That's the game . . . Tedious? Amusing? What does it matter!"

"What about the homos?"

"Back numbers! Finished! Museum pieces! The secret's out . . . Turnaround! Low-angled spot! Anyhow, all they want is to be like women with pricks for and with one another . . . They live off the reflection of their and women's mutual bedazzlement . . . The women blind themselves with the pretense that they, the women, have got it . . . They know they haven't, but they can't resign themselves to the fact . . . All this is common knowledge . . . But never mind—on with the show!"

"Someone just said to me, 'So you think women are the incarnation of ontological falsehood?' "

"Of course! Ontological, horizontological! And if they manage to make you feel ashamed you're done for! We need to invent a new nervous system for ourselves, old boy! A tough one! . . . You didn't ask to exist, and women always have to try to justify existence . . . In other words, death . . . Life! Death! Life! Death! Chug-chug! Stick to that and the rest follows . . . You have to go through them, the women . . . Not by . . . Not a little bit this side of them or a little bit that . . . Your body comes from their body? Well, it's by going back through their bodies that you have a slight chance of looking down on your own . . ."

"It isn't always very exhilarating . . ."

"You're telling me . . . But *sursum corda!* Make choices . . . Invent . . . If you let your imagination flag you descend to their level! Even the most sublime female can turn into a pumpkin from one moment to the next . . . You must remain a coach! Grow beautiful! Fly! Take off! Talk to yourself! Give your best performances when you're playing the flute to yourself! Delight yourself! Levitate! Don't have anything to do with psychology! No doubts! Not an atom of jealousy! The gods according to Epicurus . . ."

"What were they?"

"He said, 'A god is an animal that's indestructible and happy.' "

"No relaxation? No rest?"

"Not a chance! On no account! This is war! The slightest pause and the enemy penetrates your defenses, occupies your territory, presents the bill! Which is all the bigger for being late! Beware of long-term investments! Don't forget you're living on borrowed time . . . Everything's on credit . . . Never free of charge . . ."

"Never?"

"Never! Good grief! Are you crazy?"

"But what about Cyd? And Ysia?"

"Exceptions that prove the rule! You stabilize their narcissistic image . . . In passing . . . For the moment . . . By a lucky chance . . . You happen to be lucky . . . But you may be sure they make others pay . . . And twice as much . . ."

"But what about passion? Sexual passion?"

339

"Investments . . . Investments . . . Credit cards!"

"For what reason?"

"To restore order . . . A notch higher . . . A spiral . . . Against their will, actually . . . It really upsets them . . . From depravity to depravity . . . The domestic kind . . . Simmering hatred . . . The Mama tyranny . . . The long useless days and evenings . . . Premature old age . . . Gloom . . . Medusa triumphant! Inflexible law . . ."

"But why? Why?"

"No reason! Just so that it's said! The Commander! The Commanderess! To ratify the irremediable!"

"Even now?"

"Especially now! Bodies slumped in front of the deadly TV . . . No more conversation . . . Silence . . . Boredom . . . Accounts . . . Taxes . . . She and her mother side by side! The sidecar-cum-coffin! The bear-garden of the kids . . . Sound without fury . . . Fatigue . . . A race to be first to die! Yoo-hoo! The vault! The urn! The die is cast! Down the drain! A lifeless screw . . . Nothing left . . . Elementary, Watson!"

"You're too sarcastic!"

"Schlegel says, 'Irony is the clear awareness of the eternal agility and infinite plenitude of chaos . . .' "

Supposing Molière came back to life? He'd do just what he did before! Everything, with hardly any modifications . . . *The School for Women* . . . *The Blue-Stockings* . . . *The Misanthrope* . . . *The Hypocrite* . . . *Don Juan* . . . *The Bourgeois Gentleman* . . . Or perhaps *The Petty-Bourgeois Harshwoman* . . . *The Hypochondriac* . . . Or *Analysis by Suggestion* . . . That would cause a nice scandal . . . They'd complain to the court . . . Armande Béjart would play him up and finally prefer a mediocre actor . . . The drawing-rooms would thunder excommunications . . . There'd be plots . . . In short, he'd do what every writer always has done and always will do . . . Hoaxes . . . Devious revelations . . . If the cap fits . . .

Célimène . . . Arsinoé . . . Philaminte . . . And later on Laclos . . . Shall I write you a new *Liaisons dangereuses?* . . . My goodness, how innocent it all was . . . Will the Marquise fall? The other evening she did seem to turn rather faint . . . But she's still holding out . . . I trap her in a pincer movement . . . My plans progress . . . My guns are ready . . . I can tell she's weakening . . . Yesterday she couldn't resist leaving me. her handkerchief . . . The next attack will be fatal . . .

Or maybe Restif, hell for leather . . . *My Calendar* . . . Those eighteenth-century names are like silk bows: Apolline, Honorine, Rosine, Nanette, Mélanie, Fanchon . . . Now skeletons fallen to dust . . . But still charming little faces on the page . . .

S. is jubilant . . . He's always wanted to indulge his classical talents . . . It's a rest from his hazy modern opera . . . Esoteric and anticosmic . . . "Well," he says. "What's the next adventure? And the next setting?"

I tell him there's a bit more to be said about frigid women, the ones who don't even know they are frigid . . . And that includes most of them . . . Look at Mildred . . . An American . . . She paints . . . She wants to have a show . . . She invites me to her place . . . I take in the pictures on the walls right away . . . Utterly hopeless . . . "Abstract . . ." Canvasses running with foundation cream; mascara; khol . . . She loses no time in making a declaration . . . She fell for me at first sight . . . Her whole life was transformed . . . She's tall and dark and not at all bad-looking, with big black eyes she pops at you earnestly . . . A real all-purpose smouldering gaze like those in the silent movies . . . Valentino . . . A bit greasy . . . Brilliantine . . . This is all happening in a villa in Neuilly . . . It's midnight . . . I know the front door locked itself after me and she'll have to come downstairs to let me out . . . The sooner the better . . . I attack . . . An unaccompanied tango in the living room . . . A spell on the couch . . . Mouth to mouth . . . Then bed . . . She sucks me off a bit, asking if I like it . . . What am I supposed to say? Yes, yes, as if I'm consumed with lust? It's a flop . . . So then she just turns around and presents her backside . . . Well . . . But nothing happens . . . A vague embarrassed squirm . . . Then I realize she wants me to go to it like a man without bothering about her . . . To finish, and let's say no more about it . . . The john . . . And then we start to talk about serious matters . . . Her "work . . ." The possibility of some articles about her show . . . Okay, I give up . . . We lie on the bed and smoke . . . She's not in the least put out . . . On the contrary, this is only the start of the nightmare playacting . . . Of course I'll stay the night? No? But I must! That would be terrible behavior on my part! After the shock she's had! She knows, she has a feeling we're made for each other . . . It's visceral . . . Astral . . . Obvious . . . There's nothing we can do about it . . . She moans and whines . . . I think about the locked front door . . . I'm afraid she won't open it for me . . . But, thank goodness, she does . . . Phew!

In the days that follow, a volley of telephone calls . . . She goes around to all my friends . . . Organizes dinner parties that she knows in advance I won't go to . . . "But I must defend myself," she says . . . Against what? The fact that I'm not interested? But it can be turned to use . . . She'll act as if we really had had an "affair . . ." That ought to attract a few guys . . . There's no such thing as a small profit . . . There'll even be some who'll think it will bring them closer to me . . . Or, better still, that they're taking her away from me! Homo leverage . . . Magnetic . . . That would make another chapter: the females that let it be thought that . . . Gentle hints . . . Words to the wise . . . We're great friends . . . We have been . . . We might be . . . One man as bait for another . . . A man who's rather in the swim dangled before a young climber . . . I've already got someone . . . But of course it's very hush-hush, you understand . . . Because of his situation . . . His wife . . . Meaning, "I might be his wife one day . . ." After all . . . Or what about X? Yes . . . If you only knew . . . Oh no, it's not at all what people imagine! Far from it! I could tell you more . . . Much more . . . Another time . . . He has told me certain things . . . But let's change the subject . . .

Some men are turned on by that sort of thing. . . But not me . . . I'm more likely to feel sorry for the guy in question . . . No doubt he thinks he's invisible and unscathed . . . Typical masculine naiveté . . . He thinks he's It . . . That it's all for love . . . His mother always told him he had nice eyes . . . So he's loved only for himself? Just look at the silly twit!

Who was it that played me this same trick with Fals? Oh yes — Elissa . . . A real card . . . The Minerva of the philosophers in her day . . . A great gawk of a girl . . . Egyptian . . . Editor of *Toth*, the under-the-counter learned review . . . The Science of Writing . . . I remember . . . She used to see people at her place with all the shutters closed . . . By candlelight . . . A fortune-teller's lair . . . Mystery . . . Crystal ball . . . Tarot cards . . . Half Jewish, half Arab . . . Rumor had it she was a "genius . . ." She was always writing down her dreams in little notebooks . . . When you came in she'd sit you down on a divan and start reading aloud in a low voice . . . Like Aragon! It went on forever . . . Aversion therapy . . . A funny, sharp, excited little voice that she thought was melodious. . . People said she was close to ministers of all persuasions . . . Influence and Inspiration . . . The ideal Surrealist muse . . . "Do you know Elissa? Isn't she beautiful? What a face! Just like Nefertiti!" That was the cry . . . The curse of the Pharaohs . . . And what did she write? Wild, disjointed stories . . . Ravings, flights of fancy, dual personalities, reincarnations, apparitions, processions of the dead, passions in the fourth dimension, Eurydice's laments, Dido's sighs, revelations by Jocasta, messages from Isis . . . Greece by the gallon . . . Sappho in frenzy . . . After an hour I was torn between falling sound asleep and shrieking for mercy . . . Between being hypnotized and having hysterics . . . I kept pinching my leg . . . And letting out a little "ah" every so often to show I was still with her on her fantastic journey . . . In the daytime Elissa would let fall bits of news . . . The jobs she got . . . The transfers . . . The regradings . . . The falls from grace . . . The temporary favors . . . She used to gather the cream of the Paris intelligentsia together at her place . . . Academic celebrities upset by the events of May '68 used to pass one another on the stairs . . . She really was very trendy . . .

She found me odd . . . Different . . . I didn't want anything from her . . . I wasn't writing a thesis . . . I didn't make any conditions . . . We had a friend in common, Martha, who was furiously in love with her . . . Martha was very keen that I should be dazzled by Elissa . . . Bowled over . . . That it should become a real romance, a literary explosion . . . In short, she'd appointed me her delegate phallus . . . An honor accorded by the lesbian army . . . Without asking my opinion . . . That was taken for granted . . . An American on the Nile . . . An Antony rented out to Cleopatra . . . The barbarian smuggled into the secret apartments of the palace . . . So I must swoon away! Prostrate myself! Worship my empress! Unfortunately Elissa left me cold . . . The more she threw herself about on the cushions in her miniskirt, reading me her papyrus with ever-increasing fervor, the more artificial, pretentious and off the beam I found her . . . Sickeningly affected . . . Yet I always arrived with the best of intentions . . . But it was no good . . . Her mouth was too pouting . . . Her legs were dull . . . She had knock knees . . . She was extremely bony . . . Admittedly she was bursting with energy, but though that might be enough to excite professors or even a learned lesbian, for a true connoisseur— impossible . . . The situation was becoming indecent . . . Elissa would kiss me and touch me a little . . . No reaction . . . Though I can usually manage to be polite . . . It was at this point that she began to try to sell me some men . . . The last remedy . . . The ultimate aphrodisiac . . . A? B? C? D? No? What about Fals, then? She knew I'd be interested in him . . . That with him there might be a chance . . . "I've still got the bitter taste of his sperm in my mouth," she said to me once, looking me straight in the eye . . . "He's got a lot of it, you know . . ." At that I ought in theory to have given in . . . Especially as she was giving me everything for nothing, so to speak: the keys to her apartment, the free disposal of her body . . . Details of her dinners with Fals, the luxury hotels they'd been in, the jewelry he'd given her . . . And she showed me his letters too . . . The tender little notes . . . "Till this evening, darling . . . Eight-thirty at La Diligence, without fail . . ." And very indiscreet observations about his family and friends, his pupils, and even his own work, from which I could corroborate my suspicion that he thought it pointless and doomed to failure . . . Did all this make Elissa more attractive? Yes . . . No . . . There she was, all agog, a piece of cake . . . Alas . . . Taste . . . Instinct . . . The irrepressible nerve-endings . . . Poor old Fals . . . being bored to the marrow by this pseudoprophetess . . .

Martha and Elissa got to be friends with Kate . . . then Bernadette took the whole lot of them in hand . . . A feminist maelstrom . . . It was then that Kate wrote her liveliest articles . . . And the ones that revealed most about the new yet very ancient religion then on the march . . . I remember the one where she described the family celebration she held, of course without any men, to greet her daughter's first period . . . With champagne . . . To show how proud one could be to be a woman . . . How one overcame the ancient malediction . . . She mentioned that her young son was very quiet during there festivities . . . And ended by saying that he too would be reeducated in the glorious world of tomorrow . . . A world in which all the mothers and daughters would join hands and dance in a ring over the corpse of the Moloch, the phallocratic Judeo-Christian dragon of patriarchy . . . Charming, wasn't it, this notion of mothers proudly and publicly displaying their daughters' daintily soiled linen? This mass uprising of primal repression . . . Of girls freed from shame and directing their scarcely nubile bodies toward energetic procreation in common . . . Noble Spartans! You sensed in all this a neoclassical influence, of pediments, friezes, wreaths of flowers, and initiations by night . . . Unknown rites disinterred . . . The return at last of the Great Goddess . . . Demeter . . . Proserpine . . . A sheer thrill . . . I don't know who it was that passed onto Kate my idle remark that she'd never have thought of having the same sort of celebration for her son's first ejaculation . . . That was a kind of injustice, wasn't it? The first spurt of sperm was after all an event? She didn't speak to me for two years . . . She'll never forgive me . . . Women without children . . . Mothers without husbands . . . Children without fathers . . . All of them seeking husbands and fathers while proclaiming the opposite . . .

Elissa too ended up by asking me if I thought Fals might marry her . . . This was about three in the morning . . . "Marry . . ." The word was like a consecrated wafer on her lips . . . But next day, of course, it was back to pamphlets and proclamations . . .

Elissa published "poetic novels . . ." More and more unsuccessfully . . . The last one I read was a kind of hymn to Bernadette . . . Savior of the human race . . . Courtly Gomorrahism . . . Unlimited soft soap . . . Litanies to Venus . . . Metaphysical lizzerie . . . Excruciatingly inane . . . Bernadette was seen as Primeval Nature . . . Alchemy's Source . . . Radiant Goodness . . . When you know her! Malice and mischief incarnate . . . Slyness and irascibility in person . . . Ugliness itself! The devious spirit of revenge condensed; cooked over and over till it's as hard as a stone . . . Soaking up venom like a sponge! Beautiful with it, though . . . At least that's what I think . . . Yes, Bernadette's got a sort of necessary beauty . . . Better than Elissa . . . Whom everyone has gradually more or less dropped . . . It's really wicked people who are liked, not their mere followers . . . Even the American women have deserted her . . . Too undesirable . . . Too crazy . . .

Kate has distanced herself from FAM, for the sake of her future career . . . But I believe she and Bernadette still have a secret pact . . . A common strategy . . . A blacklist that's kept up to date . . . I must be one of the few people who've been on it since the start and are still here to tell the tale . . . But my name's underlined three times . . . In a reddish-brown extract of irregular menstrual blood . . . It was Flora who used this image, in a moment of abandon . . . When she too had been appointed to give me the works, but didn't hesitate, perverse creature, to betray her sisters . . . Elissa and Bernadette summoned her one evening to tell her about me . . . The walls are still reverberating . . .

What part does a perversion of pychoanalysis play in all this, you ask? A crucial one . . . Psychic manipulation . . . Personal terrorism . . . Middle-European Moonism . . . A new method of espionage and puppeteering by remote control . . . The sect is making plenty of recruits in these parts . . . Shades of Freud! Freud, so scrupulous and respectable! Apparently the Russians, themselves still at the stage of parapsychology, aren't at all displeased by this general softening of the brain . . . These harmful intranervous injections . . . Vulnerability . . . Disequilibrium . . . Craving . . . Drugs here, confessions there . . . And it's easy to see that the leaders of the organization are among psychoanalysis's failures . . . Perhaps their analysis was prematurely terminated . . . But they know enough about it to be able to profit by people's fixations or excite a weak sexuality and lead it up a blind alley . . . Quasi-impotence for men . . . Cold and paranoiac core for women . . . All connected to more and more ineffective resentment at being a shit, a washout . . . Which makes people ten times more vindictive . . . Obsessed . . . Devious . . . Low . . . The logic the sect uses is always the same . . . Parasitism and pressure . . . A strange breed of analysts, who insist on hanging onto their patients . . . Who phone them, force them to come back again, dangle promises of social advancement, paint enticing pictures of travel and authorship . . . Tell me your dreams . . . Dear me! So you know So-and-so? How did you meet him? Where? Tell me more . . . Tell me more still . . .

Easy to see why the various secret services should be interested in a potential network that's so widespread and unobtrusive . . . Economical . . . According to the latest information the Russians are in the lead by at least a dozen lengths . . . They throw in a bit of everything—spiritualism, thought-transference, metal-bending —but that doesn't matter . . . They were told Freudianism was the thing in France, so Freudianism was okay by them . . . Why not? Everything's too confused in the USA . . . Free competition . . . Charlatanism in fifty-seven varieties . . . Dollars . . . Much more tempting is something more centered, more controlled, virtually nationalized, telepathically Jacobin . . . The main thing is to stick together . . . That everything should be communal . . . That there should be something there, behind it all, governing everyone . . . Do you want to call it the "unconscious"? If you like . . . So long as there's a group . . . A general mass . . . There are negotiations by hint . . . The women's movements are especially interesting . . . Pacifist . . . Ecological . . . Anti-imperialist . . . Anti-Biblical . . . Linked to revolutionary organizations . . . So . . . All things considered . . .

Upon which you find you're under constant surveillance . . . A sort of cloud clings to you and goes in front of you everywhere . . . Like being in a diving suit . . . Unpredictable ramifications . . . There's nothing so stable as Sectism . . . It's betting on a sure thing . . . Human fears, inhibitions and regressions . . . The credulity of males . . . Nothing more widespread than Repression . . . It works ten times out of ten . . .

But, let me tell you, there's a hard gulag and a soft gulag or coolag . . . You ought not to joke about that word! What word? Gulag . . . Why not? It's too horrible! No, listen a minute, I only want to bring it to life a bit in another language . . . Philological foresight . . .

What do you hear in the word gulag?

First of all a divine name . . . The Goddess Gula . . . The Great Goddess of the Chaldees . . . Bracketed with Ninib in the Assyrian-Chaldean pantheon . . . We always seem to come back to the Pantheon, don't we . . . Gula is the heat that either kills or gives life . . . The goddess of medicine . . .

And then there's *ghoul*, from the Arabic *ghul* or *gul*, . . . A female vampire who devours the dead at night . . . Ugh!

Ghouls in the guise of attractive young women (yes, there they are again!) gather in graveyards to dig up the corpses and devour them . . . In the daytime they slit their victims' throats and drink their blood . . .

There's also *gull*, which can mean a chasm . . . *Gula*, the gullet . . . *Gully*, a large knife . . . *Gules*, which in heraldry means red, the color of blood . . .

And so on . . . I won't insist about *goulash* . . .

There's *gulag* for you . . . Human existence in a nutshell . . . And here, as in every innovative dictionary worth the name, is my trump card, a quotation from Rimbaud:

"So she will never end, this ghoul who is queen over millions of souls and dead bodies *which will one day be judged!* (Rimbaud's italics). I can see myself again now, my skin eaten up by mud and plague, my hair and armpits crawling with worms, with bigger ones still in my heart as I lay among ageless and unfeeling strangers . . . I could have died there . . . . . . What a fearful thought!"

It depends on your point of view . . . "I have seen the hell of the women out there . . ." Or again: "It really was hell, the ancient hell, the one whose gates were opened by the son of man."

You can't put it more plainly than that . . . He that hath ears let him hear . . . If he's still got his ears! If they haven't been pulled off, not by the androgynes but by the gynandres . . . Those prehistoric and posthistoric beings . . . Unthought-of before me! The secret of the zombies!

Well, well, here's Flora back again . . . New tactics . . . It's not she herself who phones or comes to see me—it's Sandra, a friend of hers she's mentioned to me sometimes . . . She's Spanish too . . . From Madrid . . . A tall blonde with blue eyes . . . Scriptwriter . . . Wearing leather, with a cloche hat . . . Something stiff about her, like someone who's had trouble with her joints . . . Arthrosis? We have lunch together . . . She loses no time in singing Flora's praises . . . "What a woman!" "But of course," I say . . . "But do you really appreciate her qualities as a *woman?*" Sandra insists . . . "But they're self-evident," I say.

"What I'm really talking about are her erotic talents," she says.

"Of course."

"I was at her place recently . . . And I looked at her as she was sitting opposite me . . . And it literally hit me in the eye . . . She's a tiger, isn't she?"

"She's a remarkable woman . . ."

"What are you doing this evening?"

"I'm not free, unfortunately . . ."

"You could have come to dinner with some friends of mine . . .

Anyhow, if it's not too late when your evening's over, perhaps you could drop in . . .''

She gives me the address and phone number . . . Of course I don't go . . .

A few days later, Flora:

"So . . . It seems you tried to get off with Sandra . . .''

"Certainly not . . .''

"She told me she could hardly get rid of you the other day at lunch . . . You insisted you had to see her again that evening . . .''

"Is that so?''

"I do understand . . . She's very attractive . . .''

Now I get it! Shooting around corners . . . Recapture through a third person . . . Flora's faithful to her religion . . . (1) It's only vis-à-vis her that I can be interested in another woman. (2) Any woman she doesn't know doesn't exist. (3) I can't possibly do any work because I spend my time screwing . . . All this because of the character she's ascribed to me once and for all, in the name of the whole sorority . . . Men are *bound* to think of nothing but sex . . . Homage to the Idol . . . How can you make a woman understand that you don't necessarily desire a woman who happens to impress *her?* Martha was furious with me for not having turned a hair when I met Elissa . . . Now Flora thinks she could control me better by engineering certain comings and goings . . . Because it's clear that I don't want to change my legal setup . . . That there's really no chance of my getting a divorce or leaving Deb . . . And being the other woman carries the right to impose customs duties . . . Taxes on luxury goods . . . Regular reports on movements . . . Anything so long as another relation doesn't spring up, independent of the customary one . . . That would be the height of immorality! A denial of Ethics! When Flora talks about ethics you can be sure her calculations aren't working out . . . Women are eminently "ethical" . . . Social . . . National . . . Sororal . . . Racial . . . By instinct . . . With a silent but absolute violence . . . You'd almost think the only mortal sin is rejecting a woman suggested to you by another woman, using various more or less indirect means . . . Including

scenes of jealousy . . . Because that's how you make yourself opaque
. . . Unavailable for the plot, the story, the affair . . .

Flora, as I've said before, doesn't want to and can't know anything about the sort of women I like . . . She invariably guesses
wrong . . . Okay, we have different tastes, that's all . . . But I have
the impression that it's been bothering her recently . . . She senses
she's missing something . . . Cyd? She wouldn't understand Cyd at
all; her charm, her liberty . . . Ysia? She doesn't even know she
exists . . . Flora's mistakes make me laugh . . . As I've always
laughed at lack of sensitivity on this subject . . . Don't neglect your
laugh! It's right about things, in advance! And one day it will be
right about everything!

We're visibly falling out, Flora and I . . . She never even asks me
to write an article for her anymore . . . Oh well, that's life . . . A
landslip . . . A question of geology . . .

Jeanne's another one who's sniffing around . . . Jeanne, the high
priestess of peculiarity . . . She's the wife of a famous painter who
specializes in erotic drawings and pictures . . . We knew each other
quite well once . . . She used to organize "sessions . . ." Which
she'd tell her husband about . . . For his sketches . . . Every so
often she'd bring him a "model" . . . Some novice for one of his
sado-masochist performances . . . Chains . . . Whips . . . Fetters
. . . Dog collars . . . That's how Jeanne holds on to her painter . . .
While she's waiting to become a Widow . . . But he's a sturdy
bloke, a peasant, suspicious . . . He holds out and refuses to fall ill
. . . These Widows! "Do you know how many of them there are in
France?" the Chairwoman asked me one day . . . "Do you realize
the influence they wield in elections?" "No . . ." "Four million,
my dear . . . Just think of it!" I do think of it . . . Of them . . .
The tedious ones . . . The ones who take advantage . . . With their
tame poets and artists and essayists . . . Going around all the galleries and publishers cannily negotiating the remains . . . Notes, prefaces, signatures with the given name plus the Name with a capital
N . . . Originals . . . Things put away in drawers . . . Unpublished
works . . . And the legitimate ones are not necessarily the worst!

There are also the mystical ones . . . The nuns devoted to pus . . . The levitators of the musical skeleton . . . Those possessed by the inspired ashes . . . The Teresas of the thinking skull . . . The Bernadettes of the rhythmical sacrum . . . The Catherines of the painting forearm . . . The Marys of the rhyming tibias . . .

So Jeanne wants to know how I'm getting on . . . If the loony sexual lobby can still count on me . . . If I can still be aroused by that little carry-on . . . She spends her time seeing people who are impressed by that kind of entertainment . . . She's nice, though; touching . . . Creative in her own way . . . Which is just as good as her husband's sophisticated "designer" daubs . . . Better . . . Tableaux vivants . . . All alike . . . A woman being crucified and pelted with eggs . . . A beautiful young man being delicately drained of a few drops of blood . . . Servants of both sexes . . . She and a few women friends sit at the table wearing no undies and are waited on by naked boys who then get down on all fours to suck them off . . . Or else a slave is brought in blindfolded and shown a beautiful girl bound hand and foot . . . They may make love . . . If the Mistress so desires . . . And so on . . . Jeanne has never asked me to take part, but she tells me about it . . . That's what she likes best . . . Exchanging information with her sodomite colleagues . . . She makes an exception for me . . . Three or four times she's tried to offer me the use, in her presence, of one of her "models" . . . Nice girls—scared, docile, anxious to succeed . . . I admit I have gone along with it on occasion, with just a few superficial signs of sadism, such as a few beltings or light slaps . . . While Jeanne masturbated . . . A few little trifles like that . . . Nothing to write home about . . . But they seemed refreshing in their old-fashioned way, at the time . . . I'm really quite fond of Jeanne and her childlike persistence . . .

"So what are you on at the moment? Your novel?"

"I travel a lot, you know . . ."

"Yes . . . I think I've got someone for you . . ."

"Who?"

"A marvelous girl . . . Who wants a writer . . ."

"A writer? Really?"

"When are you free?"

"Well, I'm leaving again the day after tomorrow . . ."

"When you get back, then?"

"Sure . . . With pleasure . . ."

She can tell I'm not very keen . . . I've moved out of reach of the radar . . . The control tower can't locate me anymore . . . She's been told as much already . . . At the SGIC monthly meeting . . . Or on her recent trip to America, by her friends in WOMANN . . . The ones who are interested . . . I hesitate to tell her her show is rather out-of-date . . . Not to say square . . . Even if she has introduced a few fashionable trimmings . . . Leather . . . But the fact is, that sort of thing isn't done privately anymore . . . There are special places for it now . . . And anyhow, once you've seen it a couple of times . . . Groups? That was all right in the sixties and seventies . . . The years of transition . . . Education . . . There might have been something in it then . . . It's a question of age as well . . . After forty the element of ugliness comes in . . . And it has to be either in the head or not at all . . . I don't say one can't have a sideshow from time to time, to keep one's eye in . . . We've become too clear-sighted; we can see the mechanisms of power and domination at a glance . . . And then it doesn't do for the people to know one another . . . As soon as they do the whole thing is blown . . . It becomes a family affair . . . And I'm just not a family person, except in the case of my own . . . "Yes, I know," Jeanne says, "you've become such a family person, haven't you? I don't understand you . . . I have no family myself . . ." This rather angrily, wistfully . . . I feel like telling her to lie down and tell me about the last dream she had . . . I could show her in ten minutes that she hasn't moved an inch away from her parents . . . But what would be the good? Still, I'd make a wonderful analyst!

Jeanne has never had any children . . . She probably thinks hates them . . . Elissa, on the other hand, had three, but for h was as if nothing had ever happened . . . Most women hav astonishing virginity . . . The train passes through them

leaving any trace . . . Apart from that echo of madness . . . No?
They're virgins, virgins! That's probably why they get so cross
about the business of the Virgin herself . . .

It's true that ever since I started this book I've detected a definite
whiff of surveillance . . . It must have been there all the time, of
course, but I didn't pay any attention . . . But write away as much
as you like, until you genuinely have this feeling — and are not just
imagining it — you can be sure you're not really writing at all . . .
Not anything interesting, anyway . . . You start out quite simply,
without any illusions . . . Then you gradually realize you're uneasy
. . . You must ooze uneasiness . . . Even while you're asleep . . .
You may say any scribbler could easily persuade himself he has the
feeling . . . And fancy, amid his laborious and pointless gibberish,
that the whole world is hot on his heels . . . Maybe . . . And yet
. . . What was that essay called? *Persecution and the art of writing*
. . . But is the persecution genuine or not? That's the point . . .
   There's a whole network made up of opinions, likes and dislikes,
beliefs, illnesses, and currencies . . . The meshes are very fine . . .
And as soon as one of them looks as if it might be going to tear, the
whole complex enters into feverish activity to close the gap . . .
Well may we speak of the body of society . . . It has its own
automatic immune system . . . Active everywhere and all the time
. . . Long before couples and families and clans and governments
. . . The antibodies fly to the danger zone . . . At the slightest hint
of inflammation . . . They sense . . . They smell . . . They divine
. . . They move toward the suspect spot with the certainty of
amoebas . . . The glands are always on the watch . . . Just try to
tack them . . . You'll see . . .
   Hello . . . I meet Jean-Luc, former revolutionary and ex-"Maoist
" He teaches in the provinces now . . . We go for a walk in the
ies . . .
   ll," he says, "I'm fine. Making great progress with my

"For your research on Islam?"

"It's more than research, old boy. As you know."

I'd forgotten . . . The Maoists' return to God . . . The spiritual crisis after the failure of '68 . . . The revelations by Solzhenitsyn on the one hand and about the Chinese concentration camps on the other . . . The great turn of the tide . . . The return of the Spirit . . . Miracle . . . The explanation of the fact that France, unlike Germany and Italy, has escaped the fascination of terrorism . . . France's potential Red Brigades are seen as a kind of celestial militia . . .

"I had an exam the other day," says Jean-Luc, "where I had to do an unseen translation of a particularly complicated passage by a thirteenth-century Arab mystic . . . Do you know, it came to me all at once . . . That shows you the power of the Archangel Gabriel . . ."

He laughed as he said it, yet he was serious too . . . But more relaxed than when he used to quote Mao . . . Others have gone back to Judaism . . . "Gone back" is paying them a compliment . . . They just suddenly discovered it . . . It was there beside them all the time but they never noticed . . . The Purloined Letter . . . From Maoism to Mosaism . . . Thus Albert, a perfectly respectable sociologist, started an abstruse conversation with me not long ago about the Tetragram . . . Others—not so many, admittedly—go back to the Christianity of their childhood . . . There's plenty to choose from . . . Sufism, Buddhism, the various esoteric sects . . .

Jean-Luc has always regarded me as an amateur, a comic-opera revolutionary . . . Who was there at the time because it was the thing to do . . . I remind him of the great "stock-taking" evening when he was playing second fiddle to Alain, the movement's most radical leader . . . Analysis of the action on all fronts: the factories! the university! the country! the unions! the immigrants! the local groups! the women! Alain is coming to the end of his speech: "But as comrade Stalin said, comrades, what matters is what grows and develops . . ."

This bold conclusion is greeted in silence . . . Respectful or stupefied, or both . . . You must admit it's stunning . . . Everyone

355

knows that one of the Maoists' great problems is to distance themselves from Stalin . . . From previous generations . . . The formal-
dehyde of the past . . . The Soviet thing . . . To invent a new
experience, the real thing, a return to the origins, the genealogical
rectification initiated by Lutz, the direct line through Marx and
Engels and Lenin to Mao . . . A high-speed train with the Stalin
carriage uncoupled . . . He's in quarantine . . . Under observation
. . . With luck, being demolished . . . So Alain was playing for high
stakes that evening . . . His reputation . . . His troops . . . His best
officers . . . His women . . . But no, his women stare at him bright-
eyed . . . They're in the know . . . Silence . . . Someone has to
sacrifice himself . . .

"Yes," I say, deliberately bringing out my usually imperceptible
American accent . . . "Yes, but I think La Fontaine says something
even more brilliant: 'Slow but sure wins the race . . .' "

You could cut the atmosphere with a knife . . . Murder in the
cathedral . . . Am I going to be expelled on the spot? But no one
sees me anymore . . . All eyes are on Alain, sitting casually by a
nice fire in a comfortable drawing-room in the Marais . . . It belongs to his current girlfriend, a little blonde psychoanalyst with
radical ideas . . .

Alain sits for a few seconds with his head bowed . . . A few
seconds of Siberia . . . Firing squads . . . Bullets in the back of the
neck . . . Electric wires . . . Baths . . . Chemicals . . . Poisoned
umbrellas . . . He turns his head toward me . . . Slowly looks up
. . . Then he laughs . . . And everyone else starts to do the same
. . . If the boss laughs . . .

"Do you remember?" I ask Jean-Luc . . .

"No, I don't," he answers curtly . . . "Are you sure? I've completely forgotten . . . Anyway, Alain was extremely bright . . . The
best interpreter of Hegel France has ever had . . . Better than Lutz,
anyhow . . . And you, what are you doing these days?"

"I'm writing a novel . . ."

"A novel? I thought you wrote for the American papers and were
only interested in avant-garde stuff . . . Like S. . . . I even heard
you'd become a Catholic, but of course I didn't believe it . . ."

"I don't need to *become* a Catholic," I say. "I am one."

"Really? Anyway, you used to be a bit suspect because of your American origins, but no one knew you were a Jew."

"But my dear fellow, I'm *not* a Jew."

Jean-Luc leans forward, not seeing me . . . Oh, I get it . . . My name once appeared in one of the movement's pamphlets denouncing the enemies within . . . I was bracketed with five or six others . . . As a "rabid Zionist . . ." Why? I can't remember! . . . It was some article about Israel . . . Did Jean-Luc write it? I don't like to ask him . . . He's probably forgotten anyhow . . . Now, lo and behold, I'm allowed to be visible again . . .

"Did you know Boris goes around saying he's a Catholic? Is that your influence? He's jumped on the bandwagon rather late in the day, hasn't he?"

"There's no law against it," I answer. "Even if it's just his umpteenth provocation . . . If that's what he wants . . . Though it'll make him more enemies than friends . . ."

"A novel, you say?"

"Yes."

"What about?"

"Women."

"Oh, really?"

He's at a loss . . . He never reads novels . . . Regards them as mere phenomena . . . He changes the subject . . . He's still as cultivated and intelligent as ever . . . A great generation wasted, really, these guys . . . But anyway they haven't gone back to the main fold . . . They've come to rest a long way away from Moscow . . . They're lost to the Left . . . To the Communist Party . . . Which quite understandably is very upset about it . . . All those cherished officials vanished into thin air . . . Nurtured in the bosom of the state for nothing . . . And now they hover about in some kind of no man's land . . . The Archangel Gabriel . . . The Tetragram . . . Psychoanalysis . . . Or else going straight out for drugs, homosexuality or drink . . . The Tetragram and the Archangel aren't so bad . . . At least they force them to read . . . And to learn foreign languages . . .

"I believe you've studied Chinese?" says Jean-Luc.

"A bit . . . For a couple of years . . . And I'm not sorry I did it . . . But it's like the piano—you need to keep it up two hours a day . . . The most interesting thing about it is learning to pitch your voice differently . . . The tones . . . And then there's Taoism, too . . ."

I recite a few lines of Tang poetry, in Chinese . . . And think of Ysia . . . In the ramblas . . .

Jean-Luc, not to be outdone, spouts three sentences in Arabic.

"But I wasn't dreaming, was I?" he goes on . . . "I did see an article you wrote as a tribute to John Paul II? About theology? Duns Scotus?"

"Yes, I rather care for the present Pope . . . And theology's very chic just now, let me tell you . . ."

We laugh . . . Funny sort of times we live in . . . When I think that . . . And that . . . And that . . . The memories flood back . . . We haven't met for ten years . . . What happened to him? What's become of her?

"We had a lot of fun though, didn't we?" says Jean-Luc . . . "That's what *they*'ll never understand . . . *They*'ve never understood a thing . . . Do you remember? 'We're right to rebel!' The great Mao slogan against *them* . . . No regrets . . . Either you were in on it or you weren't . . ."

I'm glad he's ready to pass me as O.K. now—he'd have refused implacably before . . . So I was "in on it . . ." What? Oh, the lark, the chaos, the energy we didn't know what to do with . . . The discussions, the staying up all night . . .

"I envy you your Arabic," I say . . . "What *I* might be tempted by now is Hebrew . . . To be able to read the Bible better . . ."

"Hebrew . . . Yes . . ."

Am I mistaken or was there a tinge, just the slightest tinge, of reserve in his voice? Come, come, the time for paranoia is over . . . He's quite sincere . . . Open . . . Just wants to find out as much as he can about all that was kept from us . . . By our grandparents, our parents, school, college, University . . . Philosophy the Queen of Knowledge . . . Politics-in-Itself . . .

"But Lutz!" he says . . . "What a business! And Andreas! And Fals's death!"

This is getting to be an old dodderers' conversation . . . A pastiche of Flaubert . . . Faces drifting up from the past . . . Death . . . He realizes as much . . . We call it a day . . .

We've reached the Louvre.

So long!

I turn off toward the river, he goes back into the gardens . . . He hasn't aged . . . Still something of the same old student, cocky and obstinate . . . He'll never change . . . He turns around and calls out . . .

"Don't forget to send me your novel!"

"Sure thing!"

Nine o'clock in the morning . . . Phone call from Christian, the publisher . . .

"That Chinese manuscript you gave me—do you know what it is?"

"No—I couldn't read it, of course . . . But I have a pretty good idea . . . A dissident diatribe, I should think?"

"Sensational, old boy! Just the evidence we were waiting for! How did you come to get hold of it?"

"Through a friend . . . I can't give you any names . . ."

"Sensational! Sensational! Thank you! Just wait till you see it!"

Ten o'clock . . . A ring at the studio door . . . No? Yes!

Flora descends on me . . . Shouting at the top of her voice . . .

"In Barcelona! In my own country! You're disgusting! Disgusting! And with a Japanese, I'm told?"

I don't react . . . It's too much . . . This time is really the last . . . She throws my typewriter on the floor and kicks it . . . Hurls my papers around . . . And then suddenly stops . . . And goes on in a much lower voice . . .

"A hundred times I've suggested we go to Spain together . . .

359

You've always refused . . . Invented a hundred and one excuses . . ."

It's quite true . . . I've never managed to be boorish enough just to tell her a trip with her would *bore* me . . . Will anyone ever do justice to men's incredible delicacy? To the ingenuity with which they make things up and pretend, rather than wound a woman fatally? By finally telling her the truth: that one simply doesn't fancy it . . .

But I come very close to bawling the truth at her this morning: Don't want to!!! Yah!!!

Don't feel like listening to her drone on interminably about backstairs politics, for the sake of a rather tense screw . . . Don't feel like hearing a slanted account of our relationship for the thousandth time . . . Her generosity . . . Her sacrifices . . . Her fidelity . . . My selfishness, coldness and self-seeking . . . Her constancy . . . My fickleness . . . Her magnanimity . . . My meanness . . . Her broadmindedness . . . My narrowness . . . Her morality . . . My cynicism . . . Her genuine culture . . . My hairsplitting . . . Her frankness . . . My hypocrisy . . . Her straightness . . . My deviousness . . .

Shall I do it, once and for all? Now? No, I mustn't . . . And, you never know, it might be risky for Ysia . . .

"What do you mean, Barcelona? I haven't budged from here!"

"Liar! They told me at the *Journal!* And someone saw you there!"

"I might have said I was going to Spain so that people would leave me in peace . . . And if anyone says they saw me they were just seeing things . . . There's a lot of it about . . ."

But yes, why not tell her the truth? It's self-evident . . . For example: "Have you noticed it's always you who call me? *Always?* Never the other way around? *Never!*" As bluntly as that? Yes . . . She knows it perfectly well . . . That's really why she's so furious . . . I feel very sorry for her now . . . Don't know what to do to avoid humiliating her any further . . . If only I'd fancied her Sandra, whom she provided so kindly in order to pep up our dwindling relationship . . . They could have discussed me together . . . It would have given them something to do . . . To stop desiring someone is to stop desiring their desire . . . Their projections . . . Fantasies . . . Playacting . . . The boredom, when a man and a woman disconnect from one another sexually! The immeasurable boredom . . . The sea . . . The Sahara . . . Friendship? Yes, perhaps, after moderate, not too exhausting efforts . . . And even so . . . But anyway . . .

Only a year ago Flora would have proceeded from making a scene to direct attack . . . Straight for the joystick . . . But that doesn't work anymore . . . She hasn't the strength . . . Something's broken . . . What? She looks at the papers strewn all over the floor . . . But she doesn't see typed pages . . . No . . . She seems to see blood, shit, some crawling insect . . . A spider . . .

She's simply finding she's reached the bottom of the barrel of contempt . . . She doesn't "love" me anymore . . . She doesn't hate me anymore in an interesting way . . . There's a physical inhibition . . . That impossible "novel" really does exist! And therefore I exist too . . . Symbolically . . . Whether it's good or bad . . . It's proof of my negative attitude . . . My autonomy . . . My independence . . . My nontransferable masturbation . . . Of the to her inconceivable fact that I have a life of my own . . . Another "world view" . . . It's a tangible sign that I'm really unspeakable . . . All the rest is nothing in comparison . . . Women? Gone with the wind! Changing opinions? Unimportant! No, this is the unforgivable sin . . . The ultimate betrayal . . . A novel! And readable! That everyone will be able to read! Unveiling of the Mysteries! Lecherous viper! Betrayer of Eleusis!

I didn't know I'd entered into a kind of phantom government . . . A secret society . . . And that it was my duty not to tell . . . I didn't know I was dead! Okay, there have to be writers . . . Clowns too . . . And dancers . . . Big grown-up children . . . It's very good for appearances . . . It soothes people's imaginations . . . And it's not too dangerous, is it? They're so sweet, with their obsessions, their manias, their inflated egos . . . Like Malmora . . . *Vecchio porcellone* . . . They're needed, they really are . . . Especially as they don't upset anyone . . . It's all on the surface . . . Nothing too bold . . . All in aid of the Prizes! No, no danger, they respect their Mothers too much. . . It's a well-known fact . . . I mean all the things with capital letters . . . Life, the Inexplicable, the Infinite, Man, Death, the Cosmos . . . Charming people, writers . . . You can put them here and there from time to time, like vases, and it doesn't do any harm, brightens up the place, adds a whiff of culture . . . At the end of the news or in the back pages of a magazine . . . As a "feature," a "profile" . . . A "think piece" . . . With a thoughtful-looking photograph . . . His childhood . . . His opinions about everything . . . Humble wisdom . . . Inner experience . . . In other words, keep talking—words never hurt anybody . . .

Does anyone really important write a *novel?* You must be joking . . . Flora certainly didn't agree to rub my root because I was a budding novelist! Not on your life! She was prepared to love me like herself . . . In other words, as someone important . . . In her eyes, at least . . . That is, someone who deals with genuine questions . . . Power . . . The power struggle . . . The manipulation of the setting in which writers briefly dream on behalf of all . . . Or rather, to revert to what I said before, she loved me as she might love someone completely dead . . . "I love him, therefore he's dead . . ." This is one of the two key syllogisms, according to S. . . . What he calls the two syllogisms of the hysteric . . . The first is, "He loves me, but I'm nothing, therefore he's a dope . . ." And the second, "I love him, but I am him, therefore he's dead . . ." There's also what S. calls his "great law." Which is: "For a woman, a man is nothing but an erect penis or a blank, but never a body equipped with sex organs which is something other than just a blank . . ." Write it out ten thousand times . . . After that you can go away . . .

Yes, when they really give themselves it's because they think you'll be silent . . . Or silenced . . . Dead, as far as telling the story is concerned . . . Writers, you've never known anything . . . Or not much . . . Your books prove it . . . You don't know what goes on . . .

There she stands, Flora, fascinated by the papers she's chucked around, as by a cobra . . . Now, unavoidably, she's trampling on them . . . It's against them she's making a scene now . . . Against

the principle of literature as a whole . . . I'm not here anymore . . .
My sperm should not have produced *that* . . . Or, to be more
horribly exact: "What? He's got enough of it left to write *that!*"
Accident, anomaly, nightmare . . . Biological disruption . . . Denial
of osmosis . . . Of the whole of thermodynamics . . . If only I could
not be there! If only she could burn it all up, here and now! And I
could disappear, as I came, in a puff of smoke! Baneful Mephisto
that I am!

I go over to her . . . Kiss her gently on the forehead . . . She
doesn't react . . . I lead her to the door . . . She doesn't resist . . .
She goes . . . Heavily . . . Without a word . . . Beware of pity! No,
too tiring . . . And pointless . . .

Rousseau writes of Mme. du Deffand: "In the end I preferred
the scourge of her hatred to that of her friendship . . ." Well said
. . . Turn the page . . .

"Come if you can. I'm at the Savoy. Yours, Cyd . . ."

Weekend in London . . . I stay with Cyd . . . I don't move from
her spacious bedroom . . . She has to go out on business . . . I sleep
. . . She comes back . . . We make love . . . She makes some phone
calls . . . Goes out again . . . I watch television and have another
sleep . . . Shall we have dinner here? Yes . . . Champagne and
caviar . . . Sunday morning . . . Breakfast . . . We make love again
. . . Cyd makes some phone calls . . . We go for a walk in Hyde
Park . . .

Cyd is very cheerful here, more than in New York . . .

"Guess who we're having brunch with!"

"Who?"

"My mother . . ."

She gives me a sidelong glance . . . But yes, why not? Brunch at
her mother's place . . . From anyone else but Cyd I'd take that as a
trap or an attack . . . But she bewitches me . . . Her mother lives
near Kensington Gardens . . . An only-just-elderly lady, very calm
and distinguished . . . She came back to live in England after the

death of her husband, who was a banker . . . The conversation moves easily from one thing to another . . . The Falklands . . . The birth of Lady Di's son . . . The Pope's visit . . . Spy stories . . . The I.R.A. being infiltrated by the Russians . . . We're all very much at ease as we eat our bacon and scrambled eggs . . .

"I hear you're a journalist?"

"Yes . . . But on vacation at the moment . . ."

"He's writing a novel, mother," says Cyd.

"A novel?"

"Yes . . ."

"What about?"

"Women today . . ."

"Ah! A man's point of view at last! They've changed a lot, haven't they? Or perhaps not all that much? What do you think?"

"As you say — a lot and very little . . . One has to try to describe it . . ."

"And it's always the same story in different forms?"

"More or less . . ."

"The same story as ever since Shakespeare? Only with cars, planes, computers, atomic bombs and space rockets? Comedy? Tragedy? *The Merry Wives of Windsor? Macbeth?*"

"It's difficult to do better than Shakespeare . . ."

"Do you like Virginia Woolf?"

"Very much . . . *Mrs. Dalloway* . . ."

"Oh yes! That's her best, don't you think? And her ideas about women, too? Very advanced . . . Prophetic . . . People are beginning to see that now . . . Don't you think?"

"Yes indeed . . ."

She's in the process of finding me charming . . . That's the main thing . . .

"And how's business with you, darling?" she asks Cyd.

"Fine, thanks . . . Contracts pouring in . . ."

"Oh, television! . . . Aren't you tired of it?"

"I don't watch it, mother . . . I just do it . . ."

"What about New York? Not too exhausting?"

"No . . . But it's nice to be back in London . . ."

"And"—to me—"how are things in Paris?"

"The same as ever, thank you . . . You know what Paris is like . . ."

We go back to the hotel . . . Cyd's delighted . . . Her mother likes me . . . She whispered as much to her in the hall as we were leaving . . . Everything went smoothly . . . Cyd makes love to me again on the strength of it . . . Affectionately . . . Confidently . . . We skillfully manage to disappear . . . In the mirror . . . Nothing and no one left . . .

"Do you know what I'd like, darling? Really like?"

"Tell me."

"For us to be together in Venice. For the Biennale."

"Venice, yes . . . Biennale, no."

"Yes, then?"

"Yes."

"You're an angel."

She drives me to Heathrow . . . We hardly say anything now . . . Light conversation, caresses . . . It's restful . . . She keeps on kissing me . . . These Englishwomen . . .

That was my weekend in London.

Right, now I need to hole up alone again . . . I can't make up my mind . . . What about my old trick of taking a hotel room right in the middle of Paris? Or Versailles? The Trianon? Walks on the grounds . . . No . . . I know! Why didn't I think of it before? The Plaza Lucchese, of course . . . In Florence . . . Overlooking the yellow, muddy Arno? No, room 177, with a view of Santa Croce . . . The cupola . . . The Pazzi Chapel . . .

And here I am . . . With the feeling that this time I'm face to face with time itself . . . Lord, how lovely Tuscany is! How can one live anywhere else? . . . I've cut myself off completely . . . No one but Deb knows where I am . . . Suddenly swallowed up . . . How quickly everything disappears . . . How instantly everything can be forgotten . . . I get going at once on all cylinders . . . Bed at 10

P.M. Up at 6. Breakfast on the balcony, 7:15. Work till noon. Lunch, 12:30. Two coffees in the sun and read till 2. Siesta till 4. Work till 7:30. Light dinner . . . After three days, some progress at night. Work from 9:30 till 1 A.M. Pause for breath.

Read the paper . . . Ease the wrist . . . Every detail counts . . . Breathing, digestion . . . Learning from sleep.

I'm really enjoying myself.

After five days I start going to one of the side chapels in Santa Croce every morning . . . The ones with the Giottos . . . St. Francis . . . There aren't many of us there at 8 A.M. Four old women, the almost paralyzed sexton, and me . . . The ageless little priest arrives with his battered leather briefcase . . . Kneels at the altar . . . Goes into the sacristy . . . Comes back wearing his chasuble . . . Rings his little bell as he enters . . . And starts off at a great rate . . . "Nel Nome del Padre e del Figlio e dello Spirito Santo . . . Signore, pietà . . . Cristo, pietà . . . Signore, pietà . . ." Then he hurries through the Creed and the Gospel toward the consecration . . . "Aspetto la resurrezione dei morti e la vita del mondo che verrà . . ." Then communion . . . Then the conclusion . . . "Vi benedica Dio Omnipotente Padre e Figlio e Spirito Santo . . . La messa è finita, andate in pace . . ." "Mass" means "sending away," doesn't it? You're sent away . . . Come on, then . . .

I have another coffee afterward . . . A stroll through the cloisters, and then into the Pazzi Chapel, white, gray, and blue, with its Della Robbia medallions . . . The four Evangelists, pen in hand . . . Then I rush back to my room . . . Come on, come on, get it right . . . Come on, letters; come on, sentences . . . With the blessing of the Holy Trinity . . . Of the Virgin Mary, the Apostles, the Martyrs and all the saints . . . Ah, but it doesn't come as easily as that, the grace of the Spirito Santo! And I *am* dealing with rather special subjects . . . Unorthodox . . . Dubious . . . Inflammatory . . .

But I must keep at it . . . Sit there poised . . . It might start to flow at any moment . . . Meanwhile, shift the syllables around . . . Go over old notebooks . . . Make my mind a blank . . .

I close the shutters . . . Shut the summer out . . . The hills, the olive trees, the yews, the pines, the belfries . . . Or else I go and

take a nap in the Boboli gardens, up in the Earthly Paradise . . .
Foresta spessa e viva . . . Yellow roses . . . Nobody about . . . It's
out of season . . . And then I go back . . . Two more pages . . .

Around six o'clock, a whisky . . . At dinner a half-bottle of red
wine . . . No alcohol at all during the day . . . Chastity . . . Gradual elimination of sexual activity . . .

From my balcony I can see a girl in one of the neighboring
apartments . . . Dark, about twenty, lying on her front on the bed,
reading . . . She's almost naked, wearing only a pair of blue shorts
. . . She's there all the time, deep in her book, absorbed, wriggling
her behind as she turns the pages . . . What can she be reading?
And is it worth writing anything else? Oh, now she's putting on a
record . . . French . . . An arrangement of *Chagrin d'amour* . . .

> *Under my feet the earth,*
> *Under yours, hell!*

Rapid, jerky little rhythm . . . Pause . . . Breathless song . . .
Shock of the chorus . . .

By the eighth day the body starts to live a different life . . . Light
and airy . . . A low but continuous flame . . . One thing follows
another of its own accord . . . Your memory rises up and reproaches
you for all you were going to leave out . . . It's almost like having
a magic carpet . . . What a strange beast language is . . . Loyal,
patient, long-suffering, putting up with your conceit, your self-
indulgence, your incessant coarseness, and always forgiving, par-
doning, and returning to you as if it were coming home . . . Here
it is . . . A little breath . . . If only it doesn't die out! If only it will
stay! It pauses . . . Is it about to go away? Come back, true god of
gods, light of lights! Don't be angry with me! Come back! "Remember not our sins," says the priest during mass, "but the faith
of thy Church . . ." That's it! I am a tiny little church . . . In a
tent . . . A nomad in the desert . . . Not worthy to cast his shadow
within thy walls! Careful, now . . . Easy does it . . . Here it comes
again . . . On tiptoe . . . In a whisper . . . Sweeping space aside like
a curtain . . .

"And, behold, the Lord passed by, and a great and strong wind rent the mountains, and brake in pieces the rocks; but the Lord was not in the wind; and after the wind an earthquake; but the Lord was not in the earthquake: And after the earthquake a fire; but the Lord was not in the fire: and after the fire a still small voice . . . And it was so, when Elijah heard it, that he wrapped his face in his mantle, and went out, and stood in the entering in of the cave . . . And, behold, there came a voice unto him, and said, What doest thou here, Elijah? And he said, I have been very jealous for the Lord God of hosts: because the children of Israel have forsaken thy covenant, thrown down thine altars, and slain thy prophets with the sword; and I, even I only, am left; and they seek my life, to take it away . . .''

And Elijah got his ascension into heaven in a whirlwind, with a chariot and horses of fire . . . He got it by knowing how to behave, alone on the mountain . . . "And the ravens brought him bread and flesh in the morning, and bread and flesh in the evening; and he drank of the brook.'' . . . You can find all this in the First and Second Book of Kings, one of the most disturbing and angry parts of the Bible . . . The Bible is the only book I've brought with me . . . It's quite enough . . . Elijah and Jezebel . . . A really crucial business . . . Yet another woman . . . Who understood immediately, and better than anyone, how dangerous someone like Elijah was . . . He'll undermine our "Goddess" ploy . . . Overthrow our idols . . . Slit the throats of our favorite eunuchs . . . Our beloved drag queens . . . Discredit our sorcerers . . . Our sleight of hand . . . He'll profane the shrine of the great and holy womb . . . Compromise the whole business of the loaf in the oven . . . And the whole country too, if he's allowed to get away with it . . . If we let him preach his god from on high, invisible and intangible . . . Who doesn't give a curse for the most sacred things . . . Consecrated wafers . . . Painted ova . . . And above all the primal bed . . . And the secrets of the bedchamber . . . What a horrible, cold, insensitive guy! The absolute opposite of the movie-lover we'd have liked!

I've decided to take a closer look at the business of women in that part of the world . . . But it crops up everywhere! No one talks about anything else! It's fascinating! But we're not told any of the real story . . . Even though it's quite clear and explicit all the time . . . Everything that happens does so because of or through the medium of women . . . Starting with the wives of the patriarchs! Who are highly respectable matriarchs! Listen—you want to know when Israel and the Arabs will be reconciled? I'll tell you . . . When Sarah and Hagar stop scowling at one another . . . Resolution 242! It's not going to happen in a hurry! But it all goes back to that . . . And the trick played by Rebecca! And the contest between Rachel and Leah for Jacob! Enough to make you fall down laughing . . . The World Cup! Leah kicks off with a burst of four children . . . Four girls . . . Rachel's flabbergasted . . . She's been caught un-awares in the penalty area . . . Free kick! Penalty! Corner! Use your head! To try to even things up she asks Jacob to screw her maid, Bilhah, "and she shall bear on my knees, that I also may have children by her" . . . Bilhah gives birth to a son . . . And then another! But Leah counterattacks after half-time . . . She too gives Jacob her maid . . . Zilpah . . . And, surprise, surprise, it works! Twice . . . A couple more sons! Wham! Let's see, how many does that make? Eight! After that there's some murky business with drugs . . . Mandrakes . . . From the Hebrew *dûdà'im*, from the root *dwd* or *dôd*, meaning beloved . . . The plural, *dôdîm*, means caresses . . . The hero's a bit worn out by now . . . Aphrodisiac duel . . . But Leah wins again . . . A fifth son! And another! The sixth is hers! This could go on forever . . . It's incredible . . . Needless to say, Jacob, like Adam, seems passive under all this pressure . . . It's the women who decide things . . . Fighting like tigers . . . With embryos . . . Everything points to the fact that this famous patriarchy is really an iron matriarchy! Exhausting! Jacob is a slave of the penis! A miner of balls! A prole of the prick! Leah indulges herself so far as to produce a daughter . . . Dinah . . . What a waste! Just to show what she's made of . . . Dinah's going to get herself raped a bit further on, but don't let's confuse the issue . . . Rachel is in despair! She still hasn't got a child of her own, one that's really hers . . . But in the end god softens . . . "And God remembered Rachel, and God hearkened to her, and opened her womb . . ." And who is this? Why yes, it's him! Joseph! The great Joseph, the one that went to Egypt . . . An affair to keep an eye on . . . But Rachel follows her long break right through . . . And dies giving birth to Benjamin . . . The last-born . . . How sweet . . . And where is it they bury her? In Bethlehem . . . Well, well . . .

Phew! I don't know if you've managed to follow all that . . . But the story itself is marvelous . . . Completely impassive . . . All these experiences teach Jacob a thing or two about genetic manipulation . . . And he manages to make sheep couple in the way that suits him . . . "Then all the cattle bare speckled . . ." In short, he endures the severest of trials . . . And emerges worthy to wrestle with the Angel! And to take the name of Israel . . .

Rachel . . . She was the one Jacob loved . . . Too much . . . Hence all those children of her sister's . . . But it's quality not quantity that counts . . . Q.E.D . . . Thank you, God! And good-night . . .

Look at Genesis . . . The Beginning . . . A detailed gyneco-theology . . . All the other genealogies are muddled . . . Vague . . . Look at Egypt, India, Greece . . . Only the Bible rubs your nose right in it, instead of in the clouds or in the ideal shell arising out of the waves in the heavenly light of rosy-fingered dawn . . . But there's nothing heavenly about copulation . . . That's rubbish . . . Don't look for god where he can't possibly be . . . But psychoanalysis must have been born somewhere around here? Of course . . .

What was the name of Rebecca's nurse? The ten dollar question . . . Deborah . . . And what does Deborah mean? The twenty dollar question . . . The bee . . . There's another woman called Deborah in the Book of Judges . . . A prophetess . . . Who went up to battle . . . "Awake, awake, Deborah: awake, awake, utter a song . . ." A bee that sings? The Bible, one of the oldest of poems . . . She's the wife of Lapidoth, whose name means torches, flashes of light . . . Barak lends her a hand in the commando attack on Sisera . . . Who is slain by Jael, from the Hebrew ya'el, an antelope, who took him into her tent in order to murder him in his sleep . . .

One could go on indefinitely . . . But what strikes me afresh is

the play on names . . . The interplay . . . When children are born
. . . Translations . . . Transpositions . . . Acts of praise . . . Sights
. . . Invocations . . .

So god opens wombs when he feels so inclined, supervises what
goes on, forgets, goes away, returns, earmarks for himself the first-
born, the cutting edge, and is represented as the axis of flux, regu-
lating it and intermittently watching over its vagaries . . . He's
therefore very jealous . . . Can't bear people to leave him . . . To
drift toward the female gods with whom he's always picking quarrels . . . Astarte . . . Ashtaroth, the companion of Baal, symbolized
by the sacred bed . . . God isn't pro-bed at all, though! He's very
much against! Various massacres follow . . . Woman in bed—very
significant, huh? Here . . . Only here . . . And now . . . Everything
now . . . Only now . . . Amnesia . . . Closing of all horizons . . .
Cycle . . . The eternal return . . . Not the Law . . . But the "cus-
tom of women" . . . And all the time the chosen people, chosen by
the faceless one, keep going off and worshipping gold or statues . . .
"And Israel abode in Shittim, and the people began to commit
whoredom with the daughters of Moab . . . And they called the
people unto the sacrifices of their gods: and the people did eat, and
bowed down to their gods . . . And Israel joined himself unto Baal-
peor: and the anger of the Lord was kindled against Israel . . ." We
keep coming back to it . . . The same story told ten thousand times
over . . . It's endemic . . . Magnetic . . . Viscous . . . Libidinous
. . . They can't help it . . . Always the same pattern . . . And then
Jehovah sends someone . . . A prophet, a leader . . . And he de-
stroys Baal's altar and the sacred bed, interrupts the decadent orgy
. . . The insidious routine . . . Challenges and exterminates the
local magicians, beauticians of the local tart . . . Disembowels one
. . . Stabs the others . . . Then it happens again . . . And dies down
again . . . Happens again . . . The ups and downs of desire . . . The
pull of true pleasure, which uproots people and makes them jump
around, to the horror of those, male and female, who trade in
measured-out sperm . . .

With a few exceptions, including Elijah, the main character sees
god, prostrates himself before him, is astonished to survive, keeps

his commandments, wins all along the line, and then—loses his memory! Very odd . . . Take Solomon . . . He builds the Temple . . . The Temple to end all temples . . . Helped by the Lebanese stonemason from Tyre . . . What's his name? Oh yes, Hiram . . . Not satisfied with his wages, seeing it's something that's going to last for ever . . . Jealousy . . . Resentment . . . An important matter . . . Legends about it . . . The Queen of Sheba's stunned by the Temple . . . God solemnly manifests the presence of his Name in it . . . Appears to him in a cloud . . . Everything seems to be finished . . . And then, horrors! "But King Solomon loved many strange women, together with the daughter of Pharaoh, women of the Moabites, Ammonites, Edomites, Zidonians, and Hittites; Of the nations concerning which the Lord said unto the children of Israel, Ye shall not go in unto them, neither shall they come in unto you: for surely they will turn away your heart after their gods . . . But Solomon clave unto these in love . . . And he had seven hundred wives, princesses, and three hundred concubines: and his wives turned away his heart . . ."

Solomon himself? The wisest of the wise? Note the delightful detail: 700 wives and 300 concubines! More wives than concubines! More problems than pleasures! But very well thought of . . . Great performance . . . Superprofessional! The Song of Songs . . . How decadent we are now! But finally this great glittering snare does turn away his heart to Ashtoreth, hence the decline of his descendants . . . And so on . . . Solomon has lost touch with the living god . . . Fallen asleep in the indulgence of false gods . . . He has debilitated himself . . . And I shall meet with the same fate . . . So why have I been better-behaved than he? What good will it do me?

Once you really go into the Bible you can never get out again . . . This is what's happening to me in Florence . . . I started out just trying to prepare for my next trip to Jerusalem . . . And here I am, caught up in the greatest detective story ever . . . I knew the Bible already, of course . . . But now *it* is beginning to know me

. . . And that's different . . . Now it's I who am the enigma . . . And *it* is a way of setting out all the solutions . . . My little priest reads out a passage from it every morning . . . Exodus . . . Deuteronomy . . . Isaiah . . . The Psalms . . . From the Christian point of view, of course . . . And there's the problem . . . I don't say that point of view is wrong, but for the most part it does let you off going into the origins of things . . . On the other hand the study of foundations can make you neglect the roof and the overall view . . . All full of excellent intentions . . . Symmetrically organized misunderstanding . . . Strange . . .

But of course I speak as a novelist, don't I? . . . Who dreams at night of what he's going to write the next day . . . The great scene in Sinai . . . The peals of thunder that stand for voices . . . The smoke . . . The pillar of fire . . . "And they saw the God of Israel: and there was under his feet as it were a paved work of a sapphire stone, and as it were the body of heaven in its clearness . . ." I dream of that blue stone . . . Of the solid water . . . And wake with a start . . . Thinking I've seen it . . . Touched it . . . Sitting up in bed with my eyes open, listening to the darkness, I exist less than my dream . . .

I think about the contest between Rachel and Leah again . . . Two sisters . . . When her handmaid, Bilhah, gives Jacob a second son in her stead, Rachel cries out: "With great wrestlings have I wrestled with my sister, and I have prevailed . . ." A fight with the nonangel . . . The name of his son, Naphtali, refers to the Hebrew word for "my struggle . . ." *Niphtaltî* means "I have struggled . . ." *Naphtâlî*, struggles of god . . . And so on . . .

This does shed some light . . . A woman can't see further than the end of her femininity . . . Than another woman . . . Than women in general . . . That's her approach to god . . . Violent . . . Giving birth to a child in order to crush another . . . The sexual act itself is obviously of minor importance . . . Similarly, when Rebecca decides to deceive Isaac for the sake of Jacob it's because she can't stand Esau's wives, Judith and Bashemath . . . Jacob will go and marry elsewhere . . . Sarah and Hagar—we needn't come back to them . . . And what about Eve? Who says, after Cain is born, "I

373

have gotten a man from the Lord . . ." A play of words on *qanîti*, "I have acquired," and *Qayin*, Hebrew for "Cain . . ." The habit of changing children into witticisms, again . . . As if witticisms were the other side or antimatter of generation . . . And who knows? So what about Eve, then—who gave her the idea of the other woman, the horizontal one? The Serpent? And then death began? And the wheel came full circle? That must be it . . . You might not be the only woman, says the Serpent . . . Lilith . . . So make sure you are the One and only . . . The tree of good and evil, *du bien et du mal* . . . *Du bien et du mâle* . . . Adam doesn't matter . . . A robot only just capable of thought . . . A golem . . . A puppet . . . You can do what you like with him . . . A convenience . . . A husband . . . An extra . . .

That's what you find everywhere, it seems to me . . . Women's incredible contempt for men as such . . . And their fierce admiration for one another . . . Take Flora . . . She thinks of me only as an appendage for women . . . The rest is waffle . . . Stupid? Yes, but incurable . . . And it took me a long time to realize it was their stupidity that fascinated me . . . Really? No, it's not possible! Such blindness? No, it can't be true! But it is . . . And there's a perverse pleasure in proving it over and over again . . . In watching them endlessly plant themselves on the sacred tree . . . A man is soon sized up—just an extra little bit of meat . . . So what? Phooey! Whereas a woman! If she had one of those bits of meat it would be quite another thing! Immeasurable! That's why she's been unjustly deprived of it . . . Of the real zappendice! Something much more than children . . . Hordes of children! Potential children . . . It's man who's barren, incomplete, frustrated, anxious, with his frail, inconsequential, piteously castratable phallus, tottering foolishly from one mess to another . . . Whereas a woman *knows!* She's plugged in direct to god!

It always seems superfluous to women that god should speak . . . Artificial . . . A shadow show . . . Compensatory megalomania . . . A male hijack . . . But he *is* there, really there, attending to the Great Screw . . . Which propels bodies into the roulette wheel of increasing and multiplying . . .

374

You can understand the precautions in the Bible . . . The hurried ad hoc anointings . . . The elections—early, postponed or rigged . . . What a job! And always needing to be done all over again . . . For the moment—thanks if you're still following—I'll just call your attention to the business of naming the baby . . . Of commemorating the birth with a pun . . . It's very revealing . . . Sarah laughs incredulously at the idea of conceiving at her age? So along comes Isaac, and his name means "laughter . . ." And don't tell me yet again that Sarah's age is a "metaphor . . ." No, it really is a question of her periods . . . Which have stopped . . . It's stated quite plainly in the text . . . She's incapable of becoming pregnant . . .

I can still hear Flora's sardonic laughter whenever I excused myself for not seeing her more often by saying I was "working . . ." "Tell it to the marines!" She used to stare at me . . . Women! More women! That was the only possible explanation . . . What else? Nothing . . .

How could anyone like being on their own? Absolutely on their own?

Who would credit the life I'm leading now, this agitated penance in my room in Florence? No one . . . He's making it up . . . He invents it afterward . . . It's a well-known fact that books write themselves . . . What's that you say? Jehovah spoke to Moses face to face? After forty days? And he spoke to him again in the tent of the congregation, about the ark of the covenant, with the two cherubs of gold on the two ends of the mercy seat? The voice of god . . . Live broadcast? From Heaven, no doubt? And what else, may I ask? You're surely not going to swallow that? A hoax, a hoax! Just to usurp power and lead the simple-minded by the nose! Tell it to the marines!

But I do call Deb every two or three days . . . I love the crackling and the occasional hiatuses of long-distance phone calls . . . Sometimes you're lucky enough to catch voices overlapping one another in all kinds of languages, interfering with one another, canceling each other out, multiplying, in a hurry to convey elementary information from one end to the other of the revolving satellite . . . Business . . . The Stock Exchange . . . Sell! Buy! Raise the bid! Lower it! Swarms of stereotyped phrases of interest and affection . . . Darling! *Chéri!* Honey! Sweetie! *Querido! Liebling! Carino!* Angel! The weather . . . Money . . . Everything's fine . . .

"I had a funny sort of a visitor the other day," says Deb.

"Oh?"

"A little Spanish woman—dark, with blue eyes . . . Very excited . . . She's in politics, I take it? Valenzuela? Flora Valenzuela?"

"What did she want?"

"You seem to be breaking hearts all over the place, my dear!"

"What did she say?"

"Lots of things . . . We'll talk about it when you get back, if you don't mind . . ."

"Nothing serious?"

"That depends on your point of view . . . It was a mixture of the comic and the pathetic . . ."

"Right. But for goodness sake don't let it bother you."

"I'm not in the least bothered. Are you all right?"

"Yes, thanks. And you two?"

"Stephen's got a cold . . . He's staying home from school . . ."

"Has he got a temperature?"

"Nothing to speak of."

"Anything to report?"

"The *Journal* called. They're wondering where you've got to this time."

"What did you tell them?"

"That you were having a look around in Thailand . . . Are you getting on all right with the book?"

"Not too badly."

"Oh yes—you're supposed to ring a number in Rome . . . They've asked for you three times . . . It sounds rather urgent . . ."

"Rome?"

"Yes. The man sounded upset when I said you weren't here."

Deb gives me three numbers . . . Ask for extension 333 . . . I can't think who it can be . . . Some weekly, I suppose . . . Wanting me to translate an article . . .

So Flora's going all out . . . Direct attack . . . Dive bombing . . . Raid on the rear . . . Offensive against the private sanctuary . . . Attempt at female solidarity . . . "You don't suspect . . . You don't want to know . . . But, believe me, he's a liar . . ." I can just imagine the scene . . . And I know it won't work . . . Deb's too intelligent . . . Once the first irritation is over . . . And all this just to try to spoil my landing when I go back . . . I can see how Flora imagines it . . . Revolutionary tribunal . . . Popular justice . . . Morality . . . I come in, handcuffed . . . The court's full of the women I've treated badly . . . They speak one after the other . . . I am confounded . . . All the details . . . Movements, names of hotels and restaurants, statements by chambermaids, dates, damning witnesses . . . Each of the victims tells her story . . . The vampire's crimes . . . I'm found guilty . . . No mercy . . . The cell door clangs shut on my despair . . . My sexual organs are encased in an iron box . . . It's nighttime . . . But in the damp corridors there's the sound of footsteps . . . I sit up on my straw pallet . . . The heavy door creaks open . . . Am I going to be surreptitiously murdered, like the heroes of the Red Army Faction savagely liquidated in their cells by imperialist killers? A shadow glides over to me . . . Masked . . . It's the end . . . Flora! In black stockings, garters, lace . . . She hurls herself on me, opens my iron box with a little key hidden in her bra, and rapes me, roaring with pleasure . . . I groan with her . . . This lasts several months . . . Long enough to reeducate me completely . . . To make me adore the outraged authentic deity . . . Coitus? Brainwashing . . . Every coitus another brainwashing . . . After which I'm quietly released . . . But I'm socially dead . . . Destitute . . . Entirely dependent on Flora, who uses me as a secretary-cum-confidant . . . I spend my time typing her speeches . . . I'm her tool . . . Completely at her disposal . . . Suitably humiliated . . . I get worn out . . . Old . . . I die in oblivion . . .

Speaking of which, that phone call from Rome . . . What can it be? An assignment, perhaps? Well paid? Might as well just find out . . .

"Hello? This is the Secretariat . . . Extension 333? What was the name? One moment, please . . ."

Good heavens, yes! My letter to the Pope! Enclosing my long article about him from the *New York Times!* Published in England, too, and all over the place . . . I just mentioned that I'd like to meet him some day . . . But nothing specific . . . Was there anything else? Oh yes, by the same post I sent a copy of the limited edition of my little essay on Duns Scotus . . . And my short piece on theological novelty in Joyce . . .

"Hello?" A guy speaking in English . . . "Oh, it's you! We've been trying to get in touch with you for two or three days . . . Good . . . Where are you? . . . Florence? . . . Excellent! Can you be in Rome the day after tomorrow, in the morning? . . . Splendid! Will you come straight to the Vatican, at eleven o'clock? Eleven sharp? . . . Absolutely perfect! His Holiness has granted you a brief audience . . . To be treated as confidential, if you don't mind . . . Ask for me when you get here . . ." He gives a Polish name . . . "You will be punctual, won't you? . . . All right? . . . Splendid . . . Perfect . . . See you on Thursday!"

Right . . . After all, it's not so very improbable . . . At the moment all is grist that comes to the Vatican's mill . . . So we must get ready to meet Peter's successor . . . Preceded, if I remember right, by Linus, Cletus, Clement, Anacletus, Evaristus, Alexander, Sixtus, Telesporus, Hyginus, Pius, Anicetus, Soter, Eleutherus, Victor, Zephyrinus, Calixtus, Urban, Pontian, Antherus, Fabian, Cornelius, Lucius . . . Let's skip ten centuries . . . Martin V, Pius II, Sixtus IV, Alexander VI, Julius II (hiya, Michelangelo!), Leon X, Paul III (the Jesuits! the Council of Trent!), Clement VIII . . . Let's skip another four hundred years . . . Gregory XVI, Pius X (the Immaculate Conception, Papal Infallibility, the 1864 *Syllabus* against "pantheism and Communism"), Leon XIII *(Aeterni Patris, Rerum Novarum)*, Pius X, Benedict XV, Pius XI (against Fascism, Nazism, Communism), Pius XII (the Assumption!), John XXIII, Paul VI,

John Paul I, and finally John Paul II, the first non-Italian Pope for four hundred and fifty-five years . . .

The long history takes up only a few lines . . . Scarcely enough even to start a conversation . . . I'd better brush up on the present . . . What is it the Anglicans won't accept? The Real Presence, praying to the saints, prayers for the dead, purgatory (very important, this—hiya, Dante!), the celibacy of the priesthood . . . Hmm . . . Not bad . . . And what about Transsubstantiation . . .

The number of believers . . . Catholics: 803 million . . . Orthodox (the crucial matter of the *filioque*): 133 million . . . Anglicans: 50 million . . . Lutherans: 42 million . . . Current recovery . . . They thought they were in the lead . . . Or on the way to it . . . They were wrong . . .

How many Jews? That's a decisive factor . . . Thirteen million . . . Six million in the USA . . . 3.2 million in Israel . . . 1.7 in the USSR . . . 70,000 in France . . . 390,000 in Great Britain . . . 380,000 in Canada . . . 240,000 in Argentina . . . 110,000 in Brazil . . . As Esther always says, "There are more of you, but we're the best . . ." O.K. . . .

Islam? 450 million . . . That's the other side of the coin . . .

The end of the twentieth century really is amazing . . . Recapitulation . . . Sifting . . . Montage . . . Being a novelist now is a dream! Better than ever before! So long as you dare . . . Frenchmen, one more effort! I've just read the list of best-sellers in France in a weekly that's on sale here . . . Nothing but women! Historical novels by women! Soppy . . . "The King had looked at her that day, so Mary felt she was walking on the deliciously scented air which filled the castle grounds" — that sort of thing . . . There is one American male, though . . . And an Englishman . . . And a Rhodesian . . . But the French novel-reading public hasn't chosen one Frenchman! A public that's supposed to be "literary"! These lists are a reliable guide to what a country's like . . . The books you find under their beds . . . In their bathrooms . . .

Another day's work . . . My little neighbor's still in her room, passionately devouring her mysterious book . . . Still lying flat on her front . . . And in her shorts . . . She never looks up . . . She

wriggles at regular intervals . . . Gentle, unconscious masturbation
. . . Sun . . . Florence sun . . . Divine Comedy blue . . . I take
another stroll around the Pazzi Chapel . . . Filippo Brunelleschi . . .
His art of poetry . . . His architectual testament . . . The temple of
sound . . . The absolute musical box! Without sides . . . Open all
around . . . In the air . . . A complete interspacial capsule . . . I
must ask the Pope if I can be buried there, in a corner . . . By
special dispensation . . . Under a flagstone . . . No inscription, so as
not to embarrass anyone . . . Not to make anyone jealous . . .
There beneath the blue-white-gray . . . Without any insolent gravity . . . Don't look any further . . . There isn't anything better . . .
No one has ever built anything more beautiful on this crazy planet
. . . Late afternoon . . . Bells ringing everywhere . . .

I take a morning train . . . Reach the Vatican at the appointed
time . . . Go in . . . It's like suddenly stepping out of the middle of
Rome into Tibet . . . Or rather into nowhere . . . A negative space
. . . Antimatter setting . . . I'm met immediately by a plump and
jovial little Polish priest . . . We hurry through offices, galleries,
corridors, libraries . . . There's a combination of bustle and quiet,
as in a battle . . . All the people look as if they're at war . . . And
so they are . . . A building site in the middle of a museum . . . On
the eve of ruin or renaissance . . . We go straight on, around
corners, up, down, up again, down again . . . He takes me into a
little dark room and tells me to wait . . . A wave of the hand and
he's gone . . .

I wait for quite a long time . . . Nearly an hour . . . The room's
so dark I can scarcely see the antique furniture . . . The pictures
. . . The curtains and shutters are closed . . . I must be somewhere
over St. Peter's Square, to the east . . .

The door on the other side of the room opens . . . A white shape
. . . It's Wojtyla . . . He beckons me in . . . Takes me by the hand
. . . Leads me to a chair facing his desk . . . Sits down behind it
. . . Looks at me . . .

"Shall we speak English?" he asks in English.

"Yes. Or in French," I answer, also in English.

"Or Italian?" he asks in Italian.

"Or Russian?" I say in Russian.

He laughs.

"Why not in Polish?" he says in English.

"Let's make it French," I say in French," if Your Holiness doesn't mind."

"Well," he says in French, "I liked your articles . . . They were very relevant after my visit to London . . . You know the difficulties . . . The prejudices . . . The misunderstandings about Marian dogma . . . I haven't much time, but I noticed you're also interested in literature and theology . . ."

"Yes," I say. "I think we're on the verge of great events there."

"That difficult Irish writer . . . Joyce?"

"Marvelous, Your Holiness."

"There are so many things I haven't read!" he says, just raising his right hand . . . "But not everything is in books, is it?"

He looks at me, smiling. Piercing eyes. Very compact body, not easily got down . . . Used to suffering, keeping silent, going through the mill. Tired, too . . . Sculpted . . .

"What about Duns Scotus? Our Subtle Doctor . . . You're interested in him too?"

"Very. He strikes me as very modern."

"He is, he is!" says the Pope, tapping the arm of his red chair. "Are you writing something else of that kind now?"

"No," I say. "Or perhaps. A novel."

"A novel?"

Silence.

"Listen," he says. "I have very little time, but I wanted to see you. You're young, you're a writer. You could do a great deal for the future . . . Did you know we're going to start a Papal Cultural Center?"

"What a good idea," I say.

"We'll see, we'll see!" he laughs.

I'm dying to mention the assassination attempt . . . The young

381

Turk who shot at him . . . Who's behind it? What? The Russians? How does he feel? . . . But no . . .

"Does Your Holiness still write poetry?"

"Good gracious, no! Where would I find the time? Anyhow, those poems were only youthful exercises . . . But here's the latest translation . . . Into Hebrew . . ."

He gets up quite spryly and comes around to hand me a little volume printed in Hebrew characters . . .

"A language with a great future," I say.

"You think so too? I've asked our Committee to be more active."

"The Bible in Hebrew!" I say.

"You should like St. Jerome! *Hebraicum veritatem* . . . Yes, yes . . . There's still a lot to be done" . . .

I don't like to ask him why the Vatican hasn't yet recognized the State of Israel diplomatically . . .

"It's getting late," he says . . . "Let's say the Lord's Prayer together . . . That says everything . . ."

He stands up. So do I.

> Our Father who art in Heaven
> Hallowed be thy Name.
> Thy kingdom come.
> Thy will be done
> On earth as it is heaven.
> Give us this day our daily bread,
> And forgive us our trespasses
> As we forgive those that trespassed against us.
> And lead us not into temptation,
> But deliver us from evil.
> For thine is the kingdom, the power and the glory,
> For ever and ever.
> Amen.

Then something happens . . . It's as if the Pope's voice were suddenly coming down from a height . . . He's suddenly become both higher and deeper before my very eyes . . . Deep as an abyss, yet at the same time light and transparent . . . All right . . . Every word he said felt momentous . . . It's an odd sort of prayer, when you come to think of it . . . The silence now is terrific . . . He stands there . . . Unmoving . . . I bend down on one knee . . . And feel his hand flutter over my head . . . Latin, this time:

"In nomine Patris, et Filii, et Spiritus Sancti."

It's over.

He takes me by the hand and leads me over to a little door in the wall . . . Opens it . . . "That way . . . Au revoir . . . Farewell . . ."

"Thank you," I say.

A little wave . . . He shuts the door.

The private staircase leads straight down into a courtyard . . . A hundred years and I'm on Bernini's esplanade . . . In broad daylight . . . Silver fountains . . . Blue breeze . . .

On the train I read a few articles about the way the Papacy's going . . . Always the same refrain . . . Too much politics . . . Too much spectacle . . . The Pope as superstar . . . Exorbitant expense . . . Publicity . . . Too conservative about sex . . . Homosexuality, contraception, abortion . . . Opposition to the ordination of women . . . Insistence on the celibacy of the priesthood . . . Rigidity about sex changes . . . Pilgrim of peace? Yes, but . . . And then there are the financial scandals . . . The Banco Ambrosiano . . . Poor old Ambrose! The Mafia . . . The P2 Masonic lodge . . . The dubious Lithuanian cardinal . . . Real estate transactions via the Bahamas . . . But in the end they always come back to organic considerations . . . I can't understand what kind of Pope the authors of these articles *would* like? One that runs a male brothel? Or a special gynecological clinic? Handing out pills as he used to hand out indulgences? Turned into a kind of supreme nun? No—the best thing, of course, would be to have no more Pope at all . . . To have done with this antique absurdity . . . The Virgin Mary! Infallibility! All incompatible with modern, open-minded humanism . . . No question . . . Could anyone imagine a setup more unreal and retrograde than the Catholic Church? It flies in the face of mathe-

matics . . . Ethnology . . . Physics . . . Physiology . . . Biology
. . . Astrology . . . Sorry, I meant to say astronomy . . . What sign
are you, by the way? I'm Sagittarius, with Aquarius in the ascen-
dant . . . Oh, terrific! Very fashionable! An interview with Borges
. . . Talking about the Pope's visit to Argentina . . . He refers to
John Paul II as an "important Italian official" . . . To his own
Methodist background . . . And then he's off again into the occult
. . . Am I me, or someone else dreaming he's me? Chang-Tsu . . .
Alchemy . . . Magic formula . . . Two lines from Dante, always the
same . . . The book of books . . . Babel . . . Aleph . . . The usual
performance . . .

The voice of the Chairwoman comes back to me: "The real
problems are probably quite different from what people think . . .
The emphasis is all on problems of sex and reproduction, and very
little is said about hygiene . . . It's as if it were even more taboo
than sex . . . You can't imagine how recent a phenomenon simple
elementary cleanliness is, especially for women . . . Yes, I mean
cleanliness about underwear, etc. . . . The end of the fifties . . . If
not later . . . You'd be amazed if you did a survey . . . Self-respect
. . . Respect for one's body . . . Look at all those prematurely
worn-out, let-go bodies . . . Motherhood? It's not only that . . .
It's not long ago, my dear boy, since women put soda in the water
they used to wash the dishes . . . And as for underwear! Just think
about the progress in fabrics! The invention of nylon was one of the
greatest revolutions in history . . . Ask all the grandmothers . . .
Nylon stockings! Lycra! Vinyl! Instead of that horrible "art silk
. . . " So . . . Do you read Balzac? Proust? So you know all about
Madame This's taffeta and Mademoiselle That's shawls — but what
about their underwear? Not a word! So the upgrading of underwear
is a desacralization! Very important! It's a question of chemistry too, of course, but from the point of view we're talking about
. . . And then there are deodorants! And makeup removers! Nail-
polish! Hair-spray! Bubble-baths! Creams! That's where real progress lies . . . A long way away from questions of metaphysics . . .
The battle against the priests for power over people's souls is an-

other matter altogether . . . Power in general is another matter . . . And don't forget women like to destroy themselves too—you have to take that into account . . . As if to punish themselves . . . The question of sex is quite different from daily maintenance . . . Of course the two things are connected . . . But upkeep must come first . . . Make no mistake . . ."

All this is very wise . . . It would have delighted Flaubert . . . Hey, doesn't he say something about the Immaculate Conception? In his correspondence? I must have it in my notes somewhere . . . The Immaculate Conception—not the Incarnation, but the sinless conception of Mary herself by her mother, Anne . . . Quite a different problem . . . Though everyone mixes them up . . . Ignorance! The link connecting mother and daughter . . . A crucial point . . . But quite a different thing from the fathering of the Son by the Holy Ghost . . .

Yes, here it is . . . "One of the causes of the moral weakness of the nineteenth century is the exaggerated *poetization* of women . . . I regard the dogma of the Immaculate Conception as a stroke of political genius on the part of the Church, which has formulated and negated to its own advantage all the female aspirations of the age . . ." And this, too, which I'd forgotten, from a letter of June 19th 1876, to Mme. Roger des Genettes: "Do you know St. Francis's *Fioretti?* I mention it because I have just embarked on reading this edifying work . . . Speaking of which, I believe that if I go on as I have been doing I shall win a place myself among the shining lights of the Church . . . I shall be one of the pillars of the temple . . . After St. Anthony, St. Julian, and then St. John the Baptist . . . I seem to be stuck among the saints forever" . . .

Flaubert shouldn't have been surprised — it's quite natural . . . But then he wasn't really surprised . . . He's writing in code . . . And what about Baudelaire, when he discovers the truth from the other side? An evident paradox? Or a deep-seated logic? "Who is more Catholic than the Devil? I am an incorrigible Catholic . . ." There are plenty of statements like that . . . Conscious . . . Provocative . . . Deliberate . . .

Perhaps Flaubert and Baudelaire should be beatified . . . I'll suggest it to the Papal Center . . . That would stir up the universities for a few centuries . . .

So here I am back in my room in Florence . . . One more week . . . Must try to stay braced . . . My little neighbor across the street is still glued to her book . . . But look, here's another show . . . A couple of queers . . . One's tall and hairy, with a moustache . . . The other's young and effeminate . . . Americans . . . They make love on the bed in the room next to the girl's . . . Very traditional . . . Just like heteros . . . Him on top of Her . . . Her with her legs in the air caressing His hairy behind . . . It's feeble, slow, persevering . . . Touching . . . Organic quid pro quo . . . Homos can't know what an ass really is . . . Its delights . . . Because for them there's only the vagina . . . How sad! What a narrowing of the horizon! What a shrinking of the curves! I pass them in the street later on . . . Well-behaved, irreproachable—like a pair of young honeymooners . . . Catalogues, museums . . . The splendors of Italy . . .

Can't help wondering what's waiting for me in Paris, though . . . How Deb has taken Flora's tour of inspection . . . And Flora's certainly not left it at that . . . Visits . . . Blather . . . Airports bombarded . . . Roads blocked . . . Ammunition dumps blown up . . . Bridges destroyed . . . Active revolt . . . I may find my base reduced to ashes when I get back . . . I'm not too worried about Deb . . . She'll react professionally, practically—as an analyst . . . She'll put up her prices, though . . .

I look up . . . My two nice queers are back in their room and at their conjugal coupling again . . . With sepulchral determination . . . They petrify the atmosphere . . . The Bible's very severe on them . . . In those days there were swarms of sacred male prostitutes around the temples . . . In Babylonia . . . Syria . . . They were introduced into Israel at the same time as idolatry . . . Ashtaroth again, and the bed, and its consequences . . . "Dogs," they're called in the Hebrew text . . . These two are rather like sleepwalking poodles . . . Nuts . . .

A few more days of being alone . . . More and more alone . . . Why not go into one of the neighboring monasteries? No—seriously? Disappear there . . . How tempting! Paper . . . Ink . . . A hidden bottle of whisky . . . What else? What else would a form already reduced to ashes, a reprieved skeleton, need? To be alive? Why? What for? How? To *feel* alive, you mean? With these flowers here in front of me? Before my very eyes? But the eyes that are for the moment mine belong to a different world from that of the flowers . . . To be imprisoned inside these eyes! "Who shall deliver me from the body of this death?" Cells aimed at me, against me . . . How can I get back to that which I feel as farther away than this self that can feel only what I feel? There's a veil . . . *Pulchritudo saeculorum*, as Augustine says . . . "The beauty of the ages . . ." My foot . . . I'm alone, but willed by god, a thought of god, a piece, an eternal part of the praise offered up to him . . . The voice of these speaking beings is the proof that they exist . . . The word . . . Yes, together and eternally all is said . . . You act only in speaking . . . The breath, the spirit, hovering above, gravity inverted and launched aloft . . . When our souls have crossed the insubstantial waters . . . But whom to tell? How to say it? *Dixi, et salvavi animam meam!*

We live in an age of publicity and mystification . . . Publicity plays havoc with every kind of production . . . Puts paid to theater as such . . . Brings back eighteenth-century casualness . . . That's where lucidity lies now . . . Cyd . . . Music, irony . . . What pleases Mrs. Schnook finally reigns supreme . . . No one looks further than Mrs. Schnook . . . No depth . . . All surface . . . Flash . . . Smile . . . Buy . . . The best! Washing powder . . . Perfume . . . How to fabricate *vox populi* . . . Mass desires . . . Marketing . . . Glandular manipulation . . . A very subtle science—I'm not joking . . . It calls for the keenest powers of appraisal and intuition . . . Gentle persuasion . . . Make people acclaim you . . . Accept you . . . Nothing to do with you . . . Entirely up to them . . .

But then there's the fire, the invisible flames behind it all . . .

Which can't be represented . . . The voice that speaks out of the fire . . .

I could also reflect phew! another day without women . . . Plenty of time to get back to them . . . Soon . . . The flesh is weak, alas . . . Fortunately there's a book that survives any number of readings . . . Phew, another day without Flora, anyhow! No telephone calls, no pressures, no battening, no chatter, no poisonous hints, no forced seduction, no "great session" . . . Your prick, darling! I want to see the sperm come out! Whoosh! On my breasts! On my eyes! Everywhere! I want to swallow it! Yum-yum! Take me! Again! I adore you! I love you! Suck me off! Stroke me! Screw me! And the tears of joy when she comes, poor form convulsed in a spasm of pleasure . . . Ah, humanity, humanity! The stream of time . . .

Sunset over Florence . . . Red sunlight on the narrow frieze of the Pazzi seraphim . . .

VII

One of the advantages of spending most of your time traveling is that you see the shifts in the game better . . . Take the people you meet again after a year's gap: one look at their puffy faces is enough . . . The wear and tear . . . That's why everyone's scared of strangers . . . X-ray eyes . . . Instant excavation of the Void . . . Wipe . . . Grin . . . Blank page . . . The same with words . . . Stereotypes . . . Every era has its own emphases . . . Its repetitions, its mannerisms . . . Its verbal carbuncles . . . In France there's an adverb that crops up all the time these days . . . Everywhere . . . On television, on radio, in conversation . . . *Actually* . . . "Yes, *actually*, I thought that . . . "; "*Actually*, I must tell you that . . ."; "I *actually* do believe" . . . It's an epidemic . . . All social classes, at every opportunity, men and women alike . . . They *could* express it differently . . . But no . . . *Actually* . . . Politicians, trade unionists, commentators, intellectuals, sportsmen . . . My concierge . . . My editor . . . The electrician . . . The bank manager . . . The woman at the bakery . . . Models . . . Tarts . . . TV presenters . . . Actors . . . It's incredible . . . An unconscious, unwitting password . . . A temporary abscess living a life of its own in people's mouths . . . *Actually!* A bromide . . . Padding . . . A boring balloon . . . *Actually* . . . Yet some of them are important people . . . Involved in events . . . Participators . . . Decisive, competent, well-informed . . . "Actually, we predicted that unemployment wouldn't exceed two million . . ." "Actually, the dollar has nearly risen to seven francs again . . ." Telephone operators . . . Taxi drivers . . . Middle-class housewives, such as are left . . ." A-a-actually!" Just like that

391

. . . For no reason . . . No cause . . . But what if there were no more cause? No more causality? At all? If everything went on as before, but in a kind of free fall? *Actually* . . . The reserves have collapsed . . . The main computer has blown up! "We are actually in the presence of a catastrophe . . . Before us stretches an indescribable expanse of twisted girders and smashed walls . . . You, ma'am? Do you know what happened? Were you present when the disaster occurred? Actually, I was just looking out of the window when I felt the whole building sway . . . What did you think it was? I thought it was an earthquake, *actually*."

There weren't all that many words still in circulation before . . . Now there's a downright shortage . . . We're going to have to ration ourselves on the *Journal* . . . "You and your philosophical disgressions! The facts! The facts! Just write something simple and direct! Eight hundred thousand copies!" "But I like to try to vary things a little . . ." "Good god, you know very well the readers loathe variation . . . They just want the same number every day . . . Exactly the same!" "Just to amuse myself, then . . ." "I believe you actually mean it!" The ironic use of the word . . . You feel you've been muzzled . . .

Perhaps I'm especially sensitive to this craze because I'm a foreigner . . . Maybe . . . And admittedly being a writer makes one hypersensitive about words . . . You flinch where others feel nothing . . . Everything sounds amplified and reverberates . . . As if the people speaking to you were repeating what they've hardly even started to mutter for the first time . . . You listen too hard . . . You stop listening altogether . . . You start reading people's thoughts too quickly . . . You can finish their sentences, together with their unspoken cancellations . . . Because you can hear them mentally murmuring the opposite of what they've just said . . . "Very good!" —enthusiastically . . . Followed by: "Lousy!" I show Robert one of my articles . . . "Excellent!" he says . . . By which he means: "Nothing to write home about!" Robert's the one who's just told me: "Loot's the only thing, old boy—loot . . . Business . . . All the rest is literature . . . I hope your book takes this fact into account . . . Money rules nowadays, believe me . . . Nothing else

. . . Figures working themselves out mechanically in people's brains
. . . Expenditure . . . Income . . . Estimates . . ."

Just so . . . Actually . . .

At least once a day Deb says to me, "How long is it since you
stopped listening to what I'm saying?" It's true . . . I must watch
myself . . .

So my return to Paris passes off according to plan . . . They don't
seem to have noticed I've been away . . . You can disappear nowadays without anyone batting an eyelid . . . Or die . . . Or commit
suicide . . . It's of no importance . . . Scarcely a ripple . . . At most
people who're really well-known get three minutes on the television
news . . . No time . . . Business . . . Racing results . . . Faster and
faster . . . As in the case of Werth's accident . . . Oh well, he
should have been more careful . . . It can happen to anyone . . .
Immediate profit and loss . . . It's a long time since human fate was
really important, a serious matter . . . Complicated and moving
. . . Those humane days are past! Now bodies are two a penny . . .
One down, a thousand being hatched! What do you expect? — we
don't know which way to turn! But what about someone exceptional? A genius, perhaps? Pooh! We've got stocks of genius sperm
. . . We'll reproduce him . . . Between ourselves, that's all been a
bit exaggerated, don't you think? The romantic refrain . . . But
fortunately *we* live in an age of real equality, clever dicks everywhere . . . Every man for himself, and climbing . . . Not to fail and
not to suffer, that's the thing . . .

Poor Flora . . . Her ploy hasn't worked . . . No one gives a damn
. . . Especially Deb . . . No time, no time! Psychology? Passion?
Love scenes? Scenes of jealousy? In the movies, O.K. . . . But not
in real life . . . Out of date . . . Old hat . . . *Intrigues* don't work
anymore . . . Nor do *love stories* . . . Except to sell half a million
seats . . . Or in prime-time soaps . . . With a murderer as a bonus!
And sweets! Bar of soap! It's enough to make you wonder if stories
about power and money still work in real life . . . Of if there still is
a real life . . . It's not certain, actually . . . And so? What are we to
show? How are we to keep the mill turning? What is it that will
interest people? Nothing . . . Unthinkable! Impossible! And yet it's

true . . . *Eppur, non si muove!* The earth is flat . . . Galileo comes back with the good news and gets himself burned for real this time . . . Nothing more to know! Nothing to explore! Of course, a tenth of the world's population eats a thousand times less than the rest . . . Statistics! Photographs! Mystery is dead . . . What a time to live in! The newspaper editors are tearing their hair out . . . Sales aren't moving . . . Scandals? Bah! Everyone's had them up to the neck . . . The marvels of science? People are blasé . . . Crime? Maybe, as usual, but it's getting tame . . . War? Next, please . . . Perversion? Commonplace . . . It's as if people's nerves had gone dead . . . As if they had less and less saliva . . . "It's funny," someone says to the editor, "but I sometimes wonder if they're still human . . ." Football? Yes, thank god—but for how long? The papers are going through a crisis . . . And now TV exhibits the news to everyone at the same time every evening, there's no alternative . . . Identical images . . . Minds on open display . . . So long as there isn't a power failure . . . As Cyd says, if TV were abolished there'd be a revolution right away . . . The age of cable . . .

The human race has reached its promised land . . . Overflowing with household goods . . . Still a few discrepancies? Blatant inequalities? Crying injustices? So be it . . . But paradise does exist, they've found it, the search is over . . . Air conditioning . . . Automatic pilot . . . Hello, origins, can you hear us? Caves! Tents! Cannabalism! All that in order to get where we are now . . . Hello and goodbye . . . That's the end, folks! That was our super-duper color production in stereoscopic, hot and cold, all-revealing mondioscope! Sounds and smells! Add your own feelings . . . That's not asking much . . . Compulsory emotional contribution . . .

A few years ago Flora's denunciations could have been disastrous for me . . . But now . . . Period of quiet apocalypse . . . He's been in Barcelona with a girl? A Japanese? Hell, good luck to him! When it comes down to it, Flora, the revolutionary anarchist, is the only one who still believes in middle-class values . . . Marriage . . . Fidelity . . . The family . . . The state . . . She fights them — or rather tries to regenerate them . . . But only in order to make use of them, as a clever anti-establishment parasite . . . If only the Law could be just at last! What an idea! Maybe it still impresses a few ardent and ambitious officials in totalitarian regimes . . . A Party secretary in Georgia . . . Or Lithuania . . . But I wouldn't care to bet on it! It's finished! Social blackmail doesn't get anyone going now as it used to do in the good old village days . . . The female magic of gossip is nipped in the bud . . . Just as they were celebrating victory, they abort! Beaten in the finals! On the verge of success! Hysteria all of a heap!

I've just been watching the last match in the World Cup, together with a couple of billion other viewers . . . But what's this he's doing, that Italian forward, what's his name, Tardelli, just after he's scored his goal? *Crossing himself!* Good grief! And nothing happens! In front of the entire world! Giving thanks *urbi et orbi!* Better propaganda than that of the Pope himself! Abomination and desolation! *In hoc signo vinces!* In front of the King, the Queen, the President, the Chancellor, the world press, the hundred thousand spectators in Madrid, the inhabitants of all the cities, all the vast anonymous crowds being whirled around in the cosmic darkness! Superstition? Childishness? Christ triumphant as center-forward! The limit! Celebrations in Rome! Shouting and firecrackers . . .

Deb scarcely mentions Flora's visit . . . Shrugs . . . And the same with the others . . . Two or three curt allusions from Kate . . . Inquiring looks from Robert . . . Heavy hint from Boris . . . Nothing either here or there . . . Any other clues? Yes, the Chairwoman was supposed to call me and hasn't . . .

"Do you know Paule Schreber?" asks the editor of the *Journal* casually.

"Very vaguely . . ."

"Not enough to interview her? Even after all those vacations?" (Well, well, my "vacations" really have started getting under his skin.)

"I don't think so."

"Oh . . . Because Kate said—"

"She must have got it wrong . . ."

It's Kate, of course, who'll interview the Chairwoman . . . On the Côte d'Azur for the summer . . . What's the state of play

between the sexes? The war will not take place! And other trifles
. . . Such as: extreme feminism provokes male chauvinism . . .
Time to tone things down . . . Strategic withdrawal . . . Forty days
in the wilderness . . . They're kicking the habit . . . Dropping
agents who are too compromised . . . Blown . . . "Elissa—what a
slut!" drawls Kate coldly at an editorial meeting . . . New instructions from FAM, WOMANN, the SGIC . . . Reassignment of roles
. . . New objectives . . . End of armed struggle . . . The political
line . . . "Bernadette—she's crazy" . . . That's the sort of thing
you hear nowadays . . . The heroic age consigned to the past . . .
"Virginia Woolf Centers" set up in Africa . . . Among our great
martyrs: Camille Claudel . . . Victim of ruthless killers: her brother
and Rodin . . . Female circumcision . . . The scandal of embryo
discrimination in India . . . Nationalization of Nobel sperm bank
. . . New networks . . . New-blood appointments to leadership . . .
Competition for jobs . . . Social considerations above all! I'm not
sure I wouldn't rather have the openly paranoiac pains in the ass of
the old days . . . But no . . . Never mind . . . All in good time . . .
     Actually . . .
     Talking of madness . . . I've started reading Kraepelin . . . Emil
Kraepelin, a German psychiatrist of the late nineteenth and early
twentieth century . . . Died in 1926 in Munich . . . One of Fals's
last ambiguous suggestions . . . "What, do you mean to say you've
never looked at *Clinical lessons on dementia praecox and manic-
depressive psychosis?* That's a mistake, old man . . . You really
ought to read it . . ." I agree with him across the gap of his death
. . . What decided me was a sudden encounter with Lutz in the
Carrefour de l'Observatoire . . . His case was dismissed and he's
free to come and go as he pleases at his psychiatric clinic . . . We
came face to face with one another . . . Good heavens . . . Late
afternoon . . . That massive, stooped figure looming up in front of
me . . . Those protruding, empty, chemical eyes fixed on me . . .
It's him and no mistake . . . Does he recognize me? He ducks his
head and hurries on . . . I hesitate to overtake him . . . I let it
go . . .
     Kraepelin was born in 1856, the same year as Freud . . . He's as

cold, external, and rough as Freud is sensitive, imaginative, and tactful . . . But they both have a lucid despair that ought to be shared by the modern novelist . . . He should long ago have abandoned psychology for the macabre, pitiless fantasy of real human tissue . . . Kraepelin's a first-class writer . . . Judge for yourself.

"Gentlemen, the patient I am showing you today almost has to be carried . . . He walks with his legs wide apart, balancing on the outside edges of his feet . . . He throws off his slippers, then sings a hymn, and repeats several times, 'My Father, my real Father' . . . If you ask him his name he shouts: 'What's your name? What does he shut? He shuts his eyes . . . What does he hear? He hears nothing, and can't understand anything . . . How? Who? Where? When? What's the matter with him? If I tell him to look, he doesn't move . . . Come on, look over here! What? What is it? Watch out . . . If I say that, what? Why don't you answer? Are you going to be rude again? How can anyone be so rude? You're an uncouth fellow . . . I've never seen such a swine . . . You mean to start all over again . . . Don't you understand anything? Do as you're told, won't you! You won't? You're going to be more and more impertinent?' His insults degenerate into inarticulate cries . . ."

Or again:

"The patient starts to utter monotonous, unbearable shrieks . . . You can only interrupt her by asking questions, which she always answers, but in a preposterous fashion . . . She was the serpent in the Garden of Eden . . . She seduced her husband, whose name, incidentally, was Adam . . . She has brought a curse down upon her husband, herself, and her children . . . She has made everyone unhappy, and that's why she was burned . . . She's already in hell, and therein she can see her horrible sins . . . The sky has fallen in; there's no more water, money, or food . . . She has destroyed everything; she has brought ruin upon the world . . . 'I bear the weight of the world upon my soul.' In a letter to the court she accuses herself of every possible crime; she asks to be sent to prison and signs herself 'The Devil.' "

Another example:

"She doesn't consider herself at all mad . . . Her speech is inco-

397

herent and frequently intermingled with bits of incorrect French and absurd or garbled quotations . . . 'Ingratitude is the praise of the world . . .' 'Many words, many ideas . . .' She repeats ad nauseam such phrases as 'Devil's shit in the feet of the soul; foot of the soul in the devil's shit.'

"She's sometimes cheerful, sometimes silly, sometimes erotic or irritable. She's very fond of insults and indecent sexual allusions. She chatters all the time, never letting anyone else get a word in edgewise. Her language is extremely stilted. She separates each syllable, stressing the final ones and pronouncing g's like k's and d's like t's. She speaks like a child, leaving sentences unfinished, distorting some words and inventing others, jumping from one idea to another. All her movements are heavy, stiff, and uniform. She keeps pulling faces, jumping up and down and clapping her hands. Of course she complains of sexual attacks. Her lungs, heart, and liver have all been torn out. She adds the particle 'de' to her surname."

Another:

"This patient speaks without looking at the other person, and in a sugary, affected tone that makes her seem distinguished. But for years she has been hearing voices that insult her and make attempts on her modesty. The voices are very clear, she says, and probably come from a telescope. Her thoughts are worked out faster than she can express them. Someone is tormenting her body: they have changed her womb and put it outside; they bombard her back with pains, put ice on her heart and strangle her. They injure her spine, and finally rape her. But although she complains about all this, she doesn't feel any great emotion. She does cry from time to time, but goes into morbid detail with surreptitious satisfaction, even adding an erotic element. She's always asking to be allowed to go home, but can easily be consoled for being here . . ."

So . . . Dementia praecox . . . Stupor or catatonic activity . . . Paranoid forms . . . Terminal states . . . Melancholia . . . Circular depressive states . . . Maniacal activity . . . Mixture of maniacal and depressive states . . .

Waxy flexibility . . . Echopraxia . . . Echolalia . . . Suggestibility
. . . Negativism . . .

"The patient died of consumption five years later in a hospice for
the chronically ill. She had remained stupefied, negative and affected, with occasional bouts of slight agitation."

Couldn't this really be *anyone?* Somebody perfectly "normal"?
If they were ever driven to the breaking point? Emma Bovary? This
woman? That woman? That man? The visible surface is so thin and
frail . . . And underneath — chaos . . . We're all patients trying to
convince ourselves we're not so sick as our neighbor . . . Mental
. . . Too mental . . . It's surprising there isn't more outright torture, more shit thrown in people's faces . . . The crazies confess
. . . And fall to bits . . . Just give someone too much of a shove and
he collapses into dust, epileptic, a wreck, a rag . . . Absurd to
imagine there's something behind all that . . . You could look for
an explanation . . . Try to drag it out . . . But no, the ultimate limit
is just incommunicable idiocy . . . A novelist's vision can only end
in the horrible hilarity of asylums, the decay of the sacred into the
twitchings of delirium, the decline of the supposed fairy or witch
into mere bestialized digestion . . .

Of course they've all either seen it or will see in the end . . . One
grimace filling all space and time . . . A maelstrom of feeble-mind-
edness . . . Murder or infinite compassion: you have to choose . . .
Terror or mercy . . . Pleasure or charity . . . In the middle, casually, and because one must occupy oneself somehow, you might put
Science . . .

War in Lebanon! Just before I leave for Jerusalem . . . Lightning
advance of the Israeli army . . . Beirut surrounded . . . Shellings,
bombardments . . . Tyre, Sidon . . . An old story that never ends
. . . As was only to be expected, a flood of speeches . . . I'd rather
not be at the *Journal* at the moment . . . But I just drop in to take
the temperature . . . Kate is beside herself . . . "Nazis! Nazis!"

399

"Who?" "The Israelis, of course!" . . . "Nazis?" "Yes, they've become like their former torturers! The Jews are the new SS" . . . She's off . . . "You're not going to deny it? You don't mean to defend them?" "Don't think I like seeing people killed" . . . "But it's genocide! They want to exterminate every single Palestinian!" Her whole nervous system is quivering . . . I've never seen her in such a state . . . Like an electric cable . . . Of course the Palestinians are the least of her worries . . . You have to see other words through the words, other people behind the names . . . She stops and stares at me . . . "Oh, of course, you and your origins . . ." I see! In three days I've become an American again . . . An honorary Jew . . . By assimilation . . . Dangerous to the left . . . Suspect in the eyes of the right . . . Numerous petitions are got up in just a few hours . . . Always the same names, grown old in the service of ritual protest . . . For Good, against Evil . . . Demands . . . Fierce denunciations . . . It's a French tradition—you don't see it any- where else . . . Drawing up lists . . . Scanning the columns of names to see if this person or that has signed . . . Goodness, isn't So-and-so there? Heavens, don't tell me What's-his-name has signed! No, he protests a couple of days later . . . The lobby got to him! No, it was his wife's mother . . . Oh . . . Intellectuals spotlight tyranny . . . See Plato! You're either a philosopher or next to nothing . . . What's striking here is how all the comparisons are with Germany . . . Or Russia . . . Arafat compares Begin to Hitler attacking Moscow . . . So he sees himself as Stalin, winning the Second World War and saving civilization from the brown plague . . . And here comes Goebbels! Not me — you! No, you! I tell you it's you! I've got my index cards to prove it! Night of Broken Glass! Final solution! Long Knives! Fascist! Semi-Fascist! Terrorist! Bloodthirsty hyena! Warsaw ghetto! Oradour! Sacrilege! Commu- niqués . . . Countercommuniqués . . . Feverish negotiations that collapse the next day under the shells and bombs . . . Revive . . . Collapse again . . . Warning from Brezhnev . . . Veto by the Amer- icans . . . Dogged efforts by France . . . Egypt . . . Declaration by Austria . . . Syrian withdrawal . . . Cease-fire . . . Fire! Fascist! Another cease-fire . . . More shelling, of the ruins . . . Devaluation of the franc . . . Austerity . . . Freeze on prices and wages . . . Bang! Eight floors fewer than before . . . Clouds of smoke . . . Rubble and corpses . . . Bang again! To help bring about successful change . . . Popular culture . . . American and Zionist plot . . . Carlos . . . The Red Hand . . . The Steel Crescent . . . Booby-trapped cars . . . Rockets . . . Embassies blown to smithereens . . . Qaddafi asks the Palestinians to commit suicide so that their blood may become the fuel (sic) of the Revolution on the march . . . Khomeini likewise . . . Discontent among the farmers . . . And the steelworkers . . . External trade deficit . . . Iran attacks Iraq again . . . The Sikhs rebel . . . The Vietnamese keep getting drowned trying to escape . . . The Reverend Moon solemnizes 1,500 marriages in New York and is then convicted of income tax fraud. Fire! Cease-fire! Fire!

And it's all hotted up lately because of the "revisionists" who claim that the gas chambers never existed . . . According to them they're an invention on the part of the Zionists . . . A self-seeking masochist fantasy, designed to obtain compensation . . . These Jews, they'll stop at nothing! They vanished, no one knows how, in Europe during the war . . . Six million disappeared into thin air . . . Smoke without fire . . . When people refute these new historians they only persist . . . But their refuters are starting to call the Israelis Hitlerites . . . Confusion is at its height . . . Hitler is a circle of which the circumference is everywhere and the center nowhere . . . Anyone would think that as I speak they're building ultramodern gas-chambers underneath Jerusalem . . . Under the Holy Sepulchre, for instance . . . To gas the Arabs . . . The Christians . . . The Druses . . . The Positivists . . . No, not the Christians—they're Nazis too! As is proved by their calling themselves "Phalangists" in Lebanon . . . The "Christian Phalangists . . ." Successors of Franco . . . Raping and plundering ruthlessly, with the Virgin Mary on their banners . . . The Sacred Heart embroidered on their chests . . . What? You think I'm exaggerating? I've seen it . . . With my own eyes . . . And they sort out prisoners by painting a black cross on their backs . . . A cross! The Crusades! Godefroi de Bouillon! Frederick Barbarossa! Richard Coeur de Lion!

The Jews, spearhead of the Christian invasion! Or vice versa! History turned completely upside down! Two thousand years for nothing! But Saladin is keeping watch! He will return! Allah is great! Holy war on all sides . . . Jihad! Strangely enough, we can still think only of Germany . . . And Poland . . . Auschwitz . . . The imagination has limits . . .

The *Journal* is in confusion . . . One polemic after another . . . Eyewitness accounts . . . Cris du coeur . . . Appeals to reason . . . In vain . . . They're all delighted to be able to tear each other to pieces again over this . . . A godsend! All the repression of the past forty years bursts out again . . . The long chewed-over grudges . . . Or perhaps it goes back even further than that . . . A century . . . Three centuries . . . Ten . . . Six thousand years . . . That's what happens with the word "Jew . . ." It sets the whole of time alight . . . The mummies all come out of the cupboard . . . Astarte and Cybele rise up majestically . . . The Pharaohs come and claim their taxes . . . One passion sets off another . . . Twenty thousand volumes on the subject . . . Fifty thousand theories . . . Turned over and over for generations . . . One suspected it already, but these few weeks have brought blinding confirmation . . . Horrendous rendezvous . . . Omega of the nerves . . .

I listen to a radio program . . . The various trends in French politics are all represented . . . The speakers all preempt each other . . . Politely but firmly . . . That's the convention . . . "Allow me to speak . . ." "I didn't interrupt you, so don't you interrupt me . . ." Two at least—the Communist and the Gaullist—sound drunk . . . Raucous voices . . . They don't agree about anything . . . The economy . . . Local elections . . . But then suddenly there's a deep silence . . . A way out . . . A belief in common . . . Self-evident . . . Patriotic . . . The condemnation of Israel . . . National unity is restored . . . They all agree . . . For diametrically opposite reasons . . . They're moved, childlike . . . They'll start singing the Marseillaise any moment now . . . The Jews are now Germans . . . The Germans were Jews . . . So by collaborating with the Germans in 1940 or '42, were the much-abused French really collaborating in advance with the Jews? By arresting the Jews, were they really

402

arresting potential Germans? Do you follow me? Presto! No one's guilty . . . Or rather, the innocent were already guilty . . . You see what they do as soon as they're strong . . . I tell you, the Jews ought to remain weak and humiliated . . . Or else they start turning into Nazis . . . Just like everyone else . . . Nothing new under the sun . . . Here we are again, Marshal . . . Decent faces of the French cops at the Vel d'Hiv . . . Good old bureaucratic pen-pushers with names, at least, like yours and mine: Bousquet, Leguay, Drumont, Darquier . . . Not like Dreyfus, Pytkowicz, Aronowicz or Fellmann . . . And as the Jews of today are the Germans of yesterday, one can always call one of their divisions *Das Reich* . . . And easily imagine them as tall and fair and sweaty and brutal, shutting women and children up in a church and setting light to it . . . A little church just like the one in the Socialists' "peaceful strength" poster . . . Arabs now? Before it would have been French peasants . . . Oradour, Oradour, somber plain! That's what you get for not liking Baudelaire! You're insensitive to the variations of Evil! You get the local Flowers mixed up . . . A trap! Anyhow, all that goes to show we French weren't far wrong to anticipate in the past . . . Even to overdo it a bit and expel those Nazis-to-be, including their children, to the east . . . Where they belonged . . .

Or else the scenario changes, and the Israelis are like the French in North Africa . . . Colonialists . . . And they must go through the same process as the reactionary French . . . In Algeria, for example . . . They must withdraw . . . They must accept the people's independence . . . But where are they to go? Where they belong . . . But where? Not in the USSR, surely? No, to the United States . . . Everyone knows Israel is a projection of American imperialism . . . But what about Jerusalem? And the Bible? All that? A soap opera! A cock-and-bull mythology! Human life can't be based on a book! Look what that's led to in Iran . . . *Das Kapital?* That's different! That's scientific! And then: 5,500 kilometers of Siberian gas pipeline! Five billion francs! Twelve thousand French jobs! Whereas there they're slaves!

Just as, forty years ago, I'd have been a degenerate cosmopolitan Jew, so now I find I'm a macho, Hitlerite Yankee—and still a Jew

. . . Even though I'm not one . . . But I am . . . A writer is always a Jew . . . Why? Perhaps because he will only speak or keep silent in his own way . . . No communal feelings . . . No collective unconscious . . . But in that case one has to be a supreme, an absolute Jew, doesn't one? . . . Kafka . . . Céline . . . All harking in one direction . . . Toward one place . . . The wrong one . . .

Flora would have criticized me as harshly forty years ago as she does now . . . With the same spontaneity, the same wondering sincerity, the same inescapable perversity . . . The grit in the bearings . . . The wrench in the works . . . The traitor . . . The pornographer . . . Not serious . . . Lacking in morals and meaning . . . In other words: a virus that attacks nature and prevents its uterine fulfillment . . . Forty years ago a virus was a microbe that attacked the fundamental Health of the Strong . . . Now it's a sophisticated disease that crushes the Weak . . . Swing of the pendulum . . . Whichever way you slice it, an alien germ is always alien . . . Perverse . . . Intrinsically . . . Genetically . . . No, no doubt about it, a Jew is nothing like a Negro or an Arab . . . Nor like Women or Queers . . . Nor Freemasons, the latest surprise . . . A Jew is something different . . . Meta-metaphysical . . . Of course . . . The Hebrew was neither one thing nor the other . . . Neither like this nor like that . . . Not a gypsy . . . Nor universal as people used to think . . . Universal, yes—but in a different way . . . Not in the language of "natural" humanism . . . Certainly not . . . Jews are really against nature . . . And to think we protected them against the Christians . . . And now see the thanks we get . . . They stuck secretly to their own plan . . . They don't want to build socialism anymore! They go their own way, pursue their own goal . . . By force . . . In defiance of history as organized by the rest of us . . . With their Book in the original language . . . Jargon from the mists of time! And never completely translatable, into the bargain! . . . The giddy limit! . . .

We've lost sight of the women in all this? Not at all! Remember the Report . . . Yes, you do—I mentioned it at the beginning . . . You thought it was very farfetched . . . You didn't believe me . . . You thought I was exaggerating to suit my own purposes . . . As if

404

I was writing a propaganda novel . . . A tract . . . But no . . . I
don't describe a ten-thousandth part of what actually happens . . . I
don't come anywhere near the real horrors . . . You'll see in due
course, when things start to leak out . . . They always do . . .
Fortunately . . .

In a nutshell, the first suspicions came from the United States
. . . That feminism was a form of Judeophobia . . . Plain as a
pikestaff! But no one saw it until a number of the younger, better-
informed and bolder Jewish women started to get fed up with what
they were hearing . . . It mounted from the ear to the brain . . .
The tympan . . . The divan . . . Freud . . . I gradually received a
lot of indirect evidence . . . Then letters . . . Really wild! And so it
goes on . . . That's how it is—you drag yourself across the desert,
and then one fine day a lot of oases appear . . . Everything I've
written up to now is true, one hundred percent true . . . Too true!
you may say . . . A novel doesn't have to be true . . . Yes it does,
though! It *is* the truth . . . Everything depends on the author's
nervous system . . . How much truth he can endure along the way
. . . You don't have to accept a drowsy atmosphere just because it's
been a languid age . . . I upset your scene? Too bad! Don't forgive
me! Criticize me! It won't change anything . . . I've got hold of an
intuition about things, and I won't let go . . . Baudelaire wrote:
"Manet doesn't seem to realize that the more injustice there is, the
better his situation becomes . . ." Manet realized it very clearly!
He would just have liked things to move even more swiftly in his
direction . . . Just take a good look at *Olympia*—one ruthlessness
and another, face to face . . .

It's only a beginning . . . But gradually, thanks to intrepid ex-
plorers like myself, who are not afraid of constantly having their
noses put out of joint, the whole picture is emerging . . . The
outlines of the mask become clearer . . . One can breathe a little
. . . Fem-animism is starting to break up . . . The demand for
physical fulfillment turns out to be mistaken . . . You know the
sort of thing: the Jews are not the only, nor perhaps even the chief
victims of persecution through the ages . . . What about homosexuals? Witches? Women? The old tune . . . What a bore! There

ought to be a ban on the idea of "something missing" . . . It's not you, it's me! It's us! Competition . . . Imitation . . . Physiology . . . "Difference" . . . As if there were such a thing as Identity! In terms of which people absolutely had to assert themselves! A Body of bodies!

"I was amused to see you use the Latin tag, *Dixi et salvavi animam meam*, earlier on," says S.

"Why?"

"Because the same phrase pops up in someone you'd never expect to use it . . ."

"Who?"

"Marx . . . At the end of his *Critique of the Gotha Program* . . . A very important work . . . Not as well known as it ought to be . . . As revealing in its own way as *The Jewish Question*, that confession par excellence . . . The *Critique* is prophetic . . . Do you know how the Marxist scholars translate that most Catholic of quotations? In their footnotes?"

"I have to admit I don't."

"Here, I've got a French-language edition published in Peking . . . Look: 'I have said what I had to say and my conscience is clear . . .' Amusing, isn't it? When Marx tips you the wink in Latin that he has no illusions about the future, that he isn't a Marxist yet, and that taking it all in all, and with an eye to eternity, he has a soul! *Dixi et salvavi animam meam* . . . Was he being ironical? Of course . . . That is, given his circumstances, as serious as possible . . . 'I have spoken, and saved my soul . . .' 'Clear conscience'? Oh yeah? That quotation is worth its weight in double meanings! You should have reminded Lutz of it . . ."

"Perhaps he remembered it himself, one day," I say . . .

" 'I have killed, and saved my soul?' "

"More likely: 'I couldn't speak, so I killed.' "

"Yes, that must be it . . . Bodies are paralyzed sentences . . . Sentences that get fat . . . Reflections of words, pregnant, swollen . . . Until they burst . . . We have to learn to see ourselves like that . . . To our cost . . ."

"Failures of language . . ."

"Always . . . That's why writers are so touching, isn't it? People hate them . . . Love them . . . They remind them of It . . . They never let go of the revelation . . . They hang on . . . No persecution or humiliation can make them give in . . . They'll say anything to make people get the feel of it . . . But not really *anything*, huh? . . . Just balloons in cartoons . . . The maunderings of fatigue and illusion . . ."

"And how are we getting on?"

"Making progress . . . You put as many obstacles as you can in your own way . . . But they're on your side, because we exist in antimatter . . . You have to upset everybody at once . . . Any old how . . . En bloc . . . Simultaneously . . . A triumph!"

"And where does that get us to?"

"Ecstatic solitude . . . A dark yet penetrating view of the void . . ."

"You're joking, but you forget that your name is going to be on this book . . . And it will be attributed to you, however much you deny it . . . As for me, I just disappear . . . Vanish . . . Escape the Furies . . . Nothing to do with me . . . Just send me a check . . . I resume my disguise . . . My articles on foreign politics . . . My trips back and forth . . ."

"And I go back to my *Comedy* . . . No one can understand a word of it; or hardly . . . But that doesn't worry me . . . I shut myself up, I withdraw, bang on with my syllables, swim a little, sleep . . . I thus reach the ultimate state as defined by Bossuet: 'An inner ascesis which, by a holy circumcision, produces externally a virtual isolation from all superfluity . . .'"

"I think that as the narrator I have the right to invoke the Odyssey, Canto XVII," I say . . . " 'That gods take on the features of distant strangers and go about from city to city in every possible guise observing men's virtues and crimes . . .' "

"Help yourself . . . We like quotations . . . It irritates our readers, but it educates them in spite of themselves . . . You make a funny kind of a Greek . . . But will you allow me to add another dash of Chateaubriand? From *Life of Rancé?*"

"It can't do us any harm . . ."

" 'The annals of humanity are made up of a large number of

407

fables intermingled with a few truths . . . In the life of anyone destined to be remembered there is a novel which gives birth to a legend, one of the mirages out of which history is made.' "

"Excellent . . . He used to be our parallel university . . . Our Pléiade in digest form . . . But tell me, how are the preparations for the grand maneuvers getting on? The preparations for the regular, systematic, eternal and transeternal commemoration of the French Revolution?"

"Feverishly, as usual . . . But they're hanging fire a bit . . . It gets across better when the Monarch has a particle to his name . . . The Rights of Man still work, but usually out of context . . . Apart from that, the Terror's still going strong . . . But it casts rather a cloud . . . As the Inquisition does over the Gospels . . . And Stalin over Marxist humanism . . . You can explain till you're blue in the face that theory and practice are two quite different things—you know what the guinea-pigs are like . . . They always see a connection . . . It's difficult nowadays to have a Doctrine pure and unde-filed! But you'll notice that if there *is* a god who doesn't lie about his occasional just ferocity, it's Jehovah . . . Which makes it very likely that he's the genuine article . . . Thou shalt not kill, except when I tell you to . . . Death in full knowledge of the facts, exactly defined and determined . . . The 'intermittencies' of the Lord of Hosts . . . A touch of Severity here, a touch of Mercy there . . . Admittedly he's laying it on rather thick with Beirut at the mo-ment . . ."

"I've just been reading a speech by a professor above all suspi-cion," I say. "He was taking part in a symposium about those who deny there was any genocide of the Jews by the Nazis . . . He said: 'The existence of the gas chambers is as beyond all doubt as the use of the guillotine during the Terror . . .' Comparison is no argu-ment, but you must admit this one is very odd . . . Clever, too . . . And supports your thesis . . ."

"Absolutely . . . A family riddle . . . Charade . . . My first, my second, my third, my whole . . . All those topped aristocrats! And the 'fanatics,' as they were called at the time . . . The term referred to ordinary believers and priests . . . People still joke about it, don't they, in this gentle land of ours . . . As one of our teachers said to me at high school when I told him Marat and Robespierre made me sick to my stomach—as did Fouché, Fréron, Tallien, Barras *and* Napoleon too, by the way—'Come now, don't make such a fuss! You're just being small-minded!' "

"What? Robespierre?! The Sea-Green Incorruptible?"

"Yes . . . It's strange . . . There was a mixture of purity and corruption . . . Side by side . . . Wig by wig . . . Apparently you never get what would be the perfect couple: impurity and decency . . ."

"You mean that Crime is really nourished on the Ideal?"

"Of course . . . It's obvious . . . Rousseau protecting perverts . . . I'd rather have Sade justifying the Just!"

"You and your paradoxes!"

"You think so? What if I said that Rousseau plus Perversion is the very embodiment of the tyranny that takes no account of Evil? Is unconscious of it? It's feminine, really . . . Hysteria used by filth for its own purposes . . . The eternal Héloise . . . Evil through Innocence . . . And this tyranny can only be abolished by Sade plus Consciousness . . . And distance . . . The mental representation of crime while abstaining from it in fact . . . It would be quite 'Freudian,' actually . . . Except that poor old Freud still deluded himself with Goethe . . ."

"You're dreaming!"

"Yes . . . Of a world that would at least be less boring . . ."

Three quick days in New York for the *Journal* . . . Then I'll go from there to Jerusalem . . . I stay with Cyd . . . Late afternoon . . . A long session right away in front of the glass . . . She's wearing a blue slit skirt, and kneels down, watching herself as she sucks me off and taking note of the contrast between her hands and lips and the revolting thing she's holding . . . Disgusting . . . Such a delicate face, such pretty fingers, such pure and distinguished lips messing about with that erect sausage . . . Frightful . . . We enjoy ourselves . . . I like her uncovered taut left thigh . . . She insists on our going to the john, and to swallow me as I sit there naked as if I were bound and crucified . . . I have one finger up her ass, which she clenches, and I tell her she must *think* about what she's doing . . . The actions and images are false and absurd and unimportant . . . It's her thought, formulated and hard, that I want . . . I feel her clench herself more, and tell her I'm in her thought now . . . In her brain . . . Abstract . . . In the most intangible part of her . . . I check in front whether she's wet . . . Yes . . . Very . . . A handful . . . I'm about to come very strongly, lying back, right in her mouth . . . We go on to her bed . . . She makes me come again by whispering complicated obscenities . . . About sewing . . . And my prick . . . Sometimes I can't quite make out what she's muttering . . . She's whispering to herself . . . To no one . . . To an ear that doesn't exist . . . But *I* don't exist . . . That's the whole point . . . Recipes for beauty creams; my sperm kept in a tin . . . Or to use as a makeup remover at night . . . Scenes in a doctor's office . . . Operations . . . All this tenderly, groaning, getting excited . . . Needle . . . Thread . . . White jacket . . . Naked underneath . . . Feel, judge, give an injection . . . Cut . . . Cut up . . . Mend . . . Close up . . . Surgical spirit on the wound . . . Leave a bit . . . Just a bit . . . A bud . . . A scar . . . That she'll lick from time to time . . . Show to her women friends as a sign of contempt . . . Does she hate me then? Yes! And how! Men's horrible pricks . . . That they're so proud of . . . They believe in them . . . The idiots . . . The dopes . . . Or else I'm her imaginary brother she meets from school . . . She has to take me to the toilet . . . Take my pants down . . . Help me pee . . . Kiss me a little . . . Not too much . . . Just enough for me to want it again . . . To long for it, be obsessed with it in class . . . Implore her when I get home . . . Just to brush me with her lips . . . For me to writhe and come mentally . . . Tears . . . Exhaustion . . . Or else she puts her hand under my sheet in the evening . . . Before she goes and joins Papa, the slut . . . How she'll think about me spouting in her mouth as he takes her . . . As she cries out how good it is . . .

Surreptitiousness . . . Lies . . . Lying is what Cyd likes best of all . . . That's the true side of her . . . Artless . . . Because she *knows* she's lying . . . Dangerous knowledge . . . Which makes one too sophisticated . . . Ironic . . . Lonely . . . That's what makes

her look so "irreproachable" in real life . . . A bit schoolmistressy
. . . But there's also her sense of humor and her generosity . . .

Her audacity too . . . Like the time in Paris when she arrived
with a kitchen knife and a fillet steak she'd just bought at the
butcher's . . . In her purse . . . To cut up in front of her while I
took her from behind . . . Red meat, and white sperm invisible
inside her . . . That's what she wanted to experience . . . The
canceling out, the transcending of matter . . . Let it be repulsive in
order to conquer repulsion . . . That pleasure may be beyond it . . .
Disregard disgust, boredom, emotions, wrappings, profane and
everyday relations . . . Let it be ridiculous in order to destroy
ridicule . . .

When these conditions are fulfilled she agrees to be screwed
properly, with the whole prick big and hard inside her . . . From
being a little girl, a little sister, she changes to another level and
becomes a woman . . . Violently . . . Cutting out all the preliminaries . . . And there she is in front of the mirror again, breasts
thrust out, looking herself straight in the crazy eye, a veritable
tempest . . . In one fell swoop from the microscopically slow and
ingratiating to the brutal . . . We both come together now, with life
thrown aside, gratuitous, knowing itself already a weary blur . . .

A knife in the water . . .

Afterward, nothing . . . We each go to our own bathroom . . .
She repairs her makeup . . . We smoke . . . Carry on as before . . .
It wasn't us . . . Like that it's impossible to cheat . . . Nice and
flexible . . .

Father, mother, son, daughter, brother, sister, husband, wife,
lover, mistress, uncle, aunt, nephew, niece, male and female cousin
—all screwed in one encounter! Whew!

The various kinds of homosexuality desecrated in passing . . .
Dismembered bodies consigned to the trash can . . . Circulation of
the blood, and other liquids—nowhere . . .

We begin mouth to mouth, tongue to tongue . . . Fusion . . .
And end as separate as possible . . . No long tales about families
and childhood . . . There are couches specially for that . . . Do I
even know how old Cyd is? Yes, twenty-eight . . . And I'm already

thirty-five . . . Another few years, three or four, before she gets the obsession about children? And I? How long till I start finding all this just a mess? . . . Shut up and get on with the story . . .

A walk . . . I feel like having another look at the Frick Collection . . . A mansion crammed with masterpieces . . . Rembrandt's *Polish Horseman* . . . There he is, rising up oblique and fierce out of the yellowish-brown landscape . . . Fur cap, bow and arrows . . . Apocalypse on the alert . . .

"Why 'Polish Horseman'?" asks Cyd . . .

"It's a strange picture, full of occult references, as is often true with Rembrandt," I say . . . "There's something metaphysical behind it all . . . Some religious controversy, I can't remember exactly what . . . But look how he cleaves through the room . . . Through time . . . And how he rises up from the earth . . . The soil . . . The muddy silt . . . What's he looking at? Now I remember—the Polish army helped halt Soliman's forces outside Vienna . . . Did you know croissants dated from that period? Or that Nietzsche liked to compare himself to a Polish horseman?"

"Really?"

Cyd's quite willing to believe me . . . She puts up very amiably with my little impromptu lectures . . . We come out of the Frick and walk to the Plaza for a drink . . . It's the sunny, vibrant New York of high summer . . . With the ocean seeming to stand there vertical beyond the light . . . Cyd wants to know what I think about what for her is already old-style American literature . . . Salinger . . .

"Very well written," I say . . . "Very skillful . . . And very useful evidence about American matriarchy, don't you think? The short stories . . . A shrink would say they're remarkable illustrations of the castration complex . . . *A Lovely Day for Banana-Fish* . . . *Pretty Mouth and Green my Eyes* . . . The Fifties . . . Very chaste . . . Good dialogue . . . Like Hemingway, but not so strong" . . .

We walk a bit further up Madison Avenue . . . Then go back to her place . . . We make love again gently . . . Go out into the dark . . . Have dinner at the Artists' . . . Go on to Seventh Avenue to hear a double-bass player she's just discovered . . .

412

"So you're going to stay in Paris?" says Cyd.

"I wonder . . . I wonder more and more . . ."

"Come here then . . ."

"Maybe" . . .

The rest of the time she talks about her television projects . . . She's really nice like that, in the early July heat, naked under her white blouse and skirt . . . The band has started playing *These Foolish Things* . . .

"How's Lynn?" I ask.

"She's in Los Angeles . . . She won't be back till fall . . . Perhaps a bit before . . ."

"What are your plans?"

"I stay here and work . . . And spend the weekends at Easthampton" . . .

She doesn't ask me anything about my novel . . . She doesn't really believe in it all that much . . . She loves me . . . She is me . . . She kisses me . . . We go back to her place . . . We're exhausted and a bit drunk . . . We sleep . . .

I wake up in the night . . . Cyd is breathing quietly, lying on my right arm . . . I feel as if something has turned around inside me . . . And far away in the recesses of space . . . An icy shift . . . A landslide of atoms . . . I am a black pebble . . . I see my Polish horseman disappear along Fifth Avenue, gallop across Central Park and rear up, quivering, over the docks . . . He flies, he streaks across the whole scene . . . Three in the morning . . . Great silence . . . Recapitulation . . . I'm lost in the story, here and now, eyes wide open in broad darkness . . . I get up and go out into Cyd's kitchen, open a beer . . . I lie down in the living room . . . Light . . .

"What the hell are you doing here?"

"Just ruminating."

"Aren't you sleepy?"

"I was thirsty.

Cyd goes and pours herself a whisky . . . She's a bit puffy and disheveled, her fair hair in her eyes, naked . . . She comes and lies beside me and kisses me . . .

"I'll miss you all summer," she says.

413

"I'll miss you."

"Venice in October?"

"O.K."

"I might come to Paris before . . . Will you have finished your book?"

"I hope so . . ."

"How is it going to end?"

"I don't know yet . . ."

"Well? Badly?"

"Neither badly nor well, I suppose . . . Ambiguously . . . Vaguely . . . No answer . . . After a certain point, you know, you can't see anything beyond volumes, tangents, cylinders, that sort of thing . . . Intersecting spheres, inner geometry . . . Painting without lines or colors . . . Music without sounds or notes . . ."

"Do you reckon it'll work?"

"No . . . But it doesn't matter . . . I'm really enjoying doing it . . ."

"You are funny."

She'd like it to work, for my sake . . . She'd like me to have a richer, freer, more spacious life . . . What people really call a life . . . She remembers she earns much more than I do . . . She has a wallet full of cards . . . Blue, yellow, white . . . I noticed her expression just now in the restaurant, when I took out some notes . . . Cash in hand—that's awful . . . I haven't got a bank account here? I don't exist . . . Someone like me shouldn't have to calculate . . . Yes, why can't I manage to live life as it's really lived . . . American life, of course . . . Away from it all . . . Above it . . .

She puts on a record . . . Scarlatti's sonatas, to sum it all up . . . How long have we known each other? A year? Only just . . . Paris . . . New York . . . The harpsichord somehow gets to me . . . Wings me . . . Sea-gulls . . . Wind . . .

The El Al plane is full of girls . . . Quite young . . . Thirteen years old . . . Fifteen . . . Where have they come from? Peru . . .

Lima . . . Cuzco . . . They're going to spend three months in a school in Israel . . . To improve their Hebrew . . . Their religious knowledge . . . Rachel . . . Ruth . . . Miriam . . . Sarah . . . We go from English to Spanish . . . And what are you going for? Journalist? Politics? Reporter? No? Just for personal reasons? Oh . . . And are you Jewish? No . . . Oh, don't feel bad about it! That sympathetic, encouraging "Don't feel bad!" is a world in itself . . . I'm not Jewish? Even though I'm so nice? Never mind . . . I mustn't take it too hard . . . Of course, that being the case my life is pretty meaningless, but still . . . I can and do eat my first kosher meal . . . And now we're winging our way toward Tel Aviv . . . Young Rachel tells me the story of her life . . . Or rather the journeyings of her family . . . I find it hard to follow . . . Russia . . . Egypt . . . Bulgaria . . . Spain . . . Bordeaux . . . Then Peru . . . She was born there . . . And now she's going back . . . To Palestine . . . That's to say, really somewhere . . . It's her first time . . . First time! Like me . . . *La primera vez* . . . She's very dark, fat, tiny, and looks clever . . . She's genuinely upset that I'm not Jewish . . . But still . . . Everybody can't be . . . That's how it is . . . A matter of luck . . . Divine chance? Not even . . . Am I married? Oh . . . My case gets worse . . . Children? Only one? My case is desperate . . . A boy? . . . Well, things are not so bad after all . . .

I picked up an old copy of the *Journal* at Kennedy Airport . . . I glance through it now . . . Am I dreaming? But no! Good grief! The Ministry of Culture has arranged a visit to Mexico . . . With Simone de Beauvoir and, of all people, Aragon! I rub my eyes . . . I'm afraid I must have imagined it . . . But no . . . How sublime! Beyond my wildest hopes! Just in time for my novel . . . It almost writes itself . . . What are they both supposed to do out there? Recite *The Crow and the Fox?* Dance the minuet? Give a fashion show? Introduce a performance of *Les Fausses Confidences?* An exhibition in memory of Oradour? The French Couple! Together again at last! Wonderful! Poor Sartre! Actually, there was a dago side to him . . . Nauseous . . . Suspect . . . Unpoetic . . . Not really keen on women . . . Not enough . . . Marriage of state between Aragon et Beauvoir! To boost the export drive! I'd never have dared think of it! A stroke of genius! Delighted, emotional crowds . . . World scoop . . . Happy end! I suppose there'll be meetings . . . Cocktail parties . . . Seminars . . . No, one's not supposed to use the word "seminar" anymore, according to a statement by Bernadette that I find on the next page . . . She said so at a "Feminist Constructive Assembly" . . . It's "genesiars" now . . . "Seminar" is to be deleted from our vocabulary . . . It has a Christian tinge . . . Sexist . . . Deriving from the Council of Trent . . . Yes, it's Bernadette herself attacking the Council of Trent! So all's well! "Genesiars" it is! What a brainwave!

Farewell, Elsa, so soon forgotten! Too Russian! Bye-bye, old Sartre, scarcely cold in your grave! Common Front! Red and pink! Popular Front! Beaugon! Aravoir! The minister dropped in on Cuba on the way . . . And expressed discreet anxiety as to the fate of my Catholic poet in prison there . . . Valladares . . . "An obstinate Catholic," to use the description *Les Temps Modernes* applies to the Poles . . . Speaking of whom, what's become of Walesa? Is he still in prison too? Well, if you think the struggle of Enlightenment against Obscurantism ever knows a minute's rest in this world! . . . Repression of the idiots of the family! Castro sings the praises of the Encyclopedists and the French Revolution . . . He receives the minister in his luxurious villa, wearing a pair of shorts . . . This is a special token of respect, according to observers who are in the know . . . The minister is "charmed," and notes the great things popular power has achieved in the overcoming of illiteracy and superstition, but keeps his geopolitical distance . . . Aren't they enough for him, then—the Leader's display of muscle, that Voltairean thigh, that hairy calf? They make him feel uncomfortable . . .

The plane lands at Lod Airport . . . The drive up to Jerusalem . . . Of course my friends, here as everywhere else, are progressives . . . They're embarrassed . . . This war . . . International opinion . . . The Palestinians . . . The PLO . . . The deaths among the Lebanese civilian population . . . Yes, yes, of course . . . I've always said, and am ready to say it again as often as necessary, I belong to the left, absolutely, without hesitation or reservation! There! No vocation for martyrdom! I'm for peace! For the mutual recognition of all parties! Shalom! So why is it no one really quite believes me? Why do I yet again have the feeling people think I belong to the right? And why do the clods on the right always immediately think I belong to the left? Is it just the way I talk? Or joke? Or keep silent? Or eat? Or drink? Or smoke? There's always the question of accent . . . Gestures . . . Too much like this . . . Not enough like that . . . Salt at the wrong time . . . Sugar when it isn't done . . . Enthusiasm for things other people have never heard of . . . Love of contradiction . . . Frivolity about serious matters . . . Seriousness about trifles . . . Irresponsible . . . Arrogant . . . Enough, enough! I wish someone would tell me where I stand! If I've got permission to breathe! If my life is a dream! I'm frightened . . . I don't know what they want anymore . . . To be in the right . . . To know Good is on their side . . . All right, all right . . . But how is one to make them share in the Anguish that isn't even really anguish? The Absurd isn't so bad after all, though . . . Sartre's root, that went on being meaningless before the narrator's very eyes . . . People are overflowing with Meaning now . . . With Sense . . . Good Sense . . . Conformity with a capital C . . . It gushes in all directions . . . Give us back our good old Absurd! First-rate in times of crisis . . . The least lousy thing there is in times of war, actually . . . Vanity of vanities, mist of mists . . .

My Jerusalem friends, who were expecting a great evening of discussion, are rather surprised when almost as soon as I arrive I ask if I can go and see the Wall . . . We go . . . It's dark . . . So there I am, with my papier-mâché skullcap on . . . There are heaps of them at the entrance . . . The place is lit up by spotlights . . . Piles of Bibles on tall tables covered with crimson or blue embroidered velvet . . . I go and stand among the men busy chanting, with their faces glued to the stone . . . The Western Wall . . . Kotel . . . Herod . . . Sound barrier . . . I'm standing between a young soldier who's put his machine gun down beside him and is droning away in a rapid high-pitched moan, and an elderly Polish rabbi with a raucous voice and a beard . . . I put my hand on the warm stone . . . And listen . . . Listen to the voices coming from so far away

417

. . . From living throats . . . Which ought not to be so . . . "More-over concerning a stranger, that is not of thy people Israel, but cometh out of a far country for thy name's sake; (For they shall hear of thy great name, and of thy strong hand, and of thy stretched out arm;) when he shall come and pray toward this house; Hear thou in heaven thy dwelling place, and do according to all the stranger calleth to thee for: that all the people of the earth may know thy name, as do thy people Israel; and that they may know that this house, which I have builded, is called by thy name . . ."

The First Book of Kings . . . It's Solomon speaking, inaugurating the Temple, of which this outer fragment survives . . . Sacred session . . . The House of the Name . . . Impossible . . . Spotlights on the foundations . . . With the mosques up above, in the shadows . . . Omar . . . Al Aqsa . . . The foundations of the Name . . . Its exposed roots . . . And the rapid recitation goes on, mounting up toward a cloudy absence more present than any presence . . . No need to know much about it to feel physically, in a hundredth of a second, that this is where it's happening . . . Has happened . . . And will happen . . . It's inevitable . . . Compulsory . . . Nervous concentration . . . Subatomic . . . The battery of Time . . .

"But if ye shall at all turn from following me, ye or your children, and will not keep my commandments and my statutes which I have set before you, but go and serve other gods, and worship them; Then will I cut off Israel out of the land which I have given them; and this house, which I have hallowed for my name, will I cast out of my sight; and Israel shall be a proverb and a byword among all people . . . And at this house, which is high, everyone that passeth by it shall be astonished, and shall hiss; and they shall say, Why hath the Lord done thus unto this land, and to this house? And they shall answer, Because they forsook the Lord their God, who brought forth their fathers out of the land of Egypt, and have taken hold upon other gods, and have worshipped them, and served them: therefore hath the Lord brought upon them all this evil . . ."

So here they are . . . Laying siege to their own memory . . . They have survived . . . They are alive . . . They come from every-

where . . . And I with them . . . Why? That's just the way it is
. . . It must have been written down in my program . . . I had to
come here to find out . . . Coming from farther away than myself
. . . Going farther away . . . Remarkable perseverance, now I come
to think of it . . . So have I heard something? Been heard? What?
When? How? Where? Suddenly I can't help thinking of the splendid
interior of St. Peter's in Rome . . . In the seventies A.D. a number
of inspired Jews realized the thing to do would be to make straight
for the northwest and capture the oppressor's capital . . . While the
Romans were destroying the Temple and Jerusalem . . . Osmosis
. . . A good wheeze . . . But this remains the key site . . . This is
where the building had to be done . . . Even the mosques up above
are the radar-transmitters of unity in abeyance . . .

The Hebrew hits the stone with a dull thud . . . As if the voice
spoke of its own accord . . . As if the Voice were speaking of the
voice . . . The whole body, from head to foot, is in the voice . . .
Swayed by it, traversed by it, like a mesh in a vast invisible net . . .
Synagogues have always made me think of recording studios . . .

Thou hast heard their reproach, O Lord, and all their imaginations against me; The lips of those that rose up against me,
and their device against me all the day . . . Behold their sitting
down and their rising up; I am their musick . . .

Whether you like it or not, the atmosphere here is immediately
mystical . . . A mixture of gaiety, tragedy, and wit . . . Just now
one of my friends, talking about the situation in Lebanon, quite
naturally started to quote Isaiah: "Lebanon is ashamed and hewn
down . . ." I don't want to be facile, but still . . . The air . . . Its
lightness, lack of density . . . The basket of a balloon . . . The war
of the galaxies . . . Science fiction . . .

I must get some sleep . . . I'll come back . . . I get here again at
dawn . . . I sit beside four bearded old men out of Rembrandt . . .
One of them says good morning to me . . . Shalom . . . They recite
. . . Go on reciting . . . Hand to hand fighting with the wall . . .
The huge stones have to be turned into a continual vibration of

syllables . . . I don't understand a word . . . I'm dreaming; perhaps I'll wake up . . .

Thou has covered thyself with a cloud, that our prayers should not pass through . . . Though hast made us as the offscouring and refuse in the midst of the people . . .

Now they've formed themselves into a kind of chorus . . . The oldest one stands a little way behind the rest and leads the chanting . . . The war . . . Beirut . . . Phantoms . . . F-16s . . . Bombs . . . Suffering . . . They're the stronger . . . For the moment . . . But for how long? They know the hatred against them is eternal, eternally organized, spontaneous, channeled, exploited . . . Israel, the Jew among the nations . . . The State within the States . . . Source of trouble to the marrow of its bones . . . Magnet . . . Pole . . .

My flesh and my skin hath he made old; he hath broken my bones . . . He hath builded against me, and compassed me with gall and travail . . . Also when I cry and shout, he shutteth out my prayer . . . He hath enclosed my ways with hewn stone, he hath made my paths crooked . . .

They've got a bone to pick with their difficult god . . . The watcher . . . The tax man . . . The authority that lets years go by and then comes down on you for next to nothing . . . An oversight . . . A parking offense . . . Disregarding some line or other . . . Never the right thing . . .

Wherefore doth a living man complain, a man for the punishment of his sins?

Wherefore, indeed . . . If you really think about it . . . And then, the dead always get their revenge . . . All the dead . . . As if the lot of them were virtually there . . . A terrible millstone . . . Grinding . . . There are little scraps of paper among the stones . . . In the stones, voices from inside the stones . . . You ought to see it, the stone Jerusalem is made of . . . White and yellow, sulphur ivory, glint of bone . . . A grave? Yes . . . Mantegna . . . Piero . . . The tomb, the tombstone par excellence . . . The whole city a cemetery . . . A Messiametery . . . The Name that is stronger than Death? This is where it all happens . . . In broad daylight . . . Not in the Holy Sepulchre, where fat Orthodox monks of more than doubtful cleanliness, old women oozing clammy sweetness, beckon you into a corner to sell you a dried Holy Land flower, and whisper a blessing as they sprinkle you with a kind of consecrated but diluted eau de Cologne . . . Russians again . . . And here come some buses full of Swiss tourists . . . They rush to kiss the stone that witnessed Christ's resurrection . . . Germans gone wild . . . Luxemburgers in raptures . . . Americans galvanized . . . Japanese taking photos . . . No, better to go up to the Mount of Olives, the base the Ascension took off from, the Cape Canaveral of its day, and look down from there at the sparkling trickle of tombs falling down into the valley . . . Gehenna . . . Watch out! For believers the Messiah is supposed to enter the city from this direction . . . Jerusalem, Ariel, Daughter of Zion . . . they had themselves buried in thousands along his path so as to be able to rise up at once and follow him on resurrection day . . . But it's as if they'd always been hovering over the surface of the earth, dissolved in the quivering, piercing heat . . . Stand up! Stone on stone! Oven! Host! The sweltering endless day . . . And against that day and staving it off by every possible means, an everlasting army of shades, venom, blood, shit, ignorance and deceit . . . Cast-iron error, falsehood incarnate . . . *Perduta gente* . . . The tall sky and the stone, the lights on the cool mountain invoke their own calm . . . A place for taking off . . . Or landing . . . The descending, bedecked double city . . . Ruby-red wisteria . . . The bells of Our Lady of Sion over on the hill opposite my room . . . "Dormition" . . . The last sleep of the Virgin Mary . . . Assumption . . . Right, are all the characters here? Can we ring up the curtain on the final play? The performance to end all performances? If you have a better scenario, say so . . . Call Hollywood . . . But wait—it's as if the rehearsal were already at its height . . . As if the true theater had just reopened . . . The Globe . . . Shakespeare! Nations . . . Languages . . . Colors . . . Pupil . . . Drums . . .

I'm now in a car, zooming toward Qumrân . . . The Dead Sea
. . . The Scrolls . . . To tell the truth it was my main reason for
coming . . . I've been curious about them for ages . . . To see them
. . . And the place where they were found in 1947 . . . I saw
photographs of them as a child . . . I was very struck . . . Some
Bedouins found them in the caves . . . Scripture emerging from the
rock . . . Magic wand . . . The figures of '40 to '44 . . . Very nice!
Much ado about nothing . . . Massacres over trifles . . . You didn't
know the score, that's all . . . Nothing new under the sun . . . A
harsh and blatant sun keeps the ever new very visible . . . Millions
of victims? So what? Always the same words . . . Once again the
new leaf wheeze doesn't come off . . . 1947? Coincidence? I'm
belting along . . . July 15, 1099 . . . The capture of Jerusalem . . .
883 years ago . . . 1204, the sacking of Constantinople . . . Lepanto,
1570 . . . Vienna, 1683 . . . The light beats straight down on the
bare, tawny mountains . . . Gray . . . Reddish-gray . . . Brown
. . . Purple . . . I don't know . . . Sweat . . . Bedouin tents, camels
. . . Settlements composed of futuristic blocks of flats with TV
aerials . . . Moon landing . . . I swoop down toward the plain . . .
Into boiling oil . . . Whoa, here it is, on the right, among those
holes in the rock . . . Silvery horizon, misty sea . . . Pits . . .
Hermit's lairs . . . Essenes . . . Difficult guys . . . Set opinions!
"The war between the sons of light and the sons of darkness . . ."
Scrupulous scribes, perspiring through the sweltering days . . . And
the icy nights, I suppose . . . Crouching, tracing shapes . . . Intent
. . . "As thou knowest not what is the way of the spirit, nor how
the bones do grow in the womb of her that is with child: even so
thou knowest not the works of God who maketh all . . ."

I go up again to Jericho . . . Oasis . . . Palm trees . . . Fruit . . .
The oldest city in the world, apparently . . . Excavations . . . Beside
it, perched up on a rock, the monastery of the Forty Days . . . The
Temptation . . . You know, when he's been fasting and the Other
offers him power and glory and riches . . . "If thou be the Son of
God . . ." "Man shall not live by bread alone . . ." "Get thee
behind me, Satan . . ." The whole carry-on . . . The great curtain-
raiser . . . Before the play itself . . . The director revealed by the

author . . . Don't eat or drink for forty days and forty nights and the plain unvarnished truth will be revealed to you . . . I tried it once . . . Kept it up for ten days . . . Then lapsed straight into weakness and breakdown . . . From which I emerged with a few useful lessons . . . Like being ill . . . On a drip . . . Military service . . . Exempted because of "acute schizoid tendency . . ." Silent . . . Slow-witted . . . But I knew what I needed to know! A joke . . . But this is quite another ball game . . . An attempt to see through phenomena . . . The organs . . . The circulation . . . From the beginning . . . The devil . . . Grub, screwing, dough, power . . . GSDP! Pathetic! Walking skeleton! Imminent disintegration! "If thou be the Son of God . . ." With a body? A real body? And stones instead of bread? Admittedly he comes from Bethlehem, which means "house of bread" . . . One almost wants to eat some of that stone—it appeals strangely to the mouth . . . As if made for the palate . . . Bread . . . Stone . . . Peter . . . Word . . . Bang go the glass houses! "Cast thyself down"? Be borne up by angels? Crude provocation . . . "Worship me . . ." Now we come to it . . . Proposition . . . Pact . . . Signature . . . Religion . . .

In fact the Hebrews, with their intermittent and unpronounceable god, had to fight continually against terrestrial Religion . . . GSDP! Dark hole! Crucial rectum! Medusa . . . It takes thousands and thousands of years to exhaust and eradicate it . . . Every day . . . A hundred times a day . . . Interminable . . . Neither beginning nor end . . . You can see why they insist on a good rest at least once a week . . . Sabbath! To show there's a lull . . . Not at all the same thing as Sunday . . . On the contrary, the height of concentration . . . The repose of god, who's supposed to be saying "O.K.!" to himself—unless he's begun to regret his mistake . . . "Thou shalt not be affrighted at them: for the Lord thy God is among you, a mighty God and terrible . . ." There are a thousand times as many of them? No matter, god will take care of the ebb and flow of the battle . . . And will even require the others to be purely and simply exterminated . . . Anathema . . . Against the Hittites, the Girgasites, the Amorites, the Canaanites, the Hivites and the Jebusites . . . Genocides, if you like . . . A horrible, cruel, jealous, inflexible,

423

bloodthirsty god? In a way . . . That's one side of him, the left side
. . . But he has two sides . . . Destruction . . . Benediction . . . The
Law . . . And how can you have a Law without transgression? Yes,
of course, the Christians and their grace . . . But by dint of repress-
ing the left side too much he emerges every so often as ten times
more savage . . . The god of perfect love blessing massacres? An
awkward inconsistency . . . The right side may be sublime, but
don't forget the left . . . Christians don't really believe in god . . .
They think they've been let off . . . Exempted . . . A good bargain!
No more death! So they plunge straight into the first charnel-house
ideology they come across . . . Little Oedipuses . . . They think the
Son came to eliminate the Father . . .

But the left side is not civilized! Never! No confidence at all in
civilization . . . A backstage view . . . But of course if you kill in
the name of the Law you have to account for it ten times more
strictly . . . God keeps on getting angry . . . Relaxation . . . Mild-
ness . . . Always being betrayed . . . Money-grubbing . . . Prostitutes . . . Adultery . . .

What? What's that you said? A synthesis of the two sides? Yes,
of course, that's the whole point . . .

Let's see . . . "Palestine . . ." "Palestinian . . ." Where does the
word come from? From *Philistine?* Yes . . . The Philistines, invad-
ers from Crete and the other islands, are the Pulasati in the Egyptian texts . . . Their country is called Pulastu or Pilistu in Assyrian
inscriptions . . . The name of Palastu, Pelesheth in Hebrew, is the
origin of the name of Palestine: an extension to the hinterland of a
term that at first designated only a part of the coast . . .

So which people is actually where it belongs? Who can say? And
since when? And how do you define the *where* and the *when?*
Quarrels over property, as old as the world . . . Various megalo-
manias . . . As the one in the Bible is the weightiest, it naturally
bothers the whole world . . . Some tell you: That's enough—we're
going to make History start *here* . . . No! *There!* . . . But on
reflection, perhaps it should be *here* . . . Or *here* . . . This time
we've got it right! The birth of Christ! The Hegira! The French
Revolution! The Russian Revolution! Everything looks marvelous,

to start with . . . The Rights of Man—isn't that inspiring? Posted up in every school? Yes, yes! The emancipation of the Jews, in particular . . . No, that's too much, thank you! "All men . . ." "Man . . ." "We love man," says the minister in Cuba . . . Of course, of course . . . That sounds solid enough; incontrovertible . . . Don't go telling me it's a religion . . . Tolerance! And what about women? Women too! Included in Man? Of course? That's why people can't understand why the Jews want to remain Jews . . . But professor, they say they've had their dates forever! Perhaps, but so do the Egyptians! The Greeks! The Mayas! India! That's not a good enough reason! . . . "Man" above all! Yes, yes, but they want to keep the continuity . . . Through a dead language . . . And in a way it's rather disturbing, the way they're mixed up in the story all the time . . . They're never out of it . . . Never stagnating on the sidelines . . . You can't just put them away in a museum once and for all . . . They're right there in the nervous system, hanging on like grim death . . . Always up to new tricks . . . Hence their reputation . . . And the crises . . . And, every so often, deportations, expulsions, ghettos, bans, badges, yellow stars, gas chambers . . . In the name of the Whole . . . This gives you a headache? Too bad! What do you want me to do? Given the length and complexity of the Text! Readers short of time needn't apply!

Right . . . The only way to sort all this out, ultimately, would be to define the real Beginning . . . The beginning of all mankind . . . That would be clear . . . Obvious . . . Self-regulating . . . But that's precisely where the trouble starts . . . Proteins? Gooseberry bush? Chimpanzee? Probably, but that doesn't cut any ice . . . And that's where Mama comes in, just as if she were coming home . . . Just at the right moment! Matter . . . Cosmos . . . Primal soup . . . Venus, mother of the species . . . *Aeneadum genetrix* . . . Evolution, if you insist, but common tissue . . . Tangible . . . No need for dates, with Mama . . . And she'd soon get the names mixed up . . . It's her, and that's that! The Mother of the Scientist! All men are brothers, they're all born of the same mother . . . They start to imagine that's the end of the story . . . Some hopes! Or else the real story is Science . . . Hmmm . . . Memory won't go along with it . . . "I'm a memory come alive," notes Kafka . . . "That's why I can't sleep . . ."

Sleep won't work . . . Neither will Nature . . . Death seen as a mere incident doesn't convince anyone . . . Reconciliation is always premature . . . Even if I possess the key to all neuroses, a fat lot of good that does us . . . Wisdom is given to few . . . And even so! In the past! They wanted it more! Indefatigable! Withdraw if you like, regard all this bustle as loathsome, devote yourself to contemplation . . . Poems . . . Philosophies . . . Please god let all men be sages, poets, or philosophers! But as soon as this is decreed all hell breaks loose . . .

I told you so, murmurs Jehovah . . . And the whisper becomes a roar again . . . The best-seller of best-sellers becomes peppery and devious once more . . .

That which was, is; and that which is to be, has been; and God seeks that which flees . . .

So you're abandoning Reason? Not at all . . . On the contrary . . .

I linger a while in Jericho . . . Dust under the trees . . .

By car to Bethlehem . . . Oh, there's a Catholic church! I was beginning to think that apart from Judaism and Islam there were only the Orthodox, the Armenians, the Jacobites, the Nestorians, and the Maronites . . . It's a little Franciscan church . . . Clean . . . Modern . . . Nineteenth-century . . . A daub of the Assumption, with bleating pilgrims . . . A faint sound of organ there to one side . . . Yes . . . A concert . . . Rehearsal for the evening . . . My god! At last! Music! Vivaldi! I don't know if my religion is the true one, but it's the one that has music . . . So it must be the true one . . . What? Do you mean to say Bach was a Catholic? Blasphemy! Nonsense! But it's true, it's true! Baroque, Italian . . . The Mass in B . . . The Messiah . . . The best Credo ever written for the *unam, catholicam, apostolicam ecclesiam* . . . Luther's just an episode! Venice is the source! Ah, Giudecca, I die for thee! Ten notes and everything is changed . . . Three bars and the mystery is revealed . . . If they play thirty seconds of the Gloria near my coffin I swear

426

I'll rise from the dead . . . Try it! . . . I am in the records, all of them . . . And all the cassettes . . . Yes, that's it, I'm not making it up—the Gloria for two sopranos, alto, choir, and orchestra . . . A student group . . . From Jerusalem . . . Not bad . . . Let's see if I can remember . . . Yes . . . (1) Gloria in Excelsis. (2) Et in terra Pax (chorus). (3) Laudamus te (duet: two sopranos). (4) Gratias agimus Tibi (chorus). (5) Propter Magnam Gloriam (chorus). (6) Domine Deus (aria: soprano). (7) Domine Fili Unigenite (chorus). (8) Domine Deus, Agnus Dei (aria: alto and chorus). (9) Qui tollis (chorus). (10) Qui sedes ad dexteram (alto solo). (11) Quoniam tu Solus Sanctus (chorus). (12) Cum Sancto Spirito (chorus).

I go out into the square . . . Yellow late afternoon . . . I have a tepid Coca-Cola in an Arab café . . . Watch a whole family cram themselves into a taxi . . . Father, mother, grandfather, four young children, baby in arms . . . They won't make it . . . Yes, it's O.K. . . . They kiss a brother or cousin good-bye . . . Once . . . Ten times . . . They'll never stop . . . The baby cries . . . They look very beautiful in the warm light . . . Unreal . . . "Biblical" . . . Neither happy nor unhappy . . . Just *there* . . .

Bethlehem . . . Tourism . . . Nothing . . . And yet it's the ancient Ephrath . . . Where Rachel died in childbirth . . . What was it she named her son as she was dying? Benoni, "son of my sorrow" . . . A curse . . . Which the father, Jacob, who felt he was being got at, and to whom, in Bethel, god had just granted the new name of Israel, immediately countered . . . Just in time . . . A father renamed by god renames his son as the latter's mother is dying . . . So he calls him Ben-yamim, "son of the right hand" . . . Whew! A quick switch from left to right . . . Benjamin . . . Joseph's youngest and favorite brother . . . They meet in Egypt . . . Once again a running together of places, dead people, births and names . . . Not to mention miscarriages! Or hysterical pregnancies! Or spontaneous abortions! Too many to count! As if everything happened via physical reproduction . . . Space . . . Speech . . . To arrive at what? Take Bethel . . . "House of God" . . . its old name was Luz, meaning almond or almond tree . . . The Vision of the Ladder . . . The wrestling with the Angel . . .

427

But thou, Bethlehem Ephratah, though thou be little among the thousands of Judah, yet out of thee shall he come forth unto me that is to be ruler in Israel; whose goings forth have been from of old, from everlasting . . .

Micah, chapter 5 . . . One of the twelve . . . Prophets, not apostles . . . Four great and twelve "minor" . . . Four canons of prophecy: Isaiah, Jeremiah, Ezekiel and Daniel . . . Twelve fugues: Hosea, Joel, Amos, Obahdiah, Jonah, Micah, Nahum, Habakkuk, Zephaniah, Haggai, Zechariah, and Malachi . . . Music! Music!

I come back to Jerusalem . . . I'm beginning to understand their word for describing a return . . . *Alyah*—a going up . . . It's like a forbidden city; inaccessible . . . Inside a magic circle . . . You twist and turn up toward it, knowing it's waiting for you somewhere behind the sky of mauve mountains, and suddenly there it is . . . At once a peak, and hemmed in by other heights . . . An inverted cone . . . As if balanced on its apex . . . On a point . . . Find that point! Outside the sepulchre! What a paradox, fighting over Christ's grave! What an admission! As if they wanted him to be fixed to the time and place of his resurrection . . . Chained . . . Prevented from coming back . . . This mania about places . . . "Hysteria is linked to place . . ." Yes indeed . . . The place to defend yourself against god . . . A point that's neither in time nor space? Mathematical? That's how progress was made in both mathematics and logic . . . Al-Khârismi . . . Zero . . . Nought . . . Nothing . . . *Sifre* . . . Cypher . . . Figure . . . The Fourth Crusade brought about advances in the history of map-making . . . The astrolabe . . . Via Venice yet again . . . It's as if I could see that point fluttering about before my eyes . . . Swift, elusive, burning, devastating . . . Black . . . The dot on the i . . . A blank, a space, an interval just long enough for a great silent cry . . .

A maze of narrow streets . . . I'm going to have dinner in the

Arab quarter . . . A long walk . . . There's a bar open opposite the King David Hotel . . .

I have a drink with a bored girl with fair hair . . . Kitty . . . Am I an American? Good . . . But I live in France? What a funny idea . . . I'm a journalist? A political journalist? So how is all this going to end?

"It'll sort itself out," I say . . . "Gradually . . . Imperceptibly . . . Via a thousand ups and downs . . . Never . . . And yet . . ."

"Will there be more actual wars?"

"Let's hope not . . . But as war's a permanent thing . . ."

As far as I can make out the romantic period is over, here . . . Concrete problems . . . Inflation . . . Jokes about the local currency, the shekel . . . The real currency is the dollar, of course . . . The same as everywhere else! As I've noticed more than once, it's only the French who won't admit it . . . A Frenchman who immediately translates money into dollars is a biological freak . . . Even the Russians are ahead of them in this . . .

"And what do you think about our religious revival? Fanatics, huh? Did you see El Al's suspended all Saturday flights? To respect the Sabbath! On the grounds that tradition is above profit."

"Really? I hadn't realized . . . Maybe . . . But isn't it something else?"

"What?"

"Technology . . . World scale . . ."

We're both getting bored . . . She smiles faintly . . . I drone on about New York . . . Paris . . . She'd like to go to Paris . . . She was born here . . . Polish parents . . . University . . . Keep it short . . . Two in the morning . . . I hold her hand . . . We go out to my car . . . Dark street . . . We make out . . . I can tell she's surprised when she touches my prick . . . I remember what Esther said once . . . "Circumcision makes the actual screwing easier . . . But the foreskin's better for the other things . . . Smoother . . . More flexible . . ." Pagan sweets . . . Delights of Capua . . . Of course I know it's a more metaphysical matter than that . . . And one that could be brilliantly expanded . . . Penetration of divine veils and

screens . . . Ecstasy within the shrine . . . Face to face vision . . .
Some other time! But you don't mind if I just amuse myself? If I
relax? If the traveler does something to calm his nerves?

A museum in Jerusalem . . . Garden designed by a Japanese . . .
Two sculptures by Rodin . . . Adam! Balzac! One by Picasso . . .
And the archaeological rooms . . . Here we are . . . Chalcolithic!
It's amazing what they can dig out of the desert . . . Especially now
that we live in . . . I won't say Messianic, but certainly radiographic
times . . . Come now, cards on the table! The bill! The balance
sheet! The final count! Israel, sieve of the nations! It looks like
being a long list . . . They find something else every day . . .
Objects they can't even identify . . . Civilizations that leave you
flabbergasted . . . We're on Mars, I tell you . . . The earth isn't the
earth anymore . . . It's become celestial in the last twenty years
. . . We're discovering it as if we were mutants just landed on its
surface . . . Real depths . . . Time not merely lost but completely
annihilated . . . From the original big-bang . . . To the final bang-
bong . . . Perhaps a mere breath! As brief and imperceptible as the
initial explosion was loud . . . Fffft! A light breeze, as unobtrusive
as all these scrolls of the Book of Esther in the showcases . . .
Dating from all ages, and coming from Alsace, Italy, Turkey, Holland, Morocco, Germany, and (again) Poland . . . The Book of
Esther was very popular . . . A textbook on how to survive in exile
. . . How to handle the Diaspora . . . Ahasuerus . . . The palace
garden . . . The eunuchs . . . How to become a queen . . . And
protect one's people . . . Mordecai . . . The plot unmasked . . . The
inauguration of Purim . . . From *pur*, meaning "fate . . ." Commemoration . . . The number of little Esthers that must have taken
themselves, and still do take themselves, for Esther herself! Racine!
The alexandrine of the golden age . . .

Ah, there she is! Right in front of me! The Great Mycenian
Mother! A variation on the universal Female God . . . The most
impressive representation I've ever seen . . . Just a seat . . . High-

backed . . . With two scarcely visible breasts in the vertical plane
. . . An armchair with breasts . . . Olympia . . . Phaedra . . . A
hollow throne . . . Mother Chair! Electric! The Platonic idea of a
bergère! The Assize! But the Assize (=seated) standing up, so to
speak, and laying down the law on its four legs . . . The Widow
Guillotine! Ceres SS! It's not a very big statue . . . About a meter
high . . . Elegantly enigmatic . . . Yes, it really is the right Emblem
. . . The one you see everywhere, if you leave Egypt behind . . .
And it's still there today, all over the place, all the time . . . The
Parca . . . The Form . . . The Measure . . . The concept of hips,
sculpted . . . Ishtar . . . Venus . . . Astarte . . . Presto! Summon
up the trivial popinjays! The great superfluous bodies! Cartridges!
Photomatons! Refills! Vanish! Come back again! For damn-all! . . .
So here is One of the human tides . . . The weaveress . . . The
queen of the skies on earth . . . The Eternal Executrix-Urn . . . The
great Spinster resolutely awaiting her bridegrooms . . . Van Gogh's
chair? The very same! Straw for the crib . . . Wood for the coffin
. . . But here in stone . . . A vertical sepulchre! But alive . . .
Mocking! But no — just crushing indifference! Blind, deaf, incom-
prehensibly detached . . .

Body of bodies! . . . Before you, after you . . . ? to the gnomes!
. . . Et gnomus factus est! . . . Just time to sit down, shit a bit,
have your passions and your periods, physical and moral, and that's
it! Off with your egos! . . . Antechamber of the ages . . . Surgeon's
waiting room . . . Ejectable placenta! . . . Egregious oven! . . . Eve!
. . . Even the kitchen sink! And someone actually made it . . . This
wonder . . . This monumental con . . . Petrified Beatrice! . . .
Anti-Pietà! . . . Phooey! . . .

The friend who's with me is rather surprised to see me standing
there in front of Our Lady all this time . . . He's wondering what's
the matter with me . . . What these groans and crows of delight
portend . . . Why I bend down to look at her from below, from the
side . . . From behind, from in front, and so on . . . And then all
over again . . . I'm almost panting . . . Oh, she's immovable, that's
for sure . . . It would take a miracle to detach her from the ground
. . . She *is* the ground . . . And who can lift the earth into the air

. . . She is Plane . . . She is Gravity . . . But no—determination, rather . . . Definition . . . The negative that demonstrates, makes tangible, calls into existence . . . *Omnis determinatio est negatio* . . . Omnis! Isis! Semiramis! Miss! I imagine this is the sort of stool women used to use to help them give birth . . . *Je suis belle, ô mortels, et sur mon sein de pierre* . . . I am beautiful, O ye mortals, and on my stone bosom . . . That chairback with breasts! What a brainwave! Beautiful isn't the word . . .

> How doth the city sit solitary that was full of people! how is she become as a widow! she that was great among the nations, and princess among the provinces . . .

That's the old Jerusalem they're talking about . . . In the Book of Lamentations . . . The great Jeremiad . . . In Hebrew it's called, as is customary just by the first word of the text: "How . . ." " 'êykâh! . . ." The prophet is lamenting the decay of the holy city through sin—in other words, as ever, he's lamenting the hidden practice of prostitution . . . "How" is the first word that comes to him . . . How doth the city sit! The wall of the how! By which they come to lament from the four corners of the earth . . . The holy places! Jerusalem . . . Mecca, with its black stone . . . Always that rock! And Lourdes, with all the crutches hanging up on the rock— that's not bad either . . . More vulgar, I grant you . . . You have the best sort of visions you can . . .

"Which turned the rock into a standing water, the flint into a fountain . . ."

Right . . . Well, I now propose to end the visit with the star attraction . . . Enemy number 1 of Mère la Chaise . . . The best ever . . . To see it you have to enter the Shrine of the Book . . . A special building . . . Dazzling white . . . The shape of a flying saucer . . . The Martians are here . . . The terrible little green men . . . The scrolls! The Dead Sea Scrolls! There they are, in a circular room, just like the year two thousand and one . . . All around the walls . . . And there it is in the middle, as it should be . . . In a kind of shaft ready to dive underground for protection if need be . . . Atomic shelter . . . Dread! Priceless morsel! Scroll of scrolls!

432

A secret kind of radium! At least to me . . . Isaiah . . . From right to left . . . Counterclockwise on the clock of visible time . . . Spidery characters . . . With graffiti-style eagle's talons to represent the unpronounceable name . . . Yellowed paper, dried up, scorched, eaten away . . . Hidden away in the caves . . . Isaiah! . . . Yesha'yâhû . . . Greeting to Jehovah . . . Lover of *remains* . . . Something will remain . . . And return . . . A stump . . . A trace . . . A grain . . . A footprint . . . Even if you destroy everything, there'll still be the residue of a residue of a residue left . . . Almost nothing . . . But more than is needed . . . To understand everything . . . To start everything all over again . . . As all this only goes to show . . . Son et lumière . . . The amazingness of the past . . .

. . . unto me every knee shall bow, every tongue shall swear . . . Surely, shall one say, in the Lord have I righteousness and strength: even to him shall men come; and all that are incensed against him shall be ashamed . . .

Here I am with my nose pressed against the glass . . . Like a dashboard . . . I hover around the manuscript . . . I can feel the swelter of Qumrân . . . It certainly is a strange country . . . You sense wave after wave of history . . . Ancient history . . . Romans, Crusaders, Arabs . . . Modern history . . . First the German-style buildings . . . Bauhaus . . . Then the Yugoslav . . . Then the American . . .

Who hath wrought and done it, calling the generations from the beginning? I the Lord, the first, and with the last; I am he . . . The isles saw it, and feared; the ends of the earth were afraid, drew near, and came . . .

Who could have foreseen or even suspected all this, fifty years ago? No one . . . More things have happened in thirty years than in a couple of centuries . . . And for me, more in two years than in thirty . . . Skies rolled back, unfurled . . . No danger of getting bored in the next two decades . . .

I am the Lord that . . . frustrateth the tokens of the liars, and maketh diviners mad; that turneth wise men backward, and maketh their knowledge foolish . . .

I can hear you from here . . . What about your characters? you say . . . What's become of them? We want the characters! Not the author! The characters! We want to know what's happening to them! The sequel to the cartoon! WE WANT A PROPER NOVEL! Grimaces . . . Uproar . . . Hissing . . . Yawns . . . Be patient, insatiable reader, avid readeress! You'll see them again soon . . . Of course . . . You insist on being kept safe in the story, don't you? As soon as the characters disappear for a moment you're afraid you're going to be driven right out of the book? You want to hold on to your seat? Your couchette? Your imaginary cushion? If the narrator's too solitary and free you lose the thread? You're afraid he'll drop you? Withdraw into his monastery? Once he's off on his biblical hobbyhorse . . . Disillusioned as he obviously is . . . It's hard to see how he can still go in for passions and escapades . . . And what about Flora? Kate? Bernadette . . . Boris, Robert, the Chairwoman? And Diane, Ysia, Lynn, Cyd? And that nice Deb? And what about the screwing?

They'll be back . . . Male and female . . . Just give them time to change their clothes and put on fresh makeup . . . To review their relations with me . . . Size me up in silence . . . Work out the best way to have fun with me . . . Or fool me . . . More often the second than the first, if the truth be told . . . Vampires! Just like you! Oh, you're killing me! Your systematic hostility is getting me down! Never satisfied! Always watching out for weaknesses! Longueurs! Inadequacies! Waiting ferociously for me to get stuck . . . To stall . . . To give up . . . Counting the words, the signatures . . . Only thinking about the surrounding hullabaloo, never mind what's inside . . . How many copies they're printing . . . Promotion . . . Influence . . . Will he have any? A little? None at all? Frankly, I wouldn't say this was the right moment . . . Everything's against it . . . I can see you preparing your excuses already . . .

Changing the subject . . . Deadly phrases . . . Articles . . . Dinners
. . . Phone calls . . . Rumors . . .

That's why I'm not in any hurry . . . Another couple of days
here . . . I'm just back from Haifa, a kind of Barcelona at the foot
of Mount Carmel . . . Now Jerusalem again . . . I go back to the
Wall . . . And the Mount of Olives . . . I've brought Loyola's
autobiography and *Spiritual Exercises* with me . . . I discover that
when he was still a young licentious soldier he was wounded in the
leg by a French cannonball at the siege of Pampeluna . . . And then
he was roughly handled by the Turks in Jerusalem . . . That was
his Franco-Arab experience! His pilgrimage to the Holy Land makes
a great story . . . A whole age . . . Barcelona . . . Venice . . .
Dangers at sea . . . Like Cervantes, who, like Swift and Sterne, has
never been as relevant as he is now . . . And to think that Eleanor
of Aquitaine came here too . . . Yes, in person . . . The granddaughter of Duke William, first of the troubadors . . . Crusades
. . . Pogroms . . . A whirligig of history, since it was because of the
persecutions that the Jews started to come back here . . . The
sermons of the Mellifluous Doctor: St. Bernard . . . "The Jews are
the flesh and bones of the Messiah; if you harm them, you are in
danger of hurting the Lord in the apple of his eye . . ." Well put,
but what good does it do? General unrest . . . An inferno of infamy . . .

There I go, digressing again! The *Exercises* were published in
Rome in 1548 . . . Right in the middle of the Reformation . . .
Financial scandals! Indulgences! That poor modern cardinal caught
up in a bank crash . . . Nothing new . . . Ignatius comes to the
Mount of Olives to see a stone supposed to have preserved the
prints of Christ's feet when he took off into heaven . . . The Turks
pick him up and give him a bit of a going over . . . But he insists
on going back to see which direction the footprints point in . . . Left
and right . . . To make a sketch . . . Things like that happened in
those days . . . Ah well . . . "The first thing to do in order to get
an idea of the place is to look in imagination at the synagogues,
villages and towns which Christ visited during his ministry" . . .

So . . . "I shall regard myself as an abscess or a fistula . . ." Excellent . . . "We might arrive at this idea by imagining we see our soul shut up in this corruptible body as in a prison, and man himself exiled in this vale of woe amid the senseless beasts . . ." Of course, of course . . . He sees life as governed by two contrasting movements—diastole and systole: desolation and consolation . . . Two standards: Lucifer in Babylon, Christ in Jerusalem . . . "Communication will take place if I imagine Jesus Christ present before me, nailed to the Cross . . ." A touch of El Greco? You've got it . . . But the best is yet to come . . . Paragraph 325 . . . To be reflected upon seriously before going back into the world . . . Leaving my spaceship . . . An eternal rule . . . Not a wrinkle . . . It should be spread around . . .

"Some rules to help identify the impulses of the soul as caused by the various spirits, so that we may accept the good and reject the bad . . .

"The twelfth: Our enemy partakes of the nature and temperament of women, as regards frailty of body and stubbornness of mind . . . For just as a woman, fighting a man, if she sees him hold out firmly, herself gives in and turns her back on him, whereas if she sees he is timid and cowardly she becomes extremely bold and attacks him fiercely—so the devil is always weakened and cast down whenever he sees a spiritual athlete meeting temptation with a stout heart and head held high . . . But if the man trembles and is downhearted at the thought of having to bear the devil's first assaults, there is no earthly beast more furious, aggressive and persistent against him than the enemy, eager to assuage the desires of his wicked and obstinate spirit at our expense . . ."

Isn't that charming? I told you it would be. . .

I go back to Paris in the middle of July . . . Deb and Stephen have already left on vacation and are waiting for me . . . S. is in Italy . . . Robert in Spain . . . No sign from Flora . . . Kate's "covering" the festivals for the *Journal* . . . Oppressive atmosphere

. . . Terrorist attacks . . . Bombs . . . Beirut burning on every screen . . .

The phone . . . Boris . . . I disguise my voice and pretend to be the usual American friend living in the studio during the vacation and not understanding a word of French . . .

"Tell him to read the latest number of *Scratch!*" bawls Boris . . .

"Sorry . . ."

"As soon as possible!"

"Sorry . . . Sorry . . ."

He realizes his interlocutor can't or won't get the message . . . Perhaps he's recognized my voice after all . . . But it doesn't matter to him . . . For him there are no other languages, no other words, than his own . . . Publicity personified . . . The only consideration . . . He doesn't speak English? So what? What does he care? The world is his! He's the navel of the universe . . . And this week the universe can think of nothing but *Scratch* . . . Has the latest issue reached all the newsstands? I bet he went out early this morning to check . . . He trembles . . . He can't bear it . . . He writhes . . . Who cares about English? Or Chinese? Or Swahili? He hangs up in a fury . . . What can it be now? Something political, no doubt . . . With a full-page photo, judging by the state he's in . . .

I go down and buy the rag . . . I was right! Terrific photograph of Boris . . . Taken with the man who's now the President . . . It's an old snapshot, but still . . . An extremely savage interview . . . Goes for the present government tooth and nail . . . Gossip! Anecdotes! Really good stuff! He tells about lunches and dinners with the current political crowd . . . How he's been made use of . . . Been promised this and that . . . And never been given anything . . . Not been made head of a television channel . . . Or director of the Opera . . . Or ambassador in Stockholm . . . Or minister for leisure activities . . . But the joke is that everyone will now see how the coldblooded brutes in power thought they had him in their pockets . . . That they could manipulate him with impunity . . . Use him as some sort of a parasite . . . There's literature for you! Fancy not liking Baudelaire and calling Boris the greatest writer of his generation! There must have been some mix-up with Napoleon

437

III! Left, right—what does it matter? So has Boris just gone back to the right? After having tried to turn to the left? No, no—he'll be on the left again tomorrow . . . Much to the delight of those he's telling off today . . . Nothing to get worked up about . . . Everything can be arranged . . . Adolescent excitement . . . High school . . . Nothing to it . . . Not worth mentioning . . . Valse triste . . . Just a little media jerk-off . . .

Poor Boris . . . He's out of luck . . . Fifty children burned to death in a bus! He doesn't make the front page . . . Universal emotion . . . Coffins everywhere . . . Messages . . . Opinions . . . Terror on the motorway . . . More air raids on Beirut . . . Too many dead! Too much suffering! Boris's performance seems narcissistic, frivolous . . . On the rebound: "The politicians will disappear, but my work will remain," he says . . . What work? A touching admission of fear . . . Is he afraid of disappearing with the *combinazione* itself? Of which he is the archetypical product? Ungrateful wretch!

I pack my bags again . . . Diving gear . . . A few records . . . Mustn't forget my racket . . . Books? . . . Just the Bible . . . And a Hebrew dictionary . . .

I come over all dizzy for a moment on the stairs . . . I realize I'm tired . . . Or getting old? Quite possibly . . . Do you know when you're starting to get old? It's when you begin to anticipate your own actions. Go over them quickly in your head before you do them . . . Think before you act . . . Isn't that being mature? No, it's a sign of wear and tear . . . Hardening of the brain . . . Nerve cell renewal slowing down . . . The circuits are "photographing" one another . . . To save energy . . . Admittedly I've been overdoing things lately . . . Too much time spent on planes . . .

I go back to the studio and lie down . . . Then get up and put Paul Desmond's "You go to my head" on the turntable . . . One of my favorites . . . Percy Heath on bass . . . Right away I'm in a beat-up yellow cab on Fifth Avenue, rattling and swooping toward the Village . . . Bank Street! The No Name Café . . . My New York Studio . . . The Hudson . . . The sun on the planks by the river . . .

Phone call from Cyd . . .

"Have a good trip?"

"Very."

"Find anything new?"

"Lots . . . I'll tell you about it . . . How about you?"

"I'm O.K. . . . I'm leaving tomorrow."

"For Easthampton?"

"Yes . . . But I have to go to California first."

"For long?"

"A month . . . Shall I call you from New York when I get back?"

"Do that . . . Is Lynn joining you?"

"Yes . . . She's getting bored . . ."

"I understand . . . Go easy on the chemistry, huh?"

"We'll be thinking of you . . ."

"How kind."

"Oh, I was forgetting—I love you . . ."

"So I should hope."

"How about your book?"

"Haven't had time . . . I'll be getting back to it . . ."

"Don't forget! The story! Plenty of action!"

"A thriller!"

"Kiss, kiss!"

"Same to you."

"I went back to see the Rembrandt."

" 'The Polish Knight?' "

"Yes . . . I saw it better than when I was with you . . ."

"Of course . . ."

"What do you mean—'of course'?"

"I mean, more from your own point of view . . ."

"Macho wretch!"

"I warn you, machismo's coming back into fashion! The polls say
so! The monster's back! New! Exciting! Intriguing!"

"I know! It's true! It's terrible!"

"Who, me?"

"No—you're sweet! I love you!"

"You love a male chauvinist pig?"

"Of course not! You're an angel! You know you are! You only pretend!"

"What time is it where you are?"

"Ten-thirty . . . So it's four-thirty for you?"

"Yes, a stifling afternoon . . . I want you."

"Same here."

"What are you wearing?"

"Nothing . . . It's hot here too . . ."

"Are you stroking yourself?"

"Of course! And you?"

"As I'm speaking to you now."

"Bye then . . . Lots of love."

"Ciao!"

"Ciao!"

We've tossed each other off so often over the phone, Cyd and I, including across the Atlantic, that we're not about to start again now . . . Just a reminder of nice moments . . . The blaze of the beginning . . . Abbreviation . . . Password . . . Casual smut is the modern equivalent of romantic billets doux . . . Frenzied, clammy, consumptive . . . She's just got up, she'll get dressed and go out to lunch . . . Whereas for me the day's ending . . . Dusk in Paris . . . Difficult . . . Alone? Yes, it's better . . . Otherwise you have to have opinions . . . Quote from the papers . . . Invent witticisms . . . I'm tired . . . Don't feel like *bitching* anyone . . . I've a feeling the dead are stirring . . . Skulls being swallowed up by the dark . . . How can you forget so easily, reader of either sex, that *your* skull, yes, *your* empty eye-sockets will ultimately be brought to dust, fire, and rich earth? Speeding-up process . . . The height of misunderstanding . . . I know why the French prefer to "forget" that America exists . . . For them it stands for a personal humiliation . . . LaFayette? No, the disagreeable feeling that a bigger, freer city rose up there *after* them . . . An extra day . . . It redeems the lost time with ampler, more modern resources . . . And that makes them feel provincial; they'd rather not know about it . . . And then there's the French language and nationality, both a minor quantity over there . . . A drop in the ocean . . . Hardly even that . . .

English people, Italians, Germans, Slavs everywhere . . . The Span-
iards have got the whole of Latin America, yet you hear Spanish
spoken everywhere in New York . . . Chinese too! But you never
hear French . . . Not "in" . . . What about Canada? Quebec? No,
it's humiliating—more like the accent of the Morvan . . . Just take
a look at a Frenchman in New York . . . Lost, overwhelmed, jealous
. . . For a Frenchman in France, who's never set foot there, it
simply doesn't exist . . . A mythical country . . . No family life
. . . What about the cinema, music, literature? Yes, no doubt they
exist there, but it's as if they were produced in some chemical
factory far away under the sea . . . The French have stayed at home,
and the world goes around without them . . . Six o'clock in the
evening . . . I can feel myself mingling with the crowd on Fifth
Avenue . . . It nearly always comes back to Fifth Avenue, or Broadway . . . I feel myself moving backward: more sun, more freedom
—it's still morning, broad daylight, for Cyd . . . What Italy was to
full-blooded nineteenth-century authors—Stendhal, say—New York
ought to be for French writers today . . . It's true of thriller writers
. . . But what about the others? The highbrows, the ones who
contribute to "culture"? Where have they got to?

Telephone . . . Kate . . .

"So you're back."

"Looks like it . . ."

"How was it?"

"Fine."

"Did you see any important people? Get anything new on the
war?"

"No . . . Just friends . . . Personal contacts . . ."

"No article?"

"No . . . Just stuff for myself . . ."

I can tell she's relieved . . . So long as I don't try to make the
front page of the *Journal* . . . She wants me just to withdraw slowly
. . . So people can think I've got lost in the sands . . . Oh yes,
what's become of him? No one knows . . . He's traveling . . .
Perhaps he hasn't got anything left to say . . . He's not with it anymore . . .

"Are you free for dinner, by any chance?" she asks kindly.

I hesitate . . . In theory an evening on my own is a godsend . . . But after all I ought to try to catch a glimpse of what people are thinking about me . . . Just to check . . .

"Let me see . . . Yes, I could fix it . . . Late-ish?"

"The Closerie at ten?"

"Right."

I arrange some of my papers . . . Photographs . . . Letters . . . Bills . . . Notebooks . . . Odd jottings . . . The things you write down that never come to anything . . . On the spur of the moment . . . Ashes . . . One ought to destroy everything . . . Burn it . . .

"You haven't become a Zionist, then?"

Kate's tan hasn't been a success. She looks worn. White underneath it. Bitter. Exhausted.

"Why should I have? What an idea! Would you like a drink?"

"A whisky . . . That Reagan—he's crazy!"

"Do you think so?"

"Of course! I've just had another call from Bob in New York . . . The Americans can't take him anymore! They've had more than enough!"

Bob called me too when I got back . . . I noticed he started talking about Reagan before he asked me about myself . . . A way of signaling that my friends have gone off me . . . Call me Reagan . . . Or something similar . . . God knows I couldn't care less about Reagan!

"It's time to put a stop to him," says Kate somberly, as if she had some say in the matter. "Him, Begin—the whole gang . . ."

"I see Tass refers to the Israelis as 'cannibals' . . . Some nerve," I say. "They want them put in a straitjacket . . . They compare them with Hitler yet again . . . That's going a bit far . . ."

"You know what the Russians are . . . They exaggerate . . . But still . . ."

"Yes, I know . . . But even so . . ."

"So what was it like there?"

"Well, in Jerusalem . . ."

I've scarcely opened my lips when I notice Kate isn't listening

. . . She's not the slightest bit interested . . . So I just produce two or three tourist platitudes . . . She's restless, preoccupied with her own thoughts . . . Amazing the way intellectuals use politics to talk to one another about their private passions . . .

"So you've had a row with Flora?"

"Have I?"

"It's public knowledge . . . She's going around saying you're a reactionary . . . A bureaucratic macho . . ."

"Flora's fond of phrases . . ."

"But she's furious . . . What did you do to her?"

"Nothing . . ."

"The Chairwoman was talking to me about you, too . . . In a very friendly way, I must admit . . . She thinks you're clever . . ."

Kate subjects me to a professional stare . . . You can't say *I'm* not a professional . . .

"How is she?" I ask.

"Great! But the fight's not getting any easier . . . Did you know IVG's still not reimbursed by social security?"

"Really?"

"It's a scandal! Fancy trying to save money on *that!*"

"Abortion, you mean?"

"Yes . . . Isn't it incredible?"

"Terrible . . . But things will come around . . . Of course, in a way . . ."

"What now?"

Kate puts on the expression, at once disapproving, resigned, and pleased, of someone about to be provoked . . . Agreeably, of course, in a way that only strengthens your own opinion and way of looking at things . . . I'm quite ready to provide her with this pleasure . . . To pretend that the terrible enemy actually exists . . . Like making believe with children about the big bad wolf!

"Well," say I, "if I wasn't afraid of shocking you . . ."

"Go ahead . . . I know what you're going to say . . ."

"What?"

"Go on, go on!"

"All right . . . In strictly economic terms, the suspension of the

443

plan to reimburse abortions—which I'm against, let me tell you, and which I trust is only temporary—is a sign, if one can put it like that . . ."

"Come on, spit it out!"

"Of an unconscious compensatory revaluation of sperm—"

"You're disgusting!"

"—which seems to echo the exchange rate of gold and the dollar!"

"That'll do! . . . What do you think about the cultural crusade against U.S. financial and intellectual imperialism? Against the invasion of American stereotypes?"

A straight counterattack to the liver . . .

"Very good! Really throwing down the gauntlet! Very French!"

"Be serious . . . What do you think?"

"What do you expect me to think? Nothing!"

"You're not going to write an article about it?"

"No, I don't think so . . ."

Another source of satisfaction for her . . . I'm going to keep quiet . . . No article about Israel, no defense of the United States . . . No attempt to occupy the printed page . . . That's the main thing . . .

"So what are you doing now?" she asks almost affably.

"Well . . . there's my novel . . ."

"Oh yes, that's right—your *novel* . . ."

There we go again—it's as if I'd said something indecent . . . He's getting on with his *novel!* The word produces a magical effect whenever I say it . . . Once again I'm struck by how mobile Kate's face is . . . At one moment it's animated, and then suddenly, without any transition, it turns leaden . . . Schoolmistressy . . . So you didn't learn your lesson properly? You're all right for a few seconds and then you're stuck! Awkward! No concentration! A dunce!

"And where have you got with it?" she asks coldly.

I'm not going to say "Now! Here! With you! In the middle of this conversation!"

444

"I rather lost track of my characters," I answer. "And now I'm getting around to them again . . ."

"I meant how many pages?"

"Five hundred and fifty-nine."

"Five hundred and fifty-nine?"

She looks at me seriously . . . Too long! If I've got so far, either my "novel"—probably a low-down attack on women—is very good, or else it's terrible and I don't realize it . . . In which case, curtains for me . . . "Have you seen his novel? Poor fellow!"

She hovers between the two hypotheses . . .

But I can see she's leaning slightly toward the second . . . A failure! Finished! Tee-hee!

She gets a grip on herself.

"And are you still seeing S.?"

"Yes . . . But he's away at the moment . . ."

"What's *he* up to?"

"He's in Italy . . . Then I think he's going to Australia for a couple of months . . ."

"Good riddance!"

"Why?"

"Oh, enough is enough! Have you read his last thing, on the Virgin Mary?"

"Yes . . . Strange, isn't it?"

"Crazy!"

"I don't agree . . . What is it he's trying to prove? The ultimate equivalence between the Phallus and the Word . . . It becomes evident if you imagine one woman being penetrated from within by the word of god . . . And giving birth, quite logically, to a resurrectable body . . ."

"Pull the other one! You must have something wrong with your brains!"

"This fantasy, if that's what it is, is as close as you can get to phenomenal impossibility, and so to a reality that's not simple reality . . ."

"Whatever next!"

"It follows that the Virgin Mary herself is defined as a hole . . . The absolute opposite of the Phallic Mother . . . A complete hole . . . Her body is a hole, through and through . . . Hence her immaculate conception and assumption . . . Which results in the brilliant idea of the vagina as a false hole, endlessly plugged, on which the entire mesmerized world keeps coming to grief . . ."

"You can say that again!"

"It might be the best commentary ever on sexual repression in Christianity . . . Perhaps on repression and religion in general . . . S. uses Dante as an example . . . By tracing the use of the word *mezzo* in the *Divine Comedy* . . . It can stand for both "middle" and for "belly" or "womb" . . . I think that's brilliant . . . A combination of theology and Freud . . ."

"Theology, perhaps . . . Certainly not Freud!"

"You're referring to the humor?"

"Pooh! Do you ever read that review of his? That spew without any punctuation?"

"Occasionally . . . It's a bit too difficult for me . . ."

"Admittedly there was a time when it wasn't bad . . . Progressive, too . . . But now . . . Of no interest whatsoever . . . Nothing but his own blatherings . . . People couldn't care less . . ."

"That isn't necessarily anything to go by . . . Especially these days . . ."

"Yes, it is! I only hope his publisher will draw the line . . ."

"That'd be a pity . . . It's all right to talk about Dante, isn't it?"

"Oh yes . . . And about Shakespeare too, why not?"

"Well, then?"

"You don't seem to realize! You don't begin to understand this country! We're living in an era of change . . . Long overdue . . . And more fundamental than people think . . . Everything's on the move! And fast! Hell for leather! And the intellectuals ought to go along with it . . ."

Now we've got it—she's trying to sell me the Program . . . We're at the coffee stage . . . I round matters off . . . Ask her what she's doing this summer . . . If she's going away . . .

"Yes . . . To India . . . How about you?"

446

"I'll try to find somewhere here, by the sea, to write . . ."

I don't tell her where I'm going . . .

But look who's just come in! Louise! You remember Louise? No . . . You never remember anything . . . The pianist . . . The pianist, at the beginning . . . In the old days! She's with a lady friend . . . They're trying to find a table . . . I tell them to join us . . . The friend's Austrian, a singer . . .

"Are you still interested in the piano?" says Louise. "Scarlatti? Haydn?"

"Yes! More than ever . . ."

"Haydn's very much in vogue now, you know? Not like when we used to meet before—remember? You always used to say how unfair it was . . . And do you still loathe the nineteenth century?"

"Oh, you're old friends, are you?" says Kate.

"Yes," says Louise . . . "Very old friends . . . Ten years, is it?"

I look at her hands. I love her hands . . .

"Was he already a misogynist then?" asks Kate.

"A misogynist?" says Louise.

"Doesn't she know?" says Kate, turning to me.

"Know what?" says Louise.

I steer the conversation back to music . . . Kate's furious, and finally leaves . . . I stay on with my two girlfriends . . . I drink a bit . . . Try to get them to come to a nightclub . . . They won't . . . Louise tells me to call her . . . I end up alone in Montparnasse . . . That's fine . . .

Wake-up call on the phone . . . Seven in the morning . . . Pack bags . . . A few more books? One or two Hemingways, perhaps? *Fifty Grand? To Have and Have Not?* Can't find them anywhere . . . A Miller? *Black Spring?* No, read it already . . . So? Something to keep me in trim . . . Little descriptions . . . Dialogue . . . What, though? No, there's nothing . . . Never mind, the television will do . . . Watch the current tricks . . . The ads . . . The magazine programs . . .

Train to the Ile de Ré . . . Like the note, in music . . . Off La Rochelle . . . A little bit like Long Island . . . S. has lent me his house . . . He's not using it this year—he and Sophie are going straight from Italy to Australia . . . The universities . . . "Send me a few chapters there—I'll translate them into kangaroo . . ." Our last conversation before he left . . .

"It's there! Down under!"

"What is?"

"The Switzerland of the Third World War! The golden triangle of the year 2000! The place after the catastrophe! Australia! New Zealand! Sydney, Melbourne, Auckland! Take it from me!"

"Are you sure?"

"At any rate things are better there than they are here at the moment . . ."

"Yes, so it seems . . ."

"No—really!"

" 'Actually!' "

"I'll lend you my place. Take care of the flowers! Mow the grass! Sophie will call Deb and give her the details . . . It's quite habitable, you'll see . . . It's the place where I can get on best with what I'm writing . . . Don't forget to breathe in the night air . . ."

"How are you getting on? With the work?"

"Oh, terrible! I can only crawl forward a quarter of an inch at a time, now . . . I can't even understand myself anymore . . . Can scarcely read my own writing . . . I feel as if I'd been caught out . . . I can't remember why I ever got myself into it . . . Impulse . . . Pride . . . I get to thinking everyone else is right . . . It's worthless . . . Gibberish . . . Greek . . . Chinese . . . Mumbo jumbo . . . A hoax . . . Unreadable . . . Madness . . . But I can't do anything about it . . . It's a flop . . . But it's too late . . ."

"Come, come . . ."

"No, they're right! I'm the one who's wrong . . . I always have been . . . It's the way I'm made . . ."

"How do you mean?"

"Madness! Madness! And yet . . . you know, I did believe in it!"

"I'm sure!"

"I used to believe in it! It's strange . . . You can't imagine how I thought about it . . . How hard I worked . . . Slaved, cogitated, pondered . . . I lived with it . . . Every moment . . . And I shall go on . . . But with such a bitter taste in my mouth! . . . Mind you, every so often I do feel as if the wind's in my sails again . . . But no . . . All those useless words strung together . . . I'm ashamed . . . I ought to have killed myself ten times over . . ."

"You exaggerate . . ."

"Not in the least . . . I'm dead . . . I've gone fatally astray . . . I ought to have known . . . That euphoria, that vibrant sense of certainty—they're bad signs . . . The unknown masterpiece suddenly turns into a pulp . . . Cacophony . . . Catastrophe . . . You can't believe your own eyes . . . The language! There's nothing in it! Pure mystification, and, what's worse, self-mystification . . . Absolutely ridiculous . . ."

"But what will you do?"

"Live quietly . . . Not say anything . . . Disappear, as far as possible . . . Go on writing this thing, because by now it's a nervous compulsion . . . A drug . . . My own private yoga . . . But useless, useless! Nothing to be proud of! Any other human life strikes me as more moving and authentic than my own . . . What a waste! What a mistake!"

" 'My life is nothing but an accident; I feel I should never have been born: accept the passion, the brevity and the suffering of that accident . . .' "

"Who said that?"

"Chateaubriand."

"Fine words, but only words . . . No. Things are much more sordid than that . . . Or tedious . . . Take your choice . . . According to the mood you're in . . . Admittedly, as I talk to you I can feel the old demon stirring again . . . The old pride in working all night—feverish notes, corrections, digressions, interpolations, subtractions, injections . . . Perhaps I am right, after all . . . Inventing the verbal hologram . . . Luminous sculpture . . . That includes and reorders everything . . . Each part valid for the whole . . . A new dimension . . ."

"A misunderstood genius?"

"That's it! It's best to laugh about it . . . Time will tell . . . Anyhow, let's have another drink . . . The main thing is to live as long as possible and die with one's vision at its height . . . Have a good vacation! See you soon!"

VIII

The house is hidden in a recess in the island . . . At its narrowest point; an isthmus . . . On one side the ocean, and on the other, close to, a series of inland lakes, lagoons and salt marshes like a chessboard of mirrors . . . One of S.'s great-grandfathers, a naval officer from Bordeaux, used to come here to hunt . . . An old, isolated farm, razed to the ground by the Germans in 1942 . . . The "Atlantic Wall . . ." They blew up anything that stood between their guns and the sea . . . It was rebuilt after the war . . . With a garden and trees again . . . You can see water in every direction; you feel as if it's always flowing through you . . . The island is flat and covered with cypresses, umbrella pines and vines . . . Like a raft or part of a deck . . . Pearly bluish-white light, air full of butterflies . . .

I have a large bedroom away from the main part of the house . . . My typewriter overlooks a bay-tree . . . I'll be able to watch the tide rising and falling . . . Going out, then coming in again slowly from the depths of the green horizon, often bringing the wind . . . Ho for the motionless movement . . . The navigation to end all navigation . . . But I must go it properly this time, day and night, against the dark . . .

A cheerful dinner . . . Deb, Stephen and me . . .

I've brought my old notes on Shakespeare with me . . . The ones I made for an essay I never wrote . . . In my youth . . . I just came across them again in Paris . . . News, current affairs, massacres, communiqués? I know only too well what's going to happen . . . Let's get back to the real subject . . . I feel it may be here, in these feverish, almost forgotten papers . . . What was it I was trying to say?

First, about the Sonnets . . . Son-nets . . . A mass of minutely woven rhymes cast like a net to catch the son in the will of the father . . . Or, if you like—it comes to the same thing—to catch the young man who is loved in the desire of him who lives again through and in him . . . A musical snare of surrogate fatherhood . . . A passionate meditation on time as both theater and memory . . . Plato turned upside down . . . An imitation of the Psalms? Yes, so long as you see here, suddenly reversed, a suffering god trying to recall his own image through the error of loving women . . . Homosexuality? Too easy an explanation . . . The Sonnets are above all about him, him alone, and his various incarnations . . .

The father question . . . The whole of Shakespeare lies in that . . . Incest in broad daylight . . . Pericles . . . Father and daughter . . . The riddle . . . And Hamlet too, of course . . . But people too often get Hamlet wrong . . .

Now let's suppose I'm Shakespeare . . . It doesn't cost anything . . . Darkness is gathering, ready to have its say; the wind's blowing in through the window . . . Shall I act all the plays for myself?

What does Sophocles say?

I invoke Bacchus, companion of the wandering Maenads, that he may come by torch-light with his golden mitre and vinous countenance . . .

Or more appropriately, Tiresias, speaking of Oedipus:

We shall see he is at once his sons' father and their brother; the son and the husband of the woman who bore him; lover of his father's wife, and his father's murderer . . .

Ready? To abolish time and fly through the ages?

The curtain rises . . . I am simultaneously, in no particular order, Coriolanus, Julius Caesar, Antony, Lear, Richard III, Nietzsche, Dionysus and the Crucified One, Othello, Timon, Prospero and Ariel . . . I am drama, I am nothing, atoms are unveiled, reality evaporates . . . Come, Cleopatra, you too, of course: "I am fire, and

454

air; my other elements/I give to baser life . . ." We're going to see what "giving the other elements to baser life" means . . . Distillation of matter . . . Come, with your asp like a babe at the breast . . .

Enter, suddenly, Hamlet and his mother . . . He confronts her with the comparison of the portraits . . . "Have you eyes? Have you eyes?" Can she see anything but herself? She is blind . . . Too much regarded . . . He, the son, tries to make her see him through the face of the murdered father . . . Poison dropped into his ear as he slept . . . Torpor . . . Like Adam sent to sleep by god, so as to create Eve from one of his ribs . . . Before Eden . . . Now, half decayed, his eyes blank, he returns, rising up out of the floor of the stage . . .

"Swear!"

"I swear!" (Cf. "sword.")

Can you imagine the everlasting Polonius, hidden to spy on the sexual episode he suspects is going to take place between Hamlet and his mother? Polonius has read the Greeks too much . . . The same obsession gnaws at Ophelia . . . What if the son makes love to the mother? Or at least longs to? Is it compulsory? Does Sophocles say so? Shakespeare doesn't . . . He doesn't follow that line at all . . . On the contrary . . . Though this won't be admitted for a moment by the hordes of frightened Poloniuses hiding behind their mother-cum-queen's arras! They believe with all their might in the son's desire for his mother! That's what she's told them . . . It would explain the murder . . . But no . . . First and foremost it's her! Herself! That's really why she can't tell the difference between two men . . .

Ah, the Dark Lady!

One ought to demonstrate how everything happens through plays upon words . . . Is there a single essay on plays upon words in Shakespeare? Or in the Bible? What *do* the researchers spend their time on?

When the actor is so much the author himself you get a complete reversal, the rout of all generalizations, pure panic in both community and tribe . . . Matricide . . . The secret of secrets . . . But stifled . . . Suppressed . . . Should one lift the stone and reveal the true reason? Without taking any notice of those, male and female, who'd kill themselves before your very eyes rather than allow it? The kamikaze pilots of the great mystery . . . Sacrificial sleepwalkers . . . No, it's impossible . . . The show goes on forever . . . But Shakespeare isn't in it, which is why he'll go on being performed indefinitely, amazedly . . . What is he? A vanishing point . . . Elusive sorcery . . . Alchemy . . . A wand of wonderment . . . Music . . .

"My spirit!" cries Prospero.

"All hail, great master . . . Grave sir, hail!" answers Ariel at once, the greeting of the wind.

Do you hear the tomb in "grave"? And the echo of hell in "hail"?

The Tempest . . . On an island, like an open coffin . . . Noises and a light breeze . . . Everything in the sound, the curve of the sound . . .

Another antimother affair . . . Sycorax the witch imprisoned Ariel in a pine tree . . . Of course there's nothing mythological about all this . . . Sheer realism . . . A description of rooms in the city . . . London . . . The audience would understand at once . . . Do you want to know what that pine tree really is? The tree of life and of evil? Is that what I'm telling you? Just listen!

"Its root is bitter, its branches dead, its shadow is hatred, its foliage lies, its buds the cream of vice, the fruit of decay, the seed of envy, the germ of darkness . . ."

You can find that somewhere in the *Secret Book of John*, an old gnostic treatise . . .

Brave Caliban, the witch's son . . . His dream is to "people" the island . . . The opposite of the "spirit"! Is *The Tempest* a fleeting hymn of victory over matriarchy? Yes, just for as long as the performance lasts . . . Like *The Magic Flute* . . . With no other weapons but words . . . Magic and pronunciation . . .

> *O, how this mother swells up toward my heart!*
> *Hysterica passio! — down, thou climbing sorrow,*

thy element below . . . Where is this
daughter?

That's Lear, complaining . . . (But translations are hopeless . . .
You can't hope to understand unless you can hear Shakespeare's
own words . . .) The old, mad king is trying to tread down his
mother, who makes his heart heave, and the next thing he does is
ask after his daughter . . . He's nothing but a tortured transition
between mother and daughter . . . Lear . . . Ear . . . Tympanum
. . . Hymen . . . That's Shakespeare talking to you!

Why do the French translate all this so badly? Rendering "mother"
as "morbid ferment"? To save their mother, to keep her a virgin
. . . Joan of Arc . . . They don't feel the inner action, won't take
the risk of the membrane, the bat, the vampire . . . They daren't
descend into the cave . . . They won't risk their lives physically . . .
It leaves them cold . . . Frigid . . . Deaf . . . Virgin . . . Look at
Gide, translating "wretched queen" as "ô misérable mére!" And
"mouse" as "petit rat . . ."! But Polonius is a mouse, not a rat . . .
And certainly not a "little rat"! As for the queen, she's not merely
miserable . . . The word is too weak . . . She's *wretched* . . . What
are they thinking of?

I am dead, Horatio . . . Wretched queen, adieu!

He dies . . . She is in despair . . . The rest is silence . . . It's
much better than the scene with the Sphinx . . . And Jocasta going
and hanging herself offstage . . . Here you see everything . . .
She's like a wrecked ship . . . She drinks the same poison as was
poured into the king's ear . . . Here we must understand the hull
and the keel . . . Of the Drunken Boat! The wash! Whirlpools!
Undertow! Algae! Jellyfish! Surf! Coral! Octopuses! She's holed!
She's sinking! It all happens at sea . . . The Danaides! You need to
be a bit of a sailor to read Shakespeare . . . Otherwise don't bother
. . . Wind . . . Rigging . . . Pullies . . . Cleats . . . Shrouds . . .
Port and starboard . . . The watches . . . Lanterns . . . Ghosts . . .

Followed up by Melville . . . By Céline, on the Baltic . . . I've seen the house there where he lived in exile . . . A dog kennel . . . Thatched roof . . . A boat at anchor . . . Korsor . . . Klarksvogaard . . . Apple trees in pale pink blossom above a creek where a swan was swimming . . . The Baltic, the "silent sea . . ." Elsinore . . .

Similarly, Gide translates "too too solid flesh" as *"chair massive"* . . . *"Chair massive"* Hamlet! Whereas what you hear in the words, what you *see* in the very repetition of "too," is someone literally beating against his own body . . . His own physical wall . . . Difficult to convey in words . . .

> O! that this too too solid flesh would melt,
> Thaw and resolve itself into a dew . . .

Dew . . . Something delicate, almost invisible, made by the fairies in the night . . .

Another translator, another example . . . *The Tempest* . . . Here it's more serious . . . For the play's a sort of testament, a statement of the poet's art . . . If Shakespeare writes "noises,/Sounds and sweet airs" (and you're immediately transported to the supple and contagious magic of Dowland, Byrd and Purcell's *Fairy Queen*), it isn't in order to be translated as *"résonances, accents, suaves mélodies"* . . . "Noises, sounds and sweet airs" is a simple ascending order of musical power . . . A definition of the fabric of which our little dream-like life is made . . . Surrounded, like another island, by the zero, the dark sea, of sleep . . . Itself a bubble of nothingness . . . But it can be evoked, summoned up, unfurled for a moment by the art of noises, sounds and sweet airs . . . How can you hope to seize the visions that we are if you don't use words in their very rhythms, nerves, sinews, and power to enchant?

Translation like this is an insidious kind of emasculation that isn't even deliberate . . . A mutilation of *l'homme sensuel*, impulsive and noble . . . They don't even listen to what he says . . . How he says it . . . Hamlet's father, Hamlet himself, Lear, Othello, Timon, Antony . . . Female domination . . . Such an old, old story . . . Lady Macbeth, Lear's daughters . . . It's in 1603 that Elizabeth, Queen of England, gives way to James I . . . Shakespeare will be able to increase the pressure . . . The revelations about the real monstrosity of women date from 1606 . . .

To summarize . . . Born 1564 . . . On November 27, 1582, Anne Hathaway marries him . . . She's twenty-six; he's eighteen . . . She's already pregnant with Susanna, who's born six months after the marriage . . . In 1585, twins are born: a son, Hamnet, and a daughter, Judith . . . He's still only twenty-one! She struck fast and hard . . . The tragedy clearly is the death of Hamnet in 1596, at the age of eleven . . . He has only two daughters left . . . One of whom, it's too often forgotten, is bound to be the incredible double of the dead son . . . Shakespeare's father dies in 1601 . . . The year of *Hamlet* . . . William is now thirty-seven . . .

The amazing thing is that no one seems really comfortable about the Hamnet/Hamlet transposition . . . Joyce refers to it in *Ulysses* . . . But no one reads that . . . But how can people not see, for heaven's sake, that at that particular metaphysical moment Shakespeare is midway between his dead father and his dead son? That apart from the theater, in life itself, he is the ghost par excellence, at once his own father and his own son? That he may well be wondering what it means to have these two unequal corpses, cause and effect, behind and before him? I'm empty, a vacuum, he may be thinking, and that's why nature abhors me . . . His mother has outlived his father, his wife has outlived his son . . . And as his wife married him by force and forced him to be a father, he can enter better than anyone into the lament for the murdered father, slain in and in aid of the mechanism, the mechanism of the reproduction of the living and dead, and of the living by the dead . . . Life's a dream? That's not all . . . Dream is a more fundamental life than life itself, because it allows the dead to reveal how they were, through violence, alive . . . Artificial insemination . . . The death of Hamnet becomes the life and death of Hamlet—that's how Shakespeare tells us of the horror of the traffic of the womb . . . Perpetrated in all natural innocence! Of course! The horror that has caused him to be there . . . Instead of those who belong to the same mortal sequence . . . He hides himself as a ghost beneath the stage, and like a prompter or stage manager rises up from death to settle his accounts . . . He frees his son Hamnet from the limbo where he's been imprisoned, and charges him, in adult form and sword in hand, with exposing the crime of existence . . . Couldn't William save Hamnet? . . . Did he prefer his twin with the murderous name —Judith? Well, now he will arm him . . . The "n" becomes an "l" . . . Golem fashion . . . The "Ham" remains — the âme or soul of Will . . . Mr. W.H. — to whom the *Sonnets* were dedicated . . . The ghost is Shakespeare, Hamlet is Shakespeare, but above all Shakespeare has come full circle on Shakespeare . . . Genealogy has been corrected, birth overcome . . . A play within a play, and so a crime within a crime . . . Death is now on the side of truth, the mirror of the shades broken . . . Once Hamnet Shakespeare has become Hamlet, William is really Shakespeare and fully occupies his name . . . But to no avail! "I'll drown my book!" With the letter "l" he has delivered one person from death; with the letter "l" he has allowed another to die . . .

The Tibetan Book . . . Elizabeth excommunicated in 1570 . . . The Massacre of St. Bartholomew's Eve, 1572 . . . El Greco's "Assumption," 1577 . . . *Jerusalem Delivered*, 1581 . . . Execution of Mary Stuart, 1587 . . . Destruction of the Invincible Armada, 1588 . . . Death of Shakespeare's mother, 1609 . . . Shakespeare retires to Stratford, 1610 . . . Galileo's trial, 1615 . . . You can't say it's a dull age . . . Tumult on all sides . . . The Trojan War still going on . . . Chaotic, sleazy, pointless, grotesque . . . Look at *Troilus and Cressida*, on the heels of Hamlet . . . Shakespeare really rubs it in: antilove, anti-Greek . . . Antiheroic and anti-Olympic . . . The *Iliad* ridiculed . . . The *Aeneid* a bloodthirsty farce . . . The sexual card played in broad daylight . . . A mixture of lies, crazy treacheries and elaborate vanities . . . A comedy of tragedy . . . With a compulsive coquette at its center . . . Yes, he can stroll clear-eyed about the battlefield—he knows the hidden spring, the invisible muscle, the trick of vain arousal . . .

Magic, perhaps, but here on the stage one has to submit to the concatenation of cause and effect . . . In other words the twists and turns of the generations, the vagaries of power . . . You can think yourself lucky if, like Prospero, you can rise from being a mother's boy to the detached and blasé role of a father to a daughter . . . And relinquish your daughter, your mirage, your Miranda for reasons of state . . .

After which, Prospero can abandon his own physical manifestation . . . Make the visions he conjured up melt into thin air . . . Break his wand and bury his spells twenty thousand leagues under the sea . . . And enjoy dreamless sleep . . . In short, go back to what he would have been all the time if the girls hadn't flown off the handle and become mothers, creating and murdering fathers in order to obtain sons who'll be bound to destroy the mothers themselves . . . What a to-do . . . Not to be . . . Never to have endured existing . . . Good-bye . . . Forgive me for having been . . .

I look up . . . The storm that was raging when I landed on the island has just abated . . . The bay-tree is still . . . The leaden black sky has frozen into gray slabs heralding complete change . . . High tide just about to turn . . . Just a drop in the balance . . . It's evening . . . Deb and Stephen will soon be in bed . . . The flowers in the garden are breathing . . . Clover, lavender, roses, geraniums, gladioli, daisies, begonias, fuchsia, veigelias, cannas . . . The cannas are magnificent . . . Bright fleshy blossoms . . . The catalpa and the mimosa drink up the darkness . . . The umbrella pine and the arizonas filter it . . . The grass looks as if it were turning over . . . Stephen comes to say good-night to me . . . Papa started writing as soon as he got here . . . His "novel" . . . What is a "novel"? A story? With airplanes in it? Yes . . . I'll explain it to you later . . . For the moment, no noise, okay? Okay . . . Promise? Promise . . . Deb's in great form, tanned already, rested . . . I work on into the night . . . My windowpane gets covered with brown moths, midges, mosquitoes . . . It's hot again . . . A whole evanescent life is staying up with me . . . As if from furthest prehistory . . . Small but living . . . Legs . . . Antennae . . . Stunned vibrating . . . Carbon 14 in tatters . . . In the window I can see a reflection of my face covered with insects . . . With the intermittent light from the lighthouse it makes a rather nice picture . . . Fantastic . . . The Baleines Lighthouse . . . Lighthouse of the Whales . . . Built in 1854 . . . Fifty-five meters tall . . . Two hundred and fifty-seven stairs . . . Light visible for 75 kilometers . . . Hello, Nantucket? Hello, all the three-masters ever, ghosts on the face of the waters? Lord Jim? Billy Budd? The Ancient Mariner himself?

I turn on the radio . . . As we're out at sea we can get foreign stations better . . . England's very clear . . . This is the BBC Third Programme . . . I like the unobtrusive stress on "This is . . ." As if the announcer were introducing the Queen . . . Shouted orders . . . Drums . . . But at the same time nothing overemphatic . . . No, a civilization sure of itself across the oceans, sober, god and my right, the Thames, the City . . . And then Spain . . . San Sebastian . . . The gleaming conch shell . . . The Casino . . . Palaces, terraces . . .

Voices of a summer night . . . Oberon . . . Titania . . . Puck . . . Elves . . . Lulla, lulla, lullaby! "Ahora vamos a escuchar . . ."

I go down to S.'s study . . . Look at his books . . . A seventeenth-century Bible . . . Homer . . . Aubigné's *Tragiques* . . . Virgil . . . Lucretius . . . Plutarch . . . Mme. De Sévigné . . . Sade . . . The *Complete Works* of St. Bernard . . . Well, at least there's plenty to do on August nights by the sea . . . But there are also old leather-bound books in no particular order . . . Treatises on navigation . . . The coasts of Africa . . . A physics textbook . . . A geometry ditto . . . *French Eloquence . . . Man and Creation . . .* 1860 . . . That type of thing . . . Nineteenth-century . . . What an ocean-going captain might read in his cabin or on the bridge, somewhere between Bordeaux and Singapore or Bombay . . . And newspapers . . .

"Sunday, June 8, 1862. The *Bordeaux Chronicle*. Politics, Commerce, Maritime and Industrial Affairs, Literature, Legal Announcements. Telegraph Service.

"Ragusa, June 5.

"On June 2, at Piperi, Abdy Pasha and a force of ten thousand Turks attacked Mirko and eight thousand Montenegrans. The Turks lost four hundred men, and the men from the mountains two hundred.

"On the Monday and Tuesday Dervish Pasha moved along the Montenegran frontier without leaving Herzegovinian territory.

"Rome, June 5.

"The Pope yesterday gave audience to the Infanta Isabella, former regent of Portugal.

"The cardinals of Bonald, Donnet and Schwartzemberg have arrived, together with thirteen bishops, three of whom are French and three from the East.

There at at present 44 cardinals and 278 bishops in Rome.

"Vienna, June 6.

"Trading in the fifty million new Austrian shares is now closed. They have been acquired by the house of Rothschild, the Crédit Mobilier of Austria and Messers Goldschmidt of Frankfurt at a price of 88 (88 what?).

"Turin, June 5.

"Letters from Rome dated June 3 say the French stopped two wagons containing arms near Albano. The wagons were being escorted by Papal guards.

"New York. June 5.

"M. Mercier, our ambassador in Washington, has just informed President Lincoln of the manifesto addressed by French plenipotentiaries MM. Jurien and de Saligny to the Mexican government concerning the possibility of its ceding territory to foreign states."

"*Sailings.*

"For Montevideo, direct.

"Departure July 5.

"First-class ship *Immaculée Conception*, Captain Monnier . . . Freight still being taken on, also first- and second-class passengers . . ."

(Shades of Isidore Ducasse!)

There's something of everything in the *Bordeaux Chronicle* . . . Reports on the state of the sea . . . Weather forecasts . . . Financial bulletins . . . Sales . . . Funerals . . . Letters . . . And, of course, small ads . . .

"M. Joyaux, horse dealer, begs to inform customers that he has just transferred his establishment from rue Burguet to no. 81 rue Durand (by the White Cross), and has a large number of fine horses of every variety for sale."

And there's a serial too: *Marie-Anne!*

"She received me in her bedroom; she was alone. Her lovely face was greatly changed, and her sharp bright eyes were feverish and full of restrained passion and dignity. Had anyone seen us they would have taken me for the guilty and her for the injured party."

"*Had* anyone seen us . . ." That subjunctive!

Fancy reading that in the middle of the Indian Ocean!

I go out into the garden . . . The sky's clear now . . . The Great Bear on the left . . . The beam from the lighthouse falls faintly on the whitewashed walls . . . Velvet . . . Stars . . . Hail and farewell to that brief little flutter in your chest as you sit here looking at merging sea and dark . . . Hello again! And good-bye! Dear me, here you are once more, alive and in a living body, with its veins, its nerves, its digestion and its billions of brain cells . . . Hand in the pebbles . . . In the soil where the flowers grow . . . And a stone thrown into the black water to see whether I'm dreaming . . . Where are they, all those before, and all those after, who are just the same as those before in relation to the Milky Way, that white blob of spit, that spray of sperm? Eraser, blackboard, squeaking chalk . . . No, no writing . . . Nothing legible, anyway . . . Not even a figure . . . And here am I, the millionth fool to feel it inside . . . "I will multiply thy seed . . . as the sand which is upon the sea shore . . ." The stars weren't enough . . . The desert and the beaches were needed too . . . Turned into crowds . . . Morning market . . . Stomach abscesses one against the other . . . Children shouting . . . And grannies, and yet more grannies—old dears forever and ever . . . Bags, purses . . . How much? Give me a bit more . . . Meat, fish, vegetables . . . And bread . . . All the day's shit to be produced again . . . And the same tomorrow . . . Nowhere to park . . . The noise . . . Frightened babies falling over . . . Men? Where? Oh yes, a few "old women" of a certain kind— breastless, potbellied, in shorts and underpants, shapeless, oily and red . . . Like Red Indians . . . Ravaged by the teeming ancestral "no!" Not a chance . . . Try to escape notice . . . Sidle . . . Invisible . . . Question of nerve . . . Come on, take the plunge! "Can't you look where you're going?" I've bumped into one of them . . . A "male" . . . I press on . . . You need to hum a tune to yourself at times like this . . . Drugstore . . . Tobacconist's . . . Post office . . . Three black spots . . .

I've always thought there was a nook somewhere in the night . . . To the right or the left . . . Behind . . . Quite near . . . If you leapt through space . . . Going away . . . Just like that . . . A "fantasy"! . . . Psychological surveillance . . . What was that amusing thing I read the other day? About Joyce? "Symbolic castration is to be seen in its effects . . . The image of Christ used to enable people to project a fantasy of birth without sex and thus without death . . ." And so on . . . Hold it, professor! You strike me as very sensible! In a flash you see the relationship between plumage and song, and the vain efforts of the birds in this forest to set up as phoenixes . . . How Christ, in his naive failure, must envy you for being around to tell him what sort of fantasy he'd have had! Money for old rope! Psychoanalysis makes its solemn entrance into the chief temple of the Philistines! *Sex and Death* . . . But do I hear a heckler? What is it you're whispering there at the back? That sex (masculine in French) has nothing to do with death (feminine)? What? What's that you say? It's perfectly obvious! What? It's because we're not up to sex that we die? Who do you think you are? Who's your authority? Sade? "Nothing is finer or greater than sex, and outside sex there is no salvation . . ." Help! The Beast! Call in the psychoanalysts! Save the University! But which death are you talking about? And which sex? Mine, of course, and yours . . . Everybody's: yours, mine, my sister's, my grandmother's, my cousin's, the whole family's—they've always been in teaching in one way or another!

What now? If there are two sexes there must be two deaths?

Gosh, it's true, nobody's thought of that before . . . But at first sight it's absurd . . . You don't mean to say you'd define man by saying if he can't be fulfilled sexually he dies?

A topsy-turvy version of the return of god? Better not dwell on it . . . Or everything will have to be thought out again! Overhauled! Right from the beginning! Could man have fallen, been driven out of Paradise, not just because of sex but because someone in or beside him tried to *exploit* sex? To make something out of it?

The Serpent? Eve? The image in the mirror instead of sex itself? Reproduction? Then presto, everything's down the drain? Death? And life a disease of resentment against sex that only perpetuates death? That'll do! Chuck him out!

This is how I see it . . . Sex and no sex unimaginably one outside death . . . The kingdom of death merely a slowing down and cooling off of sex . . . But it's presumptuous to claim to know it all! False arguments! Lame excuses! Misleading images! Suffer the saints and the little children to come unto me . . . But also the adventurers whose boldness has shown them the true boundaries of the world . . . There is no birth or rebirth except in relation to sex, over which death has no dominion . . . In the Magic Flute itself . . . Death? A rejection of music as such! Scandal! Pollution!

Secret meditation . . . I watch some falling stars . . . Brief orgasms no one will ever enjoy . . . Cold fires . . . Halley's comet will approach our pinpoint earth in March 1986 . . . March 8 and 12, to be precise . . . About 150 million kilometers away . . . For the first time we'll send probes into its tail . . . Gas and dust . . . The center? No one knows . . . Ice? It passes by every seventy-six years . . . So the last time was in 1910 . . . People have been talking about it since the year 231 before the great fantasy! Calixtus III excommunicated it in 1456 . . . Watch out! Achtung! Madness! Destruction! Carnage!

Stephen keeps blowing up balloons . . . Rubber rings for swimming . . . A cat . . . A swan . . . A Donald Duck . . . "Daddy— another package of balloons!" Red, white, yellow, green . . . Round, long . . . Sometimes they burst . . . He cries for three seconds . . . Then blows up another . . . They thrill him . . . He spends all his time in the water . . . Blissfully happy . . . Bucket, spade, sand pies, tunnels, drawings of airplanes in the sand—the lot . . . He started flying when he was six months old . . . From Paris to New York . . . Now of course he wants to be a pilot . . . An airman . . .

To take off, fly, go away . . . Will passengers please fasten their seat-belts? Extinguish all cigarettes? Thank you! Merci! Instead of being the wolf, as at home, I'm now Pussy Cat . . . But we still pretend to be samurais on the lawn in the morning . . . Yôôôô Rôôôô! I utter my pseudo-Japanese groans . . . He imitates me . . . Hits out harder and harder . . . He'll soon be six . . . I think about the Noh plays . . . The "marvelous flower . . ." *Kyui-Shidai* . . . "At midnight the sun shines!" "A charming and subtle style beyond all praise, emotion beyond all consciousness, visual effects beyond comparison—all these are what make up the 'marvelous flower . . .' " If only one could write like that oneself . . . With verbs for roots, nouns for stems, adjectives for petals, punctuation for pistils . . . A butterfly hovering over all . . . It's flown away! Glissade . . .

Deborah's working on her book on hysteria . . . I can hear the clatter of her typewriter . . . We have little artillery duels . . . She's preparing her lectures for Columbia . . . On Kafka . . . We discuss it a bit in the evening . . . There she is on the beach in the nude . . . Every so often we have simple, stereotyped, well organized, bitter scenes . . . Compulsory . . . All part of the tradition . . . We live à la Rubens . . . Huh? What's that you say? Oh, no time . . . *The Garden of Love* . . .

It all sounds very "cultural," doesn't it! Not really. Bathing, sun-bathing, bathing again . . . And the waves, the tennis court, the waves . . . Grilled fish . . . Solitude for three . . . It isn't right . . . Aren't you ashamed? With all that's going on . . . Lebanon! Poland! Afghanistan! Fire and slaughter! But this is how they'd like to live, all those bodies precipitated into the inferno of war by generals, by governments, by "fronts" . . . Mad with history . . . As if anything were really happening . . . Killers and blatherers . . . They revel in it, really—trampling on entrails and wallowing in human shit, with their heads full of ideas and plans . . . They say it's "important" . . . But nothing's important! . . . Except the asphyxiation, the waste . . . They vie with one another with their corpses . . . Invent "explanations" . . . Always plenty of those . . . Thesis . . . Antithesis . . . Proof . . . Counterproof . . . I'm familiar with the drug . . . The hardest of the lot . . . Whole tubes every morning . . .

When you go back over troubled times and ages of disaster—and they're all that—what's left, in the end? Pictures, books, music . . . They know that . . . That's what they really want to prevent . . . The rest is pointless . . .

Stephen's knocked out after his day by the sea . . . He eats like a horse . . . Fritters . . . Savory rolls . . . Sausages . . . Frankfurt! Strasbourg! There's cities for you! I'm going to put him to bed . . . We play for a while with his Lego and Clipo . . . I hear him say his prayers . . . Yes indeed . . . In the name of the father and of the son and of the Hole Ghost . . . No, darling, the Holy Ghost . . . Hail, Mary . . . "The fruit of your womb"—that's a bit more tricky . . . Pray for us, miserable sinners . . . Now and at the hour of our death . . .

Deb turns a blind eye to these obcurantist practices . . . Neurotic, ridiculous, square . . . Charming . . . Since I set such store by them . . .

Hey, there's Edwige on the beach . . . Used to be a feminist organizer . . . Rather decent . . . She sticks to us like a leech . . . Comes out with her rigmarole every now and again . . . The old soporific . . . Androgyny . . . How we owe everything to our mothers . . . But have always plundered them . . . Elementary impulses . . . The soul of matter . . . Fusion . . . Transfusion . . . The timidity, cowardice, fearfulness, narrow-mindedness, meanness and hard-heartedness of men, poor wretches! The age-old exploitation of women . . . Judeo-Christian patriarchy . . .

"Did you see the slaughter in the rue des Rosiers?" I ask.

"Yes, it's frightful . . . But Begin's really sick, isn't he?"

Edwige's Jewish . . . She's not very clear what she means . . . Vague ideas of persecution . . . She's not anti-Semitic, my god, but we need to rediscover what was destroyed by the Bible . . . Something else behind it . . . Another truth . . .

"Mother cults, of course," says Deb. "The Bible's always fighting them . . ."

"Savagely, too!" says Edwige. "But all that needs digging out properly . . ."

"In short," says her husband resignedly, "feminism isn't anti-Semitic—it only wants to save Judaism from itself?"

What he says gets lost in the sea, the swimmers, the children running to and fro . . . You soon won't be able to see anything for wind-surfers . . . They get upon their floating scooters, fall out and half stun themselves, swim around, right themselves, and start all over again . . .

"Did you watch the film about test-tube babies yesterday evening?" I ask.

"I couldn't," says Deb. "I think it's disgusting."

"I hear it was fascinating," says Edwige.

"Superb," say I. "I love closeups of vaginas being entered by eels . . . And all the pipes and tubes . . . Marvelous!"

"Sadist!" says Deb, laughing.

Edwige has turned pale . . . She stands up, naked, worried about the effect of her backside, and drags Deb off into the water . . . Tells her a bit of no good about me, I expect, between strokes . . . Nicely, no malice in it, just to see . . .

"Do you like to see people going around naked?" she asks me.

"Not much," I answer. "It stirs me up . . ."

She shrugs . . . Tries to draw Deb into a psychological discussion . . . Deb answers in shrink language.

Toward the end of the afternoon I listen to a jazz program on the radio . . . Someone's had the bright idea of juxtaposing what the politicians said between 1938 and 1944 with recordings made at the time . . . The voice of Thorez in 1939: "All Frenchmen who are republicans and heirs of 1789 must unite! Members of the workers' party . . . Communists . . . And the socialists, the men of Peace!" Immediately afterward there's a record of Lester Young . . . Then Billie Holliday, *Lover Man*. No spoken commentary . . . Kathleen Ferrier and Billie Holliday . . . I admit those two introduce a new era for women . . . And so for the whole human race . . . *Kinder-totenlieder* . . . *Lover Man* . . . Billie Holliday's throat . . . Lungs

. . . Sinuses . . . Was jazz way ahead of its age? Obviously! No argument . . .

I get reacquainted with my body . . . Thin it down, harden it, plunge it in the water over and over again, float it, stretch it out, lighten it, burn it, dry it, give it a more subtle license to sleep . . . It has visions at night, and others in the afternoon . . . Neither swimming nor sleeping is the same at both times . . . Different currents, different depths . . . I look at things . . . And look again . . . At a gull veering, swooping, striking . . . Green is always changing . . . So is blue . . . The cries of the birds . . . Heaps of salt, scent of violets . . . Flower of air and water, the silent undoing of the day, the tongue at night savoring the saliva of the porous earth . . . It happens slowly, imperceptibly, milligram by milligram . . . Salt by day, dew at night . . .

"We ought to retire to somewhere like this," says Deb.

"Why not?"

"It's funny, isn't it, how no one really suits us? Or wants us . . . Don't we do things right?"

"We're too intelligent. And we love each other too much."

"Listen to him! No, I think we're never in one place long enough, that's all . . . Perhaps we ought to settle in New York for good?"

"Why not?"

"I had a sort of revelation the last time I was in Japan . . . In Kyoto . . . That we were heading for the void . . ."

"Really?"

"You're not listening to what I'm saying!"

"Yes, I am!"

Stephen comes in with his kite and his construction kits . . . More planes . . . Pan Am . . . Air France . . . TransWorld Airlines . . . British Airways . . . Lufthansa . . . Swissair . . .

"Stop it, Stephen! Don't make such a noise!"

"Just a tiny bit?"

"No, that's enough!"

Deb is highly organized . . . The house . . . Stephen . . . Her own work . . . Plus the beach, tennis, the flowers . . . And being attractive . . . Sometimes in the late afternoon she comes and picks some bay leaves from my tree . . . I recognize them in the rabbit we have for dinner . . . The sea-bream . . . The sole . . . Amen to that . . .

I've brought a bit of hash with me . . . We smoke it together in the evening, under the pines . . . She soon goes to sleep on my shoulder . . . I take her in to bed . . . Then sit down again at the typewriter . . . A sentence . . . Then another . . . It's no good . . . I leave it . . . Or else it does go well, it's a good night, and I become a grain that's escaped from the mass . . . A particle of antimatter, a boson, as the physicists call them now . . . How many vagaries can one indulge in? Before one subsides? Forgets? Wakes up again? Gets stuck once more in the traffic jam?

After we make love we fall back, asleep, side by side . . . As soon as we've come we drop off . . . That's what love really is . . . Two people able to be unconscious together immediately . . . The petty war of cohabitation—You're too this or not enough that! . . . You should talk! . . . Well, what do you expect, with you!—can't compare with the pleasure of legs entwined or the smell of the skin, the cheeks, the neck you love to feel and inhale . . .

Breakfast by the window overlooking the sea . . . News on the radio . . . Shopping list . . .

We meet again among the waves . . . The roll of the swell, the slap of the spray . . . Stephen in his red ring, trying to swim . . . We all converge . . . Kiss . . . Laugh . . .

I see the *Journal* has started a big survey after the recent terrorist attacks . . . "Are the French anti-Semitic?" What a joke! You only need to collect the insinuations made every day . . . I have a French friend in Paris who called his son David . . . He isn't Jewish . . . He was thinking of the English pronunciation . . . He told me how one of his wife's friends took her aside in the maternity hospital and

said: "But you're giving him some other names too, aren't you?"
"No, just David . . . Why?" "Well, so that he can choose for
himself later on!" . . . Another woman asked, "Why don't you call
him Christian?" As if there were any connection between David
and Christian! As if "Christian" was a translation of "David"! . . .
Someone else said, "So you're giving him a Zionist name?" . . .
Yet another: "But why 'David'? Where do you get that from?"
"The Psalms . . . That's as good as Victor Hugo, isn't it?" . . . In
short, he told me, "They kept it up for three months . . . Probably
no one would have said anything if my wife and I had been Jewish
. . . With Jews — O.K., only to be expected . . . But that a Frenchman who isn't a Jew should give a child a Jewish name! . . . That's
just provocation!"

I could scarcely believe him . . . I kept wondering if he wasn't
exaggerating . . . And then I came to live here, and listened in
surprise, observed and registered . . . It keeps hitting you in the ear
. . . It may be they don't notice it themselves . . . A natural
psychological factor . . . From generation to generation . . . Rampant family stupidity . . . School silent on the subject or disapproving . . . I carried out two or three casual tests myself among the
people I knew . . . A few hackneyed questions about the Bible . . .
Really obvious . . . Such as, What were the names of the patriarchs? Who circumcised Moses? Who was Solomon's father? Eloquent confusion . . . And these were "educated" people, mind you
. . . But I'm told you'd have got the same result with questions
about Jupiter and Venus . . . Maybe . . . It's true illiteracy is in full
swing . . . Tabula rasa . . . Young people completely hopeless . . .
Old people gaga before their time . . . Writers who are ignoramuses
. . . No more Latin, no more Greek . . . So you know what you can
do with Hebrew! No more History! No more Memory! Not bloody
likely! 1984 . . . Newspeak . . . And that's where we are now . . .
Yes, but there are always the Jews clinging to their Hebrew! Openly
mumbling it, working it out aloud . . . Enough to give people
complexes . . . Inferiority complexes, now . . . Before, you could
look down on the lousy though sometimes wealthy wretches, who
wouldn't have anything to do with Apollo or Aphrodite . . . The

thousand and one wonders of Greece and Rome! *They* wanted the miracles of the true Messiah . . . But now they make people anxious . . . Science isn't good enough for them . . . They hang onto their own inner thing! They know better . . . With their dusty old book of what are practically hieroglyphs . . . That claims to throw light on their origins, and, what's more, to date everything else from them!

Anti-Semitism isn't racism anymore . . . It's sheer anti-intellectual prejudice . . . Unless you regard intellectuals as a race in themselves . . . Perhaps that's it . . . A dual system . . . But one system is enough . . . Ding-ding! Quick! Pavlov! Saliva! Spleen! Little gray ejaculation! Then O.K. again!

All right, let them talk . . . "Ideas" . . . Not one of their anecdotes is from personal experience . . . Though that would count more than a thousand dissertations . . . Just a little something that actually happened to you . . . That you noticed in passing . . . An intonation . . . A gesture . . . An insinuation . . . So that everyone can see you know what's going on . . .

S. calls . . . From Rome . . .

"Everything all right? Do you like the house?"

"Terrific."

"Strange sort of place, isn't it? What's the weather like?"

"Splendid! And you—when do you leave for Sydney?"

"I've canceled! Too much of a bore! I'm coming back."

"Soon?"

"In about ten days . . . Did you start work again right away? Are you making progress?"

"A bit . . . It's not going as fast as I'd hoped, but I'm not doing too badly . . ."

"Has the news been upsetting you?"

"A little . . . There's a lot going on, isn't there?"

"Oh, I don't know . . . Never as much as people think . . . Soon the only thing that makes us think anything's happening will be terrorism . . ."

"And have you started writing again?"

"Yes! I *believe* in it again! Rome! Bernini! Thanks to you!"

473

"The baldaquin?"

"The baldaquin!"

He sounds very cheerful . . .

"Have you remembered about the flowers?"

"Luxuriant! In great form! The roses . . ."

"And the cannas?"

"The cannas especially . . ."

"The canna is to other flowers what the sole is to other fish . . . Simple, magnanimous . . ."

" 'A hardy herbaceous plant bearing irregular flowers, with a thick underground stem and adventitious roots. Buds develop into aerial branches bearing alternate sheathed clusters of blossoms in the form of scorpioid cymes with colored bracts. Native to tropical regions, especially in North America and Asia . . ."

"Absolutely!" . . .

"How's Sophie?"

"Basking in the Assumption! The Black Virgin! Poland! How about Deb? And Stephen?"

"Flourishing . . ."

"So long, then."

"So long."

The phone again . . .

"Hello?"

"Hello? How are you?"

The voice sounds a long way away . . . I hesitate for a couple of seconds . . . But it's her all right—Flora . . . I can scarcely hear her . . .

"Where are you?"

"Mmmammaba . . ."

"Where?"

'Ma-la-ga! Are you going deaf?"

"How are you?"

"Great . . . I'm with some friends . . . Malmora . . . Remember?"

"Of course . . . How is he?"

"He's working . . . On a big novel . . . About love . . . We were talking about you only five minutes ago . . . That's what made me think to call . . . They told me at the *Journal* you were at some friends' place in the southwest . . ."

"That's right . . ."

"Are you working?"

"When I can . . . How about you?"

"Yes . . . And I wanted to ask your advice . . ."

No! Mercy, mercy! It's starting all over again . . . Just as if nothing had happened . . . Who's the best person to call up in New York about a general piece on terrorism in Europe? She's been making some contacts . . . She can't say with whom . . . "Very high-level" . . . Yes, of course, to do with the Middle East . . . And beyond . . . Don't I think that. . . ? After Beirut? And in connection with the latest developments in France? Perhaps I could call the *New York Times?* And, naturally, go over her article for her . . .

I pretend I can't hear . . . I cling to my shiny green bay tree, just in front of me . . . I moan . . . "Hold on—don't cut us off !" I shout . . . "Hello! Hello!" I hang up . . . Pick up the phone again . . . I *become* the bay tree . . . Merge into the leaves . . . The smell . . .

Flora will think it's difficult to reach the provinces in France by phone . . . Not enough lines . . . Anyhow, I realize she's worked things out . . . Quite coldly . . . I can still be of use . . . My English . . .

The mail's forwarded . . . A note from Cyd to the studio . . . She's going to Berlin at the end of the month . . . She'll be in Paris for a couple of days . . .

I go out into the sun again . . . Walk through the marshes . . . Come back to the sea along a path hidden among the grasses . . . No one around . . . I go for a swim on my own, with three gulls perched on the water nearby . . . They take off lazily, fly over me, and settle down again twenty yards away . . . A little game we play in the silence . . . The blue, faintly rippled surface is like a held breath . . . A divine skin . . . I go in, stop to look at the house from a distance . . . Stephen has just woken from his afternoon nap and is running around the garden holding one of his planes . . . "Pussycat!" he shouts . . . "Pussy-cat!" He's looking for me . . . Deb comes out too . . . "Pussy?" I watch them . . . They don't see me . . . They sit down on the bench, facing the incoming tide . . . I lie in the grass and watch them, as if I were dead and looking at them from beyond my death . . . Perhaps they'd think of me from time to time . . . Occasionally . . . Good old Pussy! A queer fish, with his funny ways, his inability to keep up a conversation, his habit of never really telling you anything, of shutting himself up on his own for hours and hours . . . Deb's dark outline looks suddenly frail in the violent, vertical afternoon light . . . She drinks her tea . . . Time out of time . . . The ceaseless cry of the gulls all around . . . I think of them as "gulls," in English . . . Long Island . . . The white-painted houses with their lawns and fountains . . . Belport, Watermill . . . Easthampton . . . Big cars leaving the humid, sweltering city every Friday . . . The New York summer, as hot as the winter is freezing . . . The same wing glittering from one coast to the other: we haven't heard the last of the Atlantic yet . . . Long drone up in the sky . . .

"Pussy!"

"Do you know about the current negotiations?" she asks.

That's very nice of her . . . She knows I don't know anything . . . She'll tell me . . . About the circulation of capital, and thus of influence . . . The way industry is getting involved in the media . . . The various parts played by the banks . . . How my own fate is decided up there on the Olympian heights of balance sheets, conveyancing and holding companies . . . Can I really say, just like that, who happens to own me at this moment? I mention a few names . . . She rolls up her eyes . . . I don't know anything . . . Have I been singing all summer, or what? Poor grasshopper! So I've no idea what's going on? The way videodiscs have been hit by financial difficulties in steel? The decline in electronic equipment because of the American-inspired invasion by the Japanese? Which affects the chain of newspapers I write for? And the highly complex geopolitical background to all this? Wars, balance of payments, interest rates, the Snake? Hasn't anyone told me? Or about the setting up of watch committees on typefaces?

"So," says the Chairwoman, "how have you managed to stay so remote from your own concerns?"

"My novel," I say.

"Of course," says she, "your novel! Sorry, I forgot . . ."

She radiates irony . . . She really thinks I'm down the drain . . .

"But it's what's happening that's a novel!" she says. "Though no one will ever write it . . ."

"Mostro the whale," I say.

"What?"

"Mostro the whale . . . Haven't you ever heard of it?"

"No — what is it?"

"It's in *Pinocchio*," I tell her. "My son's just reading it" . . .

The Chairwoman frowns . . . She doesn't like me to talk about my family . . . It sounds wimpish . . . But she tries to be polite . . .

"So?"

"The great big whale swallows all Pinocchio's nearest and dearest . . . His father, the dog, the bird, and so on — I don't remember . . . But Pinocchio has held onto a box of matches . . . He lights a fire inside the whale and it spews them all up . . ."

The Chairwoman looks at me as if I were a harmless idiot . . . A charming lad, but rather feebleminded . . . Not bad value, but unfortunately no ambition . . . Doesn't know how to sleep around properly . . . No future . . . Career kiboshed . . .

"And what about god?" she laughs.

"He must be very busy these days."

"I hope he doesn't talk to you too often?"

Yes, that's how she sees me — charming, but not all there . . .

She goes out of the room to phone . . . I see the latest books on her desk . . . *Defense of Periods*, by Raymonde Foucal . . . Amalia Joris's *Menstruation Without Tears* . . . Oh, so WOMANN has changed its line! The SGIC has undergone a strategic reorientation! The pill, contraception, IUDs, induced periods and abortion have been demoted . . . Now there's a return to nature! To fundamental rhythms! A reassertion of the value of earth! And blood! Of the old cycles!

I leaf through one of the volumes at random . . .

"Music no longer opens people up: it makes the listener impenetrable to others, deaf both literally and metaphorically . . . And if it has ceased to be the source and accompaniment of people's physical lives and of the dramatic incidents in them; if it is only a repetitive outpouring, a negation of individual existences, a mere common ground for the mesmerized masses, then it ought to be destroyed to make way for the revival of those vibrations which turn us into human entities."

I see . . . The American Satan . . . Jazz . . . Rock . . . Pop . . . Walkman . . . And Wagner . . . ? Destroy music? A tall order . . .

"The pill and the IUD allow men to keep on demonstrating their potency"—at least this author's optimistic—"but though they may sow their seed in the Danaids' barrel"—as in the "outpouring" of music?—"this potency is nothing to do with life, as their unrestrained generosity rarely produces any consequences."

The Danaids? Cause and effect? *Life?*

A new catechism . . .

We might amend as follows: "The pill and the IUD at last and for the first time allow men to be really alive, because they sow their seed in a nonbarrel which the Danaids no longer have to fill . . . This reasonable generosity demonstrates that they have been liberated from death, because it rarely produces any consequences."

We could add a line from Baudelaire: "Hate is the barrel of the pale Danaids . . ."

The Chairwoman comes back . . . I put the book down . . . She gives me a suspicious look . . . I'd better be going . . . I stand up and kiss her hand . . .

I ask Robert if he can confirm the news about the *Journal* . . . He does seem worried . . . He says we've been bought up by a subsidiary of ITT . . . Who have a lot of Arab capital . . . He says it won't change anything much . . . So I can be sure of the opposite . . . But he has something more important to tell me . . . He didn't want to mention it before . . .

"Yes?" I ask.

"Well, it happened during the summer . . . I'm writing something . . . A novel . . ."

"Really!"

"You don't mind?"

"Why should I mind?"

"I don't know . . . Your own novel . . . We'll have to make sure they don't come out together . . ."

"Have you got a publisher?" I ask.

"Yes, I signed the contract yesterday . . . A very good one . . . With Hiram's . . . They're entering it for a prize . . ."

"Watch out for Boris!"

"Do you know how he's getting on?"

"No, but he must be nearly finished. . ."

"He called me up . . . He's very excited . . . Do you know what he's calling it?"

"No?"

"*The Abyss!* Just like that!"

"Not *The Rush to the Abyss?*"

"No . . . Just *The Abyss* . . . Is yours still called *Women?*"

"Yes . . ."

"I don't like it much . . . Too colorless . . . A bit affected . . . Have you signed with anyone?"

"No . . ."

"Anyway, I don't suppose our two books will have anything in common?"

"I don't suppose so . . ."

"When does yours take place?"

"In the present . . . Everywhere . . . Simultaneously . . ."

"Oh," says Robert . . . "Mine's got a time scheme . . . A story . . . A definite scenario . . . A sequence that you can follow . . ."

I understand now . . . Robert has written the sort of novel I could never have written . . . And is looking forward to the sort of success I can never enjoy . . . He got the idea from Boris . . . Or Kate . . . Or Flora . . . It's been incubating inside him ever since he heard about my project . . . Now he can join in with the others and say: "Oh yes, his novel . . . Not bad . . . A bit difficult . . . But wait till you see mine!" And so on . . . Oh, these media people! They ought to be called medians . . . A media actor . . . A medium one . . . Mesmeric passes, hypnosis by remote control, ubiquitous powers, vampirism ever on the watch . . . Perpetual imitation, immediate echo, the image swooping on its shadowy prey . . . The living are the medians' sheep . . . Coming and going, working, thinking they really feel and have a life . . . Unsuspecting, swallowing anything, repeating whatever they're told . . . They're bound hand and foot to the medians . . . Even when they're asleep! Or dying! Or copulating! Day and night!

I'm finding out more and more how for all of them, male and female, I'm a camera, a screen, a projector, or simply a mirror . . . They want me to reflect them back to themselves, to record them . . . They ask me to be their hidden author . . . Their ever-hidden cause . . . The dummy at bridge . . . Their silent witness . . . They contemplate themselves in me . . . Reconstruct themselves in relation to me . . . Succubi! As if they were suspended in some fragmented and disembodied interworld . . . Then I appear, and their identity is reinforced . . . They tell me, in a fever of discovery, what I told them a week or a year ago . . . They suddenly announce that they're in the middle of doing what I'm supposed to be doing . . . A novel? Of course! Fifty novels! It's an unconscious compliment . . . A tribute . . . So Robert's writing a novel . . . No doubt there'll be others . . .

"I've just reread *L'Education sentimentale*," says Robert . . . "Flaubert really is the supreme Master . . ."

"I prefer *Madame Bovary*," I answer . . . "I find *l'Education* rather long and drawn-out . . ."

"How can you say such a thing?"

"It's dated . . . It bored Flaubert himself . . . The women are impossible . . . The *Madame Bovary* lawsuit had scared him . . . So this book is chaste and indirect . . . Mme. Arnoux is a terrible bore . . . And Rosanette . . . No, just read the dialogue again and you'll see . . . That vague sort of prudery's unreadable now . . . Proust wins hands down on that score . . . Though he's dated quite a bit too . . ."

"Proust? Dated?"

Robert's nearly choking . . . He's gone red in the face . . .

"I mean the way he idealizes women," I say . . . "Of course, his malice is wonderful . . ."

"You take a hard line, do you?"

Robert smiles pityingly . . . A hard line means a limited public and small print runs . . . Hee-hee! It won't get a prize! . . . But no unseemly jostling among "beings and things" . . . Silent shock . . . No need to rub it in . . . And then of course I'm an American, so it's quite all right for me to go my own crude way and write a hefty unsalable tome . . . And as I also lay on the sophisticated intellectual too thick . . . And not in an acceptable way, either . . . So I'm right out . . . Anyway, it won't be long now before the distinguished thing to do will again be *not* to write a novel . . . Full circle . . . At present, fashion has caught up with me . . . Before, philosophical treatises were all the rage . . . What, aren't you writing a philosophical treatise? Your view of the world? No . . . An autocritique, then? No . . . A novel? No . . . A play, a film script? No, no . . . What then? Poems? A journal? No? Well, what, then? Oh, I see . . .

Cyd in her studio . . . She leaves for Berlin the day after tomorrow . . . A serious session . . . Side by side for a long while in the red and black half-light of drawn curtains, whispering cheek to cheek . . . Her lips in my ear . . . All the smut she's been thinking . . . How she's screwed thinking of me . . . The details . . . Two men . . . She and Lynn . . . Tongues, breaths, sexes, a chain of bodies . . . Her whole art of obscenity ever more torrid and elegant . . . Jealousy acted as pleasure . . . As merely glimpsed in Shakespeare's *Sonnets* . . . *My female evil* . . . *As black as hell, as dark as night* . . . Except that Cyd is blonde and fair-skinned . . . And her eyes are green, like the sea I've just left, when it's stormy . . . The pleasure to be derived from a mixture of love's unimportant crimes . . . *"Then, in the number, let me pass untold"* . . . But I want to be the only one you tell all . . . The only one within you, deeper than you yourself . . . Cyd, Cydie, Cyda, Cressida . . . I think again briefly of Flora . . . That's what really frightened her— the purity of vice, the morality of its truth . . . How sad, a woman you no longer want to screw . . . How wearisome, how depressing, after the little dark death . . . A devitalizing black hole . . . Bad temper or headache or exhaustion and lassitude for three days . . . What a business, the deliberate making use of sex, its setting up, its profanation . . . With a few exceptions, and then only temporarily for the most part, women see nothing wrong in bringing the sexual organs into everyday life . . . As if it were a matter of housekeeping . . . And if there were such a thing as an extra screw, a brief relaxation to relieve the boredom . . . The hell . . . No question of Danaids! No fear! A fanatical sense of property! . . . Whereas vice is gratuitous . . . The profound tenderness of vice . . .

Happiness with Cyd . . . Skin, saliva . . . Today she wants to eat me—really devour me; as never before; to the death . . .

The number of times she'll have cried out, like this, while I'm touching her . . . All the different sighs and near-sobs . . . A wreath in the madness of time . . .

We don't speak . . . Tomorrow . . . She's got something to tell me . . .

The next day I wait for her in a café in the boulevard Saint-Michel . . . It's a lovely day . . . Paris is still empty . . . It's still a good time for driving around, idle afternoons . . . Girls with almost nothing on, and brown legs . . . Here she is . . . She sits down . . . Kisses me across the table . . . Hey, there's something going on over there . . . Three men and a woman, running . . . They're young . . . Wearing khaki jackets with some kind of tubes hidden under them . . . They're coming nearer . . . Cyd opens her mouth to say something to me . . . They're coming nearer still, getting some shiny objects out from under their coats . . . The dark girl is looking toward us . . . They're only twenty meters away . . .

I don't know which came first . . . The noise or the blow on my left arm . . . I just had time to see Cyd's mouth open inordinately wide, about to say "Well" or "What" . . . And now the syllables are printed at infinite length on the black and yellow air . . . Like shouts in cartoons . . . "Weeeeelll . . . ""Whaaaaat . . ." Or rather, just "Wwwwweeeeeaaaaa . . . " I just have time to see people hurl themselves to the ground, to hear the first screams, feel the café tables collapse and the whole pack of cards around me blow up in panic . . . Submachine guns—I know the score . . . I also know how you unexpectedly faint, with a hundred-mile-an-hour gale battering at your forehead, nose and ears . . . This is it . . .

I dimly hear the sound of ambulances . . . Open my eyes in the hospital . . . Burns on my left arm . . . A guy bending over me . . . "You've had a close shave . . . But it's nothing . . . Practically nothing . . . You feel groggy? You'll feel better soon . . . Just lie still . . ."

"Where am I?"

"Cochin . . ."

"And the friend who was with me?"

"I don't know."

"An Englishwoman . . ."

"I can't tell you . . . They took the injured to a lot of different places . . ."

"Were there many?"

"About twenty . . . They fired indiscriminately."

"Do they know who it was?"

"I don't know . . . The police are on the spot . . . "

"Could you send a message for me?"

"Of course. I was just going to ask you."

I give him Deb's number on the island . . .

A nurse goes by.

"Have you seen an Englishwoman?" I ask.

"An Englishwoman? One of the injured?"

"I don't know," I say. "She was with me . . . "

"Oh, her!"

"What do you mean?"

"Wait . . . don't get worked up . . . I can't tell you anything . . . I'll be back."

I have a first-aid dressing under my arm. The bullet must just have grazed me. I'm in pain, but lucid. A big fat chap comes in. Police. Counterespionage.

"You're an American?"

"Yes. But I live and work in France. I've got dual nationality. I'm a journalist."

"So I've just seen from your papers. Here they are. You were with a British citizen, Mme. MacRoy?"

"MacCoy," I say. "Cyd MacCoy. Yes. We had a date there."

"I'm very sorry."

"Is she badly hurt?"

"She's dead."

"What?"

"Dead. I'm sorry. She was killed instantly. Shot through the heart. She couldn't have suffered. Do you know her family?"

"Yes," I say.

"Don't you feel well? They told me you had very superficial injuries. That's why I thought I could . . . She was between you and the gunmen, wasn't she?"

"She's English, but she lives in the United States," I say. "She's a television journalist. But her mother lives in London."

"We'll inquire at the Consulate. Or the Embassy."

"Could you inform a friend of hers, too? She lives in Los Angeles."

I give him Lynn's number.

"Would you rather I came back later to ask you a few questions?" asks the perspiring fat guy tactfully.

"No, go ahead."

"Are you all right?"

"Yes."

"Were you there by chance?"

"Absolutely."

"Did you recognize anyone? Could you describe the gunmen?"

"No, I couldn't" I say. "I didn't see a thing."

"Are you sure?"

"Quite sure."

"Had you received any threats? I see from your passport that you were in Israel a month ago. Do you think that could have anything to do with it?

"I don't see how. I really don't."

"Are you Jewish yourself? I'm sorry, but under the circumstances . . ."

"Not in the least . . . But I'm feeling rather tired . . . "

"I'm sorry. Of course. Thank you. Can we reach you at home?"

"Yes."

I'm gradually losing consciousness. I ring. The nurse reappears.

"Yes?"

"I don't feel too good."

She pushes the considerate fat man out and gives me an injection. The heart. Solucamphor.

"You'll get off very lightly," she says. "Hardly a scratch. You'll be out of here in a couple of days at the most. Was it your wife who was killed?"

"No, a friend."

Oh . . . I'm sorry. Call me if you need anything."

She goes out.

This time I really go off. A merry-go-round of distortions. I start by throwing up. Twice. I can't stop. My stomach wants to get out of my body. The burn gets more painful.

I ring.

Another nurse this time. They're curious. About the tall, fair, slightly gory American whose wife was killed in the terrorist attack.

"What's the time?" I ask.

"Eight o'clock. In the evening."

"When did it happen?"

"About five."

"I'm in pain."

"It's nothing. I'll give you another jab. You'll soon be up and about. You're still suffering from shock."

I go off again. I have to find my body, which is very near yet very far . . . The left arm seems to be slowing down somewhere on the fringe . . . Cyd is turning into that arm, carrying it off . . . I can see, right in front of me, a closeup of her smiling face, so pleased to see me, and the Wwwwweeeeaaa of her lips against the background of the general mayhem . . . Tell me where you are now . . . Don't go away . . . The explosion is burning hot, we're all burning together on the sidewalk . . .

The thoughtful fat man comes back again . . .

485

"Excuse me . . . You've traveled a lot lately . . . The United States . . . Italy . . . Israel . . . And you've been to China . . . Might I ask if it was for political reasons?"

"Not at all."

"Did you go as a reporter?"

"No. Just to please myself. I'm writing a novel."

"A novel? About current events?"

"Oh, very indirectly. It's a philosophical novel, you might say."

"You've never been to Lebanon?"

"No, never."

"And you've never noticed anything out of the way about the people you know?"

"No, but there's always the chance . . ."

"Was Mme. MacCoy involved in politics at all?"

"Not as far as I know. Highly unlikely."

"I'm sorry. You do see . . ."

"Has anyone claimed responsibility for the attack?" I ask.

"Not yet . . . But it must be just another one in the series. Do you have any theory about it?"

"No. None."

"I'm sorry . . . But we're afraid France might be getting to be the same as Germany and Italy have been lately."

"It's only to be expected."

"Are you in pain?"

"A bit."

"You don't have any particular statement to make?"

"Yes. I'd like to shut my eyes."

He leaves . . .

I'm running a temperature now . . . A deep dive . . . It's a long time since I've been shaken like this in the magneto of delirium . . . Not since I was a child . . . Cell-shaker . . . I shiver, sweat, go hot and cold, twitch . . . What's coming up now in the theater of images, declamation and vociferation, the steep of strings and voices? Oh yes . . . Television . . . Wagner . . . Valkyrie . . . Siegfried . . . *The Twilight of the Gods* . . . *Parsifal* . . . The unending shout . . . The deeps of throats, canyons of color, rocks, screaming chink

486

in fiery breath . . . Lungs in frenzy . . . "Divine, frivolous and lustful rabble . . ." Yes, yes, death with a smile . . . "We shall go down laughing" . . . I can see larynxes swallowing graphs . . . Erda . . . Wala . . . GDR! Risen prophetic from her earthy sleep . . . With her penned-up widow daughters, ceaselessly crying out . . . In Bavaro-Prussian . . . In Arabic . . . Mutter! Artificial Rhine, livers of steel . . . Fricka making a scene with one-eyed Wotan . . . As Armande used to with Fals . . . Flora running through the woods . . . Lost among the shrouds . . . They want to eat Cyd's remains . . . Here, right away . . . Cannibalize, lick their lips over them . . . Come here, you too, so that they can take you away . . . The predatory sleepwalkers in free-fall . . . The yelling gets louder and louder . . . Inside my head or in the next room . . . I ring . . . The nurse comes . . . "Could you lower the sound on the television?" "What television?" Right, now it's the mourners of the wind . . . And the daughters hypnotized by their father, and the father going back to his mother, and her mother returning to her mother, and the eternal nest of them finally distorting into funereal sound . . . Ash tree of the world . . . Machine-made leaves . . . Extra-strong . . . Spring . . . Dragon . . . The lot! The ring and the helmet . . . Blood in the goblets . . . Notung! The sword! Slash slash! Withdrawal symptoms! And the phrase that comes and goes, breaks off and fades away, calls to itself like a distant echo, heralds itself with blasts on the horn, snaps apart, comes back, wavers, dies, puts itself together again, splits, comes back again . . . Thirsty ghost . . . Fluidor . . . Knights of the séance table . . . Termites in the floor . . . Sacred cows baying the moon . . . Anima! Anima! A burst of violins assault my spinal cord . . . Force eight shudder! They go to sleep, think they wake up, go to sleep again, think they're really awake at last—shrieking all the time . . . Birds speak, but that's nothing—the trees receive secret intelligence, metamorphosis is in . . . I incest you utterly . . . And send you back to sleep . . . Olympus doped, poor Greeks, charming Ovid . . . Poison, philtre, it's you I was waiting for, but it's not you, because you are me and I'm no longer I . . . The hero's rolling on the ground . . . He screws his sister . . . She sucks him off . . . He's transfixed by

487

Papa's spear, on Mama's orders . . . Her son reappears, carried by a wolf . . . Romulus! Oremus! He keeps screaming on the heels of his lost, expiring mother . . . Bringing forth of pains . . . Forceps by night . . . Conversation of owls . . . Traitor's impotent fury . . . Triumph of untruth . . . Expiration of the original sin . . . We don't quite know what it is, but the flood's inevitable . . . Biblical Wagner! It'll end badly . . . Vallallâh!

Meanwhile, my own blood is doing its stuff . . . It courses, percolates through me . . . Thuds in my ears . . . Burns the back of my neck . . . Comes back into my windpipe . . . And it's now I'm afraid . . . A little leaf! A dusty moth! I open one eye to see if I'm still here . . . A steel table . . . White walls . . . Accident . . . Cyd?

At that I take another dive . . . Guilty? Of course not! Not at all! Yes! No! You will be . . . Here they come again . . . In my veins . . . A surge of cocaine . . . *Rheingold* . . . And when the dope really starts to shout, you're on the brink . . . The outside is after you within, but there isn't a within anymore . . . You might say it's melted, frayed away, his phallus-organ, in all directions at once, smithereens . . . Leitmotiv . . . Hamleitmotiv . . . Measure for measure . . . Stop! Cut!

Pitch dark . . . The first nurse is bending over me . . . Everyone has been told . . . Your wife's on her way . . . Go to sleep now . . . Sleep . . . Fair hair, blue eyes . . . Looks as if she's from Brittany . . . Cyd's white blouse that afternoon, gray skirt . . . Concrete . . . Plane trees . . . Smile-concrete-plane-trees . . . Wwwwwwwwaaaaaa!

The music starts up again, lower, in the jab . . . The bottom notes open out . . . One might bring in the clarinets and the oboes . . . Let the orchestra let itself go . . . Bask, surge . . . Seem to be at its last gasp . . . Then revive in the percussion . . . Bong! Bong again! Muffled! Corpses coming and going on the heights . . . Celestial morgue . . . Sort it out . . . By the legs . . . What's that whispering over in the corner? Kate and Bernadette . . . Wearing the chador . . . What are they doing here? No—in Puccini or Verdi, but not in Wagner! Not allowed! They look like old peasant women from the Auvergne trying to force their way into *Macbeth* . . . With their headscarves . . . The Chairwoman goes by, very upright, in the background . . . In evening dress . . . Gutrune! Gutrune! She doesn't see me . . . "I don't know him . . . Have never acknowledged him . . . Always had a rather poor opinion of him . . ." She disappears majestically into the distance . . . Ambulances crossing bridges, sirens shrieking . . . Relays of cops tearing off space like strips of sticking plaster . . . The strings of lights go on . . . Robot gods playing billiards . . . Giant ads . . . Times Square . . . Secret agents with plastic hearts disguised as terrorists looking for terrorists disguised as secret agents . . . They kiss, groaning merrily . . . Fight with poisoned umbrellas . . . Radioactive meatballs . . . Cancer-inducing sun-ray lamps . . . End up with lasers at point blank range . . .

Now here come those of all ages who've been quartered, decapitated, hung, garotted . . . Followed by those who've been guillotined, very dignified, led by Robespierre and Louis XVI with their heads tucked underneath their arms . . . Those who've been electrocuted . . . Gassed . . . Bayonnetted . . . Shot . . . Deported en masse, with their fluorescent pajamas . . . The Gulagites, carrying huge posters of Solzhenitsyn . . . Trotsky, with the hologrammed ice-pick in his skull . . . The Poles, walking in procession behind a black virgin making lewd gestures . . . Another Russian rocket . . . A Chinese one . . . Ysia makes a rude sign at me through a window . . . And then the Vienamese, the Palestinians, the Salvadorians, the Bulgarians, the Romanians, and I don't know who else . . . Blast-off every ten seconds . . . "Come here! Come here!" Cyd's calling me . . . She's taking off from Cape Canaveral . . . Or Baikonor . . . "Come on!" The orchestra attacks now — the violins are on an amphetamine drip . . . A loudspeaker bawls at regular intervals from a watchtower: "Wagner's coming! Wagner warns you!" A writer's rocket, with an enormous pink favor on the tip of its electronic prick . . . Homer, Sophocles, Virgil, Dante, Shakespeare, Cervantes, Sade, Chateaubriand, Balzac, Flaubert, Bauderlaire, Proust, Kafka, Joyce . . . Artaud as Marat! . . . Céline, of course, with his glass of water and his noodles and his ticket: pioneer of the three dots . . . The Brottin rocket! Formerly a metro station . . . The wonders of technology! Faulkner alone and silent in the corner, drinking his tenth whisky . . . On the next stage, the philosophers . . . I can hear Fals calling to me from far away in one of the cabins: "Don't forget! Anything! I told you to be prepared for anything!" He's fidgeting nervously with some old bits of string . . . Werth gives me a pale, friendly smile . . . He's holding his mother's hand; she's draped in Japanese cameras . . . Lutz is there too, between life and death, wearing a funny kind of astrakhan cap with wires in it . . . He shouts out that the "Symbolus" rocket will never take off . . . It'll be flattened by the Israeli air force . . . By the Wehrmacht! Fals tries to shut him up . . . The Wemecht? But Lutz only yells louder . . . Wehmahcht! Wemacht! Céline stamps his foot: "Be quiet now!" Lutz stops . . . He's covered in snow . . . Holding a glass of vodka . . . And now here's Flora, trying to take off under her own steam . . . As in 1914! And in 1870! To horse! In fishnet stockings, a Wild West moll! With Garcia Marquez riding pillion! Havanas and pesetas! Both of them wearing sombreros! The guillotine victims keep shouting at them that there are no more horses, there haven't been any for a hundred years, but it's no good, they're determined to go on horseback! With a pack of tarot cards! Actually, says the Chairwoman thoughtfully, arranging the badges around her plunging neckline: SGIC, WOMANN, FAM, SOLIDARNOSC, KGB, MOSSAD, CIA, SDEC . . . Flora brandishes her sword . . . A wooden sabre . . . Garcia Marquez spurs Rosinante on . . . Fals tries to calm them down . . . "Nothing is everything! Nothing is everything!" In vain . . . He throws balls of wool at them . . . But who's this old Swabian farmer, with a beret on his head and a swastika on his back? Goethe? No . . . The old man mutters, "Only a God . . . " The orchestra slows down . . . Sighs . . . A red spotlight standing for sunset . . . "Only a God could . . ." Pizzicati by the violins . . . "Only a God could save us now" . . . "But which?" squeals his companion in mourning, a bent old woman from the Black Forest . . . "Put a sock in it,

Erda," says Heidegger . . . "Which, you fool?" she persists . . .
"Spit it out, know-all!" . . . He hangs his head . . . The violins
throw up . . . She slaps him . . . The rocket blasts off . . . Symbolus is airborne . . . Ecstasy in the strings . . . Lateral orgasm
among the bassoons . . .

I open my eyes . . . I feel better . . . Two in the morning . . .
The pain's bearable . . . Temperature gone . . . I try not to think
about Cyd . . . Resist the image of the thought and the image of
the image of the thought . . . The expression of the little dark girl
in khaki looking at us, brief glimpse of her eyes, her sure fingers
. . . Have I seen her before? No . . . And yet yes . . . No . . . But
. . . Not her—her expression . . .
    I go back to sleep.
    Eight o'clock . . . Cyd's mother comes into my room, crying . . .
We mumble inanities at one another . . . Yes, I'll write . . . Yes,
I'll go to see her in London . . .
    She and Deb pass each other in the corridor . . .
    "Well, nothing serious," says Deb, kissing me.
    "Luck . . ."
    "You were with an American journalist?"
    "Yes . . ."
    "Did you know her well?"
    "Quite well."
    "And she was killed outright?"
    "Yes," I answer. "Instead of me . . ."
    "Come now, don't be silly . . . It could happen to anyone any-
where these days . . . Are you in pain?"
    "Not much now . . . Did they break it to you sensibly?"
    "Yes, very . . . But it gave me a fright . . . Stephen wants to
know why Pussycat's ill . . ."
    "You always wanted romantic things to happen . . . Instead of
"fantasies . . .'"

491

"I didn't bargain for this" . . .

She kisses me again . . . Leaves me . . . Goes to buy a few things . . . Will be right back . . .

The nice fat guy comes back again . . .

"Are you sure you didn't see them?" he asks.

"No, I didn't . . . Just a sort of maelstrom."

"Can you tell me how many there were? Two? Three? Four?"

"Three, I think . . . But really, I'm not sure about anything . . ."

"We're told now there was a woman among them . . ."

"Really?"

"You didn't notice her?"

"No."

"Do you know Flora Valenzuela?"

"Yes."

"Is she in Spain at present?"

"I believe so . . ."

"Were you involved in political movements of the extreme left ten years ago?"

"Oh, only slightly . . . Never seriously . . . "

"Were you a Maoist?"

"I wrote a few articles, at the most . . . But that's a long time ago . . . It's been a thing of the past for ages now . . ."

"You're not still in contact with those circles?"

"Definitely not."

He goes . . . Routine . . . Deb brings me the papers . . . My name is linked to Cyd's . . . "A couple of American journalists . . ." Deb pulls a face . . . "Why a 'couple'?" "Journalese," I answer . . . The editor's office phones to ask for my impressions . . . I say I haven't got any . . . Ask them to leave me alone . . . Cyd? No, nothing special . . . I talk to Robert . . . "When are you coming out?" "This evening . . . " "I must see you right away" . . .

Lynn calls . . . She's coming to Paris . . .

It never rains but it pours? Naturally . . . You've got the right idea . . . The lousy one . . . A trend goes on in the same way until it's reversed . . . And so on . . .

"I'm afraid there've been big staff cuts," Robert says, scarcely pausing to ask how I am . . .

"Be more precise."

"Well, I think your job's been left out of the new organization chart . . . Perhaps you ought to see the unions" . . .

In short, he's sacking me . . . I'll have to get a new employer . . . A new exploiter . . . A nice spectacle I make, looking for a job with my arm all bandaged up . . . I call New York . . . Get things moving there . . .

Kate comes into my office, beaming . . .

"So, you poor old thing, it never rains but it pours! Are you in pain?"

"Not really . . ."

"Did you know her well, this MacCoy?"

"Quite well . . ."

"What are you going to do?"

"See how things look in America . . . And you—are you off to India?"

She's away . . . The whole guidebook . . . On and on . . . And then of course she's very sad . . . Butterfly, her little angora cat, is dead . . . She loved her so . . . Her eyes are full of tears . . . Luckily she has to go to Naples . . . An official conference . . . On Mediterranean cultures . . . Chaired by Garcia Marquez . . .

"What a great writer!" says Kate . . . "His last book's a master-piece! A force of nature! Such talent! And such a nice person . . ."

"I'm sure," I say. "What are 'Mediterranean cultures'?"

"Well . . . The Latin ones . . . The Greek . . ."

"What about the Arabs?"

"Oh yes, of course."

"And Israel?"

"Israel part of the Mediterranean? Oh yes, right—it doesn't occur to one at first . . ."

"So how many languages, in all this?"

"French, Latin, Greek, Arabic, Italian, Spanish . . ."

"And Hebrew," say I.

"Hebrew?"

"Israel . . ."

"Do they speak Hebrew?"

"Hebrew and English . . . And Yiddish . . ."

"By the way, how's your novel?"

"More or less brought to a halt . . ."

"How far had you got with it?"

"Almost finished . . ."

I start feeling lousy again . . . Scar forming . . . Irritation . . . Blood all on edge . . .

Robert comes back . . . Tries to explain that my job may still exist . . . But that . . . Well, I need to change my image . . . I've been rather too unilateral . . . I might be more balanced . . . If I made an effort . . . Hey, why don't I do a long article reviewing my past? A critical appraisal?

I'll help him not to feel so guilty, since that's what he wants . . .

I quote Weininger: " 'A superior mind realizes how important everything in his life has been, and that's why he's so respectful toward his own past. It's because his whole life is always present to him that he knows he has a destiny' " . . .

That ought to do it . . .

Robert pulls a face . . .

"You and your quotations," he says. " 'A superior mind'? 'Destiny?' "

"Why not?" I laugh . . .

He throws up his hands . . . I'm not in a position to follow suit . . . I feel he's full of sad and immeasurable hate . . . He's leaving me in the lurch . . . It's all happening very fast . . . Every man for himself . . . Income tax due soon . . . Everyone trying to survive—it's only natural . . . Still, I suggest one last article . . .

"About terrorism?"

"No," I say. "Poland . . ."

"Poland? But everyone's going on about that!"

"But they don't do justice to the Black Virgin," I say.

"One last provocation?"

"If you like."

"Well, I'll see . . . Call me tomorrow" . . .

That's it . . . A glance around to see what I need to take away . . . Drop in at the hospital for a dressing . . . Cyd's body has been flown to London . . .

I notice Boris doesn't call me . . . He knows . . . I've had it . . . Had the plug pulled on me . . . Down the drain . . . Casualty or not . . . The life struggle . . . The novel? Chuck it away! Chuck everything away! I'm a ghost . . . Far away, dead, worm-eaten, out to pasture, forgotten, retired, on silent leave of absence . . . It can all happen in a couple of days . . .

Lynn arrives . . . She's shattered . . . I tell her what happened . . . She talks about the summer when she went to see Cyd at Easthampton . . .

"Did she tell you?"

"What?"

"About the child, of course" . . .

She's let it out . . . She goes pale and tries to bite it back, too late . . . God! . . . "I've got something to tell you . . . Tomorrow" . . . Poor darling . . . She must have prepared what she was going to say . . . Had it all ready when she came to the café . . . Now I come to think of it . . . Yes . . . The last time . . . Affectionate exasperation . . . I ought to have understood . . .

"I'm sorry," says Lynn.

"Since when?" I ask.

"A month, I think . . ." She hesitates . . . "Your last trip to New York?"

There's a glint in her gray eyes now . . . The swift demon . . . But still, not so *soon!* But of course we're going to make love anyway . . . In memory of Cyd . . .

495

She gives me her thesis on Faulkner, which she's turned into a book . . . It looks good . . . I concentrate on the quotations . . .

"The precipice, the dark precipice; all mankind before you went over it and lived and all after you will . . ."

Charlotte's yellow eyes in *The Wild Palms* . . .

"One always tends to forget her . . ."

"Yes," says Lynn, "though she's one of his most interesting characters."

"Have you noticed how it's in *The Wild Palms* that he stresses, quite coolly, that the 'race' of women is different from the 'race' of men? Strange . . . The black issue serves to conceal the real black issue . . . Perhaps that's why I like *Pylon* so much . . . The unbuttoning of the flies on the plane . . . The settling of scores in mid-air . . . The crimson sex of the guy forced to have an erection . . . The 'eternal unvanquished' " . . .

"And you can do nothing about it: maybe you thought all the time that when the moment came you could rein back, save something, maybe not, the instant comes and you know you cannot; you are one single abnegant affirmation, one single fluxive Yes out of the terror in which you surrender volition, hope, all — the darkness, the falling, the thunder of solitude, the shock, the death, the moment when, stopped physically by the ponderable clay, you feel all your life rush out of you into the pervading immemorial blind receptive matrix, the hot fluid blind foundation — grave-womb or womb-grave, it's all one."

"I like all those phrases," I say . . . "The avenues of adjectives . . . Arpeggios . . ."

"Do you remember the words the novel ends with?"

"Which one?"

"*The Wild Palms* . . . An apparently ordinary exclamation, but coming after all the rest it has an extraordinary effect . . . A sort of summary . . . A punctuation . . ."

"I've forgotten."

"*Women — t!" The tall convict said.*

"The tall convict . . . Yes . . . That's good . . . That's it . . ."

"It says more than Bachelard and Jung's interpretations, doesn't it?"

"Everyone defends himself as best he can . . ."

"Against what?"

"I don't know what to call it anymore . . . Literature?"

"Only literature?"

"The art of turning women upside down," I say . . . "Or rather the right way up . . . What makes them tick . . . Them and everything else . . ."

We go out for a drink or two . . . Have dinner . . . We talk about Cyd, in English . . . Go back to my studio . . . Lynn undresses right away, quite naturally . . . Wants to see my wound . . . Kisses the bandage . . . She's really back with Cyd . . . It's with her, and with me in her, and with her in me, that she wants to make love . . . With Cyd pregnant . . . Another person . . . And with Cyd dead . . . Yet another . . . Forever, this time . . . Until we too vanish . . .

"I really am sorry," says S. "It's terrible for you . . . But of course no one will believe us . . ."

"They need only look at the list of victims," I say.

"People don't notice . . . If you put the terrorist attack in the book it'll seem phony . . . Invented! Too pat! . . . Are you in pain?"

"No, it's almost finished now . . . Thanks for Wagner . . ."

"Elementary . . . But we haven't got poor Cyd anymore . . . Or rather, we've got her in a different way . . . Anyhow, what would you have done when she told you she was pregnant?"

"I'd have told her to get married as soon as possible," I say. "She'd mentioned some old boy who was practically a millionaire and was dying to marry her . . ."

"Was that true or made up?"

"True, I think . . . She was very attractive, you know."

"Yes, I see, the usual thing . . . Did I ever tell you I had a daughter, like that, somewhere in France?"

"How old? What's her name?"

"Laure. Seven."

"Do you see her?"

"Sometimes . . . As if by accident . . . With her mother, in a café . . . Or from a distance . . . Surreptitiously . . . She looks like me."

"And Sophie doesn't want to have children for the moment?"

"Oh yes she does! I can tell it's going to happen at any moment . . . The *novel* puts ideas in their heads, old boy . . ."

"Novels are very dangerous," I say seriously.

"Very . . . That's what makes them so interesting . . . In moments of crisis everyone comes around to them or thinks of doing so . . . It's particularly striking just now."

"Sade in '89? Proust and Joyce in '14? *The Sound and the Fury* in '29, at the height of the depression? And *Le Voyage au bout de la nuit*, in '32?"

"Yes . . . All novels say the same thing . . . Dead-end and convulsion . . . The unique truth of sensation . . . If possible! Despite the current *castrade* . . ."

"I was very fond of Cyd," I say.

"So was I, if you don't mind my saying so!"

"We're not going to let Lynn take her place?"

"I should think not! I imagine you're going to be a bit lonely on that score for a while . . . Still, that's up to you . . . If the novel is life itself, as the instinctive despair of the nations makes them suppose, you must admit we're right in the middle of it . . ."

"We've exceeded the estimates," I say.

"Good . . . A touch of magic . . . Now we must await events . . . A novel is like a magnet . . . All the rest is iron filings . . . From the most important matters down to the smallest detail . . . Wait and see how the story develops . . . Whatever you do, don't decide on anything in advance! Algebraical iron filings . . . Taking their time . . . Grain by grain . . . You listen, you watch, you note down . . . The melody accumulates . . . Are you leaving for Venice?"

498

"Venice?"

"Had you forgotten?"

"Oh yes . . ."

"Be careful, now! Don't do anything silly! No 'Death in Venice,' mind! Be a good sport!"

"I'll try . . . But I'm feeling pretty low . . ."

"Come on, now! Life, death . . . Happiness, horror . . . We have to keep our heads above water . . ."

"With only one arm?"

"With no arms at all, if necessary!"

"Have you ever really suffered?"

" 'Suffered'? That's a woman's word . . . But if you really want to know—yes, terribly!"

"All this summer Deb kept telling me a narrator had to suffer in order to be sympathetic . . . Had to be ill at ease in his body . . . Had to bleed a bit . . ."

"She wasn't really hinting we really have to feel he knows what castration is?" . . .

"Yes."

"Of course . . . Well, you look rather good with your arm in a sling! You'll just *melt* them, old man . . . Men and women . . . All men love a woman . . . All women love a man . . . Women! Men! They'll be all over you . . . Finish you off . . . They'll love that . . . Just what the doctor ordered . . ."

"I might point out that their first reaction was to show me the door . . ."

"Just for the moment! For your own good! Mark my words! They're blind . . . God be with you!"

S. is right to stick to his guns . . . It cheers me up a bit . . . He's back at his *Comedy* again . . . He doubted, yielded to all the negative forces ranged against him, made himself scarce, buried himself . . . And now there's a minor resurrection . . . *Secundum Scripturas* . . . He puts on a record . . . Haydn's Mass . . . The *Credo* . . . He laughs . . . The brute . . . What madness, what sanity!

"Would you like a jab of Marilyn Horne?"

That agile, hoarse, rapid mezzo-soprano . . . *Orlando Furioso*

. . . That swift spiral voice . . . He listens, head tilted back . . . Tense, lithe, as if about to spring . . . Salvation through the voice . . . I remember what Deb said once, when her work as an analyst was getting her down: that when you came right down to it, all you could find in women was hatred or megalomania . . . That, in comparison, men were modest little boys taking their first communion . . . So what's to be done with the women? Turn them into singers? Sirens? Bacchantes? Write them down? It's only for their own good, anyhow . . . And then ring down the curtain?

We go back, Lynn and I, to Cyd's studio . . . One suitcase is enough . . . Not much there . . . A white plastic bag in a closet, between two sweaters . . . Coke . . . So she had her little supply here too . . . Lynn takes some . . . I pretend not to see anything . . . I keep a blue scarf that she wore in London . . . When we've finished tidying up we draw the curtains and lie down on the bed . . . And it's then that Lynn suddenly starts to sob . . . And writhe . . . Her face is ravaged, distorted . . . She arches her back hysterically . . . The bridge of sighs has turned into a shrieking muscle . . . "Give me one! Give me one!" "What?" "A child!". . . Of course . . . She reaches a peak . . . I kiss her, try to calm her down . . . She goes on moaning: "The child . . . The baby . . . The little girl . . ." So they really did talk about it . . . Imagined it was between themselves . . . That they'd bring it up together . . . The little girl . . . I underestimated the passion of their relationship . . .

Lynn would be quite willing to stay . . . She'd come to Venice with me like a shot . . . Yet again I'm amazed at the incredible cool, interspersed with tears, that enables them to adapt realistically to any situation . . . They may be moved, but they don't let that stand in their way . . . Genetically oriented . . . Only natural they should have thought I was there to perpetuate them some time . . . To give them a foundation, identity, authenticity . . . To liberate them from themselves, replace them in time, cast them as in bronze . . . To bring about the birth of little Cydlynn . . . Sieglinde! Tattooing!

500

Compulsory placenta! And so on . . . Forever . . . The wheel . . . The movement of history . . . Ever more diverse and complex . . . Civilization . . . After all, we're better than the men of Lascaux, aren't we? And especially than their women? Obviously . . . You can't stop progress . . . The individual is just an incident . . . And the male is, at the most, merely a variant of that incident, a punctuation mark . . . What? What's that you say? You, a wretched drop in the ocean, claim to be as important as the vast adventure of the Whole? A part that's greater than the Whole? You've put up a "full house" notice? You must be crazy! You'd do better to give in before it's too late . . . Psychotic . . . Sure you don't want to commit suicide? Only a bit of friendly advice . . .

Lynn is intelligent . . . Aren't you feeling up to much? She soon pulls herself together . . . We part good friends . . . We'll probably be seeing one another in New York . . .

As well as the blue scarf I take the recording of the Scarlatti sonatas home with me . . . Wanda Landowska . . . An old record, Cyd's favorite . . . Evening . . .

The phone.

"Hello? So we got your Yankee girlfriend . . . Your turn next, you swine!"

A young, fanatical voice . . . Suburban . . . Some nutter trying to be in on what's going on . . . It happens all the time . . .

Phone again.

"So? Diddums get a scratch or two? Izzums feeling better?"

Flora . . . I hang up without saying anything . . . Disconnect the phone . . . Put Landowska on the turntable . . . Bury myself in the dark with the harpsichord . . . Little operas . . . Chinese lute . . . The recording was made at the beginning of the war, when the Germans were entering Paris . . . She went on playing while the bombs fell . . . Then she went to live in Connecticut . . . In Lakeville . . . Sublime Polishwoman! I've got a review about her: "Wanda Landowska possesses the extremely rare art of being able to slow down or accelerate time; to mould a phrase by means of tiny variations, like the brush-strokes of a painter; to make an almost imperceptible pause before an important note, a modulation or change of color; and, above all, to do all this in her own inimitable way, unhesitatingly and with complete assurance . . ."

She died in 1959 . . . Born in Warsaw in 1877 . . . And Scarlatti himself? Three years of intimacy with the Queen in Spain! Maria-Barbara . . . Hence his unique, invulnerable nervous system! Gigues, Sicilian dances, staccato chords, crotchets, quavers, guitars, castanets —the whole skeleton mastered and enclosed in the feathery keys! Capers with the left hand! Rhythm above all! A thousand and one afternoons for Her Majesty! Under the trees . . . By the fountains . . . In the boudoirs . . . Mischief! Energy! Love! Nothing else! Five hundred and fifty-five sonatas! Grace or disgrace . . . A steel wire! I listen, I forget everything, peace returns . . . The peace of cool blood, there, subterranean, celestial . . . Landowska gave her life to it . . . Like Haskill with Mozart . . . Women of another world . . . Intervals . . . Saviors . . . All for the intangible . . . Cyd . . . I die under their skillful fingers . . .

IX

Dead . . . Three-quarters dead . . . Half-dead . . . A quarter dead
. . . A tenth . . . A hundredth . . . A thousandth . . . A millionth
. . . I'm back! Or rather, I land . . . At Marco Polo . . . Between
sky and sea . . . I'm here . . . In Venice . . . City of the Holy Spirit
. . . Spirit itself . . . Yes! Yes! Don't fidget . . . Remain seated
until the engines have stopped . . . Seat-belt fastened . . . I explain
it to you, calm you down . . . Hand on brow, like that . . . A
compress—handkerchief, eau de Cologne . . . Smelling salts . . .
Mint sweets . . . Relax! Smile! Forget about Combes! Comte! Littré!
Michelet! Marx! Hegel! Freud! Swedenborg! Bakunin! Jules Verne!
Aristotle! Plato! Let yourself go! I'm moving you . . . De-necro-
phaging you . . . One last effort . . . Come on . . . To finish it
off . . .

The motoscafo leaps and laps along by the San Michele cemetery
. . . Yew trees, cypresses, pink walls, gulls on the cornices, white
angel . . . The rush of the wake . . . Horizontal cataract . . . Pleated
Niagara . . . We're entering the veins of the city . . . Little bridges
. . . We're getting to the heart . . . Liquid fan, fine spray cool on
your face . . . Pale and dazzling blue . . . San Marco . . . 829 . . .
Mark . . . One of the four . . . Body brought from Alexandria . . .
On camel-back . . . Wrapped in a pig's hide . . . To discourage any
frisking by the ultrafaithful . . . Islam . . . The Evangelist bound in
pure pig! As good as a coquille Saint-Jacques! Here we are . . .
Home! Marble, mosaics, light emanating from the walls . . . Five
hundred columns!

St. Mark was born in Jerusalem . . . Died a martyr in Egypt in

67 . . . Was converted by St. Peter himself, who calls him his "son" at the end of his first Epistle . . . Said to be good at languages . . . An interpreter . . . A born translator . . . Spoke Syriac, Greek and Latin . . . From the Hebrew, of course, which by a supreme denial everyone has done his best to forget . . . "Pax tibi, Marce, Evangelista meus . . ." Winged lion . . . Ancient disaster . . .

So here's the place . . . It could be worse . . .

Now? In our day?

You must admit the earth's a vast shambles . . . Where you don't know who's who anymore . . . Who's killing whom . . . Who's behind whom . . . Who's manipulating whom . . . The whole world's full of people touting heaven knows what . . . Open grave . . . Cars blowing up in the streets . . . Buildings collapsing . . . Synagogues being shot at . . . Executions in Palestinian camps . . . Sabra . . . Chatila . . . It really did happen, that Oradour of the East . . . What did they tell you . . . "Christian Militia . . . " With a pass from the Israeli Army . . . Poor corpses that have been shot, broken, had their throats cut . . . Women and children . . . Arafat went to see Jean Paul II just before . . . Scandal . . . The Pius XII story is dug out again! Arafat entertained like a head of state in Greece . . . Photograph in *Time*: he's on the deck of the *Atlantis*, somewhere between Beirut and Athens, reading the *Odyssey* . . . Homer as publicity . . . Why not? The Pantheon against Solomon is an old story . . . No one knows where to turn now? Blood on every hand? Satan staging a comeback? Laughter from the shades? . . . "The Pope's Polish, and the Poles are anti-Semitic" . . . It's started again worse than ever . . . "Genocide" . . . "Holocaust" . . . "Israel is the real enemy of the Jews . . ." Arab summit . . . Reagan in a rage . . . Warning from Brezhnev . . . France's good offices . . . Storm in the Knesset . . . "Goys have been killing goys . . ."

The front page full of bad language! Sensation! Sensation again! Terrorism and TV! Live! Electronic crime! The picture no more than a black hole! Death in the spotlight! In the old days the battle of Lepanto, in 1571, gave Titian time to paint his picture . . . One of his last . . . A year later . . . He's in Madrid . . . Spain, Genoa,

and Venice are led by Don John of Austria . . . For the Papacy . . .
Against the Turks . . . Right . . . It encouraged painting . . . But
now . . . Point blank! One corpse follows another at breakneck
speed! Not even time to make a sketch . . . To think about the
colors . . . The artist has to react with his own nervous system . . .
To answer the intangible . . . With antinerves! With his own marrow! What a job . . . No wonder there are no more decent paintings, no more symphonies, not a sign of a tolerable novel . . . No
more art! The Devil has spoken! Assassinations and supermarkets
. . . Blue ballets . . . On the boob-tube . . . At eight o'clock . . .
Dinner-time . . . A maelstrom of consumer goods . . . Movement
of capital based on the revolution of the earth . . . No room for the
slightest resistance . . . Sold! Screened! Devalued! Chuck it away!

I think of Cyd . . . How many others like her? General unfulfill-
ment . . . The price of a life today? Minus zero . . . Minus four
billion zeroes . . . Lungs, eyes, skin . . . Words . . . Then click!
Gone . . . Nothing left . . . I dare not think of her body . . . Our
actual gestures . . . Words . . . I just hear myself murmuring
sometimes: 'Poor child, poor child . . .'' She'll end up being only a
scar, here under my arm . . . Until my torso itself disappears . . .
In short, there's nothing except birth and death . . . And life, like
death . . . At once . . . Existence wiped out . . . Explosions . . .
Blanks . . . A mist of individuals . . . You . . . Me . . . The others
. . . Dust to dust!

Mustn't forget I'm convalescent . . . That I still have to sleep on
my right side . . . That I carry my abyss about with me, on my left
side . . . My spear wound . . . My Adam's rib . . .

Talking of Arafat going to see the Pope . . . I've kept the official
photograph of the interview . . . Arafat, unarmed, turning toward
His Holiness and smiling . . . Propaganda . . . And John Paul II
looking straight at the camera . . . All white . . . His face too . . .
But that gesture . . . Only a few people will notice it . . . The right
hand over the heart, with the thumb slightly spread . . . *In petto*
. . . To myself . . . But that's what I think . . . Secret communication, purloined letter . . . Prisoner! Hemmed in by the great powers
. . . Financial scandals? Russian pressure? You scratch my back and

I'll scratch yours? Who'll ever know? But it's a dramatic photo . . .
For the initiate . . . NBC has just revealed what all the professionals
suspected: that the KGB really was behind the attack in St. Peter's
Square . . . The Pope's supposed to have written to Brezhnev before
it happened, saying that if the Soviet army entered Poland he'd
resign and go back to Warsaw . . . The American press is full of it
. . . The French and other European papers hardly mention it . . .
The suicide or fake suicide of the banker Calvi in London . . . Under
a bridge . . . Mafia gone over to Qaddafi, the drug route . . . The
files of Italy's Grand Lodge seized . . . Suspicion hanging over Opus
Dei . . . It's certainly even harder to be Pope now than it was in
Dante's day . . . The Turkish killer, Ali Aqsa, spending seven weeks
in the best hotel in Sofia . . . Revenge for Lepanto! With a revolver!
Via Moscow! Direct hit in the intestines! And what are the novelists
telling you about while all this is going on? Trifles . . . Exotica . . .
The provinces . . . While the Novel unfolding before their eyes is
the most fabulous era ever . . . And what are the critics concerning
themselves with? Whether a certain great prewar writer interfered
with little boys standing up or sitting down . . .

I looked up at the Giudecca . . . I'm at the house of some friends,
on the Zattere al Spirito Santo, not far from the Salute . . . Over
the rose-covered balcony I can see the wind's light traces on the
water . . . Boats go by from all over the world . . . Green, yellow,
gray, brown, black . . . Wood, oil . . . The *Norwegian Challenger*
from Oslo . . . The *Royal Eagle* from Monrovia . . . The *Suavity*
from London . . . The *Pacific Arrow* from Tokyo . . . The little
Luki from Palermo . . . The *Romanza* from Panama . . . The *Kaptan Necdet* from Istanbul . . . The *Evangelia* from Limassol . . .
The *Corona Australe* from Genoa . . . The *Jasmine* from Haifa . . .
The *Vispy* from Trieste . . . The *Ziemia Kielecka* from Stettin . . .
The *Ras el Khaima* from Alexandria . . . The *Orpheus* from Athens
. . . The *Ikan Bilis* from Singapore . . . And others from Odessa,
Shanghai, Barcelona . . . The shuttle transporter *Ammiana*, carrying cars . . . And the tugs, black and white, with their Latin names,
going ceaselessly from left to right and right to left, writing their
litany: Maximus, Novus, Pardus, Geminus, Strenuus, Titanus, Val-

idus, Cetus, Ausus, Squalus . . . It never stops . . . The port is running a cool fever . . .

Names and logos, they're all there . . . The great logo war has started up again, obliterating names . . . And the ghost that haunts the signs is the scarcely forgotten swastika . . . This results in a daily chorus of parallels belted out in speeches and sprayed on walls . . . Hammer and sickle = swastika? Propaganda of the Polish resistance . . . Star of David = swastika? Communist propaganda . . . You sense that no one dares write up other hasty equations that have had their day and produced their own quota of corpses . . . For example: star of David = hammer and sickle . . . Or cross = swastika . . . Or, in the future, cross = crescent = swastika = hammer and sickle = star of David . . . Signed: skull and crossbones . . . And so on . . . Anything's possible . . . Sieg! Heil!

Anyhow, the symbol thing is back . . . With the Americans, and Nixon's X, it didn't much matter . . . Asia . . . Latin America . . . But now it's nearer and more definite . . . The Jewish communities are frightened, even here . . . They haven't quite made up their minds whether the cross or the hammer and sickle is their main enemy . . . People take good care to work them up against the Christians . . . That trick's still good . . . On the other hand, the crescent might become the sickle . . . Or the other way around . . . We're on the eve of a general, nameless fusion . . . Watch out for the Name! The Name is everything! Don't let them leave yours out . . . I, the Anonymous One, am giving you solemn warning through this book . . . That's why writers have always been kept under observation, and will be more and more . . . "You're telling me," S. will groan as he edits these lines . . .

Aldo's a journalist in Rome . . . He's just gone away on a trip . . . Sonia leaves me in peace . . . She has her children . . . I have a large, comfortable room at one end of the apartment . . . Everything will have closed down by October 15 and it will be the foggy Venice winter . . . But for the moment, summer goes on getting deeper and more shrouded . . . What a year! I don't know if the water is the water of the Hudson or the East River . . . The Ile de Ré or the Adriatic . . . The gulls are the same, though their cries

509

are different . . . The cupolas of the churches? Rome? Florence?
No, that's the Redentore on the other side of the canal, where the
Jacopo Tintoretto is gliding by . . . At this moment Deb and Stephen are arriving in New York . . . Settling in . . . On the East
Side . . . 90th Street . . . I'm joining them there in three weeks'
time . . . I'll have my column on European politics . . . We'll start
a new life there . . .

"Are you all right?"

Sonia comes to see if I need anything . . . She brings me a coffee
out on the balcony . . . Sits down . . . She's a dress designer . . .
Work-room, plate-glass windows . . . She's tall and rather serious
. . . We talk about her two sons . . .

"Are you working again yet?" she asks.

"A bit . . . It's starting to come back . . ."

"Does your arm still hurt?"

"No."

"Were you very friendly with the English girl?"

"Yes."

"Are you very upset?"

"Yes . . . Crazy, isn't it?"

"A journalist friend of ours was killed like that last year . . . It's
horrible . . . As if he'd never existed . . . Worse than an accident."

"Much worse."

"That's how it is."

"That's how it is."

"What's your novel about?"

"Oh, you know—the times we live in . . . Women, terrorism,
politics, journalism, money . . . The repercussions of the Middle
East . . ."

"All that?"

"Especially women . . ."

"Why 'women'?"

"They're the main element of what I'm trying to prove."

"Are you trying to prove something? In a novel? Not very good
for sales!"

"You never know!"

She laughs . . . We've known one another a long time . . . She doesn't give a damn . . . But nicely . . . She's very fond of Deb . . . She comes to Paris occasionally for the collections . . .

"Aren't you going to miss France?"

"I shouldn't think so . . . I like New York . . ."

"But still, Paris . . ."

"Maybe I'll be back . . . Anyhow, thanks for everything."

"Right, I'll leave you to it."

But she gives me a curious look . . . The spell of the novel . . . You're there and not there at the same time . . . Perhaps you're the one who really is there . . .

Do you know what he's doing there in the Piazzetta, St. Theodore, standing on his crocodile, watching over the entrance to Venice? Where is he from? He was martyred in 406 for setting fire to a temple dedicated to Cybele . . . Beside him is a winged lion . . . I enter the cave of San Marco, revisit the Pala d'Oro, 1105, Constantinople . . . Come out again . . . It's the end of the season but there are still some tourists about and Florian's is half full . . .

"Hello!"

Louise . . . She's here for a concert . . . With her Austrian girlfriend . . . I hadn't realized she'd become famous . . . The day after tomorrow Inge is singing Zerline in Mozart's *Don Giovanni* . . . Louise is performing the *Goldberg Variations* on the harpsichord . . . At the Palazzo Grassi . . . When? At the end of the week . . . They're cheerful and lively . . . It's like seeing Cyd and Lynn again in New York . . . We get on right away and decide to have lunch together . . . God *is* with me, no doubt about it . . . Which one? The one who wants this story to be written . . .

We're going to forget everything now! We're surrounded by music and Venice! Forget everything! And the rest! And everything again! Refuse to be blackmailed by sorrow . . . Come on! Let's go! Let's have fun! I take my two musicians by the hand and rush them off through the narrow streets, jostling the passers-by somewhat—

511

we're going to go and lie in the sun on my balcony . . . Sonia is
rather surprised . . . So soon? But she plays along and lends them a
couple of swimsuits . . . Inge keeps a scarf around her neck . . .
Because of her voice . . . I look at them . . . Louise, dark, short,
rather fat . . . Inge a slim, fair, fragile Viennese . . . Whatever you
do don't go into things too closely, don't get to know one another
too much, stay safe in melody and misunderstanding . . . We'll see
. . . Later on . . . The dread psychological moment . . . The time
for transactions . . . Everything depends on the order in which
things are done . . . You either start with gratuitous sex and keep it
up, or you begin with psychological negotiations . . . The rest
depends on your choice . . . Go straight for the act itself and
everything's resolved . . . Wait, and you get bogged down in characters and roles . . . Let's raise my baton and conduct the whole
thing . . . One, two, three . . . Rondo . . . Allegro . . . Where are
they staying? At the Luna . . . Are they free for dinner? Of course
. . . I warm them up one against the another . . . I start to sing . . .
Inge says my voice isn't at all bad, in fact it's very good, what a pity
I never had it trained . . . "Vivan le femmine! Viva il buon vino!"
"Excellent!" Louise stiffens . . . Sonia, confused, fetches some fruit
juice . . . The afternoon is like a new pin, boats sail by, vaporettos,
taxis bounding over the waves . . . A sudden soft breeze . . . 'Io mi
voglio divertir!" "Not bad! Not bad!" Inge coos a bit of Zerline in
reply . . . "Vedrai, carino, se sei buonino, che bel remedio to voglio
dar . . ." But now they have to go off to rehearsal . . . They get
dressed . . . Cover up their white skins again . . . I go with them
. . . Stay with Louise, who takes me to the Palazzo Grassi . . . Her
harpsichord is there . . . We're alone . . . I kiss her . . . She doesn't
mind . . . Her tongue's still warm and shy . . . Though less shy,
warmer . . . But she has to work . . . Yes, of course . . . She starts
on the *Variations*, and is immediately quite transformed . . . Her
face a firm, imperious mask . . . She's suddenly far away, even
though there are only a few feet between us . . . She's made
enormous progress! Nothing vague about her playing now . . .
She's really right in it, to the marrow . . . The wooden coffin
responds like a cathedral . . . Liquid nave and apse . . . Vaulting

become like feathers . . . She stops, dissatisfied . . . Starts again
. . . That's it . . . She shuts her eyes, goes on . . . Everything's to
be confronted again . . . Space stands up to her, then falls back and
unfolds, stave by stave . . . The hands, the ankles . . . The movement of the neck between the arms . . . The face down over the
supple neck . . . The rhythm of her breathing changes . . . She
stops to check the spiral she has now become . . . And is off again
. . . Her back free now, the spinal cord vibrating through her
finger-tips . . . The instrument is weightless now, she's got the
better of it, it floats . . . She makes it rise up in the air . . . Like a
medium's table . . . A table in a dream . . . A couch of harmony . . .
All by herself . . . It's as if she and her harpsichord were suspended
three feet up in the air above the parquet floor . . . She's teaching
me a lesson, is little Louise . . . Alla francese! Presto! She takes me
. . . Takes me with her . . . By heart . . . She's starting to perspire,
in her cherry-red dress with white spots . . . Just now, out in the
street, I noticed several times how her white panties outlined her
firm buttocks through her dress . . . Leather stool . . . Gently she
lifts the sensual weight of her arms, which gives strength and
endurance to her wrists . . . Both fat and nerve are necessary . . .
The *Goldberg Variations* echo through the empty palace . . . Paneling, gilt . . . She stops . . . The pedal-board, released, clicks like a
loom . . . An extra note, like a wrench, like a broken horn . . . The
aircraft, wings retracted, flies off on its own into inaudibility . . .
She keeps her eyes shut . . . "Scarlatti!" I whisper . . . She pretends she hasn't heard . . . She takes a deep breath, straightens up
. . . I remember the Sundays when she held me close to her by the
piano . . . She remains in suspense . . . So that I know she's
making a decision . . . And then she plunges in and flings the Gigue
in my face . . . Turmoil, bliss . . . Hands like propellers . . . Like
beaks . . . Crossing one another, jumping, swooping . . . This is it,
pure emotion . . . She turns her keyboard inside out, does what she
likes with it, breaks it down into its components, sends it off into
flashbacks . . . This time she's smiling . . . Enjoying herself . . .
Well, I'm going to cry . . . I do . . . Cry my eyes out, stupidly,
sitting there in my chair . . . She can see me . . . But takes no

notice . . . Goes on . . . Raping me . . . Darling slut . . . Implacable . . . I don't matter anymore, and neither does she . . . Neither does Scarlatti . . . What she's playing is the merciless black rain . . . Slashing at the window panes while the sun's shining, nothing to do with anything . . . The chastisement of muddle and mist . . . The proud refusal . . . She bites her lips, clings to the sorcery . . . She has gradually become transparent, a pendulum, perpetual motion . . . She slows down by stages . . . Re-enters the procession . . . Goes off under the windows . . . Turns around . . . Calls out a last farewell . . . Is silent . . .

For a couple of minutes we don't move . . . Then I get up and go and kiss the nape of her neck . . . It's wet with perspiration . . . She smells of cut grass . . . A lawn . . . A green evening . . .

We go to the Fenice for the rehearsals of *Don Giovanni* . . . I'm now part of the company, actor among the actors, musician among the musicians, stagehand, electrician . . . Italians, English people, Germans . . . Don Giovanni's a German . . . Leporello an Italian . . . Donna Anna is Scottish . . . Elvira a New Zealander . . . Don Ottavio's American . . . The conductor's Japanese . . . That should produce a kabuki atmosphere . . . "I think we know each other, don't we?" says Ottavio . . . "Aren't you a friend of the little Austrian girl's?" "What—my wife?" says the Spanish Masetto . . . Inge arrives . . . She rehearses the rape scene . . . "Gente! Aiuto! Aiuto Gente!" "Scellerato!" "Soccorretemi, son morta!" "O soccorretemi!" She shrieks very well . . . Louise and I sit in a corner . . . All the directions are given in English . . . Repeats . . . Details . . . Sets . . . Violins . . . Spotlights . . . Basses . . . I leave, arranging to meet them in the evening . . .

"I like your two friends," says Sonia. "Have you known them long?"

"Louise, yes. Not the other one."

"How old are they?"

"I think Louise is thirty. Inge's twenty-five."

"The fair one would make a very good model . . ."
"I prefer the dark one."
"I see" . . .
I go upstairs, get out my typewriter . . . The Bible and the JB are
set out beside me . . . Have I got something to write about exile?
Psalm 119? The longest, the most structured . . .

I am a stranger in the earth: hide not thy commandments
from me . . .

Stranger . . . Hebrew *gêr* . . . Psalms, *Tehillîm* . . . Praises,
from the verb *hillêl*, as in *hallelû-iah* . . .

My soul cleaveth unto the dust: quicken thou me according to
thy word . . .

I lie down on the bed with the window open . . . I can hear the
gulls, the throbbing of the ships . . . The sudden wake of some, the
steady swish of others . . . Water lapping against stone, the bridges,
the steps . . . I start to drowse . . . The typewriter is there on the
table, against the sky . . . I ought to take a photograph of it, from
in bed . . . And call it "Convalescence" . . . Or "Scarlatti" . . .
People would ask why . . . As if it were a painting . . .
    I fall fast asleep . . . Just manage to write down "Tiepolo" before
I drop off . . .
    I'm back in the hospital, in Paris . . . Cyd's bending over me . . .
Watching over me . . . Gazing at me . . . Her lips are moving . . .
She's murmuring something . . . She points to her chest, red with
blood . . . She doesn't say anything, just weeps . . . She points to
her stomach . . . Takes my hand and puts it there . . . It goes right
inside her, up to the elbow . . . I'm going to touch what she wanted
to tell me, the little ball, nipped in the bud . . . I feel her twist
slightly under my fingers . . . She's smiling now and shrugging her
shoulders . . . Life, death, laughter, suffering—all in smithereens
. . . I draw back my arm, covered in blood . . . She bows her head
. . . No hatred . . . No reproach . . . No love either . . . Something
better . . .
    The bells wake me . . . Six o'clock . . . Exile? I'm wide awake

now . . . The heavy sleep has gingered me up . . . Whisky, Psalm 16 . . .

I will bless the Lord, who hath given me counsel: my reins also instruct me in the night seasons.

I have set the Lord always before me: because he is at my right hand, I shall not be moved.

Therefore my heart is glad, and my glory rejoiceth: my flesh also shall rest in hope.

For thou wilt not leave my soul in hell; neither wilt thou suffer thine Holy One to see corruption.

Thou will show me the path of life: in thy presence is fulness of joy; at thy right hand there are pleasures for evermore.

Blessings in the back, joy in the liver . . . That's what god really is—the rest is just words . . . Back pains, enlarged liver . . . Jealousy . . . Hell . . . That simplifies matters . . . Death, life . . . Beware of lying and murder . . . And dishonesty . . . That's all . . . And music! Above all, and forever, music! Look at everything from the point of view of music, forget about all the rest, and every moment will be your native land . . .

The bells rise up from all around . . . San Giorgio . . . San Marco . . . La Salute . . . Il Redentore . . . Cymbals and timpani overlapping again and again . . . Regularly, high up, deep or shrill, above the roofs, out to sea . . . Down below are the ordinary events— christenings, funerals, weddings, confessions, communions . . . Trifles . . .

Marx was probably right: men's social existence determines their thought . . . But it's their prohibitions that count the most, and the effort needed to overcome them . . . Baroque follies . . . Bells to mark the end of the day, above mauve canals and ever pinker walls . . . the opium of the people? Yes, that's awful . . . So I'll have all the opium myself! Free! No one wants churches anymore? Give them to me, the walls, the ceilings, the sacristies, the altars, the chairs, the frescoes, the chapels, the pews, and the lamps! Every man to his taste . . . It's extraordinarily peaceful, morning and evening, under the cupolas surrounding Venice . . . Salons and boudoirs where, as in the past, you can experience speed and light and dark . . . Locks opened . . . Earth without form and void . . . Liquid chaos . . . Darkness above the abyss, spirit brooding over the waters . . . A sacristy with a tall window, branches tapping against it, a sketch by Veronese in the corner, and the serpent in the tree . . . Seven o'clock . . . I go out . . . I'm going to evening mass at the *Gesuati* . . . And then my musicians and I will go and have some grilled fish for dinner . . .

> *Le donne, i cavallier, l'arme, gli amori,*
> *le cortesie, l'audaci imprese, io canto . . .*

I recite it to them as we walk toward the boat station, beside the still bright oleanders . . . I think of the ones in Barcelona, and of Ysia that night on the hill . . . Women, knights, fighting, love, derring-do, acts of chivalry . . . Inge and Louise sing softly . . . Zerline, Inge says, is a perverse character . . . You have to portray her as hypocritical, with lowered eyes and sidelong glances, looking as if butter wouldn't melt in her mouth but ready to trap the dissolute nobleman whose promises she doesn't believe a word of . . . She just wants to use him to send her prices up . . . Have him caught red-handed . . . The symbolic big-shot . . . Social and conjugal advantages to be got out of it . . . *He* wanted to rape *her*, but she gets the better of him! No flies on her . . . She also gets the upper hand of her Masetto, who'll tremble for it his whole life long . . . She'll make love to him when and how she chooses, reminding him of her traumatic experience . . . A future mischievous shrew . . . "E un certo balsamo che porto adesso . . . Saper vorresti dove mi sta; sentilo battere, toccami qua . . ." She's still aroused by Don Giovanni . . . Like Anna, at bay, and with her father's murder on top of it all . . . You realize she'll spend the rest of her life in mourning, being followed around by that declamatory clot Ottavio . . . "Toccami qua!" The same character repeated . . .

We pass San Trovaso again, near the Salute . . . We go as far as the Customs and come back via the wharves . . . past the *Ibrahim*

Baybora from Istanbul, with DB TURKISH LINES written upon the hull in big black capitals . . . Gray and black, with yellow lines on the funnels . . . I invite them for a drink at my place, looking at the roses and the dark water . . . I sense that Louise, for the moment, doesn't want to go any further . . . Not before the concert . . . Of course . . . Sonia pulls rather a long face . . . We sit out in the open, on our deckchairs, without speaking . . . Inge puts on her silk scarf . . . They want to go back to their hotel . . . They go . . .

Sonia goes to bed . . . I phone Deb . . . Late afternoon over there . . . "Pussy!" Everything's fine! Yes . . . When am I coming? In three weeks . . . "An airplane, Papa!" shouts Stephen . . . "Don't forget!" Another airplane . . .

Midnight . . . It's very hot . . . I go down to the balcony again . . . Sonia's there, in a pajama jacket . . .

"You startled me," she says.

She quickly tucks her legs up under her. Her bare thighs on the blue cushion.

"Have they got stage fright about tomorrow?"

"It's tomorrow for Inge," I say. "Another two days for Louise."

"Have you called Deb?"

"Yes."

"Is she settled in? Does Stephen like it there?"

"Apparently . . . They're on the East River. I prefer the Hudson, for the sunsets, but never mind."

"Aldo phoned," says Sonia. "Still all this business about Israel . . . It's the first time people have been afraid of a wave of anti-Semitism here . . . The Jews in Milan and Rome are very worried . . . You know there was a big demonstration against Begin in Tel Aviv . . ."

"It was bound to happen," I say, "He ought to have agreed to an inquiry into the massacres in the Palestinian camps before he was forced to . . . Even if it was only for the media . . . The Israelis aren't much good at handling the media . . . Strangely enough . . . Anyhow, all that will distract attention from a lot of other things . . ."

"You mean the Ambrosiano affair? Lodge P2? the Mafia? The Red Brigades?"

"Among others . . . Here . . . Other things in other places . . ."

"What do you think about Arafat being received by the Pope?"

"Nothing in particular . . . Except perhaps that Israel will soon recognize him, and vice versa . . ."

"Will the Americans stop supporting Israel?"

"Oh no . . . But the Russians are keeping very quiet these days . . . Oh, to hell with it all."

"You're right, it's a bore. What *do* you think about?"

"My novel," I say. "I'd like to end it here. Talking about here."

"End in Venice? Isn't that a bit hackneyed?"

"It all depends on the angle . . . You know what I'd like to define more exactly at this moment?"

"No."

"What the word 'sexy' means."

"No one uses it anymore . . . It's old hat. . ."

"Even so . . . Do you know what it means?"

" 'Sexy'? Not 'sexual'?"

"Not at all the same thing!"

Sonia relaxes . . . Stretches out her legs . . . It's the first time we've been alone together . . . I've never really thought of her in relation to the question of questions . . . Maybe . . .

" 'Sexy . . .' " ponders Sonia . . . "Applied to a man or a woman?"

"I think it must mean the same for both, don't you think?"

"Yes . . . Someone who knows exactly what it's all about and doesn't attach too much importance to it?"

"That's not bad . . ."

"Someone who's always been loved more than they've loved?"

"That kind of person isn't necessarily sexy . . ."

"Someone who judges from a certain remove and doesn't say anything?"

"And who knows from experience that there's nothing to be expected from women?"

"Oh yes, that's not bad at all . . ."

"To summarize: someone sexual has too much sex, just as some-one asexual has too little . . . Someone sexy can take it or leave it, come through it unscathed, knows something about it . . . They need to look a bit blasé. . . Thoughtful . . . Detached . . . Childlike . . ."

"Childlike?"

"Childlike but sensual, distant but experienced . . ."

"Yes."

We mention names . . . It makes an amusing game . . . Writers, actors and actresses, singers, male and female politicians . . . Heterosexuals, homosexuals . . . That's no longer the problem . . . The good old American word makes a useful category . . . Of course it's impossible to be both sexy and sexist . . . Sexy still has an air of mystery, it's difficult to pin it down completely . . . Someone quite chaste can be sexy . . . Someone quite depraved too . . . A pervert or the opposite . . .

"Someone who's sexual independently of any sexual reference?" says Sonia.

"Be careful—we're not talking about charm . . . A person can have charm without being sexy . . . On the other hand, anyone who's sexy usually has charm . . . But sometimes they don't . . . He or she is just sexy, that's all."

"Someone who knows how to experience pleasure? In him- or herself?"

"You talk about 'knowledge'? Yes, but without attaching too much importance to it . . . Otherwise people like that are very unattractive . . ."

"Desperate narcissists?"

"Unable to be fascinated by anything. Not even by themselves."

"They create inexplicable hostility. But it gets results."

"That's a good way of putting it — 'successful hostility . . .' They treat the body as gratuitous . . . Hence all sorts of crises . . ."

"Good-looking or not?"

"Neither here nor there."

"Truthful or not?"

"Truthful, probably . . ."

"But why are you so interested?"

"I want to define a new civilization! And that's the supreme criterion!"

"It's all very American, isn't it? Anyhow, it's bound to mix up good people and bad . . . Perhaps even torturers and victims . . . Your criterion's immoral! It doesn't apply! It's too subjective!"

She laughs . . . We don't say anything for a while . . . We smoke . . . The water slaps against the stone quay and washes over the edge . . . Just a few motoscafi on the Giudecca . . . I look at Sonia sitting in the shadow, her tall, gracefully stooped body, her chestnut hair . . . I can just see her bright brown eyes . . . She's wearing only the jacket of her white pajamas . . . She knows I know, and that I know she knows I know.

"One last drink?"

"There's some mineral water in the fridge . . ."

"I'll have some too."

I come back with glasses of cold fizzy water . . . I hold hers out to her . . . Kiss her forehead in passing . . . She's curled up again on her cushion . . . She shivers . . .

"Cold?"

"Oh no."

Silence again . . . This wasn't at all on the agenda . . . It may even upset it . . . Never mind . . . It's the silence that decides things at times like this—the weight of the air . . . After all, I did all I could to arouse her indirectly with my two girlfriends . . . At this point it would be uncouth not to do anything . . . But in fact it's she who gets up, comes over and sits on my lap, feels for my mouth . . . Stays like that . . . Stirs a little . . . I stroke her legs, her buttocks . . . She slips her hand down to open my fly, takes out my prick . . . Straddles me . . . Directly . . . Moves, starts to moan and turn her head from side to side . . . "Oh, marvelous," she whispers . . . "Marvelous, darling . . ." She moves back and forth for some time, gently . . . Professional . . . Realistic . . . Late evening . . . Interlude . . . Ideal sleeping pill . . . We both come, finally, suppressing our cries of satisfaction . . . We wait a little . . . She kisses me . . . Throws her head back, stretches and stands up, holding her hand in front of her to prevent the semen from spilling out . . . The perfect hostess . . . Kisses me again . . . "Good-night . . ." Vanishes . . .

Tiepolo! Giambattista! The underrated! The last of the great Venetians! Who shuts heaven's gate for two and a half centuries! Immediately after him, the tunnel . . . Vivaldi and he are the sunset cries . . . No one ever had a clearer premonition of an end . . . Nor ever defied it with such a dazzling outburst of nervous energy . . . The necessary explosion . . . Brought about with brushes and bows, bows bent into brushes, a concentrated mass of strings, a frantic sunburst, a dark and virulent bombshell . . . Color at the end of its tether . . . Rhythm the same . . . It's really the end, hard to take the extreme pleasure of limits any further . . . They know it, they lift the curtain on it a little, throw it overboard for later on . . . For someone else, one day . . . Perhaps . . . Or perhaps never . . . No hope in gatherings and groups . . . One for one . . . In aid of one . . . Always one . . . One forever! Never mind the different kinds of carnage! Of flattening! Of squashing into nothing! Here's another one, just the same! And another! He breathes a little, enjoys, takes pleasure, expresses himself, collapses . . . Next, please! Twenty years later . . . Fifty . . . A hundred . . . A thousand if necessary . . . Everyone's in a great hurry, but that's not right, continuity proves nothing, interruption rules . . . When you're on a vertical you can't see how a horizontal can refute you . . . All it can do, the inflatable horizontal, is prevent most bodies from meeting themselves as they meet you in the flames . . . Venice declines, but Madrid is just beginning . . . Subversion of surface and sound has taken refuge in Spain . . . Fleeing revolutionary reduction and tidying up . . . The French . . . Stendhal comes to an Italy that's deserted . . . He looks for wonders next door . . . The satanic Goya's already there . . . The diabolical Picasso is to come . . .

A mystic and a free-thinker? Tiepolo? Of course . . . He stirs up the heights and the lower depths . . . Ceilings, caves . . . St. Dom-

inic's flight beyond this globe, borne by cherubim up to the Virgin
. . . Grays, yellows, whites, blues, reflected reds, sienna . . . Venice
is a Dominican city, a city of serenity and contemplation . . . The
Serenissima . . . Seraphs are for Florence . . . For the ascension of
Christ, Mantegna's for instance, surrounded by his burning baby
reactors, au revoir . . . Here, on the other hand, everything's open,
all the time, inside and out . . . On its way . . . Transfer! Trans-
port! A house in the air, sails spread, wings and legs amid trumpets,
crowns and chariots . . . With a bound, you take space with you
. . . A fig for gravity . . . Even Titian's *Assumption* looks timid in
comparison . . . And heaven knows . . . Eppur si muove! At last!
What if she breaks loose? As a body! What if she hasn't got a soul!
Have the courage to say so! No soul! Wham! Therefore either
weight or balloon! Impossible to detach her from herself, as in the
complicated operation of crucifixion-deposition-burial-resurrection
. . . Here the frame must disappear of its own accord . . . The
surface must yield . . . Tiepolo multiplies this detachment of the
retina by a hundred . . . Which isn't to say he doesn't concern
himself with the cellars . . . On the contrary . . . Diana and Ac-
taeon . . . The rape of Europa . . . All the little gold-digging,
thieving, fucking goddesses . . . On his palette, in chinks in the
rock . . . With buoyant bulls, dimly suggested eagles, little boys
peeing . . . The pale mannerisms of someone who knows what's
what . . . Farmyard and bath-house aviary . . . Goddesses below
. . . Saints above . . . A place for everything . . . And set it all
alight! Tambourine! From deepest throats to fine ecstatic death-
rattle . . . Do you want me to draw it? All right . . . These Venetians are imperturbable! Determined to cause pleasure, all the rest
is lies, they'll never give in, they'd rather die . . . Incurable! . . .
Zattere agli incurabili—that's the name of a quay, just near the
quay of the Holy Spirit . . . Near the bridge of Humility, to make
sure there's no mistake . . . Humility, fumability . . . Glorious
bodies? What are their four canonic qualities? Do you remember?
Yes — impassibility, subtlety, agility, clarity . . . So let come what
may! Convicts redeemed on all sides . . . Rock reduced to dust . . .
Crumpled to powder . . . Good-bye stone!

I know: it's offensive, it's irritating, it goes too far . . . Superficial! Not serious! Erotomaniac! Megalomaniac! I can hear the shrinks' lobby already . . . Couch-armchair, petrification, lemurs' tomb . . . Lemurs have false ears too . . . Unions . . . Scouts . . . Abstract temple . . . All the flesh ceaselessly frustrated! The levitation all over the place! No soul! Everything physical! It was about time they were introduced to the Cogito . . . The Ego . . . Equality . . . A great leap backward . . . Compulsory castration . . . No more elite of castrati singers! The same operation for all! Universal reform . . . The State! The Moi! Hatred for all! All against one!

The surprising thing is that all these obscene paintings haven't been banned . . . That they're still here, scarcely transposed at all, in the middle of the mass . . . But in reality they are banned . . . Inside people's heads . . . No enthusiasm allowed! Flying forbidden!

I can still hear Francesca, quite pale, saying to me in Paris: "Please, no 'god'! Not at any price!" I don't remember why . . . But I wasn't going to tell her she shouldn't reveal her frigidity in that way . . . The rational darling . . . Always on the way to another massage . . . Another jab . . . What a coincidence . . . These women—they think they're living in genuine reality . . . A matter of temperature . . . They think "god" is their mummy hippopotamus they have such trouble getting out of . . . No luck with men . . . *They*'re still clinging to their mummy rhinoceros, imagining they're her horn or her nose . . . My god! My god! But there aren't any men left in Tiepolo . . . Only all that scrambled mythology and confused flights to heaven . . . Man is only a baby or an image on a cross . . . That's what he is anyway, to a woman . . . But she thinks she's detached! Launched! Put into orbit! Her desire is acknowledged . . . Supported . . . Approved of . . . And then it's turned over . . . Turned over and left to float! That's the mixture!

Louise phones.

"Will?"

"How are you?"

"Are you coming to the show this evening?"

"Of course."

"Shall we meet in the bar next door?"

"O.K."

"Are you bringing Sonia?"

"She can't come."

"See you later!"

"Is Inge feeling all right?"

"She's asleep" . . .

Sonia comes into my room . . . Perfect . . . As if nothing had happened . . . She gives me the keys . . .

"Are you making progress?"

"A bit."

"What are you on now?"

"Tiepolo . . ."

"Oh. Do you like him?"

"Very much."

"I thought you were more modern . . ."

"But he *is* modern . . ."

"You must explain it to me" . . .

She kisses me . . . Her sons are waiting for her . . . I go down and install myself on the balcony, in the bluish light . . . I type our conversation straight onto the machine . . .

To tell the truth, I'm bored by the show before it begins . . . I know *Don Giovanni* by heart . . . The rehearsal was enough for me . . . I hang about backstage with Louise . . . We talk undisturbed in a corner . . . I expound my thoughts about Sade and Mozart . . . The parallel between them . . . Suddenly a picture of my conversation with Cyd rises up before me . . . So vivid and exact that I shut my eyes . . . The Overture is just filling the red and gold theater . . . The Japanese is approaching it very emphatically, gloomily, with a slight trace of cruelty . . .

"Yes?" says Louise.

"You know we have the *Memoirs* of Da Ponte, the librettist . . . He tells how, to get himself into the right frame of mind, he spent one night reading Dante's *Inferno* . . . *Don Giovanni* was written with Dante in mind . . . Curious, isn't it? And do you know what Da Ponte wrote about Mozart?''

"No?"

I get out my notebook . . .

'' 'Mozart, although endowed by Nature with a genius perhaps superior to that of all other composers in the world, past, present and future, had not yet been able to display that divine genius in Vienna because of the machinations of his enemies. He remained obscure and unrecognized there, like a precious stone buried deep in the earth and forced to hide the secret of its splendor.' ''

"Mozart a hidden jewel? That's hard to believe . . .''

"Let's take it a little further . . . Divine genius, divine marquis . . . The music we can hear now was exactly contemporary with *Juliette* . . . Just imagine . . . The opera is performed in the background, and between the arias everything stops and passages from Sade are read aloud . . . That's one of my dreams . . . I think it would throw light on everything . . . *Juliette et les prosperités du vice*, libretto by Donatien Alphonse François de Sade, music by Wolfgang Amadeus Mozart . . . It was unthinkable at the time, but why not now? People must have thought of it a dozen times . . .''

I take *Juliette* out of my pocket . . . Louise looks at me in amazement . . . During the duel between Don Giovanni and the Commander I start to read aloud, quietly . . . Inge comes up and listens . . . Zerline herself! In costume! That marvelous, subtle little goose Zerline! With her big blue eyes . . . Louise is dressed in black . . . Shining black eyes . . . Elvire looks at us curiously from a distance, patting her wig nervously . . . Now . . . The sword and the orchestra both plunge into the body of the Law . . . Never has the French language been so beautiful and precise . . . What nobility! What lofty sentiments! What courage! What knowledge of places! What geometry!

"She was sitting near us, half naked . . . Her wonderful bosom was almost on a level with our faces . . . It amused her to have us screwed . . . She watched us, looking at the saucer tinged with our blood . . . First we were touched on the clitoris, then, very skilfully, in the cunt and in the ass-hole; both these orifices were tongued . . . Then our legs were raised and tied in place with cords, and a somewhat mediocre penis was inserted into the two openings alternately."

I spare you the rest of the horrors . . . After all, I don't know who you are . . . I've chosen one of the most impressive passages in *Juliette*, the one in which magic plays a part . . . Mme. Durand . . . Poison, echoing the affair so well described by Mme. De Sévigné . . . Mme. Voisin . . . The sylph . . . Slow, murky murders, such as one dreams of . . . Bones protruding from the ground . . . Hell as it really is . . . Acted, not suffered . . . "How revolting!" says Inge, smiling as she moves away . . . Louise goes on listening . . . I'm paying her back for her trick with the harpsichord . . . I read with as little expression as possible . . . No need for special effects . . .

"How do you see it?" says Louise . . . "As a film?"

"Perhaps . . . But it's a film we're already in, darling."

"That's enough. You're crazy. You'll disturb the performance" . . .

She kisses me on the forehead . . . We go and give Inge some support. . . She's doing very well . . . "Soccorretemi!" Don Giovanni, the German, is more than adequate . . . The Commander, Italian, is a little bit tired . . . The Englishwoman and the woman from New Zealand are superprofessionals and somewhat cold . . . Leporello is excellent . . . Sings the catalogue at a great pace . . . Masetto's too simple . . . Ottavio, the American, is definitely too much of a fairy . . . Never mind, it's a good show and the audience is happy . . .

"Pentiti!"

"No!"

The choruses pound out the final curse . . . The hero bawls from beyond the grave . . . The Japanese draws squeaks from the strings . . . Introduces the four principals . . . Bravo . . .

Inge is radiant and perspiring . . . Are we all going on to the party? What party? On the English yacht . . . It arrived yesterday and is moored in front of the Customs . . . Who owns it? A producer . . . Who? A *pro-duc-er* . . .

Inge takes us on board . . . A converted three-master flying a Union Jack . . . So crammed with people in evening dress it looks as if it will sink . . . I hold Louise's hand . . .

"Well, well—I thought you were in New York!"

A mocking voice, sharp with aggression . . . No doubt about it . . . I turn around . . . Flora . . . Dressed all in white, with Malmora in a dinner jacket . . . I introduce Louise and Inge . . .

"I think you were singing Zerlina just now?" says Malmora, trying it on.

"Are you a journalist?" Flora asks Louise.

"A harpsichordist."

"What?"

"A harp-si-chord player."

Flora looks at me. Inquiringly . . . What am I doing in Venice with a harpsichordist?

"Can I speak to you for a minute?"

We go to the end of the deck . . . Fireworks are going off in the distance . . . The Lido . . .

"Well, you look as if you're better . . ."

"It was nothing . . ."

"And the girl you were with?"

". . . ."

"Another of your conquests?"

"Listen . . ."

"And that little brunette—are you screwing her?"

"Please . . ."

"Anyhow, I don't give a damn . . . Did you know Malmora wants to marry me?"

"An excellent idea . . . Are you going to accept?"

"I can't make up my mind . . . He *is* very old . . . And stingy,

528

as you know! Still, one can't expect passion every day, can one, darling? You see how sensible I am? Are you going to the States?"

"In two weeks' time. How about you?"

"I'm going back to Spain. You know the socialists are in the process of winning there?"

"So I see from the papers . . . Only natural . . . But the Pope's going to Spain too, to try to pep up St. John of the Cross and St. Teresa of Avila . . ."

"And Opus Dei," says Flora.

"Which is apparently no worse than Lodge P2 . . ."

"You ought to come to Madrid . . . We're going to need people like you, in spite of your absurdities . . . There'll be things to do . . ."

"I'll probably drop by . . . Why not?"

"We're still friends?"

"Of course . . ."

The boat rocks slightly as we pass San Giorgio and the Redentore . . . The butler brings us glasses of champagne . . .

"I hear you were in Israel recently?" says Flora.

"Yes."

"You really have a gift for going where you shouldn't!"

"It was very interesting . . . Personal reasons . . ."

"Yet another girl?"

"Certainly not."

"You've never understood the first thing about politics . . ."

"It's politics that doesn't understand me!"

"Are you talking about Israel?" says Malmora, coming up with Inge and Louise.

"Not really," I answer . . . "There's quite enough about it in the papers."

"I'm terribly worried," says Malmora "But fortunately it's a democracy . . . And the Americans are making some progress . . . The massacre in Beirut is awful . . . But the Fez summit is a good thing, isn't it?"

"I hear your last novel is very good," says Louise. "And that it's been a great hit?"

She takes my hand . . . Flora sees.

"Not bad, not bad," says Malmora complacently.

The eternal cycle . . . Almost exactly the same scene as a year ago . . . We'll have got it word perfect before long . . .

"Do you like the Bible?" I ask Malmora.

"Huh?"

"I asked if you liked the Bible."

"Well . . . naturally . . . Why do you ask?"

"To have you on," says Flora.

"Huh?"

"A harpsichordist, eh?" says Flora, looking Louise straight in the eye.

"Yes . . . I'm giving a concert the day after tomorrow . . . Why don't you come?"

"Where?" says Malmora.

"The Palazzo Grassi . . . The *Goldberg Variations.*"

"The what *Variations?*" says Flora.

"You know—Bach," says Malmora.

"So now he likes the harpsichord?" says Flora, with a glance at me.

"Now?" says Louise.

"Anyhow, you were wonderful, extraordinary!" says Malmora, turning to Inge.

"Thanks to Will's advice," she answers.

"Really?" says Malmora . . . "I've never seen the part played with such subtlety . . . That duplicity! Would you care to have lunch with me—with us—tomorrow?"

"Con molto piacere," says Inge, with a little curtsey.

Flora edges me toward the rail . . .

"I'm at the Danieli, room 235," she whispers . . . "Will you come around later?"

Louise takes my arm . . .

"Will? It's getting rather crowded . . . Shall we go?"

I make a sign to Flora, conveying neither yes nor no . . . No, then.

"Look out for your harpsichord," says Flora, not looking at Louise.

"Oh, I always take great care," says Louise.

Inge stays on with some friends . . . Louise and I disembark at the Zattere ai Saloni . . . And here's the Zattere agli Incurabili . . . "What does *Zattere* mean," asks Louise . . . Rafts . . . There must have been rafts once where the quays are now . . . For incurables? Lepers? Plague victims? Yes . . . A boat goes by—black, with green and yellow lights . . . The moon is almost full over the Redentore . . .

"That Flora seems very interested in you?" says Louise.

"An old acquaintance . . ."

"What does she do?"

"Politics . . . Journalism . . ."

"Are you cross?"

"A bit" . . .

She takes *Juliette* out of my pocket.

"Can I borrow it?"

"Sure."

I see her back to the Luna . . . This time she kisses me . . . At length . . . Properly . . .

Seven in the morning . . . Bells . . . Chimes, a broken row of beads, a necklace unstrung, a rosary . . . Bing-bong! Bing-bong! This time I stay where I am . . . Louise phones . . . She's rehearsing . . . Sonia brings me the papers . . . I'm on the balcony, my face and my typewriter both in the sun . . . I wish I could make the typewriter bound along like the motorboats whizzing over the canal . . . Perhaps just a glance at the papers? Attack on a synagogue in Rome . . . Two children killed . . . Thirty-four people injured . . . The Italian press, especially the Socialist and Communist papers, has been violently anti-Israel lately . . . Caricatures that are blatantly anti-Semitic . . . The killers realized the atmosphere was

531

favorable . . . Solidarity banned in Poland . . . The Pope canonizes Maximilian Kolbe, a Franciscan martyred at Auschwitz — the first person to be made a saint since the Second World War . . . Beirut, Jerusalem, Germany, the mark . . . Dollar at 7.18 francs . . . War . . . The old war . . .

Hey, a piece about the "Nobel babies"! The first was born six months ago . . . A girl . . . Vittoria . . . From the sperm of a famous but anonymous mathematician . . . But I see the mother disappointed the Insemination Bank . . . They found out she'd been in prison for ill-treating her first two, "natural" children . . . And another mother taking part in the experiment doesn't want to get married now . . . Whereas it's the rule that the women involved have to be the wives of husbands who are sterile . . . Never mind, there are a couple of hundred experiments under way . . . Women are competing to get on waiting lists . . . The occasional slip-up among the ova? Such as the pairing of mathematics with delinquency . . . Nuclear physics and kleptomania . . . The head of the Bank is accused of being a Nazi . . . He admits to being an "elitist" . . . I can't understand why he's under fire . . . He's only on the same mad slope as everyone else . . . "Who fertilizes an egg can take semen from an ox" . . . It should produce some interesting results . . .

I crouch over my Hermes . . . Snuff the roses . . . Oh what a beautiful morning . . . The water, the air, the gulls . . . Glitter of light, sound of airplanes, of hammering on hulls, of ships' turbines . . .

"Yooo-hooo!"

Sonia . . . She's going jogging along the quays, over by the Salute . . . In gray track-suit and trainers . . . Am I coming too? No . . .

Imitation! Copying! Multieverything! Have I talked about it before? A matter of timing! It's not new, but now it takes on its true importance . . . Duplicates! Dubbings! Doublings! The Original in crisis! The Origyne instead! A typhoon of *likes*, a tidal wave of *ases*, magnetic clouds of similes . . . It's touching, pathetic, this insurrection in aid of sameness . . . This frenzied fraternity . . .

532

You can see why women are starting to be chary . . . They insist on selection . . . Not just any old injection from anybody! Scientific guarantees! A genuine Nobel prizewinner . . . Patented . . . Select spermatozoa . . . Proven stud . . . Copyright! Where would we be if we couldn't rely on our currency? No more names, if you like, but the great Anonymous Name, the authentic gene! Reliable! With degrees! Decorations! Established heredity . . . Mind! Cortex! The Bank announces that after the Nobel prizewinners they'll be having recourse to sports champions . . . On your marks! Get set! Go! Discus! Javelin! Hammer! 110 meter hurdles! 100 meters! 5,000 and 10,000 meters! Marathon! Pole vault! Butterfly stroke! Crawl! Ping-pong! Tennis! Rugby! Baseball! Football! Peashooters! Tossing the caber! Weight-lifting! They're going to open special surgeries in sports stadiums . . . Near the infirmary . . . They'll take the semen a week after the games . . . When the guys are rested . . . Women will start following matches closely on television . . . And make their choice à la carte . . . Husbands will be very worried . . . They're sterile by definition . . . Greece will be the model Republic again! Geneticist and Platonic! From the Gymnasium to the Symposium, from the Symposium to the Uterine Syringe! Order your Ideas by post! I must put my name down for the forthcoming celebrations on Olympia! I'll be Pindar! I'll cry up the wares! The muscles, biceps, quadriceps! The immaculate triception! The different varieties of sweat . . . The nobility of backs, legs, buttocks . . . The clearness of eyes . . . The excellence of torsos . . . There are already agencies selling plots of land on Mars . . . So you can imagine what it will be like with the fundamental plankton! And there are plenty of female customers! I propose to negotiate with the SGIC and WOMANN! They need a poet! For the publicity!

And then, after the Nobel prizewinners and the sportsmen, they could consider using musicians! Pianists, violinists, clarinettists, percussionists! For the more refined clients! It's only natural to start with Science and Sport . . . Obviously that must produce fine children . . . Like eating fish . . . But still . . . Singers! Rock! Have they ever thought of using the Beatles? Maybe not! And what about the black market? You can imagine the profits from under-the-counter capsules of sperm . . . In the country . . . The suburbs . . . Everywhere . . .

And how about painters? Writers? Hmm . . . Doubtful . . . Onanism . . . Unreliable product . . . Tired . . . Polluted . . . Twisted penises . . . Unhealthy . . .

In short, this is human revolution in a nutshell . . . Irresistible market approach . . . Exposed at last . . . Last judgment . . . Stocks . . . Hothouses . . . Underground cold storage . . . Morgues, cemeteries and charnel-houses can be done away with forever . . . Too terrestrial! Fire! Fire! At once! Crematoria pointed the way . . . For one corpse that's lost, a thousand more are possible! And better! For the galaxies! To populate the whole cosmos! Stellar West Bank! Superman! Space Odyssey! Every virgin womb delighted in the Milky Way of the future! Frankenstein! Dracula? Too bad! It all leads up to the Absolute!

But tell me this—what side will the babies belong to? There'll be a conflict of influence . . . I'm the daughter of a distinguished expert on functions . . . My father was a champion high-jumper . . . My grandfather swam the Channel . . . Mine won prizes for canoeing . . . And mine invented the electronic eyebrow! The one that split the atom just at the right moment! And mine was a hero of labor! All mutants will be numbered . . . Legion of honor! First class!

Of course, records will be a problem . . . Trying to trace family trees . . . You can't stop them from dreaming . . . They'll need a literature . . . Feelings . . . But we'll see to that! Instead of writing about any old thing, or telling for the umpteenth time about their aunt who lived in the provinces and how a biscuit suddenly brought back their childhood in Mayonnaise-on-Cucumber, novelists will work in teams to produce imaginary biographies . . . They'll labor day and night in groups . . . Be paid wages . . . There'll be new prizes . . . The Spermaton instead of the Goncourt . . . The Ovula instead of the Femina . . . And lesser awards like the Injectol, the Matricis, the Pondal, the Grand Prix of the Académie Genèse . . . The Nobel Prize will stay as it is, of course . . . But only children of Nobel laureates will be allowed to win it . . . But really only one of them will be truly mysterious . . . The one who called himself the Son of God, derived directly from the Other without any injection . . . He'll be remembered after a few centuries if they haven't destroyed all the books . . . Around the year 6000 . . . Or 7000 . . . Well done! The Messiah reappears in his glory over the grand gynecological center . . .

You think I'm joking? Not altogether . . . The trend exists . . . Down with literature! I could be the last writer out of captivity . . . The Chinese in Cognac? Or in Epernay? One of Céline's fantasies . . . Champagne got the better of him? Merely bubbles in the glass? No, it's more to do with the biological depths . . . Céline drank too much water . . . The Pléaide? . . . Not much comfort! But on Bible paper? You'd need to consecrate it first! . . . But he saw as no one else has . . . Those staccato phrases . . . And I carry on the good work! I amplify him! Correct him! He's given me his spermission! And so have the others! All of them! Fate!

Beginning with the prophets, and their visions of floating scrolls . . . To show it's been written outside the pages themselves . . . Scrolls they have to swallow, what's more . . . Take that, son of man, and eat it . . . Honey that makes you throw up . . . Sweet to the taste, agony for the stomach . . . Burned lips . . . Isaiah, Ezekiel, John, Zachariah . . . No chronology! The flying curse . . . Babylon! Paris! Patmos! The same story? Of course! Always the same . . . The same author under different names? Sure! You've got some nerve! Who do you think you are? Incredible! Unbearable! Ridiculous! Grotesque! But no one can stop you doing the same . . . Here, take the zither! Sing your own song! Write your own novel! Since you think you know how! They're all gathered together on Olympus . . . Parnassus . . . Or rather, near Elohim . . . Anyhow, all together . . . Exceptional unanimity . . . In favor of sending me . . . Special envoy . . . They've taken a vote . . . It's me . . . All the otherwise irreconcilable factions have agreed on my name . . . Jerusalem, Rome, Mecca . . . Homer, Shakespeare, Jeremiah! Mark! Desperate ills, desperate remedies . . . Wasn't there

anyone else? More talented? More genuine? Apparently not . . .
Sorry . . . Too bad for morality! Rhythm must come first! Arrows,
voices, thunder, lightning!

The funny thing is they always think it happens of its own accord
and doesn't need anyone to do it . . . And that therefore this
anyone can be got rid of . . . Jeremiah 18:18:

> They said they, Come, and let us devise devices against Jere-
> miah: for the law shall not perish from the priest, nor counsel
> from the wise, nor the word from the prophet . . . Come, and
> let us smite him with the tongue, and let us not give heed to
> any of his words . . ."

Religious psychology . . . Psychology in general . . . The community against the name, the crowd against the one, the letter
against the spirit, the seed against the exception that springs from
it . . .

I look up . . . The day has passed like the wing of a bird . . . A
red sun, to the right, over mercury-colored water . . . A few drifts
of smoke . . . A fine day, and it will be fine again tomorrow . . .
Strips of yellow, jade, purple, and orange sky . . . A bright moon
on a ground of Tiepolo gray-blue . . . And then the whole horizon,
seraphic sky and seraphic sea, all bursts into fervent flame . . . A
river of blood . . . Couples go out . . . Dark-skinned girls . . . The
dark red background doesn't change . . . In the east, calm . . .
Venice is pink, blue, black, all set on fire . . . Jerusalem is moun-
tainous, black, a mirror-image memory . . . All in the palm of my
hand . . .

Sonia takes me out to dinner . . . At some countess's . . . Everyone's there . . . Malmora, fussing around Inge . . . Flora, who
scarcely acknowledges me . . . The musicians . . . Louise, radiant,
warm from her day's work . . .

"I've just read an article by Garcia Marquez, published in Mexico," says Malmora "It's the toughest attack I've seen on the Israeli

government . . . He says Begin ought to be given a Nobel Death Prize."

"To protest against that awful Beirut business?" says the Countess.

"Yes," says Malmora. "And to express amazement that Begin should have been given the Nobel Peace Price in 1978."

"Garcia Marquez has good reasons for attacking the Nobel Prize," I say.

"Do you think so?" says the Countess.

"He'd have liked to get the literature prize himself last year . . . But he didn't . . . He'll get it this year, though—you'll see . . ."

"Still, he's right," interrupts Flora. "I like him."

"A terrific writer!" says the Countess.

"The terrorist attack in Rome strikes me as more important," say I.

"The synagogue?" says the Countess. "Those poor people."

"But on the main question Garcia Marquez is right," says Flora.

"Should writers get involved in politics?" I ask.

"Of course!" cries Malmora. "It's their duty to bear witness . . . All the time! Sartre set an excellent example!"

"So did Balzac!" say I. "No one's ever really explained why he went to Russia for a wife . . . Don't you think that's a very relevant question nowadays?"

Everyone looks at me: has he gone crazy?

"Writers are peculiar people," says the Countess . . . Then, to me: "What do you do?"

"I'm a journalist . . ."

"And France?" bawls Malmora. "What's happening in France?"

"Nothing much," says Louise.

"Some very important things!" flashes Flora.

"And what about Sartre's successors?" Malmora goes on yelling. "The new intellectuals?"

"The betting's still open,. . . says Flora. "But as yet no real favorite has emerged . . ."

"What about literature?" says Malmora.

"At a standstill," I tell him.

"No more Nouveau Roman?"

"Oh, the Americans are the only ones who bother with that now," I say. "The academics, of course . . . Who was it that was called a philosopher for senior-year students? Now there are novelists for minor degrees in Texas or Wisconsin . . . Grammatical exercises . . . Go from the present to the imperfect . . . From the conditional to the future . . ."

"What about little S.?" asks Malmora . . . "What's he up to? Still working on his Joycean gibberish without any punctuation?"

"Oh yes," says Sonia . . . "A funny guy . . ."

I make a hit with the Countess . . . Sixty, jewelry, dry skin . . . Gets me to tell her my impressions of Venice . . . Palladio . . . And then of New York, where she has an apartment on Central Park . . . A short, fat guy with glasses comes up to me . . . Knowing expression . . .

"I think we have a lady friend in common," he says, "I'm a psychoanalyst . . . In Athens . . ."

"Really?"

"Diane . . . She's spoken to me about you . . . It *is* you, isn't it?"

"How is she?" I ask.

"Very well. She's very good at her job."

"Is she an analyst too, now?"

"Didn't you know?"

No, but I might have guessed . . . I can still see the apartment near the river in Paris . . . The honey on the balcony, the day breaking . . . Diane naked under her yellow dressing gown . . . I don't like to ask whether she had her child . . .

"I'm just reading a novel by Françoise Sagan,. . . says the Countess. *"Bruises on the Soul* . . . Well, do you know, it's quite delightful! Have you read it?"

"No," I say.

I look at her . . . She's the one who's delightful . . . I can just see her reading her Sagan in bed at night, covered with face creams, in her palace with Rauschenbergs all over the walls . . . Painting, not literature . . . The usual thing . . . It's literature that tells the

truth, not "art" . . . You need words . . . To tell the difference . . .
"Bruises on the soul . . ." That sort of writing won't rumple her
hair! Everything is for the best in the least bad of all possible
worlds . . .

An American cultural adviser comes over to talk to me . . . A
tall, correctly dressed man, clearly a homosexual . . . He leaves to
go back to Tokyo tomorrow, via Paris . . .

"Tokyo?" I say . . . "Do you see the Chinese people there?"

"Yes, of course."

"Have you noticed a new representative arriving lately? Mme.
Li? Young, dark, pretty?"

"Ysia Li? Yes, certainly. Very active. She organizes opera tours,
doesn't she? Do you know her?"

"A little. She used to be in New York."

"She seems very dogmatic," says the American.

"Do you think so?"

The CIA is getting more and more inefficient, no doubt about
it . . .

"But Cyd was the one I knew best," he goes on. "We saw quite
a lot of each other in Easthampton three years ago . . . She went
into television, didn't she? She was still a student when I knew her
. . . I heard about your accident in Paris . . . I'm so sorry . . . Has
the inquiry produced any results?"

"Nothing at all," I say. "Naturally."

"The worst of it is that people get used to that sort of thing . . .
Forget which atrocity is which . . . Have you got over your injuries?"

"Yes."

"Do you still work for your *Journal* in France?"

"No . . . Enough is enough . . . I'm going back to New York
. . . Perhaps we'll meet there?"

Oh dear, here comes a Frenchman from the consulate . . .

"God, I envy you," I tell him. "It really is one of the most
beautiful spots in Venice . . . Those wistarias at the back . . ."

"Do you think so?"

539

Of course he must be rather bored here . . . Too provincial . . .

I join Louise on the balcony . . . The Grand Canal . . . Balmy night . . .

"Are you all ready for tomorrow?"

"Yes . . . I think so . . . If there's an encore it'll be for you . . . Scarlatti . . ."

"You must get some sleep . . ."

"I'm going now . . . We'll celebrate tomorrow, after the concert, shall we?"

"Really celebrate?"

Malmora goes by . . . He's still making up to Inge . . . Bending over backward . . . Turning somersaults . . . Inge makes eyes at us as she passes . . .

Flora appears briefly at the French window with an Italian journalist . . . Sees us . . . Turns around, taking him with her . . . Mustn't let him be influenced by me . . . Me and my peculiar sense of humor . . . Politics first . . . She's going to interview him . . .

"Is everything all right?" says the Countess. "Enjoying yourselves?"

"Terrifically," I say. "What a marvelous place!"

"Yes, but the upkeep! You can't imagine what a problem it is!"

Louise leaves . . . I settle myself in a deckchair in a corner . . . Sonia joins me . . . I go to get us a drink . . .

"What, another?" says Flora, meaning another woman, as I go by . . . "You need your head examined!"

Sonia and I drink our whiskies quietly in the shadows . . . Restraint . . . But she gives me a generous view of her bare legs . . . Her best feature . . . Together with her eyes. . .

"What are you thinking about?" she asks.

"The idea, which one could try to demonstrate, that all writers are really one."

"Hasn't Borges said that?"

"Among others."

"Good writers and bad indiscriminately?"

"That's where the paradoxes begin."

"But you could almost apply it to the whole of the human race. Isn't that what everyone says?"

"Women included?"

"Oh yes" . . .

We leave it . . . Drink, smoke . . . Breathe . . . Flora, Inge, and Malmora have disappeared . . . We go back to Spirito Santo . . . She makes sure the children are asleep . . . We make love on the balcony . . . Or rather I let her rape me . . .

The amorous lodger . . . The dissolute guest . . . The ladies' extra dash of soul . . . The edible traveler . . . Suits me . . . Gratuitous passage through the world . . . A meaningless world that doesn't deserve any better . . . The show isn't all that interesting . . . My apologies to universal suffering, obliged to think it has a meaning . . . And to everyone who is bored and waiting for something to turn up . . . Everyone who's got troubles . . . Beliefs . . . Ideals . . . But they'll have given up reading this long ago . . . If looks could kill . . . No mysteries? No double meanings? No symbols? Not really perverse? Quite flat? And on top of all that, the Bible? Horrors! I avoid any psychological explanations with Sonia . . . I can tell what it would be like . . . The usual little girl act . . . Or little sister . . . The father . . . The giant figure of childhood . . . Adorable . . . Inaccessible . . .

> My father gave me a husband,
> God, what a man, what a little man . . .
> My father gave me a husband,
> God, what a man, how little he is . . .

Cosi fan tutti . . . Forever . . . Two years . . . Three . . . When they bobbed up and down on the giant's lap . . . The giant who bossed Mama . . . Or so they thought . . . Golden age! Mythology! Once upon a time . . . Followed by round after round of disappointments . . . Never tall enough, noble enough, magnanimous enough! Still, I go jogging with her for a while the next day . . . We sit down to get our breath back on the broad steps of the Salute . . . Built to celebrate the end of the plague . . . The Madonna saved Venice? Yes, of course . . . What does the plague actually mean? Now, between ourselves? Frankly? Really? The plague, from the desert in Egypt . . . With which Lucretius himself ends his poem, which by some strange coincidence he began with a tribute to Venus . . . So atoms, falling into the void, turn into a black and stinking charnel house? It was only to be expected . . . In the beginning, matter looked quite wholesome and fresh . . . But . . . But . . . Here, anyhow, to emerge from the original pestilence, from the convulsive bubonic cesspit, they pulled out all the stops . . . A rounded, convoluted, ethereal façade . . . Spirals and conches . . . Stone angels celebrating the flight up to heaven . . . Twisted sanctity! Contorted salvation! The whole thing very strictly domed . . . Benediction of the halved sphere . . . Whew, it was a close thing, that putrid fever with its corpses, those heaps of debris . . . Send for the Virgin! No expense spared! Counterepidemic according to the rules! The germs exorcized! Drowned! Sent packing!

Phone call from Louise.

"Will?"

"Did you sleep well?"

"Quite well . . . Will you come and pick me up this evening before the concert? At half-past seven?"

"O.K. Relax . . . Think about something else . . . Whoever isn't against us is for us . . . "

"Huh? What did you say?"

"Nothing. See you" . . .

Back to the typewriter . . . Passage on the Songs of Songs . . . What skillful presentation . . . How to persuade a woman to make the trip . . . Not as easy as it looks . . . You have to find the right angle . . . In relation to her mother, in the background . . . You have to get to her at precisely that point . . . The navel . . . The frozen spring . . .

I raised thee up under the apple tree: there thy mother brought thee forth: there she brought thee forth that bare thee . . .

Apple tree . . . Apple of love . . . Mandragora . . . The need to pile up images of sweetness and perfumes . . . Doves, nest, milk . . . Lilies, gold bracelets, ivory, alabaster, chrysolite, sapphire . . . And spiced wine! And pomegranate juice! And cedars! And cypresses! But that's not enough . . . There must also be henna, nard, crocus, cinnamon, calamus, incense, aloes . . . No stinting! The whole gamut of sensations must be pressed into service . . . Otherwise it won't work . . . This is a very dangerous enterprise . . . Taking a daughter away from her mother! From her cataleptic double! Interrupting the Rite itself! A dreadful rite, as the text warns you . . . The Seal of Seals . . . Death . . . The furnace of Death itself! If you don't manage to sort this out with the utmost skill, heaven help you! She has to be your sister . . . Has to imagine she is . . . That you have in a way come from the same body as she emerged from, the body she belongs to . . .

O that thou wert as my brother, that sucked the breasts of my mother! when I should find thee without, I would kiss thee; yea, I should not be despised . . .

Yes indeed! It's easy to see why ten thousand incomprehensible books have been written on the subject . . .

I would lead thee, and bring thee into my mother's house, who would instruct me: I would cause thee to drink of spiced wine of the juice of my pomegranate.

His left hand should be under my head, and his right hand should embrace me . . .

I'm not going to give you a detailed interpretation . . . I personally would translate everything into the present tense . . . The transition from "thee" to "he" would call for several pages of comment . . . So there you are! Successful incest! Just the right amount . . . Wrapped in layers of myrrh . . . And do you know where myrrh comes from? *Myrrha* . . . A daughter who screwed her father with the connivance of her old nanny while her mother was celebrating the rites of Ceres . . . The angry gods changed her into the tree which bears the product that shares her name . . . Dante is severe and consigns her to hell . . . You'll find the story in that great ragbag, Ovid . . . These pagans!

Were you pleased? Metamorphosed? The Song is all yours! You are the dashing, desirable beloved!

Let him kiss me with the kisses of his mouth: for thy love is better than wine.

Because of the savour of thy good ointments thy name is as ointment poured forth, therefore do the virgins love thee . . .

This business of a name being like ointment or oil is very important . . . Think about it . . . The liquid smell, taste, sound . . . All the senses culminating in the ear . . . For the man, naturally . . . The sense of hearing which makes things flow . . . St. Bernard is always going on about it . . . Sermon after sermon! Now we're back on virgin soil again . . . I can't help it! That's just how it is! . . . Mathematically! . . . You surely don't think all these lucubrations have fallen into place by chance? That they just happened? That they haven't their own raison d'être that reason is in a hurry to ignore? If you've made people hate you, at least you'll know why . . . Of course, some people prefer to be hated . . . Why not? it's perfectly understandable . . .

Louise goes to it . . . Full house . . . They're all there . . . Even Flora . . . Malmora, preoccupied with Zerline . . . A scene from which time is already abolished . . . She starts with *The Well-Tempered Clavier* . . . Gradually infuses with passion the walls and ceilings of the palace, then little by little the squares, the alleys, the canals, the whole city . . . She sweeps through the churches and catches the organs up in the brilliant, impeccable fragility of her marginal instrument . . . It's stopped being a concert—it's a lesson in metaphysics . . . A complete course in eroticism . . . Flora yawns ostentatiously and bends over to speak to Malmora, who signs to her to be quiet . . . They're hooked . . . Unable to resist . . . I can see Louise breathing deeply . . . She's launched, even though she's still suffering the strain of beginning . . . Her hands answer for her . . . The slight drop in tension after five minutes . . . Automatic pilot . . . The reflexes come into play . . . She shuts her eyes . . . Now she's feeling all the audience's negative vibrations—that's what it is . . . You shall not pass! You'll fall! Skid! Collective malevolence . . . Inevitable . . . It's the rule . . . Wall of resentment against anyone who's on the point of escaping . . . I can feel Flora leading the unholy sabbath . . . Concentrating all her strength to stop Louise taking off . . . Black magic . . . Against the white magic of the keyboard . . . I sense Louise flagging a little, becoming mechanical . . . All right, I'll take a hand too . . . I join in . . . Together with Cyd's ghost . . . I send her waves of benediction . . . Tightrope . . . I tremble a little . . . How many girls are there all over the world at this very moment who are hot, moist, with their legs slightly parted, waiting—for what? Nothing! Nothing but Nothing! The sorcery's in the balance . . . For . . . Against . . . Flora's against . . . Entirely against . . . She's too fond of women . . . Hatred . . . I'm for . . . I'm very fond of them . . . So there it is . . . Louise has slowed down . . . She's realized she has to get around it . . . She breathes in, braces her thighs, her ankles . . . Her buttocks . . . Then plunges in again, concentrated in the nape of her neck . . . She's won . . . All Flora can do is put on a bored expression that only I notice . . . They're beaten . . . Louise presses on, enveloping them . . . She reconquers space, and the space of space and the ephemeral, mortal time that changes them into this momentary dream . . . God, how beautiful she is now, like an impassive insect, a scarab of sound . . .

She goes into the *Goldberg Variations* . . . Her round face is completely still and out of this world . . . Sleepwalking . . . She told me once that a successful performance is when you find yourself meditating in the void, and at the same time looking down on yourself from above and seeing yourself going through the necessary movements as if fast asleep . . . Mistakes are impossible . . . Not only that, but it's then that the spirit of the music really hovers over you . . . As at the beginning of the *St. John Passion* . . . In the beginning was the Word . . . At last a woman who understands that . . . Her shoulders . . . Her arms . . . In the beginning that will never end, in the nooks and crannies, in the furrows and the strokes, the endless veils and unveilings, in the mixture of sulphur and mercury, in the dark before the everlasting dark . . . Here it's grain by grain . . . From high to low . . . Right to left . . . Up to the hilt, which you have to seize . . . And pull out . . . One-two-three-four! Five-six! Seven-eight! Palalala! Lala! Lala! An upward rush! A downward thud! And then the pendulum . . . Perpetual motion . . . And then the pounding with the left hand . . . And then euphoria, joy, victory over all . . . And the left and the right overlapping . . . And the forehead, nose, mouth, and chin all swallowed up by the notes . . . Flora sneers silently . . . She can't help herself . . . Malmora taps her on the shoulder . . . But Louise is too far gone now to be bothered . . . She has hysteria on her side . . . Controlled hysteria . . . Concentrated . . . She charges, breaks through, swerves back, gets free, scatters, gathers together again, smashes, mends, starts off again, goes to extremes, comes back to the middle . . . A different body . . . Then she calms it all down . . . Goes back into the dark . . . Fires off the theme, distantly . . . Swing of the pendulum . . . All sound stops . . .

It's worked . . . They're all on their feet . . . Acclaiming . . . She seems to wake up, but I know she's still clinging to her black nucleus . . . And now it's my turn . . . She throws me an unseeing glance . . . Announces her encore in an expressionless voice . . . She's perfectly happy now . . . Scarlatti must be exulting in his grave . . . One sonata . . . They shout for more . . . Two sonatas . . . They go on shouting . . . A third . . . She can't play anymore . . . The last one's better still . . . She seems to float . . . One's rarely tired enough to attain that great repose . . . Free, lucid, subtle flight . . .

Right, a triumph—now let's go and have dinner . . . Louise goes to change . . . We dine with Inge, who's ditched Malmora . . . Just the three of us . . . Champagne . . . Sonia has got the message and gone home . . . Ciao, Flora! Good-bye, everyone! We go back to their adjoining rooms at the Luna . . . We're high . . . We send down for more champagne . . . We all mix in together merrily, right away . . . We've soon gotten rid of our clothes . . . Hands and lips at random . . . Louise is between Inge and me . . . We stroke her . . . She kisses me ardently . . . I've got strands of her black hair in my mouth . . . She lets herself be taken, starts sighing . . . "You really are crazy . . ." I can feel her warm skin . . . Inge gets up and goes into her room . . . We both come, there behind the curtain of drink, almost unconscious . . .

I wake up . . . Louise is still asleep . . . I get up and dress . . . Leave a note . . . Go for a long walk along the quays . . . Seven o'clock . . . There's the *Luki*, black and rust . . . And the *Adventure*, from Athens, being pulled along by the *Novus* . . . And the *Arnon*, from Haifa, with its name in Hebrew characters . . . Sun on the Salute . . . Sun on the sea of heaven . . . At least thirty days in one . . .

Gulls in rows seeking the warmth of the tiles . . . Coffee with Sonia a bit strained . . . It's time to tell her I'm leaving . . . Tomorrow . . . "So soon? Have you done as much work as you'd hoped?" Sarcastic . . . "Did you enjoy yourselves yesterday evening?" "We had a lot to drink . . ." I go out and head for the *Gesuati* . . . This is the time when they celebrate the Madonna del Rosario . . . They've brought out a big gaudy doll wearing a crown and holding her baby King of the Universe . . . Train and dress embroidered with flowers . . . Candles . . . Novenas . . . Nuns muttering "Ave Maria, piena di grazia . . ." Earlier on there were the *misteri gaudiosi* . . . Annunciation, conception, redemption . . . In the afternoon there are the *misteri dolorosi* . . . Passion, crucifixion, stabat mater, sacrament of the sick and the aged . . . And in

547

the evening the *misteri gloriosi:* resurrection, ascension, assumption . . . The whole thing punctuated with masses and sugary sermons beneath the wild Tiepolo of the heights . . . "Ad te clamamus, ad te suspiramus . . ." *Santa Maria Gloriosa* . . . Catholic rites . . . Litanies . . . Mysteries in broad daylight . . . They really are the only ones who've dared to say and keep on saying all this was the height of the obviously absurd, and that as a result the whole animated escapade was artificial and empty . . . Nothing to get worked up about . . . You are a mistake that's salvageable provided you believe in absolute extravagance . . . Antibiological . . . You can see why it drives the advocates of careful restraint out of their minds . . . But I'm very fond of the *misteri* . . . They give you a whiff of both heaven and earth . . . So long as you don't turn them into state doctrine, of course . . . *Famiglia cristiana* . . . Wholesomeness . . . Mothers . . . Wives . . . Soppy propaganda . . . And all the rest . . . But how can you prove that view has only a mystical meaning? Waste of time . . . No point . . . Attraction, repulsion . . . Never interpretation . . . I'll light a candle all the same . . . For Stephen . . . For my novel . . . If Kate could see me now! Or Flora, Robert, Bernadette, the Chairwoman, and the others! And Louise, who must be still asleep, dreaming she's playing . . . To you, then, Holy Virgin! With your red evening dress and your big blue cloak! To you, morning star! Gateway of light! Dethroner of the Goddess! To you, elevator of the once-and-for-all! Hole in the universe! Consolation! Exit! Vanishing point! To you, eternal absence of psychology! To you, rose and dew! Compassion! Rest! Velvet! Silk! Pneumatic softness! To you, music beyond the spheres! Crown of the galaxies! To you who let Monteverdi be buried near you, in a corner of the Frari chapel! Lucky devil! Laid to rest in his subject! Dead in his own Vespers! Orfeo of his Beata! Voice of voices!

There are some Cage and Stockhausen concerts on in Venice just now . . . "Thirty pieces for five orchestras . . ." "Trans . . ." I see Cage sitting on one of the quays, leafing through *Finnegans Wake* . . . Looking for inspiration . . . For the computer . . . With his rather foolish smile . . . American Zen . . . "Sounds like bubbles on the spherical surface of silence . . ." Stockhausen is bang in the middle of it in India . . . Alchemy . . . The Zodiac . . . Sirius . . . Music as the reflection of an age . . . A crowd at San Stefano to see them . . . I remember S. telling me how he met Pound here, waiting alone in the sun for death . . . Sixty years before, Joyce, after leaving Trieste . . .

I pick up Louise and we go for a coffee in Florian's . . . She's leaving soon for London, with Inge . . . Concerts . . . I put them in a motoscafo for Marco Polo airport . . . See you in New York? Sure! One of these days . . . We kiss . . . Wave enthusiastically . . . Hey, she didn't give me back my *Juliette* . . . Blonde and brunette . . . Vapor trail . . . Gone . . .

Around three in the morning, thunder and flashes of lightning . . . It gets to me through drawn shutters and closed eyelids . . . Sky and bedroom are both shaking, cleaving through my shattered brain . . . Hitting my bones . . . I open the window . . . The whole city is slashed, purple . . . Yet still sleeping . . . Peaceful under the storm . . . As if cut off by a window pane . . . Low, flat, struck by the series of explosions . . . Space having a nervous breakdown . . . Vertical epilepsy among the dimensions . . . The Redentore is dark, on the other side of the canal . . . Cascades of flashes . . . Photocosmos! Bombardment with phosphorus! And here comes the rain . . . A rushing torrent . . . Cats and dogs . . . I switch the light on . . . Pick up my Bible . . . Zechariah . . .

> I saw by night, and behold a man riding upon a red horse, and he stood among the myrtle trees that were in the bottom; and behind him were there red horses, speckled, and white . . .

These prophets are prehistoric, with their mania for animals . . . Their phobic horses "whom the Lord hath sent to walk to and fro through the earth . . ." They spring forth everywhere, muzzles, muscles, noses, hooves, bounds, wings . . . Waterside visions . . . The Kebar . . . The "rivers of Babel"—in other words the Euphrates and its canals . . . Teams . . . Burning chariot and its horsemen . . . All John did on Patmos was gather together in murderous fashion the divine menagerie . . . For the grand finale, the great settling of accounts that is to come . . . Or rather, that is already here . . . That never ceases to be here, in the earthquake fold of dead time . . . Zechariah has his "flying roll" or scroll, too . . . And another, very special apparition . . . An angel shows him a cask . . . Or ephah . . . Capacity thirty-seven liters . . . And sitting inside is a woman . . . Wickedness . . . Wickedness herself! And the angel closes the cask up again with its lid of lead . . . And two women with "wings like the wings of a stork" come and carry it off to be buried under the temple in Babylon . . . Mum's the word! That's it! Black magic! Thirty-seven liters of radioactive fundamental hatred there in the secret heart of the enemy religion! Black liver! Booby-trapped gall-bladder! Pile of bile! Sealed up in the cellar! Concentrated paranoia! Letter-bomb revelation! Carcinogenic nuclear package! Undetectable by geiger counter! Hiroshima mon amour!

The storm stops as suddenly as it began . . . The sky clears in twenty minutes . . . The wind withdraws . . . The moon comes out again, full, pale, like a luminous die-stamp . . .

I feel as if I don't have any right to be in Paris . . . As if I'd never been here before . . . All those years for nothing . . . Transplant rejected . . . I drop in briefly at the Journal to collect my mail . . . Kate and Robert avoid me . . . I find out Robert's just been made assistant editor . . . And Boris is to write a new regular feature . . . Kate may be going to head a TV channel . . . It's as if they couldn't see me anymore . . . Myopic glances . . . I'm no longer part of their history, of History in general . . . For them I represent one competitor fewer, so much money and so many column inches more . . . I notice Boris in the street . . . He sees me coming, hesitates . . . I cross over . . . I'm dead, just a drop of water evaporated without a trace . . . I stroll for a while along the Champs-Elysées . . . Meet S. at the Ritz . . .

"Well," he says, "have you finished?"

"Only a few more pages . . ."

"When are you leaving?"

"The day after tomorrow . . . I'll leave the end on my desk."

"Venice?"

"You'll see . . . How are things here?"

He waves his hand vaguely . . .

"Oh, you know how it is after the summer break . . . Another year starting . . . The same as before, apart from a few minor changes . . . Promotions, demotions . . . Predictable collapses . . . Foreseeable confirmations . . . The struggle for survival . . . Nothing special . . ."

"Have you managed to do some work?"

"Quite a bit . . . I seem to be hitting the lucidity I was aiming at . . ."

I give him the keys to the studio . . . And the code number, to get in through the street door at night . . .

"Will you be coming to New York soon?" I ask.

"In a couple of months."

"Will you have found a publisher for the book by then?"

"I expect so . . . Have you any preference?"

"Gallimard!" I say . . . "Of course! The Central Bank! The IMF! You can't have read what I've written!"

"Only joking . . . And how about New York?"

"That's another kettle of fish . . . We'll see . . . No film, no book! Too many digressions! And pornographic escapades! For no particular reason! And the plot doesn't hold up! And you have to think about the women's organizations! The League of Women Consumers! The Quakers! The Mormons! The Episcopalians! The Baptists! The Anabaptists! The Seventh-Day Adventists! The Pentecostals! The gay lobby! The Guardians of the Sacred Text!"

"We'll have our work cut out," says S.

"Question of strategy."

"So it's still *Women*? No change?"

"*Women*. It has to be called that . . . Leverage . . ."

"I'll be interested to see the reactions," says S.

"Don't we know already?"

"Of course . . . Terrible . . . Automatic denigration . . . Dirty tricks! Stabs in the back!"

He laughs . . . All this doesn't seem to worry him much . . . Me neither . . .

"But there'll be some friends on our side," I say.

"Who? My dear fellow, you know very well everything is negotiable . . . The surprising thing about friends and relations is not that they'll sell you down the river, but that they'll usually do it for so little . . . Quite cheap! A bad bargain against themselves! Thirty pieces of silver! To show the thing belonged to them after all! Blind reflex! Family vanity!"

We finish our whiskies and get up . . . Walk as far as the Place de la Concorde . . . Vast autumn evening, red sky . . . We cross the square and walk along by the river . . . The pleasure steamers going past all lit up . . .

"You have to admit it's a beautiful view," says S. "Won't you miss it?"

"Perhaps . . . I'll find out what I get there . . . I'll use it in the next book . . ."

"Really?"

"I've got a few ideas . . . Will you handle it?"

"Why not?"

"I'm not really a writer," I say. "You're my double in a country of doubles!"

"I wonder which of us two *is* the writer," he says thoughtfully.

"Does it ever occur to you that all writers are one?"

"From the start? From the absence of a beginning?"

"Yes."

"It's a plausible hypothesis . . . Anyway, it would explain why they all keep watch over one another so passionately . . . And language all comes down to one? The one?"

"Yes."

"They are transitory and it is One? The one and only? Outside existence? Nudging them, prompting them, coloring them according to their various capacities? And they merely modulating it? Punctuating it?"

"That's it . . . Exhalation rather than inspiration . . ."

"They've all more or less come around to thinking that in the end," he says . . . "That each of them was the only one . . . And all the rest were incapable of saying anything . . . Until the next one thought the same thing of them . . . And all of them feeling identical . . . Down to the same historical costume . . . I am Balzac, I am Cervantes . . ."

"I'm Melville and Shakespeare . . ."

"And we're all shadows of I Am . . . Who is no one in particular . . . Or not only . . . Or so improbably that it's not worth talking about . . ."

"And the Word was sent by I Am to X, that he might say . . ."

"That's the Bible . . . But be careful, now! Any cretin can think he's in on it . . ."

"Do you think so?"

"No, not really . . . There's a kind of filter . . . It's terrible . . . Always letting the same quantity through, apparently . . ."

We've reached Notre Dame.

"So here we are again," says S. "While they're all glued to their sets . . . News? Soaps? Fluctuat nec mergitur? Paris's motto . . . Tossed by the waves but never sinking?"

"Certainly tossed by the waves . . ."

"Pooh! Never let on!"

"In spite of Nietzsche?"

"Because of him, because of him . . ."

"And Marx, Einstein, Freud? Test-tube?"

"Because of them too . . . Mere agents . . . Never look back . . . Claudel's atomic pile in 1886? An incident . . . No need of conversion . . . We're almost in 1986 . . . See how alike the fins de siècle are . . . Aren't we right in the middle of a Renan phase? A reign of the Great Fat-heads . . . Of the kind of inferior rattle-pates stigmatized by Mallarmé? With their moons and their electronics and their cosmonauts? Have appetites, lies, manipulations, jealousies, ulcers, bilious attacks changed? Isn't the same vast shittiness still taking its course? Isn't the currency still blood? Suffering? Agony? Groans? And joy too? Pleasure? Expressed in what words? In what accents? Isn't it all terrifyingly and irrevocably absurd? Hypnotic? Somnambulistic? Generation . . . Corruption . . . Better stay with the writers . . . They don't tell so many lies . . .''

We separate . . . I go up the rue Saint-Jacques . . . As I pass the Pantheon I see the skeleton standing out plainly against the dome . . . Making a great airy sign of the cross . . . In the moonlight . . . To the great men and their grateful country . . . Yes, a young skeleton with a bunch of dried flowers in its hand . . . A red light shines intermittently where its sex organs would be . . . Go and see for yourself if you don't believe me! Dinner alone . . . Back to the studio . . .

Packing my bags . . . Yet again . . . I go and buy Stephen's plane, a superduper aerodynamic fighter with guns and rockets and a cockpit that opens and shuts to order . . . Of course, what matters is not the plane itself but arriving with it . . . Perfume for Deb . . . Passport in order? Dollars? Yes, here they are . . . Sunshine in the Luxembourg . . . Hey, that little brunette, reading . . . Not bad . . . Why not? Maud . . . A nurse . . . She'd like to go to the cinema? So long!

I finish typing the last few pages for S. He'll come tomorrow after I've left . . . Find the manuscript in the red file marked ''NOVEL'' in black felt-tip . . . He'll go over it and make corrections . . . Ginger up the plot . . . Tone up the rhythms . . . Invent turns of phrase . . . Up to him now . . .

I'm already on the other side . . . In some blessed old crock of a taxi with a low rear seat tearing along toward Washington Square . . . The Au Reggio Café, with Deb, as in our student days . . . And then lying on my wooden pier again by the Hudson River, with a great stretch of water shimmering the same as in Venice . . . Can one transform one's life inside one's life? Stay on time with oneself? You only need to pay attention . . . Follow the hidden heart-beat of what goes on . . . Minute by minute . . . The other dotted line . . . But one's always late . . . False images . . . One forget's one's own death . . .

I feel as though I were breathing in the tall blue darkness by the World Trade Center . . . I paint it on the inside of my eyes . . . Fondle it . . . The little cigar store on Seventh Avenue . . . The icy winter wind . . . The hurtling ocean . . . The sun piercing as a nail . . . Other games, other powers . . . All to be done again . . . Weaving a new web starting from almost nothing . . . It'll be grueling . . . But amusing . . .

I'm leaving my typewriter behind . . . I'll buy another one over there . . . Almost no baggage . . . My Hermes has been all over Europe . . . Jerusalem . . . I look at the array of rods and letters . . . The gray keys . . . Like a flight of steps . . . Five . . . Fingers . . . Figures . . . Alphabet . . . Millions of hands type on it every day . . . Dates, messages more or less veiled, negotiations, threats, courtesies . . . Could you make music with it? Soon it'll be some-thing else . . . Computers? People will get used to them . . . Keep a pen in reserve in their breast pocket for the more difficult bits . . .

What shall I do on my last night in Paris? Go out? Try to get off with someone? No . . . The Bible . . . The Psalms . . . The style that's eternal . . . Meditation by lamp-light . . . I get into the swing . . . For the Coryphaeus . . . The leader of the chorus . . . On stringed instruments . . . Flutes . . . In a low voice . . . Softly . . . David's . . . When he was fleeing from his son Absalom . . . When he was feigning madness to Abimelech . . . When he was at war with Aram-Naharaïm and Aram-Soba, then when Joab returned and conquered Edom, in the valley of Sel, slaying twelve thousand men . . . When Saul sent someone to watch his house and kill him . . . And when the Philistines seized him at Gath . . . And when the prophet Nathan came to him, after he had married Bathsheba . . . When he was in the desert of Judah . . . When he was in the cave . . . The psalm about the hills . . . David, the servant of Jehovah . . . The greatest poet of all time . . . But never quoted as such . . . Always Homer and Co. . . . For the Jews, he's a divine king . . . So it's up to us Greeks to make him enter literature in triumph . . . Laurels! Palms! In spite of Athena . . . The goddess with blue-green eyes . . . And the hordes of learned professors and customs officers . . . Latin unseen . . . Prizes . . . Academies . . . David of Bethlehem, the root of the Messiah, the loins of the Branch . . . Quoted by Christ on the cross . . . Psalm 22 . . . "Eli, eli, lamma sabactani . . ." The Just Man, abandoned, cries out to his god . . . To the tune of *Doe of the Dawn* . . .

My God, my God, why hast thou forsaken me? why art thou so far from helping me, and from the words of my roaring?

O my God, I cry in the day-time, but thou hearest not; and in the night season, and am not silent . . ."

You probably know the beginning, more or less? Though you never dared imagine that Christ *roared* on the cross, did you? But how about the end?

All they that go down to the dust shall bow before him . . .

So . . . After that comes the great question . . . Was he got out of it? Or left? Did he rise again? Or not? The betting's still open . . . Resurrection through Singing? Music? David's always complaining that people are horrid to him . . . Attack him for no reason . . . Flatter him, but really hate him . . . Accuse him wrongfully . . . That his enemies are always setting snares in his path . . . Plots . . . Machinations . . . Lies . . . Nooses . . . Traps . . . Nets . . . They give him back evil for good . . . Spy on him . . . Dogs . . . Serpents . . . False friends . . . And all because of the god he serves . . . The god whose grace is in heaven . . . Whose truth rises up to the clouds . . . Whose justice is like mountains, and whose judgments are like the Abyss . . . The god of the universe is above the universe . . . Present everywhere, in the north and in the south, in the heights and in the depths, the stars and the nonstars, in thought, entrails, hearts, wombs and embryos, and in the intentions of the tongue . . . He makes the gates of the morning and of the evening cry out with joy!

556

I am a wonder unto many; but thou art my strong refuge.

Let my mouth be filled with thy praise and with thy honour all the day . . .

What would they say about him now? Paranoiac . . . Persecution mania . . . Melancholic . . . Megalomania . . . But what about the music? What music? The Psalms! Oh, well . . . It's that that gets under their skin . . . Inevitably . . . Verbal music, day and night, directed toward the source . . . Familiar terms with the invisible . . . Words preoccupied with their own fire instead of cracking up the scenery . . .

When I remember thee upon my bed, and meditate on thee in the night watches.

Because thou hast been my help, therefore in the shadow of thy wings will I rejoice.

My soul followeth hard after thee: thy right hand upholdeth me . . .

Someone who never stops singing for that which can't be seen? Can't be touched? Yet claims to reign over all things? And what's more, insists on truth and justice, and keeps on telling you that man is a mistake, a mere breath, a nothing? You must admit it's annoying . . .

Oh how great is thy goodness which thou hast laid up for them that fear thee . . .

Thou shalt hide them in the secret of thy presence from the pride of man: thou shalt keep them secretly in a pavilion from the strife of tongues . . .

So, on top of everything else, this god has favorites? And one particular favorite among them? True, he treats them all harshly . . . But others envy them all the same . . . Their verbal power . . . But what if it were true?

557

He sent from above, he took me, he drew me out of many waters.

He delivered me from mine strong enemy, and from them which hated me: for they were too strong for me.

They prevented me in the day of my calamity: but the Lord was my stay.

He brought me forth also into a large place: he delivered me, because he delighted in me.

The cat's out of the bag . . . Especially as this god of his has never said he loves men in general . . . No . . . On the contrary! He just "delights in" this particular one . . . How unfair! What partiality! A god who's a music-lover! Interfering with the angle of atoms to save his favorite performer! Can you be surprised that it makes for jealousy among the bodies? As if bodies didn't all want to be delighted in! Stroked, pampered, reassured, fondled, rocked, before the final leap into the dust! As if he didn't deserve Death, this choice of the One out of the Many . . . Yes, Death . . . For him and for everyone, forever . . . So there!

Right, now that's the end . . . One of the possible ends . . . I sleep and yet I'm not really asleep . . . I can and I can't hear myself thinking . . . Casting off the last moorings . . . The physical ropes creaking, chains of muscle and bone, from fatigue and silent strain at last abandoned . . . Arm outstretched, then bent . . . Neck knotted, brow worried, hands cold . . . If we have bored you, ladies and gentlemen, your indulgence! The poor spirits of the air are swept away in the gathering darkness . . . Are the gulls crying? No, no gulls here, no liquid to and fro, no spray . . . A squirrel in its mental treadmill . . . Collapse into the tiny dimension of oblivion . . . So small . . . Vanishing as you watch; microscopic serried teeth of the vertebrae . . . Coat of blood . . . Shiver and fur of words . . .
Can't it be looked at straight, death? Still, in profile . . . Or

sideways . . . Fleetingly . . . You shall not pass? Yes, I shall . . .
And here one is, outside for a timeless moment, drawing the curtain
from without . . . Drawing up the ladder . . . Taking oneself off,
leaving oneself divided below . . .

Sleep is morality itself . . .

Day! Coffee, shower, call up S. . . . Errands, rain, taxi, Roissy,
"satellite" building, check-in for New York, embarkation lounge
. . . Hey, that elegant blonde, quite tall, black blouse, gray suit and
gray eyes, smiling at me . . . Do I know her? No . . . Oh yes, we
met once at the *Journal* . . . Yes, that's right, an Englishwoman
. . . The *Sunday Times* . . . Smoking? Yes . . . See you on the
plane? Yes . . . She's very good-looking . . . Marvelous skin . . .
We're at a bit of a loss . . . She pretends to be looking at something
in her bag . . . Smiles again . . . Gray gleam . . . Now boarding
. . . Red warning light . . . Immediate boarding . . .